# THE QUEENS OF INNIS LEAR

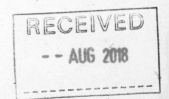

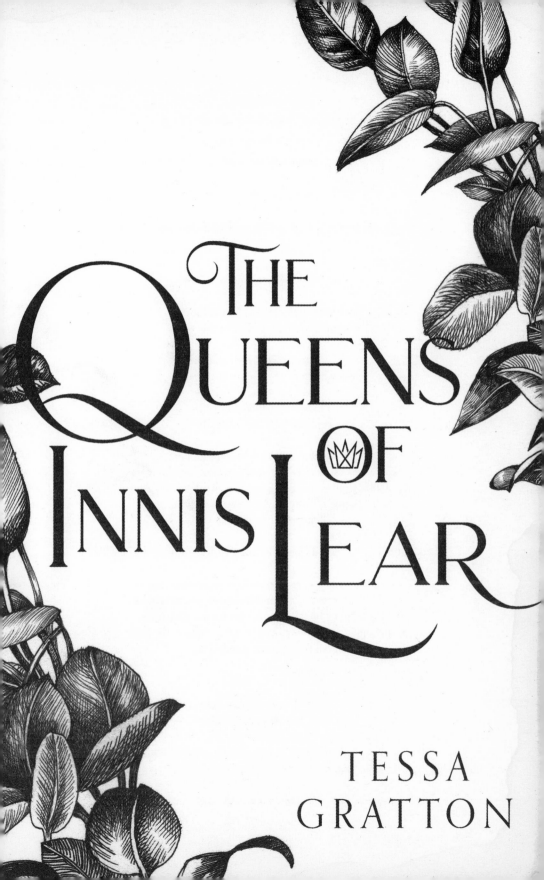

# The Queens of Innis Lear

TESSA
GRATTON

Harper*Voyager*
An imprint of HarperCollins*Publishers* Ltd
1 London Bridge Street
London SE1 9GF

www.harpercollins.co.uk

First published in the UK by HarperCollins*Publishers* 2018
1

A catalogue record for this book
is available from the British Library

HB ISBN: 978-0-00-828187-8
TPB ISBN: 978-0-00-828188-5

Printed and bound in the UK by CPI Group (UK) Ltd, Croydon CR0 4YY

MIX
Paper from
responsible sources
FSC™ C007454

This book is produced from independently certified FSC™ paper
to ensure responsible forest management.

For more information visit: www.harpercollins.co.uk/green

*To Laura Rennert,*
*who believed in this book even more than I did.*

# Part
# ONE

*IT BEGINS* WHEN a wizard cleaves an island from the mainland, because the king destroyed her temple.

The island is raw and steeped in her rage, making the people who grow there strong, and sharp, and ever quick to fight. Mountains claw upward in the north, and a black river gushes south and west, spreading fingers east into smaller streams that trip through the center of the island. The rush of water gathers up all the trees and flowers, giving them the blood to grow wild and tall, feeding the roots until they dig through the rock itself. Where roots merge with stone, new clear springs are born.

The people build stone shrines around these rootwaters, making holy wells in which to bless themselves, their life rituals, and their intentions. Soon these wells are the centers of towns and at the heart of every fortress or castle, connecting the people always to the blood of the island. Lords from each quarter of the land come together to build a cathedral in the White Forest, where their four domains kiss. That is the heart of the island.

Every generation a child from each quarter kingdom is given to the wild forest for dedication or sacrifice. One lord offers his firstborn, and that is a beginning, too: the beginning of a line of wizards so strong, the other lords rise up together and bury the ashes of the unruly family in saltwater sand.

But the magic survives.

For centuries after, the island bristles and growls, all wind and scoured moors, valleys of pasture lined with protective oak forests, and the jagged north mountains break for rubies and the western cliffs gleam with copper. There is iron in the southern marshes, too, raw mineral that whispers to those who can hear, and when it is forged with magic, it never cracks. The rootwells run strong, and the thin earth is more fertile than it should be, and so the island thrives, fed on the blessing of star prophecies and the teeming love of the roots.

\* \* \*

*IT BEGINS* WHEN a lord of the island reads ambition's reward in his stars, and rallies the strength of iron and wind to defeat his rivals, uniting all under one crown. He calls himself Lear, after the wizard who cleaved the island. In her honor, he raises a great fortress in the north, along the shores of a black lake so deep many call it the island's navel. He crowns himself on the longest night, the holiest time for star prophecy; offers his blood and spit to the island's roots, his breath to the birds and the wind, his seed to the iron, and his faith to the stars.

*IT BEGINS* FAR away from the furious island, in a place so different in name and air that the one could not recognize the other as being born both of the same earth. There, a young woman asks her grandmother for a ship with which to sail out past the edges of their empire, for she has a hunger to understand the world, to experience something not more broadly but more deeply, until that one thing becomes an entire universe. She says her curiosity is like sand in a storm, scouring bones smooth as glass. Her grandmother agrees, though suspects she'll never see this daughter of her line again. "God will bring us back together," the young woman says, and her grandmother replies to her with only an old desert prayer:

"Do not forget: you will be air, and you will be rain, and you will be dust, and you will be free."

Perhaps that is an ending, too.

*IT BEGINS* ON the day two bright hearts are born to the island, one just past dawn as a crescent moon rises, and the other when the sun is brightest, obscuring the glow of stars. Their mothers knew they would be born together, as witches and best friends often do, and though it is the first child for one and the last for the other, such does not come between them. They sit beside each other, arms stretched to touch the other's swollen belly as they grit their teeth and tell stories of what might become of their children.

*IT BEGINS* WHEN a queen sits in a pool of stars.

*IT BEGINS* WITH seven words with which to bind a crown, whispered in the language of trees: *eat of our flower, and drink of your roots.*

*IT BEGINS* AS the sun sets, the last time the final king of Innis Lear enters the cathedral at the heart of the island. This Lear has never been devoted to the roots, or paid much mind to well or wind. He is a man driven by the stars, by their motions and patterns, their singular purity and steadfastness, bold against the black reaches of night. To him, the cathedral is redundant; a person devoted to star prophecy has no need of rootwater or navel wells.

Two vast halls of carved limestone and blue-gray granite cross in the middle of the holy place, east-west arms aligned with the sky to trace the path of the sun at the summer solstice, so the Day Star rises precisely over the eastern spire; the other hall aims as true north as the ever-constant star Calpurlugh, the Eye of the Lion. In the center point where the halls cross, a well sinks deep into the core of the island, fresh and mossy, a dark channel from the womb of the earth. No ceiling caps the edifice, for what would the purpose be in closing away the sky?

When it rains, water scours the stone floor and soaks the wooden benches. It cleanses the quarter altars and fills tiny copper bowls, making simple music with only the natural touch of water to metal. On sunny days, shadows caress living vines and the poetry and icons etched into the walls, counting seasons and time of day. Clouds lower themselves in the spring to nest around the highest spires, curling soft and dewy and cool. Nothing separates sky from land here at the heart of Innis Lear.

Now it is night, and a heavy moon tips against that eastern spire. Another beginning, ready to burst.

The king walks on the soles of thin slippers, his embroidered robe dragging off his shoulders. He is old, though not old enough to look as ravaged as he does, his hair wild and damp, his eyes tight from grief. An undyed tunic falls to his knees, nearly the same pale gray as his lined face and those long fingers. Straight to the well goes this royal wraith, and he presses his hands to its stones, breathing deep of the moss, the metallic smell of the earth's blood water. A shudder wrenches down his spine, and he grimaces.

"Now," he commands, turning away.

Seven strong men come forward with a flat, round piece of granite. Carved off one of the massive standing stones that once marked this holy well, before the cathedral was erected around it, the granite glimmers bluish in the moonlight. The retainers roll and twist it awkwardly, straining against the ropes that bind it. Slowly they walk, turning it up the aisle. One of them is glad of this mission, two unmoved by the significance of their actions, three too worried to be quite as indifferent as they would prefer to be, and the last one alone wishing, with every ounce of his heart, that he'd been strong enough to stand against his king, to protest that this was wrong and unholy.

The men position the stone, and in a moment of desperate hesitation, the last retainer looks fearfully at the king's expression, hoping for a reprieve. But the king's brows are drawn as he glares at the well, as if the well itself is responsible for everything. The retainer lifts his eyes instead to the open sky above, consoling himself with the reminder that his king does nothing without permission from the stars. And so this must be fated. It must be.

Tears glimmer in the king's lashes when the granite slab falls forward, the sound of stone on stone filling the sanctuary. With a final pull of ropes, the navel is eclipsed.

The smell of rootwater vanishes, as does a slight echo that the king had not even noticed, until it was silenced. He puts his hand atop the stone cover, caressing its roughness, and smiles grimly. With his fingers, he makes the shape of the tree of worms, a sorrowful, dangerous constellation.

IT BEGINS, TOO, with a star prophecy.

But there are so many prophecies read on the island of Lear that to say so is as good as saying it begins with every breath.

# THE FOX

IN A QUIET, cool grove of chestnut trees, heart-leafed lindens, and straight-backed Aremore oaks, a fox knelt at the edge of a shallow spring.

Scars and fresh scratches marred the rich tan of his back and arms and thighs. He had already removed his uniform, weapons, and boots, piling them on a wide oak root. The Fox—who was also a man—poured clear water over himself, bathing and whispering a cleansing song that married well with the babble of spring water. He'd traced this source at the first light of dawn, glad for a forest heart from which to ask his questions.

A breeze came, tightening his skin with cold breath, and the canopy of leaves chattered welcome. Ban the Fox replied, *That's encouraging,* in their tongue, shifting his vowels to match the cadence of this Aremore forest. The trees spoke wider and more graciously here than on the rocky island where he'd been born. On Innis Lear the trees tended toward hard and hearty, shaped by ocean winds and the challenge of growing against the bedrock; not green and radiant so much as gray and blue with the coolest brown barks, lush moss creeping around in hollows, and thin leaves and needles. They spoke softly, the spreading low mother oaks and thorned hedges, weaving their words into the wind so their king could not hear.

But in Aremoria there was room and soil, enough for loud trees more concerned with bearing fruit than surviving winter storms or heartless kings. They conversed with each other, sighing and singing to please themselves, to taunt colorful birds, to toy with the people's dreams. It had taken Ban months to win the trust of the Aremore trees, for he'd arrived angry and corded over by bitter flavors, far too spicy at such a young age. They'd not welcomed an invading thistle, but eventually he charmed them, grew to be as familiar as if he'd been rooted here.

Slipping deeper into the spring now, Ban untied the tiny braids patched through his thick, dark hair. His toes sank into silt as water curled about his ankles; he kept up his idle banter with the nearby linden trees, who had a vibrant sense of humor. Finally, with his hair loose and falling stiffly at his ears and neck, Ban ducked himself entirely into the spring water.

All conversation dulled. Ban held his breath, waiting to hear the pulse of this forest heart. A deep well might serve better, but the spring was natural, built only of the earth. He needed the rhythm under his skin to properly connect, to find the paths of magic he could use to track the loathsome Burgun army and certify their retreat.

Peace and cold solitude surrounded Ban. He parted his lips to allow in a mouthful of water and swallowed it, drinking in the tranquility. He slowly stood up.

Water streamed off his rising form. A small man, with not a strip of comfortable fat, Ban was all tawny muscles and sharp edges. Dark hair blackened by water hung heavy around large eyes, the brown and dark shadow green of forests. He blinked and droplets of water like tiny crystals clung to his spiky lashes. Had anyone witnessed his emergence, it would've been easy to think Ban a thorn of magic, grown straight from the spring.

Refreshed and blessed, he crouched at the shore to dig his hands into the mud. He spread it up his wrists like gauntlets, smoothing the gray-brown mud into a second skin over his own. With it he painted streaks across his chest, down his stomach, around his genitals, and in spirals down his thighs. He slapped handprints over his shoulders, splattering them down his back as far as he could reach.

Now, fully a creature of this specific earth, adopted child of these balmy trees, Ban the Fox picked his way back into the forest. Every footstep brought him words whispered up his legs: *starwise, starwise, forward, this way, turn here, this way, starwise again, and nightwise now!* The trees directed him toward the goal he'd requested, and finally Ban reached the tallest of them, at the edge of the forest, where he might best catch hold of a wind willing to report on Burgun.

A spreading, ropey old chestnut waited, roots buried several horse lengths off the line of trees. Ban glanced all around, at the churned earth of the valley, where days ago the Burgun army had camped. No grass still lived except in scattered clusters, the rest trampled and flattened and gone dry. Abandoned fire pits were scorched scars, and he could see the heaped dirt of covered privy lines.

No men or women remained, and so Ban dashed across the narrow strip of open land, using the speed to launch himself up the trunk of the chestnut. He caught the lowest branch with a grunt, swung up, and climbed high. The tree was sturdy enough that it never shivered with his weight, merely chuckled at his tickling grip.

Three small birds burst away from his intrusion, and the chestnut warned him to mind the eastern circle of limbs, where he'd already angered some brown squirrels.

Ban climbed along the ladder of boughs, up and out, toward the highest northwestern branch. There, a line of charred lightning strike allowed him a perch with a view of the valley for miles ahead of him, and of the rolling green forest canopy behind. He pushed aside long, serrated leaves and gripped a branch at his shoulder, only as wide as his wrist, to steady himself.

Ban stood, balanced carefully.

Wind caught his hair, pulling it out of his face. He asked the tree to warn him if anything approached, animal or person, then opened his mouth to taste the flavors of the air.

Smoke, old death, and the dusty musk of crows.

Ban lifted onto his toes to reach into the air. He caught a feather, black and smooth. In the inky color he saw shifting waves of men and horses; he saw a cliffside and clouds of reddish smoke, sparkling rocks, rotten flowers, and an empty white hand.

He slid the edge of the feather along his tongue, spat onto the back of his hand, and rubbed it against the chestnut bark hard enough to score the skin bloody. The language of birds was full of dreams, and impossible for men to interpret, it was said. But Ban had learned otherwise, these six years in Aremoria, at least if he could use pain, or blood, to facilitate the translation.

His hand throbbed now, and Ban closed his eyes to recall the pulse of the tranquil spring water. Slowing his breath, he brought his heart into alignment with the forest heart, through this focus of tender skin.

The crow's many images became one: an army dressed in maroon limped far from here, a full day and night's ride, backs to him and Aremoria, facing the north cliffs of Burgun.

*Thank you,* Ban said in the language of trees, and tucked the feather into the crook of leaves where it became a gift for the chestnut. He offered to trim the dead branch, but the chestnut was pleased with its storm-gifted scar. Ban rather liked his own scars, too, for how they proved his experiences and belonged to none but him, and he told the tree as much as he returned to the ground.

Ban landed in a crouch, cold suddenly in the shade. The sun sank over the far mountains bordering the edge of Burgun lands, and Ban wished his clothes were nearer. He'd return to camp, report to Morimaros, and then eat, drink, sleep the short summer night away, not once looking up at the glinting stars.

The evening forest whistled and hummed. The trees observed the usual yawning transition to twilight: they watched animals wake for the hunt, wondered if the king of deer would drive off a lone wolf trapped here, apart from her pack, by the armies, or if that most gentle rabbit would neglect to avoid the oak full of owls. Hungry himself, Ban considered joining the fray, stalking that wolf to try his own hand at her. He smelled like the mud of the forest now, and just a slight trail of his dried blood. It would keep their advantages even.

But if he did not return to camp before darkness set in full, the king would worry, though Ban had tried for years to teach him that there was no need to be concerned with the Fox's safety in a forest.

It made his lips curl in a small, involuntary smile to think on: a man as good and bold as Morimaros of Aremoria concerned for a bastard like Ban.

So distracted was Ban, it took a scream from three young linden trees to alert him to the man who had invaded the heart spring grove.

Immediately alert, Ban crouched low to make his way around from the south, where the canopy was thickest and more shadows would hide him. Listening to the gentle prodding of trees, Ban crawled along, only his eyes gleaming.

At the edge of the grove, he lowered himself onto his stomach and slipped under a rose vine, enjoying the delicate perfume even as the hooked thorns brushed the dry mud on his shoulders.

Seated on the very root where Ban had left his belongings was none other than King Morimaros. A midsize, handsome man with short, practical dark hair and a matching beard, in the regular uniform of the army except for the long orange leather coat and the royal ring on his forefinger. Ban looked about everywhere, confirming with the trees that Morimaros was alone. Casually reading a letter.

Exasperation and a shot of fear made Ban grit his teeth and creep backward. He'd show Morimaros how stupid it was to be alone, even with the war over, even with Burgun fled.

He climbed up an oak, whispering a request that the tree hold still, and then the next, too, as he stepped across to it, so that they would not shake their leaves and reveal to the king his location. Thus, Ban walked gently from tree to tree, like an earth saint, and sank finally into the embrace of the oak under which Morimaros sat. Ban climbed down, and even when the king looked suddenly out at a cracked branch in the west, Ban was invisible to him, directly above.

In one swift motion, Ban dropped onto the king's back, threw an arm around his neck, and pulled. But Morimaros grasped his arm and bent, flinging Ban heels over head, hard onto the muddy shore of the spring. Ban rolled onto his hands and the balls of his feet, and glared at the king, eyes and teeth bright in his muddy, wild face.

Morimaros had his sword free, knees bent, ready to defend himself again. "Ban?" he said after a slow moment.

Ban stood. "You were very vulnerable, Your Majesty."

"Not so, it seems." The king smiled. He sheathed his sword and picked up the fallen letter.

"Why come out alone? I was on my way to returning." Ban crossed his arms over his bare chest, suddenly too aware he was naked but for mud-scrawled magic.

"I'm not allowed much solitude, and this evening is perfect for it," Morimaros said. He ran a hand over his close-cropped hair, a sign of slight embarrassment. "And I would speak with you privately on a certain matter, ah, pertaining to this letter." He brandished it, and Ban could see the deep blue wax of Lear still clinging to one edge.

All his skin went cold with dread, but Ban nodded because he had to: this was his king, his commander, no matter what else they might be to each other.

The Fox strode into the water and ducked down fully into it, allowing his entire body to be enveloped. It was not peace and cool calm he felt as the water brushed away mud, tickled his spine and the backs of his knees. No, it was a roar of suppressed memories: clenched fists and dismissive words; sheer peaks, crashing waves, and a howling, powerful wind; haunting sweet laughter and black eyes with short, curled lashes; tiny iridescent beetles.

Ban, the bastard of Errigal, scrubbed his skin clean and turned over in the spring, spinning once, twice, and a third time. Rising, he wiped his face, spat water, shook his head like a dog.

When he emerged, he desperately thought of his Aremore name, the one he'd earned, trying to will himself back to center.

*The Fox. Ban the Fox.*

His eyes opened to see that Morimaros offered him trousers. Ban muttered thanks and dragged them on, tied the waist up and used the plain wool shirt to wipe drips of water from his face and neck, chest and arms.

"Now," Morimaros said, clasping his shoulder, "I have wine in the crook of that root. Read this letter."

Ban followed the king, reminding himself he was trusted here, he was honored by the grand crown of Aremoria. Whatever Lear wanted, Ban would attack it from Morimaros's side. Together, the men sat.

Morimaros gave over the letter and uncorked the brown glass bottle of wine with his teeth. The writing was roughly scratched into the parchment. Ban read:

> *To the honored King Morimaros of Aremoria,*
>
> *We of Innis Lear invite you to join us at our Summer Seat for a rare celestial occasion. The Zenith Court will commence some two weeks from the writing of this note, on the full moon after the Throne rises completely to mark the ascent of the Queens of Autumn. The greatest of our island shall attend, and we look forward to introducing you to our youngest, with whom you have corresponded these last months, with hope I am certain in your heart. We are eager to set our daughters onto their star paths, and know your attendance will aid us in that desire.*
>
> *With the blessings of the stars in our words,*
>
> *Lear*

Ban managed to remain calm, despite the implications involving Elia Lear. He read through the letter again, and Morimaros swung the bottle of wine toward him.

Trading his thirst for the burn of memory, Ban took a long drink. It was sweet and crisp, very easy to swallow. Not like the wine and ale of Innis Lear. Not like the hard yearning that tugged at him even now to go back. To touch the iron magic of Errigal again. To set things right and show his father and that king what he'd become. A confidant of this king, a renowned soldier and spy. Important. Necessary. Honored.

Wanted.

"Did you know her?" Morimaros asked, interrupting Ban's sputtering thoughts.

"The youngest princess?" Ban lightly avoided her name.

But the king did not.

"Elia," he said simply, and then easily continued. "She is the star priest, we hear, preferring this to her title. Though I met her as such, once, a long while ago. When her mother died, I traveled to Innis Lear for the year ceremony. Princess Elia was only nine. It was my first time in another country, acting as Aremoria. Though my father lived still, of course. He didn't die until I was twenty." Morimaros took back the wine and sipped at it. Ban studied the king, trying not to imagine him speaking with Elia, touching her fingers. Morimaros was gilded and handsome, a strong man, and one of the only good ones Ban had ever known. Elia deserved such a husband, and yet, he could not imagine her living here, in Aremoria, away from the twisted island trees, the harsh moors, the skies overwhelmed with stars.

Ban shook his head before he could stop himself. He'd thought of her, though he'd tried to forget those years before he'd been the Fox. Thought of the smooth brown planes of her cheeks, her black as well-water eyes, the streaks of improbable copper in her cloud of dark brown spiral curls. Her warm mouth and eager young hands, her giggle, the wonder with which she dug into tree hollows with him, whispering to the heart oaks, to the roots, to the sparrows and worms and butterflies. He'd thought of her most when he was alone in enemy camps, or washing blood off his knife, or cramped and stinking for days in the hiding holes the roots made for him. She saved him, kept him quiet, kept him sane. His memories of her made him remember to stay alive.

"Did you know her?" Morimaros asked again.

"Barely, sir." And yet more entirely than Ban had known anyone in his life. She once was the person who'd known him best, but Ban wondered what her reply would be, if asked the same question today. In five lonely, bloody years, she'd not written to him, and so Ban had never sent word to her on the wings of these Aremore birds. Why would she want to hear from a bastard now, if she hadn't before? And now they were grown.

The king said, "I'll leave next week. Sail around the south cape to the Summer Seat."

Ban nodded absently, staring down at the dirt beside his toes.

"Return to Innis Lear with me, my Fox."

His head snapped up. *Yes,* he thought, so viciously he surprised himself.

King Morimaros watched Ban with clear blue eyes. His mouth was relaxed, revealing nothing—a special skill of this king's, to present a plain mask to the world, holding his true opinions and heart close.

*Home.*

"I . . . I would not be a good man at your side, Majesty."

"Ban, here and now call me Mars. Novanos would."

"When we discuss Lear it reminds me too keenly of my place, sir."

Morimaros grimaced. "Your place is at my side, Ban, or wherever I put you. But I know how that old king thinks of you. Is his daughter cut of same cloth?"

"As a girl, Elia was kind," Ban said. "But I do not know how I can serve you there."

The king of Aremoria drank another portion of wine and then set the bottle firmly in Ban's hand. The Fox recognized the low ambition in Morimaros's voice when he said, "Ban Errigal, Fox of Aremoria, I have a game for you to play."

# ELIA

THE YOUNGEST DAUGHTER of Lear threw herself up the mountainside, gasping air cold enough to cut her throat. She hitched her heavy leather bag higher on her shoulder, taking the steeper path in order to reach the top on time. Her fingers scrabbled at the rough yellow grass, and her boots skidded on protruding limestone. She stumbled and ground her skirts into the earth, then dragged herself up to the wide pinnacle, finally reaching her goal.

Elia Lear lay flat, rolling onto her back, and sighed happily despite her raw throat and the dirt under her fingernails. Above, the sky tilted toward night, edged in gentle pink clouds and the indigo silhouettes of the mountains cradling these moors. She shivered and hugged her arms close to her chest. This far north on Innis Lear, even summer breathed a frosty air.

But the solitude here, as near to the sky as she could hope to reach, was Elia's greatest bliss. Here, it was only her spirit and the stars, in a silent, magnificent conversation.

The stars never made her feel angry, guilty, or forlorn. The stars danced exactly where they should. The stars asked her for nothing.

Elia glanced up at the purple sky. From here she had a clear view of the western horizon, where at any moment the Star of First Birds would appear and hang like a diamond at the tip of the Mountain of Teeth.

All around her, the golden moor swept down and away in rolled peaks and valleys, marred by jutting boulders like fallen chunks of the moon. Wind scoured the air, hissing an upland song from the northwestern edge of the mountains, heading south toward the inner White Forest and east toward the salty channel waters. The princess could have felt quite abandoned out here, but the shadowed valleys hid roads and some tiny clusters of homes; it was where the families lived, those who cared for the sheep and goats grazing this land—some of which could be seen freckling the hills with gray and white.

If Elia looked down to the south, she would see the star tower clinging to a limestone outcrop, built centuries ago by an old lord before the island was united, for a military stronghold. The first King Lear had confiscated it for the star priests, opened up the fortified walls and left them to crumble, but with elegant wood and slate from the south he had lifted the tower itself taller, until it was the perfect vantage point for making accurate star charts and reading the signs on every point of the horizon. Elia had lived and studied there since she turned nineteen last year, and every morning she dotted white star-marks onto her forehead to prove her skills as a priest and prophet. She did not yet consider herself a master, but hoped one day she might.

This morning's marks had smeared slightly, as they often did, for Elia spent much of her time brushing errant, wind-tossed curls away from her face. Her companion, Aefa, often made sure to wrap a veil or scarf about Elia's hair, or insisted on using ribbons or at least braids to keep her hair in place, as befit a princess, if not a prophet. Elia could not help preferring to leave it free, tended by nothing but bergamot oil from the Third Kingdom, and perhaps a few begrudged decorations near her face. It put her in contrast to her sisters, neither of whom would leave their bedrooms without their costumes fixed and perfect.

Aefa was ever despairing that Elia made her worst choices whenever she did so with her sisters in mind. Such fussing was what a lady's companion was for, and as her father, Lear's truth-telling Fool, was always willing to argue, so did Aefa uphold the family tradition. It was enough to make the princess grateful for these stolen moments alone.

Sitting, the princess hauled the leather bag into her lap and unknotted the thong holding it shut. She pulled out a folded wooden frame and a roll of parchment to fix to it so she could mark the progress of star appearances onto a simple chart.

Elia'd wagered this morning with the men in the Dondubhan barracks that it would be tonight the Star of First Birds finally moved into position to sparkle exactly over the distant peak. Danna, the star priest mentoring her, had disagreed when she told him, so he watched from the roof of the star tower at this very moment, while Elia had climbed here, even higher, to see first. The dignity of winning mattered more to her than the handful of coins she had bet.

Oh, how shocked her father would be at such a wager.

For a moment, she wished he was here with her.

Her smile reappeared as she imagined refitting the tale into a shape palatable for Lear. Assuming she won, of course. If she lost, she'd never confess it to her father.

This youngest princess favored her late mother in most ways, being small and sweetly round, and warm brown all over: skin and eyes and hair that spiraled in ecstatic curls. Her father was tall and pale as limestone, with the straightest brown hair in the world. What she lacked in his looks, she made up for by sharing his vocation to the stars.

Lear would say, *The Star of First Birds is brighter than other stars, and she moves unlike any other. Out of their fixed pattern, and yet with her five sisters. The Stars of Birds fly through all the rest, influencing the shapes and constellations. When you were born, my star, the First and Third Bird stars crowned your Calpurlugh.*

She knew the patterns of her birth chart by heart, and the brilliant star at its center; Calpurlugh, the Child Star, symbolic of strong-heartedness and loyalty. The Star of First Birds was purity of intention and the Third flew near to the roots of the Tree of the Worm, so her Child Star attributes were affected—or distracted—by holy thoughts just as much as unseen decay. Her father said the influence of the Worm in this case meant Elia would always be changing others or the world in ways she could not see or predict. Elia wondered if holy bones or some other wormwork might have a different answer, but Lear refused to taint his royal star readings with such base matters, so she couldn't say. To him, the stars were beyond reproach, disconnected from death, filth, animal lust, or instinct. All the magic of the world existed beneath the stars, and beneath them magic should remain.

*Ban would know which tree to ask,* Elia thought, then covered her lips with her fingers as if she'd spoken aloud. That name needed be banished from her heart forever, as the boy himself had been banished years ago.

Disloyalty and longing twisted together in the back of her throat. It went against her instincts to deny herself even the memory of him, yet for so long, she'd done exactly that. She breathed deeply and imagined the feelings diffuse out of her with every breath, making her cool and calm as a star. Singular. Pure. Apart. She had learned long ago that stray passions needed to be leashed.

It was difficult, for Elia was a daughter of Lear. All her family were born of the same material, and all tended toward high emotions: Gaela, the eldest, wore her anger and disdain like armor; Regan was a skillful manipulator of her own heart as well as the hearts of others; and the king caught his grief and leftover love up in layers of rigid rules, though they never quite contained him. Elia, unfortunately, had loved too easily as a child: the island, her family, and *him,* the wind and roots and stars. But love was messy. Only the stars were constant, and so it was better to be exactly what her father wanted: loyal, strong, pure starlight. A saint for Innis Lear, rather than a third princess.

Thus was she able to bear the weight of Gaela's disappointed glares, and answer Regan's sly mocking with simple courtesy. She was able to swallow her longings and her worries and any joy, too, as well as the enduring sorrow that her sisters did not care for her at all. She was able to bear up under the weight of Lear's rages and soothe him instead of lashing out to make things worse as Gaela and Regan did. Able to expel any strong emotion by scattering it in the sunlight like fog off a lake, until everything she felt was naught but starry reflections.

"There," Elia whispered to herself now, as between one blink and the next, she caught the sparkle of the distant Star of First Birds. It was only a shimmer of light, and Elia stopped breathing to steady her gaze, wishing she could still the tremble of her heart, too, for one perfect moment.

"Elia!"

Twisting to peer down toward the steep southern road and the call of her name, Elia at first saw nothing but a distant flock of tiny swifts, darting close to the ground. Then she spied her companion Aefa waving at her with both arms, and beyond, a rider leaning over his saddle to press onward for the star tower's courtyard. A star-shaped breastplate gleamed in the final evening light, belted across his dark blue gambeson to mark him a soldier of the king. From the back of his saddle rose a trio of flags: one the white swan of Lear, one the maroon crown of Burgun, and one the plain orange field that belonged to the king of Aremoria.

Letters.

Elia touched a hand to the undyed collar of her dress, the space just over her heart. The last letter from her father was folded there, hidden between seam and skin. It had arrived the day before yesterday; the words he had written were not worrisome in themselves, as they were but the usual, dear ramblings he sent and had always sent. Filled with his own star chart calculations, gossip from the Summer Seat, irritation at his first daughter's martial interests, and sneers at the temper of his second son-in-law; and yet this one was far different from any that had come before.

*Dalat, my dear,* he had scrawled in his swooping, casual hand.

Elia's mother, who had been dead these twelve years.

The shape of the name remained, sharp enough to break a daughter's heart.

Getting to her feet and stuffing the parchment back into her bag of charts, Elia reluctantly turned south, picking her way down to the road. She'd much rather have remained and done her work, but knowing a new letter waited would distract her and she'd lose count, lose the patterns threaded across the sky even as she dutifully wrote them down. Never mind the letters from those other kings, Burgun and Aremoria, courting her for their politics and war. Such things did not concern her: Elia would never wed, she'd long ago determined. Both her sisters had contentious marriages: Gaela because her husband was a beast, though one Gaela had chosen for herself, and Regan because her lord's family was a generations-old enemy of the house of Lear, a threat Regan would gladly lose herself inside.

No, Elia would marry only the stars, live her life as a solitary priest, and care for her ailing father, never in danger from too much earthly love.

This latest deluded salutation from Lear was even more proof of that danger. When their mother had died, their father lost his heart, and with it everything that kept his mind at ease and actions in balance. Her sisters had turned ever more inward, away from both Lear and Elia. The island, too, seemed to have withdrawn, offering less abundant harvests and giving more weight to the cold, cutting wind. All in mourning for the lost, much-loved queen.

*Dalat, my dear.*

The star signs these past nights had offered Elia no comfort, no guidance, though Elia had charted every corner of the sky. *Can I save my Lear?* she had asked again and again.

No answer had emerged, though she wrote down and dismissed a dozen smaller prophecies: *the storm is coming; a lion will not eat your heart; you will give birth to the children of saints; the rose of choice will bloom with ice and rage.* They meant nothing. There was no star called the Rose of Choice, only a Rose of Decay and a Rose of Light. Lions had never lived on Innis Lear. Earth saints had long ago left the world. And there were always, always storms at the end of summer.

The only way to piece out the true answer was to ask the trees, listen to the voices in the wind, or sip of rootwater. This was the wisdom of Innis Lear.

Elia stopped, recalling the feel of her bare toes digging into the rough grass, sliding her fingers over the ground to hunt up crickets or fat iridescent beetles.

She remembered once Ban had taken her hand in his own and then placed a brilliant green beetle onto her finger like an emerald ring. She'd giggled at the tickling insect legs, but not let go, looking up into his eyes:

green and brown and shining just like the beetle's shell. *A pearl of the earth for a star of the sky,* he'd said in the language of trees.

In truth, she hardly remembered how to whisper words the earth could understand. It had been so long since she'd shut herself off, swearing to never speak their language again.

So long since he'd been gone.

Darkness veiled the dusty white road as Elia finally arrived: the sun was entirely vanished and no moon risen, and the star tower did not light torches that would ruin the night-sight of their priests.

Aefa stood at the shoulder of the messenger's horse, arguing to be given the letters. But the soldier said, clearly not for the first time, "I will give these only to the priest Danna or the princess herself."

"And so here I am," Elia said. She need prove herself in no way other than her presence; there were no other women who looked like her and her sisters, not across all of Innis Lear. Not any longer. Not for half her life.

"Lady." The messenger bowed. He began to unseat himself, but Elia shook her head.

"No need, sir, if you'd like to ride on. I'll take my letters, and you're welcome at the tower for simple food and simpler accommodations, or you have just enough light to return to Dondubhan and sleep in those barracks. Only wait there for my responses in the morning before you depart."

"I thank you, princess," he said, taking the letters from the saddle box.

She reached up to accept and asked his name, a habit from her youth in the castles. He told her and thanked her, and she and Aefa backed out of his way as he turned his horse and nudged it quicker on the road to the barracks.

Elia wandered toward the star tower with her letters, studying the three seals. The leather bag carrying her charts and frame, candle-mirrors and charcoal sticks, pressed heavily on her shoulder, and she finally slumped it off, settling herself down on the slope of moor beside it.

"Did you spy your star?" Aefa asked, herself gangly and pretty, like a fresh hunting hound, with plain white skin tending toward rose under heightened emotion and chestnut hair bound up in curling ribbons. Unlike Elia's gray wool dress, the uniform of a star priest, Aefa wore bright yellow and an overdress in the dark blue of Lear's household.

"Yes," Elia murmured, still staring at the letters.

A long moment passed. She could not choose one to open.

"Elia! Let me have them." She held out her hand, and Elia gave over the letters from Burgun and Aremoria.

Clearing her throat, Aefa tore through the Burgun seal, unfolded the letter, and then sneezed. "There's—there's perfume on it, oh stars."

Elia rolled her eyes, as Aefa clearly wished her to, and then the Fool's daughter held the letter to the last of the twilight and began to read.

"*My dear, I hope, Princess of Lear*— Elia, he is so forward! And trying not to be by acknowledging it, so you must in some way give permission or not! —*I confess I have had report from an agent of mine as to your gentle, elegant beauty*— What is elegant beauty, do you think? A deer, or a reaching willow tree? Really, I wonder that he does not provide some poetic comparison. Burgun has no imagination—*your gentle, elegant beauty, and I cannot wait many more months to witness it myself. I have recently been defeated in battle, but thoughts of you hold my body and my honor upright though all else should weigh upon my heart*— His body upright, indeed; I know what part of his body he means, and it's very indelicate of him!"

"Aefa!" The princess laughed, smothering it with her hands.

Aefa quirked her mouth and wrinkled her nose, skimming the letter silently. "Burgun is all flattery, and then, despite telling you he's been trumped on the battlefield, he still finds ways to suggest he is handsome and virile, and perhaps a wifely partner would complete his heart enough to . . . well to make him a better soldier. *Affectionately, passionately yours, Ullo of Burgun.* Worms of earth, I don't like him. So on to the king of Aremoria. I wonder if Ullo knows the general who defeated him also pays court to you."

Elia drew her knees near to her chest and tilted her head to listen better. The letter from Lear pressed between her two hands, trapped.

"*Lady Elia*, writes Morimaros, which I approve of much better. Simple. An elegantly beautiful salutation, if I may say so. *Lady Elia, In my last letter I made it known I was nearing the end of my campaign against the claim of Burgun*— This king refuses to even give Burgun the title *kingdom*! What a pretty slight. Certainly this king knows who *his* rival is—*against the claim of Burgun and can report now on the eve of what I believe to be our final confrontation that I will win, and am sure this shift in political lines will too shift the direction of your thoughts. In Aremoria's favor, I expect, but if not, let me add we have a nearly unprecedented harvest this year, in the south of barley and*— Elia! My stars! There is now a list of Aremore crops! He says nothing of his hopes for you, nothing about himself! Do we even know what sort of books he enjoys or philosophies he holds? At least Burgun treats you like a woman, not a writing exercise."

"Are you swinging toward favoring Burgun, then?" Elia asked lightly.

Turning her back to the silver light still clinging to the mountains in the west, Aefa shot her princess a narrow look and held the letter toward her. Elia could see it consisted of three perfectly lined paragraphs. Aefa pulled the paper right to her face and read, "*I have petitioned to your father that*

*I be welcomed in Innis Lear in the near future, that you might look upon me and perhaps tell me something of my stars.* Oh. Oh, Elia, well there. That is his final line, and perhaps he is not so dry as everything. His signature is the same as before. *Yours, Aremoria King.* I dislike that so very vehemently. Not his name, even, but his grand old title. It's like your sister refusing to call Connley anything but Connley, when everyone knows he has a name his mother gave him."

Elia closed her eyes. "It is not a letter from a man to a woman, but from a crown to the daughter of a crown. It stirs me not at all, but it is at least honest."

The huff of Aefa's skirts as she plopped to the earth beside her princess spoke all the volumes necessary.

"And your father's letter?" Aefa asked quietly.

"You might as well light a candle. I'm done star gazing tonight." Elia danced her fingers along the edge of the letter; it was so thin, one parchment page only, when it was not unusual for her father's letters to be five or six pages, thickly folded. From the leather bag, Aefa dug out a thin candle and a candle-cradle attached to a small, bent mirror. She whispered a word in the language of trees, snapped her fingers, and a tiny flame appeared. Elia pressed her lips in disapproval as she snapped the letter's wax seal in two, cracking the midnight blue swan through the wings. Aefa set the candle into its cradle so that the flame lit the mirror. This device was meant to illuminate star charts while keeping brightness from the eyes of the priests who needed to stare high and higher into the darkest heavens. In Aefa's hands, it angled all the light onto the letter and Lear's scrawl of writing.

*Elia, my star—*

For a moment the youngest princess could not continue, overwhelmed with her relief. The words shook before her eyes. Elia took a fortifying breath and charged on. She murmured the contents of the letter aloud to Aefa: "*Our long summer's absence is at an end. Come home for the Zenith Court, this third noontime after the Throne rises clear. The moon is full then, and will bless my actions. I shall do for my daughters what the stars have described, finally, and all beings shall in their proper places be set. Your suitors are invited, too, for we would meet them and judge them. Your beloved father and king.*"

"That's all?" Aefa said, rather incredulous. She pressed her face to Elia's cheek, to get a look at the letter. "When is that? The Throne is part of the Royal sequence, and they began a month ago . . . it's the . . . second? After the Hound of Summer? So . . ."

"Six days," Elia said. "The Zenith Court will be six days from now, when the moon is full."

"Why can't he just say, *come on the Threesday of next week*? And what does he mean? *All beings in their proper place*? Will he finally name Gaela his heir? That'll set the island off, though it's inevitable. She has to be crowned someday."

Elia folded the letter. "I hope so. Then in the winter we can have a new queen. Before Father loses his faculties, before his continued hesitation breeds more intrigue and plotting." She turned her eyes toward the west again, where the vibrant diamond of the Star of First Birds should gleam.

But the star was shrouded by a single long strip of black cloud cutting across the sky like a sword.

# REGAN

IN THE EMERALD east of Innis Lear lounged the family seat of the Dukes Connley, a castle of local white limestone and blue slate imported from Aremoria. At only a hundred years old, it was the youngest of the castle seats, built around the old black keep from which Connley lords of old once ruled. No city filled the space between its walls, nor abutted the sides, though the next valley south flourished with people devoted to the duke, as did the valleys to the north and west. None could deny the Connley line was expert at inspiring loyalty.

Perhaps because the Connleys were defiantly and fixedly loyal to themselves. Perhaps because they continued to study wormwork and respect the language of trees, despite the king's decrees. Or perhaps only because they were so beautiful, and strove to reflect such personal attributes in their castles and roads and local tax policies.

Connley Castle itself consisted of three concentric, towered walls, each higher and lovelier than the last, and in the center a new, white keep faced the old, black one, matching it stone for stone. At least externally, as the guts of the black keep had long since crumbled. Trees grew up from its center; vines and creeping flowers had taken over arrow slits and arched doorways. The cobbles had cracked, surrendered to the earth more than a generation ago. One ancient oak flourished at the very heart of the keep. It had been planted by one of the lords for the pillar of his throne room, back in the days when baser magic topped the island, and few cared for the path of stars. There, the wife of the current Duke Connley kept her shrines and working altars. And it was there she now knelt, stricken, among those winding old roots, surrounded by a bright pool of her own blood.

Regan, the second daughter of Lear, had come to the shady courtyard to listen to the whispers of the island trees and to recast the quarter blessings that rooted her magic to Innis Lear. Each altar was created with a slab of rock—carried by her own hands from a corner of the island in the four great directions—settled against the crumbling stone walls with permission from the oak, tied down through three seasons of growth and decay. Their lines of magic crossed through the heart of the oak tree, and its roots dove deep enough into the bedrock of the island to hear the other powerful trees, to pass Regan's words, and to collect for her the concerns, complaints, and hopes of all who still spoke through the wind.

These days there were many complaints, and while her altar blessings should have lasted a full year, the island's magic had become so withdrawn she had to bless the altars at the turn of every season. She needed living rootwater, but such holy wells were forbidden and Regan had to rely upon the witch of the White Forest for a steady supply.

Recasting and blessing the altars was the work of an afternoon, and Regan had just moved on to the final altar in the east when she felt the first twinge at the small of her back.

She paused, telling herself she'd imagined it, and had remained kneeling before the eastern altar. But the language of trees would not spring to her lips easily; Regan's attention was all for her womb, waiting, hardly able to breathe.

The delicate thread of nausea might've been overlooked by one unused to such things. But Regan had been through this before, and so followed the nausea as it turned over into a knot between her hips, then pulled tight.

The princess's cool brown hands began to tremble. She knew this pain well, and how to hold rigid until it passed.

And pass it did, but not without leaving that ache behind, an echo of itself that radiated down the backs of her thighs and up her spine, hot and cold and hot again.

"No," Regan hissed, scraping her nails too hard on the stone altar. One cracked, and that pain she welcomed. Her breath caught like a broken necklace, dragging up, up, up, and chattering her teeth. She bared them in rage and forced her breathing into long, slow rolls.

Was it her? Was this failure some greater symptom of the island cracking?

Any beast could be a mother—there were babes in nests and hovels and barnyards. It was only Regan who seemed unable to join them.

When the next cramp caught her, she cried out, shoved away from the altar, and curled tightly over her knees. She whispered to herself that she was healthy and well and most of all strong, as if she could change what happened next by ordering her body to obey her.

A pause in the pain left her panting, but Regan ground her teeth and stood up on her bare feet. Though preferring quite formal attire, even in her husband's castle, Regan had come to the altars today in only the thinnest red wool dress and no underthings. She'd left her slippers outside the arched gate and untied the ribbons from her wavy brown hair, allowing it to spill past her waist. Hers was the longest, straightest hair of her sisters, and her skin the lightest, though still a very cool brown. There was the most of their father, Lear, in her looks: the shape of his knifelike lips, and flecks of Lear's blue lightened his daughter's chestnut eyes.

Regan walked carefully to the ropey old oak tree to pray, her hands on two thick roots. *I am as strong as you,* she said in the language of trees. *I will not break. Help me now, mother, help me. I am strong.*

The tree sighed, its bulk shivering so that the high, wide leaves cast dappled shadows about like rain in a storm.

Regan went to the northern altar and cut the back of her wrist with a stone dagger, bleeding into a shallow bowl of wine. *Take this blood from me instead,* she whispered, pouring the bloody wine over the altar, where *north root* was etched in the language of trees. The maroon liquid slid into the rough grooves, turning the words dark. *Take this, and let me get to my room where my mothers' milk tonic is, where my husband—*

The princess's voice cut away at the sensation of blood slipping out of her, tickling her inner thighs with dishonest tenderness.

She returned to the grand oak tree on slow legs, sat on the earth between two roots, and slumped over herself. Despair overwhelmed her every thought, as hope and strength dripped out of her on the heels of this treacherous blood.

The sun lowered itself in the sky until only the very crown of the oak was gilded. The courtyard below was a cold mess of shadows and silver twilight. Regan shivered, despite tears hot in her eyes. In these slow hours she allowed herself a grief she would deny if confronted by any but her elder sister. Grief, and shame, and a cord of longing for her mother who died when she was fourteen. Dalat had birthed three healthy girls, had done it as far away from her own land and god and people as a woman could get. And Regan was here among the roots and rocks of her home. She should have been—should have been able.

The earth whispered quiet, harsh sighs; Regan heard the rush of blood in her ears and through the veins of the tree. She saw only the darkness of her own closed eyes, and smelled only the thick, musty scent of her womb blood.

"Regan, are you near?"

It was the sharp voice of her husband. She put her hands on her head and dug her nails in, gripped her hair and tore until it hurt.

His boots crunched through the scattered grasses, over fallen twigs and chunks of stone broken off the walls.

"I've been looking for you everywhere, wife," he said, in a tone more irritable than he usually directed at her. "There's a summons from your . . . Regan." Connley said her name in a hush of horror.

She could not look up at him, even as she sensed him bend beside her, too close, and grasp her shoulders to lift her up off her knees. "Regan," he said again, all tenderness and tight fear.

Her eyes opened slowly, sticky with half-dried tears, and she allowed him to straighten her. She leaned into him, and suddenly her ankles were cold where air caressed streaks of dark red and brown, left from her long immersion in blood and earth.

"Oh no," Connley said. "No."

The daughter of the king drew herself up, for she was empty again now, and without pain. She was cold and hungry and appreciated the temporary bliss of detachment. "I am well, Connley," she said, using him as a prop to stand. Her toes squished in the bloody earth. Regan shuddered but spoke true:

"It is over."

Connley stood with her, blood on the knee of his fine trousers, the letter from her father crushed against the oak tree's root, forgotten. He was a handsome, sun-gilded man, with copper in his short blond hair. His chin was beardless, for he had nothing to hide and charm enough in his smile for a dozen wives. But now Connley had gone sallow and rigid from upset, his smile sheathed. He put his hands on Regan's face, touched thumbs to old tears just where her skin was the most delicate purple, beneath her eyes. "Regan," he whispered again, disappointed. Not with her, never with her, but still, that was how it sounded to her ears.

She tore free of him, storming toward the eastern altar that had not been blessed this afternoon. With one bare foot, she shoved and kicked at it, jaw clenched, hands in fists, hair wild and the tips of it tinged with blood. What was wrong with her? In the language of trees, she cried, *What is wrong with all of us?*

It was her father's fault. When he'd killed Dalat, he'd killed their entire line.

"Stop, stop!" Connley ordered, grabbing her from behind. He grasped her wrists and crossed them over her chest. He held her tightly, his cheek to her hair. She felt his hard breath blowing past her ear, ragged and unchecked. His chest against her back heaved once, and twice, then his arms jerked tighter before he released his stranglehold, but did not quite let her go. They slumped together.

"I cannot see what's wrong with me," Regan said, her head hanging. She turned her hands to hold his. All her hair fell around her face, tangling with their clasped hands. She gazed at the altar, which she had only shifted slightly askew. "I have tried potions and begged the trees; I have done everything that every mother and grandmother of the island would tell me. Three months ago I visited Brona Hartfare and I thought—" She sobbed pure air, letting it out rough and raw. "I thought this time we would catch, we would hold on, but it will never now. My thighs are sticky with the brains of our babe, Connley, and I want to rip out my insides and bury it all here. I am nothing but bones and desperation."

He unlatched his hands and turned her toward him, gathering her hair in one fist. "This is the only thing that makes you speak in poetry, my heart. If it were not so terrible, I would call it endearing."

"I must find a way to see inside myself! To find the core of what curses me."

"It might be a thing wrong with me. More than a mother is required to get a strong child."

Regan scratched her fingers down the fine scarlet of his jacket, tearing at the wool, the velvet lining the edge. "It is me. You know the stars I was born under; you know my empty fate." When she said it, her father's voice echoed in her memory.

"That is your father talking, Regan."

She reeled back and slapped him for daring to notice. The edge of his high cheek turned pink as he studied her with narrowed, blue-green eyes. Regan knew the look in them: the desire, the scrutiny. She touched his lips and met his gaze. He was a year younger than her, ambitious and lacking kindness, and Regan loved him wildly. Every sign she could read in those damnable stars, every voice in the wind and along the great web of island roots had cried *yes* when she asked if Connley was for her. But this was her fourth miscarriage in nearly five years of marriage. Plus the one before they'd been married at all.

Connley drew her hair over one shoulder, kissed her finger as it lingered on his bottom lip.

"I don't know what to do," the princess said.

"What we always do," her lover replied. "Come inside and bathe, drink a bit of wine, and fight on. We will achieve what we desire, Regan, make no mistake. Your father's reign will end, and we will return Innis Lear to glory. We will open the navel wells and invite the trees to sing, and we will be blessed for it. Our children will be the next kings of Innis Lear. I swear it to you, Regan." Connley turned, his eyes scouring the darkening courtyard. Though Regan did not wish to release him, she did. She stared as he picked his way back to the oak tree and lifted up the letter. It was crumpled now, torn at one corner. He offered it to her.

Regan smoothed the paper between her hands and lifted it to the bare, hanging light of dusk.

> *Daughter,*
>
> *Come to the Summer Seat for a Zenith Court, this third noontime after the Throne rises clear, when the moon is full. As the stars describe now, I shall set all my daughters in their places.*
>
> 

*Your father and king,*

*Lear*
> 

"Would I could arrive heavy with child," Regan murmured, touching her belly. Connley put his hand over the top of hers and moved it lower to the bloody stain. He cupped her hand gently around herself.

"We will go heavy with other things," he said. "Power, wit, righteousness."

"Love," she whispered.

"Love," he repeated, and kissed her mouth.

As Regan returned her husband's kiss, she thought she heard a whisper from the oak tree: *blood,* it said, again and again. She could not tell if the tree thanked her for the grave sustenance she'd fed its roots, or offered the word as warning of things to come.

Perhaps, as was often the case with the language of trees, the word held both meanings—and more too unknowable to hear.

# GAELA

THE CREAK OF the war tower was like thunder in her blood. Gaela Lear ground her teeth against too-wide a grin, feeling like a child, gleeful and alive as she played with her toys.

But these were not a child's trinkets, they were dangerous siege weapons, marring the valley with their mechanical violence. To this eldest daughter of the king, commander of Astora's forces, they were more than mere tools: they were her treasures.

Gaela raised her gauntleted hand in a fist, then swung it down hard. Archers clinging to the inner scaffolds of the war tower loosed arrows at the targets set atop the ruined castle wall ahead, while the men hidden at the base pushed it inexorably nearer, crushing soft green grass and stinging thistles beneath its huge wheels. Wood and taut wet wool protected the soldiers from any retaliation, or it would have, if the ruined castle were in truth alive with enemy archers and men throwing rocks and flaming spears.

When the tower landed against the ruined old wall, archers covered soldiers as they leapt out to secure it in place, so a horde of miners could then rush in and use the shelter to dig beneath the twelve-foot-thick wall, until the earth was weak enough to collapse under the weight of it.

Gaela raised her hand again, signaling the nearest block of her retainers to charge, with ladders and shields high. Their screams filled the summer air like a storm. Gaela allowed herself to smile proudly as they slammed into the ruins, climbing up and pouring over the crumbled ramparts, never flagging in their enthusiastic cries.

She gritted her teeth then, wishing this were real battle, not mere posturing and practice. At her back, a ballista was mounted to the platform of a cart, capable of swinging in any direction to aim its heavy bolts. She had six of them ready, and a half dozen more were being fitted with wheels for enhanced mobility. In addition to the fifty who charged the wall, three hundred soldiers and retainers stood in rank surrounding her, in the dark pink of the Duke Astore, their mail bright as moonlight and their bucklers polished, their swords naked and pointed at the sky like the teeth of a massive sea snake. It was an impressive force, and only a fraction of the army she'd command under the crown of Innis Lear. These men all wore her husband's colors, but their loyalty belonged to her.

She did not turn her head toward the east, where folk from the nearest town had come to see the ruckus. That town sat across the border of Astore lands, on the Connley side, and Gaela hoped the people crouched behind rough limestone boulders and shuddering with the skinny trees of the ridge would spread tales of this afternoon. The moment Gaela was king, they should be prepared to submit to her, or face these very men and these very war machines.

She'd chosen this location not only for the nearness of Brideton and the border, but for the ruin specifically. It had been a Glennadoer castle stronghold three hundred years ago, before the island united under the Learish dynasty. The Glennadoers had promoted so much magic in their bloodline all others had joined together to defeat them. Glennadoers still lived now, but confined in the far north, and powerful in name only. Though they leaned toward Connley in loyalty, they were earls under the banner of Astora. This ruined castle symbolized the strength they'd lost, both by opposing a united island and by thinking magic could protect them.

Gaela's smile turned scornful. *Look at this beautiful valley, rough and growing lush despite the holy well capped off just to the north.* It was only superstition that had sent the island folk scrambling in a panic when the king ordered all such wells closed ten years ago. When she was king, she would allow towns to open their wells again if they liked, but keep the castle wells closed except on holidays, a sign of her generosity to an easily awed populace. She did not need the rootwaters, but neither did she fear them as her father did. Neither wormwork nor star prophecy made Gaela strong: she did that all herself.

"Withdraw!" she yelled to her soldiers who'd cleared the wall, knocking down targets and hanging the Astore banner: a dark pink field with a white salmon leaping over a trio of four-point stars. "Solin, you and your men reset the tower; the rest of you form up for a melee. I want to see broken shields, and for everyone in Brideton across that hill to hear your roar!"

The soldiers cried and growled, banging their bucklers against hard leather chest pieces to cause a swell of noise. She laughed, and they jumped into action at her signal.

The broad blue sky glinted off Gaela's chainmail hood, pulled up over the tighter linen hood that protected her twists of thick black hair from the shifting metal. Her dark brown eyes narrowed as that same sun glared off the sea of blades and bucklers turning the valley into a meadow of steel. Gaela posed for a moment at the edge of it, hands at her hips, boot heels dug into the damp earth. She was tall but not broad, though she'd spent her life encouraging muscles where few women wanted them. Her posture could have her mistaken for a man from behind, a resemblance Gaela appreciated.

Gaela had been anxious as a child about how different she looked from all the people of Innis Lear: her deep brown skin and thick black curls made her too easy to identify. Everywhere she went, she was not only the heir to the throne, the black princess, but that dreaded first daughter prophesied by the unrelenting stars to be her mother's death. A son would not have born such a burden. But Gaela could not escape her body, her stars, or the prophecy.

When she was six years old, she'd destroyed a stack of thin songbooks imported from Aremoria. All the beautiful ladies in the songs were pale as the moon or soft as cream or sunlight on sand. Dalat and the Fool had been learning them together, a favored pastime while the king himself focused on the alliances necessary to open the docks at Port Comlack to wider trade. Gaela had told the Fool that if he did not compose a song about the queen's dark beauty, she would gut him with his flute. So the queen and the Fool had taken Gaela and her younger sister Regan on a long walk, cataloguing all the pieces of the natural world he might put in his poem for Dalat.

The Fool was an imbecile, bringing pink flowers and bright yellow butterfly wings to little Regan, teasing her and trying to tease Gaela, too. She remembered it still, always with a scowl. *Are there green undertones in your mother, do you think? Let's compare . . .* Dalat smiled and tilted her head to allow the young man to brush a leaf to her cheek until Regan declared a babyish yay or nay. Gaela had been more determined, more precise. She had gathered walnut bark and a deep purple flower, smooth black river rocks, gleaming acorns, a shining crow feather, and a feather mottled rich brown from an eagle's wing. The last her mother had accepted like riches, and woven the quill into the tight knot of braids at the base of her neck. *Like my grandmother's imperial crest,* Dalat smilingly declared. It stood out like a horn, or a slender, delicate wing all its own. *It's still not right,* Gaela had said angrily. The Fool sang, *Poetry is about perception, little princess, not accuracy. It is about what it* means *to compare the Queen's dark and curving mouth to a powerful eagle's wing.* Then her mother took Gaela's hand, spread it out against her own, and said, *This is the only match that matters.*

But Dalat was dead, the Fool attached like a wart to the king, and Gaela had no use for poems. Poems did not create power, and Gaela intended to be king when her terrible father died, or sooner. Nothing would stop her.

The urgency of the soldiers now thrummed in Gaela's bones, lending satisfaction to her resolve. She wished she could march with her army to the Summer Seat, drag her father to his knees, and take the crown. How her satisfaction would grow at the sight of him bowed before her, trembling and afraid. *Did my mother die on her knees?* Gaela would ask. *Did you touch poison to her lips with a kiss, or put it in her nightly mug of warm honeyed milk? Did you ever trust me as she trusted you?* Of course, he never trusted anyone or anything except the vicious stars. And so Gaela would thrust her sword into his neck, and watch as he gasped and gargled, as he sank into an undignified pool of blood at her feet.

But no matter how she longed to take the crown in such a way, it was not the most direct, most efficient, or even most secure path. No, the people of Lear took their king-making seriously, claiming them fast and hewing hard to the anointment and the secret, specific traditions of the island's roots. Gaela would have to bide her time, wait for the king to name her his heir, and then give the island her blood and spit on the longest night of the year. As was right.

To do it by any other method would invite Connley to challenge her— curse him, his ancestors, and his perfect stars, and curse Regan for marrying into that line and giving the dog a stronger claim. Though Gaela wanted war, wanted a chance to release all the fury and aggression inside her heart more than most anything, she did not want a war with her sister on the opposite side.

So here Gaela Lear stood, amidst her personal army, performing for the folk on Connley's border, sending a brutal message without quite making a firm challenge.

The soldiers had formed up for the melee. With a ferocious smile, Gaela abandoned her perch and ran to join them. Her movement served as signal, and the two sides slammed together, all yelling and chaos, with some few laughing as Gaela laughed. She drew her sword and aimed for the nearest soldier; he had plenty of time to block with his buckler and sword, but the force of her charge shoved him back. She bared her teeth and twisted, shoving at him with all her might. He spun, and Gaela dove farther into the battle.

A flash of light to her left had Gaela turning hard, lifting her own buckler as she dodged under the attack and slammed the edge into her attacker's face. It caught his helmet with a clang, and he stumbled back, falling hard. Gaela swung around, just in time to see the next attack.

She lost herself in the frenzy of danger, in the cuts and blocks, in the fight to prove herself. She kept on as the battle raged, her teeth clenched, alert, pounding again and again toward the center of the horde. Pain jolted through Gaela's body with most blocks; she cried out; she screamed. She reveled. This was the nearest she'd come to war, to the desperation and danger: some men would die in this game, and some would be injured too badly to fight again for a long while. Their swords should be blunted, or wrapped. This should be less deadly, but Gaela did not care. She would survive, and she would win, today and tomorrow. It was not reckless. It was vital. Her husband could never understand how this brought her to life as nothing else did, how she needed the immediacy of this danger. This—*this*—brought her to the edge of her strength, made her feel the mettle she possessed in the very core of her bones. When she fought, Gaela knew she did not need any root blessing or star prophecy.

She was born to be king.

Suddenly, Gaela found herself in a break of soldiers, facing one man. This soldier was huge, blond-bearded with pocked scars on his young pink cheeks, and clearly he had built his uniform from castoffs that did not quite fit. His sword and buckler were borrowed from the Astore armory, and they were stamped as such. But he did not take his eyes from hers, even when she lifted her chin so the sun caught the red blood at the corner of her mouth. She smiled, and it smeared her teeth.

He planted his feet in a very strong defensive pose.

Gaela dropped her buckler and attacked.

Her two-handed grip gave her strength and leverage, which mattered as his size negated any reach advantage she'd have gained by fighting with her shield.

Blood roared in her ears, and she shouldered in past his block, nearly bashing his cheek with her pommel before he twisted and shoved her back hard enough she stumbled. With a spin from the inertia, she drove hard again, hacking at his sword, each clang of metal filling her heart with joy. He was good, using his weight, but still slower than she was. Soon they were the only fighters, all others watching the show.

It was brief but glorious, and Gaela risked a low cut up under his reach, so enthralled she was with the rhythm of their game. He blocked it, chopping with his buckler so the reinforced edge caught her upper arm, numbing the entire limb. She cried out, shocked, and dropped her sword from that hand. It swung off-balance in her other and the man pressed his advantage as she valiantly blocked again, again, and then with his boot he stomped on her thigh.

Gaela went down.

The soldier dropped everything to catch her arm, lifting her to her feet again in a smooth gesture.

He did not hold on when she was steady, and the entire movement appeared so natural, so easy, the gathered soldiers cheered.

Gaela liked a soldier who would win and still save her face. The fingers of her shield arm tingled as blood rushed back into them. Gaela sheathed her sword and rubbed her hands together, smiling for her opponent and all the soldiers. "Well fought, man. Give me your name, that I might invoke it when I speak with my husband."

"Dig," the large young man replied.

She lifted her thin eyebrows. "No other?"

"None, lady."

"Then, Dig of Astora, welcome to my army."

Just then, a horn sounded from the ridge to the west. Gaela clasped Dig's wrist, then released him and strode heavily toward the camp. Her body ached with weariness, but she was glad of it.

Osli jogged up, chainmail ringing with the movement. The captain pushed her hair out of her face, dragging it through sweat, and said, "Lady, should I order the end of the games today, or do you want them to run the tower drill again?"

"Drill once more, then have the beer shared out here on the field before everyone returns to camp." The princess smiled at her young captain, a girl of only nineteen with nearly as much ambition as Gaela herself. "Then you should join me for whatever news comes with this horn, and we'll share wine while we plan tomorrow's games. Bring that Dig soldier, and choose two more exemplary men to reward."

Osli nodded sharply and darted off as Gaela climbed the steeper section of the hill, reaching the long flat plain on the crest where her army had set up camp. Most tents were simple single-pole shelters or lean-tos, ringed wide about fire pits. The supply wagons made a crescent at the south end, and smoke rose there as folk cooked a hearty meal. Fifty men and women and ten wagons to keep her three hundred soldiers tended and fed for this weeklong campaign. She'd ordered them to act as though the supply from Astora City had been cut off, as it might be in real war.

Her eye caught the trio of horses stamping near her tent, a much larger canvas shelter with seven poles and crowned by the Astore banner. One of the horses was her own, its head lowered and rear hoof up in relaxation, but the other two were still dressed and saddled, eagerly drinking from the trough set before them. They were Astore's horse and one of his stewards'.

Gaela looked all around, and spied him there, a good distance from her, atop a promontory where he'd have a good view of the valley below. Likely he'd witnessed only the final moments of the melee, and now was eying her towers and bastilla.

She made for her tent to divest herself of mail and gauntlets with one of the apprentices, denying her husband the pleasure. A boy in a pink tabard waited at the entrance, and she dragged him in so he could undo the buckles under her left arm that held her small chest plate over the mail.

It was not quick work, and Astore slapped open the tent just as the heavy mail shirt finally slipped off her head and into the waiting arms of the apprentice boy.

"Get out," Astore said fondly, filling the front of the tent. Fifteen years older than his wife, he was blond and wore it long, in a plain, straight tail. Though he was certainly not ugly, Gaela found it difficult to judge his attractiveness, as she found such things difficult with all people. He was fit and strong, a good war leader, which had brought him to her notice in the first place. He wore a trim blond beard, his light brown eyes were edged in wrinkles, and his skin was as white as hers was black. Save the pink patches from staying too long on the sunny castle ramparts with his retainers.

Gaela stripped the linen hood off her hair as he stared at her. She then went to pour them wine from the low table beside her bed. He always was struck by Gaela when she was disheveled from battle, wearing men's trousers and a soldier's quilted gambeson, with only a smear of dark paint around her eyes. It amused her that he strove to hide the visibility of his sexual interest as best he was able, lest it cause her to turn cold. Gaela could always see it. She knew the signs, and she pushed at them when she was feeling mean. Their marriage bed was a contentious one.

"Wife," he said, accepting the clay cup of wine. She saw a letter with the swan of Lear waiting unopened in his other hand, and she sipped her wine in silence. Her heart still thrummed with the energy and joy of battle.

Astore moved around her to sit in the only chair, a heavy armchair rather like a throne that Gaela brought with her always. He watched her carefully as he drank nearly all his wine. She did not move, waiting. Finally, Astore said, "You're reckless, setting your men against each other with sharp blades."

"Those who are harmed in such games are hardly worthy of riding at my side, nor would I be worthy of the crown, to die so easily."

His grim smile twisted. "I need you alive."

Gaela sniffed, imagining the release she'd feel if she punched him until that smile broke. But she still needed him, too. The Star of the Consort dominated her birth chart, and to those men of Innis Lear she needed on her council and in her pocket, that meant coming to the throne with a husband. Though Gaela longed for war, she was enough of a strategist to know it was better that the island fight outward, not among themselves. For now, she used Astore, though her sister Regan would always be her true consort. "What does Lear want?"

"He wrote to both of us; to me he still refuses to allow reconstruction on the coastal road."

"It isn't in the stars?" she guessed, restraining the roll of her eyes.

"But it is—I commissioned a chart by my own priests. He twists his reasoning around and dismisses what seems to be obvious necessity. Possibly Connley has been whispering in his ear."

"He hates Connley more than you, usually." She sank onto the thick arm of the chair and leaned across Astore's chest for the unopened letter.

Placing his arm just below her elbow in case she needed steadying, but not quite touching her, Astore did not disagree. "I might write to your little sister and ask her for a prophecy regarding the coastal road. Lear has never yet argued with one of hers."

Gaela drank the rest of her wine and set the cup on the rug before cracking the dark blue wax of Lear's seal.

> *Eldest,*
>
> *Come to the Summer Seat for a Zenith Court, this third noontime after the Throne rises clear, when the moon is full. As the stars describe now, I shall set all my daughters in their places.*
>
> 

*Your father and king,*
*Lear*
> 

Grimacing, Gaela dropped the message into Astore's lap. She touched the tip of her tongue to her front teeth, running it hard against their edges. Then she bit down, stoking the anger that always accompanied her father's name. Now it partnered with a thrill that hummed under her skin. She knew her place already: beneath the crown of Lear. But did this mean he would finally agree? Finally begin the process of her ascension?

"Is he ready to take off the crown? And will he see finally fit to hand it to you, as is right?" Astore's hand found her knee, and Gaela stared down at it, hard and unflinching, but her husband only tightened his grip. The three silver rings on his first three fingers flashed: yellow topaz and pink sapphires set bold and bare. They matched Gaela's thumb ring.

She methodically pried his hand off her knee and met his intense gaze. "I will be the next queen of Innis Lear, husband. Never mistake that."

"I never have," he replied. He lifted his hand to grasp her jaw, and Gaela fell still as glass. His fingers pressed hard, daring her to pull away. Instead she pushed nearer, daring him in return to try for a kiss.

Tension strained between them. Astore's breath flew harsher; he wanted her, violently, and for a moment she saw in his eyes the depth of his fury, a rage usually concealed by a benevolent veneer, that his wife constantly and consistently denied his desire. Gaela did not care that he hated her as often as he loved her, but she did care that his priorities always aligned with her own.

Gaela put her hand on Astore's throat and squeezed until he released her. She kissed him hard, then, sliding her knee onto his lap until it forced his thighs apart. Scraping her teeth on his bottom lip, she pulled back, not bothering to hide that the only desire she felt now was to wash off the taint of his longing.

"My queen," the duke of Astore said.

Gaela Lear smiled at his surrender.

# THE FOX

BAN THE FOX arrived at the Summer Seat of Innis Lear for the first time in six years just as he'd left it. Alone.

The sea crashed far below at the base of the cliffs, rough and growling with a hunger Ban had always understood. From this vantage, facing the castle from the sloping village road, he couldn't see the white-capped waves, just the distant stretch of sky-kissed green water toward the western horizon. The Summer Seat perched on a promontory nearly cut off from the rest of Innis Lear, its own island of black stone and clinging weeds connected only by a narrow bridge of land, one that seemed too delicate to take a man safely across. Ban recalled racing over it as a boy, unconcerned with the nauseating death drop to either side, trusting his own steps and the precariously hammered wooden rail. Here, at the landside, a post stone had been dug into the field and in the language of trees it read: *The stars watch your steps.*

Ban's mouth curled into a bitter smile. He placed his first step firmly on the bridge, boots crushing some early seeds and late summer flower petals blown here by the vibrant wind. He crossed, his gloved hand sliding along the oiled-smooth rail.

The wind's whisperings were rough and harsh, difficult for Ban to tease into words. He needed more practice with the dialect, a turn of the moon to bury himself in the moors and remind himself how the trees spoke here, but he'd only arrived back on Innis Lear two days ago. Ban had made his way to Errigal Keep to find his father gone, summoned here to the Summer Seat, and his brother, Rory, away, settled with the king's retainers at Dondubhan. After food and a bath, he'd had a horse saddled from his father's stable. To arrive in time for the Zenith Court, Ban hadn't had the luxury to ride slowly and reacquaint himself with the stones and roots of Innis Lear, nor they with his blood. The horse was now stabled behind him in

Sunton, for horses were not allowed to make the passage on this ancient bridge to the Summer Seat.

At the far end, two soldiers waited with unsharpened halberds. They could use the long axes to nudge any newcomer off the bridge if they chose. When Ban was within five paces, one of them pushed his helmet up off his forehead enough to reveal dark eyes and a straight nose. "Your name, stranger?"

Ban gripped the rail and resisted the urge to settle his right fist on the pommel of the sword sheathed at his belt. "Ban Errigal," he returned, hating that his access would be determined by his family name, not his deeds.

The soldiers waved him through, stepping back from the brick landing that spread welcomingly off the bridge.

A blast of wind shoved Ban forward, and he nearly stumbled. Using the motion to turn, he asked the guard, "Do you know where I might find the Earl Errigal?"

"In the guest tower."

Ban nodded his thanks, glancing at the scathing sun. He did not relish this meeting with his father. Errigal traveled to Aremoria every late spring to visit the Alsax cousins and to be Lear's ambassador. He'd always lavished praise on Ban in front of others, awkwardly labeling his son a bastard at the same time.

Perhaps Ban could eschew the proper order of greeting, and ask instead where the ladies Lear would be this time of day. Six years ago he'd have found Elia with the goats. But it was impossible to imagine she hadn't shifted her routine since childhood. He had changed; so must she have. Grown tall and bright as a daffodil, or worn and weathered like standing stones.

Ban squashed the thought of her hair and eyes, of her hands covered in green beetles. He suspected most of his memories were sweetened by time and brightened with longing, not accurate to what their relationship had truly been. She, the daughter of the king, and he, the bastard son of an earl, could not have been so close as he remembered. Probably the struggle and weariness of being fostered to a foreign army, the homesickness, the dread, the years of uncertainty, had built her into a shining memory no real girl could live up to. Especially one raised by a man like Lear. In his earliest years at war, Ban had thought of Elia to get himself through fear, but it had been a weakness, like the straw doll a baby clings to against nightmares.

Surely she would disdain him now because of the stars at his birth, just as the king had. If she remembered him at all. One more thing to lay at the feet of Lear.

Ban settled his hand on the pommel of his sword. He'd earned himself his own singular epithet. He was here at the Summer Seat not as a cast-off bastard, but as a man in his own right.

Turning a slow circle, Ban made himself change his eyes, to observe the Seat as the Fox.

Men, women, soldiers, and ladies swarmed in what he guessed was an unusual amount of activity. The castle itself was a fortress of rough black stones quarried centuries ago, when the bridge was less crumbled, less tenuous. It rose in a barbican here, spreading into the first wall, then an inner second wall taller than this first, with three central towers, one built against the inner keep. The king's family and his retainers could fit inside for weeks, as well as his servants and the animals necessary to live: goats, pigs, poultry. Barracks, laundry, cliff-hanging privies, the yard, the armory, and the towers: Ban remembered it all from childhood. But it was ugly, old and black and asymmetrical. Built over generations instead of with a singular purpose in mind.

The Fox was impressed with how naturally fortified the promontory was, how difficult it would be to attack. But as he studied his environs, the Fox knew it would be easy to starve out. Surround it landside with an enemy camp, and seaside with boats, and it could be held under siege indefinitely with no more than, say, fifty men.

If one could locate the ancient channel through which spring water flowed onto the promontory, the siege would be mercifully brief. Were he the king of this castle, he'd order a fort built landside, to protect the approach, and use the promontory as a final stand only once all other hope had been lost.

Unless, perhaps, there were caves or unseen ways from the cliffs below where food could be brought in—and there must be. But an enemy could poison the water in the channel, instead of stopping it up. The besieged could not drink seawater. Was there a well inside? Not that Ban could recall from his youth, and it was surely less likely now. This place was a siege death trap, though winning such a battle would be symbolic only: if the Seat were under siege, the rest of the kingdom should already have fallen, and so what would the Seat be against all that?

Ban felt a twisted thrill at the idea of the king of Innis Lear having to make such choices. Better yet if his course here led directly to it.

He went along the main path through the open iron gates and into the inner yard where soldiers clustered and the squawking of chickens warred with hearty conversation, with the cries of gulls hunting for dropped food, the crackle of the yard-hearth where a slew of bakers and maids prepared a feast for the evening. Ban's stomach reacted to the rich smell, but he didn't stop. He strode quickly toward the inner keep, one hand on the pommel of his sword to balance it against his hip. Ban wondered if he could greet his father (he was fairly certain he remembered which was the guest tower) and then find a place to wash, in order to present himself in a fitter state than this: hair tangled from wind, horse-smelling jacket, worn britches, and muddy boots. He'd dumped his mail and armor in Errigal to make a faster showing astride the horse.

A familiar orange flag caught his attention: the royal insignia of Aremoria.

There was a good king. The sort of soldier who took his turn watching for signal lights all night long, digging his own privy pits and rotting his toes off. Who had suffered alongside his men and took his turn in the slops and at the dangerous front. Morimaros of Aremoria did not make choices based on nothing but prophecy.

Across the yard a maroon pennant flapped: the flag of the kingdom of Burgun. Ullo the Pretty. Also come to court Elia Lear, despite, or maybe because of, being trounced in battle.

Ban wondered what she thought of the two kings.

Beyond the second wall, the smell of people, sweat, and animals was crushing. The lower walls had no slits or windows, nothing to move air, and Ban longed to climb onto the parapets, or into the upper rooms built with cross-breezes in mind, because this was where court spent the months warm enough for it. From the parapets he'd be able to see the island's trees, at least, if not hear them: the moss and skinny vines growing on this rock had not the will for speaking. Ban made for a stairway cut along the outside of the first, only to freeze at the base when his father appeared in the dark archway above.

Ban waited to be noticed.

Errigal had long mottled blond and brown hair, a rough dark beard, and the face of a handsome bull he used to his full advantage. His thick braids were wound with dark ribbons, and a fresh-looking blue tunic pulled across wide shoulders that his older son had not inherited. The earl's boots were polished, his trousers new, his belt buckle dangling with carved bone and amber beads. Errigal stomped down the steps, a smile pulling at his teeth as he spoke to his companion, an almost-familiar man, also wearing the beaten copper chain of a Learish earl.

The other man was speaking, soft but clear, as they drew near. "He has always loved Astore rather more than Connley." A worn, knowing fatigue had settled in the lines about the man's clear-shaven mouth, though he was not old, yet. His black hair curled tight and short-cut, and his eyes were gray as river rocks against dark brown skin. That recalled his name to Ban: Kayo, the Oak Earl, whose family had been related to the late queen.

"So it always seemed, and rightly so in Connley's father's time," Errigal agreed, coming to ground level with Ban. "But his growing unpredictability this last year has made it rather impossible to tell which he'll prefer in dividing out his land when he finally names his heir. There is much to favor Connley and Regan now. Including my iron."

Though the matter of their talk intrigued Ban, he kept his face neutral with the ease of years' practice hiding thoughts.

Errigal clapped a heavy hand on Ban's shoulder. "Son," he said warmly, and Ban was relieved.

His companion lifted thin eyebrows. "This lad cannot be your son, too? He's nothing like his brother."

"Indeed!" Errigal said, shrugging and offering a conspiratorial smile. "This one was got in such a way I blushed to admit it in the past, but I've grown used to it by now. You know my legitimate son, Rory, just younger, born truly of my house and stars. But this one, Ban, has no less iron Errigal blood in his veins. Have you heard the name of the Oak Earl, Ban?"

"Yes, my lord," Ban said quietly, familiar with his father's abrupt conversational shifts.

"Well then, look on him as a friend." Errigal grinned, turning his body and clasping his other hand upon Kayo, forming himself into a bridge between them.

"I shall, Father," Ban murmured, turning his own eyes back to the Oak Earl. They had met before, a long time ago. In the White Forest, high to the north, before Ban's mother had shooed him away.

"I'm glad to see you again, Ban," Kayo said, offering his arm. Ban stripped off his glove quickly and took Kayo's bare hand. Kayo continued, "I'd like to hear more about the exploits of the Fox of Aremoria."

"That I can do, my lord," Ban said, letting a smile of pride creep over his face. The Oak Earl had heard of him. Not as the bastard, but as the Fox.

"The Fox of *Lear*," Errigal protested.

In their youth, Ban had once bested Rory and all the other boys their age at a racing contest, because Ban dared to leap across a neck-breaking gully instead of scrambling down and up again. The king of Innis Lear had tossed the prize of woven flowers at him as Errigal had said, "So much more willing to risk his life for the win than the others," as if he approved. It was heard by Lear, who scoffed and said Ban's life was worth less than the other boys', so he should of course be more willing to risk it.

Ban opened his eyes and jerked off his other glove. His father was weak for never standing up to Lear on his own son's behalf, but the king was the true enemy.

Unwilling to retreat, and thinking of how best to play the fox in this squalid henhouse, Ban slid his gaze toward the inner keep again. "Why are the kings of Aremoria and Burgun here?"

"Vying for Elia's dowry," Kayo said, leaning his shoulder against the black stone wall. "Though not so much for her*self,* it seems to me."

Errigal barked a laugh. "So it should be, for a third daughter."

Ban had heard as much from Morimaros weeks ago, but standing here now, so near her, the thought of her being wed made his tongue go dry. He had no right to care on her behalf.

"It will all be done tomorrow," Kayo told him. "At the Zenith Court. Lear will choose between Aremoria and Burgun."

"Tomorrow," Ban said, too hushed to sound uncaring. His father didn't notice, instead studying a party of soldiers and ladies in bright wool hurrying around behind them toward the third tower. But Kayo heard Ban's echo, and peered at him.

"Six years it's been since you saw her?" Kayo prodded gently.

Ban nodded.

"Come on," Errigal said, clapping both their shoulders again. "I want a word with Bracoch, to see the lay of alliance and whether he'll stand with Connley."

The Oak Earl nodded, but because Ban had been looking, he saw dislike move swiftly through Kayo's eyes. Interesting.

"You clean yourself up and join us, my boy," his father ordered Ban. "We've rooms up there, can't miss the Errigal banner. Be at dinner in the hall, too, if you want to see the princess before she's a wife. This one," he said to Kayo, "used to trail behind Elia, all devotion and round eyes. Now I remember it, the king even called him her dog—a tamer sort of fox he used to be, I guess!" Errigal laughed at his own joke.

"Not tame anymore, Father," Ban said.

"Ha! So like your mother! Stars, I miss her."

It was on his tongue to remind his father that his mother was easily found, but curse him if Ban would aim Errigal back in her direction.

"Farewell for now, Ban the Fox," Kayo said gently, as if he knew the storm brewing inside Ban's chest.

Clenching his fist, Ban closed his eyes and withdrew. It was appalling how easily his father set his teeth on edge, made him want to scrub his face and strip the black from his hair, be as gold-speckled as Rory. But it wouldn't have mattered: the king, and therefore Errigal, cared only for birth stars and the orders of privilege that came with title and marriage. Ban could have been more handsome and sandy and gilded than Rory, and they would still have scorned him. One truth Ban had always understood about his father: Errigal swung to the winning side, or the loudest side, or the most *passionate* side, but he was rarely static. As a child Ban had struggled to follow him, to stand next to him, and win some approval. It took years in Aremoria to realize he and his father stood opposite each other across a dark and vicious chasm called legitimacy, and nothing would bridge the gap.

A figure half the yard away caught his attention.

It was her.

Elia Lear, slipping quietly along the inside of the curtain wall, toward the royal tower. She wore the dull regalia of a star priest, gray skirts snapping around her ankles, and worn boots caked with mud. She kept her chin tucked down and her hood held low, as if avoiding attention, but a warm band tightened around his chest. It was *her.*

She was small, though she had to be twenty, as Ban was. As he stared, her hood slipped back in a gust of wind and her hair fell free in spiral curls, dark brown and copper, shining as if spun from the very metal itself. She gathered it in her hand and tugged the hood back up. Even from this distance her eyes were wide, bright, and black as polished horn beads.

He knew he stood like a dullard, or like useless statuary, and when she did glance his way, her eyes passed over him on their way to the tower. No more than he expected, for though she had grown only more lovely, Ban knew he was harder and sharper than the mischievous slip of a child he'd been. She'd never seen him with a sword before, or with his hair so short and greased, spiked with a few tiny braids. Why would she remember Errigal's bastard at all, or if she did, give him a second glance?

This sulking was not why he was here.

Ban gritted his teeth and turned away.

# ELIA

IT WAS EASY for the youngest princess to make her quick way beneath the arching iron gate of the outer wall and across the muddy inner ward, full of people going about their day. Head ducked to hide her face and hair beneath the undyed gray wool of her cloak, and otherwise unremarkable in the drab dress of a star priest, she ignored the new construction on the north wall and avoided the maids and retainers she knew, so as not to be stopped. It was overcrowded, and smelled it, for the high keep walls blocked most fresh air from the ocean, and the number of people was nearly double that of the Summer Seat's usual residents, thanks to the kings of Aremoria and Burgun.

She'd seen their banners from the high coast road as she and Aefa and a trio of soldiers from Dondubhan approached. Dreading meeting any other king before she'd reconnected with her father, Elia had abandoned Aefa and the soldiers to sneak alone into the keep, safely incognito in her priest robes. The retainers she could not avoid at the gate nodded solemnly when she bade them keep her secret.

The narrow passages of the inner keep had been built of rough black rock generations ago, tight for security and lacking windows but for regular arrow slits. Golden hay covered the stone floor of the family hall, rather more dusty than usual. Elia climbed the curling staircase up the first tower, hood falling entirely off her curls. She passed retainers lounging lazily in a guard hole, sharing a meat pie between them; one even had a smear of gravy marring the star on his blue tabard. They sprung to attention at her judgmental glance, muttering fast apologies, but Elia did not stay to chide them or make them glad it was not her sisters who'd caught them relaxing. The corridor near her father's chamber widened, and a sharp ocean breeze pushed through the arched windows cut wide enough for a face to peer out.

Several dogs piled in a corner, stinking of mud and meat. They wagged their tails at her as she passed.

Wishing she'd paid more heed to the state of the keep as she snuck in, Elia frowned. Her father had kept a clean home all Elia's life. Smelly dogs had been roped in the kennels, near the goat pens, and retainers ate in the retainers' hall on the eastern edge of the yard. She resisted the temptation to veer off into the guest tower or the great hall to make certain they were still presentable for the visiting kings. Or presentable at all! Her own people deserved a Summer Seat well-tended and bright.

Worry dragged her heels and she scuffed the thin soles of her boots on the stone floor, shoving aside seeds and dirt. Ahead, at her father's chambers, two more retainers stood, these at least upright, beards braided and belts polished. She approached with her chin up, recognizing one, but not the other. "Seban, is my father fit for me?"

"He is, Lady Elia," the older retainer said, though some sadness put hesitation in his answer. "Preparing for his next audience, but I'm sure you'll be more welcome yet."

Instead of questioning him further, she pushed straight through the door and into the chamber.

Incense sharp and thick greeted her, a familiar sticky scent from the star towers, much too cloudy here. Waving a hand before her face, Elia peered around at the trappings of her father's anteroom: the hearth burned hot, and incense spirals created the smoke that filled the air, not enough of it fleeing up the chimney. Rugs sprawled over the floor, piled in thick layers. Pillows were strewn about, along with charcoal sticks and flapping star charts. Elia picked a path through them to the arch that led into Lear's bedroom.

The king of Innis Lear stood before a tall window where the incense cleared, as a maid restitched the cuff on his outstretched arm. His dark blue robe fell from bony shoulders, a heavy hem of velvet and black fur holding the folds in place. Lear murmured to himself, a recitation of star signs in the shape of a child's poem he'd taught Elia ages ago. The princess mouthed the words with him, not interrupting lest she startle the maid with her needle, or ruin Lear's patience to let the girl finish her repairs.

This room was less familiar to Elia, though she knew the high oak bed had been there, just so since her mother lived, near the line of three tall, narrow windows overlooking the sheer cliff drop and crashing ocean to the north. A good view for the first evening stars; Lear always preferred to stand there watching and waiting for them, alone, after the queen had died. The rugs here were vibrant teals and blues and oranges, even one impossibly rich black, from the Third Kingdom; the dyes had been imported at great expense for the queen's pleasure, and though most of the rugs were threadbare now, Lear refused new ones. Only the wall tapestries were woven in styles of Innis Lear, with star-spotted trees and rampant swans. Lear's desk pushed unused against the far stone wall, covered in letters and ink pots. There the curtained door led to his private privy down three stairs, hanging over the cliffs.

"Are you nearly finished?" The king broke halfway through a verse of his poem, testy and wrinkling his long nose.

"Yes, sir," the girl replied, tying off her thread as quickly as her fingers could manage.

Elia smiled and stepped farther in, inviting her father's irritated "What now?" and the sewing girl's obvious relief.

"Hello, Father."

"Elia!"

The king regularly wore his age-spotted brow in furrowed gloom, melancholy drawing dark lines about his thin mouth and lengthening his already long, rectangular face. But now Lear smiled so brightly that his lost handsomeness shone through for a brief moment. He held out large white hands, entirely consuming Elia's small brown ones, and drew her in for an extended embrace, tucking her head beneath his chin. Elia could feel his ribs through the layers he wore, and while he'd always been thin, this was excessive. She pressed her nose into his collarbone hard for a moment, squeezing away her concern. Her father was old, that was all.

He stroked her hair. "You smell like your mother."

"It's the same oil she used," Elia said, pulling away enough to speak. She tilted her head back. Lear's own hair was flung high in a mane of brown and wiry silver. A few streaks of almost-beard marred his jaw, though he'd shaved clean all her life. "Seban outside said you're readying for a meeting? Shall I comb your hair?"

The king studied her smartly. "You are the one in need of grooming if you are to join me at this meeting. It's with your courting kings."

Elia winced. "They should meet me thus, Father, plain and myself."

"If either of them thinks you plain I'll drive them off the cliff!" Lear kissed his daughter's forehead and released her. "Tell me of your studies, my star, while this girl . . ." The king eyed the room, but the girl who'd mended his cuff had vanished. "Stars and . . . !"

Laughing softly, Elia led the king by his hand to sit upon a chair with a simple, sturdy back. "I'm glad to attend you, Father."

"My loyal Calpurlugh," he said, sighing as Elia gathered a horn comb off the narrow table along the wall that was covered in odds and ends: combs and rings, a beaten copper chain, tiny crystals arrayed like constellations, ribbons and buttons and a hood missing the loops to tie it to a tunic.

Elia told her father then the story she'd perfected on the journey south: her wager with Danna her tutor, the win, the twist—that most of the retainers at Dondubhan had sided with her despite her comparative inexperience. Lear slapped his knee, pleased, and his still-bright blue eyes closed as Elia's fingers and the comb pulled his thick hair back from his forehead and drooping ears. She wound it into a single braid and twisted it into a knot, pinning it with the same horn comb. Several of the rings on the table belonged on his fingers, especially the sapphires, and she dropped them into his palm.

"Your turn," he said, trading places with her. "I've a winning idea, Calpurlugh."

Obediently, Elia sat, hands folded in her lap.

"We shall leave you clad in this plain star priest gown, and bring you with me to this meeting with Aremoria and Burgun. Will they see their sought princess, or only a servant of heaven?"

Though her father's smile was large and infecting, Elia was not enthusiastic. "Should we play games, Father? They might be offended." Her thoughts drifted to those last letters she'd received, and she wondered if Ullo was capable of seeing past an unadorned dress, or if Morimaros of Aremoria had been honest when he said he wished for a star reading.

"And what should happen then?" Lear raised spiky brows. "A retreat? If either king is so easily put off of you, then now is the time to discover it. They will not attack us; they will not risk their trade with the Third Kingdom, nor the access to our rubies and gold and iron."

It was true Innis Lear was rich in resources and minerals, and their location put them between sea trade and Aremoria, though Aremoria could always trade overland with the vast desert kingdoms to their south and east. It was also true Aremoria would risk any trade they established with the Third Kingdom if they consumed Lear, dethroning Dalat's line, which was also the line of the empress. And Burgun couldn't defeat Lear if they tried. Alliances mattered much more to their small country. But Elia had no intention of marrying either king, and so she supposed she could play along.

"Very well, Father," Elia said, and Lear's smile spread into a wicked old grin. With a groan he knelt, reaching under the low oak frame of his bed. Before she could offer aid, he made a sound of triumph and dragged out a small clay pot.

"Is that oil? It must be rancid now." Elia leaned away.

Her father started to stand, then shook his head and gave up without much effort. He handed the pot to her. "Open it."

The orange glaze and black rim proved the pot to be from the Third Kingdom, but it was small enough to fit easily in her hands. She pried off the lid, where wax still clung from an old seal. The lingering perfume of bergamot oranges brought tears to her eyes. She was used to the smell, for her uncle the Oak Earl bought copious amounts in trades on her behalf, just as he had for Dalat over the years. But this, surely, had been a pot touched and admired by her mother. Those gentle hands had caressed this smooth glaze, cupped the base as gently as Elia did now.

Inside curled a thin chain of silver woven into a delicate net, and studded with tiny diamonds—no, merely island crystals, but in Elia's palm they glinted like shards of fallen stars. "Father," she whispered, just barely remembering Dalat's hair bound tight in a thick roll that curved from ear to ear, along her nape, and dotted with the same tiny sparkling lights.

"This will be enough of a crown, my little love, my favorite." Lear stood very slowly, but Elia was too stunned, admiring the sleek dripping silver, to notice in time that he needed aid to rise. The king moved behind her and put his hands on her shoulders. "I remember how to do it, though it has been so many . . . long years."

Elia closed her eyes, flattening her hands on her stomach. This would infuriate her sisters when they saw, for both would demand this artifact of their mother for themselves. Gaela because she felt she deserved all Dalat's mementos, because they'd been the closest, because she was the eldest and would be queen; Regan because she liked to deny Elia small things, and as ever would support Gaela's claim.

No doubt Lear had hidden it in the tiny clay jar in order to keep it to himself. And now, he set it where he willed it, upon his favorite daughter's head. *All beings shall in their proper places be set,* he'd written in his letter. A sliver of worry slid coldly through Elia's heart. But Lear's slow, steady hands soothed her, as he twisted her hair into a long smiling roll, and her shoulders relaxed. His tugs were more tentative than Aefa's, and the story he told as he worked was a story Elia had heard before: the first time Dalat had agreed to allow her husband to braid her hair, and the terrible time they'd both had of it, neither giving up for hours and hours, until Lear had made such an utter mess Dalat had burst into tears.

"I was devastated, of course," Lear said, as he always did, "but not nearly so much as your mother. When Gaela was born, we learned together, though Gaela declined to sit still, and then Regan's hair was easy. By the time you were born, I was nearly an expert, even Satiri said so."

As always, Elia wished to ask him: if he'd been an expert, why had he never taught Aefa, or Elia, or anyone, after he sent all Dalat's attendants away, letting Elia's own hair go dry as gorse in the summer?

But she knew the answer, though her father would never agree: it was the depth of his grief. And she knew, too, that sometimes Lear's version of the past was woven equally of truth and pleasant fabrication. So long as the stories harmed none, she could not bring herself to challenge them. Especially when they involved Dalat.

"There," the king said, caressing Elia's neck and squeezing her shoulders.

Elia lifted her hands to carefully explore the silver and crystals in her hair; Lear had set them in carefully, a web of starlight, she imagined, with a few tiny pins. Simple and elegant. A starry crown for a star-blessed princess.

# AEFA

SOMETIMES AEFA OF Thornhill thought she was not hard enough to survive Innis Lear, but when such doubts plagued her, she remembered what her mother would call her, and take heart.

*My little mushroom.*

Mushrooms weren't generally thought to be pretty or resilient, but they appeared overnight, kissed into being by the sweet lips of earth saints who returned to the island only for secret dancing. Or so her mother had liked to whisper when Aefa climbed into bed with her, nose wrinkled and begging for a new nickname. *Mushrooms are born of the damp earth, fed by starlight instead of the sun. They are both stars and roots, and they are never alone. When have you come across a single mushroom? Never! What a lovely thing to be, my little mushroom: never alone.*

Aefa missed her mother.

At least Alis was alive, though hidden deep in the White Forest. She'd railed against Lear three summers ago, calling him foolish and dangerous, mad in his obdurate grief and old age. Only the king's love for his Fool had saved Alis, buying her the opportunity to flee. And only the star prophecy that the sanctity of the White Forest itself must be maintained saved it from the king's soldiers. There was a refuge at its heart now, held by the witch Brona, and Alis was there, safe but unable to leave lest she be caught and imprisoned, or worse, exiled forever from the island.

That was how Aefa's clandestine meetings with the witch had begun: to pass letters for her mother. It was just as well Elia had abandoned her companion to sneak into the Summer Seat alone, for it left Aefa free to go where she wished, unseen.

The town of Sunton was a collection of stone cottages arrayed about a square and surrounded by portioned fields and shared grazing meadows. It clung in a raindrop shape along the low, sloping moors. The tip pointed toward the standing stones perched at the northernmost bluff overlooking the Summer Seat promontory, then curved against the King's Road that led all along this southern cliff coast toward Port Comlack and Errigal Keep at the far eastern edge of the island. Aefa made her way along the road openly under the sun, swinging a basket in her hand and humming one of her father's more ridiculous songs about kings and snails. She skipped across the muddy furrows in the dirt. Villagers smiled at her from their yards, women mostly, hanging laundry and sewing in the bright daylight while children dashed here and there, chasing goats and chickens. It was exactly like the village in which Aefa had been born, down to the capped well in the town square, to which she headed directly. Her memories of Firstday blessings at the holy well of Thornhill were dim, as it had been twelve years since she'd attended, and nearly ten since the wells were capped all across Innis Lear, but she remembered the scent—the dank, stony smell of moss and rootwater, and the shiver as a star priest flicked drops onto her face. She'd sneezed once, and it made her mother scowl, but her father had laughed.

The cap on the Sunton well was an old wagon wheel covered with lime wash and set with small gray river stones in a spiral pattern. Lovely and simple, and no doubt those still devout considered it a symbol of the path down and down and down to the water, as if they could still touch it. At the south rim, where the spiral began, Aefa crouched. In the cap's shadow, there ought to be a box tucked against the foot of the well. But only a small lizard darted away at Aefa's seeking touch.

With a huff, she stood. She supposed she could circle around town once or twice, or return tomorrow and hope Brona had found a chance to come.

"Aefa."

It was the witch, her deep voice fond and laughing.

"Ah!" Aefa gasped, twirling with a delighted smile. "I didn't miss you after all."

The two women ducked together, embracing. The witch of the White Forest handed Aefa a small stoppered vial before they parted. She was a powerfully built woman with strong hands and a lovely tan face; loose black curls bound under a hood of vibrant red that matched the paint touched to lips as plump as her thighs.

Tucking the vial into a pocket of her skirts, Aefa said, "The princess is already inside the keep. I wish I could have brought her here to see you. She never speaks of you anymore, or her own mother, or truly much of anything but the stars. I've not caught her whispering to any flowers or wind in two entire years, Brona."

The witch's dark brow bent with sorrow, and she gazed toward the Summer Seat. "Be sure to put the rootwater in her mouth."

"I slip it into her wine, or sometimes her breakfast. Shouldn't she notice?"

Brona shrugged one shoulder. "She likely does, she only refuses to admit so, for many, many reasons."

"Is she afraid?"

"No doubt."

"I want to tell her," Aefa said ferociously.

"And if you did, what would she say?"

Aefa imagined Elia's face, her bright, black eyes. *You have to listen to the island, Elia,* Aefa would say, and those careful eyes would lower, perhaps flick up to the sky, or to the horizon, and the princess would take one of the great, deep breaths she used to quash the overwhelming song in her heart. But then Elia would make a sad, pretty smile, and move to some other conversation, some other answer, as if Aefa had said nothing at all.

The witch touched Aefa's knuckles, and said, "She'll ask you, when she's ready. You'll make sure she knows you have the answers?"

"I snap fire sometimes, out of air, to remind her." Aefa pursed her lips. "She disapproves."

Brona's eyebrows lifted.

"She is afraid," Aefa corrected herself, barely whispering.

"That's good, little mushroom." Brona smiled at Aefa's darting glance. "Alis is well. She's cultivating a long vine of sweet peas with charming purple flowers and a tendency to giggle at bluebirds."

"Father wants to see her."

There Brona's expression closed off. "Then he should come see her. Nothing to stop him."

After a pause, the women shared a knowing grimace. There was everything to stop the King's Fool from a visit to Hartfare. The witch sighed. "But listen, Aefa, he will see her soon enough. All who were riven will soon return to their center."

Aefa's lips parted in wonder, for though the witch's tone did not alter, the words held the weight of magic. "Is that a star prophecy?"

"I do not read stars," Brona said with delicate distaste. "It is only the gossip of trees."

But the witch turned her head east, and all her body followed, until Brona faced the rising land, staring as if she could see beyond it to the ocean channel, and past even that, to Aremoria.

"Even . . . ?" Aefa whispered.

"Yes."

A thrill straightened Aefa's spine, and she danced a little in place. This would delight the princess, make the fire she was so afraid of flicker again and burn. "She'll be so happy!"

"No," Brona said suddenly, grabbing Aefa's wrist. "She won't be. But she will survive."

# GAELA

In Innis Lear it was believed that the reign of the last queen had been predicted by the stars—and had ended, too, because of them.

Lear had been middle-aged when his father and brothers died: too old to have planned for ruling, too old to easily let go of his priestly calling, his years of sanctuary in the star towers. So the first thing the new king ordered was a star-casting to point him in the direction of a bride. He needed a queen, after all, as he needed heirs of his own to ensure the survival of his line. Every star-reader on the island joined together and offered their new king a sole prophecy: the first woman to set foot on the docks of Port Comlack at the dawn of the third dark moon after the Longest Night would be his true queen. She would give him strong children and rule justly beside him, then die on the sixteenth anniversary of her first daughter's birth.

Lear arranged to be there, ready to greet this star-promised woman, and waited all night long under the third dark moon, despite icy winds so early in the year. As the first sunlight broke through thin clouds a ship came limping to port, too many of their rowers weak from struggling against the roiling ocean. It was a trader's ship from the Third Kingdom, an ocean and half a continent away, where an inland sea and great river met in a gulf of sand and stone. First to emerge were the dark-skinned captain and five dark soldiers; they were royal guards along to protect a granddaughter of the empress, who'd traveled north searching for adventure. Lear welcomed them, inviting the princess to come forward. She descended like a slip of night, it was said, black-skinned and robed in bright layers of wool and silk against the cold ocean. Glass beads glinted from her roped black hair like ice or tears or—like stars.

Lear married her, though she was less than half his age, and loved her deeply.

She died at dawn on her first daughter's sixteenth birthday, twelve years ago this winter.

The pain was as fresh to Gaela as every morning's sunrise.

Anytime she was at the Summer Seat, Gaela would make this pilgrimage, down to the caves pocking the cliffs below the keep. Dalat had brought her here at least once a year, for all of Gaela's childhood. At first only the two of them, then when Regan was old enough they were three, and finally in the last few years even baby Elia tagged along. They'd descended to the sea farther to the southeast, where the cliffs became beaches and bluffs with more ready, safe access to the hungry waves, and with an escort of heavily armed retainers in separate boats, they rowed back up the rocky coast here to the caves. Gaela remembered especially when she'd been eleven, and Elia only three years old, wrapped up against Gaela's chest so she could protect her baby sister while Dalat held nine-year-old Regan's hand. Elia had danced with all her limbs, excited and gleefully singing a childish rhyme, clutching at the collar of Gaela's tunic and at one of her braids.

Dalat had dragged the boat as high onto the beach as she could, then smiled like a young girl and dashed with her daughters to the largest cave. She laughed at the spray of salt water that splattered her cheeks, and then when they were far inside the cave, knelt upon the wet stone, disregarding the algae and saltwater staining her skirt. "Here, Gaela," she said, patting the earth beside her, "and here, Regan. Give me my littlest in my lap." When all were situated, Dalat taught them a soft prayer in the language of the Third Kingdom. It was a layered, complex language filled with triple meanings depending on forms of address, and to Gaela it always sounded like a song. She fought hard, scowling, to remember the prayer after only one recitation. Regan repeated the final word of every phrase, planting the rhythm on her tongue. Elia mouthed along with their mother, saying nothing with any meaning, but seeming the most natural speaker of them all.

Today the tide was out, and Gaela was strong enough she didn't need to row up from a beach or bring retainers to assist.

The emerald grass capping the cliffs bent in the sea wind, and she unerringly located the slip of rock that cut down at an angle, crossing the sheer face of the cliff at a manageable slant. She'd left off any armor and all fancy attire, put on dull brown trousers and a soldier's linen shirt, wrapped her twists up in a knot, and tied on soft leather shoes. Carefully, Gaela made her way along the first section, forward looking but leaned back with one hand skimming the steep rocks for balance.

As Gaela climbed down, she muttered her mother's prayer to herself. She didn't believe in Dalat's god, but it was the only piece of the language she remembered fluently, having stopped speaking it three days after the queen died.

Sun glared off the water, flashing in her eyes. Gaela turned her back to the sea, placing toes where they would not slip, and gripped the ridge in her strong hands. Wind flattened her to the cliff, tugging at her shirt. She glanced down at the steep gray-and-black precipice, toward the clear green water and rolling whitecaps. Her stomach dropped, and she smiled. The rock was rough under the pads of her fingers, scraping her palms; her knees pressed hard, she climbed down, and down, until she could hop the final few feet to land in a crouch on the slick, sandy shore.

Her shoulders rose as she took a huge breath, filling her lungs with salty air. She blew it out like a saint of the ocean, summoning a storm.

Walking along the beach, Gaela eyed the mouth of the cave: a slanted oval, wider at the base and twice taller than her. At high tide the ocean swallowed this whole beach, and only tiny boats could row in, though there was danger of becoming trapped. This cave that Gaela had climbed to was directly below the Summer Seat, but unfortunately too wet for storing castle goods, and there were times smugglers would need to be cleared out. Gaela glanced up the cliff toward the black walls of the castle, high above and leaning over in places. She thought perhaps to install stairs, or some system of ladders, and wondered, too, if the cave could be transformed into cold storage, if they could put in high shelving to keep the water off. But it seemed too complicated to be practical.

She reached the mouth of the cave and paused, one hand on the rough edge of the mouth, her lips curled in a frown. For five years now she'd only come alone, since Regan had married. Elia hadn't been welcome in the caves, not since she chose Lear over her sisters, damn her. Today, Gaela would've preferred to have Regan with her again, but her sister had kept herself away in Connley unexpectedly, even since their summons.

On her own these two days, Gaela had been assessing the state of her kingdom behind her father's back, first meeting with the strongest earls, Glennadoer and Rosrua and Errigal, and discussing a tax for the repair of that blasted coastal road, if her father did refuse funds from the treasury. It was necessary, especially that the worst erosion be bolstered before the fierce winter storms. She and Astore had been appalled at the state of Lear's accounting records in the past three years, demanding Lear's stewards find a path through the mess. The earls had promised records from their own holdings that would make up for some of the confusion. When Gaela took the throne, she'd be ready to put resources exactly where she wanted them: trade and a stronger standing army. Her grandmother was an empress, and

Gaela would transform Innis Lear into a jewel worthy of such a relationship. By the time she died, no longer would this land be a blight clinging to the sea, its inner woods a mystery of ghosts and hidden villages, the people known for superstition and old magic. Kay Oak had told Gaela that Lear's star prophecies were considered an artful, childlike folly in the Third Kingdom, where the study of stars was a science. Even in Aremoria the king was building great schools, and his father had turned his people away from magic. Innis Lear was a backward holdout.

Gaela would change it all. She would not be remembered only as the prophesied daughter who killed a beloved mother, but as the king who dragged Innis Lear away from venal superstition and filthy wormwork.

She entered the cave. The floor was sand; her boots sank into watery puddles and the meager warmth of the sun vanished. Layers of rock, slick with algae and striped gray with pale green stratification, cut away, curving deeper. Salty, wet stone-smell filled her nose, and she even tasted the delicate flavor of dark earth on her tongue. The air seeped with it. A drip like a pretty chime echoed farther back, where she could not see.

It was like standing in a frozen moment of rain, surrounded by a refreshing, cool breeze and droplets of water that never quite touched her. Gaela's mother had said there was nothing like this in the desert. And that standing here, breathing, was as near to sharing God's breath as Dalat had found since leaving her old home.

Gaela often wished she could visit the Third Kingdom, but Innis Lear was her birthright. In Dalat's home, Gaela might be allowed to govern a city, or work her way up in the ranks of the armies to general. But here she would rule over all. If she had a god, it was this island. She would make her name, and the name of Innis Lear, so strong and great that the words and spirit of them would travel to the desert in her place.

"I am so close, Mother."

Her voice remained low, but Gaela had no need to be heard. It was the memory of her mother to whom she spoke, no ghost. She had not brought a candle to light; a thousand candles burned for Dalat every night in the north. Nor did Gaela bring mementos: eagle feathers pinched her heart, but what good were they buried in this sand or tossed into the ocean? Gaela was unsentimental, and her mother was gone. Taken from her by Lear, by the reign of his stars. Nothing could bring Dalat back, no rootwater nor blood, no star prophecy nor faith in even the great god of her mother's people.

When Gaela spoke to her mother's memory, she really was talking to herself and the island.

"There are things I've done you would not approve of," Gaela said, crouching. Her bottom leaned on the craggy wall for balance, and she rested her wrists on her knees. "My barren body, my loveless marriage. You were so happy when I was young, because you loved him, and you had us, and I remember you found so much joy in so many mundane things I still don't understand. But I did what I had to do, and I'm not sorry, Dalat. I will rule Innis Lear, and Regan's children will be my heirs."

Gaela pictured her mother's face, though Dalat looked rather more like Gaela herself than she truly had; it was the best a daughter could do so many years later. Kayo had brought a small bust of Dalat-as-a-girl from the desert, and her orange clay face at fifteen was so much like Elia's instead: round and sweet and smiling. Gaela had rejected it.

"Mother," Gaela said, "I miss you. You wanted me, despite everything, but he never did. You gave me the ambitions to rule this island. You taught me I could, encouraged me to find my own way to strength, because our ancestors are queens and empresses. He pretended I was nothing, tolerating me despite the prophecy, because he loved you. When Elia was born, and her . . . her stars were perfect, he'd have named her heir if she'd been a boy. If I wasn't married to Astore and hadn't made myself into a dangerous prince, he'd try it now. Fortunately for all of us she has no ambition of her own, or I'd have to kill her. He and his stars would necessitate it." Gaela closed her eyes. The ocean outside matched the roar of her blood. Sometimes she thought that men had created star prophecies solely to benefit themselves.

"I don't understand how you loved him, Mother. He used you, and me, to prove the truth of the stars, and I will never let that happen again. My kingdom will not be defined as yours was, and I will not let him, or any of them, trap me as you were trapped. I love you, but I will not be like you."

She spat on the ground, leaving that piece of herself there, her body and water, for the sand and tide and Innis Lear.

# MARS

MORIMAROS, THE KING of Aremoria, was annoyed.

He'd been directed outside to a nearly empty garden, along with his personal escort of five polished soldiers, to await a second audience with King Lear. Mars had assumed that meant an immediate audience, an intimate discussion of his matrimonial goals, but instead he'd been waiting long enough for the shadow of the stone table at the center of the yard to shift a hand-span. The walls of the courtyard reached high, lime-washed and painted with gray trees, star shapes, and graceful flying swans, the art faded now and in need of retouching. Pine boughs and sweet-smelling lavender littered the earthen ground. Deep wooden boxes in the four corners grew with emerald moss and creeping rose vines that bloomed bloodred and creamy orange.

Though it was altogether a lovely atmosphere, something tugged at Mars's awareness, as if invisible cracks had formed in the very air. As if the roses wanted his attention.

Mars was not practiced at idleness. It led him to imagine fantasies.

He wondered if his Fox had arrived yet.

*I have a game for you to play,* Mars had said, the afternoon he'd received his invitation to this Zenith Court. *Did you know her, Elia Lear?* His Fox had lied when he answered, *Barely, sir,* with something of shuttered grief in the tremble of his words.

The Fox had served Mars passionately and well for years, discovering secrets no other spy even thought to look for, slipping into fortresses and enemy camps as if he could spin himself invisible or as quick as the wind with which he spoke. Yet that always hidden thread of angst was too easy for Mars to pluck and set against Innis Lear. Until now, Mars had held back from doing so. Things built so easily tended to be just as easily broken.

But it was time. Mars was here for one thing: Innis Lear itself, and he stood at the center of several paths to claim it. The Fox was one. The princess was another.

Waiting in this empty, albeit lovely, courtyard was not.

The king's eyes returned to the central stone table.

It was only a man's length across, and circular, cut of the same or similar hard black rock that this entire castle was made of. Mars was reminded of the stone circles that clung to this island, or the ancient dolmen to be found in the less civilized parts of Aremoria. Remnants of the oldest cults of earth and root.

That was it.

Mars, though he'd been still and standing beside one of the walls this entire time, strode suddenly to the table and crouched. He put one hand to the rough edge and peered beneath it.

The wide foot of the table was like the stump of a mushroom, built of small black rocks held together with mortar. He smelled damp moss, and despite the shadows that must perpetually cling to this underside, he saw glinting water, trickles that had seeped through the mortar. The tabletop had been set upon the foot, but not plastered in place. Like a heavy, precarious lid.

This had been a well once.

Sucking in a breath, the king of Aremoria realized he was not only surprised, but shocked in the way of a man confronting some desperate heresy.

Clutching the edge of the table, Mars stood carefully and looked around the rose courtyard again. The vines themselves, at every corner, and the lack of ceiling, should have been enough of a hint: this courtyard had been a chapel.

In Aremoria, long ago, the people had worshipped the earth, made their temples in the river caves and around natural springs. As the country grew, they built churches and cathedrals of earth, wood, and stone, always with the central well that dove deep into the heart of the world. Passages to life and death. When the worship of stars spread, Aremoria came entirely out of caves and knocked the roofs off their churches, marrying wells and starlight.

Mars remembered it being similar on Innis Lear. Their star towers rose high, but at Dondubhan where he'd once been a guest, eleven years ago, the black lake Tarinnish had been called the Well of Lear. He knew from his Fox that the White Forest was pocked with springs and wells, and the Fox's own witchcraft came from the rootwaters and worms.

But this well, in the heart of the Summer Seat of Innis Lear, had been capped off.

It shook him, though Mars could only guess at why. He had no religion himself, nor trust in prophecy and magic.

And yet.

Yesterday, Lear himself had greeted Mars outside the Summer Seat, waiting across the land bridge, seeming modest, clad in only a finely made robe, his hair unbound, and without the impressive regalia of armored retainers and cavalry that Mars himself had brought. Then, Mars thought Lear had wished to create a welcome that put little pressure on Mars to be formal, and Mars had hoped it meant the king of Innis Lear and his youngest looked kindly on Mars's intentions, to receive him so casually, as if already they were family. Then dinner had come, and Ullo of Burgun arrived, too, and Mars had gritted his teeth, holding his expression blank the entire time. Lear had behaved just as informally, giving no clear preference to either king.

Though Mars understood politically why Lear entertained Ullo of Burgun as another suitor to his daughter, it rankled nonetheless to be set on an equal footing with such a buffoon. Either it was a purposeful affront to the obviously greater alliance with Aremoria, or Lear was no statesman. Mars had taken every opportunity to remind Ullo of the folly of going against him. Ullo's response had been to flirt his way through every conversation, making Mars almost hope Elia Lear never arrived at all, to be subjected to the attentions of this featherbrained flatterer-king. Lear himself either did not mind Ullo's flavor, or did not notice. Then Lear had commented to Mars in such a way that made it sound as if they'd never before met, when they had, though briefly and now over a decade prior.

Last night it had merely irritated Mars, but now, it unsettled him.

Was the king of Innis Lear capricious, or losing his mind to his age? Something was out of balance on the island, Mars could feel it, and more than any conversation he'd overheard or participated in, this diminished holy well was proof. There'd been reports that the king of Innis Lear had shut down the wells, but in Aremoria they'd moved their folk away from holy wells and cave worship a generation ago. To the betterment of the country, and to its strength.

The difference, Mars thought, was Lear had not offered anything to replace rootwater and faith in the hearts and minds of his people. No wonder there was imbalance and unease threaded through everything. When Mars had returned home after his long-ago visit, curious and fascinated by the tightly knit faith of the Learish people, his father had, with little fanfare, dispelled his son's awe:

*That place is haunted, Morimaros, and you'd do well not to admire what-*

*ever magic granted it such power. Here in Aremoria we've given the people some-*
*thing better than ghosts and stars and trees to believe in: they have us. And if*
*you're ever to retake that island and rule it, as is your birthright, you need to*
*recognize credulity when you see it, and accept that superstition is a tool, not a*
*guarantee. Magic is untrustworthy; only loyalty matters to kings.*

A soft breeze kissed Mars's cheek, turning his attention to the open arched
gate of the rose courtyard, just as Ullo of Burgun walked through. Though
a warm afternoon, the king wore heavy fur to compliment his thick head
of hair and full beard, both no doubt intended to make him appear more
mature. Mars suddenly wished he'd managed to confront Ullo directly on
the battlefield last month, and had captured him against a ransom, which
he could then have denied, keeping Ullo locked in a fine room in the Lionis
Palace and far away from Innis Lear.

Burgun chatted with the King's Fool, whose name Mars never had
caught. The Fool wore ridiculous stripes and a toy sword in a sheath on his
back; his hair was dyed unnatural red and he had paint on his lower lip
and at the corners of his eyes. He clapped his hands and bowed extra-
vagantly toward Mars. "Your bright Majesty, we've come to entertain you
until the king arrives."

Mars nodded, unwilling to address the man simply as *Fool,* and then said,
"Ullo," to the king of Burgun. If this invitation to Innis Lear had not come
when it did, Burgun would be annexed to Aremoria by now, and in a different sort of political mess.

"Morimaros," Ullo replied, wearing a vapid smile. Behind him came ten
men in the maroon regalia of Burgun, all trimmed with fur or elaborate
golden embroidery. They wore long knives, but no mail or armor or swords.
It wasn't from politeness, Mars was certain, but the belief that finery was
more impressive than military accouterment would've been.

The Fool made directly for the only seat in the yard that was not a bench,
and thrust himself into it with the urgency of a child. He draped across the
arms, and said, "Wine not far behind, good fellows, would you like a song?"

Before Ullo could speak, Mars said, "I'd like the history of the table here."

Ullo laughed, but the Fool's smile was tinged with mystery. He said, "Only
a table, great king, and a grave."

"A grave?" Ullo said, recoiling.

To keep from rolling his eyes, Mars refused to make any expression at
all. The imbecile still had not determined that the Fool spoke only in riddles.
"For whom?" Mars asked. He folded his arms across his chest, knowing it
broadened his shoulders, and glad to be taller than Ullo of Burgun.

"Or what?" asked the Fool.

Mars nodded. He understood: this was the effect of the ascendancy of stars. A grave for rootwater.

"So serious," Ullo declared, patting his hand along the black stone table. He wore rings on all but one finger, weighing down his pale hand. "This is a celebration! We're here to celebrate . . . one of us."

Mars did not accept the volley. It was a weak charge, which would not even reach his defenses.

The Fool began to sing, and Mars considered departing. Surely it was not worth another meeting with the king of Innis Lear if Ullo was to be here as well. Perhaps courting her at all was a mistake. There were other ways to retake the island, other ways to secure better sea trade. But his father had insisted one of Lear's daughters should be the next queen of Aremoria. It might've been the first or second daughter, and then with nothing more than a marriage, Mars could have reunited the island to Aremoria. But now that he was at last prepared to wed, the only unmarried daughter was a star priest, and likely too steeped in her father's way.

He remembered Princess Elia only as a quiet girl who clutched her father's hand as if nothing else kept her tethered to this world. In eleven years could she have changed so much? Her replies to his letters had been simple and brief, speculating upon the upcoming seasons and suggesting several small prophecies for his use. Ban had described to him a young girl of vivid personality, of curiosity and an earthly beauty. Such personality had not been present in her correspondence, though when he glanced over the letters again during the ocean crossing, he'd found some hints of humor he had overlooked before. But that might only have been wishful thinking. After all, he'd been forced to idleness on the ship, too, with nothing but the gray sea and unclear paths ahead of him. Too many possibilities, not enough information.

Mars reminded himself to be patient. The worst Ullo could do was irritate him, and young Elia Lear would be here at the Summer Seat soon. One of his men had been tasked since yesterday with alerting him immediately when her entourage arrived. It was Elia he needed to win over, not her father or this Fool, nor anyone else on Innis Lear.

He remained in the Rose Courtyard, taking position with his men. With one ear he listened to Burgun and the Fool chatter and flirt, to their rather inappropriate jokes—leave it to Ullo to understand nuance only if it was sexual in nature—and songs. The rest of Mars's mind turned toward the future, and the variety of possibilities he foresaw, depending on what occurred at tomorrow's Zenith Court.

He'd been promised an answer to his courtship, and all believed the king would finally name his eldest, Gaela, as his official heir, perhaps even step down immediately. But anything could happen, and Mars would do best to have thought through any number of outcomes and actions, so that when the moment arrived, he'd have a plan, and multiple backup plans.

So the Aremore king remained, a spider carefully poised, spinning several days of the future out again and again, asking himself silent questions and answering them, busy with webs of strategy.

Then Lear entered, with his youngest daughter at his side, her chin tucked down, a small, curious smile on her lovely face, an old leather book in her arms, and stars in her hair.

Mars forgot every single thread of his thoughts in an instant.

# ELIA

ELIA WAS PLEASED to discover that her father was leading her toward the Rose Courtyard for their meeting; it had always been one of her favorite places at the Summer Seat, even since the well had been closed. She felt safe there, understood. It was a good sign for the introduction about to take place. Elia breathed carefully, practicing a cool expression, practicing being a star.

When she entered, the wind was tense, whispering little cries without words. She held tight against her chest the large tome of star charts she'd carried from her father's rooms, and glanced up, curious.

Each king had, of course, claimed a side.

To the east Ullo of Burgun waited surrounded by his own retainers in bright maroon and gold, jeweled sheaths for long knives hung from leather belts. They clustered in a friendly group, and though a few eyed the Aremores, most chatted with each other and Ullo. Just as Lear and Elia entered, the king laughed, tossing back a head of thick brown hair so his teeth glinted whitely and well. He clapped a pale hand on the chest of the Burgundian lord beside him. Sweat glistened at the temples of both Ullo and this man, laden as they were with velvet and fur-lined finery. But Ullo was pretty, and his beard seemed soft around his full, smiling mouth.

Across from him, only six Aremores presented, each of them in quilted orange gambesons, with pauldrons fixed to their shield shoulders by a red leather strap diagonal across the chest. The steel pauldrons were round as a moon reflecting sunlight. One Aremore man stood out at the fore, though he held himself exactly as the soldiers did and his costume was the same but for a heavy ring of garnet and pearls on his thumb and a simple crown etched into the surface of his pauldron. This king's head was shorn nearly bare, and a perfectly trimmed brown beard to match it spread over his hard jaw. He had blue eyes, and their long dark lashes were the only promise of softness from the king of Aremoria. And he had no love for Burgun; that was obvious from the analytic stare he cast toward the more relaxed Ullo.

With a pleased start, Elia recognized the final man in the courtyard, lounging in a chair with his leg tossed up over the arm, wearing a striped coat of several bright colors: Aefa's father, Lear's Fool. She smiled and nearly broke Lear's game by calling out to him. But she remembered that this was a volatile moment, and she needed to maintain poised calm for her father's sake—and for her own. Her smile stopped at slight.

The moment king and daughter entered, Ullo snapped to attention, and Morimaros of Aremoria bowed his head respectfully.

"Your Majesty of Innis Lear," said Burgun, stepping forward. "What a charming garden this is, and a surprise on this cold, sharp cliff. It seems roses are a perfect flower for your island, as beautiful and hearty as they are."

"And tangled," Lear said, amused. "And sharp and treacherous."

Ullo blinked, then smiled as if it were the only reaction he could think to have.

"Lear," the king of Aremoria said only.

"Aremoria," Lear returned.

Retaking attention, Ullo swept his hand toward the Fool. "Your Fool has kept us well entertained, sir, as we awaited you."

"And you"—the Fool stood to offer an elaborate bow—"entertained me beyond well, king, verging toward ill, if all things are circles." Taller and lankier than the king had ever been, he kept his hair short and spiky, dyed henna red, and dots of red painted the outer corners of his eyes and bottom lip, like a woman.

Lear embraced his Fool fondly, saying, "Your wit rarely comes full circle, friend."

"More of a spiral, I'd say, beginning and ending only in your ability to comprehend."

Lear laughed, and so did his Fool, their heads knocking together as if they were alone in all the world. Though Elia understood the joking, or so she thought, there seemed something still she could not catch.

"You've brought a star priest with you," said the king of Aremoria lightly.

Elia met his gaze: Morimaros watched her dispassionately.

"Ah, no." Ullo of Burgun bounded forward, his hand out to Elia. "This is the princess Elia of Lear. My lady, only a dullard could mistake your unique beauty for anyone else."

Morimaros's lips pulled into a line Elia could not read. She gave the charts over to one of Lear's retainers and allowed Ullo her hand, saying, "But I am a star priest, my lord, and so it was no mistake."

Ullo touched her fingers to his lips and smiled. "I am rather overwhelmed at meeting you, and apologize for any misspeaking."

She squeezed his fingers, and he released her. His eyes trailed down her neck and across her breasts with open intimacy. As her flesh went cold, she turned her face to Morimaros. "My father did bring a star priest with him. You wished your birth chart analyzed."

"We are to be honored by your very own prophecies?" Ullo said, hand over his heart.

The king of Aremoria did not react but to flick his eyes at Ullo. Elia hid another smile, believing Morimaros had stronger feelings for Burgun than for her. That should make remaining detached easier.

It was Lear who said, one arm about his Fool, the other waving at the retainers, "Here are the charts, if my dearest daughter obliges, and perhaps in your stars she'll find some preference for her favors."

"I would petition the jewels of heaven to tilt in their courses toward me," Ullo said prettily.

Elia wished Morimaros would say, *I need rely on no such petitioning,* or some such, that might put the king of Burgun down, but Morimaros was silent.

She gestured for the charts to be placed upon the well's tabletop and glanced between the two kings. "I must begin with knowing your times of birth, so we might choose the correct charts."

Morimaros paused in consideration.

"Do you know it?" she prompted gently.

"I do, lady," he said just as gently. "I only would not want to remove from Ullo the chance to be first."

"Sporting of you," Ullo snapped. "Perhaps there is some star sign now which of us should be preferred."

Casting her gaze up at the blue sky, Elia said, "I'm afraid the afternoon stars have no signs for us, influencing instead beyond our means to see."

"Perhaps a worm sign, then?"

She looked sharply to the speaker: it had been Morimaros.

"Do you listen to the language of trees?" the king of Aremoria continued. He held his expression as cool as ever, but Elia warmed at the question.

"Worm signs!" Lear cried, scrubbing the air with his arms. "None such in my court."

Elia's pulse jumped, and she forced her pleasure hard away. "Of course not, Father," she soothed.

Ullo frowned sympathetically. "Only the purest prophecy for such as ourselves."

"Indeed," Lear said. "I will be the star of this afternoon and say Ullo will have his reading first."

Elia glanced at Morimaros with slight apology, wishing she might say something to him, but in the end these kings mattered little to her.

Ullo was twenty-four years old, born under the Violet Moon of the Year of Past Shadows. Elia paged through the proper charts while Ullo leaned over her shoulder, smiling prettily in the corner of her eye, but not pressing near enough to touch or overwhelm her. He smelled of properly burnt sugar and a current of sweat, but not unpleasantly so.

The Year of Past Shadows had been full of repeating patterns in the dawn clouds, tied back to the year before, and thus given its name. Elia kept that in mind as she carefully marked a blank sky map with stars from the night of Ullo's birth, counting everything forward, wishing she knew the clouds and very worm signs Morimaros had asked after. Or had a handful of holy bones to cast. But her father did not allow bones, or any such earthly predictions, in his records. *Unlike bones and earth,* Lear said, *the stars see all, from their greater vantage point, and are not marred by subjectivity.*

The king of Burgun's birth star was the Rabbit's Heart, rising under a crescent moon to inflict sharpness on an otherwise generous spirit. Perhaps the sharpness of a crown, she assured him, so long as he did not allow it to make him bitter.

"With so sweet a lady as you beside me, bitterness would be impossible," he replied.

Elia demurred, but her father laughed approvingly, and the Fool pointed out that some bittersweet flavors remained longest in memory.

Morimaros of Aremoria would turn thirty in just over a month, several days before this year's equinox. "But it was the equinox itself the night I was born," he offered.

"Ah," King Lear intoned excitedly, putting a sour tilt to Ullo of Burgun's smile.

"That is helpful," Elia said, repeating her charge of marking down stars and counting forward as she'd done first for Ullo. The Aremore king had been born in the Year of the Sixth Birds, and on that autumnal equinox, an hour before dawn in Aremoria, it was the Lion of War that crowned the sky. Elia glanced at her father, whose eyes narrowed on the chart. "That constellation holds your counter star, Elia," he said testily.

"It is, my lord," she agreed. "The Lion of War, rampant and constant as Calpurlugh, but instead of a stationary constant, it circles the same piece of sky, protecting or confining."

Morimaros cleared his throat. He had not moved nearer to her for his reading, but maintained his stance at the fore of his retainers, shoulders back and hands folded behind him. "Is Calpurlugh not the Eye of the Lion? It has been years since my astronomy lessons, but I thought they were pieces of each other."

"Pieces that never see one another, yes," Elia said. "They are not in sequence together, but only one or the other. Depending on the stars around them, it is either Calpurlugh or the Lion that shines, never both."

"Alas," Ullo of Burgun said.

"But the Lion is bold, and on an equinox dawn as this is, he is isolated but surrounded by . . . possibility." Elia felt an unusual urge to couch her reading, for this was a lonely one, and she could imagine it heartbreaking for a man already isolated within a crown. It was not a future she would choose for herself.

Morimaros did not seem affected, though, or particularly invested in the reading. His blue eyes remained calm, and he showed neither disappointment nor pleasure, as if none of this mattered at all.

Irritated to feel she'd wasted her time, when he had requested this reading in his letter—had it been his only way of flirtation? Appealing to her interest though he shared it not at all?—Elia straightened. "I am weary, sirs," she said, "and my companion must have arrived by now. I must see her and rest after my travel down from the north."

Immediately, Morimaros bowed, accepting her withdrawal.

The Fool clapped his hands. "I would go with you, to see Aefa."

"Please," Elia said.

Lear put a hand on Ullo's shoulder, but said to both kings, "You will see my Elia again at tomorrow's Zenith Court, where all I have promised will be decided."

The king of Aremoria said, "I hope I may speak with you, Lear, further?"

Truly, Elia thought as she kissed her father's cheek, it was her father that Morimaros had come to treat with, not her. He obviously wished alliance and dowry; not a queen, not herself.

Ullo offered his hand, and she took it, glad he at least bothered to pay her personal attention, even if his eyes lingered too long on her neck, on her wrists and the line from breast to waist. Tomorrow she would be rid of both these kings.

The king of Burgun escorted her out of the courtyard, the Fool following behind with a weird, affected gate. When they emerged into the inner yard, Elia angled toward the family keep. "Thank you," she said.

"I hope we can continue our courtship, even beyond tomorrow."

"I have . . . enjoyed your letters," she acknowledged, thinking of Aefa's recitations.

Drawing her nearer, Ullo said, "I would rather your good opinion than your father's. Aremoria may be a great commander, but I rule from the heart, and I want only what is best for my people. I think you are it, and beautiful."

Though uncomfortable at the touch of his hip to hers, Elia appreciated the honesty. "I will not favor Aremoria over Burgun based on these stars."

His smile was radiant.

The Fool's face appeared between hers and Ullo's. He smiled madly, showing all his teeth. "I was born under a grinning moon, see?"

"I do," Ullo said, laughing as though charmed. He took the hint, and stepped back from Elia, bowing over her hand. "Until tomorrow, princess."

The king of Burgun and his maroon retinue passed beyond her, marching at a leisurely pace toward the guest tower. Elia wondered at the wisdom or folly of putting both kings in the same place. They clearly did not get on, and they had been at war for two consecutive summers. Had it been her father's decision, and had he done so with a mischievous mind? Or merely at the suggestion of the stars?

"I think you would make a great queen," the Fool said, touching her hair. She suspected he'd found one of the crystals pinned with the silver web. Elia turned her head. The Fool's eyes were so like Aefa's, though the white lids drooped heavier with age despite his being nearly two decades younger than Lear. She smelled spiced meat on his breath, and the earthy fresh henna in his hair.

Elia put her fingers on his red-stained bottom lip. She did not want to be any queen, nor did she feel suited to the job. "Hush, before the stars hear."

"The vault of heaven does not listen to fools," he said brightly, and danced her across the yard.

THE STAR CHAPEL of Astora was built into the surrounding mountains, formed of heavy limestone and plaster, painted generations ago with gold flake and indigo to make the first chamber like the vault of heaven. Regan Lear passed through it, unconcerned with the public sanctuary. Heads turned as star-kissed priests and the prayerful noted the middle daughter of their king gliding through sharp and smooth as a galley in calm waters. Not since her elder sister's wedding to their duke two years ago had Regan come into this chapel, but she was immediately recognizable. Against the martial Gaela Astore, who covered herself most days in armor and the raiment of men, it was perhaps a surprise to gaze upon such a sleek, feminine princess. Regan's gown was voluminous and pale as the sky at dawn, dragging behind her in a perfect half-circle of oystered layers. She wore a veil of thin silver chains woven through her curls, and looped beneath her chin from delicate brooches at her temples. A dripping crown of rain.

And most startling of all, this princess smiled.

Today was the first day Regan had been truly happy since her mother died.

She reached the arched doorway leading to the Chapel of the Navel and heaved it open. The staircase was narrow and cold, and instantly she was assaulted by the damp air blowing down from the chapel above. This was the oldest chamber in the church, carved high into the side of the mountain long before any dukedoms, when the island welcomed people into its bleeding heart.

Regan lit no candles from the small storage alcoves. In violet darkness, she steadily ascended. Her thin-soled slippers tip-tapped against the stone, echoing forward like a gentle warning. She paused to toe them off at the top of the stairs, proceeding forward in bare feet. The passage was not long, but it narrowed in the center before widening again, like a birthing canal. Or that was how Regan imagined it, her smile brightening.

The Navel itself was merely a stone rectangle cut into the mountain, with

a ledge carved along the walls for sitting. The entrance through which
Regan had arrived looked directly across the twenty-foot length and
through two narrow stone columns, outside into the dark valley below.
Astora City was a warm glow, and beyond, velvet hills lifted gently away,
before the stretch of purple sky.

A six-pointed star had been carved through the roof, allowing moonlight
and starlight to shine dimly in. It was not the proper time of year or night
to serve its greatest function, at the apex of the Longest Night Moon.

Regan moved directly below the skylight, where the slate floor had
cracked with age, and knelt beside the only adornment: a stone water basin
carved beside a deep, narrow well. The well was covered with a wooden lid,
so Regan shoved it aside. She dipped her fingers into the stale, tired water,
ruining the dull reflection of the night sky, and touched the wet blessing to
her cheeks, her lips, and then the linen over her belly. Her hand remained
there, cupping the only star Regan cared for: the new pinprick of light in
the deep recess of her body.

She bowed her head, a smile continuing to play at her lips, and thought
of the life in her, the dynamic, dangerous spark. Her breath was low and
long, deep and content. Not a feeling Regan was accustomed to, being a
woman of sharp, fierce ambition. She rarely experienced anything like peace
in her heart. Satisfaction, however, was a thing she'd recently come to know
quite intimately, and she was pleased to discover how the one could lead to
the other.

The stars grew bolder as she waited, and color fled the sky until it was
black as black could be.

Regan imagined the moments approaching again and again: her stern
sister's mouth falling open in surprise; their embrace; the tense, rough argument, followed by renewed dedication to each other. It was a thrill to
anticipate the special, unique pleasure of being of one mind with Gaela, the
most ferocious, the great pillar of her heart.

Of course she heard her sister approach.

A clatter and grunt, the oddly gentle ringing of metal, like a song.

Regan straightened her shoulders, held her penitent pose.

Behind her, Gaela burst into the room with a quiet curse.

"Sister," Gaela said harshly. Not from anger or irritation, but for herself.
Gaela wielded her words and movements like armor and war hammers.
Regan preferred her own thorns to be small and precise and subtle, though
no less deadly.

Settling back onto her heels, Regan sang out in the language of trees.
*Sister!* One of the only such words Gaela understood.

Gaela Astore fumed out of the shadows, stomped to Regan's side, and fell hard to her knees. She wore leather and wool, an empty sword belt and a skirt of mail. Her hair was twisted back like the roots of an oak, pulling her forehead wide. She was a beauty, despite herself, Regan had always thought: a slice of moon, magnificent and dangerous.

"This should be filled in," Gaela said, gesturing at the old well. "Why did you wish to meet here? After all these months."

Regan waited, patient with Gaela as with no other.

Gaela's eyes roamed her sister's face and body, coming to rest on the hand still curled at Regan's belly. "Yes," Gaela whispered. And her mouth broadened into a toothy smile.

Regan grasped Gaela's hand and flattened it against her belly, pressing their hands together there. "The future queen."

"Or king," Gaela answered, fisting her hand in the layers of Regan's skirt, and dragged her sister toward her. They embraced. For so many years this had been a piece of their goal: Gaela on the throne of Innis Lear, with Regan's children for her heirs. Gaela had been sixteen when she swore to her sister, fast and secretly, that no child would lock into her womb, she would make sure of it. *We will be king and queen of Lear,* iron-strong Gaela had promised her willow-thin fourteen-year-old sister. *No matter husbands or rivals, it will be you and me, our bodies and our blood.* Regan had kissed her cheek and promised.

Regan kissed her again now, and touched their cheeks together. She braced for the next step.

The lady-warrior took Regan's shoulders in demanding hands and said, "How long?"

"I only was certain five days ago, and so it will come in the earliest weeks of spring. You are the first to know."

"You must marry, and fast."

"We'll say we eloped already, and everyone will believe it."

Gaela's brows lifted. "Of the neat, passionless Regan Lear? I have my doubts."

"But, sister"—Regan's lips pressed a secretive smile—"they will believe it of me with *this* man. That we were forced to hide our passion from the king."

"Who is the father?" Gaela growled.

This sparked a brilliant fire in Regan's eyes: shards of brown and tan and a blue just like their father's, tossed together in a tempest that seemed a gentle brown when beheld from the distance most gave between themselves and the sly middle daughter. Only a handful of people stood close enough to know Regan had slices of her father inside her eyes. "Lear will be so furious, Gaela," she whispered, glee and cruelty warring in the thin tone. "And Astore, too. It is the worst and the best I could do."

Understanding passed swiftly to Gaela. "Oh, Regan, my love, you did not."

"Connley, Connley, *Connley*," Regan said, differently each time. First casual, then wicked, then deep in her mouth, as if she could taste him buried there.

Gaela thrust herself to her feet. "His grandfather despised our mother! His mother sought for years to marry our father! You give Connley the hope of the crown now?"

"His children only." Regan slid to stand as well. "And a knife in our father's heart."

"So, too, it will divide us, all the more because my husband and your lover are chiefest of rivals."

"It is done."

"You should have discussed it with me!"

"You did not ask my advice when you chose Astore!"

"Ah! But Astore was the obvious, only choice! He is fierce and, by our father's and other men's reckoning, worthy of the crown. The anticipated alternate, should the line of Lear fall, because of his proven strength and his blasted stars. I chose him to play the part I want him to play. He thinks already to have a crown from me. Connley will not rest with that. Does he fear you? I will not believe if you say he does."

Regan touched her tongue to her bottom lip, uncontrolled before her sister as she was before no other. "He does not fear me, no, nor I him. But Connley feels a more possessive thing for me, one that will not drive him away as fear or pity or sorrow might drive yours."

"Surely you do not speak of *love*," Gaela scoffed. "Love is no strength."

"Not even between us?"

Gaela scoffed. "This is not love between us, we are *one*. We are beyond love!"

"Are we?" Regan touched her sister's earlobe, tugged gently. She knew Gaela had a heart of iron in her chest and cared only slightly for anything she did not feel in her very bones. Worse yet was Gaela at expressing emotions that were not the fiery sort, were not those powerful feelings allowed to great warriors and kings; she disdained all things considered womanly as she disdained her own womb. Regan could not remember if Gaela had been born so, or learned it from their father, his stars, and Dalat's death. All Regan knew was that her sister had the stars of conquerors in her sky, and such men did not love well. Gaela thought she was beyond love's reach, while Regan believed herself to be composed of nothing *but* love. Terrible, devastating, insatiable love.

"So." Gaela sighed gruffly and put her hands on Regan's hips. "This is the child of two royal lines, then."

"Three, sister. Lear and Connley and the Third Kingdom."

"Connley's grandfather said it was a taint in the blood of the island, that Dalat was here."

"*My* Connley is proud of it," Regan said.

"Connley. *Connley.*" Gaela narrowed dark eyes. "You have laid yourself with him, you bear his child, and yet do not call him the name his mother gave him?"

Regan forced herself not to lower her lashes, angry at how difficult it was to hold her sister's gaze in this moment. The union with Connley would be a wedge between them; Gaela was unfairly correct. But she still protested, "Connley is himself, and so too is he his land, his title, his own ferocious crown, sister. Connley is all the crags and peaks, the rushing waters and moors of the eastern coast." Regan's voice lowered again, memories of skin and cries and a bed of earth quieting her. "Connley is so many things more than his person."

Gaela sucked in a shocked breath. "You spoke of love, but it is *your* love. You love *him.*"

Regan shuddered, skin tightening around the dangerous expansion of her heart as something quickened, much lower.

"*Regan.*"

"Gaela." Regan sighed. "Don't you see how this is our best result? Who better to father your heirs than our father's least favored duke, one sure never to align on his side? Lear will have to swallow it, he *must,* because here, listen: Connley's stars predict it! I've seen his birth chart, and the trees are adamant. The rest of the island will rejoice at the wisdom of it. Better than marrying me to Morimaros of Aremoria! Even you see the folly in allowing talks of such nature. Connley is already ours; he is entrenched in Innis Lear, sprung from our storm-wracked waves and rooted in iron. And, Gaela, his land is wild and his keep strong; his wells are far better than this one beside us. Deep and rich and flowing. They did not give up on the rootwaters as Father ordered. Do you see? Together you and I bring the two greatest dukedoms under the line of Lear. Through your rightful crown, and my growing child. We will make this island ours, the opposite of our father's foolish skyward devotions and heartless intentions!"

"Maybe," Gaela said, unusually thoughtful. Gaela, who had always favored more direct responses. At seventeen she'd bargained with Astore directly, demanding military training for herself. At nineteen she'd plotted to poison their father, and only Regan had convinced her sister of the folly of losing the king before he—or the island—blessed Gaela's inheritance. *Love him, or pretend to; let his throne be a rock of strength and a known position, while we shore up the rest of the island for ourselves, until we are ready and our methods are impenetrable.*

"I promised you years ago," Regan soothed. "I promised you that we—that I—would be his downfall. Do you remember the star under which I was born?"

"None."

Regan swallowed the bitter word. "None. I was born under an empty sky, a sliver of blackness our father cannot bring himself to love. You were born under the Star of the Consort, with the Throne on the rise. Double stars, which Father claimed negated each other for how they were webbed that night by the sheer, high clouds. But you and I know my star was already with you. The Throne and the Consort, you and me. Father could never understand, but we do. We understand, Gaela." She clutched at her belly, the tiny star she couldn't yet feel, but already burned in her heart. Regan would destroy the world for this singular star of hers, this helpless, sparking thing. When she told Connley she was pregnant, if he hesitated for even a moment, the man—no matter how passionate, how glorious—would be sliced from her life. Regan stared at her sister, willing Gaela to agree, to accept Regan's word.

She did. Of course she did. Gaela twisted around to dip her whole hand into the well. She splashed the holy water against Regan's neck.

With the sky as witness overhead, and the sleeping city of Astora below, the sisters made new promises to each other, against their father, and toward the future of Innis Lear.

# REGAN

REGAN KNEW THAT when in residence at the Summer Seat, her sister Gaela did not share chambers with the Duke Astore, but chose instead to occupy the rooms that had been hers as a child, when this castle was Gaela's favorite for its nearness to the rocky cliffs and caves their mother had loved.

Immediately upon arriving at the keep, Regan left Connley to find his supper and knocked gently at Gaela's chamber door. "It's me, sister."

The door was thrown open and there Gaela stood, regal and tall in a dark red robe fastened with a sash, thick twists of black hair loose around her shoulders. Regan slipped inside and nudged the door shut again before putting her arms around Gaela's neck and touching their cheeks together.

Gaela kissed Regan's temple and cupped her sister's face. "Your eyes are pink."

Regan, who had only just divested herself of her cloak and muddy travel boots, pushed away and wiped her hands down the front of her bodice, as if her palms were filthy. They were not. Her hands paused for a breath just over her belly, and her face lowered.

"No!" cried Gaela, whipping around to swipe a clay jar of wine off the near table with her fist. It broke against the floor. The wine splashed, staining the wooden slats.

Starting at the streams and tiny reddish puddles, at the shards of clay, Regan saw flashes of hardened brown flesh, pieces of herself sprawled broken there. She clenched her fingers into fists, bruising her palms with her nails. The hurt relieved her.

"Why?" Gaela asked in a low, dangerous tone. She leaned back against the table, gripping its edge.

"I don't know, Gaela," Regan snarled.

"Is it Connley?"

"No."

The eldest sister stared unblinking, waiting with the gathered fury of an army.

Regan refused to be cowed, returning the gaze, cool and still.

Silence stretched between them.

The very moment sorrow slipped in to replace anger in Gaela's eyes, Regan spoke again. "I consulted with Brona Hartfare at the start of the summer, and have done all I know to do, but there is . . ."

Her sister stepped forward and embraced Regan again, tighter and with a shaking intensity.

She wept, with a weariness that dragged her toward the floor. But her sister, as always, held her upright. A tower, the strongest oak, the true root of Regan's heart.

"I won't give up," Regan said, leaning her cheek against Gaela's shoulder. She drew a deep breath, awash in the familiar scent of iron, clay, and rich evergreen that clouded Gaela. A fire crackled in the small round hearth that split the wall between the rooms they'd shared as girls: the one full of weapons and cast-off leather armor, bits of steel and pots of the soft, scented clay Gaela used to shape her hair at court; the other near empty, as Regan chose to sleep with her husband now. Though there still was a trunk left behind, filled with girlish dresses and flower dolls and Regan's first recipe of herbal secrets she'd saved for her own daughters. Uselessly, it seemed.

"Sit at the fire," Gaela ordered, with her Regan-reserved tenderness.

Regan removed her slippers and lifted a wool blanket from the hearth, gathering it about her shoulders as she sank into a low chair. "I will find a way to look inside myself, Sister. To find the cause of my . . . difficulties. There must be some magic raw and strong enough to speak with my body, to demand conversation with my womb."

Gaela dropped herself into the chair opposite Regan. "If not, we must consider Elia," she said bitterly. "Those kings courting her would not work, for they would want her issue for their own people, but perhaps . . . perhaps she could marry that bold boy, Errigal."

"Rory," Regan said. "It would be a strong match, her blood and his iron magic, though the boy himself has little power, or never developed it much, thanks to his milky mother."

"I cannot confide in Elia," Gaela said suddenly, vehemently, protesting her own suggestion. "Our baby sister is too like Lear. Takes his side, always. Would she want the crown herself, instead of making her children my heirs? Or fill their heads with starry nonsense? Would her ways weaken the children? She gave up your wormwork, too, after all. Is there any of Dalat in her? Any fire of adventure or conquest?"

"And what of my Connley, should Elia's children inherit your crown? What of him, and us?"

Gaela snorted. "I care not for Connley's prospects."

Regan bit the inside of her lips to hold her expression cool and unconcerned. This was an old ritual, and she no longer argued on Connley's behalf to her sister. Connley's future was up to Regan alone. She said, "Elia can never threaten us for the crown. She has kept herself too hidden in the star towers, as our father's starry shadow and acolyte. Some will love her for it, but not enough to follow her against us. Connley would swallow her up if she tried, even with Errigal her husband."

"On that Astore will agree."

"Let us eat, then, Gaela, and have this mess cleared."

After marching to the door, Gaela flung it open, half calling already for a servant, but there stood Elia instead.

Their youngest sister froze, startled, a hand poised to knock. She wore the drab robes of a star priest, but her hair was rolled up and decorated with a net of crystals.

Gaela's fury at the sight of Dalat's jewelry flashed in the sudden tightening of her mouth, and Elia put her hands protectively up to her hair. She said, "Father put it in this afternoon, before I went to meet the kings."

Silence stuck between them, the muscles of Gaela's jaw shifting as she controlled her anger and instincts. Regan knew that set of her sister's shoulders, and she joined Gaela in standing. Regan did not hate Elia as Gaela did, but pitied her. She touched a hand to the back of Gaela's neck. "Did you choose one king or the other?" she asked Elia coolly, as if she cared not at all.

Elia shook her head. "I came to see if you had eaten."

"We're about to," Gaela said, and stepped closer to Elia, blocking her entrance.

Though occasionally Regan thought of their mother and how Dalat would prefer her three daughters united, she remembered keenly enough that Elia forever refused to believe Lear had taken part in their mother's death. She had betrayed Dalat, and her sisters. And yet she dared arrive wearing Dalat's starry accessory. Besides, Regan's womb ached, her joints throbbed, and she could not fathom allowing the cherished, naïve Elia to see such weakness. So Regan did not protest Gaela's obvious denial of their youngest sister's overture.

For her part, Elia only frowned gently; surely she'd expected this response, if even she'd hoped for better. "I'll . . . see you in the morning, then. I wish . . ." Elia lifted her black eyes and made a determined expression she could not possibly know was reminiscent of Dalat. "When you're queen, Gaela, you must let me take care of him."

Gaela breathed sharply. "If he needs to be taken care of."

Elia nodded, glanced at Regan with a tiny sliver of unforgiveable sympathy, and left.

After a moment, Gaela called in a girl to clean up the broken pot and bring them more wine, and supper. They waited in silence, until every spilled puddle was mopped up, and each sister held a fresh clay cup full of wine.

Regan sighed. "Was she right, Gaela? Will our father name you heir tomorrow? Is that what your summons said?"

Drinking deep, Gaela glanced into the fire. Her pink tongue caught a drip of wine in the corner of her mouth. "That is what we will make happen, no matter what Lear says. *I shall set all my daughters in their places.*"

"Whatever game he plays, we will stand together and win."

Together, they raised their glasses.

# ELIA

ELIA WAS LATE to dinner.

The great hall of the Summer Seat had been built into the keep's rear wall so that nothing but sky and cliffs and sea appeared through the tall, slim windows behind the throne. The low ceiling was hung with dark blue banners embroidered with silver stars shaped like the Swan constellation, Lear's crest. Rushes and rugs covered the entire beaten earth floor, adding warmth and comfort as winds howled for most of the year, even in the height of summer. Long tables spread in two rows off the king's table at the west end, and benches were full of earls and their retainers, the companions of the visiting kings, and all the resident families. A small side door to the north of the throne, hidden behind a wool tapestry of a rowan tree, led through a narrow corridor to the guardhouse and beyond to the royal tower so that the king and his family did not ever need travel outside from their rooms to the court. Everyone else was expected to enter through the heavy double doors far across from the throne. It was through the small door that Elia arrived, alone.

It was no way for a princess to make an entrance. She lacked companion or escort, had been been denied her sisters' company, and Lear himself refused to leave his chambers, trapped in a sudden fit of starry obsession he would not share with her. There'd been a time Lear loved entertaining, loved the swell of noise that signaled a well-shared feast, Elia was certain of it, though the memories were dull with age. She'd been so small, delighted at every chance to sit on her father's knee and listen to the songs and poetry, to eat strips of meat from Lear's hand. He'd liked to dot cream and fruit syrup onto her face like constellations, sometimes daring to do the same to Dalat.

Elia paused in the arch of the doorway, carefully reeling in the far-flung line of her heart. She breathed slowly, banishing memories in favor of the cool responsibility of representing her family.

She could hardly believe Lear had abandoned her tonight, when the kings he himself had invited were waiting, expecting to be fed and flattered. It spoke to the changes in him, his most capricious stars winning whatever battle raged in his mind.

Food had already been served, for which Elia was grateful; there was no need to make an announcement now, or put herself at the center of attention. She stared out at the chaos of people, the laughing and low conversations, the men and women of the kitchens moving skillfully about with full jugs of wine and trenchers of stewed meat. There were the kings of Aremoria and Burgun, seated at the high table with Connley and Astore at either end. Aremoria spoke evenly in response to Astore's boisterous laughter, while Burgun and Connley seemed to grit their teeth behind smiles. Elia could not be sure if Connley's dislike of Burgun aligned her with him for the first time.

She should go direct to the high table, she knew, and reminded herself firmly. She should be gracious and calm, perhaps tell the story of her wager with Danna, or ask after the kings' own families. Though that would invite questions in return about her sisters and father. No, she could not lead them so easily into uncertain territory. Just as she took a step, a beloved voice called, "Starling!"

Spinning, Elia held out her arms in preparation for her mother's half-brother to pick her up in an eager hug. The Oak Earl had always been a brightness in her life, rather a rarity after Dalat died. But Kayo could not help making a bold impression, with his stories from the Third Kingdom, from trading caravans and merchant fleets, deserts and inland seas the likes of which few in Innis Lear could truly imagine. He ventured westward every two or three years, carrying trade agreements for Lear while growing his own riches, but for the most part, he lived here on the island, where his favorite sister had been so happy. He had never taken a wife, instead latching on to Lear's family like a cousin. Kayo was perhaps the only person in the world all three Lear girls admired: Gaela for his adventures, Regan for his penetrating insight, and Elia because he came home.

"Uncle," she said now, carefully, as she was always careful when performing emotions in public.

"Elia." The Oak Earl leaned away, gray eyes full of gladness. He lowered his voice, bending to knock their foreheads together affectionately. "How are you?"

"Nervous, I admit," she said, breathing in the sea-blasted smell of him.

"So would I be. Do you have a favorite between your suitors?"

"No," she whispered.

"Aremoria, then," Kayo said.

"Burgun has been more interested in me," she murmured. "Courted and flirted and given me gifts."

"Is that the sort of husband you want? The sort who buys you?"

She angled her head to meet his gaze. "I don't know Aremoria at all."

"He has the more certain reputation."

"But certain of what?" she asked, almost to herself.

Kayo smiled grimly and offered his arm. She took it, and together they went to the high table. Elia introduced Kayo to Aremoria and Burgun, and her uncle effortlessly launched into a tale of the last time he'd passed through the south of Aremoria, on his way home from the Third Kingdom.

Able to relax somewhat, Elia picked at the meat and baked fruit in the shared platter before her, sipping pale, tart wine. She listened to the conversation of the surrounding men, smiling and occasionally adding a word. But her gaze tripped away, to the people arrayed before her, who seemed boisterous and happy.

The Earls Errigal, Glennadoer, and Bracoch sat together, the latter two both with their wives, and Bracoch's young son gulping his drink. A familiar head leaned out of her line of sight behind Errigal, just before she could identify him.

It might've been the drink, but Elia felt overwhelmingly as though this bubble of friendliness would burst soon, bleeding all over her island.

Or it might have been that she herself would burst, from striving to contain her worries and loneliness, from longing for inner tranquility in the face of roiling, wild emotions. How did her sisters do it, maintain their granite poise and elegant strength? Was it because they had each other, always?

Elia had never known her sisters not to present a united front. Gaela had been deathly ill for three whole weeks just before she married, and Regan had nursed her alone through the worst of it. When Regan had lost her only child as a tiny month-old baby, Gaela had broken horses to get to her, and let no one blame Regan, let no one say a word against her sister. Elia remembered being pushed from the room, not out of anger or cruelty, but because Gaela and Regan forgot her so completely in their grief and intimacy. There was simply no place for her. Though, like tonight, they did sometimes push her out on purpose.

The first time had been the morning their mother died.

After being refused by her sisters tonight, Elia had gone to Lear. He'd opened the barred door to the sound of her voice, only to stare in horror and confusion. "Who are you?" he'd hissed, before shutting the door again. Right in her face.

*Who are you?*

Elia wanted to scream that she *did not know.*

She lifted her wine and used the goblet to cover the deep, shaking breath she took, full of the tart smell of grapes.

This was worse, more uncertain, than she'd ever seen her father. Perhaps if she'd not decided to continue her studies this spring at the north star tower, and instead had remained at his side after the winter at Dondubhan, he would not be so troubled. Perhaps if her sisters bothered to care, they could help. Or at least listen to her!

*Dalat, my dear.*

Had Lear expected his wife tonight, not his youngest daughter? Was he completely mad?

She should ask the stars, or even—perhaps—slip out to the Rose Court-yard again, and try to touch a smear of rootwater from the well to her lips. Would the wind have any answers?

The Earl Errigal slammed his fist on the table just below Elia, jolting her out of her traitorous thoughts. Errigal was arguing ferociously with the lady Bracoch, and then Elia's eyes found the person she'd missed in her earlier agitation.

Older, stronger, different, but that bright gaze held the same intense promise. It was *him.*

Ban.

Ban Errigal.

An answer from the island to her unasked questions.

He was dressed like a soldier, in worn leather and breeches and boots, quilted blue gambeson, a sword hanging in a tired sheath. Taller than her, she was certain, despite his seat on the low bench. He never had been tall, before. His black hair, once long enough to braid thickly back, was short, slicked with water that dripped onto his collar. His tan skin was roughened by sun, and stars knew what else, from five years away in a foreign war, his brow pinched and his countenance stormy.

How could his return not have been in her star-patterns? They must have been screaming it, surely—or had it been there, hiding behind some other prophecy? Twined through the roots of the Tree of Birds? Had she missed it because all her focus had been on Lear and the impending choices about her family's future? Had she refused to see?

Over the years she'd forcibly rejected even Ban's name from her thoughts. Easy to imagine she'd missed some sign of his homecoming.

What else had she missed?

Elia was staring, and she realized with an embarrassed shock that he was very attractive. Not like his brother, Rory, who took after their blocky, striking father, but like his mother. There was a feral glint to his eyes, like fine steel or a cat in the nighttime. She wanted to know everything behind that look, everything about where he'd been, what he'd done. His adventures, or his crimes. Either way, she wanted to know him as he was now.

Ban Errigal noticed her looking, and he smiled.

Light flickered in Elia's heart, and she wondered if he still talked to trees.

Her breath rushed out, nearly forming whispered words that only he would understand, of all the folk in this hot, bright hall.

But she did not know him, not anymore. They were grown and distant as stars from wells. And Elia had her place under her father's rule; she understood her role, and how to play it. So she averted her gaze and sipped her wine, reveling silently in the feel of sunshine inside her for the first time in a long while:

Ban was home.

# THE FOX

AT THE HIGHEST rampart of the Summer Seat, a wizard listened to the wind. He sighed whispered words of his own, in the language of trees, but the salt wind did not reply.

He ought to have remembered the cadence here, the slight trick of air against air, of hissing wind through stone, skittering through leaves, but it was difficult to concentrate.

All he could think was *Elia*.

## ELEVEN YEARS AGO,
## INNIS LEAR

THE QUEEN WAS dead.

And dead a whole year tonight.

Kayo had not slept in three days, determined to arrive at the memorial ground for the anniversary. He'd traveled nearly four months from the craggy, stubbled mountains beyond the far eastern steppe, over rushing rivers to the flat desert and inland sea of the Third Kingdom, past lush forests and billowing farmland, through the bright expanse of Aremoria, across the salty channel, and finally returned to this island Lear. The coat on his back, the worn leather shoes, the headscarf and tunic, woolen pants, wide sack of food, his knife, and the rolled blanket were all he had come with, but for a small clay jar of oil. This last he would burn for the grand-daughter of the empress.

*Dalat.*

Her name was strong in his mind as he pushed aside branches and shoved through the terrible shadows of the White Forest of Innis Lear, but her voice . . . that he could not remember. He'd not heard it in five years, since he left to join his father's cousins on a trade route that spanned east as far as the Kingdom knew. Dalat had been his favorite sister, who'd raised him from a boy, and he'd promised to come back to her when he finished his travels.

He'd kept his promise, but Dalat would never know it.

Wind blew, shaking pine needles down upon him; each breath was crisp and evergreen in his throat. Every step ached; the line of muscles between his shoulders ached; his thighs and cracking knees ached; his temples and burning eyes, too. He was so tired, but he was nearly there. To the Star Field, they called it, the royal memorial ground of Innis Lear, in the north of the island near the king's winter residence.

First Kayo had to get through the forest. God bless the fat, holy moon, nearly full and bright enough to pierce the nightly canopy and show him the way.

It seemed he had stumbled onto a wild path: wide enough for a mounted rider, and Kayo recalled the deer of the island being sturdier than the scrawny, fast desert breeds. He'd hunted them, riding with a young earl named Errigal and an unpleasant old man named Connley. They'd used dogs. His sister had loved the dogs here.

*Dalat,* he thought again, picturing her slow smile, her spiky eyelashes. She'd been the center of his world when Kayo was here, adrift in this land where the people were as pale as their sky. Dalat had made him belong, or made him feel so at least, when their mother sent him here because she had no use for boys, especially ones planted by a second husband. Dalat had smelled like oranges, the bergamot kind. He always bought orange-flower liqueur when he found it now, to drink in her honor.

His sister was dead!

And dead an entire year. He'd laughed and sung around bright fires; he'd slept curled in camp beside his cousins during the hottest hours of the day, when the sun colored the sky with sheer, rippling illusions. His heart had been satisfied, if not quite full, even though she'd been dead already, buried on this faraway rock.

Kayo stopped walking. The edge of the forest was near, making its presence known by a bluish glow: moonlight on the rocky moor beyond. Behind and around him the forest sighed, swelling with a warm, wet breeze that nudged the trees into whispered conversation.

"Who are you?" a high voice asked.

A boy stood just out of his reach, but Kayo already had his curved knife drawn, a leg thrown back to brace for attack. In the dark, shadows shifted and danced, and the boy stood near a wide oak tree, against its dark side, hidden from stray moonlight.

"Kayo of Taria Queen," he said, sheathing his knife back in the sash where it belonged. He pulled his scarf off his head, letting it pool around his neck and shoulders. This made his gray eyes clearer, and he hoped friendly to the boy, even with his foreign clothes and skin.

"I don't know you." The boy said it with finality, despite being very small, no older than ten years, skinny, and with a snarl of dark hair. He was not pale, though his features were narrow like those of the islanders. Except the strong nose and gremlin-round eyes. Southern Ispanian, Kayo thought: those refugee tribes roaming and homeless, pushed out by the Second Kingdom's wars.

Kayo nodded his head in a polite bow. "You know of me, boy. My sister was the queen, and I've come for the year memorial."

"The princess is there already."

This information was useful, though strangely offered. Lear had three princesses, after all, though the youngest must be this boy's age. Perhaps the boy only cared about the child he knew best. Such was the way of youth. "Do you know how the queen died?" Kayo asked. He'd heard rumors of misdeeds, of suspicion, of mystery, and perhaps the child could give him the unvarnished truth to point him the way of revenge.

The boy tilted his face up to put narrowed eyes on the sky. "The stars."

"The stars killed her?" What nonsense was this?

"She died when the stars said she would." The boy shrugged, a jolting, angry gesture. "They control everything here."

The prophecy. Kayo felt a worm of discomfort in his stomach. "What's your name?"

The boy startled and glanced past Kayo as if hearing something Kayo was not attuned to. But Kayo trusted it, and turned to look behind himself.

A woman appeared out of the trees. She said in a honeyed tone, "Ban, leave me to speak with this man."

The boy dashed off.

Kayo waited, oddly reeling, his instincts rumbling trouble.

The woman stepped silently, dressed in island clothes: a cinched tunic over a woolen shirt and layered skirts, hard boots. Her hair fell in heavy black curls around her lovely tan face: a woodwoman, a spirit of this White Forest. When she gestured for him to join her on the final part of the path, so they would come out at the edge of the woods together, Kayo found himself unable to resist.

They stopped at the opening of the trees, looking down upon the Star Field. It was a shallow valley of rugged grass, covered with towers of stones and columns of seashells stacked by human hands to waist- or knee-height. Long slabs of gray rock rested as altars, etched with the uncivilized scratches of the language of trees. Candles were stuck to the stone piles, to the slabs, some fat and well made, some skinny and poor, others in clusters and still more lonely and reaching. As Kayo watched, two priests in white clothes walked through with long torches, lighting each and every candle.

Behind the two priests came a silent procession.

"It is the king," the woman said. "Lear and his court, his daughters, and some foreign guests, come to light a new year-candle at the fallen queen's celestial bed."

Kayo's brow pinched and his jaw tightened with grief. Every candle flame was a star, wavering and flickering across the valley. Though other memorial fields dotted Innis Lear, this was the grandest. The loved ones of the dead needed only supply a candle, and the star priests would light it every night. King Lear provided gifts of candles for any who asked, Kayo had heard, so that the Star Field was always aglow, always twinkling its own heaven back to the sky. A fitting memorial for a woman like Dalat.

"Come," the woman said.

"Who are you?" he asked, voice rough with sorrow.

"Brona Hartfare, and I was a friend to your sister the queen. I remember you, when you were more of a boy, solemn and secure at her side, far south of here at the Summer Seat."

"Brona," he said. It was a name that expanded to fit every nook of his mouth.

They walked carefully down into the Star Field, circling wide so as to join the rear of the congregation as it wove through the candles and standing stones to a broad slab of limestone that shone under the full moon. Brona took Kayo's hand, holding him apart from the crowd.

King Lear looked as Kayo remembered, though perhaps with more wrinkles at his pink mouth. Maybe that was the result of so many separate candles pressing together with their competing lights. His hair was brown and thick, woven into a single braid and pinned in an infinity loop. A white robe hung from his tall frame, over white trousers and a white shirt and white boots. All the royalty and many of the rest wore white, too, or unbleached wool and linen. Very little jewelry adorned them, but for simple pearls or silver chains. Moon- and candlelight turned all their eyes dark against pink and cream and sometimes sandy skins.

The king held the hand of a small girl whose curls were big around her head, some copper-brown strands flaring in the candlelight. Her focus was on her father and the monument slab they approached. Behind her came the two older sisters, arms around each other, leaning together as if a single body: one barely a woman, soft and graceful; one strong and dark as Dalat. Kayo caught his breath at her—the eldest, Gaela—whose face was so like her mother's had been. He remembered Gaela as a whip-strong child, competing with the sons of retainers and lords in races and strength, wearing pants and her hair cut short to flare exactly like his own had done. He'd enjoyed teaching her wrestling holds and a better grip for her dagger, but the girl had taken it all seriously, no games or teasing allowed. Now her hair was longer and braided into a grand crown, and though she wore white, her clothes were a warrior's white gambeson and pants and boots, and a long coat decorated with plates of steel too far apart to be useful. Her sister Regan dressed like a fine lady, despite being only a slender slip of womanhood.

Kayo's memories of her were so much gentler; Regan had been ten years old when he left, though already reading and writing as well as a scholar. She had the least of Dalat in her, outwardly: the palest brown of the girls, with brown hair thick and smoothly waved.

And the little one, whom Kayo had hardly known: her small round face pulled into sadness, her tiny fingers caught in Lear's as the king knelt at the memorial slab, tears obvious on his cheeks and chin, glittering in his dark beard.

Kayo felt tears pinch his own throat, crawling up into his nose. He clenched his jaw, and Brona leaned into him, her shoulder against his chest. She smelled like fire and rich moss. What a comfort to breathe her in, her hair brushing his mouth, though how weak of him to let her feel his trembling.

A star priest with a flickering torch lifted his arms and called out a prayer. Kayo could only just hear the sounds, not comprehend the words: he was unpracticed these days. The rhythm, though, was familiar, the crying, sharp intonation the priests of the island used to speak with the stars. All the gathered company murmured and mouthed along with the priest, except for one young man several steps back from the king's daughters. This was a prince in the burnt orange of the kingdom of Aremoria, the coat sleeves wrapped with white in deference to the mourning traditions of Innis Lear. He wore a solemn expression and a heavy, jeweled sword, a simple band of gold at his brow. No older than Gaela Lear.

As the prayer lifted, Kayo pictured Dalat, imagined her here in a dress of the finest red cloth, spiked through with orange thread and a brilliant turquoise like the surf of the inland sea. Red and black paint on her eyes and mouth, streaked into her hair. Her eyes were stars, and the hundreds of candles here glowed only to reflect her glory.

Kayo looked to see the king bow his head and clutch at his youngest daughter's hand. The little girl's brow furrowed in pain. Her fingers were squeezed too hard, but she said nothing, and did not pull away.

# AEFA

Aefa was inordinately anxious as she entered the great hall of the Summer Seat the morning of the Zenith Court. She'd left Elia with her father, despite arguing hard for several long moments in the corner of the king's chamber. But Elia insisted upon arriving with Lear, unconcerned by the visual it would create, and the statement it would make, particularly to Gaela and Regan. "My sisters have already made up their minds," Elia insisted, which was true. "I will stay at my father's side, because he needs me." Which was also true, no matter how Aefa wished otherwise.

At least Elia had allowed herself to be laced into a new, bright yellow overdress, one that pulled at her hips and breasts pleasingly, because, Aefa said, "You have a much better set of *both* than either Gaela or Regan." Elia had pursed her lips, embarrassed, but it was *also* true. And Aefa had spent over an hour with the princess's hair, creating an elaborate braided knot at Elia's nape, twisted with purple ribbons and the net of crystals. She'd smeared red paint on Elia's bottom lip and dotted it at the corner of each eye, and insisted upon a silver ring for every finger and both sapphires for the thumbs. Aefa lost the shoe debate, but Elia's reliance on her old thick-soled leather boots was at least practical. Though Aefa thought she should look into several more pairs, just as sturdily made, but perhaps dyed gray and black to better compliment a variety of gowns, or even plain priestly robes and stubbornness.

It was ridiculous how focused Aefa allowed herself to be on such matters, but better this than spinning her mind tighter and tighter around all the dreadful gossip she'd gathered last night. The rumors about the king and his temper were terrible: he frequently lost his way in conversations, or would say one thing and then directly do the opposite. Not in any way that seemed politically motivated, or even with the casual carelessness of men, but more like he'd asked for roasted bird only to rage at its presence, insisting he'd always preferred venison and to say otherwise was treason. Lear had punished two reeves last month for skimming profits, but there'd been no hearing: the stars alone had cast judgment, via a single prophecy the king himself charted. Most of the court thought the reeves guilty, but so too did most think that wasn't exactly the point. The clerks were afraid, and admitted drunkenly to a steward, who told Jen in the kitchen, that they'd been working with Gaela and Astore on the island's finances without the king's permission. But what else should they do, when the king did nothing? Retainers were enjoying themselves, for the most part, secure in Lear's goodwill. So the king had a happy army, at least, if a lazy one. Then Aefa'd heard all the crows were gone from the Summer Seat and Sunton, and honestly she couldn't remember the last time she'd heard one. It shouldn't have been the worst of the news, yet she couldn't shake the eerie nature of it.

Aefa had longed to sit Elia down and unload all the anxiety that had built up in the people of the Summer Seat, and in Aefa's own heart, but Elia's eyes had never once welcomed honesty this morning, instead tripping again and again out the window, toward the horizon, distant and cool. So Aefa kept her mouth shut, though she did not hesitate to touch Elia's wrist, or linger gently with her hands on the princess's shoulders. That was how it always was between them: a silent promise, evidence that sharing comfort could be a strength, when Elia was ready to see it.

She'd also poured every drop of Brona Hartfare's rootwater into Elia's morning milk.

Because without Elia, Aefa was not part of the family enough to use the private doors, she let herself in to the great hall by the much heavier forward doors. Dragging one open, she was glad enough at the retainer in dark blue who held it while she slipped quietly in, that Aefa winked at him in her more usual manner.

The Fool sat in the king's throne, far across the hall from Aefa, wearing a tattered blue dress with trousers beneath, rings in his ears and paint on his lip and eyes. He cradled a shallow bowl in his lap, in which Lear's tall bronze and ruby crown sat like stiff porridge.

If she'd not already been walking on edge, the sight would've cut her feet to ribbons.

Aefa mirrored her princess by taking a deep breath, pasting on a bright but neutral smile, and so made her way down the central aisle to her father.

The courtiers and guests had arrayed themselves throughout the hall in the patterns and pieces of their island and alliances: Dukes, earls, and ladies, the alders and reeves from nearby towns, and further representatives of all the king's retainers, too. They divided into groups of friends and cousins, to either side of the throne dais, depending on if they favored Astore or Connley. All the feasting tables were gone, and benches lined the long walls, pressing the thick tapestries back. Light blazed in, white and salty, from the tall windows along the west and south walls.

Of great interest to Aefa were the kings of Aremoria and Burgun, waiting separate here by the far end with the door, their retainers and escorts in clusters five men thick. Ullo of Burgun gleamed in ermine and leather heavy enough to add a glisten of sweat to the overall shine of his smile and bright teeth and slick long hair. He caught her eye, and before Aefa could so much as raise a brow, his glance fell to her breasts. She scowled and thought to herself that he wouldn't recognize elegant beauty if it landed him on his ass.

Across from Ullo, firmly set among his men, Morimaros of Aremoria flicked his eyes over Aefa, too, information gathering and nothing else. As if she were a strip of land that he must face his enemy upon, and he would quickly sum up its boundaries and flaws. Just like his letters. She let her smile quirk up on one side, recalling his dry descriptions of Aremore agriculture. Unlike Ullo, he did not flaunt his crown, but matched his retainers in leather armor, just lacking their orange tabard with its lion crest. The only sign of richness were the heavy rings on his strong hands.

"Aefa!" called the Fool from the throne. She bowed elaborately at her father, and skipped a step or two, before slowing to a more respectful pace: Near the throne dais stood the eldest daughters, Gaela and Regan, shoulder to shoulder.

They were terrifying.

It galled Aefa to be afraid of them, but she'd never shaken it.

Strong in body and tongue, Gaela had spent her earliest years with soldiers, driving herself hard enough to grow wide through her shoulders and solid flank, to hold her own against nearly any warrior. Even now, in a gown of blood red and purple, the oldest princess wore a bright silver pauldron over her shield shoulder, made of chain mail and steel plates. Her black hair was molded into a crown with streaks of white clay, and laced with dark purple ribbons. Aefa needed to talk with Gaela's girls about the styling. Earrings shaped like knives hung from her lobes, tiny little threats.

Beside her, Regan was rather like a knife herself: pointed and sharp. Regan's brown waves fell under a cascade of glass beads and pearls. She wore a high-waisted gown with layers and layers of cream and violet velvet that would be impossible to keep so pristine. Her slippers had tiny heels, and her girdle was woven of silk and lace. Keys and coins and an amethyst the size of her fist hung from it. Regan wore a ring on every finger, and her nails were colored crimson. She was jarringly beautiful, like jagged crystal or vengeful ghosts.

Aefa managed a moment of steady pleasure that she'd inadvertently put Elia in complimentary colors. It would anger the sisters, but be just as much a statement as Elia arriving on her father's arm.

The sisters' husbands waited to either side of the dais, and there was not enough space between them given the depth of their rivalry. Astore loomed to the right, grinning and loudly conversing with a handful of men out of the Glennadoer earldom, and their retainers in attendance, too. Across the other side of the dais were the Earl Errigal and a dark, quiet slip of a man in the sky blue of Errigal's banners. With them was the Earl Rosrua. With Astore, the Earl Bracoch.

Oh, stars and worms. Aefa paused in place, realizing the man with Errigal had to be that son she'd heard so much about—the bastard. Brona had been correct in her warning of his return. Elia never spoke of him directly, but everyone in the king's service Aefa had ever met during her time with the princess was more than happy to do so. Before she could say—she wasn't quite sure, but something—a hand caught gently under her elbow.

"Aefa Thornhill," said the Duke of Connley, "allow my escort to your place."

He was six or seven years her elder, and as handsome as his wife Regan was beautiful, but in a fully Learish way: sharp white cheeks and coppery-blond hair slicked back from his face, pink lips that might've just been kissed, and eyes as blue-green as the ocean around Port Comlack, steady under a serious brow. Someday his face would be cragged and rough, but now it was perfect. His blood red tunic fit the sort of shoulders a girl longed to climb. Too bad he always gave Aefa a shudder; she couldn't help but imagine him stripping her down, past clothes and even skin, to her very bones, if she ever said the wrong thing.

"Thank you," she said, with no hint of a flirt.

"Elia hasn't arrived with you," he said, solicitous but quick, for it was a brief walk to the throne.

Aefa smiled like it meant nothing. "She attended the king all this morning, so presumably will come with him."

"Presumably." Connley smiled back at her, a charming wolf in the woods.

Yes, there it was, the shudder. Aefa disguised it with a curtsey, relieved to be already at the dais. "Lord," she said steadily.

"We hope your lady proves as considerate of your father's needs after this morning, and into the future," Connley said, gently squeezing her elbow.

He stepped back and nodded in a way that was not quite a bow, but managed to suggested such. "And her own."

"I'm sure she will be," Aefa said, mildly irritated through the general chill of his presence.

"Someone will make sure of it," he said quietly, and she had no chance to react, for there was her father, leaning off the throne.

"My girl!" the Fool crowed. "Tell me: what is this crown in my lap made of?"

"Love," she called back. "Love and rubies."

"The bronze is for the love, then?"

"The bronze is the island metal, the rubies its blood. What else is love but mettle and blood?" Aefa grinned.

The Fool lifted the crown, as if to offer it to his daughter.

"The crown of Innis Lear is not made of love," said Gaela Lear, soft and challenging. "It is made of dying stars, and lying mouths."

Just then a great triple knock sounded throughout the hall, echoing through the wooden north wall. A signal that the king approached.

"Not for long," Regan answered her sister. "Get up, Fool, and make way for the king."

THIS IS WHAT *they say* of the last King of Innis Lear's Zenith Court:

The day held itself bright and bold, a brisk wind rising off the sea in fragile anticipation. All had assembled by the noon hour, but the king arrived late. He shoved in through the slender private entrance with his youngest, favored daughter at his side. They swept directly to the throne, and few noticed Kayo, the Oak Earl, brother of the fallen queen, follow behind and settle himself at the rear of the dais.

Lear wore ceremonial robes crusted with deep blue and star-white embroidery, brushed and glistening. His gray-and-brown hair shocked away from his face, hanging down his back, and his scraggly beard had been shaved. Kingly gold and silver rings weighed down his gnarled fingers, and a sword with a great round pommel carved into a rampant swan hung from a jeweled belt at his hip. The youngest princess was a delicate slip of daylight as she took her place beside the throne, across from her two vibrant sisters.

The king smiled. "Welcome."

Courtiers returned the greeting loudly, with calls and cheering. They expected great things from the next hour: a future queen, and a resettling of alliances. And hope. For far too long Innis Lear had faltered and run dry; for far too long there was no named successor; for far too long privilege and fate had danced unfettered as the king drifted further and further into the sky.

Lear called out, "Today is an auspicious day, friends. As my father obeyed the stars, and his father before him, so I bow to them now by offering this announcement: The stars have aligned to provide your king the understanding that his reign comes to a swift end. It is time for me to divest myself of cares and responsibilities, to pass them on, as time passes, to younger and stronger persons."

Murmurs of general accord and interest skittered about the hall, but no one interrupted as Lear continued, "Therefore we must see our daughters settled before the end, which comes at Midwinter."

Yes, here was the moment of destiny:

"Astore, our beloved son." Lear turned to his eldest daughter's husband, who nodded firmly.

The king then looked to the middle husband. "And you, our son Connley." The Duke Connley murmured, "My king," and nothing else, for all knew the lie of any love between them.

The king continued grandly, "You have long held discord between you, and we know that when we die very likely war and strife would erupt between you as you each would try to claim more of the other's."

"Father," said Gaela, "there is a single sure way to stop such an outcome."

He held up his hand. "To stop this, we will divide our lands now between your wives, according to the stars, and our youngest daughter, Elia, whose suitors have waited patiently to hear her choice."

"And would wait longer still, good Lear, for the chance," called the king of Burgun with a smile in his voice.

Lear returned it. "Indeed."

The king of Aremoria said nothing.

Kay Oak stepped forward, a hand hovering protectively near the youngest daughter's shoulder. "Lord," he said, going briefly to his knee. "Your kingdom wants for a single crown. Why—"

Lear cut him off. "Worry not! We will name our heir now, as the stars have prophesied. And our heir will be crowned at dawn after the Longest Night, as has been since the first king of our line." Lear looked at Gaela, his ferocious and tall eldest, then cool Regan, the middle child, then Elia, his precious star, finally in her turn. That youngest stared rigidly at her father. She did not even seem to breathe.

Did she suspect what was to come?

The king spread his hands again, chest puffed and proud. "The stars of heaven proclaim the next queen of Innis Lear shall be the daughter who loves us best."

In the silence, nearly everyone looked at Elia, for all knew she was the king's favorite. But Lear had not said, *the daughter I love best.*

Though all three women were practiced at projecting to the world the face they chose, each gave something away in that moment: Gaela her hunger, Regan her pleasure, and Elia her utter disgust.

"Eldest," the king said, "it is your right to speak first."

Gaela laughed once, loud as a man. "My father, my king," she called, moving before the throne to perform for the entire court. "I love you more than the word itself can bear." Her voice made the phrase into a growling threat. "My devotion to the crown of Lear is as great as any child ever bore for her father, more than life and breath, and I will defend my love with all the strength and power of Lear and Astore behind me. The truth of my words is in my stars: I am the Consort Star; I rise to the Throne of Innis Lear."

Nodding with elaborate satisfaction, Lear said, "And you, Regan? How do you answer?"

Regan did not immediately move to join Gaela before the throne, but her husband put his hand on her back and gently pushed. She spread her hands in a simple gesture of supplication. "I love you, Father, as my sister does, for we share a heart and we share stars. I ask that you appraise me at her same worth." For a moment, her words hung in the air. Connley's hand slid up the brown arch of her neck, and Regan frowned, then smiled up at her father as if she had only just now realized some vital truth: "Yet, Father, in my deepest heart I find that although Gaela names my love, she stops short, for there is no other love that moves me so much as my love for you."

The king smiled magnanimously at Regan, then Gaela. The sisters glanced at each other, as if they could sharpen their smiles against each other's teeth.

"Well said, daughters," said the king of Innis Lear, before looking to his youngest.

She stared back.

"Elia, our joy?" the king said tenderly. "What will you say?"

Silence thundered throughout the great hall.

Courtiers leaned in, to hear the first breath she took in answer. All she had to do was be honest, and the island would be hers. All she had to do was tell the world what it already knew: she loved her father, and always had.

But when Elia Lear spoke, she said, "Nothing, my lord."

"What?"

Lear's calm demand echoed in the mouths of others. What had the princess said? Why? What was this game? Did the king and his daughter play it together, or was it a trap?

Elia spoke up. "Nothing, my lord."

Lear smiled as to an errant puppy. "Nothing will come from nothing. Try again, daughter."

"I cannot heave my heart into my mouth, Father. I love you . . . as I should love you, being your daughter, and always have. You know this." Elia's voice shook.

"If you do not mend your speech, Elia," the king said, glowering, "you will mar your fortunes."

Swallowing, Elia finally took a very deep breath. She smoothed hands down her skirts, and said, "If I speak, I will mar everything else."

Lear leaned toward her. A wild thing scattered in his usually warm blue eyes. Wild and terrifying. "So untender?"

"So true," she whispered.

"Then let truth be your only dowry, ungrateful girl," he rasped.

Elia stepped away in shock.

The king's demeanor transformed like a rising phoenix, hot and blasting and fast. He pointed at Elia, finger shaking as if she were a terrible specter or spirit to be feared. "You false child. You said you understood me, you saw the stars with me. . . ." Lear threw his arms up, catching fingers in his silver-striped hair. "This is not Elia! Where is my daughter, for you are not she. No princess, no daughter! Replaced by earth saints, cursed creatures!" He shook his head as if appalled, eyes wide and spooked.

"Father," Elia said, but before anyone else could react, the king cried out: "Where are Aremoria and Burgun? Come forward, kings!"

Elia did not move, rooted to the rushes and rugs, trembling, as if holding back something so great, that to move would be to unleash it.

"Here, sir," spoke Ullo of Burgun. "What now?"

Lear smiled into the stunned silence, and it was clear where Regan had gotten her dangerous expressions. "My good king Burgun, you have been on a quest for this once-daughter of mine's love, and you now see the course of it. Would you have her still?"

Ullo stood to one side of Elia. He bowed and glanced at her. She gave nothing in return; her specialty today. When Ullo straightened he said, "Your Highness, I crave only what was promised to me: your daughter and the price of her dowry."

"My *daughter* came with that dowry. This girl is . . . not she." The last was said in a hush of awe or fear; it was impossible for any to tell.

Ullo took the princess's rigid hand in his, drawing her attention up to his overly sad expression. "I am sorry, lovely Elia, that in losing a father today you also lose a husband."

Elia choked on a laugh, and the great hall finally saw anger press through the cracks of her composure: "Be at peace with it, and not sorry, Ullo of Burgun. Since fortune and dowry are what you love, ours would not have been a good union anyway."

Far to the left, the Earl Errigal sputtered to hide a great laugh.

Ullo snatched his hand away and, with a pinched face, snapped for his retainers and took his leave.

A half-emptier great hall remained.

"And you, Aremoria?" Lear intoned with all the drama he was able. "Would you have her? As I've nothing but honor and respect for you, great king, I advise you against it. I could not tell you to partake of a thing I hate."

The youngest princess faltered back from the vitriol, knocking into a wall of leather and muscle: the king of Aremoria. His even, shrewd gaze leveled over her head and landed fully on her father.

"It seems, Lear," Morimaros said, calm and clear, "Quite strange that this girl to whom you previously vowed the greatest of affections should in the course of not even an hour strip away every layer of love you once felt. What incredible power she has to erase a lifetime of feeling in one rather quiet moment."

"When she was my daughter, I thought her power was that of the moon when it darkens the sun, as her mother's was," Lear said, sour and sad. "I thought she would be my comfort and queen, as her mother was. Now she is nothing, worth nothing."

Morimaros turned his gaze off the king and put the full weight of it onto the daughter. "This woman is her own dowry."

"Take her, then," Lear said nastily. "She is yours, mine no longer or ever again."

"Father," said Elia.

"No!" The king covered his eyes, clawed his face. "No father to you, for you cannot be my daughter Elia. My daughter Elia should have been queen, but she is nothing!"

"No!" Elia cried. It was the loudest she had ever been.

Even Gaela and Regan seemed surprised: the one grimacing, the other with her lips coolly parted.

Kayo said, "Lear, you cannot be—"

"Silence, Oak Earl. I loved her most, yet when I need her, she turns on me. She should have been queen!" Lear flung himself back onto his throne so hard it shifted with a groan.

Kayo strode forward and went to his knees before the throne. "My king, whom I have ever loved and respected as both my liege and my brother, do not be hasty."

"Would you put yourself in my furious sights now, Kayo?" demanded Lear. He turned to Connley and Astore. "You two, divide this island between yourselves, in equal parts. All of it to you and your issue with my daughters. Gaela and Regan both be all the queens of Lear! There are no others!"

"Lear!" yelled the Oak Earl, slowly stretching to his feet. "I will challenge this, I will speak. Even if you tear at my heart, too. I chose this island and your family—our family!—long ago. I have defended your countenance against rumors and detractors, but now you are acting the madman all say you've become. My service to you—and to Dalat—insists I speak against this wildness. You are rash! Giving two crowns will destroy this island, and for God's sake, Elia does not love you least."

"On your life, be quiet." The king closed his eyes as if in pain.

"My life is meant to be used against your enemies, Lear, and right now you are your own enemy." Kayo ground out the last between his teeth.

"Get out of my sight, both of you—go together if you must, but do not be here."

"Let me remain, *Brother* Lear."

"By the stars—"

"The stars are false gods if they tell you to do this thing!"

Lear leapt to his feet again with a cry of rage.

Astore dove between the king and Kayo. "Be careful," he said to the Oak Earl.

But Kayo shoved him away, angry as the king. He cried, "My sister, *your wife,* would hate you for this, Lear. She died for your stars, man! Was that not enough? And now you give over your kindest, best daughter? How can you? How *dare* you? And divide your island? Do this and you undercut everything wise and good you have ever done! One heir is all! Make one of them the queen, or this island will tear apart, and do not abandon Elia, who loves you best!"

Lear put his nose to Kayo's, making them two sides of a raging coin. "You say you chose us, but you do not act it. You do not believe in my stars, you do not cleave to my will, and despite always saying otherwise, you have taken no wife or rooted in your lands here. Always half here and half away, Kayo! You said you were mine, but you never were. You never were!" The king's mouth trembled. "Go to the god of your Third Kingdom, Kayo. You have the week to be gone, and if you are seen in Lear after that, you will die for heresy."

The king's shoulders heaved and pink blotches marred his cheeks. Before him Kayo bowed his head.

Silence dropped like rain, scattered and in pieces all around, smothering everything.

None in the great hall moved, horror and shock rippling throughout.

Gaela bared her teeth until Astore put his hand to her shoulder and squeezed, his eyes wide; Regan had bitten her bottom lip until blood darkened the paint smeared there already. Connley put a hand to his sword, though whether to defend the panting Oak Earl or the wild king it was impossible to say. Beyond them, the Earl Errigal's face was red, and he held a young man tightly by the arm. That young man stared at Elia, fury alive in the press of his mouth. Retainers gripped weapons; the creak of leather, and gasps and whispers skidded through the air.

It was all a trembling mountain ready to erupt.

They say Elia alone remained calm. The calm of the sun, it seemed, that need do nothing but silently stand. She reached out and put her trembling hand against Kayo's arm. "Father, stop this," she said.

"I do not see you," Lear snarled.

She closed her eyes.

Kayo said, hard and firm, "See better, Lear."

Then the Oak Earl turned and swiftly hugged Elia again. He cupped her head and said, "Stand firm, starling. You are right."

Again, Elia Lear remained silent.

Before going, Kayo said to Gaela and Regan, "May you both act as though everything you've said today were true, if you have any respect for your mother's heart."

The entire court watched him stride away from the throne. At the rear he paused, turned, and flung a final word at the king: "Dalat would be ashamed of you today, Lear."

With a flourish, he departed, and his going burst open the threads of tension that had held the Zenith Court together: it erupted into noise and fury.

# ELIA

ELIA STOOD ALONE in the center of chaos: she was as still as the Child Star, fixed in the north. All around her men and women moved and argued, swelled and pressed, pushing and pulling and departing in snaps of motion.

Pressure throbbed in her skull; her heart was a dull, fading drumbeat. Sweat tingled against her spine, beneath her breasts, flushed on her cheeks. Emptiness roared in her ears, shoving everything back—back—back.

Her stomach and lungs had always served her well—breathed for her, turned her food into spirit, given her song against fluttering nerves—and now, now they betrayed her.

As her father had.

Suddenly Elia bent at the waist, clutching at the empty pain in her stomach. She opened her mouth, but there was no cry. Only a silent gasp. Her eyes were not even wet.

She turned and ran, brushing past the king of Aremoria, ignoring the call of her name from too many familiar voices.

*She had done nothing wrong!*

In her hurry, she took the long way out the main doors and across the yard, stumbling toward the family tower. She clutched at the retainer stationed at the entrance but said nothing as she passed, up the stairs, up and up, one hand hitting hard against the black stone wall. She did not pause, blinded by shock, until she reached her room.

Rushing to the window, Elia stared out at the cold ocean and panted. The wind slipped in and tickled her skin, scouring her with unease. She closed her eyes and listened to the warning—too late! The voices obscured themselves in her ears; she was too out of practice with the language of trees.

The old magic of Innis Lear, bleeding through its roots, carved into the bedrock of the very island, a language of the hunt and fluttering leaves, a magic Elia had abandoned. She'd cut herself off from that comfort long ago, choosing instead the stars and her father. Choosing the cold, lovely heavens and those constant, promising stars.

The earth changed, human hearts changed, but the stars never did. Everyone Elia had known who listened to the trees and leaned in to the roots of magic had left her.

She had thought it was enough to be her father's truest star.

She'd thought it was a test, and if she remained that true star, all would be well. She'd thought her father understood her, that they knew each other better than anyone else.

And, a voice whispered from deep in her heart, she'd thought she was better than her sisters. Pride had kept her from breaking in the Zenith Court. Pride had kept her from saying something ridiculous to placate her father. From simply opening her mouth and playing the game.

"Love shouldn't have to be a game," she whispered to herself, and to the uneasy ocean.

"Elia."

She spun, stumbling in surprise. The king of Aremoria had followed her.

"Your—Your Highness." Her voice seemed foreign, a raw rasp emerging from her throat. As if she'd been screaming for hours.

He frowned, though it barely shifted his stolid face. "Your distress is understandable."

Elia did not know how to reply without shrieking.

The king took a deep breath. When he sighed, his broad shoulders relaxed under the orange leather of his coat. "I am sorry for what your father has done. We will leave in the morning. Pack only what is personal. When we arrive in Aremoria, my sister and mother will have you supplied with any needs."

She opened her mouth but said nothing. The king waited, watching her with steady blue eyes. She looked away, at the walls and furnishings of her room. It was perhaps smaller than a king might expect. But it was warm and bright from the cream-and-yellow blankets and tapestries she and her mother had chosen, embroidered with spring green vines and pastel wildflowers like a woven spring day. Elia could see Dalat here still, a ghost smoothing her hand along the pillows, telling a story as she tucked Elia into the bed. The wooden ceiling was crudely painted with star patterns against a day-blue sky, a gift from her father so she could recite their names as she fell into sleep. Light and ocean breeze slipped through a single window. No glass panes had been put in, for Elia preferred a heavy shutter she could open when she wished. She'd been so happy in this room, and then so alone.

Finally, she glanced back to the king. She thought of what he'd said in her defense, and was grateful. "Thank you, Your—Morimaros. I am grateful for your—your aid. But I cannot marry you or go with you."

Surprise actually found a long pause on his face. It parted his lips and lifted his brows. Both bare hands opened, and he twitched his wrists as if to reach out. "But, Lady Elia—"

Elia shook her head, distant from her own body. "I cannot—cannot even think of it."

"Ah," Morimaros breathed. Understanding smoothed away his surprise. "You are grieving. But go with me, in the morning, to Aremoria. You need time and distance from Lear's terrible judgment, and I would give it to you."

She had no idea how to tell him this did not feel like grief. She hardly felt at all. This nothing inside her was like a windless, dead ocean. Where was the crashing? Where were the waves and whitecaps, the rolling anger and spitting sorrow she should be feeling?

"I . . ." Elia removed her hands from her stomach and spread them, elbows tight to her ribs. "I don't know."

Morimaros took one step: long, for his legs were long. He was so imposing Elia had to hold herself still so as not to move away. A soldier and a king, a handsome man ten years older than her. *This woman is her own dowry.* At least it sped her heart up from the dull, slow shock.

"Go with me, Elia Lear," Morimaros said gently. "What might I say to reassure you? I promise to welcome your mother's brother Kay Oak if he desires."

"Why?" Elia leaned her hand on the windowsill, not facing Morimaros, but not giving him her back either. Was *Elia Lear* even her name anymore? "Why do you still want me, Your Highness? I bring nothing with me, none of the things you would have gained. No throne, no power here. And perhaps this madness runs in my family and I'll lose myself with no warning someday."

"I intended to gain a wife, Elia, and that is still my intention. I do not need your father's riches, and if I wished more land I could take it. What I want is a queen, and you were a queen today."

The compliment forced her head away; she looked outside at the rolling blue ocean where it blended into the hazy sky at the horizon. Why was he so kind? She longed to believe him, and yet found it nearly impossible. Was that her father's legacy? "I wasn't a queen," she whispered.

Morimaros grunted.

She said, "Queens mediate, they solve problems and make people feel better. I did none of those things, sir."

"I would prefer a queen who tells me what she believes to be true."

This time Elia smiled, but not happily. It was a smile of knowing better. Until this afternoon she would have sworn that was her father's preference, too. Did all men know themselves so poorly? "So you say until I contradict you."

He smiled, too, and she recalled thinking before that only his eyes made him seem softer. She'd been wrong; a smile did it as well. "Perhaps you are right, Elia, and all kings prefer to be pandered to."

She began to apologize but stopped herself. He made the distinction himself: he was not a man, but a king. What other option did she have but to go with him in the morning? She was lucky he claimed to understand and was willing to give her some time at least. To overcome this *grief,* as he called it. She'd been disinherited, her titles and name stripped away. She was not Lear's youngest daughter.

Her lungs contracted.

Where else could she go besides with Aremoria? Her mother's people? Was that where Kayo would choose? Despite growing up with stories from her mother and uncle, from Satiri and Yna, despite being surrounded by the beautifully dyed rugs and delicate oils, the clothing and scarves and books, Elia still could hardly imagine the Third Kingdom. And it was so very far away from her beloved island, her cliffs and White Forest and moorland, and from her father whom she could not just abandon. He would need her again, before the end. Before long. Elia's heart was here, and she could not just run away from her heart.

But she had to go somewhere, and this king seemed so genuine.

Putting her hands back to her stomach, Elia folded them as if it were a casual move, not a thing designed to keep herself from cracking. "I will go, for now."

Instead of smiling triumphantly or at least as if her answer pleased him, Morimaros slipped back into his impassive formality. He bowed to her, deeper than a king should. She bowed as well, unsure whether she was steady enough to curtsy. She said, "My girl, Aefa, will go with me."

"As you like," he said crisply. "It will be good, though my mother and sister would be happy to provide help or companionship for you."

"She's always expected to be with me, and would have no place here alone." It occurred to Elia that Aefa might prefer to go to her mother in the White Forest. But it was spoken aloud now, and Elia did not wish to take it back: without Aefa, she'd be alone.

Morimaros nodded. "Sleep well, then, if you can, Elia. I will leave you to prepare."

At the last moment, Elia took Morimaros's large, rough hand. Her fingers slid over a garnet and pearl signet ring; her thumb found his palm, so chilled there against his warm skin. "Thank you," she said, her eyes level with the tooled leather shoulder of his orange coat.

He hesitated for the space of two breaths, until Elia grew nervous and would have taken her hand away. "You are welcome," the king of Aremoria finally said, covering her entire hand with his.

And then he left her.

Before the door swung closed behind him, Aefa appeared, shutting it firmly with herself inside. Tears sewed her lashes together.

"Oh, Elia," the Fool's daughter whispered thickly. "Your father."

Elia held out her hands. Aefa hugged her, crying, and it was Elia who tried to offer shelter from her numb, absent heart.

# THE FOX

If Errigal expected to have to drag Ban to an audience with the king, he was disappointed. During five long years in the Aremore army, Ban had learned to not put off unpleasant tasks, for they tended to only become more unpleasant with the stall. Besides, Ban had a job to do here, and meeting with the king at his father's side was one of the first steps.

And so, though facing Lear was the last thing Ban wanted, he swallowed his rage from the Zenith Court, and tried to be grateful this meeting would take place in the retainers' hall over a meal.

Unfortunately, Ban had forgotten how quickly his appetite deserted him under the king's critical gaze.

The retainers' hall of the Summer Seat was long, like the court, but lacking a roof. Built of timber rather than stone, it was more like a stable, Ban thought, with rows of benches and tables and a high seat for the king. Gulls perched on the walls, waiting to scrabble for leftovers, and the king's collection of hounds slunk under legs and begged with open mouths. Lear's retainers all wore the king's midnight blue and carried fine swords, and they drank from goblets etched with the rampant swan of the king or striped in blue. A raucous, messy place of men, at least it was kept clean in between meals and celebrations by the youngest retainers and hopeful sons. Ban had spent plenty of mornings tossing pails of water and slop over the side of the cliff just outside the arched entryway, spreading fresh hay and rushes, and scrubbing the tables of spilled wine and grease. His brother, Rory, had chafed under the drudgery, but Ban appreciated any sort of work with immediate, provable results.

Tonight, the retainers' hall was subdued, given the day's events. It rubbed Ban poorly to enter at his father's side and witness hushed conversations and side-eyed glances, despite plenty of flowing beer. This was not how the king of Innis Lear's men should present, as if nervous and cowed! Not under any circumstance. The proud Aremore army would never have fallen prey to a scattering of nerves. Some smiled welcome at Errigal; others offered tight-lipped warnings. But Errigal scoffed and stormed up the side aisle to where the king himself slouched in his tall chair, the Fool lounging beside him in a tattered striped coat with his head against Lear's knee.

"My king," Errigal said expansively.

"What, sir, do you come to bother me with this night of all nights?" The king rolled his head back to stare up at the sky, too bright yet for stars.

Lear's hair remained as wild and ragged as it had been at the Zenith Court, his face still drawn and blotched with drink or anger or tears. A stain of wine spread like a heart-wound down the left side of his tunic.

Errigal knocked Ban forward. "Here is my son, Lear, come home from a five-year foster with the cousins Alsax in Aremoria. Ban the Fox they call him now, though he was only a bastard, or simply Ban, here."

Ban's shoulders stiffened as he bowed, turning it into a jerky motion. People here had called him Errigal's Bastard, not just any. Ban stared at the king's woolen shoes, wondering what he could possibly say that would not get him banished or killed. *Play the role, Fox,* he reminded himself again. *Be courteous, and remember your purpose here.* He'd earned his name, exactly as he'd promised himself he would. These people *would* respect it.

A groan sighed out of the king before he said, "Yes, I remember you. Ban Errigal. You were born under a dragon's tail, bright and vibrant but ultimately ineffective."

"I have been effective, King," Ban said, straightening.

"Perhaps for the limited time you burn brightly." Lear shrugged. "But it *will* be a limited time, and you will change nothing."

Ban worked his jaw, chewing on every response before he could spit it out.

"His actions in Aremoria have been exemplary, by all accounts," Errigal said.

"Aremoria!" Lear roared, surging to his feet. "Say no more of that place or that king! Stealing my Elia, my most loved star away!"

The Fool leaned up and sang, "Stolen with the same stealing as the clouds steal the moon!"

Lear nodded. "Yes, yes."

"No, no," responded the Fool. He was a long, lanky man, in a long, lanky coat of rainbow colors and textures. Silk, linen, velvet, strips of leather even, and lace, rough wool and soft fur, patterned in places, woven in plaid in others: a coat such as his marked him a man outside of station or hierarchy. The Fool was all men and no man at all. He wore the remains of a dress beneath the coat, and so maybe he was all women, too. And none.

The king frowned mightily.

Ban said, "I thought you had no daughter Elia, sir."

Errigal choked on a furious word, and the king whirled to Ban. "A smart tongue, have you?" Lear demanded.

"The boy meant nothing by it," Errigal said.

Ban met the king's gaze. "You are wrong, Father. I did mean much."

"Always defiant," Lear said.

Ban held his tongue.

"Always ablaze," Errigal said, forcing a laugh. "Like his mother, he's got that passion of—"

"Bah." The king waved dismissively at the earl, turning his back on Ban.

A moment of silence was only punctuated by the rustle of retainers listening as hard as they could. Ban felt their eyes on his spine, their focus and newfound attention. He would not bend or quail. This was the start of the work he must do to earn respect here, where they only knew stories of him, and his bastard name. Even if it meant bowing to this king's obsessions or anticipating his moods.

Errigal nudged him, and Ban caught the angry spark in his father's determined look. He was expected to speak again.

Fine.

Ban said, "You should call Elia back."

The room behind him erupted in curses and gasps, cries for his removal. Ban braced himself. Errigal gripped his elbow. The Fool lifted thoughtful, bushy brows.

But Lear collapsed back into his high seat. Sorrow, weariness, and a bitter curl of his lip painted the king in starkness. He turned a bony hand over, palm up. "Do you know, pup, what stars I was born under?"

"Yes, sir."

Lear nodded. "And you know how my wife died?" The old king curled his fingers closed, holding his fist so tight it trembled. The knuckles whitened.

"I do," Ban said through gritted teeth.

A murmured prayer floated throughout the hall, asking blessing from the stars against royal calamity. The layers of soft words were so like the language of trees Ban nearly forgot it was only fearful men muttering.

"You do not. Only I know," the king said hoarsely, finally opening his watery eyes. Pink tinged the edges. "I have lost so much to my stars. Brothers, retainers, my wife, and now my precious daughter."

"You did not lose her; you sent her away."

"*She* chose. *She* betrayed."

Ban threw his arms out, but before he could cry his disbelief, Errigal stepped before him.

"You are heartsick, my king," Errigal said, "and my boy is travel-worn, desperate. Let me take him and soothe his feathers."

"You cannot calm a creature such as this! More like to calm a storm," Lear said, wiping his eyes.

At last, a thing Ban agreed with. The king's shifting moods troubled him: not only for Elia's sake, but for the unpredictability they brought. It was difficult to plan someone's downfall when their actions could veer off course at any moment.

Lear shook his head, pressed his hands to his eyes. "Oh, oh, I must go. I must . . ."

The Fool stood, bending his tall body nearly in half to lean near the king and murmur a thing in his ear.

"Errigal," the king said, allowing the Fool to help him to his feet.

"My king?" Errigal moved forward to take Lear's other arm.

"I'll not have your bastard in my retainers. I cannot breathe when he is near. His stars offend. Take him elsewhere."

A tremor of absolute fury shocked through Ban, crown to toes. He'd not have served with the king's retainers if his life itself depended on it.

Errigal shot Ban another warning glance but said gently to Lear, "One of my sons honoring you so is well enough acceptable for me, sir. I can use Ban at home."

Ban bowed sharply, breath hissing out through his teeth. Without another word he left.

WHAT BEASTS FATHERS were, Ban thought darkly, head down, boots skidding on the rushes as he hurried on.

Outside, he lifted his face to the flat, still-blue sky. He'd rather get off this terrible promontory to find shade in the cool trees of the island. There was a place he knew, where the island reached up with ancient power, where surely Ban could dig his fingers into the ground and rekindle his heart's lines.

But Elia. He grimaced, worried for her, though he had no right. She'd recognized him at dinner last night, and had smiled wondrously, as if so very glad to see him. In that moment, Ban had forgotten Morimaros of Aremoria and all the years in his service. He'd forgotten Errigal and the shame of bastardy. All he'd been was the boy who once made her a crown of wind and flower petals. She'd smiled then, too, and kissed him.

"Boy, stop," Errigal growled, catching up to plant his arm across Ban's chest and stick his nose in his son's.

"The king has gone mad, Father," Ban said calmly.

Errigal tilted his head as if he hadn't yet decided on an opinion. "Kayo being banished was a terrible mistake, but the rest . . . that girl is an ungrateful whelp, and irrational for not bowing to this easy request made by king and father. Better she's not given the crown, though he said it was his preference."

A furious growl hummed in Ban's throat, making his father smirk. Errigal said, "There's that passion I remember."

Ban jerked back, but Errigal clapped his hand onto Ban's shoulder. "Ah, am I ever glad the stars chose not to make me have to worry about such things as dividing my land between children."

The cool relief in his father's words made Ban stare at his father with a creeping wonder. Errigal did have two named sons, after all. And only one of them had already earned fame and respect in war. In the beginning, the entire point of his success in Aremoria had been to show that Ban was as worthy as his brother.

Errigal caught Ban's frown and looked surprised. "What! Stars—my boy, you thought . . ."

Nauseated, Ban turned away.

"Son." Errigal roughly threw an arm around him, pulling him back. "You have my name, you have a place in my ranks, and surely you know your brother will always welcome you—Rory is incorrigibly kind, and he has always liked you. He pestered me constantly this last year to bring you home."

Ban said nothing, understanding that he would always be subject to charity here, in this place where he was supposed to belong, where he'd been born, where his mother's roots thrived. This place and its laws and its king did not want him. Ban had made the right choice when he gave his word to Aremoria.

"You're a good son," Errigal continued, his hesitation not born of uncertainty, but of the earl's deepest enemy: emotional honesty. "Everything a man could want in his issue, but for your origins." To save the moment from too much intimacy, the earl forced a hearty laugh. "I've often said it was the great pleasure and zeal at your getting that formed you into such a passionate, skilled warrior. I wouldn't have it another way."

Ban forced his shoulders to relax into Errigal's embrace. *Play the role, Fox.* "Thank you, Father. Your praise is much appreciated."

"Ha! Good." Errigal shoved Ban along, finished with the moment of fatherly affection.

Ban did not hesitate to desert the field.

THE SUN SANK, and the king studied his youngest daughter as she studied the sky.

Lear lounged upon the rug he'd brought, a half-empty bottle of wine gouged into the damp earth beside him, his wool-encased elbows bent to support his weight, his bare ankles crossed. He watched his daughter as she tilted her head and spoke some phrase the wind kept from him. She clapped suddenly, in delight, as if she alone could see the precise moment the gentle pink clouds became loose violet haze. Her hair bobbed in its own rhythm, like a cloud itself: an ecstatic, curling puff of copper and brown. It strengthened the king's aggrieved heart to see her, his favorite, intent upon the final moments of twilight, so ready to mark which star might first appear.

But then the princess fluttered her hand at the young boy crouched a few paces from the hem of her dress, and as the boy glanced up at her his face went from scowling and concentrated to relaxed and smiling. She had that effect on many, though the king would rather it not extend to Errigal's bastard. The boy's legitimate brother yelled and skidded half the meadow away, a wide stick held up like a sword in a very good offensive position to fight off invisible enemies. That one, the king thought, was destined for great purpose. The stars had clearly stated it on the night of his birth. He was the king's godson, named Errigal, too, though to distinguish him from his father the earl, everyone called him Rory. Would that Elia showed her preference to the gilded Rory, who was so beloved by the sun and saints of the earth that he bore the marks of their affection: dark red freckles all over his skin. As if his body were made an earthly mirror to the firmament itself.

As the king stared fondly at his godson, his youngest daughter clapped again, and he saw her fall to her knees in the churned dirt where the bastard boy had turned over a heavy field stone. The flat granite stood upright for a moment, then tipped away from the children, landing with a solid thump against the meadow grass. The king's daughter laughed, and the boy bent over the fresh filth, digging with one hand, touching the princess's hem with his other.

Lear's daughter scooted nearer the bastard and dug her hand into the mud with him, dragging out a long, fat worm. "Elia," the king said, frowning.

His daughter glanced at him, thrusting out the worm with a smile of triumph. It was pale and slick-looking in her eleven-year-old hand. No elegance or rich gleam like the sorts of ribbons that should curl around her noble wrist. The king shuddered at the grotesquery and opened his mouth to chide her, but she giggled at something the bastard muttered, turning away from her father.

The boy, wiry and smaller than his gilded brother, smaller than the king's favorite daughter even, though they were of age, splayed his left hand. It was nearly as dark as the princess's, though less smooth, less bright: she was a statue molded from fine metal, and he a creature built of mud and star-shadow. The king had always thought so: the boy had been born under a dragon's tail moon, and forged in an unsanctioned bed. What a disaster for Errigal, the king had always said, always counseled his friend the earl against such passionate dalliance. But some men refused to govern their bodies as they would their minds.

The bastard displayed on his outstretched hand a shining emerald.

No—merely a beetle shimmering all the colors of a deep summer day. The boy plucked the beetle from his hand and placed it upon the princess's.

She squealed that the tiny legs tickled her skin, but she did not toss the insect away.

The king watched through narrowed eyes as their heads leaned together, temples brushing until her puffed curls and his black braids blended. "Elia," the king said again, this time a low command.

She tossed him a smile and glance, then showed him the emerald beetle clinging to her finger like a union ring, as Dalat once had presented her own hand to Lear, so long ago. "See, Father, how its shell shimmers like a pearl," she said.

It pained the king, vividly reminded of his queen, his dearest queen who had loved Innis Lear, had seen beauty in every piece of his island, even in him. The king blinked: his queen was dead, no longer able to love him, or his island, or anything at all.

"Insects are not suitable rings for princesses," he said, harshly.

Surprise shook Elia's hand; the bastard gently caught the beetle as it fell.

The princess dashed over to her father. "But there were stars in its eyes," she whispered, pushing aside hair from her father's ear.

He murmured fondly, softening as he always did with her, and pulled her gently back to her proper place, seated beside him on the woven rug. Where her mother, too, had sat.

A cool evening wind brushed its way through the meadow. Elia leaned her head against his shoulder, both of them tilting back to watch the sky. The king told her quiet lines of poetry about the wakening stars as the bastard lowered his fingers to the earth so that the beetle could crawl off him and back into the dirt. Always the boy kept the princess in the corner of his eye. The king was aware. And displeased.

The brother, Rory, stomped over, sweating and triumphant. "Ban!" Rory threw his pretend sword to the ground, scattering grubs and beetles in one swoop. "What is that terrible thing?" He scuffed his boot near a curled white creature with several thin legs. The bastard did not answer.

The king called for Rory to come to the rug, to join him and his daughter, to look at the darkening sky. "The first star you see will be a portent of your year, children, for tonight is halfway between the longest night and the longest day. Cast your gaze wide."

Delighted, the princess rounded her black eyes and tried to see the entire sky at once. Rory, a year younger, flopped down at the king's feet and knocked his skull against the rug-softened ground. He peered directly up to the dome of heaven, focused on one spot.

The king watched them both affectionately. His youngest daughter and his godson, intent upon his will, intent upon the prophetic stars. As he bid them, as was right. He could abide the bastard for the evening, since his presence pleased Elia.

His daughter gasped and said, "There!" Her little hand shot up, pointing near the horizon.

The king laid his old white thumb against her burnished brown forehead. "That, my daughter, is Terestria, the Star of Secrets. Terestria was so beloved by the stars that they drew her up with them when she died, so her body was buried in the blackness of the night sky instead of swallowed by the earth. I would make for you, my Elia, my dearest, a grave of stars, if you were to die before me."

His daughter smiled in acceptance while Rory squinted his face more tightly to find another star above. The bastard gripped his brother's discarded sword-stick and jammed it into the ground.

"You won't find stars in the mud, boy," the king admonished.

Elia frowned but Rory laughed, while the bastard dropped the stick and stood still as a tree, staring at the king with eerie light eyes. "I'm not looking for stars," he said.

"Then go from here, for we are about the stars tonight, and your petulance will mar their shine."

The bastard's jaw squared stubbornly, then he dropped his gaze to the princess, who clutched her dress, caught between the king and the boy. His eyes lowered, and the boy turned away without a word. Good riddance.

"I found one!" crowed Rory, leaping to his feet. "Ban, look!"

The king angled his head up to see.

"That, godson," the king said, "is the Star of the Hunt, also called the Hound's Eye." He declined to elaborate, but Rory didn't care, elated to have captured the sight of such a glorious-sounding first star. He ran after his half-brother, crying Ban's name and inventing fulsome meanings for the Star of the Hunt.

Easily, the king put both Errigal sons from his mind, curling around his favorite daughter, his Elia. *She* needed him, *she* trusted him.

The king held his youngest in the shelter of his love as he described the portents revealed by how the stars appeared tonight, through the vivid purple and pale blue evening. He would raise her in their clear light, he promised, to be the starry jewel in the crown of Lear, a radiant heir to the skies and proof that wisdom and purity would forever outshine base emotions and the filth of mortality.

# ELIA

THE LAST MEAL Elia took at the Summer Seat was only wine, a dark red that had been her mother's favorite, borne in a cool carafe by her sisters. Elia could not read their faces, and was too tired to guess their intentions. She wanted them with her so badly she ignored her suspicions and let them enter.

Regan set three clay cups upon Elia's small dining table, and Gaela poured them to the brim, chasing Aefa away with a haughty scowl. Both had removed most of their finery from court: Gaela had on her deep red dress, but without pauldron or symbols of armor, and only clay held up her crown of twisting hair; Regan's fingers remained jeweled, but she'd taken off her elaborate belt and had most of her chains and ribbons pulled out of her hair, to be bound in a simple knot at her nape. Elia had not changed at all, though Aefa, still crying herself, had washed the smeared red paint from Elia's lip and eyes.

She wished it had been reapplied, to face this moment.

"To returning," Gaela said, holding her cup in the palm of her hand.

Regan finished the blessing. "When the old fool is dead."

Elia knocked her cup over with a shout, spilling wine across the pale table like a wave of fresh blood. Her anger surprised her.

Regan stood abruptly, though the motion sloshed her own wine onto the wrist of her very fine gown. "Elia," she snapped.

Gaela only laughed. "What a fine mess, baby sister." She drank her full cup of wine. Then she slammed her hand flat down into the puddle, splattering tiny drops onto Elia's face. They hit like tears on her cold cheeks. "Drink some."

Regan flicked her wine-covered hand at Elia, too, as if to add her irritable benediction to Gaela's.

A laugh tugged out of Elia, though it was tremulous and dry and annoyed. Her sisters were terrible, but so desperately themselves.

She did not wipe her skin, but leaned forward and poured more wine into her toppled cup. Lifting it, she said, "To peace between us, and sisterly love, and reconciling with our father."

Her sisters drank with her: Gaela with a raised, wry brow, and Regan smiling her untouchable smile. Regan said, "Reconciliation will never happen. We are queens now, Gaela and me. He declared so himself."

Not until the Longest Night, they weren't, Elia knew. But this set them as near as possible. Wine swirled in her belly, and Elia pressed her hand there. She risked herself by saying, "He asked me, when he first sent letters from Aremoria and Burgun this winter, if I thought I would make a good queen. I should have known then, that he was planning something like this."

Gaela laughed, but Regan peered closely at the youngest of them. "And do you think it?" she asked.

"Compared to what?" Elia asked, letting Regan see the challenge there. The burned-out, desperate challenge. *Compared to my cruel sisters?* she thought at Regan.

It was Gaela who sneered now. "Do not put yourself against us in this; we have strength at home, while you are only yourself. It would be a butterfly against birds of prey."

Elia was too used to the lack of sisterly support to be surprised or even newly injured. She lowered her eyes to the spilled wine, gave Regan and Gaela a moment to understand she was not truly challenging them; she was only so tired, so raw. So afraid for their father, for her future. She had done nothing at all, and yet her life was torn away. She could barely breathe, had felt lightheaded and breathless all afternoon. "I do not wish to be the queen of Innis Lear. I only wish to be home, and take care of him."

"He does not deserve you," Regan said.

"What will you do with him, then?" Elia asked. "Be kind, I beg you."

Gaela said, "We will disband his retainers but for some hundred or so of them, and share the burden of housing him and them between us."

"You could stay, Elia," Regan said seductively, "if you marry some harmless man of Lear, and never stand against us."

"Some harmless man?"

"Perhaps Rory Errigal," Gaela said.

"No," Elia said quickly, thinking instead of Ban, though she'd not let herself do so for years. It was only brotherly affection she held for Rory.

"No, Gaela," Regan agreed. She tapped dangerous fingernails at the edge of the spill of wine. "You only want her to eek Errigal's iron and loyalty away from my Connley with that, dear sister."

Gaela smiled. Regan smiled.

Elia swallowed a heavier drink of wine.

"And so," Gaela said, "Elia cannot remain here now. She must stay in Aremoria until Midwinter, and so keep herself out of the minds of any who remember Lear wished for her to be the next queen."

"If you return before the Longest Night we will take it as a hostile act," Regan added.

Sighing sharply, Elia finished her wine. She would be drunk soon, and she welcomed it. She felt exhausted. The brief silence among them was strangely comfortable, until Regan said, "Beware of Morimaros."

"What?" She thought of his hands, the garnet and pearl ring, the rough, pinked knuckles.

Gaela said, "They say in Aremoria that the greatest king will reunite our island to their country. That what was sundered will be returned. Morimaros's ambition will lead him to desire Innis Lear for his own. You must prove to him we three are Lear now, and we three are strong."

Elia pinched her eyes closed. "Are we? You just told me my presence here threatens you."

"Elia!" snapped Regan. "It is what we will *make* ourselves, do you understand?"

"I understand," Elia said, leaning forward, "that my sisters played some vicious game today, that my father disowned me and believes he hates me, and I must *leave* my *home* because of it."

Both her sisters smiled again, so familiar and yet unknowable to Elia. Regan's was small and cold, Gaela's wide enough to display her shield of white teeth.

"Why do you hate him?" Elia whispered, grasping at anything to make her understand why she was empty and broken, while her sisters triumphed.

Regan leaned in so Elia could see the tiny flecks of blue in her dark eyes. "Why don't you?" she whispered back.

The wine gurgled in Elia's belly. She touched a hand there, setting her cup down hard. "You won't be better than him. The two of you will let the island break into war. Worse; you'll encourage it between your husbands. How can you? How can you wish for such a thing?"

Gaela said, "We will encourage what we must to achieve what we desire."

It was mysteriously said, low in voice, and most unlike Gaela. Elia stared at her eldest sister, the one whose face reminded her of their mother; or else she'd been told so often that Gaela resembled the queen that she'd invented some memory to account for it. She did not know what was real. "I want Innis Lear at peace. I want my family whole," Elia said.

Regan reached for Gaela; their palms met, and they clasped hands.

Elia understood: they were whole, but apart from Elia, because Elia had been too young to choose against Lear when their mother died. Her sisters could only give her so much now, too many years later. Elia said, "I don't want to be here."

"You'll go soon enough," said Gaela.

Elia shook her head. She felt hollow where she was supposed to be overwhelmed: flooded with anger, or burning with grief. She hated the numbness, but she did not know how to change it or chase it away—and if she thought about anything else it was her father's grimace as he took away her name, as he said—as he said—

She was shaking all over.

Her sisters dragged her onto her feet and suddenly embraced her. Elia covered her face, surprised, and pressed into Gaela and Regan. "You take care of him," she said, muffling her own order. "You do as you promised today and love him. Make those words true."

"Do not teach us our duty," Gaela said, pinching Elia's hip.

Elia gripped the hard arm of her eldest sister and the thin ribs of her middle sister. When was the last time they'd stood thus? When their mother died? No—when Ban Errigal had been sent away and she'd believed it her own fault, she'd come to Regan, begging for some plot to get him back, and Regan had taken her to Gaela's room. They gave her wine like this, though she choked on it like the child she'd been, and they told her to forget her friend. Told her to hope for nothing but that he come home someday, stronger. *That is always the way,* Gaela had said. *Go, but return home stronger.* And Regan had said, *If you are lucky and willful and brave. Lear would have us weaken away from him, but we will never do as he wishes, Elia. We would rather die than give him what he wants, even if all he wants is his stars.*

"Go, but return home stronger," Elia whispered now.

"If you can," Regan said.

Gaela snorted, amused. "If she can."

Elia pulled free of them. Stumbling to the door, she wished to cling to a single memory of a time she'd felt like their sister, part of them equally, a true triad, a triplet star, anything. The memories were there, faded and locked away in salty cliff caves, under the high table on the Longest Night, and in a cottage at the center of the White Forest. But in this moment she was untethered, shorn from her father and family because there was nothing in her sisters tying her heart secure.

# THE FOX

FAR OUT PAST the Summer Seat, against the cliffs facing the fortress, a ragged half-circle of stones stood like the bottom row of a monster's teeth, growing up out of the patchy moor. Thirteen stones, twice as tall as a man but not half so wide, worn raw by the salt wind.

Ban should've loved it. A temple of roots and rock, biting hard against the sky.

His boots scuffed against grit and gravel. The wind brushed through, humming around the stones, drawing thin purple clouds off the ocean. Heather clustered on the south sides of a few standing stones, bowing gently in the twilight. Ban reached out to the nearest stone, mottled with coins of black lichen and paler moon lichen. The rock was warm, purring like the wind.

Stepping fully into the half-circle, he tilted his head up. Purple and great swaths of rich indigo crawled across the sky, letting through only the strongest stars. A full moon glowed over the easternmost standing stone. The top was slanted, and Ban walked until the moon was pierced by its higher, sharper tip. This had always been his argument with Errigal and the king as a boy: the patterns Ban saw depended on where he stood. One needed the perspective of the earth to understand the stars.

Errigal had cuffed him and the king explained disgustedly, "A man should stand where he is supposed to stand, and from there see the signs and patterns around him. That is how you read the stars."

Ban's brother, Rory, had obediently taken a place beside Lear, grabbing Ban's skinny wrist and dragging him there, too. "With me," Rory said, hugging Ban's shoulders in his arm and putting their faces together. "Look, brother!"

Then, Ban had smiled with Rory, leaned into the embrace. He'd tolerated the lesson so long as Rory had hold of him.

Elia would pace around and around the stones, counting the space, writing down her numbers to later draw a map of the circle. Lear had been proud when his daughter overlaid the stone map with a simple summer star map and showed how clear and smart the ancient star readers had been to lay this circle out just so. *See, Ban? The earth itself made into the shape of stars!*

*Show me,* Lear had said, dismissing Ban as irrelevant.

Now, Ban turned his back against the center stone and slid down to crouch at its base. Flattening his hands on the cold ground, Ban whispered, *Blessings for Elia Lear,* in the language of trees.

The words scratched at his tongue, and the standing stone warmed his back. Ban drew a breath, sinking against the earth and the stone, relaxing his body. His eyes drifted shut. He listened.

Chewing waves tugged out from the island with the vanishing tide. The purr of stones and the beat of his heart. Wind kissing his cheeks, scattering seed husks and dark petals across the gravelly earth here. Distant whispering trees clustered around streams and the thin Duv River that flowed from the northern Mountain of Teeth, through the White Forest, catching on boulders and the roots of ancient oak and ash, slick with spirits. Ban whispered, *My name is Ban Errigal. My bones were made here with you.*

*Ban Errigal,* the trees hissed quietly.

The island's voice should have been stronger. It should have spoken to him last night, even far out on the Summer Seat ramparts. Or perhaps Ban was spoiled by the vibrant, glorious tones of Aremoria.

*Innis Lear.*

Here he smelled late summer roses and dry grass, salty sea and the tinge of fishy decay. Stone and earth, his own sweat. Maybe his memories of being a boy-witch here were thin; maybe the island always had spoken so tightly.

But no: Ban was certain. Lear had done this. The fool king had weakened the ancient voice of the island when he forbade the rootwaters from flowing. Both earth and stars were needed for magic: roots and blood for power, the stars to align them. Without both, everything was wild, or everything was dead. Here, it was dying.

Ban couldn't—he wouldn't let it happen. Not to the trees and wind. Not to this hungry island that birthed him. The only thing in his life to never let him go, to never choose someone else.

Kneeling, Ban drew off his thin jacket and then untucked his linen shirt and removed it, too. Dropped both in a pile beside him.

From a small folded pouch on his belt, he drew a sharp flint triangle and pressed the edge to his chest, over his heart. *Blood,* he whispered in the language of trees, slicing fast. Blood welled as the sting flared. It dripped a thin, dark line down his chest. Ban allowed it, but caught the stream upon his finger just before it reached the waist of his trousers. There, against his skin, he smeared it into the jagged language of trees, writing *Innis Lear* with marks like naked winter twigs.

His chest ached with every breath, a low fire heating his skin and heart. Ban pressed his palm to the wound, caught trickling blood, and then clasped his hands together until both palms glinted scarlet.

*Here I am,* he said to the wind, and leaned forward onto his hands and knees, giving the bloody prints to the earth. *My power, and your power.*

*Ban Errigal,* the island trees hissed. *Ban the Fox, the Fox, the Fox.*

The slice over his heart bled onto the ground, a dull dripping, a narrow thread of life between him and the island.

The puddle shaped itself into a crescent, tips reaching away.

Ban opened his eyes and looked into the crimson pool. He saw a word marked there, something close to *promise.*

*I promise,* he whispered tenderly. *I swear to you.*

Wind flew off the island, a cry of trees, rushing past him, dragging at his hair, and tears pricked suddenly in his eyes. The wind snatched his tears and shrieked off the cliff, crashing down, down, down to the rocks and sea foam.

*WELCOME!*

Ban smiled.

He leaned back onto his heels, holding his bloody, dusty hands before him. *Light,* he said.

Five tiny silver baubles of moonlight blossomed over his palms.

He laughed, delighted.

A soft noise echoed in response.

Then a human voice: "You've become a wizard."

Ban lifted his head. Elia Lear stood across from him, part of the violet shadows. He wondered how long she'd been watching. Did she still understand the language of trees?

The moon washed out her eyes and dress and found the reddish glints in her dark chainmail curls. It turned her face into a gold mask like the kind an earth saint would wear: black eyes, slash of mouth, wild ribbons and scraggly moss and vines for hair.

Balancing the tiny stars still in his hands, he stood up slowly, his heart somehow lighter. That had always been her gift to him: she cut through all the angles of his anger and need, to a hidden spark of peace. "Elia," he said, then, "Princess."

Elia's face crumpled, becoming human again, in painful motion. "No more," she whispered. Her fingers pulled lines into the front of her gown.

Ban went to her and caught up her elbows, leaning in to offer her comfort. The balls of light dropped slow as bubbles, fading just before they hit the earth again. Elia clung to him, despite the blood and dust on his chest and hands. He put his arms full around her, his heart gasping between beats.

"Ban Errigal," she whispered, her cheek pressed to his shoulder. "I never knew if I'd see you again. I hoped, but no more than hope. It is so good, so very good, to be held by you now."

"Like the last time," he said, low in his throat, forcing the words out, "your father made a terrible decision."

She shuddered against him. Her hair teased his chin and jaw, smelling of spicy flowers still. Elia pulled away, though slid her hands down to his. She lifted one, touching the blood.

"Wormwork," he said.

"It was beautiful." She raised her eyes to his.

"The earth has its own constellations."

Elia touched his chest, and Ban's entire body stilled. Her finger skimmed above the heart-wound.

He said, "Your father makes wormwork filthy, severs himself and all of you from the island's heart for nothing but the sake of pure stars and insincere loyalties. It's hurting the magic. And the island."

She pushed away from him, going to the nearest standing stone. Elia scratched her fingers down it, hard enough to flake off tiny edges of silver moon lichen. "There have been more poor harvests than good these past years, since you left. I've heard of sickness, too, in the forests, and fish dying. Fish! I thought—I thought when Gaela was queen it all would revive. That there was nothing to do but wait. The island does not love him, but we can all survive without love, for a time. All places have bad years, hard seasons. Especially an island like ours."

"Does Gaela speak to the wind?" Ban called softly.

Elia shook her head and walked to the next stone, then the next, until she reached the center stone that he'd been crouched against. She wrapped her arms around it as far as they could go. "I can barely remember the language of trees."

He nearly smiled but was too sad. "In Aremoria, the trees sing and laugh."

"I thought they did not have magic there."

"It is unused, uncultivated, but still present. A current under all." No one he'd met in Aremoria spoke to the trees, which made it seem like they'd been waiting just for him.

Elia pressed her forehead to the stone. "My father . . ."

"Is wrong."

"Let's speak of something else."

"Ah." He thought hard for a neutral thing to say, stepping closer. The ocean wind streamed around him, and he felt the humming again, from the air, from the stones, from the moon. "If you stand here, and leap from one foot to the next"—he demonstrated, widening his stance comically—"back and forth, it looks like the moon herself is leaping."

Seeming surprised, Elia joined him. She took his dirty hand and hopped, her eyes up on the hazy sky.

The moon bobbed as they did. It was like six years vanished between them, and they'd never been apart. Elia gripped his hand, and he smiled at her, watching her face when he could instead of the moon.

Slowly, slowly, he became aware of the feel of her cool hand in his, the sliding of her skin against his skin; the motion tingled and burned up along the soft side of his wrist, pooling in his elbow, tickled all the way to his heart with a thread of starlight. It was no imagined poetry that made him think it, but magic, tying them back together as he'd sought to tie himself again to Innis Lear. His blood between them, and this shared dance.

Ban thought about kissing her.

He stumbled, jerking at Elia's arm, and she laughed. "I know what you were looking at, Ban Errigal."

She could not, he hoped, know he'd had such a thought as he'd had, to take something from her she had not offered. "I enjoy making the moon move," he said.

"Not very respectful," she chided, but without much force behind it.

"I have no respect for this place."

It killed their moment of pleasure, and Ban regretted that, though not what he'd said.

Elia went still. "Maybe your disdain can cancel out his worship," she whispered.

"I'll take you away from here," he heard himself say, and knew he meant every word. He meant this more than any promise he'd ever made to Aremoria. "We could leave now. My horse is in the Sunton stables; we'll go and be long away by dawn. From there to Aremoria and beyond, any place we like."

The princess stared at his mouth, as if reading his next words there: "Two nobodies, just Ban and Elia. We could do anything. Come with me," he said, almost frantic. This was the moment, the tilting, reaching moment that would change everything. *Choose me,* he thought.

But Elia turned away from him. Said, looking to the stars once more, "Everyone would blame you, say terrible things about you."

"And so the sun rises every morning." The bitterness staining his words stung even his own mouth. Did she know what it had been like for him as a boy? Did she ever notice her father's jabs? No, he told himself, more likely Elia had loved him the way children love what they have, and forgot him the moment he was gone. Why else did she never write to him?

"I can't, Ban. My father will regret this, I know. He must. He will see . . ." Her eyes closed, but her head was still tipped back to the sky. "He will see a new sign in the stars, and forgive me."

"What kind of forgiveness is *that*, if he only does it for them?" Ban flung his hands at the stars.

Moonlight caught the tips of her short, curled lashes. "Forgiveness is its own point," she insisted.

He stared at her, wondering if anyone could be so good. Wondering if she believed herself. "I can't forgive him," he said. "For what he's done to you. To me. I don't want to."

She opened her eyes and faced him, revealing a vivid ache in her gaze. "I think . . . I used up my heart completely this afternoon. There is no space for any new feeling to take hold, Ban. Only for what already lived there, and rooted long ago."

"I was there."

Elia nodded. "As he has always been. And you are here now, and that is . . . it is such a balm to see you."

"Just in time for you to leave, to trade places with me in Aremoria," he said angrily, wanting to remind her sharply that Morimaros of Aremoria was not rooted in her heart. But he said no more, shocked at his conflicted loyalty. Morimaros deserved much better from him.

She shook her head sadly, disapproving of his anger. Then she asked, "Why did you come out here, to this place you dislike?"

"To escape our fathers," he muttered.

"There are many ways to do that. Are you looking for a prophecy? It is what this place is for."

"You should know better. I came to invite myself back to the roots of Innis Lear. To the voices of the trees and stones. Since there is no well from which to drink." He stalked to the eastern stone, where the moon hung a handspan above it now, and the Star of First Birds sparkled just to the side. As he approached, the stone grew and grew against the darkening sky until it swallowed the moon whole. Ban put his hands flat against it and pushed.

It did not budge, of course, but he ground his teeth and shoved, straining with all his strength. His boots slid roughly.

Elia appeared beside him. "Ban?"

Suddenly he stopped. He flopped against the cool face of the monolith, sweat seeping off his skin and into the porous granite like the stone drank up his sacrifice. "I want to tear it all down," he whispered, panting. He would destroy Lear and ruin his father for their relentless devotion to uncaring, unflinching stars.

She leaned beside him, flat against the rock. For a disorienting moment, he remembered lying with her on the ground like this as children, facing each other to watch the slow progress of a snail.

They stared at each other as the night deepened and the stars lifted themselves to cast hazy light over the frazzled edges of Elia's curls. Ban thought again of kissing her, touching her mouth, her neck, the ringlets of her hair. He tried to think of nothing else, just her. To calm himself with her image, her breath near his breath. She *was* Innis Lear to him, all the goodness and potential of this forsaken land, and now the king was sending *her* away. If he accomplished his goals here, might he follow her home to Aremoria, and find welcome and peace where she was, both of them with Morimaros?

Then Elia said, "These stones have always been here. They can't be destroyed."

"Someone made this place."

"The earth saints, long ago. They're grown into the ground now. Indestructible." Elia sounded defeated, but sure.

"Like a father's love?" He could not help the mockery.

She broke in half, bending at the waist. "I don't understand it, Ban. I don't understand how he let this happen. What did I do?"

Rage cut through him, turning the starlight to sparks and fire.

"Nothing," Ban whispered. "You did nothing wrong. I will prove it to you, somehow, how easy it is to ruin a father's heart. To turn them against a beloved child."

The idea blazed in him: he would show her.

He would use Morimaros's game to his own advantage. If he could convince Elia, draw her over to his side, the world would be right, for the first time, no matter how terrible the truth might seem. Elia of the Stars and Ban of the Earth, bridging that terrible chasm. "You'll see, Elia, that it's not a flaw in *you* making this happen, but in Lear himself. A flaw your father embedded into the heart of this island. Fear and absolutism. When you understand he has no power over you, then you can be home. *I* will make you a home with this proof."

Elia pulled hard away from him

"Don't be afraid. Be bold, like you were today." He slapped his hand on his chest. "All I have is what I was born with, no star promise, and it's made me bold, won me what little I have. It's what will push me further, allow me to take what is mine. That is what I want. What do *you* want? What is yours? What is it that makes you bold, Elia? Bold enough to look your father in the eye and be honest?"

She shook her head. "I don't know."

"Find it."

"Help me."

"I can't, Elia. You have to do it yourself. I went to Aremoria and found who I am. And now you could do the same. You aren't your father or your sisters or your mother. Who are you?"

Elia touched the back of his hand. "Who am I?" she asked softly.

In the language of trees, he said it again: *Who are you?*

And she replied the first words he'd taught her, twelve years ago: *Thank you.*

*Elia Lear,* the island whispered, but she stared at him as if she did not hear its voice at all.

Ban left her at the stone and went to the edge of the cliff. Before him yawned a black, churning chasm of rocky teeth and hungry waves. Eating away at the island. Someday it would eat through enough that the earth where he stood would fall on its own, cleave apart because of that hungry sea. The stone circle would fall, destroyed and invisible to those cold stars.

# Part
# TWO

## FIVE YEARS AGO,
## EASTERN BORDER OF AREMORIA

THE ONLY THING the king of Aremoria disliked about himself was this weakness he had of avoiding the hospital tents for hours or even days after battle.

It was not that he was bothered by injury, violence, or gore; no, he met with plenty such on the battlefield itself. His aversion was, he believed, a weakness of heart, and one he would need to conquer before he could truly lead Aremoria. Mars did not like to see the damage he'd caused to his own men. The permanently scarred or disabled; the dying; the sleepless moans; the cries of specific, prying pain. Their hurt overwhelmed him now as it had not when he was merely a prince and a soldier by their sides, not bearing responsibility for the damage done in the crown's name. Mars saw the pinched eyes, the twisted mouths, the clenched fingers, the shallow breathing, and the soft pleading for mothers, wives, and children, and he could not keep from imagining those very people—mothers, wives, children, and fathers, too, cousins, friends, grand-folk, who would be immeasurably violated by the loss of a single soldier. Because of him.

Consequences lurked in the hospital tent, hungry and violent.

When Mars lay on his mat to sleep and his mind raged with possibilities, with shifting roads ahead, with history and borders and numbers and supply trains, with political operations and flag signals, all the complex trappings of running a campaign, the king of Aremoria knew how to hold it all in hand. It would build from a collection of pieces, as if each were a star scattered in its shifting—but accurate—place in the sky, and the work of a leader was to draw connections and patterns. The sky was a maze, and he must find, for his people, the way through. Consequences were only myriad pinpricks of light, distant and maneuverable.

And as Mars charged into battle, every soldier, every horse and spear, every shield and boot and arrow, the muddy, churning ground, the rain or blinding sun, the pain and sudden gutting surprises, the glint of swords, the splash of blood, the battle rage singing in his ears—that was what mattered most. He was a sword himself, a spear of light driving at the fore of his army to slice apart the enemy. Battle was a fork in the branches of the tree of war, and the options Mars saw meant only one thing or the other. Success or retreat, life or death—for himself, for the soldiers, for Aremoria. Consequences were immediate, dreadful, echoing, triumphant.

Then, home in his capital, Lionis, everything was words and plans, elaborate banquets and scheming with friends against enemies, marriages and lines of succession and blood knotting into ropes of generational manipulation. It was family and keeping them safe. Consequences linked together and spread out in spokes through cities, towns, farms, like a living system of royal roads. Mars could see the turns and breaks, the bridges that needed repair or would need it soon. His mission then became balance: strength and nurturing, losses and gains.

In most every aspect of his life, consequences were a map that Mars could manipulate. He could change things, make choices to improve the outcome, reach for the good, better, best results. There was always hope: Aremoria will be better for this step I take, for this word I pronounce, for this path I lead us down.

But in the hospital tent, Mars could affect nothing.

Change *nothing*.

Here the consequences begged, wept, died in simple rows, inside a blood-spattered tent, and it was too late for any king to make a difference.

And so Mars had allowed himself to avoid it, pretended his importance overshadowed his cowardice: Morimaros of Aremoria was needed in a great many other places, and because he could not help the dying, he shouldn't prioritize them.

They'd been at war with the neighboring kingdom of Diota since his father had died three years ago, and Diota pressed its advantage against the possibility of internal Aremore divisiveness. But Mars had brought his country to heel quickly and hoped soon to earn the Diotan king's surrender. This most recent battle had cost Aremoria, though, and Mars was uncertain how to attack next.

The morning had dawned clear, despite the great billowing clouds of smoke rising still off the stony valley where the dead of both sides smoldered after the midnight burn. Now, Mars stood several paces back from the flap of the hospital tent, wishing the sun shone brighter. Knees locked, arms at his sides. He was a man of nearly twenty-five years, a successful soldier, and a king. This should not have been a struggle. He was stronger, better than this. No coward. But the tent's entrance was a black maw, a triangle of shadows that promised only angst in the shape of soft moans and clipped voices, the stench of rotting men and the tang of blood. It would've been worse last night, worse with desperation and bone saws. Screams, running healers, everyone giving orders or obeying them, staunching blood, stuffing poultices into gaping wounds, setting bones. Prayer.

He'd had his own injuries tended to inside his tent while he took reports from staggering, tired captains.

Novanos's boots crunched the gravel as Mars's second approached the tent. For a fleeting moment, Mars was relieved, carried off by a shameful hope that the other man had some urgent business to distract the king from this unpleasant duty. But Novanos stopped at Mars's shoulder and only took a deep, gentle breath, held it for three counts, and let it slowly free.

Mars allowed the ghost of a smile to appear and drew in a similar breath, forcing his shoulders to relax under the heavy mail and leather coat he wore. He tapped the side of his fist against Novanos's. The man was exactly his age, and related through a series of cousins, though had no official claim to royal lineage because of complicated marriage contracts. Watery blond hair kept long enough to tie back, now dark and slick from bathing, and Novanos's orange uniform was clean. This was not the one he'd worn to battle yesterday, as Mars's was: still tarnished and muddy and smeared with browning blood.

"Over here," Novanos said quietly, leading Mars down the side aisle. The tent stretched long, built of strong wooden poles and canvas roof layers that lifted away in patches, and could be angled for more or less light, and to let out smoke, or keep away rain. They passed sleeping soldiers on pallets by the door, those least injured but still requiring hospital rest. Partitions separated the surgery from the resting area, and from the leftmost aisle, which was reserved for the most dire and immediate wounds. Men and women, as well as some older children, moved throughout with water and bandages, hot food and blankets. The healers, in their bleached tunics, were intent on their patients, but aides and nurses all stopped as Mars passed, bowing or saluting if a hand was free. They knew him by the simple crown etched into the bright silver of the pauldron on his left shoulder. Otherwise he did not stand out, being rather unremarkable, he thought, with his typically Aremore brown hair shorn to the skull, matching beard, blue eyes, and suntanned skin. Mars pasted a calm, confident expression across his face, aiming to project sympathy instead of the swelling grief he truly felt.

Many of those at the fore of the tent would live and be well, barring crisis. Some slept fitfully; others tried to salute from their pallets. He murmured to them to be still, and gave each his thanks for winning the day.

None showed him a hint of anger or mistrust. How it humbled Mars to know that even as these men and few women lay in torment and fear, they were glad to see him, he who was the cause of it.

He knelt at the side of an older soldier with a gray speckled beard shorn from half his face. A raw, but stitched, wound crawled like a centipede up his chin and cheek, and his head and jaw were wrapped with a bandage to keep him from speaking. Mars gripped his hand and nodded encouragement. Beside him Novanos waited patiently.

Standing, Mars leaned in toward his friend as they continued. "I did this to him," he confessed.

Novanos's drooping eyebrows lowered further. "That is rather melodramatic, sir."

"No one has ever accused me of that before."

"The Elder Queen has no doubt considered it." Novanos spoke softly, but left no room to disagree.

Mars paused with every soldier he passed. The king touched hands and hair, nodded, smiled grimly, commented on the patient's obvious prowess, or admitted to being impressed by the promised scars. His head ached from holding himself calm, from clenching his jaw beneath his encouraging smiles. He thought of his father moving through throngs of people, doing the same. Mars wanted to sit at every bedside and ask for names and families, share stories and intimacy in return. He'd been able to do that, in the past. When he'd only been one of the captains, not known by any but Novanos to be Prince Morimaros. Since his father died, and Mars was forced to shed his anonymity, the soldiers held a distance between themselves and him that Mars could not help hating.

His father had thrived in the same light, his stern countenance steadfast, remote yet never cruel or untender. *A king is a symbol,* he would say. *The crown is your burden because it makes you the representative of all the causes and consequences of a lifetime, and longer. Good and bad. A man cannot be friends with* why, *Morimaros.*

*You have friends among your people,* Mars had said.

*I love many people, and am loved, both as a man and as a king. But there is no person in the entirety of Aremoria whom I truly call friend. There cannot be friendship without the balance of power. And in that we are not equal to any in this land, because our word is the law, and our word can send any man or woman or child to their death.*

Young Mars had flinched, realizing the king's word applied to him, too.

He'd searched out Novanos and asked if they were friends; Novanos had stopped his sword exercise mid-swing and given him a look like congealed porridge. Mars had laughed, supposing only a friend could turn such a face upon a prince.

But in the hospital tent, Mars always realized his father was right.

Mars could not pretend to be a friend of soldiers, wounded or not. He was the crown. He was why they were here. If he refused such a responsibility, or avoided it, there was no worth to his own life, no worth to those lives snuffed out in the name of Aremoria. So the king would bear it.

He made his way into the quiet, darker section of tent, where the more seriously injured lay. Novanos discreetly directed his king to the darkest corner, nodding down at a soldier who could not have been much more than a boy.

"Shall we wait for his end, or will he wake?" Mars studied the heavy bandages about the soldier's middle, the swollen eye, the razed skin of his cheek, the splinted arm.

Novanos paused, as near uncertain as Mars had ever seen him. "Before he lost consciousness, he said the earth hid him."

The king frowned at the strange claim. "This is who brought the intelligence?"

"And the Diotan commander's underwear. His return made quite the stir in the men of his division. They'd thought he deserted, as he was gone for nearly four days."

Mars knelt beside the boy. He had light tan skin, sallow from injury, and his nose and hair put Mars in mind of the refugees from southern Ispania. "He can't be more than sixteen."

Novanos shook his head. "If that. He's the runt of the Alsax cousins."

Surprise pinched the corners of the king's eyes. "The one who was fostered from Innis Lear?"

"Of Errigal. But not the earlson; the bastard."

Mars grunted.

They stared at the unconscious boy.

"They call him the Fox already," Novanos said quietly. "But not for his spying. They say he's the only soldier safe to leave in a henhouse."

It made Mars's smile turn to amusement, then sympathy. "He prefers men?"

"I believe he's merely celibate."

"Can he read?" Relieved, Mars's mind shot directly to one of the recent treatises he'd examined on the art of channeling sexual urges toward a purer focus on the battlefield.

"My lord," Novanos said dryly, "I will not allow you to hand this boy one of your tracts of ascetic nonsense."

Mars laughed softly, only a quiet huff of breath. "You know me too well," he murmured.

"What will you do with him? Some honor, I hope, or a medal."

"At least." Mars stared at the slight boy. If he earned the boy's trust, and if the boy proved loyal, cunning, and stalwart, then there were any number of potential paths to take forward. Toward the promise Mars had made his dying father. "When he wakes, I . . ."

The boy stirred. He opened dark, muddled eyes. "My lord?" he said in Learish.

"I am Morimaros," Mars said, in the same. Though the language they spoke on Innis Lear had been born of Aremore, in the centuries since the island was formed the two dialects had drifted very far apart.

"The king!" The boy switched to Aremore proper.

"Be at peace." Mars crouched and put his hand on the boy's hot forehead. "If you would speak, tell me how you survived, how you found the information about the Diotans."

The wounded youth stared blearily at Mars for a moment. He whispered something that Mars did not understand, then nodded, to himself or to something Mars could not see.

"I am a wizard," he said.

Surprised, Mars only waited. Perhaps the soldier was delirious, or perhaps it was a Learish thing to say. There had been wizards once in Aremoria, but they were no more.

Ban coughed, and a healer appeared with water. The boy drank, winced, and said, "I was injured, and so went to the trees for succor, my lord."

"To the trees?"

"They listened to me, and I to them," Ban said, eyes bright with fervor. "They spoke differently than the forests I am used to, but they offered me solace, as their Learish cousins would have." He whispered something else, and this time Mars recognized some of the hissing; it was part of the prayers for the dead on Innis Lear, a piece of the blessings still carved onto the oldest star chapels in Lionis. The earth faith was mostly purged from Aremoria, but not the original buildings, though most now had more governmental or ornamental function. Mars had read much about magic and earth saints when he was young, still enamored with ancient romances.

"The language of trees still exists," he said.

The Learish soldier nodded. "I asked the trees to hide me, my lord. They protected me, keeping me alive, feeding me water, holding me in among their roots beneath the ground as I healed, until the Diotans had made camp over me. I was already in the center, already behind their lines. And the trees then helped me keep to shadows; the wind blew to cover the sounds of my movement. That's how I found the commander's tent, and his maps, his orders, and that letter from his king."

"And his underclothes," Mars said.

Ban smiled slyly.

The king of Aremoria studied Ban, called the Fox to tease, and wondered if it was fate that had already given him his name. Mars said, "Do you think you could do it again?"

The boy stared back, lips parted, dry and cracked and needing succor. "That and more, with the help of your earth and roots," he finally murmured.

"Good." Mars put his hand on Ban's uninjured forearm. "Make yourself well, then come to me."

Mars stood to go.

"Your Highness," Ban said, "you . . . believe me?"

Lifting his brow, Mars said, "Should I not?"

"I . . ." The boy's eyelids fluttered; he needed rest, food, time to heal. "I am not used to being taken at my word."

"Because of your parentage?"

"And due to the stars under which I was born," Ban said. "They—"

"Stop. I don't care about your birth chart. I care what you are. What you do. And what you've already done. And especially I care what you will do next, at my side."

It might have been fever making the soldier's eyes glassy, or tears. He tried to sit up, and Mars crouched again, gently pressing him back onto the cot. "I see what you are, Ban the Fox. Heal, and then come be yourself for me."

"Myself," the boy whispered, nodding. A low sigh escaped him, whispering like breeze through winter grass. With Novanos close behind, Mars allowed himself to finally escape the hospital tent, back out under the sun. He blew a soft whisper, like Ban the Fox had done, and wondered what it would feel like to speak to the land itself.

And he wondered if the wind and sky and roots of Aremoria would reply to the crown.

# ELIA

IT WAS INSTINCT, perhaps, that woke Elia Lear every morning before dawn, then drove her from the luxury of her bed in the Lionis palace to perch on the ramparts of the westernmost tower and watch the stars fade and die.

From this pinnacle, Elia could see the entire valley of Lionis. The rising sun caught the water of the great, wide river first, gilding its slow current. The river curled through the city, golden beneath the slips and ferry boats and barges, beneath the fine slick passenger vessels and grand royal cannon ships. The capital city spread white and gray up either bank, climbing with winding cobbled streets and narrow terraces into the steep hills. Called the Pearl of Aremoria, it gleamed in the sun like mother shells and the lips of sea snails, built mainly of chalk and pale limestone, with pink coral roofs and slate shingles.

Atop sheer chalk cliffs that cut up from the inner elbow of the river was the king's palace. Its outer wall rose high and strong, capped with brilliant white crenellations, like a massive, toothy jaw ready to swallow the interior whole. Five towers marked the edges of the main building, lifting high and supported by elegant curving buttresses. Glass windows winked in the pink dawn light, and shadows slid off the steep blue-slate roofs. Courtyards and gardens created a hive of privacy, along with small crescent balconies hooked against the pale walls.

Every morning Elia faced Innis Lear as the sun obliterated the stars, though every morning she wished she could bring herself to turn any other way.

Dawn breeze off the river now chilled her wrists and bare fingers, ruffling the curls of hair she'd picked loose from her sleeping braid. This tower seemed nearer to the sky than ever she'd been, though Elia had once visited the Mountain of Teeth with her father and sisters on the Longest Night. Then, surrounded by jagged stone and ice along the narrow pilgrim path, by snow and low clouds, she had felt the sky descend to meet her.

Gaela had grimaced to show the mountain her own teeth, and Regan had howled at the power of it. King Lear had spoken twisting star poems, while Elia had cried in silent wonder.

She thought of it now, and at every dawn, stuck in reverie, unwilling to step outside of it. As if to unlatch herself from the memory would be to forget, to let go. To begin something new.

Elia Lear was terrified of a new beginning. This dawn moment was not the start of a day, but the end of a night, or both, or neither.

Her father refused to wake before dawn; he hated to see the stars die.

She'd made the mistake at first of pretending everything could be normal; she woke in her bed and remained there, then ate her breakfast of cheese, fine cold meat, and delicate bread, allowed Aefa to dress her body and hair, and attempted to go about a lady's day. As if Elia chose to be in Aremoria, as if she had not been cast away from Innis Lear. The result had been sudden, severe moments of pain throughout the day, brought on by unpredictable words, a glance, or merely the sight of a bird the likes of which she'd known before. Elia could barely control herself at those times, shaking with the power of this inner tempest.

To calm herself, she thought of her mother, and her childhood, before Dalat died, before her family fractured. In those days, Elia had been allowed to wake slowly, so long as she was fed and bathed by the time the queen expected her—waiting in the solar if it snowed and iced, or the garden if it did not—for several hours of reading, writing, and history lessons together. The queen had encouraged her youngest in learning, as she'd done with both elder daughters, and Elia was the one, finally, to appreciate any story, no matter how foreign or strange. Both had cherished their time alone, before a quick lunch with the king, and afterward Dalat would leave Elia to the star priests, for further lessons. The queen had spent her own afternoons supporting her husband's rule: attending the king's hunt, meeting with his clerks, inspecting new spices and goods from Aremoria or the Rusrike, or sometimes even the Third Kingdom. Often, Dalat's duty had included embroidering with the other ladies of the keep, sharing the sort of gossip that greased the wheels of any government, and collecting information to use in other cases.

When Elia had been very lucky, she'd been allowed join her mother at this womanly task, so long as she worked quietly and did not repeat what she might learn. Her elder sisters joined them occasionally, hand in hand. Regan had excelled at the art of sewing with gossip, keen enough to participate despite her relative youth. Gaela had worn trousers and a soldier's gambeson more often than not, and excitedly would explain to Dalat and the ladies what the earl Errigal or earl Glennadoer—or even the ladies' own retainers—had taught her recently, of defense and the sword and the way of men. Possibly Gaela had not yet realized how vital her occasional dropped detail was to the women's network.

Elia did: she could always see the patterns of their world.

In the evenings, the whole family dined in the great hall, included in a warm mess of retainers and servants, along with visiting earls and local barons, or the sons and daughters of their neighbors; whomever had come to the long gray wall of Dondubhan Castle, crossing the Star Field to pray for the spirits of their dead. And after the meal, if Elia was not too sleepy, the princess was welcome to curl beside her parents as they listened to a harpist or oliphant player, poetry in at least three different languages, or the Fool's riddles. Elia's head would lean upon her mother's or father's lap, and the youngest Lear would drift away to the sights and sounds of her family at peace.

The memories felt like a story now, a tale of earth saints and music and happiness that had lived in some other princess's heart.

On the sleepy ramparts of Lionis Palace it hurt Elia less to think of what had never changed: Regan's pinched smile when she sipped hot coffee, for Regan loved the bitter drink; Gaela slipping a small, sheathed knife into the hidden pocket of her gown. She thought of Aefa dotting red paint down her cheeks and making a poem from any three words Elia offered. She thought of the scrape of a quill against paper, the smell of pine boughs covering the hall at Dondubhan, the lapping waves of the Tarinnish. She tried never to think of her father.

She thought of Ban Errigal.

*Be bold,* he had said.

She thought of the stars—but no, *no,* they could not be relied upon. Not her birth chart or dawn signs, none of it. Not even Calpurlugh.

When the wind blew, she listened for the whisper of Aremore trees. They did not speak to her. Whether she'd gone deaf to the language, or they refused her on some rooted principle, she did not know. Ban had said the trees of Aremoria laughed, but she had not yet heard them.

The tempest inside her raged, and Elia bound it tight.

All she could do was breathe.

Carefully breathe, in and out, and tell herself nothing was over.

# GAELA

In over a decade Gaela had never been so glad to be back in Astora. Rain had plagued her for the entire ride north from the Summer Seat, and a three-day journey had stretched to a week, thanks to her father's old bones and the hundred retainers lengthening the party. Lear's men were not nearly as efficient as Gaela's own, and by the fourth day, she'd left camp before they'd finished clearing their tents.

As she rode into the city, all Gaela wished for was a hot fire, a hotter bath, and an entire bottle of that dark wine Astore always kept cellared. She supposed she'd have to dine with him, the husband who'd left the Summer Seat a day before Gaela, and no doubt had been home and settled and working since the Sixday of last week.

Water dripped down her scalp, for Gaela had lowered her hood as her horse took her beneath the heavy city gate. Behind her came her captain Crai and her personal retinue, then the hundred Learish retainers in dark blue tabards, and several wagons with all their goods and belongings. Gaela would already be slipping into her private bath by the time the last stragglers made it to the outer garrison where they'd be housed.

Astora City filled this small mountain valley in patches of cream and gray. Most buildings and houses were whitewashed and roofed with slate tiles, though some bright yellow glowed where thatched roofs leaned short and happy against their more elegant neighbors. There was no order to the roads and blocks of homes, though taverns appeared at regular intervals. One could find clusters of blacksmiths sharing wide stone yards, and then a row of tanners' alleys had tucked themselves by the south plateau, where wind rarely blew their stench throughout the rest of the city. The old castle keep and the newer castle stood tall and proud at the northeast corner of the valley, where a mountain pass led out of the Jawbone Mountains, and a strong arm of the Duv River poured in with fresh water, churning several mills. Only three water wheels had been kept turning lately, for the villages that brought their grain here had so much less such to bring. So it was across the island, Gaela had discovered when working with her father's stewards, collecting numbers for her return to Astore territory. The island of Innis Lear was in for a lean winter, again.

The old castle keep was a square of thick walls and arrow slits, poorly ventilated, but Gaela's husband loved it passionately, knew every history of its stones. His grandfather had begun building the more refined new castle with technology from Aremoria; it would perhaps be finished with construction by the time this Astore was a sixty-year-old graybeard. But it was more than livable already, with taller ceilings and fewer drafts, a magnificent hall and bright solar he used for his office. Yet unless Astore died in battle, he'd sworn he'd die in the black keep, as all his ancestors had managed to do. Perhaps he would, but not until Gaela was crowned. She needed him still, as she'd needed him after Dalat died, when she dragged herself and her sister Regan here to command the duke to put her among his retainers and teach her to be a warrior king. As she'd needed him when she was twenty-one and finally forced to admit her father would never officially name her his heir so long as she was unwed.

Now she was officially an heir, but Regan remained childless at Connley's side, and so Gaela needed Astore still to prove the relevance of her stars. But not for long. Soon she'd not need any of these men who saw her stars over her self. Once the Longest Night arrived, Gaela would kneel in the black waters of the Tarinnish. The island would bless her body and heart, and she would seem to give herself to it. Then, only then, could she kill Lear.

The uncomfortable old keep was where she'd put her father and his top men, too, though she herself had rooms in the new castle.

Gaela lifted her gauntleted hand as she entered the wide yard between the two seats. She nodded to Crai, who knew what needed to be done now for her father's welcome. They'd sent runners ahead this morning, so all should be well prepared. And Gaela gave her horse over to a groom, grabbed her saddlebag and helmet, and headed straight into her own castle.

At her rooms, Osli waited. "Welcome home, lady. We've heard so much about what happened. Is it true, Lady Elia's gone to Aremoria?"

"Bath first," Gaela said, and pushed into the front room.

"Yes, it's ready. The girls started it as soon as we knew you'd entered the city gate." Osli took her sword belt, and two house maids stripped Gaela down as Osli carried the weaponry to its rack. Gaela went naked to the tub and climbed in, already grasping the rough soap. She flattened her lips and leaned back into the steaming water, but only gave herself one long moment before making a lather to wash herself swiftly and thoroughly.

"Elia?" Osli nudged, dragging a short stool near the tub.

Gaela sat up and waved over one of the house girls, who began the careful work of unbinding the mass of twists weighing down Gaela's head. She'd not washed it since leaving for the Summer Seat, except to scrub at the scalp with clay powder. Now, they'd mix the clay with rosewater until it was a smooth, refreshing paste to be massaged into her head and hair. Gaela carefully closed the door to memories of such moments with her mother and Satiri.

"Elia is in Aremoria, yes," Gaela said, relaxing under the girls' ministrations. "Regan and I share the inheritance, according to Lear. And he's come home with me, until the Longest Night." She groaned in approval as one girl dug fingers hard into the muscles at the base of her skull. "Then I will finally be king."

"And Regan's claim?"

Gaela glanced sharply at Osli. "She will not challenge me, but will be my royal sister, as ever. Her word, too, shall be law. Our husbands will accustom themselves to this arrangement, or kill each other trying."

Osli said nothing, and Gaela peered at the young woman's face: oval-shaped with a small nose, with the sort of skin that pinked if the sun but glanced at her. Brown hair short as a boy's. Those thin lips turned down.

It was five years ago Osli had presented herself to Gaela in the shift and apron of one of the house staff. The girl had lifted her chin and met Gaela's eyes proudly. She'd said, "I do not want to serve you in this fashion."

Gaela, well acquainted with communicating without clearly voicing her needs, had heard the message behind the words, and smiled. "How would you serve me instead, girl?"

Osli did not return the smile. "As a warrior, like you."

After a brief study of Osli's hands (strong and big) and posture (solid though skinny), Gaela jerked her chin toward the door. "Take your things to the barracks, then, and if you can make your way back to me by that route, you will get your wish."

It took only eighteen months before Gaela saw her again, beaten to the dust of the arena, but learning. A year after that, Gaela made her a captain, both for the girl's sake as well as to stir up Gaela's own ranks. Not once had Osli asked for help or expected special treatment for being a woman. She followed Gaela's example as best she could, served well and without complaint, and for that Gaela now spoke. "Ask me what you will, Osli."

"Folks are saying the bad harvests are because the king stopped taking rootwater, and stopped giving his blood to the island."

Gaela shut her eyes and leaned in to the house girl's massage. "Who? Who are you listening to that says such things? My retainers? My husband's?"

"My father," Osli confessed.

"Your father wants the wells open again."

"Yes. He's lost more sheep this year, and it could be coincidence, but those who still hear the voices of the trees . . . the things they say of the king . . . my lady, I only wonder what you intend."

Gaela sat up swiftly, sending waves of hot water lapping over the wooden edge of the tub. "Do I not give my blood to this island?"

"You do."

"Was I not born under a conqueror's sky?"

"You were."

"Do you doubt I am fit for the crown of Innis Lear?"

"Never!" Osli grasped the rim of the tub. "Never, my lady. It is only your father, and he is here now. What should I say of him, what should we say to him?"

"Say nothing of him, and nothing to him. He is old, and I am his heir. The time of witches and wizards is passing, Osli. We will be as great as Aremoria one day, as great as the Third Kingdom itself. They do not need magic, but only strength in their rulers and unity in their people. I'll keep this island unified, under my rule, with my sister at my side. With me, you shall see it."

Gaela held Osli's steady gaze, willing the captain to let go of hundreds of years of superstition, to see how star prophecy was only a tool, and the rootwater just water. The island was an island, and earth saints, if they'd ever been real, had left long ago.

The young woman nodded eagerly. Gaela smiled.

A knock at the door jolted Osli to her feet. She answered it, fetching back a message from Astore that he would see his wife before they joined the king at a feast.

Gaela resigned herself to it, though she told Osli to pour a cup of wine for both of them to enjoy as she finished her bath. She drank deeply, imagining how it would feel when she wore the crown of Lear, when she sat on the throne at Dondubhan. How many days after the Longest Night would she wait before Lear died? An hour, or a week? Perhaps if Gaela chose to be merciful, she would grant Elia the goodbye none of them had been allowed with their mother.

When she drained the wine, she stood. "The split gown," she ordered, "with that dark blue underneath."

Stepping out of the bathtub, she was rubbed down with cloth, and then another girl spread cinnamon oil along Gaela's spine and arms and belly; it stung every tiny open scratch, and Gaela relished it. That was why she preferred cinnamon. And that it cost her husband.

These were the small prices he paid for ever having loved her, for thinking she was his.

The dark blue wool underdress slithered over her loose and long, its hem curling about her bare ankles. The girls tied the cream gown on over it, arranging the split skirt carefully with ribbons that tied it in place. Laces pulled it against Gaela's breasts, leaving her collar and shoulders bare for a thick silver necklace that pretended to plate mail. Her hair they twisted wet and bound low at her nape, with tiny silver combs tucked around the thick knot.

With fine fresh lady's boots tied onto her feet and her Astore ring on her right thumb, she left her rooms and sought out her husband. A satisfying hour since he'd sent for her.

Astore waited in his study, a bright room just off the great hall that should've been a solar but that he'd cluttered with scrolls, maps, dusty books of war philosophy, and his own journals. South-facing windows were thrown open to the early evening sun, for Astore preferred to write by daylight.

Gaela did not knock before entering. Her husband sat behind his desk. Letters were scattered about, and several ink pots. A dagger for cutting wicks and opening seals weighed down a pile of the thin paper he used for jotting notes and observations.

"Ah, wife," he said, coming around the desk. "While I waited long and longer still for you, I wondered if we should leave immediately tomorrow and take Brideton? Before Connley can even blink? It could be done in a pleasant afternoon, I think. What word from your sister? Did they go straight for Errigal, or stop at home first? And Elia, will she be cold enough to refuse the king of Aremoria, or shall we prepare for him, too?"

Gaela did not answer, but only lifted an eyebrow. Astore stopped suddenly, a step away from her, and dragged his hand down his beard.

"My stars and worms, woman, you're beautiful."

She tilted her chin just slightly higher. Astore closed the step between them. His mouth brushed the hollow of her cheek, and he breathed hot against her ear. Gaela held still as a hovering hawk. She hoped he would not force his desire now; she did not have the mood for it, nor for arguing.

One of Astore's hands settled on her hip.

"Regan will take her husband home to Connley Castle first, and we will all settle in to this new arrangement," Gaela said softly, though not tenderly. "Then they will to Errigal."

"Damn them for sharing a coastline."

"Do not worry on it, Astore. The throne will be mine, and if you still refuse to trust me on that, let us march to Dondubhan tomorrow and I will sit myself upon it before all the island. I will drink that black water, and be queen in all ways."

His hand tightened on her hip. "Do not be so arrogant or impatient, Gaela. There are rules and traditions, and we will have the throne, in four months."

"I make the rules, Col," she snarled, leaning in to him, lining up their bodies. "The traditions will be mine to change."

"Some things are carved in stone, like this island itself. There is blood in the roots, and you must respect that. Innis Lear was built on magic, and united with it. With magic it can be sundered."

Gaela glared into his heated brown eyes. "The blood of this island is in me, Col Astore, and in your veins. None will take the crown from us."

"Half your blood is from a desert. You have to show the people here that you bleed rootwater."

She grabbed the collar of his tunic and made a fist. "How dare you suggest my mother's line does not belong here! My birth was predicted by Lear's stars, and her death confirmed it: we are intimately woven into the breath of this island." The final words panted out of her, and Gaela struggled to remain calm.

Astore kissed her, hard, and nodded against her mouth. "Yes, my love, that ferocity is pure Innis Lear," he whispered, tugging at her.

"Let me go." Gaela tore free, sighing deeply. "We must feast with Lear and his men."

"Wait until the Longest Night to take the crown," Astore said firmly. "You need the stars, Gaela, and the rootwater. You need the rituals. The people do."

"I know," she snapped.

He took her elbow and pulled her out into the corridor. Gaela did not bother to wipe the anger off her face, though she took his hand and held it in her own; she would not be led.

Noise rose from the great hall, raucous and pitched like a brawl. Gaela frowned, but Astore put on a smile as they entered from the stairs directly connecting his study with the hall.

Lear's Fool danced a ragged, ridiculous dance to the clapping of half the hundred men crushed together—many were her father's, though some wore the Astore pink. Food already filled trenchers, and the old king sat in Astore's tall-backed chair, eating a leg of pheasant, laughing at the Fool.

They'd begun the feast without the very lord of this castle. Gaela clenched her jaw, shuddering beneath a wave of fury. What if she cut his throat and all that hot blood poured out over the high table? If she drank from a cup of wine splattered with Lear's blood, would it be as good as bathing herself in rootwater? What would the island say then?

Astore squeezed her hand, as if he knew her mind. "Patience," he murmured. Then he kissed her temple and grinned out at the hall as if they had intended this, calling for more wine and a loud welcome to the magnificent King Lear and his retainers.

Gaela held her peace. She had patience, yes. The patience of a wolf; the patience of red-hot coals, tucked under black ash where their fire could not yet be seen, not until it was needed.

And then everything that did not get out of her way would burn.

THE ELDEST DAUGHTER of Lear descended upon the village of Hartfare like a conqueror: back straight, shoulders spread, clad in glistening silver mail and a midnight blue gambeson over quilted trousers, thick-soled, polished boots, with a long cape rippling behind her, the Swan Star crest of Lear embroidered on it in brilliant white. Her sword hung at her hip and her shield was slung over her shoulder, reflecting dappled sunlight in flashes as her thick white horse chose careful, sure steps. She had no paint on her face, despite Regan's insistence that it was required before considering oneself fully armored. Her dark mouth was set firm and frowning in her dark face.

The princess shifted, stretching taller atop her horse as nausea gripped her hipbones and dragged long fingers down her lower spine. She rode eyes forward, straight into the central square, ignoring the villagers' raised hands and surprised bowing. They knew her; who could not recognize Gaela Lear, the black princess, the warrior daughter of Lear? In the corners of her eyes she noticed as those who had never seen her—or had not seen her since she'd grown tall—now marked how like a man she seemed. How like a soldier she sat, breasts bound as flat as she could make them, allowing the chainmail and gambeson to curve as over a man's strong chest. The bulk of the sword belt at Gaela's waist made the dip of her hips more discreet, and her thighs were as strong as many men's. Her life studying war in Astora had changed her.

She reached the far end of Hartfare, where the witch of the White Forest kept her cottage. The perfectly trained horse stopped as Gaela leaned back in her seat. Dismounting, she ordered one of the gawking boys to see to rubbing down the beast if he wished to keep his staring eyes. She swung her heavy shield off her shoulder and propped it against the mud brick wall of the house.

"Brona," she called out sharply, a warning before pushing open the door. She ducked slightly under the sloped thatch.

"Gaela," the woman said happily, crouched barefoot by the fire. Brona's mass of black hair was tied in messy knots down her back, and she wore heavy ruffled skirts and a loose shift that did not want to stay on both shoulders. The sunlight spilling in from the windows seemed to dance around her. Though the woman was almost twice Gaela's age, around her Gaela felt still and old as an ancient spring.

Brona stood, smiling. "Don't you look glorious and intimidating. Come out back with me."

And with that, Brona vanished through the rear room of the cottage. Gaela followed more slowly, nudging aside bundles of hanging herbs as she passed through the longish, dim herbary toward the glint of daylight.

Halfway through, a familiar pain clenched in Gaela's womb. Refusing to bend, refusing to whimper, Gaela bared her teeth to the empty room, hissing breath at the drying rainbow of flowers and herbs. Dust motes shimmered in the sunny air like tiny spirits.

Gaela snarled silently, impatient to walk again. She was not meant for this.

The first time she'd bled, years ago, it had begun with days of lethargy and fever, until finally, with the first hot drops on her thighs, she ran to her mother in a panic. Dalat had hugged her and smiled, chiding Gaela for not listening the many times she'd been warned this would come. But Gaela never thought those warnings applied to her; they were for girls like Regan who would one day become women. Gaela had been absolutely certain she would never cross that threshold.

Her body had betrayed her. And continued to do so, no matter how she fought, prayed, cursed, ran it ragged, or pretended.

The pain loosened its grip, slinking into the hot muscles, waiting.

When she emerged into the elaborate garden, there was Brona waiting with a sprig of some gentle green plant in her hand. "Here, child. Chew on this."

Gaela took it, tearing off a bitter leaf. She studied Brona as the tip of her tongue numbed pleasingly. She wanted to argue over the word *child;* she was past twenty years old.

Brona nodded, though Gaela had said nothing, and touched Gaela's cheek briefly in fond greeting. "You've not come here since your mother died," Brona said.

"This is no place for me," Gaela said harshly.

Sorrow warmed Brona's glinting brown eyes, but she nodded. "I know."

Gaela was uninterested in reminiscing, or in regret. She would not discuss her mother or her mother's death, not with anyone but her sister. She said, "I am here now because I need something from you."

Brona nodded. The wind blew through the canopy overhead, tossing blotchy shadows over the garden, and tiny crystals and bells hanging from the branches chattered and sang together. Gaela missed the controlled sounds of the barracks, of the practice grounds in Astora.

"I'm engaged to marry the Duke Astore," Gaela said.

The witch only lifted her eyebrows, not in surprise, but to indicate she continued to listen.

"I need . . ." Gaela hated how difficult it was to say what she'd come to say. It was a weakness to be afraid of the words, doubly so because her very *need* was a weakness. But there was no alternative: only the witch of the White Forest could help her, even if Brona wouldn't understand. Not even Regan understood, so how could a witch like Brona?

"He will want to touch me," Gaela managed to say, quiet and low. A shudder coursed through her at the thought of it, of his hands on her waist, her breasts, and—memory triggered another sharp pain in her womb. Gaela could not hold back the gasp, and she pressed her hands to her belly, furious at her body's betrayal.

"Sit, and let me make you a tincture," Brona said gently.

"No medicine." Gaela would not use any restorative herbs to face this regular battle. It was hers to suffer, and hers to defeat.

Brona frowned and slid her arm around Gaela's waist, rubbing the heel of her hand against the layers of gambeson and mail, into the small of the princess's back. "All this weight you carry. Your mother spent this difficulty naked as a babe, so she could be rubbed and soothed."

"I remember," Gaela panted. Dalat had withdrawn from court during these times to share the experience with her daughters and ladies, but that was not Gaela's way. She crouched, alleviating the tightness in her back, but not the ache inside, not the viscous pain filling her hips like a cauldron of poison. The mail shirt dragged at her shoulders, shivering gently. It was a comfort to Gaela: her true, epicene skin.

In silence they waited together for Gaela's pain to pass. She breathed deeply, forcing her body to relax as best she could, and the witch held her cool hand against Gaela's neck, patient and maternal.

Gently, Brona said, "You need not marry if you find the thought of sexual congress so terrible, Gaela. If you cannot bring yourself to lie with a man, do not."

Gaela snorted at a woman like Brona offering such advice. "You know my stars, and you know Innis Lear. I will never rule if I am not married," she said, upset at the raw quality of her voice.

"I see," Brona murmured. "Then what is it you need from me?"

"I won't bear children."

"I can help with that, yes."

The princess shook her head. Her brow pinched with misery. "No, I do not mean I want your potions or skins or abortifacients. I want this inside me destroyed. Burned out or removed, or erased with your magic, Brona. I want you to make me a man."

In the bright afternoon, against birds calling high and pretty from the edges of the forest, with the sounds of Hartfare warm and welcoming all around, Gaela's voice was hard. Harsh, and determined as fire.

Brona said, "This is not what makes a woman, or the lack of which that makes a man."

"Do not be pedantic or poetical with me, Brona. Do not philosophize or moralize. Only tell me if you can."

"I can."

Gaela said, "And you will?"

"You might die of it."

"I am prepared to die in battle."

Brona's expression darkened. "Good, for that is what this shall be. A battle inside you, and all you will have is the strength of your heart. Your determination."

"I can conquer my body," Gaela whispered.

"Hm." Brona frowned, nodding at the same time, studying the warrior in a thoughtful yet daunting manner. It relieved Gaela to be reminded that Brona was an authority in her chosen work, and yet it still brought a swift pinch of annoyance that anyone could still elicit such timidity in her at all. "You will need some weeks to recover, perhaps. Are you ready now, or shall I come to you?"

Gaela's instinct was to insist on an immediate surgery. She was ready, had been ready; she needed this as she'd needed almost nothing in her life. But then she thought of Regan's fury if Gaela were to go into this alone, were to leave without a word. Regan did not get to make this decision for Gaela, or even with her, but that did not mean she would not be there to squeeze their fingers together, to clench her jaw in shared pain, to hold Gaela through the worst of it.

Sweat broke along Gaela's hairline, and she said, "I need Regan. Come with me now, and do it at Dondubhan, so I may be sick where she is."

"And nearer to your mother," Brona murmured.

"No, this is nothing to do with her. She would not . . ." Gaela stopped. She touched her fists to the damp earth of the garden.

"She wanted you, Gaela. Your father was afraid of the prophecy, but Dalat

wanted her girls, no matter what. Motherhood was a gift to her, not a curse."
Brona touched her tan hands to the backs of Gaela's. She was so much paler
than Gaela, though not so pale as Gaela's father or her future husband.

*This is the only match that matters,* Dalat had said.

Perhaps her mother had the luxury to think so because she'd grown up
in the Third Kingdom where everyone was rich and dark and proud. Where
Dalat and her daughters would have belonged. But Gaela knew that to
most people on Innis Lear it mattered more what she did *not* look like
than what she did. She did *not* look like her father; she did *not* look like a
king.

Gaela would not give up her mother's skin for anything, but she could
make herself into a king for Innis Lear.

It had been nearly five years since Dalat's death, and Gaela alone of all
the daughters felt it hard and sharp still, for she alone had grown up with
a mother, been sixteen when she died—as the star prophecy had promised.
The grief filled her with rage sometimes, and she embraced it as a hot, scouring ocean wind, keeping her clear and focused on what she wanted: the
throne.

Gaela opened her mouth to say so to Brona, for Brona had known Dalat
longer even than Gaela herself had. They'd been friends, dear friends, and
if anyone missed Dalat as fiercely as Gaela, it would be the witch.

"How can you bear to be parted from your son?" Gaela asked instead.
"How can you allow yourselves to be separated?"

"My son?" Brona's face was near enough to Gaela's, as the two women
knelt there, that Gaela could count the hair-thin lines of smiling and
sorrow and age skirting Brona's eyes. Gaela nodded, and Brona squeezed
her fists. "I would prefer he be here still, with me. But mothers must let go,
someday. He carries pieces of me inside him, and words I've given him. He
will make or break himself, as all children must. Your mother would say
the same."

Gaela lurched to her feet. "I must make or break myself."

More slowly, Brona stood. She stepped back from Gaela, enough to take
her in with one sweep of her gaze. "Yes," she said, "Make or break yourself,
Gaela Lear, and take this island with you."

"I will break myself in order to make myself," Gaela whispered, shivering suddenly with pain and promise.

*And perhaps then this island, too.*

# THE FOX

THOUGH HE COULD never think of it as home, Ban found he rather admired the oddly shaped Keep of the Earls Errigal.

The Keep had been destroyed in his grandfather's grandfather's time, when the island of Lear had been a chaotic cluster of tiny kingdoms. The then-king of Connley had sacked Errigal Keep, knocking two of the black stone walls down with the unmatched strength of his war machines, gutting and burning the inside and executing the inhabitants in waves until Errigal surrendered. King Connley brought every little territory to its knees in this way, and made the island into his own; he renamed himself Lear— after the wizard who had cleaved the island from Aremoria—and turned the former kingdoms into dukedoms. The new line of Lear forced Errigal to swear allegiance and promise never to rebuild the Keep into the great stone fortress it had been.

But Ban's grandfather's grandfather had been a clever man, and he found a flaw in the wording of the vow. Instead of erecting a new manse on the opposite mountain as was expected, he rebuilt the once-foreboding Errigal Keep—but not with stone. The angry gray ruins still reached out of the mountainside, rough and cracked like a shattered shield, but within those arms now rose a new castle of pale wood and lime mortar. There were wings built half of that ancient old granite, half of thick trees polished and striped with grayish plaster. Random wooden towers peeked over the ruins to peer in every direction, and one great tower rose spindly and strange from the center, with only room enough for three men to stand lookout. Errigal Keep gave the impression of a proud old carcass, dead and laid to rest here on the barren mountain, with only wintery blue banners for memorial.

Ban was caught between grudging admiration and irrational anger at the efficiency with which his father ran the Keep. Errigal's retainers were sharp and well-behaved, especially compared to King Lear's more ragged men whom Ban had observed at the Summer Seat. They patrolled the mountain and the Keep walls, and they held to their rotations with a moonlike timeliness. Errigal himself was free to hunt or play cards or seduce women or sit on his ass with a tankard of wine if he wished. In the evenings, soldiers and their wives gathered with Errigal in the long dining hall for hot food and plenty of beer and fire. They told stories—the same stories they'd told when Ban was a boy—or sang or gossiped or heard what news from Lear or the mainland countries Errigal had gotten during the day.

Earl Errigal was quite liked and respected here despite, or maybe because of, his bullish, loud strength.

But he was doing something wrong, for the navel well in the rear garden of the Keep had gone dry. Though capped off years ago as the king had instructed, several of the residents had secretly continued to use it for holy rootwater. Folk in Errigal understood the language of trees, and even if they strove to obey their earl as he sternly maintained the king's decree, they could not let go the faith of their mothers or the old Connley lords.

Yesterday, one such woman had found Ban in the navel garden, contemplating the plain wooden cap over the well, and admitted to him mournfully that it had been dry two years. No rootwater, even at the spring bloom. Those who wanted rootwater had to venture into the White Forest for a natural spring, or do without. *Most have turned to the star chapels,* she whispered.

Exactly as the king had intended.

Ban scowled, remembering, and climbed atop a wide boulder that jutted out the side of the Keep mountain. He looked out on the rest of the valley.

The town of Errigal's Steps scattered down the slope below the Keep, full of wattle-and chalk-daub houses, a star chapel, bakeries and cobblers and tailors and butchers and, importantly, more weapon smithies per muddy road than any other town in all of Innis Lear. Even Aremoria bought swords from Errigal, worked with the iron magic unique to this valley.

To the south of Steps was a long peat marsh where the iron ore came from, kept narrow by the short, jagged hills of the region. From the Keep lookout tower it was possible to see the ocean on a clear day, or to trace the winding Innis Road that crossed the marsh and headed from that eastern coast all the way west to the Summer Seat.

From here Ban should've been able to look north and see the edge of the White Forest of Lear, full of giant oaks and white-limbed witch trees, heavy ferns and flat daggers of slate cutting up from the earth, creeks where drowned spirits played and meadows where flowers unfurled to the moon.

When last he'd stood on this very boulder, as a fourteen-year-old boy, the canopy had waved farewell. But now, though he was taller and stronger, the forest seemed farther away.

Errigal would not have cut the trees back, nor would the trees have allowed it if he'd tried, nor the witch who lived in the forest's heart. The forest had withdrawn on its own. The trees had leaned away from the island's edges, pulling tightly together as if for safety. For comfort? Ban did not know, because he had not yet forced himself to approach the White Forest to ask. He needed to. He needed to hear the whisper of those trees. To drip his blood onto their roots again. To visit his mother.

"It's time," called Curan, Errigal's wide-shouldered iron wizard.

First, Ban would do this magic.

He hopped off the boulder and made his way down the slope toward the bloomeries. Five brick chimneys squatted on a flat ridge, each spewing short, white-orange flames and billows of smoke. They burned iron ore down to its purer parts to be worked into swords in the town. Two apprentices tended each chimney, most of them men younger than Ban, though one of the two women was older, having come late to her calling. For nearly nine hours today Curan had overseen his students take turns with their round bellows, heating the chimneys and coaxing the fire with urgent spells. They'd begun well before dawn, shoveling in oak charcoal and heavy chunks of iron ore, and Ban now studied their results, listening to the crackling, furious dialect the fire spoke.

As a boy, he'd known Errigal was the home of the greatest swords. For generations a wizard here had passed on his understanding of how earth, tree, and fire came together to make the strongest iron, the purest to be found. And the smiths worked charms and promises into the finished blades, so Errigal swords never shattered or chipped. They made spearheads and daggers, too, faster and less protected, but it was the swords that were desired by kings the world over.

So desired, it seemed, the stars themselves had revealed to Lear he need not forbid this sort of earth magic.

Curan had been the first person the Fox approached upon returning here, to learn what he could of fire and iron, and whether they could be harnessed outside this isolated valley. In a place like Aremoria, even. Morimaros wore a blade of Errigal steel that had been his father's and grandfather's. The king paid a steep price for every piece of it he wanted for Aremoria. This intelligence was not the only item on Ban's list, but it was a good place to begin: learning to make for himself a quiet magical sword, deadly and strong.

"Here, boy," Curan said, grasping Ban's elbow. "Smear the mud on your forearms, chest, shoulders, and face. It will keep the heat away while you reach in and pull out the bloom."

A wide bucket of gray mud waited, and two of the apprentices had already begun slathering it on. Ban tugged his shirt off and obeyed, welcoming the cool, heavy feel of it through his fingers. For good measure, he slid it through his hair, too, slicking it back. He and the apprentices became animate clay men, eyes glinting, and teeth, too, when they laughed at each other.

He drew a spiral over his heart and said, *My heart is the root of the island,* in the language of trees. Curan nodded approval; it had not been one of his instructions.

"You all remember the charm?" the wizard asked. "You may need it more than once, for the iron these days is sleepy. For every six blades we used to forge successful, we get only one good, living bloom now." His gnarled blond hair was braided back in three ropes, tied together with pieces of iron coins and silk. A leather apron protected his chest, painted and sewn with marked spells for steadiness and even heat. The apprentices and Ban nodded, ready.

Together they went to the first chimney, where the ore Ban had harvested himself cooked. With a long-handled hammer, one apprentice knocked the thin layer of clay away from the door at the base. Heat flared out, licking with fire, followed by a thin stream of melted slag, red-hot. Ban lifted tongs and positioned himself to reach in with them, blinking at the heat drying his eyeballs and cracking the mud on his skin.

"They will be hard, the chunks of iron, but the surface gives, like a sea sponge or loam beneath your feet," Curan said.

Breathe in the fire, out a long hissing spell: words in a hard, symmetrical pattern the iron enjoyed. Ban crouched and angled the tongs into the furnace mouth. Fishing through the roast, his nose filled with hot burn and smoke, Ban whispered the spell again. He closed his eyes, listening to the fire. It spat merrily at him, happy to be so furiously hot: *Dancing from heaven, hot as stars,* it sang.

He whispered the secret name of iron, and finally his tongs clasped onto something that felt right. He pulled. The iron dragged at the guts of the chimney. Ban coaxed it, sweat on his lips and trailing down his neck and sticking at the corners of his eyes. The bloom of iron worked free, born from the desperate heat, and Ban smiled.

Backing away with that glowing hunk clasped in the tongs—white-hot, orange, and dark, shadowed black—he turned to the stone altar slab on the ground. He set the bloom down, but did not release it from the tongs.

Curan tapped it with a short hammer, gently. *Iron,* he said in the language of trees, then shaped the words for *fire* and *earth*. Flecks of orange-black fell away.

"Good," he said.

Ban fixed his stance, holding the tongs with both hands and his shoulders back, and he began the slag charm. As he spoke it, Curan and the apprentices hammered the bloom of iron, working the slag away, the impurities, in a heart rhythm, a rhythm the wind picked up and Ban felt in the soles of his feet. He'd not touched anything like this since he was a child, working magic with his mother, or dancing with Elia. Alone as a wizard in Aremoria, he had not been offered such a chance, either.

The iron formed under their hammers into a long, soft rectangle, shining like a sun.

*I burn!* the iron cried in triumph.

Ban laughed at its joy, feeling an echo of it rumble through his arms.

Curan gave him an understanding smile, though one of the apprentices' brows creased, as if he did not hear. "It speaks easily with you, Ban Errigal, and very clear," the wizard said.

"It called to me from the marsh, when we were harvesting," Ban said. "I asked the roots for my own material—the quietest, strongest ore. To become a sword for a Fox."

"The island listened." Curan clapped his hand on Ban's bare, muddy shoulder. The iron wizard frowned a moment but said no more, going to oversee his students remove blooms from the remaining chimneys.

"I hear that bright magic!" called a distant voice in a happy yell.

Ban turned south, toward the path from the Innis Road.

A soldier approached on a fine-shouldered chestnut mare, in the dark blue coat of Lear's retainers, but unbuttoned over a dirty white shirt. His sword belt slung over the saddle and tapped his horse's shoulder with every trot. The soldier unbuckled the chin strap of his leather helm and tossed it to the rocky earth, swinging off the saddle before even pulling his horse to a stop.

Vibrant hair flared off his skull, half stuck down with sweat. "Stars and granite!" cried Rory Errigal—the brother barely behind Ban in age, but always ahead in legitimacy. Rory raised his arms wide as if he could make love to the whole valley. "What a fine place this is, and finer still to be home at last!"

The heir to the earldom was buoyant and as bulky as his father, with a thatch of red hair and matching red freckles thick over the rough white skin of Errigal, the same color as the coarse sand of the beaches. His thin beard and eyelashes were fine yellow like early morning sunlight, brighter still when he smiled.

And Rory Errigal smiled always.

Even at his grim bastard brother.

Ban fought against the tug of a smile on his own face, wondering how long it would be before Rory saw and recognized him. They'd served together in Aremoria for two years, until Rory'd been called home last year to serve in the king's retainers. They had not seen each other since.

"Curan!" called Rory. "Hello!"

The wizard nodded at the two young men and one woman currently working another bloom free of another fire, then turned to face the young lord, wiping his hands on his leather apron. "My lord Rory, welcome home."

"I wasn't quite sure what the trees were saying as I rode in, but I see now they were welcoming new iron." Rory strode over, having dropped the reins so his horse heaved a sigh and meandered slowly after him, casting several long looks toward the Keep and her eventual stable.

"You're out of practice listening," Curan said.

"So it happens with the king's retainers." Rory shrugged as it if they were not discussing forbidden magic. *Always so certain he is untouchable,* Ban thought, amazed.

Rory said, "This is your crop of apprentices? Is Allan still here? I heard he married and left our valley."

"Allan is—"

"Saints' teeth!"

All the wind seemed to quiet, even, and the hissing of fires and clang of hammers, at the shock in Rory Errigal's voice. His powerfully blue eyes widened. "Ban?"

Ban reluctantly passed his tongs to another student and wiped his hand over his cracking, muddy hair. "Hello, brother."

Before aught else but a merry cry, Rory threw himself forward, flinging his considerable muscle mass against Ban. Ban stumbled; Rory caught him with an elbow around the neck, and like that the two brothers hit the ground in a full wrestle.

If they were to greet each other in the way of dogs, so be it, Ban thought viciously, and fought back hard. Ban was not as strong or bulky as his brother, but he was fast and smart and practiced at these games. He would not let Rory have this easily.

Rory grunted a laugh of surprise the first time Ban almost slipped free, their legs still tangled and bracketed together. Ban twisted his entire body to gain the upper hand, but he could not quite keep hold against Rory. They rolled, scraping hands and knees and chins on the rough mountain path, and Ban tasted blood in his mouth. He hissed like a badger or a furious snake, and Rory cried out, *"For Errigal!"* before throwing his shoulder into Ban's gut with another laugh.

Breath snuffed out, Ban heaved and gasped, half thrown over his brother's shoulder, then managed to turn his flail into a firm stomp of his boot against Rory's thigh.

Rory fell.

They both went down.

Rory tried to throw Ban out of his way, but managed to land partially atop him anyway, and Ban flung out his arms, flat on his back and barely breathing. Blood slicked down his chin from a cut inside his lip.

Overhead, the sun and tapestry of clouds turned slow, dizzy circles.

They'd been like this as boys, after Errigal stole Ban from Hartfare and his mother when he was ten: wrestling, running about together, climbing trees, foraging, playing at swords, often with the youngest daughter of Lear as a pretty third. While Elia had loved Ban despite his situation, Rory hadn't seemed to even notice what that situation was. It had frustrated Ban, then, but he'd loved his brother for never making him feel small.

Ban blinked. It was a long time ago, years and several wars since. But Rory likely remained as unaware as ever of the bitterness in Ban's heart. The privilege of ignorance—yet one more advantage never accorded to a bastard.

Rory groaned and turned his head to look at Ban from one eye. "You learned some tricks!"

"Give me a sword and I'll win," Ban gasped. He couldn't move his legs, trapped as they were under his brother.

"Ha!" Rory shoved up with his hands, pinching Ban's legs in the process. Ban was delighted to see a smear of blood on Rory's cheek, dirt ground into it.

He sat up, felt the heat of battle expanding through his core, and the promise of bruises and pulls he wouldn't truly know until he woke up the next morning. It was good, and refreshing. Familiar, too.

Ban offered Rory his hand. The brothers leveraged their weight to stand up together.

Curan crossed massive arms over his chest. "You can be done for the day, Fox, in perhaps an hour."

Chagrined, he agreed.

"You're learning iron magic?" Rory's voice held, predominantly, curiosity, yet also a tight hint of a darker thing.

"I am," Ban answered cautiously.

"Well! I need a shower." Rory clapped his hand too hard on Ban's back. "And to see Father and tell him my news."

"News?" Ban repeated.

"Gossip more like, and letters from Astore."

"I'll go right after you, when I see to my bloom."

Rory smiled, nodded to Curan, and headed for his patient horse.

With unaccustomed fondness, Ban watched Rory lead the mare down the unobtrusive rocky path to the Keep's rear wall.

A wind blew suddenly out of the north, bringing a voice from the White Forest: *Ban,* it called. *Ban Fox, Ban Errigal, Ban, Ban, Ban!*

He looked, along with Curan and every one of the apprentice iron wizards.

*Son!*

His mother called him to her. Ban grimaced, avoiding Curan's curious eye. He was not ready to go to Hartfare, not yet, not before he set his games in solid motion. Brona would tease the truths out of him, attempt to convince him to stop. That, Ban would not do.

Shrugging off his thoughts, Ban turned to care for the iron.

BAN TOOK THE worn, black stone steps up to his chambers two at a time, eager to bathe and find his brother again. The Keep bustled with sudden preparations for a feast in Rory's honor, to welcome him home.

There'd been no such feast for the older Errigal son's return.

Ban shook away the hurt as best he was able, careful not to rub at his face or run fingers through his hair: dried mud flaked off as he moved, despite his having put his shirt back on over the streaks and cakes. The pain did not matter: this was a game, not a destiny.

The door to his chamber hung slightly open, and Ban went silent. He put one hand on the hilt of the long dagger strapped to his belt, carefully pushing the door open just enough so he could slip inside.

Rory stood, his back to the door, flipping through one of Ban's thin books. The earlson's wide shoulders were dotted with tiny drops of water, fallen from his washed and combed hair. He'd dressed himself in a clean tunic of pale blue, edged with leather and fine black silk from the Rusrike. His boots were polished deep brown, and he wore copper at both wrists and rings on his thumbs. A sapphire shone on the hand turning the thick vellum of the book cradled in his other hand.

Glancing around, Ban saw nothing else strange: his low bed was exactly as neat as he'd left it, pillow-free and plain; a trio of shields leaned like giant dragon scales below the open window; his desk was covered with books he'd hardly unpacked, though they'd arrived from Aremoria two days previous; the hearth was cold, for he'd not built a fire in it since coming home two weeks ago. Instead the space held boughs of juniper and a cluster of dried roses, two honeycomb candles, and a slice of oak polished to a shine he used for rubbing spells. Three of the five tiny ceramic bowls for offerings were empty, but one held salt and one a smear of white-burned ashes.

In the corner by his bed, an arched door led to a privy shared between his and Rory's rooms; it was held open by a footstool, and beside it sat a wide wooden tub full of steaming water.

"Brother?" Ban said quietly.

Rory startled, fumbling the book he inspected, but he caught it and spun. "Saints! Ban, you're quiet as a ghost."

Before Ban could answer, Rory laughed at himself. "Of course you are, Fox of Aremoria. The stories got even better after I left." He slapped shut the thin volume: a book of Aremore poetry, Ban saw, carefully copied out by Morimaros to use as a code key. Rory dropped it back onto the desk with the rest. "I had your bath filled for you, as soon as I was done with my own."

"Thank you," Ban said, unbuckling his belt to set it and the dagger onto the bed. "Have you seen Father?"

"Yes, and we're feasting tonight."

"Yet you're in my room, not out flirting with the entire Keep."

Rory smiled with more than a little wry acknowledgement. "I haven't seen you in longer, so here I'd rather be."

Ban paused as he crouched to remove his boots, gazing in surprise at Rory. "Just over a year." He'd not thought his brother would miss him so, based on their farewell in Aremoria, and the lack of letters between them.

"So long!" Rory threw his head back and heaved a sigh.

With a small laugh, Ban finished undressing. He dropped his dirty clothes onto the floor and tested the water: perfectly hot. He climbed in, kneeling so the water hit his chest. It was a luxury to bathe in his room; usually he used the colder baths in the Keep barracks. Ban closed his eyes, relishing the tingle of heat. He cupped water up to his face, splashed it through his hair. Dirt changed to mud again, and he stripped it off his scalp, rubbing down his face and neck.

"You have more scars than I do," Rory said softly, sinking down onto the bed. The ropes beneath the thick mattress creaked.

Ban met his eyes, unsure what to say.

Rory was unusually serious, almost sad looking. "Some of them are wizard marks?"

"I bled myself here." Ban touched a small lightning-shaped scar on his left shoulder. "And here." He lowered his hand into the water, where a line of scarring cut horizontal across his belly, just over his navel. "But most are from war."

"Impressive."

Ban grimaced. "Better not to have any. I get caught too often, blade through my armor."

"You don't wear armor sometimes, though, isn't that right? Because you're a spy and a wizard?"

"True, some. I have very good leather armor that doesn't make the noise of mail or plates."

The look Rory gave him insisted on Ban agreeing to the impressive nature of his scars, and Ban felt compelled to say, "Morimaros hardly has any scars at all, for he is so good a warrior."

"Father wanted me to marry Elia, before the foreign kings offered," Rory said, so abruptly Ban scrambled to follow the thought path.

He frowned. "I . . . can see how it would've been . . . advantageous. Better for Errigal to join our power to the king's line that way, through Elia, than keep our contract with Connley. It might've made you king, eventually."

"You loved her," Rory said, ignoring the shift into politics, "when we were children." His red hair caught the sunlight streaming in the window, reminding Ban of the fiery strands in Elia's curls.

Ban's eyes lifted east, toward the ocean, toward Aremoria. For a moment, he was stuck: no breath, no momentum, lips parted, thinking of her.

She would surely have his note by now.

"You still do," Rory said softly.

Ban refocused, reaching out of the tub for the cake of soap perched on a small washstand. "I saw her, at the Summer Seat. Before she left with Aremoria."

"And?" Rory leaned his elbows on his knees, oddly urgent.

"It's been over five years. She'll be safe with Morimaros, that's what matters right now."

"Did she truly deny Lear her love?"

Ban attacked his brother with a hearty splash. "Hardly!"

Standing and wiping water off the front of his tunic, Rory asked, "Then what?"

"The king has lost his mind; how do you not know that? You've served as his retainer for a year!" Irritated, Ban scrubbed at his arms with the soap and, in a fit of frustration, ducked down under the water. Small waves heaved over the sides of the tub.

"You should be careful what you say about the king," Rory said, once Ban had emerged.

Ban scowled. "Why?"

"He's your king."

As if it were that simple.

"He was never mine," Ban said, low and dangerously—half because he believed it, and half to shock his brother.

"Ban!" Rory loomed over him. "He can't hurt you anymore, the way he once did. You're the Fox now, and a wizard, and learning iron magic, too? I've only been home for an hour, but I already see how everyone in this Keep adores you, and you could take whatever you wanted of Errigal, with nobody to stop you! Why be afraid of King Lear?"

The earlson's breath panted from parted lips, his hands held out where he'd flung them in his angry enthusiasm.

Ban sat naked in the tub of cooling water, gaping up at his brother. It was too near Ban's actual intentions for him not to be impressed.

Suddenly, Rory closed his mouth, two dark spots of red flushing his cheeks, blending all his freckles together. He stomped toward the door between their bedrooms.

"Wait!" Ban surged out of the tub.

Rory stopped, glancing over his shoulder with his bottom lip between his teeth.

"Rory, I . . . just wait. Let me . . ." Ban glanced around for a clean shirt, or a robe or cloth.

With a little helpless sound, Rory returned. "You don't have to do it."

Ban stepped out of the tub and grabbed a shirt from his trunk. He patted himself dry before pulling it over his head to hang down over his thighs. "Do what?"

"Earn a place here. You *have* one." Rory said it like it was the most obvious thing in the world. "You'll always belong here, with me," Rory continued. "My brother, captain of my soldiers, uncle to my sons, a husband to some fat, gorgeous wife, whatever you want. And if anyone says a slant word about it, I'll make them regret it."

The words played dully on Ban's heart. They were meant well. Rory wanted to reassure him, to display his affection. But the very fact that Rory felt he needed to say it, needed to show him, only proved that Rory, finally, could see the bastard brother's lesser position.

Ban smiled, but it was tight. A fox's smile, narrow and sharp, with hidden teeth. "I know, brother. This is where I belong."

"Good. *Good.*" Rory clasped Ban's shoulders, shook him once, and let go. "I'll see you in the hall for the feast. Drink hearty, for I plan to compete with you story for story, and I won't let you get away with burying me under the Fox's exploits."

"You have a bargain," Ban said softly.

His brother departed, and Ban slowly dressed, a realization blossoming with every movement.

Rory was the widest chink in Errigal's armor.

Though sickened to think it, Ban could immediately see the spiral of an elegant, simple plan.

Limbs heavy, a frown pulling at his mouth, Ban skimmed his fingers through his ragged black hair and prepared to sacrifice his brother.

Sister,

I well hope your first week in Gallia has helped you calm yourself. Our father certainly is not happy with the outcome of his mad policies, which should make you feel relief or comfort, but I greatly suspect will only worry you more. Ever were you loyal and blind to his flaws, both as a father and king. Never mind, for he is neither to you now.

I will not horrify you with further talk of his death, but despite his new wildness that takes no rest, his seeming loss of composure, he will not change his mind about the crown or you. Both Regan and I are his heirs; we will work it out between ourselves. Mulish inflexibility is the name of his birth star, and where you used to out of kindness call it tenacity, I will name it truly now: the old man indulges in simple childish tantrums. Already my own retainers resent his contradictory orders and the slovenliness of his men. Would that you were here, for you alone might calm him and talk him out of his furies. My captain found him burning his eyes staring for hours at the sun in the sky yesterday afternoon. But you cannot return. As I said, we will read it as hostile intent, little sister. The crown is mine, but once I am confirmed, you will be welcome. So long, that is, as you do not marry Aremoria.

Keep yourself to yourself, and be strong. Give him no reason to bring his army here, or think he can take Innis Lear. When you return, we will find you a husband worthy of you: one of the Errigal sons, perhaps, for by then Regan will come around to it. One loves our father, and so you must get on well; the other is a fine warrior, and you thought you loved him once already. So.

This letter goes with the Oak Earl, and comes with a promise of his speed and safety, the one of which I can expect, and the other of which I can personally assure. It will not be long before we meet again, little sister.

*Gaela of Lear*

❖  ❖  ❖

*Elia,*

*Though our martial sister likely would not share my assessment, things are well for now in Innis Lear. This time of transition will not be so dire as some would predict. Though the harvest has gone poorly the past two years, I hear signs from the wind that we will do better this year, that the island rallies itself under my and Gaela's joint rule. The first day after the Longest Night, the navel wells will be opened again.*

*It has never been a strength of yours to see what is not obvious, to be aware of the edges of words, the double and triple layers in all purposes, but you must turn your attention to developing such skills. I should have taken you greater in hand after our mother died. Taken you farther from his influence. In our grief and unforgiving natures, we allowed you to be coddled, as perhaps is right for a young girl, but no longer for a woman or sister to queens. Now you must look past what you are told, what you are given, and you must rely on your own mind, your own heart. Suspect Aremoria, but give him enough that he maintains hope of alliance through you. If you love him, do as you will, but accept the consequences. That is what I have done. The consequences may be severe, little sister. Marriage to Aremoria would allow him an avenue through which to take the island, unless you stand against it. And remember, if you are his, so will your children be, and belong to the roots of his kingdom.*

*Probably you are amazed at these words, and narrow those eyes at my lettering to see if this is truly your sister Regan's hand. Worry not: I harbor my doubts that you will be able to do these things. This is no confession of hidden affection or respect. I love you as I always have: reluctantly, and knowing we might someday be rivals for this crown. Gaela assumes that in your core you are made of the same mettle as we, but I assume nothing, and it has served me very well.*

*Guard yourself, and guard us. Guard Innis Lear. If your own eyes, Morimaros of Aremoria, trace these words of mine, take them as the threat they are.*

*In sisterhood,*
*Regan of Connley and Innis Lear*

❖  ❖  ❖

*To the Princess of Lear and Maybe Queen of Aremoria,*

*Let this be a comfort, an assurance to you, dear lady. We love our poor King Lear greatly, and know in time he will forgive whatever fault* he has seen in you and bring you home. Until then, consider our cousins in Aremoria to be as your own. Their name is Alsax. My son Errigal, who you have known as Rory, would speak for them I am sure, as he fostered there with them for three years. Our other, less spoken of, son, whom you also know, was with them longer. He carries a reputation there himself, as the Fox.

Good lady, look to the heavens. Surely the answer to all our terrible times must hang there. As the stars and dread moon have given life to misfortune this season, so shall they bear the means of our triumph.

Earl Errigal

❖　❖　❖

My daughter Aefa,

I know you will share this with your lady, she who is intimate with all your thoughts, though perhaps not prepared for what I would prefer not to speak of. As such, I keep my words brief, though already this introduction has drawn out what might've been the truth of brevity into a surplus of concision. So.

I am well.

The king, less so.

I fear he suffers for his unwise decisions to send away both his brother and his daughter. His faith in his stars is shaken, bent, and I cannot tell if breaking it will also break him, or, like bursting a boil, relieve us all. He waits for providence to save him, as he ever has, but he speaks more of Dalat. Both speaks of her, and speaks to her, apologies and regrets, though I cannot discover the core of them. Tell your lady—hello, darling child—he loves her still, and it is a wound in himself he sought to heal when he made all his daughters choose, not a wound in her. He believed in two things: stars and Elia, and to his foolish mind both seemed to turn against him in unison, while the two more like to join in opposition to his will stood hand in hand with smiles in their hearts.

We go tomorrow to Astora, but I know not how long it will last. The eldest daughter of Lear is strong in everything but patience, and Lear As He Is would try even the patience of the sun. I fear soon the king will drive himself away from Astore to Connley, where you know as well as I his welcome will not be assured. But he is not in true danger immediately, from anything but his own stricken madness.

*Daughter, I would have you home, but I more would have you wise, and wisdom should keep you in the rich bosom of secure Aremoria. One day soon I will riddle the king into rightness, or he will see a star sign that allows him to pretend I did no such thing, and we will be together again all.*

*Your father*

# ELIA

ELIA LEANED INTO the corner crenellation of Morimaros's westernmost tower, letting it dig into her stomach painfully.

Sheer clouds slipped over the sky, like dawn lifting a cowl to shutter the stars before they vanished entirely. She stared out from her isolated perch, searching into the last curve of nighttime. It was still dark to the west, over unseen, distant Innis Lear. Stars twinkled, drops of ice on smoky glass; the Salmon nosing over the horizon, the Net of Fate beside it, stretching out toward Calpurlugh, the Child Star. Her star.

Her tutor Danna would always say messages that came with the Salmon needed fast response. Then there would be variations to the prediction specific to the day of the season, measured on distance to the equinox, the exact angle at the starbreak over the horizon; all kinds of details she could not calculate without paper and charcoal, without digging into a sheaf of schedules and seasonal records. If she asked, all such would be provided. For Morimaros's mother, Calepia, and his sister, Ianta, were determined to give her anything to make her smile. But Elia would not ask: she refused to live her life this way anymore, governed by star sign.

Yet she woke every morning and could not help searching the sky for only those most obvious of signs: star streaks or vanished stars or the rings around the moon.

There! A star shot just past the Salmon's nose and vanished. As did the final twinkle of Calpurlugh.

A tiny cry escaped Elia, and she bent fully over the crenellation, pressing her cheek to the cold limestone. What was she to do with her days? These terrible aching storms gathered in her stomach all night long. Releasing them out into the dawn was the only way to function, to politely eat her breakfast, to join the Elder Queen and princess for hot chocolate and study in the airy Queen's Library. The only way to face all the Aremore lords and ladies, the bakers, soldiers, maids, all of the cheerful court who believed she would marry their king, yet judged her lacking.

At her feet, Aefa shifted and murmured. Elia held her breath, not wishing to wake the girl. Nearly every morning Aefa dragged herself up to this tower, too, without much complaint, and waited in sleep or silence while Elia mourned. After the first time, Aefa brought the feather quilt from Elia's fine, spacious bed, and—damp stones be damned—made herself a nest. The other maids and even the few guards who passed or noticed were appalled enough that Elia could see it on their otherwise well-trained faces. Things were more formal in Aremoria, with layers of etiquette and a carefully established hierarchy of service, lordship, royalty, and the delicate dance between. The courtiers overlooked Elia's Learish manners, but with a raised brow or shared glance; Elia was a foreigner. And although they were more used to dark-skinned people from the Third Kingdom here than on Innis Lear, somehow, that made it worse.

She wanted to go home.

Pressing her cheek harder to the stone, Elia imagined being able to leech the castle rock up and into her body, fashion it into armor, into a beetle's iridescent carapace or better: a chrysalis in which to take refuge until she was transformed. Take strength from that, not those unfeeling stars and their shattering prophecies. Make herself a shell of Aremore stone, a shield to protect her heart, still rooted beneath Innis Lear.

"Lady Elia," said a low voice from just around the curve of the tower.

Though she startled hard enough to knock her nose to the stone, Elia managed not to whirl about. She did nudge Aefa too roughly as she rose and turned more slowly to face the king's Soldier in Charge of Royal Security.

La Far was the saddest-seeming man she'd ever seen, and Elia had thought it before she'd even spoken with him. She suspected he was not truly sad, that it was only the way his eyebrows drooped to either side and the perpetual searching frown on his scarred, peachy face. The king's age, La Far had risen through the military ranks beside Morimaros, and had recently taken over the palace guard. He slipped in and out of class hierarchies, coarse and warriorlike in his scoured orange leather armor, or elegant in the velvet jacket of low Gallian nobility, his rich accent capping off the trick. Aefa idolized him for this smooth facility—for that, and for his very clear blue eyes—for she wished to learn the art of being both servant and low lady. Her father, Lear's Fool, held a position of high regard and shifting nature at home, after all. But Aefa was too stubborn and unable to hide emotions behind artifice.

The girl scrambled to her feet, swearing under her breath so softly Elia only knew it from the tone and her maid's habits. Elia drew her shoulders tall and smiled dimly. "Good morning, La Far."

"The king has sent for you."

Her heart clutched briefly. "So early. Is something wrong?"

"You have a visitor."

"Who?" Elia asked, pressing her folded hands at her sternum, refusing to cast her gaze skyward for a hint of what was to come.

"I do not know, but your presence was requested immediately."

"She's got to dress," Aefa said, feather quilt bundled tight in her arms like a bulky babe.

Elia glanced down at her gown, the same she'd worn yesterday. A pale green thing, one the Elder Queen Calepia had insisted brought out some illusive flecks of green in eyes Elia had always understood to be solid, impossibly dark brown, seeming black from any distance. In Lear she'd only owned four dresses at a time, besides her priest robes, and two were for mud and rain and riding. Here Elia was expected to change from morning to evening, and keep a wardrobe of countless fine clothes provided by Calepia. She'd intended to return to her rooms to change before going out into the palace proper.

"The lady seems well dressed to me," La Far said, his eyes lingering at Elia's feet where her heavy boots peeked out from under the folds of skirt. "Well enough for this king."

"Oh my," Aefa said, disagreeing clearly with every part of her being. La Far studied Aefa with his sad eyes, and the Fool's daughter wrinkled her nose. "Let me fix her hair, at least."

Elia touched her hair helplessly, not knowing how she looked. "Aefa, it's all right."

"They'll judge *me*, Elia, if you don't look as perfect a queen as theirs, and fit for Morimaros," Aefa said firmly.

La Far nodded, and so the girl dropped her blanket and climbed onto the crenellations to kneel there, precarious and frowning. The soldier's eyes widened enough to briefly banish the sorrow, but he caught himself back from clutching Aefa's elbow in support. Aefa grabbed a handful of Elia's hair and started undoing the loose, messy braid it had been pinned into. Elia's scalp tugged as Aefa used the same pins to make thick twists and quickly wrap them into a bun, complaining under her breath that there was no oil at hand to pinch into the ends. Elia closed her eyes and thought of her father's blotchy anger, the cold detachment on Regan's face, Gaela's proudly curled lips, and the incandescent passion sharpening Ban Errigal's mud-green eyes as he pushed with all his strength against the ancient standing stones. She was well versed in ignoring dull pains.

Elia thought of Aefa, too: wearing her heart aggressively for all to see because she thought pretense was as impractical as poetry. And she thought of Morimaros, the opposite; Elia had rarely seen emotion on his face, though it was sometimes to be heard in his voice. Three days previous, they'd walked in a garden, and when he said he'd like her to be happy in Aremoria, it had been with such a quiet, thin tone, as if he was barely able to speak. *Surely I don't make you nervous,* she'd said, and the king replied, *Surely not,* but the self-deprecating humor had warmed Elia's whole body.

"Done, though it will barely do."

Elia opened her eyes as Aefa spoke, and she was surprised to find La Far watching her openly. The soldier nodded once. "Thank you," she said to Aefa. "I'll go to Morimaros and you take that blanket back, have the morning to yourself if you like."

Aefa paused only long enough to gather up the quilt again and use the motion to hide a quick squeeze of Elia's fingertips. Then she dashed off, glancing back over her shoulder to take in all of La Far from behind. When she noticed Elia notice her do it, she flushed bright pink. She dove into the dark arched stairway.

La Far offered his gloved hand to Elia, and she placed hers lightly atop it. The guard led her carefully to the steep stone steps and turned nearly sideways to support Elia as she came down after him. He did not require talk of her, for which she was grateful. The narrow tower stairs spiraled tightly, and it was dizzying despite the growing light coming through the archer slits. They'd been carved through to the outer wall with whimsy: not just plain thin rectangles but cut like simple flowers or candle flames. So many parts of the Lionis palace surprised her thus. Cornerstones carved with curling trees, tapestries of nothing but flowers instead of bold lines or rampant animals or hunting scenes. Windows of cut, colored glass and ceilings painted with clouds and tiny saints and winged lions.

Elia and La Far went from the tower into one of the vast hallways lit by tall candlesticks with as many silver branches as a tree. The floor was elegant lines of polished wood, lacking the coat of rushes atop soil or stone that was still used on Innis Lear. Such was the display of Aremore wealth and power, she supposed, though it all felt distant, impersonal. *Formal,* perhaps, was the word. In Lear she'd eaten meals at long tables with her father and sisters, with earls and retainers, with priests and apprentices, but also with the families of the retainers and castle servants. Elia knew the names of the dairy girls and the familial relations strung like a net between every person in her father's households. This Aremore castle did smell only of roses and river wind. But Elia had loved the scent of pine boughs brought in to cover the winter floor, the cling of perfumed hair and candle fat of Innis Lear.

La Far took her past the Queen's Library and into the luxurious corridors where the king kept his personal rooms and greeting hall, to his study and private dining room. They veered left, on an upper level of the main building. She'd never been inside it yet, though she'd seen the balcony from the central courtyard directly below.

"Sir," La Far said as he opened the heavy door by shoving with his fist.

"Novanos, good," Morimaros called from inside the study, and the soldier handed Elia in, remaining himself at the entrance.

Though the tall room immediately engulfed her with its rich red and orange colors, it was impossible for Elia not to see King Morimaros first.

He stood like a soldier at attention, hands clasped behind his back so his shoulders showed even wider. Here in his castle he rarely wore armor, but his orange leather coat was thick enough to serve as such if needed. As ever, Elia was struck by the hardness of him, from his boots to the dark hair sheared so close to his skull. In the past two weeks she'd become rather amazed at the control with which he made every gesture, from unbuckling his sword belt and looping it over the back of a chair to kneeling for a hug from his nephew Isarnos. Morimaros limited his speaking to the fewest possible words, and although he was unceasingly polite, he never hesitated to get physically close to her if he wished to tell Elia some quiet thing or point out a private joke.

This morning dawn light angled through the edges of the balcony windows onto the bright wooden floor. It streaked toward Morimaros like an eager friend, but he waited just outside the direct rays, avoiding the gilded light. "Elia," he said, and nothing more. His dark blue eyes flicked along yesterday's dress, but unless he owned a dozen identical orange leather coats, Morimaros wore the same thing every day and so wouldn't judge her as harshly as others might.

She bowed her head, but before she could offer a word, Elia noticed the other man in the room.

It was her uncle, the Oak Earl.

"Kayo!" Elia cried.

"Starling," he said, sweeping toward her.

Embracing, they remained silent for a long moment. Elia pressed her cheek hard against the rough leather knot-work on the shoulder of his coat. But the king watched, so Elia slipped her arms back to her sides and tilted her face up to Kayo's. He did not let go of her shoulders.

It seemed he'd aged a decade. Was that new steel gray in his tight black curls? Reddish shadows pressed under his eyes, and he watched her with a pinched brow. Kayo managed a smile. "You look horrified, starling," he said with wry humor in his voice.

She shook her head and touched her fingers beneath his weary eyes. "Banishment is not a mantle that suits you."

"And so I shall shrug it off. I return to Innis Lear immediately."

Shocked, Elia looked to Morimaros.

The king said, "He will not be talked out of it."

"Uncle." Elia took one of his hands from her shoulder and gripped it tight. "Your death rides on it. Stay here with me. I know you're welcome."

"You are," Morimaros said, as if he'd said it before.

The Oak Earl shook his head, though Elia thought painfully, wistfully, that he no longer carried any such title. He was only Kayo. Like her.

"I want to go home. But I cannot. My sisters . . ." She paused, surprised by her own low vehemence. "They ordered me to stay away until they're crowned."

"I will do what I can, starling, rest assured of that."

"Kayo, stay with me here in Lionis. My father promised to kill you. And though a month ago I'd have sworn he never would, I don't know what goes on in his mind now. What if he would go through with it for his stupid, terrible pride?" She caught herself curling her fists against her stomach to hold in the growing ache, and forced her hands to smooth down the soft skirts of her gown.

"Innis Lear is my home, Elia, and I love Lear as my brother. No matter what he says as a king, I have never betrayed him in either guise. I won't begin now, when he is lost in a storm of confusion."

Elia said, "Uncle, I want you to be careful."

"I have your sister Gaela's help," Kayo admitted, bitterness tainting what should have been a hopeful thing. "She's promised to break any sentence on my head. More for her disdain toward Lear than for any belief in me, but at least I've yet allies."

"Good. Gaela can protect you. She's stronger than he is now."

Kayo's eyes lifted toward the ceiling. "We are as strong as the people who love us, Elia, and nobody loves Gaela Lear."

It punched her, and she stepped back from him so her hip knocked into the king's heavy table. "Regan does. I do," she said. Her uncle's mouth pulled in regret, but Elia shook her head, refusing any arguments. "Though I have little enough strength to offer."

With a weighty sigh, Kayo said, "She will not accept strength from love, then. And she should, in this mess of a time. Your father threw everything into turmoil by removing you, by naming them both, and by giving himself into their care. He is still technically king until they're crowned at Midwinter, so Astore and Connley will plot and scheme until the last moment if your sisters let them, with no one left to side for Lear." The Oak Earl shook his head. "They've never stopped such scheming before now, I don't see why they would now. But maybe it's in their letters. I've brought you some. From Gaela, and Regan, and, strangely enough, from the Earl Errigal. Also one from the Fool to his daughter."

"Errigal?" Elia took a deep breath. The study smelled of cinnamon and sweetness. Probably from whatever was cooling in the ceramic mugs on the table. She'd written several letters to Ban, but she'd never had the confidence to give them to anybody for delivery. All had ended up ashes in her hearth.

Kayo turned away to rummage in a worn cloth bag. He pulled a flat bundle of letters free and offered them by reaching over the curve of the table. Elia accepted, hugging them to her chest.

"Elia," Morimaros said, "I would like to know what Errigal has to say to you, but it is only a request."

She glanced at the king. His close-trimmed beard hid what subtle expression she might've otherwise found in the clench of his jaw or the fair skin about his mouth. There was nothing but control to see in his eyes. He was standing very near.

Unwrapping the letter bundle, Elia nervously freed the third letter, closed only with a smear of wax and her name scrawled by a hand she did not know well. Elia set her sisters' letters, and the one for Aefa, onto the table and unfolded Errigal's.

A tiny slip of paper fell out of the middle, fluttering toward the floor.

Fast as a cat, Morimaros caught it. He looked up at her from his crouch, proving his eyes did not stray to the note. But Elia nodded her permission. The king read it; his lashes flickered in either surprise or displeasure.

Her heart beat too hard as Elia took it back from him. His hands were calloused and the knuckles pinked and rough. A warrior's hands, but for the pearl and garnet ring. That ring had anchored her to the earth, when her father cast her away.

"What in heaven is that?" Kayo asked.

Elia glanced at the small scrap. Scratched in the hash-marks of the language of trees, it read:

*I keep my promises. B.*

"Oh," Elia said.

"My turn," her uncle said, gently taking the paper. "But what is the meaning? I never learned to read these ancient marks."

Elia did not have to glance again to translate, "I keep my promises. From Ban."

Morimaros said, his chin tucked down and brows together, "The Fox?"

Elia shook her head, but Kayo said, "Yes, though he is most known in Lear as the bastard of Errigal."

"We were friends when we were children," Elia murmured, more nervous to open Earl Errigal's letter itself now than before. Then the king's inquiry struck her. She looked at him, startled. "You know Ban Errigal?"

"I do. He served in my army for years, and earned his epithet well. What promise?"

The last line was so evenly slipped in, Elia hardly noticed it at first, and nearly spoke unfettered truth. Ban had promised to tear her father down. *I will prove it to you, how easy it is to ruin a father's heart.*

The full truth was that Elia was not certain exactly what Ban had so furiously sworn. Heat grew in her neck, in her cheeks, and Elia was glad it could barely be seen, not in the same indecorous way she could see the gentle pink flush reaching up from Morimaros's beard, the longer it took her to answer his question.

Elia said, "He promised to do what he could for me, from Innis Lear." Truth, but not all of it.

"To fight for you?" Morimaros said quietly. A tension pained his voice, and Elia remembered what her sisters had said, that this Aremore king would take Lear for himself if he was allowed to. Elia stared at Morimaros and realized it was not nations or war at the fore of the king's mind.

An answer stuck in her mouth as her eyes stuck on his.

Kayo broke the silence. "The young man is angry at the world, sir. I've spoken with Ban, and he carries a fire that will burn down whatever he sets it upon. If he will put it to Elia's cause, she would benefit."

The king did not look away from Elia. "You need your friends," he said.

Though Elia was not entirely sure what had passed in Morimaros's heart, unbidden relief cooled her own. She did not take the scrawled note back from Kayo; instead she broke the seal on Errigal's letter to finally read for her uncle, in concession to the king of Aremoria.

But she did not need to be holding the note to feel its weight, or to remember perfectly the fast, flawed lines of Ban's writing, the deep cuts in the paper where he'd pressed too hard. Only a few words of the ancient language, and yet they might as well have been cut into her skin.

*I keep my promises.*

# AEFA

THE ROYAL KENNEL was tucked into the northeastern curve of the secondary wall of the palace. A two-story structure built with pale wood and shingles, with a round grassy yard, it was warm all the time and smelled of hay, hairy beasts, mud, and the leavings of hectic but well-trained dogs. Aefa loved it, for kennels were the same in Aremoria and Innis Lear, so she found homesickness alleviated. And besides, dogs were a refuge of loyalty, love, and honesty in a world that nurtured the opposite.

Though Morimaros kept his raches and bloodhounds comfortably, as befitting their status as the king's dogs, it was his nephew, Isarnos, who adored the animals. And as Isarnos was the reason the king could delay marriage as long as he had, Morimaros gave his heir almost complete run of the kennels.

It had been Aefa's flirtation with one of the young prince's tutors that led her to the knowledge that there was a litter of puppies, and Aefa's considerable charm applied to royal grooms gained her access to the whelps. She'd visited every other day this past week.

The litter's arrival was one of several pieces of intelligence Aefa had collected, with nothing more than the casual acquisition of friends. Another week in Aremoria and she'd determine who to pursue for more dedicated personal cultivation, based on a prioritized list of Elia's needs. After all, Aefa understood charm to be her best tool for acquiring a web of allies and informants, as she'd learned last winter at the Dondubhan barracks. She'd let the adorable legitimate Errigal son seduce her, and in return she pinned him to his pillows to interrogate him on how he made everybody like him so rotting much. He was good looking, and so was Aefa; he was charismatic, and so could she be. Therefore, what could he teach her?

Plenty about sex, it turned out, and then even more about Lear's retainers and the state of politics under the king. But he had been unable to teach her how to gain access where she was lacking. Rory Earlson had never had to learn. He simply *had* access; he'd been born with it, and he rarely noticed its effectiveness as a tool or a weapon. Aefa was not an earl's son, or even an earl's daughter. Her parents had been seasonal servants at Dondubhan until her father's humor caught Lear's attention; because of that and the lucky virtue of sharing a rare birth star with the king, the Fool was raised high. Though the king himself promptly forgot his Fool had ever been less than the equal of, say, a valued, honored retainer, the vast majority of the king's household certainly remembered. Here in Aremoria, Aefa was again fettered by status, even elevated as a princess's most trusted companion.

Aefa shook her head, hoping to shed the bitter taste in her mouth. She crouched down in a pool of her own skirts, surrounded by fluffy, slithering puppies, each large enough now to argue and snap over space on the girl's lap. Aefa smiled and teased them, rotating the little creatures as fairly as she could manage: they each got a verse of poetry along with some scratching. The mother of the litter, a beautiful chestnut dog, leaned nearby, watching with sleepy brown eyes, her feathery tail thumping slowly against the wooden floor. She was sleek and long-legged, with a wide head but a longer snout, and not nearly so rangy and shaggy as the deerhounds preferred for hunting on Innis Lear. A little page boy swept the length of the smooth wooden floor, humming along with Aefa's hushed rhymes. The windows were grated, but open to the afternoon, and a fine cool cross-breeze blew through smelling of river and crisp city fires.

The only two things marring Aefa's happiness were missing the island under her feet and her inability to decide how—and who to use—to best curry favor for Elia. In terms of pleasurable seduction, La Far would have been Aefa's personal choice, though he was more than ten years her elder. The way he moved, and the vast heaviness peering out of his eyes, intrigued her to the point of distraction. Consequently, he was a poor choice, if her purpose was Elia's benefit, not merely that of her own loins.

Then there was Ianta, the Twice-Princess and King Morimaros's sister. The woman was fat and delightful, and she'd winked at Aefa three days ago, and she was rich and in a perfect position to influence the king. But she, too, was old, and a widow, and the way she flirted with the lord of Perseria gave Aefa pause. Her sights, perhaps, should be set lower.

One of the younger sons of the Lady Marshal, maybe, or that cousin of Lord Ariacos who worked so closely with the Third Kingdom trade commander. Or the Alsax heir, if he was as unencumbered as his Errigal cousin. Any of them could provide valuable intelligence to aid Elia's cause first in Aremoria, and then on Innis Lear.

Aefa only needed to narrow down exactly what that cause might be. Elia herself would not say, which was usual. Though, her companion thought, it had to be one of two things: return home alone, or marry Morimaros and establish herself outside Lear. Aefa's instincts told her Elia would never agree to marriage before settling her father, before returning home to see everything on the island put right. Though marrying the king here might be the safer choice, it would not allow Elia to pursue what had before seemed her only goal: a life of contemplation and peace, close to the stars.

Aefa could not put down the gut feeling that Elia had to go home. That her fate could not be found here, but only submerged in the rootwaters of Innis Lear.

"Aefa?"

"Elia!" Aefa said, lifting a dun-colored puppy in both hands so its round little paws flailed like it might run through the air. "Come sit with me, and tell me what the king wanted."

The princess climbed the rest of the way onto the second floor. She nudged aside the puppies, allowed their mother a good long sniff at her skirts, and settled beside Aefa, legs curled beneath her. Elia snuggled a smooth, dusty puppy to her neck, and while it pawed at her breast and nuzzled her earlobe, Elia told Aefa about Kayo's arrival, his news, and the letters he'd brought. She read aloud the letter from Errigal first ("Patronizing old dog!" Aefa spat), then Gaela's ("Terrible as always, and you cannot marry Rory Errigal, for so many reasons!") and Regan's ("Pitiless and yet almost kind; she must be pregnant again!"), and finally they read together Aefa's own letter from her father.

"Oh, Dada," Aefa moaned softly.

Elia set the Fool's letter into her lap with the others. "He means that my father truly believes I betrayed him; either that or the stars did. The stars showed him I would do one thing, and I did another, therefore one or the other of us must be false."

"How can he think that it's *you*?" Aefa asked, viciously enough the mother dog lifted her long head.

"Because the sun sets every day and rises again at the proper time. The tides sway and shift in exact patterns; the moon and the stars do not vary. So of course it must be his daughter, because daughters—and sons, and fathers, and all men—have inconstant hearts." Elia said the last sadly.

"Not you, not Elia Lear."

The princess offered a restrained shrug.

Aefa huffed, her entire body jerking as she clenched her fists and tried not to shove the puppies away so she could stand, offended on her mistress's behalf. With exaggerated care she removed several puppies and got to her feet, allowing the last two to roll off the hem of her skirt. "Aren't you angry?"

Elia glanced at her hand, fingers dug into the silky ruff of a puppy. It wiggled, and she released it, drawing her hand more gently down its short spine. "What good will anger do?" she asked quietly, eyes down.

"It's something! Get you on your feet and fighting!"

"Fight? Fight *what*?" She raised her gaze to Aefa, whose cheeks were round, flushed cherries. "My frightening sisters? My father's madness?"

"I can't tell you what to do. A princess outranks her maid."

"There's no such difference between us any longer, Aefa."

The Fool's daughter planted her fists to keep from flinging them up or tearing at her hair. "Don't pity yourself, Elia. I won't tolerate that."

Elia's brow tightened, then she said, "It's only the truth, which you hold so dear. I'm not a princess. My father, who was the king, said so."

"Do you truly believe that? And would it matter? Your father could tell me that I'm not my own father's daughter, but nobody can change my birth. He can strip my *name* away, perhaps in Innis Lear at least, but he can't change *me*."

"I am changed, though," Elia murmured, hardly moving her lips.

"How?"

"I . . . I've lost something. Something that made me know myself."

"You hardly smile anymore." Aefa dropped suddenly to her knees, scattering the pups. She gripped one of Elia's hands, pinching rings and knuckles together.

Elia put her other hand over Aefa's. She pulled a simple ring of silver and amber off her thumb and slid it onto Aefa's first finger. "Faith," she said, not looking up to meet her friend's eyes. "Trust? I thought my father was the truest star in the sky—strange and capricious, but true. Years ago I chose him, Aefa. I chose to be his, against my sisters, because he was so very broken by my mother's death. I made myself into his perfect star, believing him to be true. But he isn't! If not that, then what? What can I believe in if I can't believe the stars will rise? How can I trust myself or you or Morimaros or my sisters or Ban Errigal or anyone?" Her voice was tight, high, and fast.

Aefa jerked on their grasped hands. "You can trust me because I tell you so. Because I have no agenda other than you and me and our families, our country."

Finally Elia met Aefa's green gaze. "I don't know how. I believe you, and yet . . . after all these years, how do I let you in? How have I never done so, before? What if I lose you, too, Aefa, as soon as I let myself love you?"

"Then you'll survive." Aefa leaned in swiftly to kiss Elia's lips. "You'll mourn, and you'll survive. That's what love is. It shouldn't break you, not like your father broke, but make you stronger."

Elia stared. She touched her lips. "Maybe it's me," the princess whispered. "I'm broken somewhere inside, in a place that used to be—that I thought always had been—solid and strong. This is what he's feeling too, my father. Even if everyone hates it, he and I were there together. I was his star, the beacon leading through the storm of his loss. Now I am gone, and he has lost his way again. He lost me."

"He threw you away!" Aefa tugged on a free strand of Elia's hair, fierce and hissing. "You did nothing!"

"I never *do* anything, it's as you said. I'm always the buffer, the balm and comfort! A bridge, perhaps. But the bridge doesn't soar or even move; it never even sees the end of the river. I thought the stars were enough, that choosing them for him was enough, but I've spent my entire life doing nothing. Studying what others do, what the stars say we should do. Reacting. Being what I'm supposed to be. I held the course, tried to be kind and listen, but did you know? Even the trees do not speak to me now. I spent myself with the silent stars and forgot the language of trees."

"You can relearn," Aefa murmured, stunned.

Elia shook her head. "I should have refused my father's decree. I could have stayed, and gone with Gaela or Regan to hold my place against him until he saw me again. I should not have let his mad dismissal push me away or their disdain and exclusion intimidate me. I should have done something. But I don't know how to act, Aefa. I only . . . am still." She paused, then whispered, "I should have run away with Ban."

Aefa pulled away and lowered her chin to stare suspiciously. "You should have done *what* with *whom*? The bastard of Errigal? The Fox of Aremoria?"

Elia fluttered her lashes and glanced down. "There was a fifth note," she confessed. "From Ban Errigal, yes."

Aefa made a strangled gasp.

"The king has it now. It said, *I keep my promises*, marked in the language of trees. At least I can still read it." Elia added the latter quickly, as if it might cover up the first part.

"What promise?!" Aefa shrieked.

"He promised to show me how easily changed a father's love can be. To prove somehow this was not my fault, but a fault of weakness in our fathers."

Aefa narrowed her eyes and mouth. "I can't decide if that sounds brilliant or dangerous. Very likely both, then."

"That describes him, Aefa. Brilliant and dangerous."

"Oh? *Oh?*" It excited Aefa: she'd been hunting for signs of attraction or desire in Elia for over a year. *Why wait for such things to be decided for you?* She'd always asked. Elia always replied, *I will be what I am.*

Aefa touched her princess's back.

Shaking her head that she was all right, Elia took a deep breath.

"We can fix this," Aefa said. "What do you want to do?"

"Be bold." Elia lifted her face and gripped Aefa's hand. "Aefa," she whispered, holding tight to her friend, "I don't know how."

"Elia," Aefa said back, strong and firm. "Choose."

"Act. Yes. I'm going to—to do what Regan says."

The Fool's daughter laughed, once, loudly and with disbelief. "You are."

Elia roused herself to her feet. "Come with me."

They went quickly down from the kennel loft, then swept across the courtyard and back into the palace proper. Without allowing Aefa a moment to pick the straw out of her hair, Elia marched them into the castle proper. She asked a guard where the king was, twice. Aefa hurried behind, until they reached the wide polished doors leading into Morimaros's grand throne room where the king was holding a hastily assembled council session.

Aefa bit her inner cheek, knowing that meant some news had come, or something disrupted the usual calm order of the Aremore court. She hoped it was nothing to grieve Elia further, and Aefa wished she could go inside with her princess, a living shield or at least support.

In their path was a small boy, his ear pressed to the throne room doors, his eyes squeezed closed in concentration. Isarnos, the king's nephew and current heir. At seven, Isarnos was already a magnanimous charmer who spread his attention to every living creature in Aremoria, based on the menagerie often trailing behind him. Today two bright green-and-yellow birds with hooked beaks perched on the sconces over his head, and a trio of cats stalked them in circles like slender, furred vultures. A harried-looking nurse and an animal handler with thick leather gloves and a pail of waste waited several paces from the doors. There was no sign of Aefa's friendly tutor.

Aefa wondered what they'd find inside, to compete with the spectacle facing them out here.

"Isarnos?" Elia said gently.

His eyes flashed open. "Elia! That is, my lady. Princess. Have you come for the council? They began without you, but, oh! Your cousin is inside."

"My cousin?"

Isarnos said, "The man from Innis Lear but who looks like he's from the Third Kingdom."

"Kayo," Elia said, frowning.

Isarnos's eyes widened at both of them, as if worried now he'd misbehaved. The boy was slender and pale, paler than Morimaros or the Elder Queen, paler than his own mother, Ianta. His father had been from the north, a warrior prince from the winter countries, and had died in battle three years ago. A terrible year that had been for Aremoria, perhaps like this one was shaping into for Innis Lear.

Aefa glanced at the palace guards standing on either side of the door, studiously ignoring the interaction of peculiar royalty. One stared straight ahead; the other flicked his eyes to Elia and away.

"It's all right, Isarnos," Elia said to the young prince.

Then she gently nudged him aside and threw open the door.

# MORIMAROS

MARS PREFERRED THE throne room empty. Cavernous and quiet, lacking all these lords and ladies and soldiers who comprised his council, those now arguing loudly their concerns.

As a boy, Mars had liked nothing more than to climb onto the long, oval council table when no others attended the room, spread on his back, and stare up, imagining great stories for all the saints and ancient kings of Aremoria. An old mural filled the entire high ceiling with bucolic rolling hills, flowering trees, and fluffy, whimsical animals with wings and horns. In the bright blue-painted sky were shining earth saints and smiling spirits, with glass embedded where their eyes should have been to show their alien magic. Though the mural depicted daytime, the most glorious of constellations shone like diamonds: the Lion Rampant, the Star of Crowns, the Triple Mountain, the Autumn Throne, and a moon in every phase. A perfect canvas for his imaginings. But if his father caught him, Mars was dragged off the table to the single gilded throne set onto an orange dais at the far end of the room. His father's throne.

The king would put Mars upon it and say it was better for Mars to imagine the world from that location.

Now that Mars was king, he left the throne empty when he could. One wall of the enormous chamber was entirely arched windows overlooking an elaborately sculpted garden, and it was here he chose to stand.

The nobility and military of Aremoria arrayed behind Mars were divided in four parts: those who thought the moment to retake Innis Lear was at hand, as the island hung between several rulers like an unstable, overripe peach; those who counseled waiting until next summer even though there would be a new-crowned queen by then, to give Aremoria the winter at least to recover from war with Burgun, to celebrate victory and peace; his sister's contingent, who suggested he marry Elia as quickly as possible and watch the island from a distance to see where the pieces fell before acting; and then Kay Oak, who alone argued for Aremoria throwing support behind Elia herself, without marriage, to situate her on the throne of Lear and reap the awards of alliance. Alliance not only with Lear, but potentially the Third Kingdom.

Not for the first time, Mars wished the Third Kingdom would agree to a permanent ambassador here in Lionis. Aremoria's interests were constantly stifled by the empress's insistence that all trade deals be brokered in her territory. His frustration was probably her goal. If Aremoria grew much richer or stronger, there would be a clearer path to rivaling the empire's dominance over their neighboring continents. Mars had to send ambassadors to *her*, receiving none in return, or get nothing. Two countries cushioned the borders of Aremoria and the Third Kingdom, and Mars's father had occasionally toyed with attacking Ispania or Vitilius in an effort to expand south and southeast against her. But Mars had an excellent relationship with the king's council of Vitilius, one he was loathe to risk, and Ispania had been conquered and reconquered by the Second and then Third Kingdoms, each time eventually earning independence again. The familial connections between the Third Kingdom and Innis Lear put a handful of his best people on the side of careful marriage and no military involvement should Mars decide to take the island. Nobody wanted to risk the wrath of the empress, but all wanted more power for Aremoria.

The best solution, he thought, was to get the granddaughter of the empress as a wife and queen of Aremoria. Marry Elia, and then take Innis Lear against her elder sisters. After his time there, Mars believed the old king had done him a favor by closing off those holy wells. Innis Lear was ready for change. The people needed it.

As the discussion waged, Mars stood at the grand garden windows, his back to the council, hands folded behind him, staring out at the rows of juniper bushes below, trimmed into spiraled cones. Despite the fraught conversation behind him, his mind was full of deep black eyes and the tremble of the princess's hand as she held the letters from home.

He had wished to pull Elia against his chest and hold her, comfort her, promise anything she asked. He had wished to take the letters and burn them if she was afraid to read.

"It is not only trade to think about, but security," Efica, Lady of Knights, broke in. "Burgun holds Innis Lear in his sights, too, and if Aremoria does not seize it, Burgun might try, and with the sponsorship of the Rusrike who have long hunted an opportunity to best Aremoria."

Mars's sister, Ianta, asked whether Regan or Gaela might consider a stronger alliance. Kayo insisted Elia was the best and only true road for Aremoria, and Mars silently berated himself for not insisting that the exiled princess be here for this council. She should be speaking for herself. Let them all know what she would even consider with regard to marriage and alliances. But her spirit had seemed withdrawn these past weeks, diminished from the humorous young woman he'd so briefly met at the Summer Seat. Still, she had not lost that quiet core of resolve holding her spine tall, as if she truly were leashed to the stars. She mourned; she longed for her home and father. That was what he told himself.

Mars would not push too soon. But he wanted to marry her. Regardless of how it would necessarily shift his tactics in taking Innis Lear. In fact, Mars found he could not stop circling his thoughts back and back and back around to it: as if nothing else mattered to him as much as Elia Lear.

He could not recall a single time in his adult life when he'd been so tilted by his heart.

Perhaps the strangeness on Innis Lear had infected him. Perhaps she was a fracture in his careful crown.

She would not be happy to know he'd sent Ban Errigal to destabilize her island. To undercut Errigal and find a means of putting an Aremore leash upon the powerful iron magic.

*I keep my promises.*

"Take the island now, Morimaros," said Vindomatos Persy, one of his northern dukes. "And negotiate your own new sea trade with the Third Kingdom after. They will enter a new bargain, for they crave Innis Lear's copper. And use the possibility of marriage to a daughter of their empress's line for better leverage."

"Is that the sort of king you would have my brother be?" Ianta asked.

Mars could well imagine his sister's expression, as cool as her voice, but likely with a mocking lift to her golden eyebrows. Novanos had reported that of late, Ianta and Vindomatos played a courtship game, though it remained unclear if Vindomatos desired Ianta herself, or to marry his daughter to Ianta's son.

Silence dragged on behind him.

"It's the kind of king our father was, Ianta," Mars said. Their father had always encouraged Mars to view Innis Lear as a lost piece of Aremoria that needed to be reclaimed. There was an old prophecy, though one not officially espoused since forsaking religion; it claimed that the greatest king of Aremoria would reunite the island to the mainland.

Mars did not believe in prophecy, but he did believe in the power of his people, and their loyalty. Aremoria would rejoice if he regained the island. Especially if he did it with minimal loss of Aremore lives.

So he said nothing else, waiting for someone to press with a cause. Ianta said no more, and Mars thought he should tell Ianta of Ban's mission. It would swing her arguments to know his man worked for their interests on the island, outside of Elia and marriage.

One of the councilors tapped a boot impatiently against the marble floor. Another sighed. Mars heard the tick of a glass touch the tabletop, and the soft gurgle of pouring wine. He still did not face them.

"Sir." It was Efica. "You should marry her, first. Hold off Burgun that way, and it will be an opportunity for all our people to celebrate. Project strength."

With that, he agreed. Rather desperately.

Kay Oak said, "Your majesty, it will go better for Aremoria in the long term if you marry an acknowledged queen of Innis Lear, not an exiled princess."

"That's true, though if she gains power, when you marry her the power would still be yours," Dekos of Mercia said.

"No, I—" Kay tried to say, but Vindomatos interrupted loudly.

"If we act now, before they've consolidated their rule, it will be easier and faster, with less loss of Aremore life."

Before any else spoke, one of the entrance doors clicked and suddenly swung open. Mars turned, alert for danger, though an urgent message was the most likely interruption.

Elia Lear halted a few paces into his throne room, chin up, mouth determined, eyes wide on him. Seeing her again was a revelation.

It always was.

Taking two concerned steps toward her, Mars said, "Lady Elia?"

Straw clung to the hem of her mint-colored dress, and her brown hands were so stiff and straight at her thighs it had to be an affectation. The throne room and the people in it fell away into a gentle roar in his ears, and Mars wondered if she'd like to go with him now down into the garden, and walk among the junipers.

But Elia instead turned to face the council table.

Kayo half stood out of his delicate chair, chagrined. Elia's nostrils flared as the Oak Earl winced, and Mars recognized, finally, her anger. Her spark. His heart flew high with hope.

Elia walked to the edge of the table, stared at every member of his council; they gazed back unconcerned, curious, irritated, and a few as chagrined as Kayo, depending on their arguments.

The princess touched the corner of the map spread across the oval table, held down by weights sculpted into ships: an elaborately painted Innis Lear and its surrounding ocean, with the shores of Aremoria just visible.

"Are you discussing my island?" she asked, too softly.

"Elia," Kayo said, fully on his feet now, sounding conciliatory.

She held up her hand for him to stop. Carefully, she turned to face Morimaros again.

"Yes," the king said.

"You should not discuss Innis Lear without Innis Lear present. Not only is it insulting, it seems tactically unsound."

His heart went wild at her offended tone, and his eyes ranged over her face as if all the pieces of it were separate, as if he could read her as clearly as any battlefield; she was a mystery in that moment. His lips parted, but the king maintained his silence.

The princess's chest lifted faster; the only signal of the depth of her upset. She lifted her brow as if to encourage him. *Yes? Speak?*

As if he needed her permission.

"You are correct," Morimaros said. "I apologize, Princess." He ignored the shifting motions of his council; indeed, he only suddenly recalled their presence.

She said, "I was grieving when I took the haven offered by the Aremore crown, and I thank you, Morimaros, for the sanctuary provided so generously by your court, and for the time to appreciate my wounds."

Mars nodded once. Any more and he would cross the small distance to her and touch her: take her wrist, brush his hand along her jaw, put his cheek to her curls.

Elia stepped nearer. "I am finished hiding."

It was a concession, to having been weak. Mars admired her for it.

She said, "I must be Elia of Lear today and tomorrow, and more than I was last month." Her eyes slanted toward Kay Oak to include him, before fixing her gaze again on Mars. "And this council should know that Innis Lear is not as vulnerable as we seem. We have a royal bloodline, born of the island roots and blessed by the stars, who will fight for it, and people unwilling to be conquered."

Her voice only trembled slightly.

Mars stepped nearer. "That is good information to have, Lady Elia," he said with equal formality. "Perhaps this council should adjourn and you and I will continue our conversation alone."

"Yes," she said.

Mars reached for her hand, and she gave it. He raised her fingers, barely grazing them with his own, and bowed once more. Without straightening out of the bow, Mars lifted his eyes, and smiled slightly for her; a smile no one else could see.

# FIVE YEARS AGO,
## HARTFARE

Kay Oak walked alone.

Despite the perfect afternoon, the peaceful clouds so high overhead, every breath was agonizing.

He'd not rested since leaving the wedding ceremony at Connley Castle, but instead taken a horse and ridden hard west, unthinking, a weight like murky water pressing down and all around him, darkening his vision. The horse moved under his urging, into the White Forest, and Kayo only knew to aim for the center, the heart of the woods, where there would be sign in the form of tattered cloth hanging from branches.

He'd never been to Hartfare, and not spoken with Brona in years. Not since that night of his sister's year memorial, when the witch had told him everything he'd missed while working his trade routes. When the witch—this island—had broken his heart. But he knew the path to her lost village, as everyone did, from songs and rumors.

The blue cloth markers appeared, and he allowed the horse its head for a while. Once they reached the village, he slid off, dropped the reins, and walked on, past curious women and children, and some few men, past barking dogs delighted to meet someone new, past cottages and finely tended gardens and smoking fires. They pointed silently the way to the witch, knowing without asking why Kayo had come.

The door to Brona's cottage was shut, and he leaned against it, slumping with his forehead to the grainy wood. Beneath his forehead, the door shifted, opening. Kayo stood, lips parted, dark eyes wide.

Brona was there, luscious and tall and numinous.

He said, "I didn't know where else to go."

She took one of his hands and led him inside, closing the door behind them.

Daylight poured in through small, square windows, and the fire was low in the hearth. Brona wore a plain blouse and striped skirt, with a bodice loosely holding it all together, tied with violet ribbons. Her feet were bare.

She put him at the long table near the fire, on a bench, and silently set about making a plate of food. Kayo slouched wearily, staring at her, feeling dull and undone.

But his pulse had slowed, and gradually his breath evened.

Brona gave him a small crescent pie stuffed with turnips, onions, and savory gravy and set a jug of ale between them, along with two cups. She poured, and they drank.

Kayo ate the pie carefully, letting the simple flavors ground him, and watched Brona's face. She remained as beautiful as she had been six years ago: dark hair unbound around her tan, freckled face; soft everywhere but the corners of her eyes and the sharp slash of her black brows. Her mouth was too plump not to think of ripe figs.

He'd not tasted a fig since leaving the Third Kingdom.

A shudder passed through Kayo and he finished his food, licking the last crumbs from his thumb. He reached for the ale and drank. All while the witch studied him.

She poured a second helping of ale and said, "I have heard Regan's wedding was beautiful, though they infuriated the king by sharing a bowl of rootwater."

"They did, and it did," he said slowly, suspecting the trees themselves must have whispered the news to her, for no human messenger could have beaten him to her door.

The witch slid his cup nearer to him and cradled her own. "I am here, Kay Oak."

"I . . . don't know what to do," he said. "Tell me what my sister would wish me to do. All is falling to pieces, and I don't know that I've done any good here." His own voice was unrecognizable to him, tight with desperation. He hid his face in his hands. Both his elder nieces were married now, to enemies that would tear apart this island—and he couldn't see how to stop them. Particularly that slick son of salt, Tear Connley. Kayo slammed his hands flat on the table. "And by my sister's word, I cannot tell Regan why it is so wrong that she married Connley!"

"I know," Brona murmured. She put her hands atop his. "I know, Kay. And Regan would not listen, if you could."

He dragged in a deep breath. "My land is dying. And the lands around mine, too. The shepherds must take their flock higher and higher, farther inland toward this forest, because even the moors do not make thick enough blankets of food. The past two years my cows have birthed fewer and fewer calves. The trees blossom only half the time, depending on how far they live from the heart of Innis Lear."

The witch nodded. "The island pulls inward, to consolidate its power since our king closed the navels and ended all the root blessings."

"What is to be done? I feel this island in my bones, Brona. I feel the promise I made to Dalat, and I despair."

"As do I, Kayo."

"Brona . . ."

"Wait, and be strong. It will be the right time, when Elia is older."

His pulse gasped. "Elia! Elia is a shadow of herself, and untouchable. I should take her, spirit her away to the home of our mothers, and save her, if that is the only possible thing."

"What would she be in the land of your mothers?" Brona asked.

"A granddaughter of the empress, beloved at least, and encouraged to thrive. Her father, stars protect him, strangles her with his devotion."

"But what would her potential be?"

"Whatever she wished. You cannot know what it is like in the Third Kingdom. Women are . . . you are the strength and hearts of the world. You rule it and we know why, there deep in the desert."

Brona smiled a little.

Kayo pushed on, "Her people are there, too. Elia would be among her own. Less rare, but less burdened, too."

"Does she want to leave?"

"No." Frustrated, he made his hands into fists. "But she can't know what it would be like. She's never known anything but Innis Lear. She's only fifteen, and you haven't seen her of late, Brona." He leveled his eyes on hers. "Her heart broke when Errigal and Lear took your boy away from her. They loved each other, with nothing to gain from the loving but love itself. Have you ever loved that way? I do not know how. Lear does not. There are too many layers of loyalty and lies and half-truths for adults to love so. But Elia had it, and might have carried it into adulthood if not for breaking them apart. And now there is a deep mistrust inside her, worse than her sisters' fury or her father's fanaticism." Kayo snapped his mouth shut and closed his eyes against a wail. He could not speak of this with his brother Lear; the king refused all mention of Ban's name in his presence, and even more so the suggestion Elia had been *influenced* by a bastard with terrible stars.

The Oak Earl looked again at Brona. "Don't you see? I must act."

"I do see," she murmured, standing. She moved away, and Kayo felt the loss of it, though she only went to a box tucked to a corner shelf beside the hearth and brought it back.

Carved of dark wood, the box was etched with the hash-marks that represented the language of trees. Kayo understood some of the spoken words, but he could not read nor write it, beyond a basic fertility blessing he'd learned to use as the earl over all those dying moors. He'd never been sure the land truly respected him; he'd asked an old grandmother to teach him to tend the needs within his borders. Was the decay some fault of his own; was he too foreign in his thoughts and wanderings to care for the roots? The grandmother had ignored his anxieties in a practiced way and chided him for not knowing the simplest blessings. For a little while, his land had thrived. No more. Kayo understood in his bones that the king's rejection of the rootwaters had forced the island to consolidate its power here in the White Forest, and yet—and yet he could not help wondering if, had Kayo himself been somehow more devoted to Innis Lear, never left to travel, rejected the ties to his homeland, the roots would thrive. The witch held her part of the island healthy and whole. Why couldn't he?

Brona lifted the lid to reveal a stack of worn, gilded cards and a small silk bag. Without speaking, she removed the cards and shuffled them, then handed them to Kayo. He awkwardly did the same, looking at images of crowns and stars, feathers and claws and worms and roots.

Brona took them again and laid out all twenty-seven cards in four circles, spiraling out from center. Then she upended the silk bag into her palm and breathed into her hand. She whispered a blessing in the language of trees and dropped the bones across the spread of cards.

Each of the nine bones hit with a hard knock, vibrating the table in little ripples that ought to have stopped long before they did. Kayo shivered, staring.

"This is always how they fall, Kay Oak," Brona said after a long moment. "Whenever I throw them for Innis Lear, and for Elia Lear. The Crown of Trees, Saint of Stars, and Worm of Birds aligned atop all nine cards of the suit of stars. Choice, heart, and patience in the core." She shook her head at him. "Even now with you here it does not change."

"What does it mean? I do not know the bones. They've been forbidden nearly as long as I've been back."

He could not stop staring at the silver lines painted along the roots of every tree card and the perfect blue of the worms. The edges of Brona's cards seemed soft and worn. Some paint was smeared away, and a drop or two of old brown blood stained a card with a lovely black bird sliced perfectly in half, but still flying.

"It means we must wait for Elia, if the island would thrive forever."

Kayo made a fist against his knee. "We cannot wait! Elia despairs, and our land does, too."

"The land will cope, and the heart of the White Forest beats so long as I am here, enough for now. So long as there are folk around the island whispering to the wind, we can be patient. And many do, Kay Oak, despite the edicts of the crown. Including Regan Lear."

"Regan Connley," the Oak Earl corrected.

"Regan Connley, then."

"Which is this card?" he asked, pointing at the bird in two pieces, curious but afraid.

"Oh," Brona breathed shakily, the first indication that her calm was hard-won. "Oh, Kayo." She came around the table to him and perched on the edge, taking one of his brown hands in hers. "Why does it call to you?"

With her near, he felt soothed, and her fingers stroked his wrist so kindly as he spoke. "It has not fallen, though it is cut in two pieces, straight through the middle. It lives in pieces."

"That is the sacrifice the bird makes," the witch of the White Forest whispered. "Not to be cut in half, but to keep flying despite it."

Her words broke open the thing inside him, and Kayo bent over, eyes squeezed closed against the tears pulling fire down his cheeks. "Brona," he choked. "Oh no, oh no. I can't. I never meant to—I am not—" He gripped her hips, pulling her nearer, and buried his face in her lap.

She petted his head, the three weeks' worth of thick black curls growing against his scalp. She bent around him, kissed the knob of his skull, murmuring soft nothings as he cried.

Moments, hours, uncountable tears later, he stopped. His breath skimmed along the stripes of her skirt, and Brona lifted the corner to wipe his cheeks. "Remain here for a few days, my oak lord," she said. "Remain here, and be in pieces. You do not have to fly when you are in my house."

He nodded, clutching her hands. He needed it. He needed her. "Yes," he said, voice hoarse.

# GAELA

IN THE LONG history of their contentious relationship, there was but one thing the king of Innis Lear and his eldest daughter, Gaela, had repeatedly managed to perform together magnanimously: a deer hunt.

Today was a glorious occasion for it, dawning bright and cool, with slipping hints of autumn in the taste of the wind. Gaela arranged it all, including an afternoon field lunch, and lent her father a brace of hounds as his own remained at Dondubhan. She rallied her captain and best scouts to her side, as well as a handful of her newest recruits, including that mountain Dig when she learned he could understand the whispered language of trees. It was a good tool for a successful hunt. Possibly the only thing the language was good for besides getting beneath her father's skin. The large youth shifted uncomfortably on his horse: he'd need to acquire the right seat if he was to join Gaela on the battlefield.

Lear lounged on his tall charger as they headed out, fully at ease despite the length of his limbs. His hair flared in wild chestnut and silver strands, flapping across his mouth when he talked to his own captains, men in the dark blue tabards of the king's retainers. They were a stark disruption of formal Astore pink and the muted green-and-gray leather of Gaela's scouts.

At first, riding with little intention, the party made its way over meadows laced with late-summer flowers and grass heavy and darkened by seed. Clouds played a game with the sunlight, rushing to cover the sun's face and reveal it again, cooling the air then making it burst with warmth. The shifting light kept Gaela alert, happy, and it distracted the hounds, who liked the rush of wind and flickering sun more than the promise of the chase.

Gaela's scouts listened to the trees when Lear had his face turned away, and took off in search of deer.

The king called for a pouch of wine that he shared around with his men, and declaimed the start of a poem from the ancient days of Innis Lear, about war bands and star prophecies and honor. It was one Gaela enjoyed, as it lacked simpering platitudes or the usual meandering narrative that too often caught itself up in repetition and meaningless action. She did not join the retainers, though, who recited the refrain along with her father, or take a turn with a verse. A small smile played on her mouth as she scanned the blue-and-emerald horizon, these edges of her island, and allowed herself to settle into the moment, into the knowledge that it was hers.

And so Gaela was the first to note the scouts had circled back to signal they'd found a deer path. She lifted her hand to interrupt Lear's verses. But while Gaela's own men and her captain Osli fell quiet, Lear himself shook his head and finished his lines. He raised them louder, along with the voices of his retainers, until the last couplet became a shout. It was followed with applause and great cheering until their horses stomped in displeasure.

The scouts held up their second flag, along the western edge of the tiny woods, signaling the charge had to be now or never.

Freeing her bow from over her shoulder, she nudged her horse on.

Wind blew at her face and she crouched in the saddle, urging the horse faster and faster. Behind her thundered her hunting party. Gaela no longer cared whether they caught their prey; this flight mattered more, the connection and movement of her body and her horse and the earth below, hard-hitting and wild.

She pulled up at the edge of the woods, where her scout Agar bowed in his saddle, and the trees clicked and whispered. Agar said, "It's a young buck; we should pause and look elsewhere."

Gaela frowned and barely skimmed a glance up at the layers of greenery and edging yellow leaves.

"What's this?" called Lear from behind. "Why end the charge?'

"A young buck, Father," Gaela said. "We will turn back."

"But the morning stars were full of firsts, and this is our first deer sighted, so it must be our first kill." Lear threw out his arm, pointing the way into the forest.

Agar said, "It's too young, my lady."

"We look elsewhere, Father," Gaela said. "To maintain the health of the forest."

"Bah!" Lear laughed through a scowl, as if he himself could not locate the most pressing emotion. "Bartol! Clarify the star sign for me. Was that not the Star of Sixes and the Eye of the Arrow Saint this morning, hanging on to brightness as we must now hang on to our prey?"

A pale-bearded retainer with burn scars and the white dots of a priest bowed in his saddle, just behind Lear. "Yes, my king."

Lear glanced triumphantly at Gaela. "We go!"

"Father," she growled, holding her horse still with one hand, placing the other with hard-fought calm upon her wool-clad thigh, "a too-young buck has not bred, and will not even have prize antlers for you, this time of year. Go for another; I will not bless this charge."

"I bless it myself," Lear reminded her, raising his hand to turn his men onward, waving them into the forest.

Gaela argued no further, but she lifted her chin and flattened her hand toward her own people. In all the years she'd learned the hunt at her father's knee, he had taught her to care for the forest's needs. To never play such an ignorant, reckless gambit with a herd, only for the pleasure of the moment. The stars, he'd said then, approved of a careful hunt, blessed the relationship between hunter and prey. The stars, the stars, the blasted stars.

"Lady?" Osli murmured, hardly moving her lips.

The prince turned dark eyes on her captain, then shook her head. "I return to Astora. Have the picnic if you like, but tend my father, and hope that young stag keeps itself alive."

Gaela spun her horse and urged it to run back up the rocky slope of moor. Though aware of Osli commanding a set of retainers to go with their queen, Gaela ignored them. She bared her teeth and leaned over her horse's neck. Lear's retainers should've known better, especially the ones who'd been with him for years. Especially that blasted Fool, though the gangly, ridiculous man had not come a-hunting; he fit poorly on a horse with all those long limbs.

They should have defied Lear when he got like this; they should've known that serving him was not about giving in to his every lazy, irresponsible whim, but helping him be a strong king. If he wasn't capable of it—which he was not!—they should serve Gaela. They should serve Innis Lear. The crown. Gaela would not want her men to ignore reason should she give a mad order. She wanted Osli to speak to her, to be honest with her opinions, to be strong. Gaela would surround herself with retainers and counselors as strong as she was. That foundation would make her rule greater! What were sycophants and cowards but a sign of rot and sickness?

Gaela nearly reared her horse with the vehemence of her sudden stop. Were there tears on her face, so much colder than the sweat of her fury? She blinked hard, commanding them to fall and be gone.

Chuffing and shaking its head, the horse beneath her danced in place. Gaela hissed soothing words, patting its neck, hunching over it. What madness were these raw, impulsive emotions? Today was but a single act of disrespect in the long story of her father's bad deeds; why should it enrage and upset her so? He'd disrespected her before. He'd taught his retainers to be just like him. She already knew all of this. She ought to have been over the hurt by now.

In a few short months, Gaela would be king of all Innis Lear, she and Regan both, anointed and blessed at Midwinter, and their father could never do such things as this again. The stars would cease to carry any weight at all under the crown.

Gaela rolled her shoulders and sat, her face hard as iron.

Four soldiers, including Dig, had caught up to her frantic ride and arrayed themselves behind her. She met each pair of eyes; all responded with naught but well-displayed control, and perhaps slight concern for her. Gaela nodded her head slowly, and the soldiers returned the gesture.

She turned her horse and started on again, now at a smooth jog, neither urgent nor at ease. As the horse's hooves pounded evenly over the earth, she breathed and refreshed her own irritation, but at a calmer pace. Gaela did not allow stray thoughts, but concentrated on the path ahead, the return to Astora.

The city finally appeared as they rode over the crest of a foothill, filling the valley with color and noise, thin streams of smoke slipping up and up like silver ribbons. Gaela sat high and tall as she led her soldiers down to the city wall and beneath the crenelated gate. Through the city, then, nodding when she thought to at the few citizens who waved or called out; Gaela was a welcome and usual sight here.

Gaela said nothing to Dig or the rest as they reached the keep, only thrusting herself off her horse and tossing the reins to a groom. Without comment or command, she stormed through the narrow front door of the new castle and up the high stone stairs, her pace speeding into nearly a run through the claustrophobic hallway, lit only by fired sconces and thin arrow slits. Finally she slammed through the door of her private chambers.

Heaving a breath, she shoved the wooden door shut and fumbled at the hard ties of her hunting jacket, eager to be free of the confining leather.

"Gaela."

It was her husband's voice, loud and surprised.

Her head flew up; Astore was in the process of coming around her desk, dropping some letters.

"What do you do in my room?" she snarled, striding toward him.

Astore caught her shoulders and shook her once. "Gaela. What is wrong?"

"Are you reading my correspondence?" she demanded.

Her husband shocked her into silence with his kiss.

For a moment Gaela did not respond, too surprised at his bold theft, and

Astore clearly took it as acquiescence; he softened his mouth and moved his hands to her face, cupping her jaw tenderly.

Gaela pulled away. "What are you about, Col?"

The Duke Astore's lips were crushed, so quickly drawn in pink. "You seem distressed, wife," he said, using the title pointedly, as if admonishing her to remember she'd entered into this relationship willingly.

She knew very well the choices she'd made. Gaela lifted one hand to carefully wipe her bottom lip with her thumb, then said, "My father insisted upon hunting a deer the scouts called too young, too new. He has no concern for the health of the forest."

Astore's hands slid down to settle at her hips, as they were wont to do. "I too worry on his mind."

"You rather understate the issue, Col. He is mad. And his behavior makes everyone around him so, too. He should be released of obligations to retainers. I should send them all away. A break would do them good."

"And better to win them to us."

"So long as they listen to my father, they will not join me. So we stand." Gaela shrugged free of her husband's grip. "Tell me now, husband, what you did at my desk, here in my own rooms without me."

The duke met her gaze. "I was writing you a note. I leave immediately for Dondubhan."

"What has happened?"

"Connley sent his men already into Brideton and Lowbinn, so I will establish our name in Dondubhan immediately, not wait for closer to Midwinter."

"Good, good." Gaela grinned. "Keep Connley in his place. I would go with you, but better, I think, for us to be both there and here. You can be Astore there, and I will be the almost-queen on my own, here, not to be seen stepping too soon."

Astore took Gaela's wrist. "That was my thought exactly. We do still make a good match. Despite your faith in your sister."

"Let go," she said softly.

"You've avoided my bed since you returned from the Summer Seat."

Gaela denied it with a sneer.

"Soon you will be the ultimate regent, before even your sister Regan, for this halved-crown will not last. We won't allow it. You will have what you have sought, and I would have it with you. This would not be possible without me to balance your womanly stars."

"I know," she said, truthfully: she never would have married at all if there had been another way.

He kissed her again, lowering his hands to her waist, then curled them around to hold her firmly. His mouth was urgent; he pressed their hips together. She did not resist, but gave nothing either. How her life might've been easier if she wanted this. Wanted him. Or anyone.

"Gaela," he said, half into her mouth, then leaned away. His brow knit, darkening his pale eyes with shadow. "What is wrong with you? I know you have no lovers, not even that girl Osli whom you cherish so close to your person. You do not seek pleasure or companionship elsewhere."

"I have no need of it," she said, dismissively.

"Everyone does."

Gaela shrugged and stepped away from him. She went to her desk, skimming her hand along the letters there; indeed one lay open and half written in his hand. "I am not everyone," she said with pride, glancing up at him briefly.

"That is why I married you." Astore stood with his hands at his hips, angry and admirably regal. His broad chest pulled at the wool tunic he wore and the gold-worked chains hooked from shoulder to shoulder. A large topaz hung from his left earlobe, glinting like the rings on his fingers and the hammered copper at his neck.

"Take a lover, Col. I'll not stop you."

"You are my wife. I want *you.* That is also why I married you. To make you mine, Geala Astore"

"I am not yours." Gaela snorted a laugh. "Rather, you are my shield, as you said: your stars are necessary to make me queen. That is all."

The duke came to her, grabbed her arm, and dragged her to him. "You are mine because you want that crown as much as I do. You came to me when your mother died so I would make you strong. Make you a warrior. And look at you." He leaned in so his beard tickled her chin. "You are a warrior, and will be a ferocious queen. *At my side.*"

Gaela fisted her hands in his tunic and said through clenched teeth, "Yes, you will be at my side when I am queen; it is done. So why do you press this between us now, Col Astore?"

"We need an heir. There can be no more waiting. Seven years of marriage, and we have achieved our goal. The crown. Now we must keep it, and to keep it we need a child. Children. You cannot have convinced yourself otherwise, somehow."

She thrust away from him and sat upon the edge of her desk. "Regan—"

Astore raised his hand between them, rigid and flat, pointing at her with all fingers. "Regan is not our ally in this," he said firmly. "If she bears a healthy a child, and you have none, Connley will rally people against us, no matter how securely we get the crown now."

"My sister is more my ally than any other."

"*I* am your ally. She chose against you years ago when she married Connley!"

It was not in Gaela's nature to argue on a person's behalf if she believed that person's motives to be clear. And so she stared at her husband, bland and cold, as she said, "You should have learned by now you cannot come between Regan and I."

"She is your blindness." Astore grabbed her knees and forced them apart, moving into the space. She pulled her lips back like a threatening wolf, but her husband transferred his hands to her thighs and pressed his fingers hard enough to bruise.

"Be careful, Col," she warned.

"What will you do without an heir? Regan seems incapable of producing one. Even if she and you consolidate our rule, if we all manage it, what then? What of Innis Lear in twenty years, or thirty?" He continued to threaten with the weight of his hands on her thighs.

"We will bring Elia home," she said through her teeth, not clawing at him or kicking him away; she'd not let him see how infuriating she found his behavior. How degrading.

"Elia!" he scoffed darkly. "Her children may well belong to Aremoria already! And why would you rather her children be your heirs than your own? Than mine?"

"My bloodline includes my sisters, Col. What difference in which of us continue it? In my grandmother's empire it is always the empress's niece who inherits after her. They make a stronger map of blood and alliance that way." Gaela could feel her rage building, the spikes of it striking harder against her armor with every moment Astore touched her and every word he argued.

He said, "This is not the Third Kingdom, and I would have heirs, sons and daughters of my own line. You condemn not just Innis Lear with this folly, but my blood."

"I do not care about your blood, you fool."

"You had better start, or stars help me—"

"Stars!" she yelled, finally shoving him away and leaping to her feet. "The stars should have provided this future for you long ago, if they're worth anything at all. I know my stars; they promised great posterity would spring from me, which is a great joke, for you could lie with me every day for eternity and never get me with child, and it has always been so, since before we married."

He smiled meanly. "You cannot escape some of your stars, when at the same time you use others of them to gain a crown. I studied your birth chart; I looked at all the signs. You are fertile, Gaela, you are passionately so."

She put her hand flat on his chest. "No. I changed it. I did this to my-self. I make decisions and act upon them. I do not allow stars or prophecy to dictate my choices. They are a tool, nothing more."

"Did what . . . to yourself?" Astore blinked.

"I am incapable of bearing a child, by choice and by necessity, Col. Brona Hartfare burned my womb out of me before you put your seed anywhere near it."

Astore hit her.

The blow bent her around, and she caught herself with her hands against the corner of her desk.

"Lies!" he yelled.

Gaela's skull rang, more with shock than any pain. She blinked. And then she turned, punching him in the gut. She followed with a slap across the side of his face.

Blood touched the tip of her tongue then, and she spat onto her floor. "Oh, Col," she said dangerously, quietly.

He grabbed her by the throat.

So they stood. Gaela sneered, tilted her chin up, and welcomed his stare. "Do what you will," she said through her teeth.

"Is it because of your mother?" Astore asked. A vein pulsed at the curve of his temple, hot pink where she'd hit him.

She wrapped her hands around his forearm. "It is because I will wear the crown, and I will get it like a king. Not as a mother and wife, but as the firstborn child, as the strongest. It is no fault of mine to be forced to per-form this illusion of being your wife, to pretend to be what a woman of this island is supposed to be, in order to gain power among you and your peers."

Astore dropped her suddenly, faltering back. He sank onto a short wooden chair with rounded arms. "Barren," he said, with the ghost of a bitter smile. "What a schemer you are, Gaela Lear. You won this war before I even knew there was a battle to be had."

She stalked toward him and leaned down, planting one hand on either arm of his chair. "And for it, you will be king, too. Be glad."

"Never," he muttered. "When we have the crown, when Connley is de-feated, we will revisit this, wife."

Gaela smiled and wondered if they both would survive so long.

# THE FOX

BAN WAITED IN the hallway outside his father's chambers, near a window and a low bench set into the smooth wooden wall. This was part of the new Keep, built of wood and plaster, with windows that opened to the southeast. Ban removed the letter from his coat. He'd written in as close to Rory's sprawling hand as he could manage.

Leaning against the sill, Ban pressed his forehead into his arm and breathed unevenly on purpose, as if desperate to rein in a great hurt. *Slip under the enemy's defenses.*

This plan would lead to getting the iron magic for Morimaros. It would prove to Elia exactly the fickle ease with which a father might overthrow a child's love. It would undercut the stars King Lear adhered to so fanatically.

All Ban had to do was sink to the level they expected of a bastard. It shocked him with an unexpected thrill.

*Base* and *vile*, those were the words the king had used, the words Ban's own father had never argued against. Well. They might have been meant to put him down, but Ban had learned of baseness and vile creatures when he hunted and tracked, when he cut his sword into the guts of another man, when he dug into the ground to bury a comrade or cover the shit of the army. He had seen how the earth accepted base and vile things and transformed them into stinking, beautiful life again. Flowers and fresh grasses. Colorful mushrooms and beds of moss. That was magic. Could the stars do such a thing? Never. Only the earth—the wild, mysterious, dark earth—knew such power.

Ban's power.

He had spent the winter he was seventeen in the estate of his cousins Alsax in northeastern Aremoria, just near the borders of Burgun and Diota. That past summer he'd continued fighting alongside the foot soldiers in Morimaros's army, all while quietly working directly for the king. He did all his soldier's work and every low job the Alsaxes expected of him without complaint, then instead of joining his fellows for food or drink after a shift, would slip away to do Morimaros's bidding. Often that meant infiltrating the lands of the opposition, whether that was Burgun border towns or the manor houses of rebellious Aremore nobles. He slept hungry with herds of sheep, in precarious nests beside red eagles, and in a womb of heartwood when he found a tree who trusted him entire. Always exhausted, always thirsty. When Ban was missing from the army for days at a time, La Far spoke with his Alsax commander and smoothed it over, though it took a long while to trickle down to the foot soldiers that he was more than just a slippery deserter.

But at the end of that summer's campaign, the king had invited Ban to spend an entire two months in Lionis, working with Morimaros and La Far together on sword craft and riding and any martial skill Ban thought to ask after. It had been one of the best times of his life, for he'd been trusted and treated as though he deserved nothing less.

When he returned to the Alsax estate for the winter, it was with the king's own letter in hand. By the king's orders, he was not to be put with the foot soldiers again, but allowed to use the cold, muffled, snowed-in months for nothing but magical study, and given a room of his own to accommodate it.

Ban was determined to return to Morimaros as great a wizard as possible: his service to the king was the only thing forcing others to recognize his worth, and so he would shine no matter what else tarnished him.

Though some old books had been written on the subject of wizarding by observers of the art, there were no practitioners in Aremore, and Ban was left without access to a teacher. Instead, he chose to learn from the trees and beasts themselves, and studied mainly through experimentation. His small corner room on the top story of the pale limestone estate smelled constantly of pine and wax; musty bats and sweet winter berry poultices; the vibrant, spicy ink made from the heartblood of trees; and fire. He worked on a wolf-skin rug turned leather up to be drawn on with charcoal; there he etched out words in the language of trees and drew circles and root diagrams to guide him. Usually a half-empty plate of cheese and bread and cold, dry meat sat nearly forgotten beside him, and a bottle of wine he never bothered pouring into a cup. When working, he wore little besides heavy wool trousers dyed the brown of the winter forest, so he might easily paint charcoal runes across his chest, or cut the shape of his name against his collarbone.

Thus Rory found him when he shoved through the door joining their rooms, stumbling slightly from all the impassioned sex and the nearly empty bottle of wine he'd so recently partaken of. Flushed and unfocused, he blinked at his older bastard brother, surprised to find Ban even less clothed than himself and covered in streaks of ash writing in the language of trees. "Are you doing magic?" he cried.

Ban frowned from the center of the wolf-skin and settled his hands on his knees. The fingers of his right hand were blackened. In his left he held a trio of black raven feathers. He did not have the patience after midnight to walk his brother through his attempt to whisper a secret to a distant cluster of ravens with a thin rope of pine smoke.

"I am, yet it is late, and I should rest." Ban eyed his little brother: the loose trousers and bare feet, the fur-lined robe and tousled hair, the long pink scratches distorting the flare of freckles down his neck. Ban pressed his mouth together. Rory had barely been here two weeks and already had a lover—or three.

"I want to know how to do magic," Rory breathed, kneeling beside Ban.

This wizarding belonged to Ban, it was the only thing of his own, and he did not want to invite Rory to share it. Rory already had so many things that should have been his older brother's. Ban said, "Listening to the wind demands quietude of the heart, peaceful breathing, and willingness to be still, brother. None of which are skills you cultivate."

"Your heart is not quiet, either, brother."

"I can see your flush right now."

"You just disapprove of my nightly activities." Rory's smile was all teasing and smug delight.

"I do, but that makes my words no less true. You'll never learn magic if you fix your attention and passion so firmly on a course of loud spirit."

Rory nudged Ban with his elbow. "So that is why you eschew the naked entertainments? For your magic?"

"That, but for the more obvious reason, too."

"What?" the earlson laughed.

"You could father a *bastard*," Ban hissed.

"If he's like my brother, Ban, it would be quite the thing! I welcome it."

The bastard scowled, but his brother threw an arm about him, still laughing, and quite obviously meaning every word. "Never fear, Ban, no power in the heavens or the roots could get my lover with child by me."

Ban began to sneer a reply, but caught the angle of his brother's smile. "Is that a man in there?" he asked, hushed.

"Erus Or," Rory confided. "He is *strong*."

"You have to stop, you have to be careful." Ban gripped his brother's arms. "Didn't you hear of the man Connley executed for the same?"

Rory shrugged him off. "I'll be fine. This is Aremoria, not home. Besides, Connley killed that man because he was married to Connley's cousin and betrayed her, not because he betrayed her with another man."

Unsettled, Ban went to the window and gripped the cold stone sill. Even if he desired to, he could never take such risks in his position, despite Morimaros's favor, despite his success in war. All Ban had was the thin iron rod of his reputation.

And there was his golden brother Rory, laughing with the carefree certainty of his own invincibility.

This plan of Ban's now, three years later, would do all it needed to do: ruin Errigal and tear into the island's foundations, work toward Morimaros's goals and prove to Elia she'd done no wrong. But most of all, it would hurt Rory, stripping away his easy confidence. Ban was a wizard revealing the truth of the world to show Rory that people are terrible sometimes and unfair, that one does not always deserve what one receives, and that there are consequences to living carelessly.

That, Ban was willing teach his brother.

The snap of leather warned Ban that his father approached, clumping up the stairs as if already upset. That would work in Ban's favor. He crumpled the letter in his hand and put both fists over his head, elbows jutting at the window casement.

"Ban!" Errigal snapped. "What is this?"

Ban straightened, his eyes down anxiously, and hurried to tuck the false letter away, in a pocket close to his heart.

The earl was alone, dressed in casual linen and wool, a sword belt strapping his tunic down, sheathing a plain soldier's blade. Errigal put his fist against the pommel and glowered. "Why did you put that up so quickly, son?"

"It's nothing," Ban said, giving a tight shake of his head. His lip throbbed where he'd cut it wrestling Rory.

"Oh ho? Then why seek to hide it from me?" Errigal came forward, large hand outstretched. "If it is nothing, then nothing shall I see."

Ban grimaced to hide the thrill of battle rising again in his veins. "It is only a note from my brother, and I've not finished reading it. What I've read so far makes me think it's not fit for you to see."

"Give it to me, boy, or I'll take great offense." Errigal thrust his hand out again.

"I think it would give offense either way."

"Let me have it."

With seeming reluctance, Ban withdrew the letter. Eyes cast down, he added, "I hope—I truly believe, Father—that Rory wrote this only to test my virtue. He hasn't known me since he left our cousins, with me still in Aremoria last year, and only hears what men in the king's retinue say about me: that I am a bastard and therefore not trustworthy."

Errigal made a growling noise of frustration and snatched the letter. He so violently unfolded it that the edge pulled and tore. Ban crossed his arms over his chest and knocked back against the wall, easily pretending anxiety. This was the moment this would tell him if Errigal was as terrible and easy to turn as Lear.

As his father's mouth moved along with the words he read and his large eyes narrowed, as his lips paled under his beard, Ban suddenly realized there was a sick thread of disappointment wound through his spine. Some part of him had hoped Errigal was better. That the earl could not believe so easily his own son would betray him. It was that same cursed piece of Ban that had yet to stop yearning for approval from his father. Ban clenched his teeth.

"*This reverence for age keeps the best of us out of power,*" Errigal read in a broad, disbelieving voice. "*We don't receive our fortunes until we are too old to enjoy them. Because we wait for our fathers to—*" The earl's hand twitched. "*We must speak of this together, for you would have half of his revenue forever, and live beloved of your brother.*"

Silence fell, but for the cool wind bringing the far-distant clangs of smithies and a howl out of the great forest. Errigal slammed the side of his fist to the wooden wall. "Conspiracy," he whispered, staring past Ban out the window. "Is this— Can this be my son Rory? Has he the heart to write this . . . I would not think so."

Ban put his mouth into a careful frown, though he wanted to hit Errigal, to knock him down and step on his throat, to show him exactly how much this hurt.

Errigal glanced sharp and hot at Ban. "When did you get this? Who brought it?"

"I found it in my room." Still he did not latch his gaze onto his father's, knowing his fury would shine through.

"Is it his hand? Your brother's hand?"

Ban shook his head. "Were the subject good, I would swear it's Rory's writing, but being what it is . . . I cannot say yes. It does not seem written in his words, even."

"It is by his hand."

The words sounded like death blows, dull and hard and promising raw blood to come.

The earl crumpled the letter. All his blunt teeth were bared. "And a feast prepared for this ungrateful whelp! Ah! Find him, so I can disabuse him of this notion his father is too old and weak to govern."

Ban held his hands out to stall Errigal, and let him see the anger now. Errigal could read it as he liked. "Wait. At least until you can hear from his own mouth what he intended with this letter! We do *not* know if he wrote it, we do not know if he meant it—maybe he is testing *me,* as I said."

"Ban!" Errigal ground out the name through clenched wide teeth.

"Father." Ban put hands to Errigal's broad shoulders. "Don't do as Lear did. If you go violently against Rory and it's merely a mistake, that is a gap in your honor, not his. Look at the chaos Innis Lear is experiencing already, with Kay Oak banished and the princess, too. Connley and Astore are ready at each other's necks. We need Rory to be innocent of this."

The earl's jaw worked, his hairy brows dipping in uncertain anger. "All this is a disaster, you are right about that. If my own son . . . ah. He cannot be such a monster."

"He cannot," Ban murmured, only half in guilt.

The two leaned together at the window, both breathing hard, though for different causes.

"Ah, Ban." Errigal sagged, and Ban dropped to the floor, kneeling. "Child against father—it is not natural. It is against the stars, and yet the stars warned us. These eclipses, these signs of division, of friend against friend, loves lost, what can we do? Heaven and earth, I love that fine, wretched boy. He must be as good as you, as loyal. Look at his stars! He was born under such good stars." The earl thumped his head back against the wall and shut his eyes. "Discover the truth, Ban. Discover it."

"I shall, Father," Ban said, pressing his forehead to his father's fist. He let his mouth twist and his eyes burn where the earl could not see.

Stars. Always the stars of birth. The blindness of old men, the weakness of their faith. Easy weapons to turn against them now that Ban understood power better.

Hurrying down stone stairs worn in the middle from generations of soldiers' boots, Ban made his way to the kitchens where he knew Rory to be already, flirting with the cooks and maids as they prepared the feast.

Ban paused just outside the bend into the sweltering kitchen, catching his breath. He heard his brother's voice trail brightly up the stairs from the larder instead. A young woman pressed past Ban, carrying a full platter of steaming bread. She smiled at him, but Ban's attention was all for the story his brother told.

". . . and though battered and bruised, Ban the Fox had clutched in his hand the underwear of the commander of the Diotan forces!"

The triumphant words spread into a shout of laughter and cheers from surely a dozen throats. Ban stepped down, steadying the sword at his belt. A cluster of young people—retainers in Errigal sky blue, two servant boys in their aprons, and even some young women covered in flour and smiling under sweat-curled hair—surrounded Rory, all of them crushed into the space around the long butter table, ducking their heads around the jars of butter and cream hung on hooks to keep free of rats and insects.

"You were supposed to be telling stories of your own exploits," Ban said softly, affection warming his belly beside stinging guilt.

"Ban! Ha! Worms!" Rory held out his arm. "You tell them a story about me, then."

Ban smiled tightly, aware that though his presence didn't quite crush the spirit of the room, he most definitely quieted it. They'd accepted him, to be sure, but he had not earned their ease. "Rory, I have an urgent matter for your ears only."

"After, then," Rory promised, grimacing wildly for his audience. He snaked through them, coming up to Ban. "What it is, brother?"

"Wait," Ban said, leading Rory up into the kitchens again, and out one of the rear corridors toward the strip of earth between the kitchens and the inner stables. The evening sun shone, still high enough to glare over the outer black wall of the Keep. Ban put his shoulder to the rough wall and pulled Rory very close. "You spoke with Father as soon as you returned today?"

"Yes, I told you that, just before bathing."

"And not again? Not recently?"

"No." Rory's brow wrinkled.

Ban nodded as if confirming suspicions. "Did he seem well? You parted on good terms?"

"What is going on?" the legitimate son eyed Ban crown to boot.

"He's furious at you for something," Ban said evenly.

"Furious? At me? What for?"

"I don't know, but he raged at me for it, just now."

"I must go to him. Discover the cause."

"No, Rory, wait. He is in a killing manner. You should leave for a few days."

"Leave! I just arrived!"

Ban took a long, calming breath. "Let me be your ambassador. Go to Brona's house where you know you can be safe. I will send to you what I discover, and when you should return."

Rory bit his bottom lip, as he'd done in uncertain times as a boy. It struck a blow to Ban's conscience, but not so deep that he altered his words.

"Trust me, Rory," he said. "Go."

"Some villain has done me wrong," Rory said softly.

For a moment, Ban thought he'd misjudged his brother and that Rory saw through the pretense and accused him. But no, Rory just took Ban by the shoulders and dragged him into a crushing embrace. Slowly, Ban brought his arms up. "Go armed," he murmured, and Rory jerked.

"Armed?"

"You cannot be too careful—these are strange times. Fathers against children . . ."

"Like the king," Rory whispered in a hollow, suddenly fearful tone. "He spoke of the eclipses as portents, and our father, too, was on edge over the whole business. Banishment and disloyal daughters, and some eclipses. He must be hunting danger—oh, worms of earth."

"Yes," Ban said through gritted teeth. Their ears pressed together.

"I go, but with your love, brother," Rory said. "And you remain with mine."

Ban hugged his brother, learning something himself. This was the lesson: while Ban had used his father's greatest weaknesses against him—mistrust, bullish ambition, and obsession with star-signs—against Rory, Ban had used only virtue.

# ELIA

THE BALCONY OFF Morimaros's study was a round half-circle protected by a short marble rail carved like a trellis of fat-blooming roses. The stone blossoms trailed down the side of the tower toward the central courtyard, where Elia supposed sometimes the people of Lionis would gather to hear their king. She touched both hands to the rail and leaned out with her face raised, imagining all of Aremoria below her, a crown wound through her elaborate braids, and voluptuous layers of an orange-and-white royal wedding gown spilling over her body. Or perhaps she would wear the dark blue and white of the house of Lear. But then, she could hear Aefa insisting, Elia had always looked most beautiful in the colors of fire.

Like the sunset spread across the great spill of city hills before her.

It was a breathtaking sight, unlike any beheld on her island. Elia had believed she'd understood summer and the end of summer, before. Innis Lear held the season rather in reserve, parting warm mists and rain for moments of crystalline sunlight, and cool, lovely afternoons of wildflowers and breezes. It was a flash of a smile, appreciated more because of its fleeting nature.

But Aremoria did not let that smile pass or fade without worship. The countryside grabbed at the shortening days, made itself rabid with color. Elia was used to rusty autumn oaks and crisp browning leaves, not this wilderness of vivid green and gashed, bloody purple, nor the narrow strips of yellow as bright as topaz. The white city reflected the sky, and the rolling hills were emerald and golden fields as far as she could see beyond the city walls. Aremoria was violent with life, while Lear froze and ached at the precipice of death. She did not like to think—would not think—that lately the island seemed to court decay harder and longer, barely relinquishing winter in time for any spring.

How Elia missed her island, even so; how she longed for the desperate, dangerous beauty of churning seas, and the naked enduring mountains, and the hungry shadows of the White Forest. She tried, for a moment, to compose herself, to close off the ache for home.

"Elia," Morimaros said from just inside his study. "I'm sorry for being late."

Before she could turn, the king of Aremoria came behind her and put his hand delicately against her back. The touch held her open, somehow; sharpened her yearning.

"Lady, are you so unhappy here?" he asked. "I see only sadness when you look out at my city."

She did not answer, breathing deep for calm and concentrating on the warmth of his hand. His thumb skimmed her skin, at her spine just over the collar of her dress. She had no wish, still, to marry, but how easy it would be to take what he offered, to turn herself over to this strong king, to let herself be subsumed under his power. The way she'd been subsumed under her father. Was this why Regan chose Connley, because he was so vibrant he could fill all the cracks in her spirit?

Elia turned and looked into his eyes. His expression left no room for whimsy or prettiness, and she wondered how a vibrant place such as this could have carved him into the serious, thoughtful man he was. But pride showed in his features, and a thin tension she was about to wind tighter. His orange leather coat hung open and casual, the tunic below untied at his neck. He wore no sword belt. The sunset lit his gaze and put fire along his bearded jaw.

"You are beautiful," he said abruptly.

It caught her off guard, for she'd not known Morimaros to fill his own silences as if nervous. The thought that he was nervous alone with her, here on this balcony in the heart of his country and castle, was humbling as well as a thrill. Could she affect him as he did her? Could her voice set his heart pounding? She'd allowed Aefa to pamper her between the interrupted council meeting and this dinner: she bathed for too long and rubbed oil into her skin as well as her hair, until she felt soft and careful and made of the finest materials. Together they'd found a dress of sunny yellow and an overdress of meadow violet to compliment her best ribbons and lace wound into her freshly braided hair. It was sturdy and intricate enough to last a long while, especially if she wrapped it in a scarf to sleep.

Elia tried to bridle her racing thoughts, staring still breathlessly at Morimaros. "Thank you," she managed.

He politely touched his hand to her elbow, guiding her around to the small table set for two, where he pulled the cushioned stool for her. She sat with her spine too rigid for comfort as the king leaned beside her to pour a clear yellow wine into her glass. He poured for himself, as well, before sitting across from her. At that silent signal, a duo of footmen emerged from the study with plates covered in cheeses, smears of jam and honey, and thin slices of smoked and salted fish.

Sparrows fluttered overhead, and Morimaros explained that he would come here as a boy to read his father's treatises and lessons, and had begun feeding the birds. His sister named this balcony Mars's Cote because of it. Elia watched how his mouth relaxed in the telling, as he spoke of his family with such obvious affection. This king was charming, but she felt a sadness reminiscent of envy. She wished she could relax into sharing a meal with him, to think merely of enjoying his company as if she too belonged here, another sparrow come home to roost and be comforted. But Elia could not forsake Innis Lear.

"The news from my sisters is not good," she said, setting down a thin layer of unleavened bread she'd spread with apricot preserves.

He frowned, his glance flickering west, toward her island.

"My father has not changed his mind, or given any sign he means to. I fear—I fear my exile is not temporary."

"From where does his madness spring, do you know?"

Elia took a small, hasty sip of wine. She set it down and folded both hands around the stem. "You have heard the story of my mother's death?"

"That it was predicted by the stars."

"That day, after she died, I have never felt such inconsolable despair, and I was so young. It was all my father, his feelings, and then my sisters both, spilling out onto me, all around me. My father gave what he could to me, and the island, but mostly to me."

Morimaros took a breath, as if to speak, but remained silent.

"I was all he had, and the stars took so much from him. My mother, his brothers to make him king, his vocation. Can you imagine what that leaves a man, who then must try to be the king he is destined to be? The stars have been his only, only constant. Of course he can't unlock himself from their prophecies, for fear of losing everything again."

"Still," the king said darkly, "he chose them over you, and set his kingdom on a path toward upset."

"Better to push me away than have me torn from him because he does not do as the stars decree." Elia forced her eyes up from the goblet. "Do you intend to invade Innis Lear?"

"If I must."

The answer hardened her heart, squeezing out the prick of disappointment she felt, too. "What would make you think you must?"

His mouth pulled down. "Do you know what I saw, those waiting days in your father's court?"

She met his eyes, nodding permission for him to continue, though she did not think she wanted to hear.

"A thin, rigid power, cracking in all the wrong places. Your father is a terrible king."

Elia gasped in shock. "You know so much better?" she said angrily.

"I had a better example. My father was a good king. Perhaps your father was once, but no longer."

She gripped her own arms. He spoke so matter-of-factly! Loyalty and love warred inside her against the need to understand, the need for change. She said, "My sisters are strong."

"Dual queens will not hold, not when they do not act in complete accord."

"They will, on the matter of keeping Innis Lear independent from you."

Morimaros shook his head. "I had letters today, too. From Gaela and her husband Astore, as well as Connley. None of them agreed on their approach to me or even what they want from Aremoria."

"What did they say?" she asked, too tentatively.

"Gaela warned me to keep my distance, saying that any action from me, including marrying you, would be seen as hostile. Astore asked me to back them against Connley, and offered me assurances of alliance if I do, when Astore is king. He suggested we might work this out as men, which I took to mean he does not trust his own wife, though perhaps I misread it. And Connley declared that he holds the loyalty of the Errigal earldom, and if I want iron from them, I must back *him*. As his wife does, though her sister might protest. This period before Midwinter is already hanging over disaster."

Elia shook her head, disbelieving. "And so you must invade? To *save* Innis Lear?"

"Innis Lear once was part of Aremoria."

"Eight hundred years ago!"

"I would see our lands reunited."

"Innis Lear will not choose you if you invade. Not the people, and not the roots. Not even if you think you're saving us."

"Aremoria needs the minerals buried in your mountains, needs the trade advantages. Aremoria needs her western flank secure, and Innis Lear is a volatile neighbor. But"—Morimaros inclined his head nearer hers—"none of that makes my words any less true. Innis Lear will destroy itself if left on this path. A ruler must recognize this and make a choice, where land cannot choose or act."

Elia stood up and returned to the edge of the balcony, but faced Morimaros. She studied him, his hard handsomeness, the certainty in his eyes. Nothing about him suggested he did not believe everything he said. Her sisters were right. Gaela and Regan both—the king of Aremoria saw weakness in Lear, and he would blow through, expecting little resistance, unless Elia proved otherwise. And so far all she'd shown Morimaros was her own grief; none of Innis Lear's strength, none of what she knew to be true about stars and roots, or even what her father had ever done well, what would make Innis Lear thrive. She thought of Lear's expectant face, the strain with which he coaxed her to answer his terrible instruction at the Zenith Court. Star prophecy was woven into the bedrock of her island, but it had led them before to ruin.

"You don't understand Innis Lear."

"Perhaps." Morimaros came to her. "But I understand rulership, and I understand balance."

"You do not respect prophecy or the songs of the Aremore trees. There is no rootwater in your city wells, no voice for the wind or roots of this land. Ours may cry out for help now, but unless you embrace what those of Innis Lear require, you could never be our true king. Not unless you submerge yourself in the rootwater at the dark well of Tarinnish, when the stars are brilliant and ready on the Longest Night, and prove the island accepts you. Your blood and the blood of the island, one blood bringing life." Elia felt breathless, imagining it from the handful of stories she knew about how Innis Lear made its kings.

He would never. He couldn't.

Slowly, Morimaros reached out, giving her ample time to avoid his touch, and took both her elbows in his hands.

"Innis Lear is a mess, with no strong head, no direction. It is not because your father closed the holy wells, or because he gave all to the stars. That is only *how* he did it. By offering the people nothing else to believe in when he forbade access and censured their faith. He gave Innis Lear no common enemy, nor any common hero, nothing to unite his people and keep them bound to their crown. He rejected *them,* preferring the distance of cold stars to the warmth of his close blood. And your sisters? They may be individually capable of ruling, but what of giving your island a hero or myth or anything to heal the wounds inflicted? And what of their husbands? They are all too selfish to understand the weight of a healthy crown. And if your sisters could somehow come to deny their own desires, cast off such quarrelsome husbands and devote more to the island than their own wounds, would the people of Lear agree to follow them, women who have been nothing but angry and cold? You see, I know much of the history of strife over the crown of Lear, Lady."

Elia stared in shock. How dare he say such things about her country, her family? She clenched her jaw, then said firmly, "My sisters are determined, Morimaros. They will fight, and the people will accept them, because they are daughters of the island. Gaela is immensely powerful, like a saint already in her reputation, and Regan is known to commune with the roots. There is more than belief on Innis Lear. It is magic, real magic in our blood and in the song of the trees. My sisters *are* the new story of Innis Lear. And—and if nothing else could bring Connley and Astore together, it is the prospect of Aremore invasion."

"I would use all of this to your advantage." Morimaros drew her closer to him by her elbows, as near into an embrace as he ever had. "Make *you* the new faith. I would make your sisters and their husbands understand the only thing to stop my invasion is their sister Elia on the throne of Lear."

Elia shook her head, denying the thought of it, even as her skin warmed. "Me? That is impossible. I was never built for it, Morimaros. I am a priest, no more, and hardly that, any longer."

"I cannot believe that."

"Then believe that I do not want to be queen. I never have wanted such a thing. I want my life to be my own."

"We do not always have a choice in that matter. Even kings."

"Do not take that choice away from me," she commanded, or tried to: her voice shook.

He studied her for a moment. "Your uncle, the Oak Earl, wants the same as I. He argued in my council today that Aremoria's best move is to put you on the throne of Innis Lear, and have a friendly neighbor, open trade without offense to the Third Kingdom. That it is what your father wanted, what he expected to have done at the Zenith Court."

Horror stalled her voice. Elia closed her eyes. "I do not want to be queen of Lear. I do not want to vie with my sisters for the crown. I do not want to face their furious disdain. I have never wanted this. I want my father safe, and at peace for the last years of his life. I want—I want to do some good. Let me write to my sisters, negotiate with them. For my father, and for peace between them. They will choose one to rule: it will be Gaela. As is her birthright. If they know you are not readying your warships, they might relax enough to listen. To calm their husbands."

"You believe your sisters can create balance? Can make Innis Lear strong? And do fair business with me? I do not see it."

"And yet what do you see in me that makes you so certain I should be a queen, so certain you can trust me?"

"*Elia*." His voice was hot suddenly, lacking his usual reserve. "I saw it the day we met, in small things, things you would not remember because they were so naturally part of you. And I saw it blossom when you stood before Lear and did not play his game. Not for power or aggression or anger, but for love. You can bring people together, instead of dividing them. That is what strength is. And what love should be."

Elia, fighting tears, said, "Then for love, let me try to save my father, and resolve these things between my sisters to make a strong country before you wreck it."

"I will not be the one to wreck Innis Lear."

Desperation compelled her to say, "Don't go to war, Morimaros. Say you won't, and I'll marry you. Make me your queen, keep me here in Aremoria, but never go to war with my sisters."

The king released her suddenly. Some strong emotion rippled across his face. "You would marry me for your island's sake, but not my own?"

"Your sake?" Elia's heart clenched, and her fists followed. "I thought marriages between kings and queens were for the sake of alliance. I thought you wanted my position and leverage over my island, Your Highness, not my heart."

"I find . . . I would have both," Morimaros said.

She stepped back, her hip pressed to the stone rail.

Her sister Regan's voice hissed at her, *Use this to our advantage, little sister. Use his heart to gain what you need.* And Gaela's triumphant, disparaging laugh echoed.

The king waited as she thought, his eyes taking in every detail of her.

Shivering, Elia said, "I would prefer that, too. Both, I mean."

Morimaros leaned in to her, bringing his hands up to cradle her neck. His thumbs touched her jaw. They were so close, too close. He was all she could see of the world, and his desire to kiss her was painted clear on his face. She hoped desperately he would not. She couldn't imagine what she would feel if he did, or how his kiss would change her. She only knew that it would. She wasn't ready.

"I see many possible consequences to your father's choices, your sisters' choices," Morimaros said softly. She smelled the sweet, clear wine on his breath. It made her want to lick her lips; his nearness pressed her anger in too many directions. The king continued, "Your choices are more mysterious to me."

"Everything I do is so simple," she whispered. "I only want to live and practice compassion, and follow the path of the stars and earth saints. I cannot be responsible for the lives and deaths and rages and regrets of others."

"I want . . ." Morimaros leaned away from her. He shook his head and turned to gaze at the shadows that overtook his city, turning it violet and blue and gray with deep twilight.

She waited, but he did not continue. As if the king of Aremoria did not know what he wanted, or could not quite bring himself to say the word aloud. "Tell me what you want."

He leaned on his hands, gripping the stone rail of the balcony. His head dropped, urging her to touch his arm. She did, then slid her hand down the orange coat to place her fingers delicately atop his. Turning his hand up to put them palm to palm, Morimaros said, "I want . . . to only care about what I want, Elia Lear."

The words were both heartbreaking and offensive, and yet when her name was in his mouth, it sounded like a queen's name.

She withdrew her hand and left him below the new-pricked stars, understanding something more about rulership, and rather less about love.

Sister,

I would rather we be together than entrust these words to you by messenger, a fallible man who may read or lose or take too long. But always has it been so, and so always have I put ink to paper and written regardless.

There is a bird haunting my dreams, sister. A great predator clutching the windowsill beside my bed, or standing at the center of my northern altar, talons scoring the granite so that it bleeds. The bird stares at me, stares inside me, and I ask what it sees, but its hissing words are in no language I understand. I think it is an earth saint, perhaps, in the guise of a tawny ghost owl. I shall ask the forest when I pass through, for we are soon to Errigal Keep.

Connley Castle and the surrounding lands are secure. My husband sent runners to every village and town, to the star towers along the coast, and to his retainers near Brideton especially, darling sister. Be sure to tell your husband. You will not catch us unaware.

If only they would settle between themselves by the trust in our hearts. Do you—

Gaela, I do not know if I can bear a child.

I cannot send this. Regan you cannot send this. I

❖    ❖    ❖

Sister—

We go to Errigal Keep soon, so send your next communication to me there.

Connley Castle is secure, and all our land. My husband sent runners to all our villages and towns, to the star towers along the coast, and especially to his retainers near Brideton. We will not be caught unawares by Astore, dear sister. But you must expect as much.

It is likely we will remain at Errigal until it is time to travel north for Midwinter, when you and I will meet again and finally become queens together. Keep our father if you like, or send him here, where it may do the Earl Errigal good to be forced to reckon with Lear's deterioration. Bracoch may join us, and I understand from Connley that Astore is heartily courting Glennadoer.

I have opened the navel wells throughout Connley lands, and I suggest you do the same in Astore, no matter your apathy. It is the best way to Glennadoer's heart, for that family has always bled like wizards.

There is an owl haunting my dreams—a great, tawny ghost owl that must be a messenger or an earth saint. Connley's cousin Metis told me of a stag that lay down along the Innis Road the same afternoon as the Zenith Court, its branches of antlers pointed toward the center of the island. Write to me if you hear of other such things, that the island is waiting for us.

I have written to Elia. I hope you are correct that she will find it in her to stand as we bade her stand, and not give in to the will of a different king.

                              Yours above all, sister-queen,
                                        Regan

# REGAN

Regan, Lady Connley, almost-queen of Innis Lear, stood naked but for a thin white shift hanging off her shoulders and down just past her knees. It brushed her hips, her small belly, the tips of her breasts, dappled by early morning shadows that cut like lace through the canopy of the White Forest. She wore no paint nor jewels, no slippers, and her brown hair fell free in soft waves. Her eyes fluttered under closed lids, her mouth relaxed in a low, gentle prayer in the language of trees.

She greeted the forest, saying her name and her mother's name, and the names of her father's mother and grandmothers, then a litany of favored earth saints. On long, bare feet, Regan walked over mossy rocks to the edge of a creek. Crouching, she touched the water, listening to the reply of the trees.

*Welcome, beautiful witch. We know you.*

This was the realm of Brona Hartfare, but Regan had come to use the power of the White Forest without the help of Brona; the woman had tried before, to no avail. The babe Regan had lost last month was the culmination of the elder witch's best efforts. Everything going forward was up to Regan herself. And produce a child she must: the future of Innis Lear depended on it, as well as her relationship with Connley. He loved her, but if she did not bear the next ruler, he would focus all his determination on taking the whole island from Astore. And he would not care if Gaela was lost in the process.

Connleys had once been kings, and he'd see it so again, one way or the other. It worried Regan, as much as it inflamed her, his noble rage and confidence the sunlight to her darker, inconstant shadows. They would merge and unite into a glorious dawn, but to protect her family, it must be through Regan's issue. Her husband insisted. *At Midwinter, you must earn the blessing of the island over your sister, which should be simple. You are the queen of the island already—you hear its voice, you bleed with its holy rootwater. There is no other way.*

*I do not want to take it from my sister.*

*At the cost of what, Regan? Always waiting for Astore to rise up, for Gaela to be restless and bite, to wipe my name from history, without our own blood to give this land life. And what of your dreams? Perhaps when you are queen, when you are the star-ordained and island-blessed queen, the rootwater and stars will give us a child. Have you thought of that?*

Regan had not, though she saw that Connley had for a long time been convinced. She'd not thought he kept anything secret from her. She said, *Let me have this time, then, to get with child again, to show you I can, that I will. Before the Longest Night.*

He had agreed, but he insisted they come to Errigal Keep, for Connley to treat with the earl and secure the long-held alliances between their families. In preparation for war against Astore, just in case the tides turned. Or even as guard against invasion, if Elia bent as he assumed she would. They already had Glennadoer with them, as Connley history demanded, and they would do best to remind Errigal of this loyalty.

This land of Errigal's was a barren landscape, raw with iron. Regan worried at her chances of conceiving here at all, much less carrying a child. Yet, it was just beside the White Forest, the most pure of heart of the island: in some places the trees leaned together so ancient, groping, and thick, no star or moonlight ever shone upon the churning black earth. Things unknown to the stars might be born here. And that ancient star cathedral waited somewhere inside it, ruined and alone. If Regan could find it, and uncover the holy well, perhaps that rootwater could restore her womb. Perhaps her dreams would bring peace instead of urgency or despair.

There had to be something she could do, that no healers or witches had heard of before. If she was an ally of the rootwater, the forest should tell her.

Regan stepped into the cold creek, relishing the shiver as her thighs tingled with raised hair and her spine chilled. She knelt, her knees parted enough to welcome the water inside her. No sun pierced through the arcing boughs of the oak spread over this narrow section of creek: all was shadow. Regan buried her hands in the water, digging into the silt and pebbles below. Tiny fish darted away, and she heard the call of a frog. The voice of the great oak mingled with the wind and he said, *This is a cleansing place, daughter. Welcome.*

*Take away my impurities,* Regan replied, splashing water up onto her face. It dripped down her neck like icy fingers, spotting her shift so it stuck to her collar and breasts. The creek water pressed around her hips and at her belly, finding the curves of her bottom and tickling the soles of her feet.

For a moment, she wished she'd brought Connley here to bury his seed deep inside her, under this oak and in this creek.

Regan dragged her hands up her thighs, pulling the wet shift high. One hand moved up to press between her breasts, over her heart. The other slid into the darkness where her pleasure lived. She opened herself with her fingers, whispered coaxing words to the forest, calling on the Tree of Mothers, the Bird of Dreams, and the Worm of Saints. Bending over herself, Regan shook and gasped, never stopping her prayer, until she rattled with passion and her words were hoarse, hissed in the language of trees and sounding exactly like wind through branches, on long moorland grass, against the rough peaks of the mountains. It was a plea pushed through her teeth, heavy with desire and love and longing.

Regan became more than she was: a piece of the forest, with roots and branches for bones, vines of hair, flowers where her lips should be, lichen hardening her fingers, and a black-furred bat unfurling its nighttime wings inside her womb. It fluttered and scratched, then shrieked as Regan shrieked, spilling her magic and her delicious pleasure into the creek, into this vein of the island.

Water covered her body as she stretched on her back, only her lips and nose and eyelashes above the water, and her toes. She was river rocks, around which the creek slid, shaping her smoother, polishing her skin to a luminous brown-gray.

*Tell me where to find the forest's navel well,* she said, her voice echoing in her skull beneath the sound of water. *Or tell me how to see what is wrong with me, I ask you, roots of my mothers, trees and birds of this island, please, that I may bear a child who will love you, rule you, and be yours in return.*

*Ban!*

Regan frowned. The name sounded sharp in the language of trees.

Was this her answer?

*The Fox is coming.*

*Beneath our branches, in the shade of our voices.*

*Iron and smoke, teeth and longing.*

*The Fox!*

Regan sat abruptly. Water sluiced off her, and she got onto her hands and knees, crouching. She stared all around at the blue-green-gray light, at the trees and bold late flowers crawling up toward the sunlight, embracing some linden and rough ash nearby. Three bluebirds danced, teasing each other; a squirrel chittered at her; there a flash of shadow from some other silent bird, a ghost owl, she thought; a soft buzz of insect life. Neither fox nor man to disturb her solitude. Then—

Flickering pale gray.

She stood, watching a line of several moon moths fly southwest, toward Errigal Keep. Too many to be natural, and as she studied them, three more arrived, flitting down from the canopy like snow.

Regan climbed out of the creek and the water painted her linen shift to her body, an earth saint rising from summer sleep. Quickly she took up the long jacket she'd arrived in, sliding her damp arms into the sleeves, pulling up the hood around her heavy wet hair. She left her leather-soled slippers here, nestled in moss, and followed the moths in silence.

They led her on a brief, easy path away from the oak and the creek, toward a clearing that sloped between two gnarled cherry trees.

A man stood in the center, his back to her, his shirt discarded with his sword belt and short black jacket. Scars etched his tan skin, carving his muscles into war-strong weapons. Sweat glistened in the curve at the small of his back. His hair was half in tiny braids.

Two dozen moon moths, white and creamy gray, perched upon his shoulders, and he allowed it, remaining still as a deep-rooted tree. They gently brushed their wings up and down, bestowing tiny kisses. Like he was an earth saint, too.

So the forest had answered her.

Regan smiled as he tilted his head, listening to the moths. This young man was a witch. She pushed the great hood off her head so the cool forest air could kiss her wet hair.

Ban turned in one smooth motion. Half the moths rose on a breeze, fluttering around his head; the others remained clinging to his skin, and flourished their wings.

This was the Ban Errigal she only remembered as a scrap of a bastard child, loving her baby sister. Now grown handsome in a wild, tight way, like a hungry wolf prince. One arm slowly streamed blood from a slash just above the elbow.

Ban the Fox, they called him at the Summer Seat.

Ban the Fox, who was beloved of the forest.

Ban the Fox was her answer.

*Lady Regan,* he said softly in the language of trees.

*Ban . . . the Fox,* she replied in the same.

The cherry trees all around them giggled, dropping tiny oval leaves like confetti.

"You're a witch," he said, awed, "as well as a soon-to-be queen."

"And you a soldier as well as a witch."

He bowed, unable, it seemed, to take his eyes off her.

Regan glanced again at the mantle of moths he wore, sending her own few to alight on his shoulders.

Shrugging as if their tiny feet tickled, Ban said, "They bring a message from my mother. She reminds me I've been home weeks, and not visited her."

For a moment Regan peered at him, as if he were a trick of the White Forest, and then she remembered: "Brona Hartfare is your mother, and I was near when you were born, for my sister Elia was born that same day, while both our mothers resided at the Summer Seat."

A thing shuttered his eyes, though he did not even blink, when she mentioned Elia's name. All instincts urging her to slice into that, Regan stepped forward. "You and Elia were childhood lovers."

The moths burst off him, though Regan did not note even a twitch or shift in his posture. He said nothing, holding her eyes with his.

"I only meant, young Ban," she soothed, "that once my little sister trusted you, and so would I now."

He swallowed, barely, and glanced down her body to the water still glistening at her ankles. "You aren't wearing shoes."

"I was in the stream, just north of here, begging the forest to lend me aid. The old oak who drinks from that stream said your name, the answer to a question I didn't know to ask."

"What is wrong?" Ban stepped nearer to her, the youthful concern in his frown and pulled brow a contrast to the reactions Regan usually garnered from men.

In answer, Regan joined him at the center of the cherry grove and knelt upon a tuft of short, teal-gray grass, flaring her coat around her like a skirt.

Ban sank to his knees. "Tell me what I can do, my lady."

Regan held her hands, palms up, to him, and he slid his against hers. The pocket between their palms warmed, filling with a tingling spark.

"We are suited," Regan said, giving him her kindest smile. One she rarely practiced in the mirror, for lack of necessity. "Both of long, powerful bloodlines rooted to Innis Lear."

He nodded, fingers curling about her wrists.

She noted how roughly attractive he was, again, this near and with his lips parted, the muscles of his chest taut. At least five of his scars were put there for magic. There was an untamed, informal note to the crease of his mouth, the haphazard braids, the thick bands of muscle. The bed of Regan and Connley never had required elegance. His wildness would complement theirs. She said, "I would like to continue my bloodline, Fox, but cannot carry a child well enough that it survives."

Here her voice hitched, and she allowed it.

"I'm sorry," Ban murmured. "My mother—she has tried to help?"

"Yes, but only with conception and enhanced potency. I need now to dig into myself, to see deep enough I might understand how to fix myself. And Brona will not go into me like that; she would not risk my life as a man might."

The young wizard leaned away, though he did not try to let go of her hands. "I do not . . . I will not go inside you."

"My husband would destroy you if you tried, Ban Errigal," she said, "and I would help him. That is not what I meant." Regan smiled her most dangerous smile, as she found it very telling what he assumed.

Ban cleared his throat. Wind shivered in response, whispering all around them: *good good good,* for the trees of Innis Lear approved of this alliance. "You don't seek power, either, then? For Brona is that—powerful."

"You are rooted with magic, but not only to Innis Lear?"

"I allied with Aremore forests," he answered simply.

"And you are iron. You are." Her nails dug at the soft insides of his wrists. "You are forged unlike me, unlike your mother. I would reap your insight, your ideas. Your power."

His chin lifted: pride at her words. Regan hid her own tiny smile of triumph in favor of a quiet, pleading frown. "Help me, Ban the Fox."

In reply, he bowed over their joined hands, turning them to kiss her knuckles.

# THE FOX

BAN EMERGED FROM the cool cover of the White Forest at the side of Regan Connley. His heart raced, more hare than fox.

He continually glanced at her from the corners of his eyes; she smiled knowingly. Her fingers at the edge of his sleeve were cool and bare, and she wore now a dark red over-dress and leather slippers they'd fetched from beside the creek. She was slightly taller than he, and six years older, and beautiful like the sun on winter trees. As he glanced at her, a small, fluttering sigh escaped her lips. Although Ban knew—absolutely knew—it was an affectation, he felt an answering flutter at the base of his spine.

Meeting her as he had, both of them nearly nude, and her glistening with water in a sleek white shift, with magic sparking in the air and sliding between them back and forth, it was no wonder he felt the bite of infatuation. At least he could recognize it.

And Regan had asked for his aid.

She'd appeared to him like the spirit of an elegant ash tree, an earth saint of old, a witch. And, Ban thought, a queen already. When he stood beside her, the unsettled roots of Innis Lear seemed to calm. Despite everything, it calmed him, too.

Once they'd both retrieved their discarded clothes, once Regan had swiftly wound her wet hair into a low knot, and once she had helped to bind the wound still glistening on his shield arm, Ban asked her why she and her husband had come to Errigal.

"To visit your father," she said.

He steadied his hand under hers as she stepped over a scatter of rocks pressing up through the path. "To assure yourselves of his allegiance to Connley, you mean."

Regan smiled quickly, then it vanished. "Is it strong?"

"From what I know, yes."

"He was distraught when we arrived this morning. I left my husband with him, as Errigal said something about his son's betrayal? He must not mean . . . you?"

It was simple to put grief and unease on his face, both being what he felt. "My younger brother, Rory, the one not a bastard. He was discovered to harbor a desire to be earl sooner than my father is like to die, and . . ."

The lady's fingers curled around his wrist. "I am so very sorry, Fox."

"I was out in the forest, hunting after his trail." Ban shook his head, looking down. It was half-true, for last night he'd pointed Rory in the direction of Hartfare, where he could find shelter. Then Ban returned home, to lie to his father that Rory had fled. Errigal's rage and grief had been wild, and this morning before dawn, Ban had left his still-drunken father, to lead several parties of men out hunting Rory's trail. It had been no difficulty to whisper at the trees and ask a handful of crows to divert them all from any path that had his brother's trace. By the sun's zenith, they'd all split off, and Ban was alone. He took the opportunity to sink into the forest, to give some blood to the roots of the trees and say hello. Messages had arrived from his mother, on the wings of moths and kisses of wind. Then Regan had come.

"Did you find him? Did he give you that wound on your arm?" she asked.

Ban nodded, though he'd done it himself, knowing how to cut to make it seem enemy-inflicted. He sighed to make his voice breathy. "We fought, but he got away, running."

Regan paused to touch his cheek where Ban had used his long knife to flick some drops of blood.

She smoothed her thumb down his rough jaw, then continued on.

Together they walked out over the moor toward Errigal Keep, past the iron chimneys. Their linked hands stretched between them. At the gate to the Keep, a bloodred flag for Connley had joined the winter blue banners of Errigal.

Ban needed to make a report for Morimaros.

But first, he would meet the duke, and lie to his father.

He escorted Lady Regan through the ward and into the old great hall, but that was not where the duke and earl were to be found. No, they'd retired to the former library, which had been Errigal's study since his wife returned to her family some ten years ago.

The small windows overlooked the northernmost, narrowest section of the ward, from the rampart wall and up the rocky, barren mountain toward sheer blue sky. It was stark and beautiful, and very much emblematic of the iron backbone of Innis Lear.

Errigal slumped in his large chair beside the hearth, where a massive fire danced and snapped. A wide cup of wine was cradled in his lap; Errigal shook his head and muttered quietly. Connley stood at the windows.

When Ban and Lady Regan entered, Errigal hardly twitched, but Connley turned immediately.

The duke was a tall man, though not broad, with a fine posture and a gleaming wardrobe, several years older than Ban. Sunlight from the window brought out the rich gold in his hair and highlighted a break in his long nose, found the sharp corner of his lips. Connley wore no beard, and needed none—with such a charming smile he would wish nothing to hide its edges. Though striking already, the cut of his red velvet tunic only made the duke seem more bold, a daring figure with gold and jewels across his chest, at his belt and on his fingers, and in small chains around the ankles of his boots. The duke's sword rested in a strapped sheath that did not protect the blade from wear, but showed off the shine and perfection of its steel. Ban judged him both proud and dangerous, recalling stories of Connley's cold temper: anger or betray him, and your life would end swift and sudden. Loyalty, it was said, held together Connley bones.

Having him here would surely help Errigal turn entirely against Rory, though also make this game a more deadly one for Ban's brother. He would have to work hard to keep Rory far away from the duke's reach.

Ban bowed then, his scrutiny complete; Regan strode across the wooden floor toward her husband.

In his arms, she became as shining and perfect as the sword at his side. Not a witch, but a sleek weapon for drawing rooms and the great hall, a perfect halberd nailed to the wall as the promise of penalty, the seductive weight of implied violence. The duke kissed her lightly on the mouth, and Ban thought of her trouble carrying a child. It must weigh heavily on both of them. He would help, if he could, for it would not interfere with Morimaros's plans. He tried not to wonder at his own motives.

Regan turned in Connley's arms to say, "Here is Ban the Fox, my love. He escorted me out of the forest."

"Ah, Ban!" Errigal lurched to his feet before the duke could speak, dropping the cup of wine. "Did you find that traitor, who was my son?"

"Sir," Regan said coolly, "your son here bleeds. I tended his wound as best I could, but it should be seen by your surgeon."

"Ban! Did the villain do that to you?"

It was easy for Ban to appear overwhelmed, trapped here in the middle of these three. Duke Connley stared at him with sharp blue-green eyes. Ban said, his gaze on Connley, but with words for his father, "He is responsible, sir, yes, but . . ."

Errigal's face went red under his beard. "That traitor! Ah, Connley, what a time for you to be here. And yet, I was right: I told you I was right to fear the worst. My own true son fled for treason—for plotting to do me harm!— and still here my natural son stayed behind, loyal and what! Injured for his brother's vile sake."

Ban clenched his teeth over his father's bloviating, but he fought to keep contempt from his voice and expression as he spoke. "I found him, Father, I found my brother and accused him—I could not help myself—and in- sisted he return with me. I said he must answer to you for what he wrote against you, and he said . . ." Ban shut his eyes as if feeling some inner pain. In truth, it was no acting: he felt that bite, though he had not expected to. Holding the king of Aremoria clear in his heart, Ban continued, "He said if I brought him home he would say it all came from me. He would put the invention to my name, and be believed—because Rory is your legitimate son and blessed by the stars, and I a bastard who hides under a dark sky."

"Oh, treacherous rogue," Errigal spat. "Let him fly as far as he likes; he will be found."

"Indeed," Connley said. "All our strength is for your use, Earl."

"I am sorry, Father," Ban said.

Errigal became suddenly woeful. "My old heart is cracking, I think. I know what the king felt, surely, when your once-sister denied him, Lady Regan. How merciful he was in his justified rage."

Ban turned his face sharply away.

It was Regan, a moment later, who put cool hands on his cheek, strok- ing tenderly. "There, young Ban," she said. "You have served your father well. The traitor deserves none of your pain."

He looked into her cool brown eyes, the color of shallow forest streams. "Thank you, my lady," he murmured.

Regan soothed him with a sorrowful smile. "Did your star-stained brother not spend this past season among the king's retainers?"

"He did," Errigal answered.

"Perhaps, then," the king's daughter said, "though I am sure it is no comfort, I can offer some reason: the king's retainers have become coarse and greedy under my father's tutelage. They likely put young Rory onto this idea, to get the revenue he would earn as Errigal upon your death for themselves."

Ban sucked in a quick breath. What a simple motivation the lady offered; he wished he'd thought of it himself. Lay the blame at the king's feet! He wanted to kiss her fingers, but he kept his gaze low so she did not notice his sudden glee. This daughter of Lear would help him ruin her father, whether she knew it or not.

She said, "Come, let me take you to whatever surgeon can see properly to your wound."

The duke caught her eye. She nodded, and Connley said, "Then, Ban the Fox, you must return. I've been discussing some matters of the future of this island with your father, but I think you should hear them. You've shown yourself true." Connley took his wife's hands off Ban, but clapped him on the back, asserting his approval. The duke's handsome face was too near to look away from without seeming weak or rude.

"It was my duty, sir," Ban said humbly.

Connley smiled. "For such loyalty, you will be ours."

Ban shivered at the layers of meaning to Connley's words. "I shall serve you," he said, bowing, "however else."

The duke released him, and Errigal poured himself and Connley more wine. Errigal shook his head again and again, and drunkenly sighed. "What cursed stars are trailing in our skies."

Again, Connley's and Regan's eyes met, and Ban nearly read the message they shared. It did not favor the stars, but bloodier desires. Regan offered her hand to him, and Ban leveled his breathing before taking it. He kissed her knuckles, his mind churning with ideas for how to help her. Perhaps there were some details of his plotting that should be left out of the report to his king.

For good or ill, this was the place Ban had landed.

# GAELA

GAELA CLIMBED OUT of her bed and flung a thin robe around her shoulders. Her face ached where her husband had hit her, keeping her from rest. The sky was dark, and Gaela's rooms even darker, lacking stars or candlelight. Her bare feet were cold as she stepped off the rug onto stone, slipping her arms into the sleeves and tying the robe securely at her waist. She lifted her hands to check the scarf tied over her hair remained firmly in place.

The Astore ruby ring gleamed on her finger, and Gaela cradled it as she went to the narrow window. Once an arrow slit, the sill was wide where she leaned, but narrowed to a bare hand-span. A long pane of smooth glass had been set into it, and Gaela beheld the small, dark courtyard from here, but it was impossible to see in from below.

She tilted her head to gaze at the velvet sky. She could make out no stars, and so the sky was a solid shade of purple-black. Did Regan stand under this same sky whispering angrily to the trees? Desperate to find her fertility? Or did she lie with her husband, enjoying the sweaty torment and cursing herself for taking pleasure in what refused to serve her?

There had been a wildness in Regan's eyes at the Summer Seat, though Gaela doubted any other noticed but perhaps—perhaps—Connley himself. It worried Gaela greatly. She'd seen that fanaticism in another face: their father's. Though they had always intended a joint rule, with Gaela the king and Regan mother to the next, Gaela now suspected that the sooner she consolidated her power and convinced Regan to give over the crown, the better for all. Curse Connley for agitating Regan, and Lear for declaring both his elder daughters equal heirs in his rash fury.

In the black courtyard below, a pale figure moved.

Behind him, two Astore servants trailed, recognizable by the color of their tunics.

It was her father, drifting like a ghost.

A thing tightened in her gut: irritation, fear? Gaela preferred the former, but the chill of the latter was undeniable.

Drowning it in a flare of ready anger, Gaela shoved her feet into fur-lined boots and pulled on a long linen tunic before replacing her robe around her. She picked up a knife and walked unflinchingly through the dark to the door of her chamber, swinging it open to the surprise of the dozing page awaiting any sudden orders in the night. The girl sprang to her feet and stammered a question at Gaela, who shushed her and ordered her to remain.

The prince swept past, an elegant, strong storm of vivid shadows and flashing pink wool.

A narrow stair led down to this small private courtyard, shaped like a long triangle with one corner bitten out. Some benches were stacked at the short end, and near the point an ancient well dropped through the foundation and rock, toward water far, far below. Once it had been a spring for intense root magic, and always had Regan collected bottles of it when she visited. Now it was capped off.

Gaela found Lear standing still beside that well, his head craned up to stare at the sky.

She joined him, ignoring his trailing servants. Clouds spread, obscuring the stars.

"You should be in bed," Gaela said, refusing to glance at her father's face. In this pit of a starless courtyard, he was the only pale moon.

"I cannot find Dalat!" Lear whispered.

Gaela jerked away. Her hand tightened around the knife. If he whirled too fast toward her, she could say he'd attacked. She could gut him, and say his mind was truly gone.

"Her stars aren't there anymore. What does this mean?" Lear sounded curious only, not panicked.

"Dalat is dead," Gaela said in a voice just as lifeless.

Lear turned his head. "She isn't supposed to die until your sixteenth birthday."

"That was twelve years ago, Lear."

"No, no, no," he whispered.

He seemed sane, despite the dark glint of this starless night in his eyes, despite the gnarled spray of his gray-and-brown mane. His gaze as he looked at his daughter was not wild, nor unfocused.

That was worse, Gaela thought, than if he'd been clearly lost to madness. But sounding rational, sounding calm—how deep did that mean his mind had fallen? If she killed him, if the servants hadn't been here, she could pry open the well and dump his body in. How would *that* be for a royal sacrifice to the rootwaters! She suspected even Regan would not argue.

"I haven't done it yet; the stars aren't right," he said. "So she can't have died."

"Done what?" Gaela cried, gripping him by the shoulder and thrusting the knife under his chin. "What did you do?" She'd known, suspected so long! And her father had never denied it, never defended himself.

Lear cringed away. Gaela held on, keeping him upright, as the servants rushed closer, one gasping, another rigid with censure. Let them be displeased or afraid. A king would not be judged. She slowly lowered the knife, dragging the cold blade against his neck.

"You look like her sometimes, firstborn," Lear said, frowning, in a voice of darker curiosity now. As if unaware of the knife, the danger to his person. "Except my Dalat was full of love; you've none."

"I loved my mother, and you destroyed that. If I have no love left, that is your doing."

"Yes, probably, mine, and our stars'. And these stars' . . ." Lear pulled free of her, and Gaela allowed it.

The old king sighed hard enough it shrugged his bony shoulders. He turned from his daughter, shuffling away on bare white feet. The servants dashed after, one—the younger—glancing back at Gaela with mingled shock and sorrow.

Gaela was left alone in the black courtyard. She sank onto the rim of the well. The rough black stone glinted with dampness, though the wooden lid was locked in place and it had not rained.

Silence blanketed her, and darkness, and Gaela wondered if it had been a dream.

# ELIA

THE QUEEN'S LIBRARY in Lionis took up the bottom three stories of the east-ernmost tower, a cheerful round room with more books, scrolls, and curi-osities than should have been available in all the world. Three half-moon balconies jutted out of the shelves at the second-story level, complete with small tables and cushioned stools for taking coffee. Elegant ladders lent access to all the shelves, even those spreading up past the second story, though of course it would be inappropriate for a high-born lady in a gown to climb such a thing. Aefa, though, and the queen's and princess's ladies, were often sent scurrying up like squirrels to fetch certain items when nec-essary.

Though many plush and low chairs were set about the main floor for reading, and several lounging sofas presented near the fire, all polished of light wood and pillowed with velvet, the Elder Queen Calepia and her daughter the Twice-Princess Ianta most often sat around the wooden table in the very center, casually discussing news and court dramas; sometimes with visitors or guests but most often alone, content in their familiar space. Some-times they invited Elia to join them, but she preferred most mornings to perch instead with Aefa on one of the balconies, visible but not quite available.

Elia cupped her coffee and breathed in the rich, bitter smell. Two days into her Aremore exile, she'd received a gift of it from a Third Kingdom trader who wished her to remember his name. *To give you a taste of home,* he'd written, not realizing it would hurt her to her core, because Innis Lear was her home, not the floodplains and deserts of the Third Kingdom.

That was the seed of her disagreement now with Aefa: they argued with pointed whispers over how Elia should handle the constant deluge of notes and letters from Aremore people approaching her. Aefa could not see any reason to refuse a visit with the coalition of foreign traders taking place to-morrow at their meeting hall near the harbor. Elia did not see the point.

She wanted to go home and couldn't bring herself to care about anything else as much as everyone around her seemed to.

"Only some of the traders are from the Third Kingdom," Aefa said again.

Elia gripped the delicate cup in her palms. "But they are the most dominant, you know it. It would be a meeting with so many of them. I'm not . . . them. And I am not ready for their expectations."

"They might be part of your mother's family, you can't know! What if they would help you? Broker something to convince Morimaros not to be rash? You said yourself he did not *want* to invade us." Aefa spoke fast and harshly, to keep her voice from growing in pitch. It had happened yesterday: her inadvertent exclamation had drawn the Elder Queen and Twice-Princess's attention, thus ending their ability to converse unwatched for the afternoon.

"Aren't you curious to meet them?" Aefa insisted.

"Are you?"

"Yes!" Aefa laughed in disbelief. "Wildly. I've never been closer to them than the time we rode past Port Comlack when one of their ships was at the docks."

Elia recalled that afternoon: her father had rushed them on, promising there was nothing but painful memories to be had in visiting with Dalat's people. Merely the drop of her name hurt, and so Elia had believed him. Kayo did all the negotiating for Lear when it came to the Third Kingdom.

"What of the Alsax then, will you see them?"

"They are related to Errigal, involved in the iron trade," Elia said rather darkly.

Aefa heaved a sigh. "You aren't shunned, Princess. You can have guests and friends. And family."

Elia bit her lip, thinking of how many Lionis courtiers treated her: as if they knew who she was only because of how she appeared. That her brown face marked her personality, marked her desires and humor. She'd never dealt with such things on Innis Lear. As silly as it sounded, at home she'd only been an oddity, an easily identified princess, a girl isolated, true—but by her family situation, not the people. She was their princess, and she desired what they desired, found amusing what they did. Here in Aremoria, a weight of political history had convinced the people they knew what she was before she acted or spoke, despite knowing nothing true about her except her name and looks.

Aefa did not, quite, understand. Nobody looked at Aefa as they did Elia.

Could she even imagine trying to be queen here?

"My sisters would be furious, Aefa," she said, her forever excuse.

Aefa's eyes narrowed, recognizing it.

"I'm not ready to earn their ire." Tentatively, she reached out and touched Aefa's bony wrist. That quieted her friend, who was unused to such physical affection from Elia.

She set down her coffee. It had been four days since her dinner with Morimaros, and three since she'd written to her sisters. They would be getting the letters today, or soon.

*Sister,* she'd written, copying the same letter twice, careful not to alter a single word and set her sisters to thinking she schemed between them. *I remain wife only to myself and to the stars, and negotiate with Morimaros of Aremoria for the independence of Innis Lear. He sees the fractured nature of our government as a weakness, and not one he necessarily wishes to exploit, but one that by nearness makes his own country vulnerable. He is convinced, for now, to peace, but it is only temporary: so long as our father runs mad and nothing is settled between us all, his threat will hang over us. I trust this king not to be overly combative or hawkish, unlike his council, but his patience toward the cracks our father created will not last forever.*

*Send our father to me, here, to await Midwinter with me. Allow me to tend to his age and mind, while you both adjust to your new roles and strengthen Innis Lear. End the fighting between your husbands, and force them into accord, either divided or together. Show me and this king there is hope for a strong, independent Innis Lear.*

Their answers would tell her much about their intentions.

"Lady Elia!" called the Twice-Princess Ianta from below. "Come join us!"

Grateful to put an end to this discussion, Elia nodded to Aefa, who bent over the balcony rail to wave affirmatively.

Elia gathered herself and her cup of coffee, and followed Aefa into the narrow hall between bookshelves, to make their way down the even narrower spiral of stairs to the main floor.

At the round table, the Elder Queen and Morimaros's sister sat, drinking spiced, hot milk from their pearl-rimmed mugs.

Calepia, like her son, presented an excellent example of straight shoulders and thoughtful, irrefutable authority. She wore the red and orange and white of Aremoria almost exclusively, with silver bracelets beaten wide, armorlike, to remind any who approached that she was yet a force of the law. Gray filtered through her rich saffron hair, and instead of covering it with veils or circlets as would most women, she had her ladies wind in white and silver ribbons, putting an accent on her age and making her hair all the crown she needed. Again like her son, her pink mouth was generous and soft when unperturbed.

The daughter, Ianta, had not inherited that mouth, nor the smooth sun-kissed skin. She was paler and less gorgeous than her mother and brother, narrower in face and expression but also rounder in body, with a happiness and prosperity that spilled out of her in ready laughter and fleshy confidence. She seemed comfortable in her natal roles—mother, sister, daughter—as much as she had pacing the marble floors of the throne room. Ianta could defeat even Gaela in presence, Elia often thought, though it would be like a clash between natural seasons: smiling, full-petal summer against bloody, crisp, martial autumn.

Elia bowed her head to Calepia, and smiled good morning to Ianta.

They bade her sit, and she did. Aefa took up a maid's position near the door.

The Elder Queen began a charming story of her children when they were young, fighting over a single slim volume of animal poetry from the Rusrike. It had been a simple war of one hiding it from the other, until found and hidden from the opposite. Ianta had kept it the longest, for she hid it inside her dress, straight down the back, both to help her sit straight and because she knew her brother would never presume to search her clothing as she wore it. Finally, Mars had negotiated for the location, offering up the greatest prize of all: his willing defeat. In giving up, he'd regained the book, and though all the courtiers amused by their antics knew he'd admitted his loss, he held his chin up and tucked the book under his pillow. Calepia laughed lightly, nostalgic with love. "He always was the best strategist."

"Win the war, never the battle," Ianta said, in the tone of one who's heard it many times before.

Elia hid the tightening of her smile behind a sip of coffee; the story seemed a threat, though Elia was certain if one looked constantly for such things, they would be found. She couldn't tell if the Elder Queen meant her story as a warning, or only offered it up as a way for a potential daughter to learn more about her maybe-future husband.

Likely, it was intentionally both. Everyone connected to a crown played games; that was the nature of it, she was learning, and so Elia needed only discern who played them for power, and who for love.

"My Morimaros would say this, frequently," Calepia explained to Elia.

"Mars's and my father," Ianta added. She paused, then spoke again. "My brother told me you read his birth chart for him at the Summer Seat."

"I did."

"How delightful. We don't have them done in Aremoria anymore. Or"—she winked—"we aren't meant to."

The Elder Queen said, "Your father himself taught you prophecy and the stars?"

"He did. My father was his father's third son, and he spent his youth preparing to be a star priest. It was not his preference to leave the chapels and rule, but one does what one must for family and country."

"And then he used his influence to rebuild the domination of the stars under his crown," Twice-Princess Ianta said. "To overthrow the earthly ways of your ancestors."

Calepia answered with a wry note, "There must be some benefits to becoming king."

Elia glanced up, wary of being tested. But Calepia's attention was on her daughter, and the two Aremore ladies shared some private humor.

"Tell me of my son's stars," Calepia said.

Elia hesitated briefly. "His Lion of War is a glorious but lonely birth star."

Calepia made a strange purr of annoyance, then said, "My birth chart gathers dust in a corner of my treasury, inked in gold and set with some tiny rubies. It's rather more worth its weight in jewels than usefulness, here."

"What were you born under, if I may ask?" Elia said.

"The Elegance," the queen said with a suggestion of hidden pride in the corner of her mouth.

"A star of resolution," Elia said, digging through her memory for more. "And diplomatic promise. Do you know what the moon was?"

"I don't remember." Calepia sipped her spicy milk, eyeing Elia over the decorative pearls. Elia did not press.

"I had my holy bones cast once, at a festival," Ianta said. "Do you do that?"

Elia shook her head. "The holy bones are the most direct connection to the wisdom of earth saints, and my father forbids them in his court."

"In Aremoria, girls will play spinning games where you turn in circles the same number of times as years you are old, then stop and pick out the first star you see, and that is the star of the boy you're meant to marry."

Smiling, Elia said, "I have seen girls say a boy's name the same number of times as it is days since the full moon, then toss stones to see what constellation they fall into, for the same outcome. It is not such things my father dislikes. He minds nothing that comes only from the stars. It is seeking signs in the shape of a flock of geese or in the scatter of autumn leaves that he believes . . . taints the perfection of star prophecy." Once, Elia had been quite skilled at throwing the bones, thanks to Brona Hartfare, but she'd not owned a personal set since her father discovered her huddled in a corner of the winter residence at Dondubhan when she was twelve, giving secretive readings to a handful of his retainers. He'd forbidden her the bones because they were low and filthy, but the incident had begun their more serious star lessons together. She said, "Father disbelieves anything that is only a reflection of stars—like the cards—could offer true providence."

"And do you believe in the providence of star paths, Elia Lear?" Calepia of Aremoria asked evenly, without judgment.

Elia opened her mouth; the answer was not forthcoming. She was wary of seeming a superstitious fool to these ladies. Though they were kind, they also were vetting her, since their son and brother clearly wanted her for a wife. They would wish to know if Elia could be convinced or compelled to give up the stars if she married Morimaros. There was no state religion in Aremoria any longer, none but king and country.

But Ianta answered first, in a wistful tone. "It has always seemed to me that the moon is a powerful creature. When I look at her, no matter her shape, I feel something." She touched a hand covered in rings over her heart. "Perhaps a power pulling me down my path."

"Perhaps," the Elder Queen said, "you feel something born in your own self."

"That is what my brother would say. He thinks the sky too distant to know what's best for us," Ianta told Elia.

Elia nodded. "I once knew someone who would argue that the roots of trees or the leavings of cows are closer to knowing our destinies than the cold stars." She wondered where he was at that moment, what he was doing. How he worked to keep his promise.

Ban.

She could at least think his name now, surely, without suffering.

Ianta laughed bright and hard. "Ha! I should like to meet this friend who thinks of cow shit as a divining tool."

"I think . . ." Elia folded her hands. "I think that the stars might see farther than we can imagine. Maybe when we're born they do see how we will die, or how, overall, we will conduct our lives. Like a shepherd on the top of a mountain can see how the flock turns in the valley below. But it is the hounds and children nipping at the heels of the sheep that determine the immediate way. So we must make our own choices, and consider the stars only advisors. Not judges or rulers."

"Wise, child," Calepia said.

From the door, Aefa said angrily, "Would that your *father* were wise *before* he was old."

All three ladies at the table glanced at Aefa, who stood with her fingers laced against evil prophecy. The girl raised her nose in the air unapologetically, but her defensive posture cut hard into Elia. Aefa was right. And Elia wanted to scream suddenly, to clutch her stomach and bend in half, to hit something. To shake her father until he took it all back.

Elia gripped her cup of coffee so hard it trembled and spilled over onto the polished table.

She gasped, and the women turned back to her; she wanted to scream even louder. Her face burned and her jaw ached from clenching. She thought she should apologize, but her voice would not agree.

"Oh, saints, Elia," Ianta said, thrusting herself to her feet and pointing at a boy in the orange lion tabard of the palace. "This calls for something stronger than milk. Fetch three—no, four—glasses, Searos." With that, Ianta swept up her layers of red skirts and made for the nearest library shelf.

Elia and Aefa stared, but Elder Queen Calepia only leaned against her straight-backed chair and drawled, "She's thrilled, Elia. My daughter has been near bursting with wondering when you'd finally thin out that incredible armor you wear around your heart."

"I'm sorry," Elia whispered, braced for disdain or disappointment.

"Apologizing!" Ianta cried from the shelf, where she was moving piles of leather-bound books to dig behind them. "It's been weeks! I didn't know if I would have to fill you with wine and start asking terribly pointed questions. Mars has said many things, and all of them made me want to wrap you up in pillows and silk quilts to keep you from further harm."

Calepia said, "Daughter."

Ianta spun around with a long bottle in hand. "Cherry brandy."

"Oh, no," Elia whispered.

"Oh, yes," Aefa said. "You need it."

Elia met Calepia's eyes.

The queen gave her a soft, sorry smile. "Ianta, Elia is safe here, and we know it, but how is she to know it? How is she to trust us when everything she trusted before was taken away?"

Though the queen directed the words at Ianta, she watched Elia, and Elia knew they were for her.

"You are safe here, Elia Lear," Calepia said.

Safe.

These ladies offered safety to her as Morimaros did: like conquerors. Elia could accept it, sit here in their extended haven. *Safety.* But what would she be asked to exchange, what was the trade? Kindness and honesty were easy things to give when you were secure. Promises were *safe.* But safety was also inaction; it was a privilege granted, not won. Elia should've been safe with her sisters, yet she could not depend on it. Because they did not trust her— allow her—to be at ease with them, had not permitted her to share comfort. She had never been safe with Gaela and Regan, and they would never be on her side.

Admitting it, even for a moment, broke something open inside Elia, and it pushed out from her heart like a great wind. The hairs on her arms raised.

"Thank you," she said to the queen and her daughter. "I think I'll accept your brandy."

Ianta smiled large and rejoined them with her bottle, pouring it all around.

Elia sipped the sweet cherry brandy to cover the cold rain in her stomach. She asked, "What do you believe in, here in Aremoria, if you don't have stars or earth saints?"

The Elder Queen said, "Our king."

"Is he so . . . worthy of it?" Elia forced herself to ask.

Twice-Princess Ianta leaned toward her. "If he reunites Innis Lear and Aremoria, he will be considered the greatest king we've had in a thousand years."

Elia froze.

"That is how Aremoria holds faith," the Elder Queen said, more gently. "My husband's father, King Aramos, proclaimed an end to the crown's reliance on the stars or the land. He said we were stewards of the land, partners with it, not subject to it, and certainly not subject to the stars, which never suffer with us. He did not raze any chapels or close any caves or springs. He merely told the people they did not need to worship or sacrifice."

"It worked? The land . . . did not . . ." Elia thought to say *cry* or *rebel*.

"It worked. But Aramos did something else to unite everyone behind him: he gave Aremoria enemies. We had always had border wars; there has always been pushing and pulling against Ispania, Burgun, Diota, even the Rusrike at times—and of course, your own island. But Aramos made our enemies definitive. Instead of being Aremore because we live with this land, because our families always have, we are Aremore because we fight to keep Aremoria. We are Aremore because we are *not* Ispanian, Burgundian, Diotan, or Learish. Do you see?"

Elia did see, and was horrified.

By this, Morimaros had to invade Innis Lear, or lose a piece of what made him who he was. The golden king of Aremoria. Their destined leader. A would-be god to his people. And when Elia had asked, Mars had offered several strong reasons he should invade. Political and martial, and economic, even going as far as arguing that it would be the clear best choice for the future growth of Innis Lear. But he had not revealed this reason. This *destined* one. Draining the brandy, Elia clutched the cup and looked straight at Ianta. "In Morimaros's council meeting, did you urge him to invade my island? And was this why?"

Ianta lowered her cup. A tiny hint of brandy stained her bottom lip before she licked it away. "No," she said. "I urged him to marry you instead."

"He might do both."

Calepia nodded. "Indeed, if you let him."

*Why is it me who must allow or stop or end or choose?*

But the words did not leave her, for she knew the answer: it was because no one else would—or perhaps, no one else could. Her sisters chose long ago to make themselves rigid, and her father chose to give all to the stars. Morimaros had chosen his path in becoming king, and even Aefa had chosen, and would choose again, to stay with Elia and support her. Everyone was pointed in some direction, of their own choice.

Always Elia had been aimed and set by others. Accepted what was given, absorbed into their wills—especially, though not exclusively, her father's. She'd borne any consequence by detaching from her own heart, unwilling to examine her actions in case they might clash with the need to be still. Elia let the stars decide the course of her life, despite her bold words framing them as distant guides.

She was exactly like her father.

Elia stood and poured more brandy for herself. She lifted her cup. "To choosing for ourselves."

One of King Morimaros's soldiers appeared at the library door. He saluted crisply and murmured a message in the ear of the nearest lady-in-waiting. The lady passed it to the queen's ear, who then glanced at Elia with slight surprise. "You have a messenger come urgently from Innis Lear."

Already! It couldn't be from her sisters yet, unless letters had crossed. Had something happened? Worried, she set her cup on the table and turned to face the door. Before she could proceed, a travel-worn young man pushed in, one with reddish hair and a face more freckled than not. *Beloved of the stars.* "Rory!" she said, shocked. "Errigal. What are you . . ."

The heir to Errigal dropped before her, knees hitting the floor hard enough the sound echoed like a knock on death's own door. "Elia," he murmured, hands reaching out, eyes cast down.

She took his face instead, forcing him to look at her. Dread filled her heart. "Tell me what has happened."

Behind her, she heard Aefa quickly explaining that Rory was somewhat of a cousin to Elia: that she'd known him since they were babes, and he was as honorable as any man. Trust Aefa to be ready to defend against even a hint of censure cast on her princess. Though Rory was known to the court, as a cousin of the Alsax. Elia found it hard to focus on their words over the frantic beat of her heart.

Elia took Rory's hand. He was a good friend, and she'd seen him more frequently this past year than the last five, since he had come the retainers' barracks at Dondubhan, near where she'd studied at the north star tower. Rory was broad and handsome, freckles overwhelming his face like the most crowded arm of the firmament. His characteristic slouch was appealing instead of indolent, promising friendliness, not malfeasance.

But now he stared up at Elia, haunted. She reached for her cup of cherry brandy and offered it to him. He drank it all.

Beside Elia, Aefa thrummed with expectation but held her tongue. Elia felt herself calm, but it was a patience borne of dread.

"My lady," Rory said haltingly, then bowed to the Aremore royalty. "I . . . I apologize for interrupting." His short, yellow lashes brushed his cheeks, and he frowned mournfully, then opened his eyes and met Elia's. "My father has disowned me, El."

It was a sharp kick to her heart, and she clenched her hands together. "How did this happen?"

"Truly, I know not! I am betrayed, that is the only thing I am certain of. Ban came to me and said— Ah, god!" Rory shoved his fingers into his hair.

"Ban?" Elia prompted, avoiding Aefa's pressing eyes.

"Perhaps we should go elsewhere?" Aefa whispered, careful of the royal women at their back. Elia shook her head, her stare locked onto Rory.

The earlson said, "Yes, my brother, Ban. He came home from—well, from here, you might know—and he warned me that our father was furious at me, for some fault Ban had not yet discovered. I wanted to go to Father immediately, but Ban swore him to be unsettled and murderous, and entreated me to lay low for some time. I agreed, though only because Ban promised to calm our father's fury. I left to go back to my friends among the king's retainers, allowing Ban to stay behind to uncover and mend any transgressions in my favor. I planned to beg Lear for aid, as my godfather and liege—but my heart was weak, and I grew fearful thinking of your circumstance, that you might understand and give me shelter. The king had banished *you,* of all the truest, kindest ladies in the whole world! Why would he find sympathy for me if there was even a breath of possibility I'd scorned my own father? Ah, stars, Elia! What has changed our fathers so hard against us? A thing in the sky? Or a cause of the wind?"

The words poured out of Rory, fast and near incomprehensible, though she understood their core. She leaned forward and took Rory's large hands. His fingers were rough, his knuckles scarred and thick. Elia looked up at him. "I am so sorry."

And Aefa said, "Was it only the word of Ban Errigal that made you flee?

Only a promise from your brother?" Her voice was tight, and Elia knew what the girl was thinking: Ban had promised already to prove to Elia how easy it was to crush a father's love. And here was Rory, banished from his father's heart where previously Errigal had only words of pride and easy trust. Alarm rang in Elia's blood.

"Yes, my brother," Rory said wearily. "I thank my stars for him. Whatever the cause of my father's anger, Ban warned me, saved me, most like. He cared not that it would likely make him again the object of our father's wrath. A traitor! That my own father would believe it of me—of my stars."

How had Elia forgotten so easily the complete words Ban had spoken? Having been consumed instead by his exhortations, by his—his raw belief in her—she'd neglected to think on the objects of his rage, and passion, and pain. His fierce vow—in her name—to prove how fickle was a father's love, that Lear's madness was not a fault in Elia, but in the stars. That Ban would tear apart Innis Lear, as her heart had been wrecked.

*I keep my promises.*

If Ban Errigal was working against peace, Elia's simple letters to her sisters would be like whispers against a gale.

"Well, Elia?" Aefa demanded. Her tone drew Rory's attention, and he glanced between them, confused.

Holding her voice calm, too aware of the threat to Innis Lear in the form of the Aremore ladies, Elia addressed Rory as if he were in her command already. "You must remain here, for now. I am certain you will be welcome with me at this court, or with your Alsax cousins at their estate. For your own safety. If you have a death sentence on your head, you must be careful in how you address this, and I must be careful my sisters do not see your flight as a desertion."

He nodded, neck loose, mouth woeful. "What a disaster these stars have been. Elia, you should write to Ban, to see if there has been news."

Elia flicked a glance at Aefa, whose lips were pursed so tight they seemed a little pink bow. But they could not share any suspicions regarding his brother, not without breaking Rory's heart further or revealing weakness to the Aremore court. She would write to Earl Errigal himself, instead. There would be nothing bizarre about that, as he'd written her first, and she'd yet to reply. Perhaps she could mend the damage on her own, without wounding either brother more. "I will."

"Thank you," Rory said, then he flung his arms around Elia.

Because she knew not what else to do, Elia allowed him hold on to her as tightly as he wished.

BY THE TIME he was old enough to understand anything, Rory Errigal understood this: the best way to learn what mattered, in any place or among any people, was to make friends with the women. The oldest women, the youngest, and those with the most secrets. In Errigal Keep, Rory began with the kitchens, using his smile with innocent abandon, and repaying extra cookies and kindness with a willingness to sweep up messes and offer information about his father's schedule in return, and even once taking the blame for a broken cup that was his mother's favorite. The housekeeper had made certain Rory's punishment was mitigated as best she could. He moved on to his mother's companions next, instinctively knowing when to smile and bring them buttons they thought they'd lost, or mention how he'd noticed his mother admiring a particular shade of blue recently. He made himself beloved of the townsfolk, too, carrying little cups of holy water from the Errigal navel well to the homes of newborns, just because of how the families would cheer. And because they trusted him after.

He was an only child, the earl's son and heir, pride and promise of Errigal's future. It was easy for him to love, easier to be generous. What Rory had, he had in plenty enough that sharing cost him nothing.

Until the day his mother left, and Errigal brought Ban into his life.

That day, Rory finally understood some things could not be shared. Sharing was what drove his mother to Aremoria, to live with her sister forever. Rory had too many friends in the kitchens and rear halls, among the wives and children of Errigal's stewards and retainers, among the bakers and hunters and barrel makers of the Steps, not to hear again and again that his half-brother was a bastard. Discovering Ban's birth had offended Rory's mother so greatly, she refused to look upon Errigal's face or the stones of their home ever again.

He understood his father should not have shared this particular thing, because it hurt his mother, but all that was overshadowed by how entirely wonderful it was to have a brother.

Ban was older, smarter, quieter than Rory, and afraid of absolutely nothing.

For years, the two played at adventures together. Sometimes they snuck into the White Forest, where the spirits whispered secrets to Ban, and then Ban told Rory where to aim his arrows. Sometimes they hid together in the guard stations at the Summer Seat, peering through crenellations to search for sea monsters or an enemy army. Sometimes Ban convinced Rory to do wild things like leap into the deep black waters of the Tarinnish, and sometimes Rory had to punch one of the retainers' sons for calling Ban a bastard.

Rory thought for a little while that he was in love with the princess Elia, but it didn't take him long to realize his feelings were only a reflection of his beloved brother's.

The month every year all three were the same age fell in the early spring, and it was Rory's favorite. Ban and Elia had not yet had their anniversaries, so remained fourteen, but Rory's passed, letting him fly older like a loosed arrow to meet them. Errigal brought his two sons north to Dondubhan after the ice broke, to be with the king and journey to the Summer Seat together, not realizing it wasn't the chance to spend time among the king's retainers both boys longed for, but Elia. Though to be sure, Rory, at least, delighted in the soldiers just as much.

Since they'd seen her at the Midwinter festival, Elia had grown to exactly Ban's height, as Rory pointed out to them when the three dashed off early on their second morning together, across the moorland to the ruins of an old watchtower settled around the eastern shore of the Tarinnish. Ban frowned at Rory's declaration and stopped walking. Wind ruffled the dark water of the lake, and the first yellow flowers spotting the moor nodded. Then Elia put her toes against Ban's toes, her hands in his hands, and leaned in until the tips of their noses kissed. She blinked, and Ban blinked, and suddenly Rory felt terribly alone.

He flung his arms around them both to make up for it, and Ban, who'd stopped allowing Rory to push him around with his greater size years ago, released Elia to tackle Rory. They went down, wrestling hard and fast, until, as usual, Rory ended up on top. He laughed in triumph, and Ban growled like a cat. Elia said, "Oh, be careful," bouncing excitedly on her feet. She clutched the skirt of her dress.

Pride at his win made Rory blush, and he leapt to his feet again, rubbing dirt off his cheek. He stood before Elia exactly as she and Ban had stood, only Rory was taller and had to bend to put their noses together. She was beautiful and smelled like spice cakes and flowers, and her faded red dress was ever so slightly too small for her growing body, tight at her hips and little breasts. Rory knew why he felt as he did, knew what his parts were telling him, thanks to all those years of being friends with the women in the kitchens and the town, his familiarity with all manner of gossip and talk. And Rory also knew that it was just how the world worked, and he wanted to love his body and everyone's, because despite his parents' problems, or because of them, Rory remained generous.

And so Rory kissed Elia.

He kissed her, and he smiled, touching her face with both hands before stepping away. Elia stared, lips parted, and then her black eyes darted behind him toward Ban.

Rory glanced over his shoulder and saw perhaps the worst thing he'd seen in his entire life: Ban, his brother, still as stone, and staring at Rory as if the wind had frozen, the new-budding meadow flowers had withered, and the sun had turned black. As if everything Ban was or could be had been snatched away, and it was Rory's fault.

"Oh," Rory said, then grimaced. "Oh."

Ban did not move, nor did Elia.

Heaving a sigh of intense martyrdom, Rory said, "I don't have to do that again."

The words snapped Elia out of her daze. She touched her mouth, then touched Rory's chin. She said nothing, but her agreement was clear. Strangely, Rory didn't mind, because she smiled, and so they were still friends.

Elia walked to Ban. She took his hand, and put it against her heart. *You know,* she said in the language of trees.

Though she spoke to his brother, Rory knew also. He saw it suddenly in Ban's every breath: love and love and love.

It didn't break Rory; instead it seemed to knit something tighter inside him. Ban would be happy, and so Ban would stay.

With a smile and a merry yell, Rory grabbed up a flat stone and flung it into the lake. He marched along, toward the ruins, expecting they'd follow or not.

That night, after dinner and the king's Fool's fantastic recitation of a battle poem, one that Rory knew several verses to already, he followed Errigal when the earl retired. He very seriously, very earnestly, told his father that Ban and Elia would be a good match, that their babies would be iron strong and star bright. Errigal turned red but said nothing.

A few weeks later, Ban was sent to Aremoria.

Part

# THREE

# THE FOX

LAST NIGHT A crow had perched outside his too-narrow window, yelling bloody murder: Ban could no longer ignore his mother.

So he'd left before dawn, taking one of his father's lanky horses.

Once through the black gates of the Keep, Ban gave the horse her head, urging her up the rocky path toward the White Forest of Innis Lear. The horse leapt forward, eager to race, as if Ban's jittery energy translated through seat and saddle. Ban leaned forward, his cheek near the horse's neck, and they shot into the trees with a crack and slap of branches and yellowing leaves.

As Ban traveled, he built thin layers of emotional armor around himself, to perhaps hide from Brona all the hope and fury and fault that roiled darkly in his heart like gathering storm clouds. He knew himself to be an excellent liar, having spent years as the Fox, but as a boy, his mother had always seen right through him.

For a long while the horse made her own way along a deer path and then a creek bed, dashing then walking again, hopping over fallen branches, picking her way carefully over mossy ground. Ban only kept her nose pointed north and west, toward Hartfare.

Around them the forest woke, chirping and buzzing with the last of summer, the flies and bees and happy birds whispering a welcome to him. He murmured back to the rich shadows and voluptuous greenery: low ferns glistened with dew, moss and cheerful lichen climbed the trunks of the trees, and the thick canopy of leaves turned the light itself glassy green. Here, inside the White Forest, was the only place the island's roots still held any joy.

This was what needed most to be restored, once Lear's oppressive rule had ended, once his legacy was torn apart. The heart of the island would thrive, and its rootwaters spread to every edge once again. Ban would make it so himself, and Morimaros would allow it, because the king of Aremoria understood balance, and could be made to understand the workings of root magic on Innis Lear, even if there was no faith under his crown.

And it would be easy, if Ban's father's state was any indication.

Last night Errigal had wrapped his heavy arm around Ban's neck and said, "If it were not for the year between your birth and your brother's, I might wonder if some earth saint had not switched you in the night. You my true son, and Rory the cur he's proved himself to be."

"Peace, Father," Ban had said through clenched teeth. "You still do not know his true heart."

Errigal had thrust Ban away. "You keep defending him and I'll charge you as an accomplice, boy! Deny you both!"

"I am no accomplice, my lord, I only wish to find him." Ban touched the hilt of his dagger, for he wore no sword to dine with the duke and his lady. "It is hard to believe this villainy of Rory. Because he is my brother." It should have been what Errigal said: *I can hardly believe this of Rory, because he is my son.*

But Errigal only tore at his beard and cried, "What could brotherhood be to him, when fatherhood is so clearly insignificant?"

And Ban was forced to be silent, or spitefully call out his father's hypocrisy.

The duke of Connley had distracted Errigal with an argument on economics then, and putting men north, as close to Dondubhan as they could without directly challenging Astore. Regan added an elegant opinion here and there, reminding them it was Gaela they should avoid challenging. Ban had wished to leave, but the lady's eyes settled upon him, despite her attention to the arguing. He'd struggled to keep the truth of his anger off his face, to be only her wizard, showing no emotion more than mere irritation at his father's drunkenness. In the end, he lowered his gaze, afraid she would perceive too much.

Now, Ban thought again of her lovely, cool eyes, her grace, and what a dangerous presence she carried, what determination and poise.

It was disloyalty to Mars to even consider the idea, but Regan Connley, Ban thought, would make an excellent queen. Better than Gaela, who was a suit of armor, a blunt, deadly weapon, and better than Elia, who was not a weapon at all.

Though if anyone could manage to sharpen her into one, it was Morimaros of Aremoria.

In the forest, bluebirds fluttered in Ban's path, following him, and flickers of pale light caught his gaze as the moths returned, marking the forward path. Ban gave the horse's withers a friendly thump and pulled her back, angling her in the direction of his mother's village.

Hartfare was supposed to be difficult to find, except to those who understood the forest or could hear the language of trees. It was no den of outlaws, but a haven for people who did not fit in the towns and cities or keeps and castles of Innis Lear. Some were like Ban's mother, foreign in blood or clinging to the old earth ways; some had lost their homes and families; some had been otherwise unwanted; some made outlaws by political slant rather than malicious intent; some merely preferred the gentle heart of the forest and did not mind living close to the wilds and saints and spirits of the dead.

Ban had lived there the first ten years of his life, unaware of the reputation he'd been born into according to the greater world of men and kings. Hartfare was an adventure for any young boy, but unlike many there, Ban knew his father. Errigal had been a bright, blustery, frequent presence, rushing into Ban's life like a spring flood, then out again on a galloping steed. He'd been a handsome warrior, a laughing, loud nobleman who made Ban's mother laugh in turn, louder than any other. And like most children, Ban had assumed nothing would change, that always he'd be helping his mother in the garden, running with the other children after small game, or mushrooms and wild onions, up all night to listen to the creaking voice of the forest. That he and Brona would be a permanent duo, Ban growing into a natural extension of the witch of the White Forest, the shadow-lady of Innis Lear. He would always be her son, a witch he hoped himself, and Ban would then dream of his own shadow-names and power. It was Brona who drew attention and trade to Hartfare: Errigal and Errigal's like, bold visitors from every corner of the island, or more often sneaking men and desperate women who needed, begged, and paid for Brona's magic.

Then Queen Dalat had died, and soon after Errigal took Ban away from Hartfare, to live with the king's court under an open, starry sky. Brona had not argued. She'd cared more for the fate of Hartfare than his own. Though she'd loved her son, she'd not chosen him.

It had seemed, at least for a time, that Ban had been chosen instead by his brother, and by Elia. But they too had not cared to keep him close, had not fought against his banishment to Aremoria.

What would Brona see in Ban now? As a grown man, after so long apart? He still felt too much like a misbehaving boy dragging his feet. Was there any chance she would approve of him using his Learish magic in Aremoria? Would she be furious he'd waited weeks to come to her hearth? What might she be like now, with the island's roots so withdrawn and unhappy? Could he even trust his memories of her, as they were the memories of a child?

Ban put his shoulders back and pushed his cloak off his left shoulder to clearly reveal the sword strapped to his hip. It did not do to hide his weapon; only thieves and criminals—and spies—did not display what strength they held. His mother hadn't seen him in years, nor he her, but he could not bring himself to pretend. There was no point in slicking back his choppy hair or trimming it into harmony. No point but to relish the scars on his face and hands, the hard lines war and wariness had cut into his features at too young an age. Brona would see through any lies regardless, unless she'd lost that sharp acumen for judging men. He hoped not—it was why Ban had sent Rory to her in the first place. She would keep him safe no matter what news she had from Errigal Keep, because she'd see the blunt honesty and goodness in Rory himself. The glorious sun to Ban's wan moon, brothers separated as much by their birth as by their spirits.

*Ban Ban Ban,* said the trees. *You're home!*

They fluttered leaves, reached for him; they chided him for staying away and they sighed piteously because no one spoke to them anymore outside the forest itself. *The navels are gone!* they cried. *Our roots are thirsty, but only the witch feeds us. Only the witch loves us.*

*Lady Regan loves you,* he said.

The White Forest replied, *Regan, poor Regan, she needs us but she does not love us.*

*Both,* he said, frowning. *She needs you* and *loves you.*

The trees hissed and sighed. One whispered, *Elia,* and another, *Saints of earth,* but before Ban could find it, find that tree who said her name, the echo had vanished and all the forest sang together joyfully.

The Hartfare path appeared as if in a dream, at the edge of a narrow clearing and marked with several tatters of blue wool, as if strips of some dark sky had become caught in the reaching branches. Hardly more than a hunter's lane, but enough for the horse to recognize. The way to Hartfare, once found, lasted only a mile or so before spilling both horse and soldier into the village.

Ban slid off the horse and stood, amazed at how it had grown.

There were perhaps forty cottages, ten more than when he'd last been here. Some little huts for livestock, rows of gardens, and the public house, and his mother's herbary. It smelled and sounded as he remembered— splatter of mud, clang of metal, and his father's laughter and his mother's quiet singing; Brona smearing blood off his palm from a shallow gouge and saying a charm, something Ban could not quite remember, but it made him feel glad. The memories were as distant as dreams, but surely they were real because dreams would not smell like crushed flowers and shit.

His horse stomped her foot and shook her head so the tack rang against her neck. Ban patted her, murmured soothing nothings, and unlooped the reins. He brushed floating moon moths out of his way as he hobbled the horse, and while some eyes on his back prickled his awareness, he lifted off the saddle and blanket to rub her down quickly and let her loose to graze.

Turning, Ban spied two young women peering at him from the nearest cottage window, and an older man kneeling in a patch of long peas, studying him, too.

The road through the village was thick with mud, and a pack of hounds ran out, barking and braying, with a boy calling frantically behind. Ban put his hand on his sword and stomped at them, splattering mud. He did his best to smile at the boy, and let the nearest hounds sniff and lap at his gloved fingers, shove their long noses in his crotch, nearly knock him over. They smelled filthy and wet and terrible. But he liked rough, loud dogs.

The moths did not, and wafted high into the air.

The boy stared at Ban, or rather at Ban's sword, eyes brown like walnut shells and skin swarthy, marking him one of the clan from far south in Ispania, and so related distantly to Ban and his mother. Ban wondered if the boy was a bastard, too, and if his only hope was to join service as a retainer. He said, "After I speak with Brona, I'll show you to use the sword if you like," and the boy grinned gap-toothed and nearly tumbled over one of the dogs.

There were people *everywhere*. Ban strode faster, before there were more interruptions, before he lost his nerve.

The herbary where his mother lived and worked was built of wood and mud bricks, with fresh thatch from which some small tufts of pink flowers grew, despite the late season. The door was closed, but the square, squat windows were open, and Ban heard his mother's voice singing in the side garden.

It shook him to his boots, for she sounded so much the same he nearly forgot his own age.

"Mama," he said, not loud enough to be heard; more for himself, a reminder, a grounding. And when he spoke, some relief blossomed in his chest. With a growing smile, he strode around the corner and found her shooing some chickens out of her sweet pea vines.

At his step, Brona spun, black hair loose, skirts twisting at her bare calves. She held two small dark plums, waxy and ripe. They'd been his favorite as a boy.

"Welcome home," his mother said, offering the fruit.

Ban took one, but the moment his finger brushed hers, he dropped the plum, frozen.

She was as imposingly lovely as he remembered.

Brona wore her waves of black hair loose and only a thin sleeveless shift hanging off one tan shoulder as if she'd just been awakened, though it was very late in the morning. Her skirts clenched at a waist caught like a bridge between heavy breasts and heavy hips. Red flushed her cheeks and her mouth; her eyes were dark and wet as the mossy forest outside. Horn and amber beads hugged her wrists and bare ankles. The tops of her feet were mud-speckled, and her toes vanished into the grass. She was exactly as Ban remembered, unbound and free, made of the very earth; the memory was a visceral wave of delight followed by the hot awareness that he could see her now the way his father must have. When he left he'd only been a boy and had only a son's eyes. Now he was a soldier, and understood the hunger of men.

"Ban," Brona breathed in a thick sigh.

"Mama," he said, just as full.

She closed the distance, and her hands found his rough cheeks. Brona slid thumbs along his jaw, toyed with the thick, uneven strands of his hair, tugged at the leather jacket he wore. She put her palms to his chest, and there were tears washing her eyes. "What a man you look."

Swallowing, Ban touched his mother's waist, wanting to pull her close and hug her until he forgot everything of the past month, or the past ten years, everything but whatever herby soap she put in her hair and the always-sharp smell of her, as if the dry flowers hanging from her ceiling and the herbs she grew and harvested, boiled, waxed, crushed, and turned to tinctures had permeated her skin and blood. Pretend she had kept him, chosen him. But instead he said, "I don't only *look* like a man."

Her laugh was wry. "As irritable as ever. Ah, I've heard so much, so many things of my son, the Fox."

Pride swelled, but Brona swiftly quashed it by adding, "Also, I've heard how long you've been on the island without attending to your mother."

"I—I'm here now."

"Not to stay."

It wasn't a question, and she did not sound sorrowful over it.

"Hartfare is not a place for me," he muttered, wondering if his mother regretted her choices, or if they were worth the specific freedoms that came with her craft. She was respected, but only in the dark, and never by men concerned with stars, those who made their laws. Brona had never married, yet never seemed sorry or lonely—Ban could dredge up no memories of her angry, no matter how hard he tried, and she'd only been sad the day Errigal took him away. Sad, but not fighting to keep him.

"Is there any place for you, my Ban?"

He only could stare at her, feeling at the edge of some new understanding. It was too big to allow in without feeling all the corners and inspecting the angles. But at the center was his mother, once a girl like Elia, making choices. And having them made *for* her by the world. Ban thought he might need to sit down, and he tried to mask his perception with another frown.

Brona's eyes crinkled, and she kissed his lips. "Ever serious, ever dour, just as irritable. You get that from none of us! Perhaps some old man on your father's side. Ah, I missed your sour face, but I would like to see a smile before you go again. Come inside."

His mother took him by the hand and led him into her home.

Lit only by calm sunlight, the cottage was full of sweet smells. Ban's vision adjusted quickly, but before he could relax, he saw a man sitting half up out of the bed in the far corner.

The Oak Earl, undressed and rumpled here in his mother's house.

Ban felt his entire being jolt again. He gripped Brona's hand too hard, and she bent her mouth in disapproval. "Ban," she chided.

"What are you doing here?" he said, low and dangerous, to the Oak Earl. Kayo was handsome and famous, strong and by reputation a good man. But here he was, spoiling this place with his casual familiarity, *and* he was supposed to be banished alongside Elia, fled to Aremoria.

Keeping his eyes on Ban, Kayo slowly pushed aside the blankets and stood. As he bent to get his trousers, he kept his movements deliberate, unthreatening. One leg then the other, and he fixed his trousers in place never having unlocked his gaze from Ban's.

Brona made a snort of incredulity and pulled away from her son. "You, my boy, are gone too long and are too grown to pretend you have any place judging me."

"Not . . ." Ban's mouth was dry. He swallowed, painfully aware it was babyish hurt clogging his throat. "Not judging, Mama," he rasped.

"Judging," she said firmly, stressing it with a firm pat on his cheek. "Call it protecting if that makes it easier for you. Either way: don't."

He folded his arms over his chest, hiding the clench of his fists, and slid another glare at the Oak Earl.

Kayo ran hands over his puffed curls, forming them back from his face. "Thirsty, Ban?" he said.

Brona padded over to her hearth. "I'd just put water to boil. Sit, son."

He obeyed woodenly.

Sunlight, cool forest breezes, and three moon moths drifted in through all the cottage's open windows. That, as much as the hanging flowers and herbs, the crackling fire, the layers of rugs, all worked together to make this a home, warm and welcoming. Gentle floral and bitter smells pinched the air, and the benches set beside Brona's long table were overlaid with patches of deer and dog and bear fur, softening the seat. Ban leaned his elbows on the rough table his mother used for both eating and working. He remembered being laid out across it once, some women from the village holding down his legs and arms, while Brona sewed up a bone-deep slice on his chin. The scar was still there, and Ban realized he'd touched it only when his mother smiled softly at him, placing a half-eaten loaf of oat bread out for them to share.

Kayo sat across from him, his back to the fire. He reached out and tore a piece of bread. The Oak Earl watched Ban with a suspicion and heavy regard that Ban could not believe he'd earned. There was no way Kayo knew anything of Ban's plotting, no matter what Rory'd confessed. Ban glared back, and said again, "What are you doing here, Oak Earl?"

"Ban," Brona warned as she shoved her feet into slippers.

Kayo chewed his bread, then flattened his hands against the table and leaned in. "What promise are you keeping to Elia Lear, Fox?"

Ban reeled back. "You read my letter? You—I trusted you with it!"

But the Oak Earl did not look at all chagrined. He said, "The lady showed it to me, and the king of Aremoria, too."

No longer hungry, Ban did his best to hide himself behind a veneer of invulnerability. He lifted one shoulder as he'd seen Lady Regan do. "I see. So the lady will marry Morimaros?"

"Who else should she marry, Ban? What else should she do?" Kayo casually ripped more bread, and behind him Brona knelt to take her pot off the fire, hands wrapped in leather mitts. She glanced at Ban curiously as she poured them all tinctures of honeyed water. The clay cups warmed fast, and Ban sat again, clutching his and inhaling the familiar, sweet steam. He shook his head, answering Kayo with silence. His mother sat beside him, near enough their arms brushed.

Brona put her hand on Ban's knee. "She needs to find her place, too," she said, like a portent.

He let his hand fall atop hers. All Ban's thoughts and feelings were awhirl, and he wished it were possible to receive word back from Morimaros, instead of only sending it. The king was so far from Innis Lear, in body and spirit. Had he lost trust in his Fox? How had he taken the note for Elia? Ban studied his water: the flakes of whatever petals or dry leaves Brona had steeped that floated atop the surface, the shiny ripples, the wavering steam. He drank, and the heat diffused down and throughout his body, relaxing him.

"She was glad to have word from you," Kayo said. "Elia was. Though she grew anxious about it, when she told Morimaros you'd promised to aid her cause."

"And what cause is that?" Brona asked.

Ban lied, fiercely, "To bring her *home.*"

His mother's dark eyes softened, and she squeezed his knee. "You love her."

"I—" Ban looked away from her again. "We were friends when we were young."

"And now it is more, because you are children no longer."

"It is *not* more," he insisted. "I don't do that. I would not. I'm not like . . ."

"Like me?"

"I was going to say like my father," he said. "But if you want, yes. You as well." Ban turned his blame toward Kayo, too. Kayo, unmarried, rich, titled, and previously so favored of the king. Worse than Errigal, Ban suddenly thought, for Errigal at least was honest with his affairs. "You returned here so fast, Oak Earl." He could not keep the accusation from his tone, and did not want to hear it might have been Brona drawing Kayo back. Did not want to think of Elia, drawn to Aremoria for anything but protection.

"There is much to do here," Kayo answered. "I must to the king, though he banished me. I fear for him in his daughters' hands, for Gaela and Regan hold him in no regard."

"Does he deserve for them to?"

Kayo frowned. It aged him past his forty years. "He was your king, Ban Errigal, no matter that he stepped down from power."

"He was only ever a terrible old man to me, and never had, or even tried to earn, my respect. And even if he had, it would be lost now after what he did to Elia—to his family. To this island." Though Ban struggled to argue evenly, he knew his words shook with passion and rage.

Brona said, "And like what Errigal has done to his first son?"

Yes, Ban nodded. *Yes.* "Where is my brother?" he asked softly, for it was all he could do now.

"Rory?" Brona leaned away. "How should I know?"

Kayo said, "We've only heard the news, from hunters and traders. It was everywhere when I landed on the island three days ago."

"What? No." Ban glanced between the two, and saw the truth of their protestations. "I sent him here. I told Rory to come here when I ushered him out of the Keep—for his own safety, of course. I said he could hide with you, Mama, that he could be secure and wait for—for me to settle our father down. If such a man could be settled at all."

She shook her head no. "I've not seen him, nor has anyone in Hartfare."

Ban opened his mouth but said nothing. Did Rory truly not trust him, to hurry off on his own?

"I leave tomorrow for Astora," Kayo said. "I need to assess the situation there—I'm worried Astore doesn't have the resources to defeat Connley, even with Lear at his side. Because Connley has Errigal, and much of the island itself listens to his wife. But Connley cannot be king." Kayo glanced at Brona, a telling, secret glance of shared knowledge, and Ban ignored it, before their intimacy infuriated him again. Kayo swung his gaze back to Ban. "Come with me. We will join with Lear and make our plans. There are others, too: Rosrua is unhappy with the events of the Zenith Court, and Bracoch. Glennadoer will side with Connley, because of his father's line. But with Lear, Oak, Rosrua, Bracoch, and Ban the Fox of Errigal, we can be a strong alternative to Astore's might and Gaela's ruthlessness, and you must know we need to oppose Connley."

Ban frowned. He did *not* know it was necessary to oppose Connley. Why would Connley be a worse king than Lear or Astore? Perhaps Innis Lear needed a dangerous, wary king for once, who did not blindly obey the stars. A king with a witch for a wife. Nearer to the earth saints than the cold stars. "Why do you speak of kings, when Gaela and Regan are queen?"

"Not yet, they aren't. Not until Midwinter. Not until the ritual is complete. Until then everything is in transition. It is a twilight time. And they are merely heirs, married to these ambitious, antagonistic men, who will not sit by and let their wives rule without them."

Though Ban was not ready to underestimate Regan, he nodded for Kayo. It was too perfect a position to waste: Regan trusted him with her most intimate secrets, and now here was Kay Oak confessing his own plans. Ban was being put in the center of it all. He asked, "You think Lear will accept your help? He was even more furious at you than at Elia."

"This is where Kayo is supposed to be," Brona said, in a voice Ban well remembered: her witch's voice. The smooth, deep tone of invocation, when she said something she'd heard from the roots, from earth saints and holy bones.

Kayo sighed. "Ban, I love Lear as a brother, and long ago I chose this island for my home. I gave up everything else I might've been: my name, my family of Taria Queen, my skills as a trader, and the wide road. Everything, boy. For Innis Lear. For the king who is not a cruel or stupid man, but only a hurting, and lost one, who allowed himself be defeated by such things. And I am here for Elia." Kayo glanced out the window at the bright day. "Lear is my king, still my sister's husband. The father of my godchild and her sisters. For the good of Innis Lear and its people, this must be settled fast and well. We cannot have a two- or three-way war. That would open us up too much to Aremoria, and I've spoken recently with Morimaros and his council. He will surely take Innis Lear if we don't get a hold of it before Midwinter."

"Morimaros is a good king, a better commander," Ban said. "I served in his army. If he chooses to invade our island, he will win it."

Brona said gently, "You know what is right, son; you've always been rooted by it, here."

"Have I? You said to me once, *This is your fate*—then so easily you sent me away. How can you know Errigal did not change the way I was grounded, or that Aremoria did not cure me from caring about this chunk of battered rock? I have made choices in a different language than that of Innis Lear, been saved and adored by strange trees whose words shift and laugh. What if I don't choose Innis Lear now? It has never chosen *me*."

He cut himself off, before he openly admitted his loyalties, before he gave too much away.

His mother studied him a long time; Ban focused on the rhythm of his breath and the crackle of the fire in the hearth.

Kayo said, "We're not asking you to choose Innis Lear. We're asking you to choose Elia."

"How?" he demanded, more urgently than he should have.

"To keep your promise and fight for her. If you will help bring her home the right way, you must be on my side in this, and on Lear's, until Elia herself is ready."

"Ready for what?" Ban asked.

It was Brona who said, calmly and simply, "To take the throne."

# TWENTY-ONE YEARS AGO,
## HARTFARE

FEW PEOPLE WOULD think to look for the queen of Innis Lear here inside this tiny cottage, tucked into the heart of the White Forest. Fewer still would expect her lounging in supreme contentment on a low, straw-filled mattress beside the hearth.

But Dalat was indeed at Hartfare, spending the week with her friend Brona, the witch of the White Forest. Both of them were heavily pregnant and ready to be finished with the experience.

Brona cupped her belly and crouched to relieve the pressure in the small of her back. She wore a long shift, sliced up the center to open in front so she could easily touch her naked skin, or press back with the heel of her hand when the baby elbowed her or stretched. Her ruffled skirt cinched the shift closed again under her belly, low around her hips, and covering her thighs, knees, and bottom. Still, it was nothing modest by anyone's standards. A heavy wool cloak weighed on Brona's shoulders, keeping in what warmth she could; this was early spring, and even the fire was not enough to heat bare skin. Cold, damp air slicked beneath the door of the cottage and at the open windows.

But the witch refused to bundle up and so lose the ability to splay her hands around her son whenever she liked.

The queen groaned, shifting onto her side where she lay on Brona's bed. "Help me get my feet up, shk lab-i," Dalat said, beckoning to her second daughter.

Regan Lear, six years old and quietly precocious, moved immediately to lift her mother's feet.

That simple gesture caused a flutter in Brona's heart. She could not wait to hold her son, to feel his touch outside her womb.

Dalat, because she was a good friend, saw Brona's hunger. "Soon," the queen said softly. "You'll have him. We both will have them."

It was Brona's first child—and her only, she knew, through careful wormwork—but this would be Dalat's third. Brona had not asked if the feelings changed: the anticipation, the pain, the longing, the exhaustion. Dalat's face was older now than it had been when Gaela was born nearly eight years ago. The queen was thinner beneath her cheeks, despite health and happiness, but her skin still shone, her smile was vivid, and the merriment that lived in her deep brown eyes promised adventure, as much as it always did. When Brona spent time with Dalat, the witch felt as though she'd experienced so much more than even her own wild life on this angry island could provide: long sea-voyages, storms and illness, foreign ports and magnificent palaces built of shining white stone, points of lapis blue set into necklaces and coronas of gold, vast prairies of rolling, shifting sand, and poetry that dropped from the tongues of men and women like diamonds.

"Is the baby hurting you, Mother?" Regan Lear interrupted Brona's musing, sitting down on the mattress beside her mother's head to put a cool brown hand on the queen's black braids.

"Ah, only a slight bit," Dalat admitted.

"But I didn't."

The queen smiled and poked a finger against Regan's ribs. The girl bent away, pressing her mouth closed against laughing too brightly. Dalat's second daughter wore a more formal dress than even her mother, long and dyed bold purple. Brona knew—because she had repeatedly cast spreads of holy bones on behalf of each princess of Innis Lear—that this one carved her place already, as a partner and prop, mother or lover, perhaps even a witch herself. A consort, but never a true queen.

That destiny belonged to the unborn princess, or perhaps that first daughter, the ferocious warrior who even now cut across the lane outside Brona's cottage, wooden sword in hand, meeting the boisterous Earl Errigal stroke for stroke.

Brona groaned as she settled onto the floor, her knees bent and splayed to the side, soles of her feet together. The princess eyed her suspiciously, judging the witch's improper attire, but Brona wrinkled her nose and smiled; Regan mimicked the exact same position with the limber ease of childhood.

"Are we casting bones now?" Dalat's daughter asked, leaning toward Brona eagerly, yet managing to keep her voice smooth.

"As the princess commands," Brona replied, holding out her hand.

Regan hopped up to fetch Brona's bag of bones, reverently offering them to the witch before resuming her seated position.

"Would you like a reading for yourself?" Brona asked.

The princess's brow wrinkled as she thought. She glanced at her mother and Dalat lifted her eyebrows and nodded, giving Regan what permission she liked. But the princess, all of six years old, touched her flat little stomach and said, "For the babies."

Brona painstakingly shifted her own seat until she leaned the small of her back against the mattress, where Dalat could put a hand between her shoulder blades, connecting the friends in spirit. Then the witch removed her cards and bones from the leather pouch. She set the bone, crystal, and antler holy bones along her thighs and began to shuffle the cards. Closing her eyes, Brona thanked the stars and worms of her heart for a friend like this queen, vivacious and cunning and gentle, who loved her enough to tuck herself away from the king and his kingdom—all the business Dalat herself saw to on behalf of her absent-minded husband—in order to comfort Brona through her first pregnancy. The witch sighed deeply as she shuffled, casting her thoughts too inside her, toward her little son. Brona listened to the threads of light and earthly shadows weaving around him, those that stretched toward Dalat behind, weaving about the queen's third daughter.

The witch of the White Forest held her eyes shut as she spread the cards in a spiral. "Choose a bone," she instructed the queen and the princess. Both did, the former taking the crystal saint of stars, the later picking up a pale bone carved like a leaf: the Worm of Birds. Brona tossed the remaining seven bones across the spiral of cards. "Now," she said, "please put your bones down where you will. Dalat, yours will be for your daughter, and Regan, if you will bless my son with your casting."

Regan's eyes lit up with pride and she bent over the spread in contemplation. The queen put her saint of stars bone against the card for the Bird of Dreams. The princess glanced up at her mother, then Regan reached out, nearly setting the chosen worm bone against the Tree of Thorns card—but a hesitation shifted her hand eastward, and she placed it instead against the linked corners of two others; Tree of Ancestors and Bird of Rivers. "Is that all right?" the princess whispered.

"Of course," Brona whispered back. "You have rootwater in your heart. You know where these bones belong."

The princess nodded slowly.

The witch slid her gaze over and around the cards. "What do you see, little witch?"

"I don't know."

"Look, and feel, and listen, and there will be something."

Regan glanced to her mother.

Dalat encouraged, "Go on."

"Here," said the witch, pointing to the Bird of Dreams card. Silver lines of moonlight wove throughout the feathers of an elegant songbird, and its shadow was a raven of stars and blood. "What does this card your mother chose tell you about your baby sister, with words or in feelings."

The young princess pursed her lips.

"Do not think too long," Brona counseled.

Regan closed her eyes and breathed slowly, lips parted as if to taste the fire-warmed air. "I can't trust her," she whispered.

"What!" Dalat frowned.

"She's not real!" Regan glanced at her mother in a panic. "I'm sorry, that's . . ."

"Of course she is real."

The witch hummed, studying the delicate crystal saint of stars where it lay against the card, connecting the wings of the moonlight songbird and its bloody raven shadow. "She is only a future now," Brona said. "Nothing but a promise, growing and wanting. But that future she is will be made by our pasts, entwined together—our pasts and our loves and troubles. She is a dream."

Seeming relieved by the longer, magical explanation, Regan looked to her mother again, for forgiveness.

"I am willing to love a dream," the queen said.

Regan hugged herself. "I don't know how."

Dalat flipped her hands, calling Regan onto the mattress with her. The princess climbed carefully against her mother, and Dalat wrapped her arm around Regan as her middle daughter curled around the bulge of the queen's belly. "Imagine her, Regan, my pretty shk lab-i. Imagine what she might be."

As mother and daughter dreamed together, Brona Hartfare glanced again at the spiral of cards and scattered holy bones. Her gaze drifted, bland and unfocused, as she waited for the symbols and names to paint her a story, for the voice of prophecy to whisper.

Suddenly, the witch stopped breathing: neither queen nor princess noticed, for the witch had simply fallen silent, unmoving, and alone. Because in honor of Brona's son, Regan Lear had put the Worm of Birds bone between the cards of the Tree of Ancestors and the Bird of Rivers.

For months, Brona's son's name had echoed her dreams, been whispered in long, ragged songs by the wind and roots of Innis Lear. His heart, blood, and magic would resonate, would echo up and up, outward and even deep into the bedrock of Innis Lear until every inch and crevice of the island knew his name. Knew him, and loved him.

But with the Worm of Birds there, his future of power and love instead became his doom.

Brona flicked her eyes to little Regan Lear, so innocently snuggled against her mother, whispering in babyish confidence.

Such a young girl could not know what she'd done, what she'd revealed like a curse.

Holding her belly in one hand, the witch of the White Forest swept her other across the holy bones, scattering the cards toward the fire.

# MORIMAROS

MARS SPRAWLED BACK at the top of a mighty Aremore hill. Beside him gleamed a pile of armor: helmet, greaves, gauntlets, and breastplate; beneath him, a thin blanket. He'd not bothered to remove the shirt of mail and so Mars, too, gleamed in the sunlight. Before him stretched his legs, his muddy boots just off the blanket. Mars tilted his head back to peer at the solid blue sky. Sweat darkened his hair, especially where the straps of his helmet had pressed. He longed for a bath and clean clothes after over a week in the field, but this was pleasant anyhow.

Ianta and her son, Isarnos, had come out with La Far to meet the king and his men for a picnic lunch, and the breeze was gentle, the cool wine relaxing. Nearly enough to help Mars clear his thoughts.

He'd joined his army ostensibly to inspect their winter camp, but truly because he needed time away from the princess, to build up defenses in his heart. To think without her presence diverting him, always. Instead, she had loomed even larger in his mind. Mars thought of her first when he woke at dawn, for he knew she, too, would be awake, and high on his ramparts saying farewell to the stars. He thought of her again when the wind brushed through curling leaves just beginning to turn the same dark copper that streaked her hair. His boots, all the boots in the army, reminded him of hers, peeking from beneath her dresses, a flower suddenly revealing thorns.

Leaving had made him long for her even more.

He sighed, and Ianta patted his knee sympathetically.

"What's that you have, my prince?" Novanos asked Isa, and the prince leaned around his mother and stretched a skinny arm across her lap, offering something to the soldier with grubby hands. He carefully opened his palm to accept it, then showed the small yellow rock to Mars.

The king smiled. It was one of the ribbed stone beetles often found trapped in the cliffs or the limestone of Lionis Palace. Old stories said they were ancient animals transformed by earth saints into rock, as punishment for a crime that varied by the family telling it. Mars reached to pluck it from Novanos's hand. The beetle was the size of his thumbnail. He said, "I spoke with a man from Ispania who thinks this is a natural process, a thing that happens to some creatures when they decompose, the way our flesh rots and falls away."

"I'm eating, Mars," Ianta said.

But Isarnos climbed onto his knees and eagerly poked the stone beetle. "Do you think if we could break inside it, there would be a hollow where its flesh rotted? Or turned to dust, or is all still there, preserved perfectly?"

"Maybe it is beautiful crystal like a geode," Novanos suggested.

Isarnos gasped in delight.

"Break it open and find out." Mars gave the beetle back to his nephew.

"Then it will be ruined, if there's nothing but stone."

The Twice-Princess nodded, dabbing her mouth with a cloth. "Then have it gilded, and save it forever. Always full of secret possibilities."

The young prince stroked the ribbed shell and leapt to his feet. "If I find more, I can break one open and still have another to keep!"

Mars laughed, well pleased by his nephew's strategic and forthright conclusion. The boy dashed through the line of soldiers enjoying their own lunch just down the hill, dodging toward the saddled horses. Most of the men remained with the camp, completing the necessary winter adjustments; this was only an honor escort so that the king did not ride alone.

Novanos got up, too, and trailed after the prince. He shared a glance with the Twice-Princess that told Mars he was facing an inquisition.

"So, Mars, how are your troops?" Ianta scraped soft cheese off the platter between them with her finger, and popped it into her mouth.

"The army is bedding down in the east. They've repaired Fort Everly's spike wall, and should be wintered well. I'll ride north toward Burgun next, but not get too close to the old line. Wouldn't want to upset them unnecessarily yet."

"Are you going to the west coast where the navy is?"

"I will have to tell them to nest or remain prepared for assault if I do."

"You haven't decided yet?" Genuine surprise lifted his sister's voice.

Mars ran his hands over his skull, scrubbing at the thick hair. It needed a new shave.

"Tell me what troubles you most, big brother." Ianta poured a little more wine into Mars's cup.

"If I want Innis Lear more than anything, I should go and take it now, when they're divided. That will be best for Aremoria, with the least risk to us."

"But there's something you want more?"

"Aremoria should be—*it is*—my only concern."

"You *are* Aremoria."

"Father told me how this would be. That being king separates me from all else. That my love—my attention—belongs to my people first, and to myself, rarely. "

"Even the sun is affected by the clouds, by rain and the moon."

"But are the sun and moon lovers?" he said, amused at the turn of the conversation, but also inexplicably hurt by it.

Ianta laughed. "I suppose you'd have to ask the sun and the moon."

Glancing up at the sky, scalded silver and nearly impossible to behold by the brilliant sun, Mars nodded.

His sister said, "You could be lover to Elia Lear."

"She is her own sun, no moon for mine."

Ianta clapped her hands as though she'd caught him in a trap. "Her own sun! Mars, are you in love with her?"

Fiercely uncomfortable, he sat up. "If I take Innis Lear now, she'll hate me."

"Aremoria will be stronger if you have a queen," Ianta murmured, wheedling. "Haven't you thought of that? Maybe stronger with a queen than with a conquered Innis Lear."

"I have an heir."

"Isarnos is *my* heir, too, you know, and I might want to protect him from your throne."

"Or give him to Vindomatos's daughter?"

Ianta shrugged. "I wouldn't mind retiring to that north duchy. And strengthening our ties along Burgun's border. Aremoria wants for you to have your own queen and your own heir."

"If Elia marries me, I could maybe have Innis Lear, too, in the end," Mars said.

"And if you go for her island first, she might never willingly marry you."

"Willingly!" Aghast, Mars stared at his sister. "I do not want a queen unwilling, Ianta, and I'm . . . offended."

"Then put the navy to nest for the winter," she pressed.

This was no counseling, not Ianta's usual give-and-take questioning, meant to help Mars decide what his choices would be. She argued vehemently for some agenda. Mars said slowly, "By the spring, when we can sail again, her sisters might have consolidated power. It will be harder to invade. More resources spent. More of my men will die."

"Or they'll kill each other, those elder sisters, and Elia will hand the island over to you. There are several ways this can go."

Mars drank his wine, brooding into the cup. Word had come from Ban the Fox, sealed on the wing of a raven, that his mission proceeded slowly but surely. Rory Errigal was unseated, and Ban positioned like creeping poison near his father's heart. Near enough to cause whatever ailments he wished, to stir trouble ahead and sow discontent further. That seemed more like fast work than a slow infiltration to Mars, but given the resentment that always lived in Ban, perhaps disrupting the earldom was a thing he was only glad to have reason to do, and so had already known exactly which thread to pull. And if it went faster, then the king's spy could return home sooner.

He missed Ban, the quiet surety of his dark presence, like a shadow always reminding Mars to *be* the sun. They had not been friends, exactly, but as close to it as a king and a bastard wizard could be.

*I keep my promises,* his Fox had written to Elia Lear.

Mars rejected jealousy, for not knowing which of them he was more jealous *of.*

He said instead, "Those sisters will not like it, if she marries me."

"But they wouldn't attack Aremoria for it. They can't. And in the end they can only make conquering their island very difficult. Sue for peace at great expense to themselves, and they are inexperienced queens, taking over a very weakened kingdom, if even half of what you've said is true."

"It would be good for Innis Lear to be part of Aremoria. Our strengths would balance. I wish I could convince Elia of that, too."

"I like her, Mars. I like her very much. And I'm sure she likes you. She's hurt and looking for a path to choose. We could convince her to choose you, to choose Aremoria. She needs someone to trust, Mars. To love, and to be loved as *you* could love her."

Mars put down the empty wine cup and for a moment watched the wind tease the corners of saddle blankets and the thick manes of the horses down the slope from him. Soldiers ranged in pairs, some eating as they walked, others alert for orders. But all seemed to appreciate the afternoon break. It was perfect here: warm, gilded, all the bold colors of Aremore. "You think I should use her hurt, her losses, to my advantage."

"It's just a tool, like everything is, your method to get what you want. And in the long run, it would be to Elia's advantage, too. You're a good man; you will be good for her."

"You're biased," Mars said with a wry smile.

"Yes. But also right, in this case."

"She wants to save her island, Ianta. To win her, I might have to prove my willingness toward alliance over assimilation. Toward supporting her without the ties of marriage, until her sisters have ascended, or until Innis Lear is strong again. That is what she wants most from me: an opportunity to see her island secure."

"Which is directly opposed to what you, you-as-king, you—*Aremoria*—want. Because it will make you truly the greatest ruler in a thousand years? Strengthen the lore of our dynasty?"

Mars sighed, knowing exactly what his father would say to this equivocating.

His sister leaned back onto her elbows. Her voluptuous curls tumbled around her shoulders. "That makes me want to throw this wine in your face. You don't believe in destiny."

"It isn't that—it isn't magic, or myth." Mars touched the grass beside the blanket, stroking it; the blades had been warmed by the sun. "It is completing what Aramos began. Taking all the stolen parts of Aremoria back. Making Aremoria whole. A single banner. Ours. Mine."

"Innis Lear was lost to us nearly a thousand years ago. It might just belong to itself by now."

"If I don't at least try, what have I accomplished with my reign?"

"Mars!" She leaned over to smack his arm, but winced as her fingers snapped against his chain mail.

It had been a ridiculous thing to say: he'd completed the defeat of Diota after his father's death, and put Burgun back in its place. He'd restructured the system of loans and guild marks in Lionis. He'd begun to build a new port for trading ships in their south city Haven Point. He still didn't have a permanent ambassador from the Third Kingdom, however, nor a queen to bear his heirs. And at least three barons along the Vitili border kidnapped Aremore folk regularly, and Mars's representatives could find no proof the nobles were involved. There were always problems with the stray cats. The roads in the north were appalling. He was a terrible falconer. Oh, and that draft in the queen's solar. There was plenty left to achieve.

"Have you thought you might accomplish peace?" Ianta asked gently.

The king startled.

"If Aremoria is not at war, you can invite your naturalists to Lionis, as many as you like, a menagerie of them. Bring that one you mentioned to Isa, to cut up all the stone beetles in the world. You can teach Isa yourself, or make Royal Libraries in every city like you wanted as a boy. You can go kill those border barons with your own hands."

"I should do all those things *and* take Innis Lear."

"If you make peace, you can take your time with Elia Lear. And her island."

He frowned. He should tell his sister about Ban. That Aremore had already dealt the first hand against Innis Lear. Against Elia.

"You have to be happy, Mars. If you let yourself be unhappy, it will spill out into your choices," Ianta said.

"Are you happy?" Mars looked hard at his sister, locking their eyes together.

"When I can be," she said. "It was difficult after my husband died. But I had our son. Mother. You. And an entire country to love."

"I love Aremoria," Mars said through his teeth.

"Then let Aremoria love you back!" Ianta cried. With a great sigh, she put her hand to the back of his neck. "Go talk to Elia. Tell her what you want most, and why. Tell her everything, and see if she is willing to meet you even halfway there."

Mars's stomach churned, rather like it did in the moments when his body-man buckled on the king's armor before a battle. When Mars had already made a choice among too many possibilities, and was prepared to take that first step leading soldiers to their deaths.

# THE FOX

THE SKY WAS bloody with the setting sun by the time Ban returned to Errigal Keep. From gossip in the stables, he heard that his father had retired, drunk and without dinner, to his bedchamber—with not one, but two women. Aggravated but unsurprised, Ban made his way toward the guest wing, where Connley and his lady had been settled. He had a letter in his coat from Elia to her sister Regan, given over from Kayo as Ban left his mother's house.

There was no such message for himself.

The afternoon had been spent discussing war in all its possibilities. His best place, Ban argued, was at Errigal, where Regan and Connley were. *They trust me,* he told Brona and Kayo, insinuating he might mitigate the duke's urgency to act until Elia returned. None doubted Connley and Astore would face off for control of the island, unless they could be united against Aremoria, or brought to heel under Elia.

Elia as queen! It was an idea both appealing and abhorrent to Ban. She could be glorious. As a boy, he'd loved her generous nature, her ability to empathize with anything—her terrifying sisters, the smallest worm, even him—but would the crown of Innis Lear not leave her crushed and wilted under the weight of responsibility? And without Aremoria and the strength of Mars's army, would she have the might to defeat her sisters? What would Mars take, in exchange?

But Brona insisted the alternatives promised worse. Gaela was believed to be strong and competent, besides being the eldest child and perhaps rightful heir, and her husband Astore was ferocious and his family a respected ancient line. He'd taken up residence already at Dondubhan, sending a very clear message of their intent. But Gaela ignored star prophecy—understandably, some said, because of the role her stars had played in her mother's death. Her vocal disdain for wormwork and the navel wells did not invoke confidence from the suffering families who worked the land. Many doubted that the holy well at Tarinnish would accept Gaela as its dedicated queen on the Longest Night. She was too martial, as singular thinking as her father, though toward a different power. No matter how strong she was, if the rootwaters refused to claim her, she would never have the trust of a majority of her people, leaving the throne weak and susceptible to sedition.

Regan, on the other hand, was known to understand the language of trees as well as any witch. The rootwaters would accept her, but could she rule? She was not trusted outside the Connley lands, and was considered to be cold and imperious in a way that did not endear her to or inspire the Learish people. However, she was the only of the two sisters to ever carry a child, and there were many who'd grown tired of the uncertainty of the royal line. She'd lost the babe—a boy—and two others before birth, but she had at least proved she could conceive. Gaela had been married for seven years with nothing to show, and Lear himself had never gotten a son, natural or otherwise. As for Connley, his reputation was strict, but his own people admired and trusted him; his justice was known to be fair, if swift, and where Astore was mighty, Connley was learned. He'd received a rather intense education from a variety of tutors throughout his childhood.

Ban's mind had wandered to the grove of cherry trees, and to Regan's determined pain, as she had laid out her body's flaws for him. He could not ignore the instinct that Regan was a piece of the island, and it would accept her. Elia was all of the stars; she'd proved as much to him. But that had not always been so. Perhaps Elia could still bridge the distance between stars and roots. She had both in her, if she could only reject her father's fanaticism, if she could see what Ban saw. He'd said, rather desperately, "Surely Elia embodies as much doubt, if not the same sort, as her sisters?"

"Elia is hope, she is possibility," Kayo had said, and Brona had agreed. Because she had lived always at her father's side, appearing only briefly as a star priest, she was a figure of speculation and wishes, not reputation. But there were rumors now, ones that Kayo had encouraged at home and abroad, that Lear had intended to name her his heir at the Zenith Court. Brona felt Elia should be present on the Longest Night, to stand before the holy well as the intended heir. And she reminded Ban that aside from Elia, the linchpin in the inevitable war between Connley and Astore would be Errigal.

The power of that earldom, with its iron magic and weaponry and standing, could sway the entire island in either direction. "That is why this business with your brother is so devastating," the Oak Earl had sighed.

"It undercuts the reputation of Errigal," Ban said, showing anger instead of the dark triumph he felt. "For the people don't care that my father's always been a brute, that he never leads, but only agrees and imitates the whims of Lear, because he's friendly and generous, too. And so now they only care that there's division between Rory and Errigal, a division that mirrors Lear's sudden madness."

"It's unnatural," Brona murmured. "Child against parent."

"*Parent against child* you mean?" Ban snapped.

"Either way," Kayo soothed, "it is up to you, Ban, to remain true and canny. To be the Fox you've made yourself into. Help Elia as you promised, by bridging the break between Connley and Astore, while you have Connley's ear—and find out more of their feelings toward Elia's rule, what they might do if Morimaros backs her claim. I admit that as Elia's uncle and also as Oak Earl, I would rather Aremoria remain an ally only, than a husband and conqueror. But it might come to that. And beware, Connley's line is dangerous as snakes. I go to Astora first thing in the morning, because from my last conversations with Astore and Gaela I know they both want war, though for different reasons. Astore would like to crush Connley for their divisive history, and Gaela wants the test of battle, no matter the cause."

"Do they not care that the island's magic is fading?"

Brona had stared at Ban in surprise, then smiled with all the sorrow of a decade. "It will survive until the island unites again, under a crown of stars *and* roots. I do everything I can to keep it vital. Everything."

He'd looked at her, and understood she meant all her choices as a mother, too. He knew, but it didn't hurt less. "Regan Lear loves the roots."

"She does not weave star and root together: she knows no balance in passion nor magic. But Elia knows the language of trees as much as the sky. You taught her, my son, to love the roots, and she also loves the stars. See?"

Kayo nodded. "She is what we need for Innis Lear."

Ban thought of their certainty again as he knocked on the outer door of Connley's rooms, the letter from one sister to another as cold as ice against his fractured heart. A maid of Regan's retinue answered quickly, and Ban had only to say his name before he was ushered in to wait by a narrow hearth. Though he'd been prepared to state his purpose, the maid was only gone a minute before she returned: Ban was to join the duke and lady in their bedroom.

Though put off by the unusual intimacy of such an arena, Ban went in at the maid's side. The girl slipped back out and shut the heavy door.

"Ban Errigal," Connley said eagerly from the wide, raised bed. Woven blankets surrounded him in disarray. The duke was unclothed. Shocked, Ban darted his eyes across to Lady Regan, who stood at the ancient stone hearth in a loosely tied robe and held a goblet. Her hair tumbled around her shoulders.

Ban bowed stiffly.

The lady seem to float as she went to the round table and poured a third goblet of clear red wine. "Good evening, Ban," she said in her cool, lovely, all-knowing voice.

"Highness," the Fox murmured, as the duke too got out of bed, pulling a robe over his shoulders. He did not tie it closed, but let it hang in long, silky lines, framing his nakedness like dark blue pillars. Connley stood calmly and reached toward Regan, who placed the closest goblet of wine into his hand. Connley walked to Ban, and Ban struggled not to back away. He'd been near unclothed men before, but never one who used his naked-ness like this, as a weapon. This was a message: *You are no threat to me and mine; even naked I am not vulnerable to any danger you could present.*

The Fox drew himself up and accepted the wine Regan offered. "Lord," he said quietly.

"Join us, Ban. We've longed to speak with you outside your father's rather gregarious presence, especially after the news my wife has given about your witch work." Connley placed himself elegantly into the carved chair to the right of the hearth. The lord casually flipped the end of his robe over his thighs as Regan sank onto the arm of the chair, as straight-backed as the furniture itself, and as luxurious.

Ban sipped the light wine and sat across the hearth, doing his best to control how he moved and what his face revealed. He'd have rather knocked back the full goblet to relax himself in this sultry, unexpected space. The final rays of sunset carved burnt shadows against Ban's eyes. Firelight flick-ered and candles, too, set onto the windowsills and in head-height nooks built into the old stone walls. This room was part of the old Keep, made of the ruins of Errigal, and appropriate, for it had been a Connley who'd first razed the place so many generations ago.

Regan said, "We missed you today."

"I visited my mother," Ban answered gruffly.

"How is Brona?" Regan's smile warmed ever so slightly.

"Well." He couldn't stop searching for double meaning in everything. No more than he could ignore the bounty in front of him: the bared inner curve of Regan's breast, the strong lines of Connley's lower stomach. Ban took another drink.

"Several times I remember she brought you to Dondubhan. You met Elia when you were wee things, before you were born, even," Regan murmured, her hand floating down toward her belly. Ban felt a bite of sorrow for the lovely, dangerous lady. The problem in her womb was clearly not for any desire lacking between husband and wife.

But Regan dismissed her melancholy with a delicate flick of her fingers. "My mother and I both have been fond of Brona and her potions."

Connley finished his wine. "But we want you just for us," he said bluntly.

Ban's fingers tightened around his goblet, his skin all a-tingle. A hissed chuckle from the fire made him think there was residual magic in the room.

The duke continued, "You have promised wizarding and wormwork for my wife, but that is not all we want of you."

"My lord," Ban said.

"We want you, Ban, as Earl Errigal, once we are crowned. Not your loutish father. You are more to our style. Cunning and resilient. Your reputation is subtle and strong, and proves you could be a fine leader of men."

Relief and astonishment dried out his tongue. Ban sipped the wine again, staring at Connley.

"Well, Ban?" Connley prompted.

"I . . . I never meant to be Errigal, or a leader of men," he said, stalling.

Both Regan and the duke smiled identical sleek smiles.

Blood rushed in Ban's ears, rather like the furious whispers of a forest. He wanted to smile with them, exactly like that. They were completely united, as Ban had never been in his life, with anyone. Not his parents, not his brother, not Morimaros. Elia, almost, perhaps, but she had been taken away before they could make anything as complete as this.

"As far as we are concerned," Connley said, "you are already Errigal. Your father is vexing in his grief, a drain on this Keep and unfit to look past his personal stake to the greater ones of Innis Lear. He is inextricably attached to the wretched once-king. It will only be a moment before this earl steps beyond his means and we, in our power as Connley and as heir to Lear's crown, will instate you. We care not for your bastardy. Your actions prove better than your stars."

"My lord," Ban said, unable to find further words. Only Mars had ever so directly discounted the circumstances of Ban's birth.

"And more," Regan said, her eyebrow lifting elegantly. "We offer you our youngest sister, furthering the alliance."

"Elia?" he breathed. "She is in Aremoria. She will marry Morimaros."

"We have counseled her not to, for it would weaken Innis Lear's position. And Elia loves this island. She never before wished to leave it, and

never would have, we think, had not our father driven her away in his ad-
dled state." A wrinkle appeared about her nose, the only sign of Regan's
disgust. "Elia will return home, make no mistake, and when she does, she
would be a good wife for the powerful Earl Errigal. A tempting offer to
you both, because she loved you, once."

Though some part of him was sure he was being manipulated, Ban could
not help wanting all she offered. It was greater and more ambitious than
anything he'd dreamed of, to be at Connley and Regan's side when King
Lear breathed his last, to welcome Elia home and then have her for his own.
His wife. To share with her the way these two shared with each other, in
heart and body and mind. Legitimately. To put down roots together here
on Innis Lear—where with Regan and Connley—the island would thrive,
the stars cease to command.

Drunk more on wishes than wine, Ban's head spun. He tried to imagine
himself as an earl, rather than a wizard; a man at the center, not a boy on
the outside, or a spy set apart. But for Ban to be Errigal, Rory could never
be pardoned. This lie that he was a patricide must remain.

Caught up in the heat of his hopes, Ban reminded himself that there
were always casualties of war, as he knew far better than Rory. His brother
had served only as idle commander, while Ban had been sent as cannon fod-
der. Before he'd saved himself, proven useful to another, better king. What
sweet revenge it would be upon the hated Lear for Ban the Bastard to father
precious Elia's children. Morimaros be damned.

With his wine halfway to his mouth again, Ban froze in sudden horror.

Elia was not his to long for. Her children were not his to claim. What
would she feel if she heard Ban's thoughts? He had wanted her to choose
him, wanted to be chosen by her. She was not a pup easily traded between
kennels, as Ban had been. She was meant to be prized—not just as a daughter
or sister or wife should have been, but on her own. As herself. Ban swallowed and lowered his goblet so it rested on his thigh. He thought of Elia's
face, the night of the Zenith Court. *Who are you?* And then, who was Ban?
*Two nobodies.* What did he want?

What a magnificent mess swirling around him.

Morimaros wanted him here to gain Errigal's iron for trade at the least,
and prepare for an Aremore invasion if possible. Likely wanted Ban at his
side, in case of a war, and even if Mars got Elia for his queen, he would
expect his best spy to protect them both with his knowledge, if not his
magic. Kay Oak wanted Ban to be a bridge between the sisters, and between their lords, until Elia could be brought home as queen, in accord with
her father's mad heart. But Kayo had no further plans for Ban, and Ban

had no interest in following the Oak Earl's path, forsaking his own life for the plans of Lear. Regan saw Ban's magic, as Mars did, but she saw beyond its usefulness to her. She understood it. She believed in it, and loved the roots and forests as he did. And she and her lord wanted him to unseat his own despised father, to marry Elia, and serve Innis Lear through his own heart. As himself.

He did not know if Elia wanted him at all, for anything.

Ban glanced up at Regan, then expanded the look to her husband. "I will join you. But not to win Elia's hand, or even to earn my father's title, which will be at your service still. I will do it because it is *right for Innis Lear.*"

Even as he said it, the Fox was not sure if he meant to betray Mars, or only to embed himself deeper where he'd been planted.

Regan rose, her brown eyes glittering, and she came to him. She took his goblet and set it aside. As Connley watched, she pulled Ban to his feet and put her mouth against his. She tasted sweet and sharp, her lips like flower petals, her tongue darting. It felt more like an earth saint's blessing than a woman's kiss.

Then she drew away. "You are so noble, Ban the Fox. We are glad to have you on our side."

Connley joined them. He kissed Ban's cheeks, first one, then the other, and then his mouth. There was more heat than had been in his wife's touch. "Hail, Errigal," the duke murmured against Ban's lips.

Ban could not help the shiver that tore down his spine.

"Finish your drink, Ban, and tell us what the Fox of Aremoria would do next," Regan said.

The letter from Elia Lear to her sister remained inside Ban's coat, discarded across the arm of a chair.

"YOU CAN'T HIDE from me, Ban Errigal!"

The princess sang out her call, smiling all the while as she picked her way across the mossy meadow. She avoided crushing any of the tiny white sparflowers, but kicked at every dandelion gone to seed. Her trusted boots remained by the creek where she'd been dipping her toes, waiting for her sister Regan to finish collecting caterpillar husks and wildflowers. The water had been cool, the silt soft underneath her feet, and Elia wished to throw off her light summer layers and revel like a river spirit.

But the hanging branches of a willow had brushed her shoulders and said, *Ban is near.*

Not having seen her friend in several months, Elia splashed to shore and asked the trees for direction.

This was the edge of the White Forest nearest the Summer Seat, on land her uncle the Oak Earl tended. Wind-stripped moors and hard grazing land, except for under the trees, where it became a bright place with quiet meadows full of young deer and hanging sunlight, creeks spilling from fresh springs, and very few spirits. It was easy for Elia to listen to a whisper here and there, to trace a straight path toward Ban. Her breath came light and full, as she tasted the height of summer on her tongue, happy for quite a long stretch, and happier still to know who it was she chased.

When she came to the line of slate and limestone rocks turned upside down, the worms and sleeping beetles exposed, Elia said his name aloud, twice—once in the people's tongue and once in the language of trees. No answer came back to her. But she saw the imprint of a narrow boot, thin-soled and supple enough to show where the ball of his foot hit and the toe brushed after. She traced the curve of it, and went the way it pointed, humming to herself a song with nonsense words like her father's Fool would sing, but changed them to flower-names and root words, in a long cheerful pattern that all the birds appreciated. A half-dozen bluebirds and sparrows hopped from their nests to flit along behind her.

The meadow of sparflowers and white-puffed dandelions glowed with traces of sunlight and floating seeds, yet all was still. Someone had told these grasses and trees to be quiet.

Elia smiled. She was just fourteen and none on the island were better than she at listening, for none but she both understood and rarely demanded a response. That was Ban's role: he asked, he spoke, he commanded. His mother, the gorgeous witch Brona, meddled and manipulated, twisting vines and flowers to her will with teasing and fair exchange. Regan had just begun to pull at roots, to weave them into hopes and messages, pouring her blood into the barren space left behind.

So Elia listened now, from the center of the meadow, her little brown hands caressing the grasses gone to seed, and the tufted dandelion heads, the kiss-soft petals of delicate white flowers. Her hair moved and shifted as she cocked her head, a mass of free copper-brown-black curls. She wore a gown her sister had once owned, and so it was three intricate and expensive layers, but all of them some kind of yellow, and Elia was everything summer-warm in the world.

One of the trees at the north side of the meadow shivered. It was so slight, so quiet a sound, Elia knew anyone else would not find him.

She leapt up, dashed to the alder, and put her hands on the grayish trunk, rubbing her fingers along the tiny horizontal markings on the bark, so like the written language of trees. Down the middle a fold pressed together, nearly four feet tall. *Open up,* she whispered, and the bark shivered, giggling at her wishes. Elia kissed it, and again. *Open up, please!* Though there was no true word for *please* in the language of trees.

*Elia!*

It wasn't the tree complaining, but Ban.

She laughed. "Come out! I've not seen you in so long. Are you taller?"

The tree shivered again, and the fold opened like arms, revealing a triangle of a hollow between two wide roots, and there she spied him half crouched in the darkness.

He grimaced at her, wiping mud from his cheeks. But she leaned in too fast, and fell against him with a little laugh. They crushed together in the musty hollow, laughter echoing up to the tree's heart. All the branches shook as they tickled the tree from the inside. Elia held tight around Ban's neck, and he lifted her to her toes and dragged them both out.

They collapsed into the meadow, knocking elbows and knees, quite breathless. Ban smiled because sunlight found Elia's horn-black eyes, making them shine, and she smiled because she had her hands on his tawny cheeks. "Hi," she said.

"Hi," he said back, rather gruff for a boy.

Elia sat. Petals and dandelion seeds fell out of her hair. "Why didn't you come see me? How long have you been near?"

Ban absently caught the leavings as they drifted from her hair. His own was long and rough, knotted in places from old braids he never untied, greasy as young men without parents are so skilled at maintaining. His fingers were already talented, though, and they danced as he wove petals and seeds into a wide ring with a strand of wind.

"Ban," she said softly, touching the corner of his mouth with one finger. She pushed it gently up.

"My father told me to be more proper and keep my distance from the king's daughters."

"And you obeyed?" Horrified, Elia could only laugh again.

A slow smile crept across his face, showing off sharp little teeth. He tossed the ring of wind and petals at her, and it looped around her nimbus of hair. "If you're to have petals in your hair, my lady, they should be a crown."

She stood, then curtsied. Spreading her arms, she tipped her head back and asked the wind to bring her shadows and flicks of stars. Wind ruffled the canopy, and shadows collected in her palms. She clapped them together, and they exploded into a spiky circlet of wavering, reaching gray fingers. With a laugh, she snapped with one hand, and there sparked to life tiny white ghost lights, which she dotted about the crown like diamonds. Then she set it gently upon Ban's unruly hair. "My lord," she murmured, holding out her hand for his.

Accepting, Ban stood with her. He was a breath taller, and his rangy little-boy shoulders had broadened beyond hers. The plain linen shirt hung open at his chest, and Elia admired the soft line of his collarbone. She touched the point of the open shirt, skimming her hand up his sternum to flatten it over his heart. Ban cupped her elbow and slid his other arm around her waist.

The meadow hummed, and the bluebirds and sparrows and a few mourning doves chirped and sang.

Elia Lear and Ban Errigal danced. Slow, and with a rhythm none but those who heard the language of trees would recognize. Stops and starts, careful spinning, a pause and a turn, then looping a spiral out and out to the edges of the meadow; back again, the opposite way, and their quiet feet stamped words into the grass and sparflowers, knocking seeds into the air, and spinning through layers of light and shadow and light again.

Breathless at the end, Elia wrapped her arms around his ribs, laying her body against his. Her small beginning breasts flattened on his chest, and he lovingly touched her hair, fluffing it and caressing the ends before finding her bare neck and drawing her closer to him.

Elia's heart beat fast as a rabbit's, and she saw all the colors of the forest in Ban's eyes, just before they drifted shut and their mouths touched, dry and hot.

His pulse floundered, too, where she felt it through his back, in the sensitive palms of her hands.

As they kissed, tasting with lips and only the tips of tongues, sweet and lapping like kittens, the forest sighed. Her crown of petals and wind dissolved; so too did his circlet of shadow and light.

Strands of wormwork and the thin light of daytime stars sparkled as they reached for each other, but fell short and dropped instead to the ground. Little imaginary flowers, born of bruised hearts and silly hopes, blossomed for just a few brief moments, lifted in pairs like the wings of tiny moths, then sank home to the earth and died.

# ELIA

ELIA KNELT BEFORE a tower of white roses and breathed a gentle sigh onto the nearest fat-faced flower. It bobbed back at her, and she whispered, *I am Elia the daughter of the king of Innis Lear,* in the language of trees.

She'd been practicing every day, for the week and some since Rory arrived in Aremoria. So her tongue might be ready when the time came to go home, at Midwinter. If only she could return now, before the crowning, and solicit the opinions of the trees and wind and perhaps even the birds—but she did not know what ramifications would follow if she defied her sisters so directly. Elia would not ask those unfeeling stars that awaited her nightly.

Not yet.

Sunlight transformed the garden into a brilliant cluster of jewels, heating her until sweat prickled her scalp. A red skirt flared around her legs, a pool of contrast against perfectly cut emerald grass, and the bodice attached kept her from slouching, with all its stiff embroidery. The collar clung to the edges of her shoulders, and tight sleeves ended at her elbows in ribbons. It was simple, but beautiful, the compromise she'd found these past weeks with Aefa, who would have Elia dolled up in impressive, elaborate costumes if she could.

Amber beads gleamed from her braids, which she'd allowed Aefa to add after the girl begged her to think of the king. *At least let me rope in amber so Morimaros might admire the flare of fire.*

But Elia had no idea when he would return, and besides, she'd come here to this garden to be left alone, asking that the gate be locked behind her until she was finished. Nearly a week ago, Elia had written to Errigal in defense of his second-born son. To Ban, she'd written and rewritten, as unsure of her words as she was his motives. She tried telling him the truth: that knowing he'd been here in Aremoria before her made her less lonely.

Then a half-truth: that she wished she'd not wasted their time together on grief and rage. That she wished she had asked him of his experiences since they'd last met, what he'd accomplished in Aremoria and what friends he'd made and whom he had grown to love. And then, a lie: that she could not believe he had betrayed his own brother, just to prove something to a woman he no longer knew.

In the end, she had written, *Do not keep promises by causing more pain*, and nothing more.

Her sisters had not replied, though surely they would have received her previous missives.

There still was time, Elia told herself, to avoid war, though she could not help but worry. Gaela and Regan would never agree to any path that offered succor or forgiveness to Lear. They'd never allow him to retire here in Aremoria, even if it meant they could rule the island without him or her or the threat of invasion or rebellion. They wanted Lear close, to witness his decline, to watch him suffer and die. His penance, for presumed transgressions. She supposed their familial drama would not be so terrible, except that they sat at the center of an entire kingdom. Most families did not have to worry about their passions and arguments rippling out into war and famine and disease.

Would it be different if Dalat had lived?

Elia hardly remembered her mother's voice, or face, but she remembered Dalat had liked to get dirty in a garden, or milking goats—*"There are a dozen reasons for a princess to know how to milk a goat,"* Dalat murmured, *wrapping Elia's tiny brown hand around the pink teat.* Yet Dalat had also enjoyed the hours it took to create her elaborate hair, drinking wine and gossiping with her companions as they pampered her. The queen had suffered harsh pains when she bled, and allowed only her daughters and favorite women around her at such times. Elia learned to link her mother's sweat and pain with intimacy, while Gaela learned her ferocious warrior's grimace from the same, and Regan learned to hide any agony she felt behind a solid mask of ice, because pain was not for your enemies—or even your husband—to see.

Elia was too young when the queen died to hear the rumors that some enthusiastic star-reader, or even the king himself, had forced their prophecy to come true. But she heard it later, from Gaela's own sharp tongue. Shocked and incredulous, Elia had defended Lear, and her own beloved stars, making them her point of constancy in the lonely roaming island court.

*You're such a baby,* her sisters had said. *His baby.*

That moment was the end of any chance the sisters might have had for a close-hearted relationship. It was clear to Elia now, though they'd never spoken of it again. The divide with Gaela and Regan on one side, and Elia and Lear on the other, had begun that day in earnest, and gaped wider and wider as the girls grew, fairly or not. Gaela allied herself with Astore, first as ward, then as wife, and though this might've been a chance for Regan and Elia to connect, Regan gripped even tighter to Gaela. And when Regan married Connley against Lear's direct wishes, his anger became the final divide between them all. Elia had grown so used to it, she'd accepted the fallout as if she'd never expected anything else.

People died every day, and their loved ones mourned, then lived on. Why could it not be so with her own family? Elia had been just as gutted as the rest of them by Dalat's death, but it amazed her, even so, that one person could have so much power to break so many strong people, just by dying.

*Did my father murder my mother for his stars?* Elia whispered to the roses. She didn't want to believe it. But then, it could perhaps explain Lear's behavior. How easily and angrily he'd banished—and disowned—her, his favorite daughter. *His baby.* She had disobeyed his stars.

A breeze ruffled the grass, tickled the nape of Elia's neck, and brought up such sweet autumn smells from the garden. But no voice came with the wind, no hissing answer from the earth. Either these foreign lands did not know, or would not answer a girl who'd abandoned the tongue of the earth for the stars.

And she'd forsaken it so readily. Because her father commanded it. Had she fought him at all? Had she struggled to keep a memory of Ban, had she begged to continue loving the trees? What was the last tree word she'd spoken? Elia hardly knew. She remembered grief and weeping and then finally the emptiness, but could not recall any fight.

Today was the first zenith since her father disowned her. Elia had never before sat alone beneath a zenith sun.

Just a month past, Ban Errigal had crouched at the base of a standing stone and called tiny silver lights to dance at his fingers; when Elia was a child, she had done the same. Once, it had been easy. She'd seen Aefa do similar, snapping fire, though the princess always would turn away, refusing that they could outshine the stars while so far from the sky.

Elia placed her hands in her lap, palms up, gently cupping the air. She took three long, deep breaths, and whispered, *I would hold the sun in tiny mirror, a ball of warmth between my hands.*

Her eyes flew open in apprehension. She scrubbed her hands together, then put them flat on the grass. She leaned forward, bent on her hands and knees, digging her fingers through the thick green grass to the cool earth beneath. Perhaps the trees of Aremoria would not speak to her, but Ban had made magic here. There was a voice to find in the roots of this land. There had to be.

*My name is Elia, once of Lear,* she said. *I'm listening again.*

The scrape of footsteps on the crushed shells of the narrow path leading here from the arched gate shocked Elia up from her crouch. She twisted, staring toward whomever had interrupted her, angry at Aefa and the royal guard who had allowed it.

Morimaros of Aremoria stood some several long strides away.

She supposed, bleakly, none would have even tried to stop *him* from entering.

"Elia?" he said, very quietly. "Are you well?"

"No," she said sitting back on her bare feet. Her empty boots slumped together in the shade of a soft lamb's-ear plant.

The king came to her and went down to one knee. He was fresh in trousers, boots, shirt, and short burnt-orange tunic, untied at the collar. Water glistened along the lines of his trim hair. Elia fought an urge to brush it away, to skim her fingers against his temple and skull. Was hair that short stiff, or soft? Warm as summer grass? Did it tickle like fox fur? Would his beard, exactly the same length, feel the same? Against her cheek or mouth?

It occurred to her that Morimaros would allow it, if she reached to touch. Her heartbeat sped, and she folded her hands together. The king blinked, and the sun caught his lovely lashes.

"I thought you were gone, still," Elia said.

"I returned, just now."

"The sun is in zenith today. It's a full month since the . . . since my father unnamed me."

Morimaros's mouth made a sad shape. "And you've no word back from your sisters."

She shook her head. "Nor have you?"

"No, but those I trust have confirmed that Connley took two towns along his border with Astore, one that spans a creek and is known for mills, and the other that has been officially in Astore's territory since before the line of Lear. And Astore has seated himself in Dondubhan, like a king, to await Midwinter. Connley and Regan are in Errigal now. Shoring up the backing of that earl and his iron."

"You know much."

The king nodded.

"And I have no network of friends or informants, but would rely on my sisters or what I might hear from the Fool or Earl Errigal or . . ." she shrugged helplessly. "You see why I fear so little support, if I tried to be queen of any land."

"I do not."

"Morimaros—"

"But . . . I understand that is how you feel at the moment. So I will tell my navy to prepare for the winter spent at home."

"Thank you."

Morimaros shifted, almost as if uncomfortable, but Elia couldn't believe it. He was in his palace, in his capital city, powerful and strong. His dark blue eyes looked randomly about the garden: the rose towers and beds of velvety lamb's-ear and summer blaze, the tiny red trumpets of the war leaf, the bleeding-spade flowers deep purple with spikes of red, the black-heart bushes with their black limbs and thin green leaves so pale they neared grayish-white.

"Do you enjoy flowers?" he asked.

Elia lifted her eyebrows.

The king grimaced. "You've been spending much time here, while I was gone." He looked at her hands; dirt made dark crescents in the beds of her ragged nails.

"I was trying to speak with them," she said, prepared to defend herself if he found her ridiculous.

Instead, Morimaros nodded. "Ban preferred trees for conversation."

Elia glanced away, warm for thinking of both men at once. "Your flowers will not talk to me, nor the junipers in your center courtyard. I am out of practice, I think."

"Or merely out of your home," he suggested with clear reluctance.

She put a hand over her heart.

"Elia," the king began, stopping after her name.

Impulsively, she lowered her hand to his rough knuckles. Her finger skimmed over the large ring of pearls and garnets. The Blood and the Sea. The ring of Aremore kingship.

Morimaros hardly breathed, she noted, as she walked her fingers gently along the back of his hand to his wrist. He turned it over, and she touched the softest, palest part of his arm, where his pulse lived.

"Elia," he said again, more of a whisper now.

"Morimaros," she replied, wishing she could say it in the language of trees. *King of this land,* she whispered instead.

*Our king,* the garden whispered.

Elia startled, snatched her hand back, and flung herself around, staring at the roses and garden entire.

The king leapt to his feet, alert for danger.

"It's all right," she said, climbing up, too. "I only heard them, I heard the flowers speak. They like that you are their king." Her voice did not shake, though her spirit did, and her heartbeat, too.

Morimaros cleared his throat, his own hands now folded behind his back, in that favorite pose, that made his shoulders broader and expanded the force of his presence as if he'd put on a blinding golden crown.

Still with a quiver in her heart, Elia met his eyes. The energy there, the intention, parted her lips.

He said, "I want you to marry me."

She caught her breath, and then said, "You want, or Aremoria wants?"

"Both."

"You told me you cannot care what you want for yourself, that you are ever the crown." Elia glanced away, then forced her gaze back.

"I went away with the army to stop myself from caring, to focus Aremoria again at the fore of my heart. It did not work. I thought—think—of you always." A grimace pulled at his mouth again.

"And that is terrible," she said very seriously.

"No! But I—" he stopped as she gave him a small, wry smile.

"I shouldn't tease you," Elia whispered.

Morimaros laughed once: a breath of humor, then gone. "I am glad of it."

"I told my father I would never marry," she said suddenly. "He let you write to me, for some purpose of his own. Politics, I assumed, and I asked him to stop, before expectations could be set, but . . ."

The king's face stiffened.

Shame lowered Elia's eyes again, though it was more her father's shame than her own. "I should not have to be a wife. I have spent years training as a priest. I should be an advisor, not a queen. A diplomat at best. I know nothing about strategy or holding a land secure. You have said that I bring people together, and I do believe I can; but that is because my people respond to an unwavering devotion and practice of faith and—and in my reliable prophecies and star-study. Things you do not have in Aremoria. Maybe I have some natural humor, and I think I am—I try to be—often kind. But my sisters devour me so easily, and so would I be consumed here, as your queen. No strength to you, no light of my own; merely something to be protected and displayed."

"I would not let you be consumed, and you would learn to assert yourself. You have fewer enemies here than you think."

"Because I am in exile, with no power. The moment this place thought I had any power, particularly over you, I would be destroyed."

"You do have power over me," he said.

Her head tilted up again, Elia smiled sadly. "You see something when you look at me that I would like to feel."

A tiny noise of frustration hummed from Morimaros's throat. "I would protect you. I can."

"I don't want to have to be protected, Morimaros," she said, biting back her own frustration. "That is a trap, too."

"Then . . . encourage you. Support you. We could find a way to be . . . partners."

"While I abandon Innis Lear?"

"Elia, you told me you want peace, and to be compassionate, and to follow the stars. That you do not *want* to be the queen of Innis Lear. I am not asking you to do that, I am only asking you to marry *me*. Marry me, and then keep up your studies, if you like. I will never allow Aremoria to obey the stars, but that doesn't mean I would forbid you, or anyone, from listening to them. Be a queen at my side, one who is a diplomat, who is an advisor. Mine. My wife and own guiding star. I won't ask you to make choices over people's lives. I won't make you responsible for anything you don't want. Bring your father here, or we'll sail forth and claim him. You can care for him, here in Aremoria. I will give you everything, all you have said you want in this life. Just with a husband, and here, in my home."

Tears pricked her eyes, because it *was* everything she'd claimed to want. This king—no, this man—was offering her all of it. But her heart clenched. It twisted, and she knew she could not concede. Elia could not forsake that rough island that had borne her, as much as her parents. Not now that she felt the lack of it, that she finally understood how she'd cut herself off from the rootwaters years ago, before her father banished her. Innis Lear was broken, everyone kept saying so, and Elia had never even noticed. She was as selfish as her sisters. If she abandoned the island, her history, as readily as her father had tried to strip her name, would she ever be able to know herself? Was that why her family made such terrible decisions? Because none knew themselves, but only knew how others defined them, be it the stars or husbands or fathers? Bad enough Elia was forced to wait here until Midwinter, until her sisters allowed her to return. Bad enough to be the youngest, weakest of them. Bad enough her father—who loved her—had also lost himself. If she cut herself away from all of it, Elia knew her regrets would forever haunt her, and her unhappiness might poison this golden land, as her family had done to their own.

But how could Elia of Lear even begin to explain it all to the king of Aremoria? She said, "You would give me all I ask for, Morimaros, and then—and then still could take the crown of Innis Lear from us. Marriage would not stop war."

"There are many possibilities, not all war. Not all—"

"But you would not be satisfied with only me. I know what they say here about reuniting Aremoria and Innis Lear. You want to be the greatest king in a thousand years. That means taking my island for your own."

He said nothing.

"You might try to give it back to me, like a gift. If I were your wife. Your queen. Is that what you think?" Elia blinked, and tears rolled down her cheeks, clinging to the line of her jaw. "Do you see? You are above me."

"What? No." Morimaros shook his head in emphatic denial. "You are already royalty, the daughter of kings and—and empresses. Never beneath me."

"That's how I feel. Disempowered, with no authority. If I marry you as I am, it would be like locking that into place." The realization took Elia's breath away. This was it: the core truth. She had to make herself into—something. Her choice. Before she could hold any power over herself or others. "I can't abandon Innis Lear to you, and marrying you now would do exactly that."

"I'm asking only for you, Elia. And nothing else."

"You know that isn't how it works. You are never only you, and I—I don't even know what I can be!"

"I'm sorry," Morimaros said, low with regret. "This is still too soon. I'm making everything worse."

He turned, but Elia grasped his elbow. The tears fell into the air. "It is not too much. I am not breaking again. Tears are not a sign of such calamity." She curled her hands around his wrist, pressing his hand to her heart. "I cannot hide here with you, I cannot be small when Innis Lear needs help. I—I cannot let you be my strength. I let my father be that for me, let him protect me, hide me away, coddle me, so that I would not be sullied with the emotions of life, or face any distress. So that I would not become my sisters. I won't make such a mistake again. My giving my all to one man, even one I might learn to trust, is how he alone was able to take everything I thought I was."

"I wouldn't do that. I'm not your father."

"I promise you I do not see you as such a king as he. But I . . ." Elia lifted his hand and kissed his knuckle. She let herself breathe against the back of his hand as his fingers trembled. She turned his hand over and kissed the center where the skin was softer than where Morimaros would grip his sword.

At the touch of her lips to his palm, Elia shivered. Heat spiraled in the small of her back. When she breathed, she was suddenly aware of the press of her breasts against the stiff bodice, and her bare feet against the tickling grass. She had not felt so alive in her body in years and years, not since—

Gasping, Elia let go. She backed away, hands clamped together over her heart.

"Elia."

That was all he said, without demand, or even longing: only her name, hovering there like a soft moon moth.

"I can't marry you," she whispered.

His short beard ruffled as he clenched his jaw, but it was only hurt in his eyes. He did not ask for more explanation.

That was what made Elia offer it. "You're the Lion of War, and I'm the Child Star. Never together, despite Calpurlugh being fixed, always there in the north. When the Lion appears, Calpurlugh is consumed and vanishes."

"Do not make this choice based on inconstant stars, Elia Lear," he warned.

"It is my heart making the choice, and the stars are only . . . the reflection of it. The poem I grasp at, to try to explain to you."

Morimaros lost all emotional expression. "The sun has no friends," he said dully. "Nor kings, either."

Elia did not understand the words, but she did understand the feeling behind them. Loneliness had been the star at her back, for these last years. "I'm sorry, Mars." She took a long breath of rosy air, shocked the garden could remain so bright and colorful, when the king of Aremoria had gone dull and gray. "Someday—" Elia began to say, but Morimaros held up his hand.

He said, "I interrupted you here. I should withdraw."

Though it hurt him, she could see, Elia did not stop him from leaving this time. She sank onto the grass, bowed over her knees, and covered her head with her hands. Grass scratched her ankles, the tops of her feet, and her nose. It smelled of earth, dry and thick, and of roses nearby. Elia breathed carefully, letting the perfume soothe her. There was one other piece of her refusal she could not have shared, for it terrified her: she would not marry a man who loved her, especially one as truly good as this one seemed. Her father had loved her mother, and then her death had destroyed him, though the stars had made him expect it all along. Elia knew her stars, too. Her loyalty had been fixed at her birth; there was no breaking its orbit. She could not risk causing such harm to Morimaros.

And Elia would not allow herself to find refuge at the expense of Innis Lear.

Aefa appeared and knelt at her side; Elia knew her friend by the gentle touch at the nape of her neck, and the stiff sigh as fingers picked at something on her shoulder. "The king looked wretched as he passed me. What did you say to him to carve such a mask?"

Elia leaned sideways so her temple touched Aefa's knee, and her friend pulled her fully against her lap. The wool of Aefa's skirt was soft on Elia's cheek. "I did not say yes."

"He proposed again?"

She nodded, then buried her face against Aefa's thigh.

"Very demanding king," Aefa said with a sniff.

"I hurt him."

"Well, he doesn't understand."

"Neither do I," Elia let the edge of a whine taint the words.

"Yes, you do."

"Yes, I do," she murmured to her friend with a sorrowful sigh.

*I have to go home,* she whispered to the flowers of Aremoria. *Now.* But they remained silent, ruffled petals shining like pearls in the zenith sun.

# GAELA

IN HER OWN home, Gaela preferred to wear simple soldier's attire: brown and gray leather, with some bits of mail or plate as the situation required, short skirts over trousers or only the trousers. A jacket that tied tight across the front for binding and armor. All finely made, but basic and plain.

Since her father had come to stay nearly a month ago, she'd learned an unfortunate lesson that her choice of clothing allowed Lear's retainers to snub or ignore her, in seeming obedience to Lear's own wishes.

She might snap for their attention or threaten to throw them out, and this or that retainer could bug out his eyes and be all apologies and smooth pretense, that he'd not realized it was her. Obvious lies, Gaela knew, as there was no one like her in all of Innis Lear.

Not since her mother had died.

But rather than act a fool for her father, or a furious brat in her husband's eyes, Gaela now chose upon rising to put on a gown and glittering belt hung with amber and polished malachite, to have her girls weave velvet and glass into her hair, slide more than only the Astore ring onto her fingers, paint her bottom lip and the corners of her eyes. As if she attended a refined court every day, as if fashion and elegance were her best morning concerns. No retainer could pretend this Lady Gaela, this queen-to-be, this duchess in her pink-and-midnight gowns, her skirts lined with outrageously beautiful teal wool, a diadem crowning her black hair, could be mistaken for any less than herself.

So did she sweep into the rear court of Astore's old castle, hunting her father and his commander.

Not five moments before, Gaela had come upon her captain Osli, back pressed to the stone wall of an unused hall between the duke's study and the old solarium. It was a fine place to hide, and Gaela would never have found the young woman if she hadn't been looking to use the solarium herself, to store the few of her mother's things she'd brought home from the Summer Seat. Gaela refused to find displays for the beloved objects until Lear and his men moved on to their time with Regan and Connley.

The captain of Gaela's personal retainers had, for the first time, hidden from her. Osli had gasped, straightened, and turned her eyes across to the opposite wall, clearly willing Gaela to walk past, ignore her—to allow Osli the privacy she'd come to find.

And Gaela would've granted it, if not for the reddened new bruise cutting an inch along her captain's right cheekbone.

This was no battle wound or accident from the arena: Osli's uniform held no dust or mud, and her knuckles were not red from hitting back. Only a single drop of blood marred the collar of her dark pink gambeson. Gaela stopped instantly.

To Osli's credit, the girl did not bend her face to her shoulder to hide the wound, nor flee. She would not cower, as Gaela would not have. Her eyes had closed, though, and so the captain could not see the flash of horror and concern that slid through Gaela's eyes before transforming into pure, cold anger.

"Who did that to you?" Gaela demanded softly.

Osli kept her lips pressed shut.

Gaela admired the determination but would not allow it. She intended to utterly destroy whoever had hit Osli. "There are times for honor in silence," Gaela said, standing near enough she could see the roots of Osli's hair. "This is not such a time. I will know, and you will tell me."

"My lady," the captain said, brave enough to meet Gaela's dark eyes. "It will do no good."

The smile that spread on Gaela's mouth was not kind. "I do not intend to try for good. Tell me."

Osli's jaw muscles shifted as she clenched and unclenched her teeth.

Gaela grasped Osli's shoulder, squeezing the thin leather cap of the uniform sleeve. "None shall know you told me, none shall know I have discovered it at all. Your life will not be made harder in our own ranks, or in your command. You have my promise on that. But I will know."

"Esric," Osli snarled, suddenly alive with fury. "They—they cornered me, said they could *fix me*! There is *nothing wrong with me*. I told them that if they were men they'd not be threatened by my strength. That's when he—I would've hit him back, but it was so vicious, and I was so full of rage. I'd have killed him if I started, and I would not have your retainer responsible for the death of your father's."

Such a swell of affection and pride filled Gaela that her grip became too ferocious, causing Osli to gasp.

"It was well done," the prince said, releasing her young captain. "I will finish it for you."

And Gaela strode toward the rear courtyard, where she knew Lear's retainers could be found, lounging and lazing even at this early time of evening.

In the yard a ring had been built, messily formed of ropes, with retainers—half unjacketed—holding the corners, all while two shirtless, barefooted men wrestled in the middle. Gaela paused on the final stair as a cheer rose, the unmelodious noise made of half groans, and several voices calling new bets. Lear was seated close to the wall, and he clapped and tossed a handful of dull coins at the men. A cacophony of vulgar behavior.

Esric was her father's commander, and Gaela did not doubt that Lear had witnessed the entire attack and done not a thing.

Gaela stepped down and called, "This game is over."

She was ignored, and that would not stand.

The eldest daughter of Lear walked to the nearest corner, shoved the retainer aside, and grasped the rope he held. She jerked it, pulling the next man off balance hard enough so he fell to one knee.

Protests rang out at the interruption, before the men noticed who had ended their revelry.

"What, Gaela!" her father cried. "Why so full of frowns?"

"Your men are all insolence, sir." She thrust the rope to the hard-packed dirt of the yard. "All hours, in all ways, and I am grown sick of it."

"Insolent! For sporting with ourselves?" Lear giggled.

"I have spoken to you of their slovenly ways before, and yet you refuse to take them to task. I will do it for you now." Gaela leveled a glare at the nearest man, then swept her gaze over them all, eyeing Esric especially. "Mend your lazy, arrogant, unbridled behavior, or be gone from Astora by morning."

Lear flew at her. "You cannot order my men. These are mine, and my will shall order them."

"Then order them better, as a commander, and not an old fool."

It was too much; Gaela knew it the moment she spoke it, but she faced Lear proudly.

"Do you call your father a fool?" Lear said with stealthy anger.

From the benches, a voice called, "You so readily did give away all your other titles!"

For a moment silence struck the yard, but for the song of evening birds and the rustle of the city just beyond the wall. Gaela could not look away from Lear to identify the speaker, not until Lear himself slid his eyes that way, with a tattered slight smile.

It was his own Fool.

"What title would you regain for me, then?" asked Lear.

"Lear's shadow?"

Gaela fought a shiver of foreboding.

"And who is this standing, then, here with us?" Lear flapped his hand at her, and she leveled the Fool with her dark gaze, daring him.

"Your daughter, Uncle, and the queen-in-waiting, if waiting be a battle."

"That is right," Gaela said to her father. "This Fool knows better than you what we are, and what we will be. Understand me: your retainers are not welcome here any longer, soaked in this dreadful behavior. Wrestling in mud and betting on themselves! Lusting after my maids and those living in the city! Think not that I am unaware. Striking my people, and making servants of their betters. A king would never have tolerated it before, nor shall I now. Get them gone if you cannot control them."

Lear brought his fists up, trembling with exhaustion or rage or some mix of the two. "I will go with them, if they are to be tossed out with so little joy and care!"

"So be it!" Gaela yelled.

"What is this storm?"

All glared at the newcomer: Kay Oak, muddy from travel and stinking of horse. Gaela wished to welcome him, the uncle who shared her better blood. But the once-earl put his hands on his hips and very clearly turned a face of comfort to the king. "Your Majesty, my kin, what troubles you?"

"My wretched girl turns me out!" wailed the king, with no hint of his so-recent fury at the Oak Earl, nor even a hint of familial recognition.

"Patience, lord," Kayo said, turning to Gaela with disbelief. He stripped off his heavy riding gloves.

She covered her annoyance with a shrug. "If he insists, so it must be."

"Gaela." Her name was all exasperation in Kayo's mouth. "You owe him a daughter's fealty. See how unfit he is."

"I owe him nothing but what he has already received. How do you stand here now, defending him, when he banished you, cast you aside, like there was nothing he owed to you? Like you were not brothers. What for?"

Lear blinked. He scrubbed at his eyes and dragged those offending hands into his wild hair. "Banished?" he murmured, and his mouth curled up into a sneer. "My betraying brother! Would he dare show himself?"

"Ah no, Lear! Ha!" the Fool danced up and between Lear and Kayo. "This is not your brother but mine, a darker Fool than me, but still *a fool*."

Gaela laughed harshly. "He is at that."

"Why are you turning your father out?" Kayo asked her.

"Lear has heard my accusations of misrule and chaos sown in my home, and does not defend himself or his men. So I judge them unfit for this place."

Lear cackled, a child unattended, and aimed his words to the sky. "Regan will welcome me, and Connley!"

Kayo frowned. "Connley cannot be trusted, Your Highness."

"But my other, brighter daughter Regan will take me in. Her love has always been true."

"You are mad," Gaela said wonderingly.

Lear fell silent. All around, retainers barely breathed.

Kayo's frown encompassed the entire yard. "Be kind, Gaela, you see how it is with him. He needs you to be a daughter."

"As I needed my mother?"

The Oak Earl said nothing, shattered—as he should have been—by the reminder.

Gaela held her hands out, uncaring now for her uncle's opinion. He was as in love with inconstant Lear and as stupid as Elia. "If Lear needs my council, he should listen to me. Father, I care not where you go, but you will not stay here, not with all your rowdy men. Revel in kinship with the beasts of the field, or ask some poorer of your lands to house and feed you! Discover whether you are truly beloved of these people. I think you will be surprised."

Kayo's eyes were shadowed, so low and glaring was his brow. "Would your people shelter *you*, Gaela?"

"I will withdraw my protection of you, Kayo, if you do not watch your tongue."

"They would shelter Elia."

Gaela bared her teeth. "I will shelter my people, because I will be their king."

Lear stepped nearer to his eldest daughter, peering into her face. "It is no wonder I find no comfort nor nurturing grace here; this daughter has none in her. She is dried up, barren of life, deprived of motherhood for being her own mother's death omen."

Gaela slapped him.

The king staggered back, and around him blades grated free of sheaths.

Kayo hauled at her arm, crying her name. She swung, knocking Kayo off her.

She faced her father and his circle of retainers, and all Gaela saw was a rotting old man who had always been sick: with star prophecy and loss and bitter fanaticism. Her stomach churned; she thought she might vomit, but

Gaela Lear did not show weakness. She did not shy from battle. She would calm herself, then strike deadly, as a commander and king. Gaela seethed, sweat on her temples, and hissed a fatal verdict to her foolish father: "I do not care what you do, live or die, only do it out of my sight. Go to my sister if you would, throw yourself at Connley."

Lear reeled back into the arms of his men, all dragging away, gathering what they could to leave. The Fool flapped his coat but said nothing, staring at his king as he stumbled.

"Why do you hate your father so deeply? It cannot be from Dalat's death, not still. It was not Lear's fault," Kayo insisted.

"He has never denied his guilt, and you were not here to see otherwise." She turned her hot brown eyes to her uncle. "You were not here, and so could not save any of us."

His mouth went rigid. "That is my great regret, and for it I will not abandon him."

"What about *us*?" Gaela shoved herself toward him, glaring right into his dark gray eyes. "Do not abandon *us,* Uncle. Let that old man go."

"He needs my loyalty."

"You should obey your new, better king!"

"Yet you are not that, Gaela Lear. And perhaps never shall be."

Fury darkened Gaela's sight with spikes of crimson. She grabbed her uncle's collar, drew her knife, and slashed it across his face.

Kayo cried out, thrusting free of her grip. He stumbled, hands up and pressed to his cheek and eye. Blood poured through, as red as Gaela's anger.

*A king had no need of brothers, nor uncles,* she thought viciously, and cried, "This Oak Earl is no more. As the king before me stripped him of his titles, *so do I.* If he is seen upon my lands again it will be his death. Now get him out of Astora."

Gaela turned and raged back into the halls of the castle, mortally bruised, with her mother's name on her tongue and a curse in her heart.

KAYO OF TARIA Queen did not know how to be a farmer. His people were caravanserai and noble governors, though he supposed perhaps five hundred years ago his ancestors might have herded goats along the dry steppe of the Second Kingdom.

This wave-racked island squished beneath his boot; vibrant green moss and lush short grass surrounded him in this valley, marked by scatters of tiny yellow and purple flowers whose names Kayo did not yet know. He thought he recognized a mountain thistle—he could understand a fellow creature's need for such a protective layer. Kayo tugged his own bright purple coat tighter, looking beyond the meadow to where, at the curve of the shallow stream, a cottage was tucked. Smoke lifted from the chimney; he was expected. Kayo wrinkled his nose at the long-haired cow chewing at a large bale of hay, and wandered toward the hill behind the cottage. It was bare of trees, but bright green, too, and little white sheep made slow grazing trails. Despite the verdant mossiness, it smelled most like stale rain and mud. Dampness clung to Kayo's nose, and his short black curls seemed thrice as thick.

"I've made you an earl. My Oak Earl," the king of Innis Lear had said to him, four days ago at the Summer Seat. "Found you a steward and good stone manor. You'll oversee several villages, and their reeves will report to you. The land is yours."

They'd walked along the yard together, during the break between rains that morning, in search of where Elia had hidden herself. "Thank you, Lear," Kayo said carefully, rubbing his hands together against the dank ocean wind. It was late spring, but his bones had not yet thawed from the long winter. He'd months ago given in to Learish fashions, wrapping himself in wool and dark leather, and a fur-lined coat with a hood. His headscarf clung around his neck; Kayo couldn't quite bear to leave it behind.

He'd been given a choice: stay, become the Oak Earl, and sever ties of family to the Third Kingdom, rooting himself permanently to this island and the fortunes of the Lear dynasty. Or go. Be a caravan master, wander and travel, serve the empress, but lose privileges of family on this island, become no more than an honored guest when he chanced to pass through.

Traditions and training pulled him toward the Third Kingdom, where he'd lived half his life, where he'd spent years building a reputation as a negotiator to run his own caravan on behalf of the empress one day. But a part of him had belonged to Innis Lear since he'd been sent to foster with Dalat as a boy. She'd been more a young mother to him than a sister, and her foreign husband had welcomed Kayo without fuss. This island had been her home. She'd loved it here, the fluffy sheep and harsh wind, the eating ocean and hearty, temperamental people. The roots were so deep and mysterious, Dalat said, she felt as though God had put her here, in a place where her curious spirit would never fall to satisfaction.

Kayo felt the same sense of mystery, though it unnerved him where Dalat had been intrigued.

*Kay Oak of Lear.* The witch of the White Forest had named him so the night of the first anniversary of Dalat's death.

*My Oak Earl,* Lear himself had said.

They did not communicate, the witch and the king, of that Kayo was certain. So how did they call him by the same Learish name? What mystery of this island's roots explained that? Did the trees whisper names into the king's dreams?

Lear had put a hand on Kayo's shoulder, there in the front courtyard of the Summer Seat. The king was some thirty years Kayo's elder, and it was apparent by the silver in his loose brown hair, the wrinkles making his long face longer.

"Kayo, I know yours to be a difficult decision," the king said. A seriousness focused his blue eyes in a way Kayo was unused to; usually Lear appeared more dreamy, looking through people and walls. "To choose one loyalty over another, exchanging family and name for family and name. But I must insist, just as I must consolidate what I can now. There are those on this island who would challenge me. And my girls. And for that, I would have you stay. Be mine."

Kayo frowned, knowing plenty about those who would challenge the king. But Lear smiled and continued, "I've had a prophecy read for you, and your stars are rather interesting, Kayo. One thing is certain: we will be great friends so long as I am king. So"—Lear winked like a mischievous child—"tell me you will stay, and be my brother."

It was said on Innis Lear that their king had been born under two constellations: the Twin Star, and the Star of Crowns. One promised he would be pulled in many directions, and the other that he would be king. But as the third-born son it had been very unlikely he would rule, unless tragedy struck the crown. So he believed, so all believed. But the last great king, his father, trusted in the prophecy and named Lear his heir, but Lear was a boy and full of dedication to the stars. He left the island instead, to study in the greatest star cathedrals on the continent for years. His brothers had remained, learning the laws and the people. When the king grew ill, Lear was sent for, and he returned, taking up his heavenly work in the chapels and towers of Innis Lear. The great king died, and his final wish was that Lear take the crown, witnessed by his first and second sons, witnessed by his retainers and earls, witnessed by dukes and healers. But Lear refused. The stars were his vocation: he was crowned *for* the stars, not by them, he argued. How better to serve the people, the kingdom, than as a royal star-reader, the most gifted and precise of them?

In only three short weeks from this refusal to take the throne, both his brothers were dead. By accident, and by sudden illness. Lear had no choice but to take up the crown in the midst of tragedy, and never again questioned the will of the stars—if he had not, his brothers might well have lived. His devotion had been a thing Dalat admired in her husband, for her heart, too, was devoted to a singular faith.

But Kayo's was unsure. He questioned God and also the stars, constantly, and could think of a dozen interpretations one might apply to the Twin Star and the Star of Crowns that would spool out very differently than Lear's. As he'd learned, the way everyone on Innis Lear must learn, what stars meant and how the prophecies worked, he'd come to realize they could function as a decision-making tool. When he faced a choice, a prophecy could suggest one path, and upon hearing it, Kayo immediately knew if he agreed or not. The prophecies made clear to Kayo not truth or destiny, but his own mind.

As for God—well, God created Kayo curious and questioning, so God could handle the inquiries.

"What is the prophecy?" he asked.

"The Star of Third Birds touching against the horizon at the same place as the Root of the Oak, and the silver-smiling Moon of Songs, Kayo, crowning its course almost exactly. You and I travel this life together: me on a certain, constant path, you moving parallel to, but *with* me, until my crown sinks below the horizon. I can have it drawn out, if you like. The shapes are fluid, and repeating, in the way your people put in your art so much. Yes, she'd have liked it, too," the king murmured, and his body stilled in sorrow.

Kayo shared the moment of remembrance by putting his hand on Lear's shoulder. Dalat shouldn't have died so young, no matter the reasons.

"I remember you had only twelve years when you came to be with her," Lear said softly. "Just older than Elia now."

"We should find her," Kayo said, honestly glad of an interruption. He longed to set eyes on his youngest niece again. It had been months, for at the start of winter he'd gone with the elder two sisters to Astora, where ferocious Gaela chose to foster herself. She'd been training with Astore's retainers, and invited Kayo there to teach what he knew of fighting, which was not too much. He was trained to protect a caravan and his own body, not attack mounted or steel-armored soldiers. Gaela had taken his tutelage, and asked a hundred questions about the queens and empresses of the Third Kingdom. Kayo tried to turn all his responses back to Innis Lear, to Dalat and how Gaela could use the history of the empresses to shore up her education and eventual rule. Regan always listened, too, and sometimes Astore, though the duke laughed at putting women in charge. He said, "Unless they make themselves like our princess Gaela, it seems a waste of women's talents."

Kayo was not fond of the Duke Astore. The man was proud, and a bully, and Kayo had been reluctant to leave Gaela alone there under his domineering influence. But the ever-loyal, ever-cool Regan had reminded him, "No one does a thing to Gaela that she does not permit. Besides, Astore is strong, as are his stars. He understands how the throne of Innis Lear works."

Kayo had understood then: Gaela intended to marry Col Astore. He tried to tell Dalat's firstborn that she should not join herself to a man already married to himself, that she needed a husband who would support her in all. Gaela frowned as if Kayo had begun to turn blue. "Astore holds the most power on Innis Lear aside from the king. I will make his power mine, and support myself." She said it as if any fool could see.

He'd sworn on the memory of his beloved sister to protect her daughters, but it seemed to him the elder two hardly needed his help.

The valley where Kayo now stood was at the southern end of the tract of land Lear had granted him. Beautiful, though he knew that except for these three months when the flowers bloomed, it would be swathes of pale yellow and a gray, dripping green under cold blue skies and sheer clouds. He would miss the red and gilded desert.

"Be mine," Lear had said.

He meant, *Give up your allegiance to your grandmother the empress. Let go of Taria Queen. Be only Kay Oak, brother to the king, uncle to three ferocious and cool and gentle princesses. Sink your name into the rocks of my island.*

Yet the king had asked, not ordered. And the king did not know the secret Dalat and the witch of the White Forest had begged him to keep.

The king merely expected a man to want a title, to want the friendship of a king, and the ties of family, to prefer this mossy island to the vast deserts, fertile riverbanks, and desperately sharp mountain peaks of all the lands of the Third Kingdom, despite the milky people here, despite their confusion of force and strength. They did not even believe in God here, only in whispering winds and the navel of the earth and the cold promise of dead stars.

But Lear was right. Kayo did want a title. He did like being respected on sight and never asked who his mother and grandmother had been, as if only their names made him matter. Here he mattered for being himself.

That alone almost convinced him.

They had found Elia Lear playing alone at the Summer Seat's navel, a well that ran straight down forever into the dark depths of the rock beneath their feet. It was a plain well, in the center of a courtyard where roses crawled up the painted walls. A single woman, pale-skinned and unadorned, sat upon a bench mending trousers. It was not one of Dalat's attendants. And Kayo realized in that moment he'd not seen his sister's women at all. He touched Lear's forearm, pausing before they entered the court.

"Where is Satiri? Where is Yna?"

Lear's stark eyebrows lifted. "I sent them home."

"Why? They'd been here for nearly twenty years! This was their home. They were *hers*."

"Yes," the king whispered. His face bent with grief. "So I remembered any time I saw them. They had to leave."

"But . . . Elia is alone." Horror made him release the king too abruptly. Dalat had made a thriving home here, surrounded herself with friends both born of Innis Lear and brought from the Third Kingdom. It had been a braided compromise, now all undone. He looked at the king, up at the sheer sky, then to Elia, a brown little nut of a girl.

"She has *me*," Lear said. "She is my daughter, and she has me. And all her people, those of Innis Lear. And we must have you."

Kayo shook his head once. "But her mother, her sisters, they're not here. And now her mother's people are gone from around her, too?"

"We are enough, Kayo. We will make it so."

Even Kayo would not be *enough*. It wasn't fair; it unrooted the girl before she could understand or choose on her own. "You should let me take her to visit her mother's people."

The king looked dazed. "No. Maybe—someday, but no."

Frustrated, unsure why he felt so violently upended, Kayo called out, putting all the warmth he could muster into his voice. He strode ahead of the king and opened his arms. "Elia!"

The girl smiled brightly, then quickly the smile dimmed into a softer one, as if she'd checked her own instinct. Kayo's heart rolled. He lifted her up and hugged her, swinging her a little so that her toes knocked against his knees. A small giggle pressed against his neck; the princess was wet. Her dress stuck to him, her skin was clammy, and the kiss she put on his cheek was cold. Kayo set her down. "Were you out in all the rain?"

"Yes," she admitted shyly. "It felt good, and I thought I could hear the roses, whispering about . . ."

"About what?"

"Nothing. Hello, Father," she said, smoothing down her dress. The tilt of her chin and wide black eyes were so like Dalat's that Kayo was struck speechless. The girl's hair was bound back plainly under a soaking wet green scarf.

"Elia, you should find shelter when it rains, and this well . . . it is dangerous." The king touched one long finger to the black rocks of the well.

"I won't fall in, Father," she said, hiding her laugh, but not that she found him silly.

The king maintained his frown.

"Come here, Elia. Let me see you." Kayo knelt, holding Elia's shoulders. He put her exactly at arm's length. "You're taller since the winter, aren't you? And beautiful as your mother. Are you well?"

She nodded, staring into his eyes. "Your eyes are so very gray," she said with a little awe.

"My mother's second husband was a Godsman," Kayo said, then corrected himself: "My father, that is."

"Oh," she said. "A Godsman." She touched his face, and Kayo felt such a swell of affection for her, tears blurred the edges of his sight. "It's all right, Uncle," she said calmly.

"I know, starling."

"Or it will be. One of those. I helped Father look at your stars, did you know?"

"I did not!" Kayo let his brows rise. "You must be very skilled."

"I like to draw the patterns. What is a Godsman?"

Kayo smiled sadly. "Holy men, a tribe of them, but I cannot tell you more, for their secrets are held close—even from their sons, if we do not become one of them."

King Lear said, "What do you think, Elia, if we call Kayo our Oak Earl?"

"I don't think it will make up for not being a Godsman like his father."

A thing pinched his heart, and Kayo gripped her shoulders a bit too tightly.

Elia leaned in and hugged him. "But we've never had an Oak Earl on Innis Lear before."

Without hesitation, Kayo had said, "Then I will be your first."

So he would learn to farm.

Kayo walked now across squishy bog, east toward the center of his land. His land. He wondered how long it would be before he would be used to stewardship of something so entire as land; a piece of an island. Would it change him, to finally have a place all his own, stationary and complete? His mind shied away from it, rather imagining his ownership fell upon the revenue or produce only, the parts that were defined by a king or a man, not the land itself, which only God, surely, could claim.

Though on Innis Lear, they said the land claimed itself. The trees had their own language, some of which Kayo had learned. The wind whispered and the birds sang messages from the stars to the roots or the roots to the stars. Kayo took deep, questing breaths, as if to bring the island into himself.

That witch last year had said, *The island's roots and wind of our trees know what Dalat of Taria Queen and Innis Lear has asked of you. The trees know your worth.*

Kayo found a copse of trees, small and spindly, with white and gray bark. Their narrow leaves shivered and tittered together, flapping pale green. He touched a ruffle of leaves, and asked, "Can you understand me? I need a place to begin."

Wind fluttered the end of Kayo's headscarf, where it looped casually around his neck. He unspooled it reverently, kneeling at the base of one white tree. His trousers soaked up muck and cold water. The scarf had been a gift from his mother when Kayo reached his majority. All his life he'd been of both Taria Queen and Innis Lear, moving from one to the other over the three-month-long journey. Tied here by adventure, love, and his sister, tied there by blood and tradition.

The headscarf was vibrant ocher, and edged with teal silk. Precious and too fine for daily wear, it overwhelmed his eyes, making them like empty mirrors in too much sun; but teal, Dalat had told him once, was his best color.

Kayo of Taria Queen pressed the scarf into the cold, unfamiliar earth. He used his hands to dig a nest for it between two ghostly gray roots, and buried it there.

When he stood up, he was Kayo, the Oak Earl, so named by the island, a princess, and the king of Innis Lear, called to walk a parallel path with his brother, until the day Lear's crown lowered beyond the horizon.

# REGAN

REGAN BLED STEADILY as she sewed downy owl feathers into the hem of a linen shift.

She chose, like her mother would have, to be surrounded by the women of Errigal Keep during her monthly blood, and they were arrayed in front of her now: the chatelaine Sella Ironwife, married to the wizard Curan, and their two daughters; three other ladies who were cousins to Connley; and one younger sister of the former Lady Errigal, who had stayed behind when the lady departed to Aremoria, perhaps in trade for the missing elder. For their benefit, Regan had chosen a careful position, seeming to lounge on a low cushion, skirts arranged voluptuously all around.

In truth, Regan perched carefully and uncomfortably upon her knees, a shallow bowl between her legs to collect what blood she could, in preparation for the wormwork she and the Fox would perform in less than a day. The occasional gentle drip could not be heard over the chatter of the assembled ladies, who sewed and embroidered and mended.

The ache in her belly was nothing compared to the pain of miscarriage, and the tightness in her legs as Regan held the wretched pose with a gracious smile was well worth the reward of discovering what ailed her womb, and the hope that it could be fixed.

And Regan enjoyed the presence of other women, who, though they did not know of the dead spirits that plagued her nor of her desperation and feral sorrow, would understand if they did.

When she had daughters of her own, Regan would build them a room like this, with women like this. Friends, maids, cousins, witches, allies, enemies, all of it, but only women. Regan had experienced such a thing when Dalat lived, when Elia was such a baby still, and when sometimes Brona Hartfare had spent weeks living in Dondubhan or the Summer Seat with Dalat, as her companion and advisor. Together they attracted other women like crows to sparkling glass beads. There Regan learned the seeds of magic, and learned, too, to read the holy bones. Brona never hesitated to whisper answers and new questions in Regan's ear, and though Dalat did not believe in the stars as magic, or the earth saints even as tiny gods, neither did the queen say it could not be so. Dalat prayed to a god of her own, an expansive desert deity of love and vengeance, who apparently favored family and loyalty and heat. But Dalat had wished her daughters to be truly of Lear, and so to Regan, her mother would say, *My God is all and has no name but God. God is more than stars and trees and worms, and is all those things, too. I pray, but with action and choice, and God knows it, no matter where I am, because God is in me, and in you, and everything.*

*Does God speak to you?*

*Not with words.*

*The island must be stronger, then, Mama, to have its own voice.*

Dalat then smiled, cupped Regan's chin, and said, *That depends on what strength is,* and would offer no more.

Maybe if her mother had lived, Regan would understand better what kind of strength Dalat had believed in.

The argument ongoing between Sella Ironwife and Metis Connley touched on strength, too: they disagreed over the behavior of one of the apprentices, who'd been lately seducing another. Sella found it unprofessional, while Metis was in favor of strengthening lines of iron magic, so if two apprentices formed a union, all the better. Regan agreed with Metis: they needed all the strong magic on the island they could find, to counter the cold stars.

The debate was halted by a sharp knock, and Regan granted permission for the doors to be opened. Into the brightly lit room came a dirty retainer wearing the dark blushing pink of Astore.

Going still against the desire to stand, Regan lifted her cool brow but rather suddenly realized it was a woman retainer. "Osli."

The woman bowed like a man, and brandished a rolled letter, sealed at both ends with thick wax. "My lady Astore sends this letter to you."

Regan extended her hand, glad as always for word from Gaela, and even more to remember that, despite choosing the life of a man, Gaela still put women around herself. "Go take your rest, and then join us, Osli. You are welcome."

"I would rather stay in the barracks, my lady."

"Gaela would join me."

Osli hesitated, then bowed again, in definite agreement. "I will wash and rest, then, first."

Regan turned her attention to the letter, snapping the small leaves of wax holding it rolled shut. Around her the women went quiet, though it was a quiet of patient politeness and continued work.

*Our father leaves Astora,* Gaela began with no salutation, as usual. *I expect when Osli reaches you, he will be near behind, if not already through your door.*

*He is truly mad, and called me by our mother's name, then in the next breath cursed her line. He has said unforgivable things to me before, but now he is lost in it. His retainers are wild, attacking each other, myself, my people, because he does not keep them under control. Ask Osli and she will tell you more, though I am sure you already know these true ways of men. I will follow this letter with another, but for now, my captain will be away to you with all haste.*

Even as Regan skimmed her sister's writing, she could hear through the open window a change in the rhythm of the wind and noise of the Keep. A distant shout of greeting flared hot and died in an echo. The warm breeze sighed against her neck.

"Leave me," Regan said.

Though it was gentle, every woman obeyed her command instantly, none pausing to ask if they might help, or lend comfort.

She finished reading.

*Do as you must, Regan, and I will see you soon.*

Alone, Regan set down the letter, and gathered up her skirts to step carefully away from the bowl of blood. She went into her attached bedchamber and bound herself up with linen and moss before returning to collect the bowl. A slight pool of viscous blood was layered across the long, shallow bottom. She fervently hoped it would be enough, as she poured it into a round glass vial and stoppered it.

And then came another bright rapping on her door, bringing the urgent announcement that the king had come to Errigal Keep, and a request from her lord Connley that Regan would greet him.

She called in her girls and had them see to the repair of her hair, pinning a few loose curls back into the sleek, swept knot at her nape. They added jewels to her fingers and hung pearls from her girdling belt.

Then Regan walked out of her rooms in the oldest wing of the Keep and toward the new hall, where Connley waited for her.

Lear was there, ranting quite freely.

But when his daughter was announced, the old king went quiet. He stood before the throne, his arms thrown out and his wild mane of hair nearly white and gray as storm clouds. He wore a tattered robe that once had been rich velvet, now showing wear at the elbows, and strips of the fur lining hung off the collar like a dog had nuzzled it rather ferociously. Perhaps he'd not changed since the last zenith. It was magnificent to see him fallen so low, he who had killed her mother and made his daughters beg for their portion in front of the entire court, all because of some misunderstanding of the stars.

Perhaps Dalat's loving and vengeful God was everywhere indeed.

"Father," Regan said, crossing into the hall. Beyond the side door she'd used, the hall widened into broad whitewashed walls, striped with blackened beams of oak like ribs. Dining tables and benches had been pushed to the sides and fresh rushes spread over the cold stone floor. A narrow line of woven rugs in Errigal's winter-sky color made a path toward the royal chairs at the end of the hall. Errigal himself hulked beside Connley, large hands clenching and relaxing in an obvious sign of anxiety. So unlike his lord, who sat regal in one of the wide, low-backed chairs. Regan's husband glanced at her, warning in the bright turquoise of his eyes. He was prepared to play his hand for dominance here, against Astore, against Lear. Her father's Fool waited with the raging king.

Lear's faded eyes fixed on his middle daughter, and he stepped to her. "Regan," he said with the soft pleading of a child. She liked his need of her, his coming here though he had always avoided her since she married.

"Yes," she comforted just as gently, reaching with both hands for his. He gave his over: dry and wrinkled and long.

Regan's nostrils flared at the old smell of him; he mustn't have bathed since leaving Gaela's lands, or even longer. Oil turned his hair glossy at the roots, and food stains marred the collar of his robes. Pity almost stabbed her, but Regan avoided its blade and let go of Lear before he could embrace her. She addressed him firmly. "What is the cause of your early coming, lord?"

Lear frowned. "Your treacherous sister has cast me out!"

"Gaela? For what reason?"

"Reason! That viper has no need of it, for she is a thankless child, and as unnatural as a woman can be!"

From the royal chair, Connley said, "We will not tolerate insults to our noble sister."

The old king reared back.

"Father, peace," Regan said, bringing herself to touch his shoulder, understanding Connley's first move. "We love our sister and want to understand the strife between you, for strife with her is often as well strife with me."

"No, you are not so hard-hearted as her, my girl, nor have turned your heart into cruel armor where there should be only soft comfort."

Regan spied a tear in his eye.

So too she spied wine laid out on one of the side tables. "Sit here, with me." She led him to the bench and sat first, holding her back straight against the tightening of her womb.

He joined her and drank a great gulp of wine.

"We *are* glad to see you," Regan said urgently. "Believe it, Father."

"How can I, when you defend your serpent sister?" the king cried.

Connley came to join them, Errigal behind. The Fool made his way to the vacated royal chairs and skimmed his hand against one, but watched Regan with a knowing eye. And there, slipping in through the back entrance to lean in the shadows, was sweet Ban Errigal, her canny Fox.

"You are welcome here still," Connley said to Lear, taking the wine Regan poured him.

"She forced my retainers to leave, and so I had to go with them!"

"My lord father," Regan soothed, "be at peace, for Gaela surely had reason if she complained of your men. After all, do you truly need so many?"

"Need!" the king roared.

The king's Fool sang, "Having more than we need separates us from the beasts of the wild, missus!"

Connley pointed around at the Fool. "Have care how you speak to my lady."

The king let his head fall back. "Truth speaks clear to any, regardless of rank."

Regan laughed prettily. The sound was crafted for admiration, to redirect the conversations of men. "Father, this argument you have is to do with your retainers, not us, or even our sister. If they behaved as Gaela has said, she was right to turn them out—but you mistake if you think she intended to turn you out as well. You could return to her, without your men, and she will welcome you again."

Connley added, smiling smoothly and with his teeth out, "You gave yourself into your daughters' care at your Zenith Court last month, lord king, and so allow them to *care*."

"Care! My Gaela has betrayed me. Bit me where I only thought to have kisses." Lear shook his head, and his hair fluffed like an aged lion's mane.

Regan stood. Her hips ached, and her heart beat hard at his whining. What need did she now have to pretend to feelings she had not? That moment had come and gone, and along with it Lear's power over her. "What must that be like, to be betrayed? Perhaps my mother would be able to tell me, did she live."

"Yes," Lear whispered. "Yes, she would. Oh, she loved you, and me, besides. And still, she was betrayed."

Regan willed herself to cold calm. "You admit this now? You agree you killed her, now you are so close to dying yourself?"

"What? No." Confusion bent his brow, though whether honest—or sane—Regan knew not.

"Who betrayed my mother?" she demanded.

Lear said, "You have, and your sisters, in the face of the sacrifice she made."

Regan pressed her lips closed against white-hot fury.

Errigal cleared his throat, soft and uncomfortable with emotional weight. "Remain here, sir, with your men. Errigal welcomes you, as you always have been."

"No." Connley took his wife's hand. "Lear—you may stay, but not all your men. We will not welcome more than our sister Gaela would allow. We'll not undercut her authority in the matter. For now we will rule together, and our word is your law."

"I would rather sleep roofless!" the king bellowed. "I would rather sleep in a barn or pasture with sheep, than sleep one night under a roof with such an ungrateful daughter!"

Errigal took Lear's elbow. "My king, come away to rest with me."

"Do you turn out this lying wretch and her snake husband?" The sorrow and hope in the king's wet, wide eyes took Regan's breath away. She clutched her Connley's hand and waited for Errigal to save or condemn himself.

Errigal grimaced. "Lord, no. Connley is my patron, you know, a duke by your own word, and your queenly daughter's husband. They must be welcome here, by the will of the stars. And your own. As are you!"

As Lear tore free, a piece of his voluminous sleeve caught on Errigal's belt: it ripped, and the sound seemed to shock him further. "Ah! Ah!" He reeled toward his Fool.

"Come, sir, stay," Regan said again, feeling the swell of some mean, yet familiar, power. "Let us take care of you, for you are old and need us desperately. There will be a fire for you, and wine, furs for your shaking limbs, and look here, I am certain you can have Errigal's star-reader at your disposal. Rely upon our generosity, for I will be as good to you as *you were to my mother.*"

"I am king! My will is as sure as the constellations above!"

Triumph surged like a cold waterfall. "King no more," Regan said. "But only titled father. And stars can fall, while roots grow."

"I gave you all," Lear said.

"And in good time," Regan answered.

"Who will you pass our crown to, then, my barren daughter?" the king asked, softly, almost as if he were sad. "You and your star-cursed sister, my empty girls."

Regan stepped backward, unprepared.

Ban Errigal strode out of the shadows, ready to draw. The duke of Connley held his palm toward Ban, low and warning, anger in his tight jaw.

"Get out," Regan whispered.

"What?"

"Get out!" she cried.

"You are not welcome where my wife has declared it." Connley backed her with his body, firm at her side. He always had, even when, as now, it crashed his own driving game. He would be a curtain wall around Regan's heart.

The king threw his hands up. "Ah, heaven! What star is this, rising above worm-eaten branches? First my Elia and now the others!"

Errigal put his arm about the old king. Blotches of red showed against the earl's rough white cheeks. He said, "I know this pain, royal sir. Stay and I will share its burden."

"Yes, stay I shall, with my men at my side."

Regan would not bend, not now, not while her womb clenched with desperation, and while her own father, having seeded this pain, stood condemning her, throwing her greatest tragedy against her even as he warped and twisted his own into destiny. She would never forgive this, as she had never forgiven Dalat's absence.

Stars had ignored her birth, and so Regan was *free,* was aflame, burning cold as any star or sword of destiny. She said, "You will stay by my mercy only, Father! Your star is eclipsed. You and you alone—*none* of your men—can here remain."

"Then I will not stay!" Lear pressed knobby hands to his face and spoke more, but it was unintelligible. He threw off Errigal's touch and spun to leave the hall, crowing and crying for his Fool.

*He is truly mad,* Regan thought, lightheaded herself, as if floating apart from her body—but for the constant ache, ache, ache of her womb.

Errigal paused in his trailing the king to say to Connley and Regan, "I'll make sure he sets his head down in some safe place, my lord, my lady, have no worries on it."

"Not in this place," Regan cried, sick at the poison of his nearness.

"See him out, and no more," ordered Connley.

The earl frowned before hurrying in the king's wake again.

Regan saw Ban the Fox in the center of the hall, gripping his sword and staring after the king with something like horror and something like glee. She went to him and touched the hot back of his neck. He startled, but relaxed when he realized it was her. "Good riddance," she murmured. Her thumb stroked below Ban's ear, and he shivered.

The great hall door shut behind the three older men, its dull echo making the following silence more profound. Regan felt as if she'd been scathed clean with a rough knife. Ready for new growth.

She should have done that long ago.

"He'll take the king to Hartfare," Ban said.

Connley joined them, a sneer of disdain nearly ruining his handsome face. "Not with all those retainers."

"What did Gaela want from this?" Ban asked, though gently, as if truly asking himself.

"Power," Regan murmured, heady with it. Though she thought of the line of distress in Gaela's letter, and wondered if Gaela had truly thrown their father out instead for not knowing how else to react. Her elder sister was a strong fighter, but not always strategic in the moment of passion. But Regan would not reveal that weakness to Ban the Fox. Not yet.

"To discover what you would do?" Ban answered himself.

"And what *shall* we do?" Connley asked. "We must discover Errigal's true allegiance—to us or the old king. That will affect our course. We need Errigal firmly before we can act against Astore."

Ban turned to them. "You know my own."

Regan nodded slowly, dragging her thoughts off her beloved sister and toward the future. "I have bled all day, so tonight we will go to the heath and make your magic. Tomorrow, we will deal with Gaela, and my father, and yours, and with everything else that will come."

"You are ready, lady?" Ban asked, earnest eyes studying her.

"Completely."

"I will go to prepare," he said sharply, and with Connley's nod, left them.

Regan did not move. She thought of little but of the angry White Forest her father certainly walked into, where the stars had no power, and of the black sky that would appear overhead soon, when the sun sank. The waning moon would obliterate the stars.

Connley pressed against her back, wrapping his arms around her middle. "Are you all right, my love?"

Leaning into him, she shook her head. "No. But . . ." She reached up to touch his face, skimming her fingernails along his jaw, to his ear, and finally into the thick crop of golden hair on his head. She squeezed it into a fist, and he hissed his pleasure. "But I will be."

# ELIA

IN SOME PLACES, Lionis felt like a labyrinth, so unlike the flat mud roads and shadowed moors and jagged rocks of Innis Lear.

Here, the stone-paved street was narrow and clean, surrounded by garden walls twice taller than Elia, snaking a steep incline just below the palace on the south, and stacked with many-storied houses of the same bright limestone of the street and gardens, all agleam in the late morning sun. As she walked between Rory Earlson and Aefa, Elia fought the urge to wince; the light made her eyes ache. Bold autumn flowers rioted over the tops of some walls, spilling their vines off window boxes, or growing tall off balconies. Arches spanned from wall to wall, supporting the gardens and houses, giving the street a glowing, cathedral presence. She understood why someone would desire to live here: if forests were carved in stone, they might feel rather like this neighborhood.

They'd been to visit Rory's Alsax relations in their city residence, where his great aunt lived with two of her seven grown children. Mistress Juda was first cousin to the current Errigal, and eager both to help Rory mend things back in Lear, and to meet Elia, who had yet to venture out to any trade enclaves in her time in Aremoria. But with Rory's arrival it had seemed less prudent to ignore the Alsax invitation, especially as Elia needed now to apply herself to finding a way home that did not directly involve Morimaros or his crown. The only thing that might mitigate Gaela's ire upon Elia's premature return would be the lack of Aremore support behind it.

Elia had soothed ruffled feathers, used honesty in her requests and reasons as much as possible, and did not hide her desire for peace and alliance between the two lands as well as between her own family lines and those of Errigal. For her part, Mistress Juda used delicious food and a very fine Alsax wine to negotiate. In the end, they agreed to the use of a barge, as long as no unhappy political ramifications would land at Juda's door. Elia's thoughts had drifted with drink as they began to leave, so much so that when Juda asked for a star blessing, Elia had found herself unusually caught in silence. Several generic blessings and prayers crowded her throat, along with those more specific to the moment: right now, invisible behind the sun, the Stars of Sixth and Fifth Birds swooped, and the curving row of stars that were the Tree of Golden Decay and the clustered Heart of Ancestors would be angling west. The patterns were there, waiting for Elia to name them in meaningful prophecy, but she could not. Would not.

Everyone had stared at Elia until she took a breath and laughed ruefully at herself. "I only can give you my own blessing, Lady Alsax, and my promise: as you are generous and ambitious and loyal, may those virtues together water the roots of earth and sing along with the stars."

"Thank you, Your Highness, I accept it with honor," Juda said, rather solemnly. "Good luck to you. This son of mine will send word when the barge is ready, and guidance to where you should be."

They left then: Elia, Aefa, and Rory, with four royal guards waiting outside in their orange tabards. Elia kept her face down against the bright sun, watching the uneven limestone cobbles under her feet. Her ears gently pounded; whether from the sun or alcohol or ignored star prophecy, she could not fathom. Aefa held her hand, and Rory marched just behind. He said, "I wish so much I could return with you now. Innis Lear is where I belong, too."

"I know," Elia replied over her shoulder. "And you will return, I'll see to it. That is one of many things I must see to at home."

*Home* was such a strange word, one which she'd not contemplated often, when she was secure in having it. Blinking up at the bold blue Aremore sky, she imagined instead the harsher color of Innis Lear, cut always by wind. Elia listened, but she heard nothing other than the sounds of people, wheels, the bark of a little dog a street or two away. *Home, home, home,* she murmured in the language of trees. Though nothing responded, the words made her feel ever so slightly happier. She could barely contain her anticipation, her longing to speak again with the trees of Innis Lear.

"Where will you go first?" Rory asked her.

Elia hummed, wistful and tipsy. "I had thought to go to Gaela, but then. . . ." She paused, unwilling to voice her anger and fear at the prospect of facing her father again. "If Regan is in Errigal as you say, I could go there first, to speak with your father on your behalf, and see how my nearest sister fares."

"Yes! And Ban will help you—he must." Rory stepped between the women, throwing his arms about both their shoulders. Elia slipped hers around his waist, but Aefa grunted and glared at him. He grinned back, holding her gaze until her eyes narrowed wickedly.

"Not in your dreams," Aefa teased, bumping her hip to his.

The earlson's smile faded. "The king spoke of his dreams sometimes, this last year."

Elia squeezed his waist. "My father?"

"He would get lost in speech, and begin talking as if he'd been having an entirely different conversation with entirely different people. Your father, Aefa, was very good at covering it, but we, his retainers, always knew. I'm sorry we didn't . . . do anything."

"What could you have done?" Elia asked.

"Told someone? But Gaela knew, and so did Regan. They always had men in with your father's men. Watching for opportunities against him." Rory sighed angrily. "I should have made myself a spy for you."

She touched her cheek briefly to his shoulder. The wool jacket was warm from the sun. "I was only a star priest, what need had I to know?"

"You're his daughter. I would . . . I would have liked to know if my father was . . ."

"Dying," Elia finished for him, very quietly. And with him, Innis Lear. She'd known nothing of either. Or . . . she'd not wanted to know, thinking herself content in her selfish isolation.

The trio walked on, and the guards led them to steps that cut sharply up toward the next street. It was empty, but for doors sunk below the cobbles and painted blue. A trickle of water in the runnel smelled clean. Overhead, great clouds of green ivy clung to the roofs. When they emerged, it was into a wide courtyard tiled with the same limestone, and there was the high first wall of the palace. It seemed to be a rarely used entrance, stationed with only one stoic guardsman.

They passed into a side yard of the palace, arranged between a series of smaller walls with iron gates that could be dropped to trap invaders at several points. It had been planted with boxes of crops the kitchen staff could manage, and did not need full sunlight. The impression was of long, narrow lanes of gilded green, for nothing blossomed now, and all but some squash had been harvested. Atop each wall guards paced, though few and far between, for any true invasion would be seen days and days before the palace itself was in danger. It was the impression of strength that mattered here, and Morimaros could afford it.

With the wealth of Aremore, he could raise enough of an army and navy to bowl through Innis Lear without anyone in Lionis noticing the absence of men.

"You should go straight to the Summer Seat," Aefa said suddenly. "Claim it. Declare yourself."

Elia turned to disagree, but as they walked under the final gate and reached the inner south courtyard then, a young man in livery dashed toward them. The royal guard, and Rory, too, tensed.

"Highness, Lady Elia." The young man dropped onto one knee. "The king would like to see you, immediately."

Startled, Elia nodded, and glanced farewell to Aefa and Rory.

She was led into the palace, quickly enough to spark anxiety. Something must have happened to require such a summons.

To Elia's continued surprise, the young man brought her to the king's private chambers. The door was open between two royal guards. And La Far, waiting outside. He nodded to her, glancing in through the door. She followed his gaze to see stark limestone walls and thick rugs lit by the lowering evening sun, and Morimaros at an elegant black-oak sideboard, his back to Elia. The king's signature orange coat was missing; he stood in a long, crisp white linen shirt, belted at the waist, over his usual trousers and boots. No royal adornment but that ever-present ring, the Blood and the Sea. Pouring a small crystal glass of port, he moved to the window and sat at its cushioned edge, sipped, then stood, and sat again. He gripped the glass so hard the tips of his fingers whitened.

Suddenly terrified, Elia ducked around La Far to step inside. "Your Majesty."

Morimaros dropped the drink.

It hit the hardwood floor, in the narrow trench between the floral rug and the limestone wall. The crystal chipped the polished wood, and red port splattered the stone.

La Far shut the door behind her, closing out prying eyes.

Elia came directly across the rug to the king, blinking at the glare from the sun out the window behind him.

"Careful," he cautioned, holding his arm down to show her the slick spill of port.

She took his hand to little resistance. The edges of the cut crystal had impressed thin pink all along the insides of his fingers and palm. "Tell me— what has happened?"

He nodded, and holding her hand led her to the sideboard.

"No, thank you," Elia said to the row of decanted wine and liquors. "But I will sit."

There was a tall hearth, set below the shield arms of his father's bloodline and a pair of crossed broadswords. Two cushioned chairs nestled beside the hearth, across from a small sofa of embroidered silk from far abroad. This front room was very formal. Everything about Morimaros was outrageously dignified.

They sat on the sofa. Their knees might've brushed together if either allowed it.

Morimaros lifted Elia's hand and kissed it gently. The warmth knocked a dull, heavy stroke against her heart. Whatever was about to happen, she suspected they would never be able to surmount it. He shifted on the sofa, and their knees did touch then. "I want you to know how I admire you, Elia Lear. I wish I could go with you, when you return home."

"How did—"

"I thought you might ask the Alsax eventually." The king looked at her evenly. "And my guards do report when you leave the palace."

"I must go home." Elia squeezed his hand, taking careful note of the hardness at the pads of his fingers. *Never forget this is a warrior king.* "There is . . . as you know . . . a sickness on Innis Lear. I think it comes of the break my father caused between root and star. That is the seed of it, at least, planted the morning my mother died. She was his everything, Morimaros, so much so that without her he was untethered, wild in a way no king—no father—should be." Elia lowered her eyes to their joined hands. "It has perhaps been a poison that I fell to as well—I have always feared, since then, to . . . love. To be loved."

The king of Aremoria said nothing, but stroked his thumb gently along her knuckles. She could not tell which of them it was meant to comfort.

Taking a fortifying breath, Elia continued. "In his pain, Lear devoted himself with singular purpose to the stars. It was his only way to live, to exist, and he was determined to make it pure, without earth or wind, without the navel wells. That fanaticism has broken him, and his mind goes only to the sky without roots to bind him to the land. But I let go of wormwork, too. I let myself be what my father needed, and nothing else. Or what I thought he needed."

"It is not your fault, Elia, what has happened to your father. His choices have been his own."

"That may be, though I bear some of the weight of the results. I feel—now I *feel* too much, I haven't let myself in so very long, and . . ." Closing her eyes against the surge of emotions, all too tangled to name, she forced herself to finish honestly. "Innis Lear is where I belong, Morimaros. I must go home and ask the island what it wants, what it needs. To unite the stars *and* the roots. I know you don't believe in the importance of such things, that you've managed to break free of it in Aremoria, but Innis Lear is alive and wild. I would die to keep it so. And listening to—hearing—what the island needs is a thing I can do, that I have done, that neither of my sisters can, or will. They, and our father, have always decided who I could be, but not anymore. I will take a seat at our table. Do something to heal my island, and perhaps my family."

The words settled in her gut, in her heart, and Elia suddenly breathed easier. As if she finally had listened to—and heard—herself.

Morimaros said, "I know. I understand, Elia, though it may seem like I couldn't possibly. I . . ." He stopped, lips parted, as if he'd run out of words, or nerve.

Her black eyes widened.

"Elia, I wish . . . I would never leave your side if . . ."

"If you weren't Aremoria." She covered their joined hands with her other, but did not raise her eyes to his. She would protect him, if she could.

"Yes."

Now she did glance up. "Aremoria cannot be at my side for this."

"Yet." Releasing her, Morimaros stood and returned to the sideboard. With his back to her, he said, "I must tell you something now that will change your opinion of me. And it's taking all my courage to be so honest."

"I can't believe that."

He turned. "That it takes all I have to convince myself to disappoint you?"

"That you can disappoint me at all," was her steady reply, though doubt already dripped through her. He'd been so nervous when Elia arrived, though she'd forgotten, in the face of her own realizations.

The king stared at her as if she'd hooked him through the spine. Elia struggled to hold his deep blue gaze, to not cover her ears, or leave, while he regained himself. From the end of the sideboard Morimaros picked up a thin stack of letters, the top of which was unfolded. He brought them to her, and handed her that first one.

She held it carefully in both hands. At top were three lines of nonsense, written in Aremore. But below was a translation in a different hand, with dots and letters marking it, as if decoded:

*The iron is mine. R and her husband trust me. I am at the center of everything, as you commanded. All occurs quickly on the island, too fast to wait for winter to set in. You must act now or not at all. There will be a final crown for Innis Lear long before Midwinter.*

Panic shot Elia to her feet. The letter fluttered to the carpet. "What is this? When did . . ."

"It arrived today. I can arrange passage for you tonight, and you can be in Port Comlack just past dawn."

Her mind whirled; everything tipped out of place. "Who is this from?"

Morimaros did not answer immediately, though his eyes lowered, in sorrow or perhaps shame. Then he met her gaze again and—

"Ban the Fox is my spy."

Elia instinctively rejected the current implication. Slowly, she said, "I know. That is . . . how he worked for you, here in your army."

"Yes. He is a wizard, which suits spywork very well, when you can involve the trees and birds."

"A wizard," she whispered. "Birds. He . . . no. No. *He* did not send you this message . . . upon a bird's wing. No. He wouldn't, that's different from working for you—in your army. Here. Ban is of Innis Lear. He has ever been ours." *Mine,* her wailing heart added.

The king winced.

Only a small expression on his face, but for a man like him, it spoke volumes, and Elia put her hands to her mouth, fingers playing over her lips as if she might find the proper sequence to shut them forever.

Morimaros said, "I sent Ban to Innis Lear last month, before I arrived to pay you court. He was not summoned home. I asked him to study the cracks of your island, to report on potential room to maneuver, for better trade and even possible invasion, especially with regards to the iron magic of Errigal where he was raised. A king who expands production and controls those swords could protect whatever borders he established, would not have to worry about upstarts like Burgun ever again. I told him to destabilize what he could, as I would approach from a more courtly flank. Ban . . ." Morimaros cleared his throat. "Elia. I am truly sorry."

"You've already begun the invasion of my island," she whispered, voiceless so she did not scream. "You lied to me, saying there was ever a chance of peace. You've been lying to me since before I even met you. Every letter. Every kindness."

The king did not defend himself.

This quiet betrayal was not so violent as what her father had done to her, but it stung. Though Elia deserved it, for believing the best of everyone. Morimaros of Aremoria had betrayed her. Ban—her Ban!—had, too. What hope could she possibly have that her sisters would not treat her the same, would not betray her, too, who had never even pretended to be her ally?

Perhaps that was better: at least with her sisters Elia had always known where she stood.

She clenched her teeth against hurt. She should not let herself be too surprised by Morimaros. He was a king, after all, and a man. And he would do as men—as kings—do. It only mattered what he needed to get for himself, for his country, for his satisfaction.

And Ban, too, was only a man.

Hurrying to the window, Elia pressed both hands flat to the clear glass. Outside was too pretty, too glorious to be real. She needed harsh gray wind and bending old trees. She said, "Ban did this to Rory. To his father. On purpose, for you, though he pretended it was for me. He took your mission and twisted it into his own revenge. Do you know how much he hated my father, and his own? You gave him sanction to destroy them."

"Yes. I knew all of this, and I used it."

"He kept his *promise*," she said. It was not dismay or grief tainting the word, but a hissing disgust.

And she turned to watch it hit Morimaros.

His expression did not alter, still and calm, and only barely ashamed.

Anger, and the loss of something very small and very pure, threaded itself though her ribcage, seeking her heart to take root.

Elia willed the swelling ocean flat.

"So Aremoria has agents inside the heart of my island," she said. "And the king is not so noble as he pretends."

"I have not lied to you about my intentions, nor my desires," Mars insisted. "I do what I must. I am many things at once, the high and the low, the root and the stars. My kingdom is strong because I know how to breathe high clouds, to take sunshine in hand, while wading my feet through the shit. That is how a land flourishes, and its plants and flowers, birds and wolves and people. Not with magic, or old superstitions, but with a leader who will do everything, give everything, to it."

She stared at him, and watched the space between them widen. She knew he was right about the duty of kings. It changed nothing.

"I am in love with you," he said, in the same determined tone.

Elia laughed once, in disbelief only that he would say so now. When it could not have mattered to her less.

She shook her head, pressed her hands to her stomach, and turned to leave.

"Elia."

"No, Morimaros," she said. "I must go, for I have some shit to wade through, and I will not have your company."

He did not try to stop her again.

\* \* \*

THEY SAILED FOR Innis Lear at dusk, to make the crossing overnight.

Elia stood at the prow of the small galley, holding the worn rail with one hand for balance against the waves and the thrusting of oars. The sailors chanted a low song to keep their rhythm, a soothing Aremore lullaby that seemed to have no beginning and no end. Men dropped out and slipped back in at any time of the cycle, in harmony or low melody-free intonation, creating a never-ending, comforting mess.

Besides the twenty-odd oarsmen, she was only joined by Aefa and the king's most trusted soldier, La Far. Every Aremore man would be left on the boat, when they made land: if La Far even stepped off without her invitation, she had threatened to arrest him on her own authority. Though she had little power to keep that word, La Far gave her the respect of believing it.

So by themselves, Elia and Aefa would go, despite neither knowing anything of traveling alone, or of camping without bags packed by priests or retainers waiting to serve. At least they would be together.

As she struggled to remain awake at the front of the ship, Elia set her plans in order: First she would listen to the wind, speak to the trees. She'd bare her heart to the roots and stones and swear to die for Innis Lear.

Next she would find her father, work out Rory's safe return with Errigal, and then she would meet with her sisters to set them on a sane course of rule. Make peace in Innis Lear between the two of them and their dangerous husbands. Crown them immediately, before Midwinter, for Elia bled of two royal lines and was a star priest besides; if anyone could ordain true queens without the long dark of Midwinter, it was her. She would convince the rootwaters to accept them, sort out the lore from truth, rally Innis Lear to respect their joined rule—after all, Gaela and Regan had said to her once they shared their stars, so they could share this crown.

And Elia would do all that before thinking ever again of the king of Aremoria, or how his rare touch had lifted her spirit.

Of Ban Errigal's future or pardon, Elia was uncertain.

The moon waned yellow and gray in the eastern sky, peeking in and out of long black clouds that blotted out nearly half the stars. All around the waves flashed silver, tickling the shallow hull of the galley with wet kisses. Aefa knelt beside Elia, her temple pressed to the wooden rail, eyes shut, valiantly holding back her sea illness. On the journey to Aremoria, seemingly years and not weeks past, Aefa had vomited heartily over the side of Morimaros's grand royal barge. Elia suspected her friend's newfound resolve had everything to do with La Far's presence, as he twice already had brought the girl fresh water and a cool compress for the back of her neck. In the moonlight, his sorrowful face took on a solemn, holy cast.

But Elia could not think so peacefully when looking at La Far. He reminded her too much of Morimaros, and then she would think of his spy. Ban the Fox, whom she did not know at all.

*I keep my promises.*

Anger curled its clutches again around her heart.

Elia would discover the extent of Ban's loyalty to Aremoria. His eyes, his hands, his promises had been so real, so intensely true at the Summer Seat: she could not believe they were only lies, meant to distract her or manipulate her toward Morimaros. They had meant everything to each other, once. She'd seen it in him again, that night when he asked, *What makes you bold?* It was not a thing to say to a woman you wished out of the way, to convince her to give herself and her island into the protection of an enemy. Elia had to believe he had not betrayed her completely.

But if he was truly Aremoria's man, she would cast him off her island forever. Elia's breath quickened. She had to know.

"Ban Errigal." Aefa's voice was rough, like sand that had seen no tide. "You're thinking of him."

Elia startled, then knelt beside her friend. "I am," she whispered.

The girl glared, her eyes bright with a feverish glint. "He is a bastard traitor!"

"Yes." Elia grasped Aefa's hands, clutching them tightly. They put their foreheads together, and the princess whispered, "Was he ever expected to be otherwise? What king of Lear has trusted him, what loyalty was he afforded by those who should have held him dear? He was made this way as a child."

"Do not hold Ban higher than Morimaros, Elia," Aefa begged quietly.

"I cannot think of that king," she whispered harshly, even as his final words to her thumped and thrummed in her skull.

"Ban does not deserve to be in your heart if you cannot put that king there, too. I do not see how you blame Morimaros for all, and Ban Errigal for none."

Elia kissed Aefa's knuckles. "Because I understand Ban's pain, and I understand who he—who he was, at least. And perhaps who he might have been, had he not been ripped from us. But Morimaros I cannot forgive. He sent a spy, his stolen weapon, against my island, then spoke to me as if we could be partners. As if we might even be more."

"He is a strong king; you saw his court, walked his city. He is good, and so he must have believed his reasoning was also good. And he didn't know you when he first sent Ban. You hardly gave him anything of yourself in those letters." Aefa managed a weak smile. "Remember how much he talked of farming?"

It churned in Elia's guts: simple, personal hurt. She'd though Morimaros was incapable of this deceit, which was ridiculous of her, naive and stupid, perhaps, but still—she hurt to be so wrong. "I will discover Ban Errigal's truth apart from Aremoria, and his choices, and judge him for them, whatever they may be."

"He was gone for five years, and you spent perhaps an hour with him, at the most desperate, vulnerable moment of your entire life, and so you trust him? This is folly!"

Elia held on to Aefa's hands. "I loved him before, Aefa. Before any of this, before you came to me. You don't remember. You were not yet at Father's court. My father was terrible to him, and then he—with Errigal, too—earned Ban's hatred. Even I . . . I let him go without a fight. I cannot . . . I cannot be surprised he fell into admiration for a king like Morimaros. I did myself, as did you! You condemn Ban for the same, but his betrayal did not come from nothing. Innis Lear betrayed him first, because his birth stars say he is worthless, or at least less, and so our men would believe, refusing to see their part in the ruin of their sons. But he . . . Oh, Aefa, if you could have seen the conviction in him that night. How he looked at me. He has power, different from Morimaros, from my sisters, from my father."

Aefa squinted her light eyes and brushed damp hair off her face. "But you do want to see him again, personally."

"I do."

"Uh!" Aefa laughed like she was annoyed, and shoved Elia gently. The princess rocked backward, only catching herself by letting go of Aefa and scrambling. It was very ungainly, very lacking royal grace.

La Far appeared immediately, formed out of the shadows and sea spray. He caught Elia's elbow and steadied her. "We have a few hours left, lady. Perhaps you might try to sleep."

Allowing him to lift her to her feet, Elia smiled a small, polite smile. "Thank you, but I do not sleep well at sea, and I would like to be aware of the moment we come again into Lear's waters."

Aefa dragged herself up by the rail, and La Far belatedly offered an arm to her as well.

The soldier watched both young women for a moment, and his sad frown nearly revealed some amusement—or perhaps it was pride. Then La Far reluctantly nodded, and Elia stopped herself from wrapping her arms around her stomach. Instead she nodded back as nobly as possible. She would not return to Innis Lear with her eyes cast down.

Though afraid, she lifted her gaze.

She turned again to face the prow, to face the northwestern horizon where soon would be a black gash against the sea and stars. A black gash of rock, of mountains and moors and gullies, of roots and ancient ruins, of wild dark forests and jeweled beetles.

A star blinked in and out, revealed and covered and revealed again, hanging there bright as a pearl. Elia did not want to care, did not want to think on it, but she knew and felt she had always known: it was the silver face of Saint Terestria, the Star of Secrets, giving her homecoming benediction.

Elia would not leave Innis Lear again.

Brona Hartfare had always known the day would come when Errigal arrived in her village not for a fuck, but to claim their son.

Against that inevitability, she cultivated an appreciation of the smallest moments. Flashes of connection, of love, of growth. The sun on a single, crisp green spring leaf as Ban pinched it between his dirty little fingers, to put into a basket for roasting. His rare laugh—not the slow, soft one he let loose for silly rolling beetles or a perfect splatter of bird droppings, but the one that startled everyone, even himself, with its sudden burst of strength. The first time he hid from his mother in her very own forest, emerging from the bark of a low, dying oak tree after she'd passed by. A shine of glee in his eyes, so like her own, and nothing like Errigal's. Often, Brona wondered what he would become after he left the bosom of Hartfare, out in the world where people took too much from one another and rarely gave back to the roots.

Only his passion would protect him, and that at least Ban had received from both his mother and father.

If there had been a way to keep those feelings from ever souring to anger, Brona would have sacrificed anything. But no matter what time of year, or under what moon she threw the holy bones, Brona could see no path that did not paint her son in bitter colors.

His birth anniversary was six days passed when Errigal came. Because of cycles of seasons and stars, it had been that very early morning when the dragon's-tail moon under which he'd been born, ten years ago, hung against the dawn, burning painfully silver in a seeping pink sky. A sickle to harvest Brona's heart, which always before she'd kept as her own.

Ban still slept, now, curled in the garden despite the frosty morning. He'd settled into a hollow of dirt and roots where the squash vines would be later in the year. A tiny fire burned in a shallow obsidian bowl Brona's grandmother had brought with them on the flight from Ispania. The flames danced against the black stone, alive by a thread of magic linked to Ban's breath and the power of the White Forest. It kept him warm despite being slight, for the magic kept his own body working.

Brona sat on a stool, leaning against the mud brick wall of their cottage, wrapped in a thick wool blanket and cradling a little bowl of her own. Hers held the last of their winter honeycomb.

Light slowly spread through the garden, waking the roots and tiny shoots of grass that worked toward the sun. A few of her hardier plants held green: the holly with its sharp leaves, and a small juniper tree Brona kept to remind her of Dalat. The overwinter cabbages and onions were beginning to peek up now that the spring had come. The garlic would soon follow, and turnips. When the light touched Ban's messy thick hair, then the line of his cheek, Brona let a tear fall, catching it with the honeycomb.

An instant later, she heard him coming, that enemy of her peace. Errigal must have left his Keep long before dawn. He would not plan to stay long, then, intending, certainly, to travel far away from Hartfare before the day was finished. His footsteps were as stomping and broad as ever, eager and careless. And as usual, he'd left his horse at the fore of the village.

Brona pinched off a coin of honeycomb and left the bowl near Ban. She went around to the front of her cottage.

Errigal smiled to see her. His breath flared in small white puffs, and the rising sun glowed in his golden hair and rough beard, lighting the star charms he'd braided in, glinting off his rings and the bright tooling along his thick belt. Wind pushed aside treetops and the sun hit full in his face; Brona's lover did not hesitate or quit his smile, and the brilliant morning turned his eyes into shards of pure light.

She greeted him at the arched trellis that marked the entrance to her yard, putting the coin of honeycomb up to his mouth.

Errigal parted his lips, and she slipped it in, allowing him to bleed the comb of its sweetness in a few quick presses of his tongue, and then to lick the remains off her fingers.

All told, Brona would have greatly preferred him to be here just for sex.

"What charm is in this honey?" he asked, wrapping his arm around her waist.

She smiled mysteriously. Let him think what he liked, but Brona offered honey so she knew what to expect when she tasted him herself.

"Ah, love." Errigal laughed and picked her up easily, leaning back to prop her against his chest. He did not kiss her, but only held her there, one arm around her waist, the other cupping her bottom. Brona put her arms around his neck and waited. "I've come for Ban," he said.

"I don't want you to take him." Her voice was soft, but commanding.

"He's my son, and should be raised with men and retainers. He's been coddled here enough."

The witch said nothing, but tilted her chin down in disapproval.

With a sigh, Errigal let her slide down his body. "I know you don't coddle him, but you are a woman, and this is a woman's place here, women and witches, orphans, runaways, those with no lords. My son will not be such a thing."

"You don't mind it in me."

"No, girl, I don't," he said, though she'd not been a girl in ages. He kissed her, and Brona allowed it, opening her mouth to his. She curled her fingers around his belt, tugging with exactly enough force to invite, and stepped back toward her cottage.

"Distracting me will only delay our departure," Errigal said, kissing her eagerly.

Brona lifted one shoulder as if she cared not, and dragged him into the cottage. She would take this from him, and then he would take her heart away in return.

The finest thing about Errigal had always been his enthusiasm. Coupled with stamina and an instinct for generosity, it made him the best lover she'd ever had. Even if not for having made Ban, Brona would have welcomed Errigal back and back again to her bed, whenever he liked. His life outside Hartfare was no care of hers, for she'd learned long ago to revel in what joy she could find, and embrace love in every form. Innis Lear did not nurture such things, but scoured them away; it was the nature of the island, to be pulled between hungry earth and cold stars.

Brona considered herself an emissary of that wild, starving earth, and devouring the power of the Earl Errigal, taking it into herself, was a blessing, a ritual itself, to weave the stars and roots together again.

Nobody else was even trying, not since the last queen had died.

Sweaty and smiling, Errigal stretched beneath her when they were done, and Brona perched atop his hips, settled exactly like a witch on a throne. "This is the end," she said.

Errigal reached up and skimmed a finger along the curve of her breast. "I don't like that."

"Then leave my son with me."

"No."

Brona put her hands on his chest and dug her fingernails in, sliding her palms along the soft hair hiding his milky skin. "This is the end."

He nodded but wrapped his hands around her wrists. "I'll take care of him."

No, he would not. Brona knew this deeply. Errigal did not see Ban, did not understand his needs or how to foster joy in the slivers of passion that cut wildly inside their son.

"Brona, I will," Errigal insisted.

She climbed off him, taking a blanket with her, wrapped around her shoulders.

"He is mine, and I will care for him as a father should." The earl made a mess of noise pulling on his trousers. He tugged his beard as Brona held silent, and she saw the moment he decided to make a threat. "You have no choice in this. I'm taking him."

That was true. Brona knew too well how precariously Hartfare existed: a heart of root magic and runaways and those hiding from King Lear's stars. A word from Errigal and Lear would raze it to the ground. So far, prophecy had saved them, stars that promised the island needed this tiny center of roots. So far, Lear accepted it. But only so far.

"I know," she whispered. "But it wounds me, Errigal."

His bullish, handsome face crumpled, and he came to her. "Ah, girl, I would not hurt you if I could."

"You do now."

"So it must be." Errigal kissed her, wiping his thumbs roughly along her cheeks, though Brona did not cry.

"Father."

Both turned to see their son. He stood in the doorway, small, skinny, with a tangle of dark hair and solemn eyes. Dirt darkened the left side of his face and streaked his shirt. His toes were bare. Quite the forest goblin.

"What a disaster you are!" Errigal laughed. He swooped down and embraced Ban. "We'll get you cleaned up a bit, then on to the Summer Seat with me. Your brother is there, and we'll find you a sword, how do you like that?"

The boy's gaze found Brona, over Errigal's wide shoulders. "Do you like the Summer Seat, Mama?"

"I do," she said. "It is full of magic, and there is a great maw of stone teeth near it. They will be strong for you, Ban."

He frowned. "You aren't coming."

"Brona's place is here in Hartfare," Errigal said, standing. He put a possessive hand on Ban's knobby shoulder.

"So is mine," Ban said, his gaze still locked on his mother's, pleading.

His father ruffled Ban's hair. "No, boy, no. It's with your father, and brother. It's with the king and his men. You've been here with the flowers too long, and need to be able to see the starry skies."

Ban drew away, finally looking at Errigal. "I want to stay in the forest. I want to stay with my mama."

"Ban." Brona knelt before him. One hand gripped the blanket tight around her shoulders, and one stretched out, but hesitating to touch his dear face. "You must go with your father."

Hurt pinched Ban's brow, and his small mouth puckered. "You don't want me to stay."

"Oh no, oh roots and worms, darling, no." She threw her arms around him, heedless of her nudity, only desperate to hold him tight and prove his fears wrong. "No, Ban. I would have you stay. But this is your fate, to be in both worlds. You must go away from me now because your father loves you, and would have you share his world."

Ban did not believe her; that much was clear. He stood still in her embrace, not returning it. The hook in her heart cut even deeper.

Errigal pulled the blanket around Brona again, crouching beside her as if to support her, as if they were united in will.

"Come on, Ban," the earl said. "Do as you're told."

The boy broke free of his mother's embrace. He turned his back to them, going for the trunk of their clothes, where Ban's only coat splayed across the top, flung there yesterday in childish abandon. The boy, older today, put on the coat, scrubbed the dirt from his face, and shuffled around for his boots.

Errigal began to speak, but Brona touched his hand. There was nothing to say.

Before they left, Ban let his mother kiss him; it broke the seal he'd put over his heart, and so her kiss made his tears fall. He cried quietly, hugging himself, wretched and unmoving, until Errigal clapped him on the back and told him to stop, that a new home was nothing to grieve.

When the sounds of their footsteps had faded and she was alone, Brona walked out of Hartfare and into the White Forest, naked and heartbroken and covered in the last of Errigal's love. She washed herself of everything in a cold, haunted stream, in the shade of an ash tree.

To the ash, she whispered,

*Don't let Ban forget the wind and roots. Don't let him forget me.*

# THE FOX

Ban had never done magic quite like this.

The air was still and quiet over the rocky moorland, here where the hill pushed out of the White Forest like a cresting whale. Silver clouds stretched over the dark sky, brightened by the soon-coming sun and by the moon that hung still in the west, off-center and almost full. Regan Connley, clad in a thin linen shift, sat along an arrow of exposed granite as sleek as she and exactly her size. Her back to the east, she cupped a shallow bowl in her lap and bowed her head over it. She whispered in the language of trees, the words blowing tiny ripples against the surface of pooled blood.

Ban snapped his fingers and called fire to hand, setting the flame down fast against the patch of pine, thistle, rose, and thick paper tinder here at the south end of the granite. The fire caught and crackled, flaring white-orange before settling in to curl the long stems and petals. Moving east-ward himself, Ban sang a low song to the wind and trees, hissing a word or two for the fire. He trailed a line of mixed sand and oak charcoal behind him as he went to the north and then the west. When he reached the south-ern point again, Ban paused to call fire again, drawing it along the entire circle.

"Now," he said quietly. Connley heard him and stepped inside the circle.

Only the three of them attended this predawn witchery, and Connley solely because he'd insisted: *I am as involved as you, and I am your other heart. Without me not all of your spirit will be there.*

Ban found it unbearably sentimental, until he saw the mutual intensity in the eyes of husband and wife, and realized they both believed, completely.

*What would such a partnership be like,* he wondered, and then caught a fleeting memory—Elia's hands holding his own, tiny moonlights dancing between and around their fingers.

Glancing up at the fading stars, the wizard knew it was time. Ban stripped himself of clothes and shoes before stepping into the circle. Wafts of thistle smoke and rose teased his shoulders as he crouched at a pan of orange mud from the iron marsh and drew words onto his chest and stomach, and his power rune at his forehead, heart, and genitals. He coated his forearms with the mud, and when he said *Shield me,* the mud dried in a quick snap, to near ceramic hardness and hot against his skin.

At a tearing sound, Ban looked up to see Regan reclined against the granite, and her husband kneeling beside her, using a small dagger to cut into the front of her shift. He sliced it open from the center of her breasts to the low mound at her groin. Parting the pale linen, Connley kissed his wife's soft belly, then left his hand there as he kissed her between the breasts and again on her mouth.

Ban joined them at Regan's feet while Connley moved to her head, and he handed the lady the bowl of her womb blood. She set it on her belly, fingers curled around the rim. Her chest rose and fell slowly and evenly.

The duke met Ban's gaze, asking silently again his earlier question. *Will this hurt her?*

Two hours ago, when they left the Keep, Ban had answered, "I don't know. It is not designed to cause harm, but there is wildness in the roots of Innis Lear, and the spirits we call will not be concerned with safety."

"If it hurts Regan, I will hurt you," Connley had promised, simple and calm.

Ban then replied, "If it hurts her, I will already be hurt."

That had seemed to console the duke, though he watched Regan now with a hovering possessiveness.

Overhead, the stars had gone pale in the cool purple sky, and the moon hung behind Ban, its pregnant lower edge just kissing the horizon. Exactly right for beginning.

From a small basket at Regan's feet, Ban took three long primary feathers, tawny and pale, from the wings of a ghost owl. He lifted them in the air, and in the language of trees called the name of the bird, taught to him very reluctantly by a cranky old oak at the edge of the forest.

Regan added her voice to Ban's, and then Connley did, too, his unpracticed tree tongue sure enough for their work.

The three named the owl again and again, growing louder as they drove the word higher into the sky. Nine times and nine again, then finally at the end of a third cycle, they fell silent.

Ban closed his eyes to listen.

Wind whispered around them, and the fire snapped happily, reaching with tiny sparks up at the sky.

There: the high, hissing screech of the owl.

Ban got to his feet and spread his arms so the feathers caught the wind. *Here,* he called in the language of trees. *Here we are, old ghost.*

It swept down, silent and pale, its luminescent creamy underside feathers presenting like a shard of moonlight against the sky. The owl circled, and Ban called its name again. Regan put her fingers in the bowl of blood and then used the drops to trace the bird's name against her sternum, while her husband panted in silence, excited and afraid.

Opening its tiny pink beak, the owl screeched again, showing Ban the dark maw of its gullet. Then it flared its wings and stretched out feathery long legs, talons flexed.

"Brace yourself," Ban murmured, just before the owl landed against Regan's belly, flapping its long, soundless wings for balance.

Regan squeaked in pain, but did not move, even as the talons clutched into her flesh and the bowl of blood rocked. Connley grasped her arms.

*A gift for you,* Ban said to the owl, holding its gaze: deep black eyes against a heart-shaped white face. Its tawny shoulders melted creamier down its back and along its wings, a splash of brown scattered down its underside.

The owl made a softer sound, a clicking trill, and walked to the bowl of blood.

It lowered its white head and tipped its beak into the bowl.

*Fire bind us.*

The moment the owl touched the blood, Ban whispered the words, making the line of their burning circle flare a brighter white; along the lines of sand and char, higher flames burst like tiny yellow autumn leaves, wavering in a breeze.

The owl shrieked and launched forward, batting the bowl away with its wings. Blood splattered across its white face, and across one elegant wing; blood slid in a branching line down Regan's hip and ribs.

Ban reached out and grasped the owl's torso between both hands, even as it slashed at him with its talons. He commanded, *Be still, ghost owl,* and said its name again.

The charge rang against the walls of the diamond, and the fire shrieked its own wild laughter. Regan sat, pressing hands to her bloody stomach, against both freshly dripping blood and that previously wrung from her cold womb. Her husband put the small dagger into her hand and pushed Regan to her feet.

In Ban's arms, the owl settled, wings limp, talons flexed but still. Its eyes hooked on his own, black and starry.

Regan joined Ban, slid one hand around his, and then firmly pierced the dagger through the owl's back.

Its wings spread in a beautiful arc, and blood dripped down its tail.

"Now, while it still lives," Ban said. He held one wing, and Connley took the other in firm hands. The duke's face was paler than normal, too, drawn with temper and concern. The men held the owl up by the wings, and Regan grasped its head, then cut free its perfect black eyes.

Ban led Connley as they lowered the owl, carefully, respectfully, to the earth as it died.

The lady walked to the granite slope, gory eyes in her palm. As her wizard and her husband watched, Regan set the dagger upon the stone, and then one by one, put the eyes in her mouth and swallowed them whole.

She knelt, back bent, head low so her loose curls fell all around her arms, hiding her face. The sun pressed up in the east, sending a ray of gold across the horizon, and the half-moon blinked, overcome. Wind nudged them all, waving hands through the fading fires of their diamond.

*Hurry now,* the wind said, and Ban knew if Regan saw nothing before the orb of the sun lifted itself completely over the earth, she never would.

Connley stepped closer, and Ban grabbed his forearm. Though the duke cast him an angry look, this was Ban's power. He was the wizard, and his word ruled the moment.

A gasp from Regan, and both men jolted forward but stopped themselves. Her hands flattened against the gray, speckled granite, and blood dripped once off her chin. It was all they could see, but her hair shook and her shoulders trembled. She moaned softly and high, bending over herself. Words in the language of trees fell from her lips, but Ban could not understand them; they were too quiet, too jumbled and full of teeth.

Ban's heart raced, loud enough to make a language of its own.

The fire blew out, though there was no wind remaining.

And Regan suddenly rose, threw out her arms like wings, and screamed at the bright morning sky.

Connley broke then, rushing to his wife. "Regan, Regan," he said, and dragged her off the stone altar, holding her about the waist as she twisted and cried. Tears pink with blood marred her cheeks, and she gouged her temples with her nails. Blood colored her bottom lip.

Waiting, impatient, Ban clenched his jaw.

Connley held her as she wept, as she curled in upon herself, and then finally, Regan spoke. "My insides are covered in scars like dark roots, and

I cannot see past them, to mend myself! I need another." She whipped her head around and stared at Ban. "Another guide, one with stronger, better eyes."

Fear slithered coldly down his spine. He glanced to Connley, then shook his head. "Rest now."

"Come, my love," Connley said, embracing her. He kissed her jaw.

Regan clawed at him—but not to push him away. She clutched his neck, pulling him all against her, shoving their foreheads together. Her voice was raw as she begged, ordered, and kissed him with her bloody mouth. And the duke of Connley held her tighter, nodding, promising nothing, everything.

Ban turned his back, shaking with weariness and sorrow. Regan deserved better. He was a scout and a spy, a wizard who knew how to seek and see. But he couldn't help her more, not without seeking his own mother, or some other witch who knew more of the putting together than taking apart. He started down the promontory alone, toward the deep morning shadows of the White Forest. Thirst drew Ban toward a spring he knew, and behind it, sleep called his name in the voice of wind and roots.

He would have let himself be pulled underground, to be revived as always by the embrace of the trees. But before he could reach them, the earth beneath his feet trembled. Dry golden grass bent awake, shifting and whispering; the White Forest fluttered, bowing toward the sunrise and the southeast.

Raising his face toward the morning sky, Ban heard a longed-for name on the wind, bright as a star, as if all the island gave it welcome.

*Elia,* said Innis Lear. *Elia has come home.*

## FIVE YEARS AGO,

## DONDUBHAN

*WAKE UP!* SHRIEKED the wind.

*Wake wake wake!*

The sharp cry threw leaves against themselves and against the walls of Dondubhan, rattling shutters and adding their slapping words until the chaos startled Elia awake.

"What?" she gasped aloud, then said again, *What?* in the language of trees.

*away they're taking him he will be gone forever you have to go now go now go*

She could taste his name in the wind's panic.

Ban.

Flinging herself out of bed, Elia grabbed her over-dress and pulled it on, then dragged her boots onto bare feet and rushed out her door. She ran through the narrow black hall of Dondubhan, listening hard for the pull of the wind, dodging early-risen servants and retainers.

A woman jerked back as Elia passed, and Elia stumbled. The woman— a retainer's wife, her name on the tip of Elia's tongue—took Elia's elbow and shook her head. "Your Highness, whatever you are doing, please slow down. You are a wild creature, and whatever you want, this behavior will not help."

Elia gasped and panted, pulling at her arm, but the woman stared at Elia's head, eyed her up and down, and Elia put her free hand up to her head. Her hair was half pulled free of the loose cap she often slept in, blast that old habit she had of picking at it in her sleep. Her overdress was skewed, untied at the waist. Nodding, Elia quickly tied it closed over both hips, glad at least that her night shirt was long and warm wool. The woman—Rea! That was her name—pulled a ribbon out of her own hair and offered it.

"Thank you, Rea," Elia said breathlessly, taking it. She saw Rea smile, pleased to be known, but that was all, for Elia tore down the hall again, arms up to throw off the cap and twist the unruly curls quickly back in a painful knot with this single ribbon.

She burst out into the front ward of Dondubhan, glancing up: sheer clouds cut the sky into patches of pink and pale blue with the final moments of dawn. She listened, and the wind said, *Horses.*

Elia hurried through the inner curtain wall, toward the long second ward, where the barracks were built against the external wall and then the stables beside them. She dashed quickly across packed earth, and there, at the gaping gate that led beneath the ramparts and out into the moor, were Errigal and her father, as well as Rory, and a dozen retainers in the winter blue of Errigal. All dressed and ready to travel, except for Lear, who wore an informal robe of midnight blue.

"Ban," Elia whispered, seeing him at last; a slight, dark figure in Errigal's shadow.

The wind fluttered banners that hung off the crenellations overhead. *she's here she's here*

Ban looked around his father's broad body and saw her.

Elia did not care about the consequences: she ran and threw herself at Ban, arms around him desperately. He was ready, holding her tight back. "I didn't know," he whispered fast in her ear. "I'm sorry. I would have warned you."

"No," she said, clutching at him. "Why do you leave?"

"Elia, stop," her father said, putting a hand on her shoulder and squeezing.

She shook her head, buried her face in Ban's neck.

"Let the princess go, my wayward son," Errigal commanded, jovial, as if this were all a humorous mistake. "You've parted before, and this is no different."

Ban shifted, loosening his grip, but Elia put her cheek to his. *No,* she whispered in the language of trees. *Mine.*

The king jerked at Elia. "Now, daughter," he said, voice deep with authority.

"It is different," she said, leaning away only slightly. She looked into Ban's eyes. Pain haunted them, and she knew she was right.

"The boy goes to Aremoria," King Lear said, "to join his cousins' retainers. It is a good position for a bastard, especially for one with his stars. It is the best he can hope for in this world, and both of you should appreciate that."

"It's too far! He won't be able to hear the island wind at all." Elia whirled to face her father. "He is part of Innis Lear, Father. Don't send him away. Let him join the retainers here and learn amongst his own people."

Lear's nose wrinkled. "My retainers are all star-blessed; this boy is not. His wrongful birth and dangerous stars offend us. And he must be farther away, so as to end the influence his stars have upon you. Your stars deserve more from you both."

Horror opened up her face. "Father!" she breathed, eyes wide, having never before realized how deeply he scorned Ban.

"You're jealous," Ban said quietly. "Elia doesn't love you best, and she doesn't hate wormwork like you do, because she's not a coward."

The king stepped forward, hand raised, and Elia threw herself between her father and Ban, ducking, waiting for the explosion of pain.

It did not come.

"Get away from him," Lear said, dangerously soft.

Fear slid through her blood, freezing her still and silent.

Ban was wrenched away from her as Errigal dragged him to a horse. "Get on, boy," he growled, rough in his attempt to boost Ban up.

Lear took Elia by the back of the neck and held her. "This is the right thing," he said. "The dragon-tail moon set too near Calpurlugh on your birthday, too near those base roots—that influence will ruin you. And if it poisons your heart, it will poison all the island."

Tears fell hot and straight down Elia's cheeks. She said no more, staring at Ban.

He returned her stare, face ashen in the dawn light, and Elia remembered leaning against the rose-vine-covered wall in the garden only yesterday, Ban's head in her lap; she'd toyed with the ends of his thick hair and traced the shape of his lips. He'd said, *Tell me a prophecy for us,* and she'd replied, *I am the stars to your roots, Ban Errigal. Together we are everything we need.*

But if she'd taken the time to think through the star patterns as they had been, instead of answering merely as she wanted, would she have foreseen this? In enough time to change it?

Why hadn't she taken the star-signs seriously before now?

Had Elia lost her way in the worms and roots? Could her father be right about her focus?

She moved her lips in the shape of his name.

Rory was beside her, suddenly, taking her hand. "I'm sorry," he said very softly, voice thick with regret. "I'm so sorry, Elia."

She nodded. Of course he was sorry; he'd miss Ban, too. But not like she would, not as if his heart were sliced in two. Then Rory was gone, joining his brother and father, and Errigal's party left through the thick gate.

The wind teased at her ears, licking her hair, and said, *Don't let me go, Elia.*

Elia could not speak a response, in any language. Her heart too full of tearing, crashing pain. She gasped and held her breath, held everything still.

Her father's fingers dug into the muscles of her neck, and he sighed. He petted her then, gently. "You'll understand one day," Lear said. "I adore you, my star, more than anything, and the heavens do as well. The stars will protect you, they and I. You'll need for nothing else."

The more she tried to speak, to shape some farewell in the language of trees—words the wind might deliver to Ban—the faster her tears fell, the thicker her throat grew. Elia thought that if she spoke those words—any words now—she would burst into a thousand shards of hot glass, never to be repaired. Would Ban die in Aremoria? Would she ever see him again?

She took another deep breath, held it, and slowly, slowly let it go, breathing away all the pain, pushing it out to the rising dawn. Every breath sank deeper into Elia's cracks, into the dark spaces behind her heart, into her stomach and blood and bones, and as she exhaled the hurt was expelled, too, leaving only starlight inside her.

Her father said, "Yes, my Calpurlugh, my truest star, things will be set right. You'll see. Better to let him go now, than when it is too late, when it would have irreparably ruined you. I know. I know. We might bring him home someday, if ever such a path is discovered by the stars."

Lear put his hand against the crown of her head, and Elia closed her eyes, choosing to believe him, because the alternative was to die.

# Part
# FOUR

# ELIA

THE ISLAND TREMBLED when Elia Lear set foot upon it again.

Dawn cast her a pale violet shadow, reaching ahead along the white beach. Tiny grains of sand shifted, slipping toward the waves as if drawn by an invisible tide.

*Elia Lear,* the island whispered, first to itself, then to her. *Elia is home!*

In the three days since, the island had not yet fallen silent.

All she needed to do was listen.

For years Elia had been only watching, as if her eyes were all: watched the stars shift in their perfect patterns, watched her father study and proselytize and grow ever frailer, watched her sisters expand and retract and conform to expectations and to losses, watched her own self diminish until she was nothing, reflecting only her sisters' disappointment, her father's obsession, a sky with a single fading star in the north.

*What about the stars taught you to forget the wind?* The island pressed. *What was the moment when you stopped hearing us whisper?*

As Elia sat on a cliff now, overlooking the churning sea, listening and listening and listening to the voices in the wind, she could not pinpoint such a time in her memory.

The loss had been so gradual, she did not even realize.

A slow-forming mist, a wasting disease.

The island told her stories to fill her aching chest: that Elia's first words in the language of trees had been *thank you.* She had once known the names of every tree along the road between Dondubhan and the Summer Seat, and made a rhyme of them when she was twelve. Her favorite game had been finding constellations in the splatter of lichen on an old tree. She wove a cloak of emerald beetles, to wear beside a young boy with a shield of golden butterflies. Hearing the stories in the voice of the wind brought them back to her, and Elia cast her memories further and deeper, recreating a legend for herself until she found the answer to the island's question.

Her father had said, *We might bring him home someday, if ever such a path is discovered by the stars.*

So Elia had stopped listening to the wind, had taken fully to the stars in order to hunt down that path, with calm and focus and trust. Until she was so calm, so focused, so filled with trust in the stars alone, that the island's voices quieted, and fell away. This was what the island revealed to her, now that she could hear again: though she had still walked with her feet against the roots, Elia had let her father put boundaries on her magic, built ramparts so subtle and strong she had thought they'd been her own design.

*He did not do it on purpose,* she whispered in the language of trees.

*But he did do it,* the wind said.

*I let him,* Elia said, *I did not notice. He was my refuge, a strong father who loved me, who chose me . . . over my sisters.* Leaning back against the ragged grasses and gorse of the cliff top, Elia stared at the afternoon sky, at the billowing heavy white clouds, and wondered what the stars would say, if they could speak back to her. How their voices might sound.

The wind rushed, the wind tugged.

*Tell me about Ban,* she said.

*Ban is loud.*

Elia laughed, loud, too, and surprised herself at the boldness of it.

"Talking to yourself?" Aefa called, gasping as she climbed the steep path. They'd made their stay here in a small abandoned cottage suggested to them by the people of Port Comlack, where they'd first walked together upon arrival. Of course Elia was eminently recognizable: she'd even frightened some of the townspeople with her sudden appearance, for they'd all heard startling tales of her flight to Aremoria and Lear's wild Zenith Court. Though efforts had been made to accommodate Elia and her attendant, to feed them and offer beds and even once an entire house for their use, Elia had said no, though with much thanks. She'd said she came home to make things right, but needed only solitary rest, and did they know of an unused place for her to sleep, a place that had become nearly part of the land again? Where she might commune with the voice of Innis Lear?

Until the island claimed her, Elia deserved nothing from its people.

"Yes," Elia said to Aefa now, still spread on her back. The sharp blue sky burned her eyes. "I talk to myself, though I think the island is listening."

Strange she'd seemed, no doubt, to those she encountered, but enough still believed in the spirit of the island, and honored the earth saints, that they liked to hear the daughter of their king, the one given to the stars, speaking with the roots.

She and Aefa had been directed to this old lookout, abandoned when a newer lighthouse was erected on a promontory slightly more northward, one which could see farther up the coast from Port Comlack. Built of stone into one room, the old cottage perched at the edge of a limestone cliff slowly crumbling into the sea. Crusted in salt, it held only an ancient hooded hearth, a table, and a bedframe she and Aefa filled in with collected grass, to sleep on together. Elia had boiled water and scrubbed it all down, chapping her fingers, while Aefa concocted thin soup from supplies La Far had pressed upon them, and tended the fire. The first evening, Elia had stared out the window, listening to the hiss of wind and crash of waves. The ocean did not speak a language she knew, though she wondered if words concealed themselves in the rush of salt and water.

After Aefa fell into an exhausted sleep, Elia wrote letters to her father and Ban Errigal in the ashes atop the hearthstone, then wiped them away.

She did not yet know the words to write to her sisters.

All the first night, Elia had remained awake, shoulder pressed to Aefa's spine, and stared at the heather thatching that hung thick but tattered between rafters. Moonlight streamed in the window, and Elia listened.

The sun rose, and she wandered outside onto the cliff, to listen more. The island chanted long strings of words and offered poems about things she'd known but forgotten, and things she'd never guessed about the lives of bumblebees and blackbirds. The island knew her, and gave her tender songs; it gave her the truth of where to find a new vein of rubies in the north; it gave her a word for the fleeting light between shadows in a windblown forest; it gave her the death of a beautiful ghost owl, blood spilled into the earth with violent magic; it told her a joke she did not quite understand. Elia laughed anyway to make the island happy, for in every other way Innis Lear was miserable.

This was a fractured island, an island of one people torn between loyalties and faiths, all in conflict: what mattered most? A king must at least hear his people, who in turn hear the island, but Lear had cut it all away, and listened only to the stars. The trees had not grown strong new roots in years, not since they'd had a king who spoke with them. Her father had closed off the rootwater so the people could not share it, and the island forgot the taste of people's blood and spit, so how could it recognize its own? The wind raged or sagged, uncertain and frustrated without strong trees to chatter with, or clever birds to lift high. It forgot the patterns to dance for the best seeding, how to keep animals ready for the change of seasons. Her sisters, the island whispered, did not trust the wind, not even the one who longed for rootwater, the one who bled onto the roots of the island as if she could provide all the sustenance it needed. As if they could be replenished by one who took ever more than she could give, wrapped in her own loss.

*We remember when all of you were born, and your mother laughed, singing a song with words we do not know, but that is broken now.*

*How do I weave it all back together?* Elia asked.

And the island said, *Be everything.*

An impossible answer to an unfair question.

So Elia listened throughout her second day, until Aefa returned again for the night, from another foray into Port Comlack and along the outer edges of the farmland nearby. She had asked all she met after the king or his Fool, for rumors and loyalties and even just opinions, about anything, learning only that a contingent of Lear's retainers camped at the south foot of the White Forest.

"I have fresh fish!"

Smiling, Elia listened to the wind flutter Aefa's skirt as the girl collapsed to the ground, and it teased Elia's earlobes with tiny fingers, tugging her hair. The princess smelled the fish then, and said, "I'll help you prepare them."

"Already clean, ready to cook, for neither of us knows better." Aefa plopped beside Elia, the bag of fish in her lap. "We'd end up choking on tiny bones if we tried ourselves. We are helpless in some areas."

Elia rolled her head to touch it to Aefa's knee. "Me more than you."

"True, but that's a princess's prerogative."

The girls cooked their fish on the hearthstone at the cottage and ate it messily together outside. Aefa asked when they would go, and Elia said, "Soon. Our fathers are safe, for now. The trees say both Lear and his Fool are in Hartfare with Brona and Kay Oak."

"With my mother, then, too," Aefa said happily, raking the coals she'd kept glowing as they ate.

"Aefa . . ." The princess hesitated, reached out and touched her friend's knuckles. "You've never stopped making fire."

Aefa's eyebrows flew high. She snapped and whispered *fire* in the language of trees, and a spark lit at the tips of her fingers. It burned for a flash and went out.

"Are you a wizard, too?" Elia whispered. She did not think so, but she had to ask.

"No. I only make fire, and honestly, sometimes when I'm not with you it doesn't work. But I couldn't stop."

"Why?"

"I needed to remind you that such things are possible."

Elia slept that night weary and relaxed, falling away to the island's low, rough lullaby.

Again at dawn, Elia wandered down into the lowlands, where the grass grew tall over the edges of the Innis Road, that long path leading from the Summer Seat in the southwest to Errigal at the southeast. Once the road had been set with granite, but now grass and weeds grew up over it, and the flat stones were sunken into the earth. Heather pulled away in all directions, streaking over the hills and valleys like low purple mist, and boulders and rough rocks jutted up, ruining the land for farms. This was grazing land, or land for digging up great star stones. And then for collecting well caps, too. It was harsh and beautiful and Elia's favorite part of the island. Unlike the rocky cliffs of the Summer Seat, unlike the furious ocean, unlike the emerald hills north at Dondubhan, or even the thick, wet shadows of the great White Forest, these southern moors gave her the feeling of flight. The wind gusted, nothing slowing it down. It roared with vivid life.

When Elia had given her heart to the stars, she'd stopped loving her island, too.

Dark clouds gathered far to the north: a storm brewing at the far end of the White Forest. By this afternoon, it would rage. For now, the wind sang, brushing her hands against the bearded wheat: she remembered how she'd loved the sensation when she was a girl, how it would make an almost-conversation, a loving murmur between her skin and the earth. The breeze blew, drawing her attention back again: there halfway up a sweeping hill stood a hawthorn tree, bent and scraggled by pressing, constant wind. She climbed to it and grasped the peeling old bark. Most leaves had dropped away, and the bright red haws already budded along the twigs and branches.

The tree shuddered under her touch. Elia shivered, too. *What would you tell me, ancient lady?*

*You were missed,* the tree croaked out, slow and so very quiet.

Tears pricked her eyes, and Elia closed them, pressing the side of her face to one rough line of trunk. She knew the tree did not mean only this month, since she'd gone to Aremoria: it meant since she was a child, since she sang magic and practiced duets with the roots. She felt sad for herself, and for her father, who had never done such things. And then sad for everyone who did not listen to trees, who lived alone and in silence.

Kneeling, Elia cried harder. She touched her cheeks and put her tears from her fingers to the hawthorn. Her weeping shook her shoulders, as the hawthorn shook, too, and she bent over herself. This was not the overwhelming, unknowable grief from before; no, she understood now what she had lost, and why. A wild tree grew in her heart. Its roots wove throughout her guts, thick with worms of death and rebirth; it stretched its crown up into the bright, open space in her mind, where she worshipped the shining stars.

The hawthorn shifted its trunk, bending around her, making a lap for Elia to curl against.

Elia cried, and she let go of so many things, even those she had no names for, so she called them instead by the trees' word for the light between shadows. And let them all go.

When she finished, Elia lay quiet and soothed, scraped empty as bark peeled in a storm. She thought she might finally be ready to fill herself up again with a new thing, this time born of her own choosing.

The hawthorn whispered, *Are you ready?*

Elia shuddered, and kissed the hawthorn tree. *Ready to what, grandmother?*

An urgent wind tugged at Elia's curls, drawing her attention to the gathering storm.

The island answered, *To become a queen.*

# THE FOX

BAN THE FOX did not hold his liquor well, or much at all.

It was perhaps the thing that made him most aware of his relative youth, despite having aged so fast in Aremoria's frequent border wars.

Leaning against the smoke-stained wooden walls of what passed for the Errigal Steps public house, Ban was surrounded by soldiers and retainers, those belonging to his father and those from Connley. Once again, the morning had been spent in war exercises, and Ban was exhausted. He'd led three charges and organized the overall structure of the games, both to prove his martial worth to Connley as well as to instruct the duke's army in the techniques he'd learned during his fostering in Aremoria. But island soldiers were unused to facing cavalry or mounted spearmen, and the new methods were harder to teach than Ban had expected.

He tried not to imagine what Morimaros would say if he found Ban exposing their army's weaknesses so readily. Even if the Fox did it to further ingratiate himself to Connley, in order to spy on behalf of Aremoria, it was a tenuous rope to walk.

Ban would rather be looking for Elia. Knowing she'd returned, but not contacted him or Regan, made him burn with eager desperation.

The pub spent most of its time as a middle-sized forge, but once the sun set on certain days, the smith had the front walls taken off their basic hinges and opened it all up. The fires kept everything warm, even tamped down for the night, and the two families who competed for the best brew in the Steps would bring barrels. Everyone was supposed to fetch their own cup to this sometimes-pub, but Ban was instead lent one by Med, the captain of Errigal's retainers, a rugged, black-bearded fellow who'd spent all day dogging Ban's heels, critiquing the Aremore method of spearing. It had been good work, and Ban found that when the storm clouds had gathered in the north, darkening the noon sun, he'd wanted to build on the relationship.

So though it was only early afternoon, Ban had called halt to the games for the day, and asked the ironsmith to make an exception to his sunset rule. The man agreed—anything for their Fox, he said—and so here some of the haphazard army stood, enjoying an afternoon off at the pub.

The retainers did not treat Ban like a foot soldier, but like a leader. Whether they respected him for himself and his knowledge, or only did so in Rory's absence, Ban didn't know. But he wasn't ready to walk away from it.

It had been a rough few days in Errigal: Regan was inconsolable, her husband curt toward all, and Ban's father had gone rather quiet, stress apparent in his every movement. Ban had never seen Errigal so tense, so lacking his usual gregarious, sweeping gestures and obnoxious likability. It had to be anxiety over the king, and Rory's betrayal, but Errigal refused to confide in Ban. Errigal barely brought himself to enjoy the war games, and when he did, he and Connley used Ban as a buffer between them.

This beer was thick as soup, colored like mud, and tasted like home in a way Ban hadn't realized he'd needed. He remembered sharing its like with Rory some ten years ago, laughing hard enough to choke—but quietly, for they'd invaded the kitchen, poured as many cups as they could carry between them, and snuck sloshing into their father's study to consume it. Ban also remembered vomiting in the fireplace.

Ban pushed aside the thought of his brother, the memory of bile too familiar. Another letter from Gaela had come, late last evening when only Ban, Connley, and Regan remained at the hearth. Though he'd tried to let them alone with it, the duke had told Ban to stay.

Regan had read her letter quickly, fingers pinching the paper with sudden emotion. "She asks if Kayo has come to us, and speaks of Elia as if she's heard from the girl!" she said. "What is this? That Elia would write to Gaela and not me? And I the one who . . ." She whirled to her husband, letter thrust out.

Connley had taken it then and read, lips pursing, one brow lifting. "Your younger sister wishes for Lear in Aremoria? Made a blatant threat of Aremore invasion? Does Gaela write this to drive suspicion between you and Elia?"

"Maybe." Regan paced away, tapping her long fingers against her skirts as she went. "But Gaela would not toy with mention of an Aremore invasion. Of all things, we are united in that. But yet . . . no letter for me from Elia. Perhaps it is Elia who would break my bond with Gaela in her favor, or that of her gallant King Morimaros."

Connley smiled. "I would not have thought the girl had such duplicity in her. If so, perhaps we were too quick to discount her power."

A sudden thought had spurred Ban to open his mouth to speak, but he hesitated just as Regan glanced at him. He looked down fast to the edge of the rug upon which the lady stood. Her sleek pale gown had dragged some rushes off the stones and onto the braided wool.

"Speak, sir," Regan said.

He had Elia's letter for her, still. He could've handed it over. He should have. But if he did, how might've he explained his lateness in delivering it? Said he'd withheld it at first because Regan had so set him in awe he'd forgotten, or confessed his prior allegiance to Morimaros? The very consideration of such action had shaken him. No, he must not admit to anything. Yet.

Ban had thought furiously as he met her gaze. "Did you not give your letters to Kay Oak to deliver, as I and my father did? And is it not likely Elia used the earl to pass her messages back? Perhaps it is not your sister who spurns you, but your uncle."

"Ah!" A spark lit Regan's eyes. "He would favor Gaela, of course, having no love for my lord."

"If the Oak Earl believes Gaela to be stronger, better for Innis Lear—or rather," Connley had said darkly, "if he believes Astore to be better, he would undoubtedly seek to tilt favor. And we do know the Oak and I have never been friends. Though he seemed always to dislike me before I even knew his name."

A fast, thin jolt of something closely related to panic pumped through Ban's heart then: it had been the battle joy, the thrill of a plan coming together. Though he'd had no plan at all. "Kay Oak has returned from Aremoria," Ban said. "I saw him when I visited my mother. He wanted me on his side. He said, *Together we would make a strong alternative to Connley.*"

The duke had grabbed Ban's arm, hard, the one he'd injured when enacting the drama of Rory's betrayal. The healing scar ached like a fresh bruise. Connley said, "Why did you not mention this, Fox?"

"I denied him." Ban had held his treasonous arm rigid, but did not pull free. This near, Connley's eyes were like verdigris. "I do not wish to sow discord, and also I thought he had no more allies here. I am not a politician, my lord. Just a soldier."

Regan had stroked her husband's jaw with her knuckles. "Sir. Harm him not."

Connley released Ban and tugged his gray-and-black tunic straight. Blood rushed back into Ban's arm, promising another thick bruise by morning. Regan took her husband's place, leaning suspiciously close to Ban.

"There is something else, though," the lady had said silkily as she gripped

Ban's chin, tilting it up so he met her uncompromising gaze. "What did you write to my little sister, Ban the Fox?"

"What?" Connley snapped.

"He said, *as I and my father did.* You wrote to Elia, Ban. Tell me."

Lowering his lashes as blood heated his face, Ban had whispered a version of the truth.

"I told her that at least one person on Innis Lear still loved her."

The duke had snorted, amused.

Hollow and cold, Ban had thought, *Is there no one I have yet to betray?*

A day later, surrounded now by laughter, gray sunlight, and the conversation of strangers he did not know how to befriend, Ban scowled and drank the last of his beer. Sour with guilt more than alcohol, Ban found the old retainer Med and returned the borrowed cup with his thanks. It was several minutes before he could extricate himself from the praise, and from the retellings already spinning about the morning's battle games, eager faces adding what legends they'd heard of the Fox's exploits in Aremoria. The captured underclothes he'd used to humiliate the enemy, the disguises, the vandalized Diotan flag. Ah, saints, how Ban had lived: rushing and surviving by his desperation and skills. Someone began a cheer, "Long be the Fox!"

Drunkenness muddied his thoughts, as Ban felt pulled in too many directions. He'd sworn to Morimaros of Aremoria because that king had respected him enough to ask for his skills, and not command them. Ban loved Elia, but perhaps only a memory of her; he hardly knew her now. But Regan and Connley, they were like him: ambitious and powerful, and they understood the roots and needs of the trees! Connley had tried to open the Errigal navel well yesterday, arguing with Ban's father that it might make the iron sing freely again.

The duke and his wife would never give up speaking to the trees, as Elia had. When it had mattered most, Elia had chosen her father's path, taken all her solace from the stars. She'd let Ban go, never fought to stay at his side. Yet, when Ban's heart ached at seeing the closeness between Connley and Regan, it was Elia he thought of: Elia's black eyes alight with flitting magic, her solemn whisper, and the sad, broken cry Ban'd heard ripped from her throat that night at the standing stones.

What could he still do? For her, or for Regan, or for the poor magic of this island, left to sink into itself while the cutting stars glared down.

Morimaros of Aremoria couldn't help these Learish roots, either, not the heartblood of this island, no matter how strong was his own land.

And what did it mean that Elia had come home? And now? The island had told Ban, but not anyone else, not even Regan. And worse, since the morning of their intense wormwork, Ban was having an impossible time conversing with the trees, as if all their attentions were elsewhere! Not on him, no; he was never chosen first. Never the most beloved.

Ah, stars, Ban was a mess.

This was why he did not drink. Even the voices of the wind had slurred. Or perhaps it was the susurrus of the coming rain, the air full of mist already.

He should return to the Keep for shelter, where Connley and Regan likely had already nestled, at a hot fire, together. He thought of their bond, their burning passion, and their gestures beckoning him to share. Sweat broke along his spine, and in his drunkenness he imagined going to them and giving them everything they seemed to want, from his body and spirit.

Shame stopped the too-vivid dream. They would likely reject him anyway, if it came down to it. Laugh that he'd taken their flirtations too far. Choose each other always, abandoning him. Everyone did.

Ban lowered his eyes to the uneven lane. Straw and dry grass had done its best to harden the mud into a level path, but he still needed to pay heed to the way. The noise of the public house faded behind him, replaced by villagers eager to shutter their windows and get all the animals inside. Ban cut away from the row of smithies, aiming up the foothill toward the mountain. Here the Steps were mostly short houses of chalk daub, except for the stone star chapel that waited at the edge of the town, at the highest point before the sharp incline and the earl's road that lead only to the Keep itself.

Ban slowed his footsteps as he approached the chapel. He'd spent hours in this particular chapel as a boy, his only appearances, then, on his father's lands, at every anniversary of his birth. Errigal would demand his presence, and so Brona would bring him, in order that Errigal could lord over a star-cast for his bastard. The priests knew how to sweeten their patron's generous nature even further, for every casting complimented the last: Ban Errigal had been born to impress the world from below. The left hand, the power behind power; always the second, the almost-as-good. His castings had been presented counter to Rory's, the gilded, the legitimate.

What a sorry fool he was, Ban thought, pausing at the long, thin window of the star chapel, that such old insults still affected him so, made him crave approval. Pathetic: he truly was no better than was expected of a bastard.

A movement up the path from the Keep flattened Ban back into the shadowy crook of the chapel door.

Errigal! Ban knew the coarse gait, despite the cowl pulled low over his father's face. He darted silently around the sharp corner stones and waited while Errigal knocked softly on the wooden chapel door, and it was answered. The earl went inside, and Ban came back around to the long window. Unlike most in the Steps, the chapel was set with glass and so impossible to discern sound through, and all he could see was the blur of fire inside. Frustration made him grit his teeth, wishing to slam the butt of his sword into the glass.

Seething, Ban sought to calm himself with deep breaths. He had been drinking, and it would not do any good to let that get the better of him. The Fox was needed to think it through: Errigal had no reason to come in secret for a star-casting. Everyone knew the earl was as devout as Lear had been. But to pull a cowl over his head as if in hiding, before any rain fell to necessitate such a thing, meant Errigal was up to nothing loyal and good. What a fool, and useless at subterfuge, Ban thought scornfully. If his father had secret business, he ought to stride calmly here and pretend he was only arriving for a casting.

No, Errigal had business here that he feared Connley discovering. Or that he wanted to keep from Ban himself.

Anger shot through him again, and Ban swung around to the entrance. He grabbed the handle and barged inside. The door was lighter than he remembered, and his enthusiasm slammed it back against the inner wall.

Errigal and the star priest shocked apart, but not before Ban saw the paper pass between them, Errigal to priest.

"Ban!" cried his father. "What is this?"

Filling the door with his presence, Ban replied, "What is *this*, Father? What need have you, the Earl Errigal, for secret meetings with star priests?"

The priest was a young man, hardly older than Ban himself, with a cloud-pale face and glossy black hair caught in a simple tail at his neck. He stared at Ban, firelight reflecting annoyance in his eyes, and brightening the constellation tattoos on his chin and left cheek. "There is no proscribed time for a casting," the priest said softly.

Ban snorted.

Errigal did, too, exactly the same. He sent his bastard son a long, weary look. "I have letters from Alsax, from Elia, and there is one for you."

Eagerness pushed through all else, and Ban reached out for it. The priest handed him a tiny square of folded paper.

*Do not keep promises by causing more pain. E.*

That was the extent of it.

His ears rang and he stared, not understanding.

"Your brother is there," Errigal said darkly. "The princess writes to me that he fled to her side. And also that she would have her father with her in Aremoria."

Ban stopped listening for a moment, realizing Elia guessed exactly why and how Rory had found his way to her. *Do not keep promises by causing more pain.* She rejected his evidence. She preferred to forgive her father than to see the truth.

Ban said, "But Aremoria cannot have both Elia and Lear."

"Yet we must do something. We must find a way to help our king."

Maybe it was bile, maybe it was hatred, maybe it was love; Ban swallowed it. He grasped the plain round pommel of his plain sword in one hand, forced the other loose against his thigh. "Help the king? Connley forbade it."

Errigal waved the priest away and dragged Ban inside, kicking the door shut again. "That is why, don't you see? Connley forbids me—*me*, his most loyal retainer—to tend the king? He and his lady will not do it, Gaela Astore will not either, and so I put the king himself to bed in the mud-brick house of my old mistress? That will not abide."

"Her bed was good enough for you once," Ban snapped.

His father clapped him on the shoulders. "Don't be dull, boy. This is no insult to Brona, but to our island, our king himself."

"He causes insult, Father. To all of us, to the island."

Errigal growled wordlessly, brow lowered, mouth pressed tight behind his beard.

Ban needed to rein the situation in, control it, before he lost sight of himself. So the Fox put on a stare of disbelief and said, "Connley has been your patron. A good one, too, who recognizes what must be for the good of Innis Lear. And you—what are you doing? What does this priest have to do with it? Will you tell me and let me help you?"

"Ah, boy, I follow the sun of loyalty to my king, and the moon of careful deceit. It is not in you to aid me in that."

"Not in my stars, you mean? That I cannot follow your same sun and moon?" His play-acting was nearly consumed by the truth of his bitterness.

Errigal hugged him suddenly, hard and rough, with his large arms a vise pinning Ban against him. "You keep yourself clear of this, for I do not know what they may do if I am caught out. If I go, Ban, if I die, you must find your brother—call him from his cousins—and make him come home to take his title, over my dead body as he had professed to want."

"What?" Ban shoved at Errigal, honestly surprised.

"I know," the earl said darkly. "It would not be my preference now, but the line must hold. Rory must keep his place, and rule then as Errigal. It's in his stars, you know, and meant to be as such. We must end this terrible cycle of child against father! This disaster with Lear and his daughters has shown me, Ban. I should have known, and looked past my rage to find forgiveness. In truth, for what comes, Rory is what I would have."

"Only he."

As always had been before, Errigal fondly patted Ban's head, cupped his face. "You're strong and good, Ban, but not my true line, not the star-ordained right of Errigal. Would that you were, Ban. My son, firstborn by season, if not bed."

"But Rory wished to murder you," Ban managed to say, the words grit and sand in his throat. "At the end of it all, after everything you have said, wishing I was your legitimate . . . You would still rather a patricide and traitor, a murderer, as your heir. You are so resolved to choose other than me."

"Ah." Errigal lifted his eyes as if he could see through the roof to the stars. "We are men, Ban. We kill, we send men to kill and be killed. We are all murderers here."

Ban put his hands to his eyes.

"Do you cry?" his father said, incredulous.

"I am drunk," he muttered, wishing his father was mad like Lear, not this constant, certain coward, this devotee to rules of destiny. Errigal was such a rotting follower. Ban needed him to be magnificent, like—like Connley and Regan. Like Mars. How could a woman like Brona have ever admired this man?

Errigal laughed his hearty, generous laugh. "Good. I heard such good things of you today on the battlefield, and I am proud to have you back on these lands."

"Tell me," Ban choked out. He dragged his hands down his face. "Tell me at least, the contents of that letter. If I am a good son, as you say."

Nodding, Errigal said, "I had word, too, from Alsax, here. They say Aremoria will set his navy to winter down, but he and Elia have been negotiating over his invasion of this—our!—island. And now the stars, too, say it will happen: the king of Aremoria will come here before the month is out. And also, the prophecies say that we must get Lear to Elia. She will keep him safe; she is all the hope we have left."

"Then Morimaros will have both king and daughter, and plenty of reason to attack. What if sending the king there is exactly what brings the invasion?"

"Perhaps, but Lear needs his crown back! The stars are clear."

"Give the crown to Elia, at least."

Errigal spared his son a pitying frown. "She is only a girl."

Only by years of constant practice was Ban able to keep calm. But barely. He said very pointedly, very slowly, "Did you tell Connley?"

"No, bah! That man is slave to his cruel, cold wife, and she would have me stocked, or killed, for treating with Aremoria, even if it is on behalf of Lear himself. Oh, my poor king. My letter aligns us—Errigal—with Elia and Morimaros, if that king will clear the way for Lear to reclaim his throne. You should be glad to hear it; I've heard tales of you riding proudly at his side."

Ban stared at his father, thinking it was true: he should be glad to hear it. War coming to Innis Lear, and from an army Ban knew well, an army he had a place in, still, if he kept his first promises to Morimaros, if he let his admiration for Regan Connley fall away. If he pretended he did not hate to hear of Elia married to Aremoria. But . . .

Ban would die a thousand humiliating deaths before he stood by and watched Lear put on the crown again.

He would not let it stand. Ban refused it, summarily.

If Errigal, who even yet preferred a son he believed to be a traitorous murderer over his proven, reputable, strong natural son, had to be a casualty of Ban's schemes, Ban supposed that was only the final evidence of his father's stars.

ANGRY WINDS SLAMMED against Errigal Keep as the sun lowered against the horizon, obscured by the coming storm. Only a few desperate rays shot free, reflecting off the silvered western hills. Black clouds, roiling air, and tiny spitting raindrops were a proper manifestation of Ban's mood.

Standing at the open doors of the great hall, he stared out into the crescent yard as dust in the cracks between stones became mud, as men dashed from black gates to stables and tower doors to black gates, at the change of watch. As soon as the sunset hour rang, the gates would swing closed for the long, stormy night.

Behind Ban, a house girl prodded the fire into a grand blaze; soon this hall would be full of retainers and families, seeking shelter together and warmth and some food. "Go," Ban said to her. "Fetch my father here, and when he's come, and after the duke and his lady arrive, shut the door."

She bobbed and fled, though he'd been gentle in tone.

"Fox."

Curan the iron wizard walked across the stone courtyard, unhurried, disregarding the force of the wind and splattering rain. A flash of light caught on the iron coins braided into the wizard's blond hair. In his hands he held a sword.

Ban's new sword. His breath picked up its pace.

"Here, young lord," Curan said, and Ban ducked with him into the great hall.

Taking the sword, Ban drew the blade and handed the plain sheath back to Curan. Ban lifted the sword: the steel gleamed like a shard of sunlight through the storm clouds.

*I burn!* whispered the steel.

A smile of absolute joy lit Ban's mouth. *As do I!* he answered, and cut the blade through the air.

It *laughed,* and Ban asked, "You forged her yourself?"

Curan nodded. "She was ready, and you are sure to need her."

"I do already." Ban squeezed the leather-wrapped hilt. He set the edge of the blade against his left forearm, holding the sword flat to inspect every inch.

Thunder rumbled overhead.

The vibration made the sword ring, settling down through Ban's bones. His pulse raced, and he knew, absolutely knew, for one clear moment, that he would die with this sword in his hand.

This sword would destroy; it would cleanse; it would change everything.

No, it was Ban himself who would do all those things. Soon.

Now.

As if prompted, Connley and Regan swept in exactly then. Ban could hear her skirts against the rushes, and Connley called, "Ban the Fox, we've come, as you asked."

Ban turned. Wet wind shoved at his back as he made his way forward. "My lord." Tension edged his voice. He glanced at the iron wizard, who nodded and left.

"What ails you, sir?" Regan asked when they were alone. She reached for him with a lovely hand decorated with several slender silver rings that set off her winter-brown skin. Today she wore a silver-threaded violet gown, edged in white fur he suspected came from his animal namesake. Despite Regan's distraction, her grief—the pink rimming her irises—Ban thought she was everything a queen of Innis Lear should be: powerful, sharp, beautiful, like a raw ruby mined from the guts of the island, set into smooth iron.

The lady touched his face tenderly. "Tell us," she coaxed.

Connley put his hand against Ban's other cheek, casual and intimate. "Tell us," he said, more commanding.

Ban removed a letter from his coat. Unlike the last time he'd betrayed a family member with a letter, this one he'd not needed to forge. Once Errigal had returned to the Keep, the Fox had stalked the young star priest out of the Steps. He leapt upon him, killed him quickly, and took the letter Errigal had written to align himself with Aremoria, Morimaros, and Lear.

"My father has betrayed us," he said, relishing the sharp stab of guilt and the thorny pull of triumph all at once.

Connley took the letter and spread the paper so his wife could share the view. She read more quickly than he did, or perhaps rage blinded Connley. Before Connley did more than drag fingers through his fine slick hair, Regan lashed out, catching Ban unawares. Her nails cut his cheek; her rings would leave a red bruise. "He names you, too, in this dangerous missive, Ban Errigal," she said.

"Regan," Connley said, voice strangled. "The Fox brought this to us."

Ban held his gaze on Regan's, face hot. "He does name me, but that man cannot speak for me anymore than your father can for you."

Her smile was a vicious creature. "Well said, Fox."

The duke crushed the letter in his fist, strode to the strong fire, and cast it in. "We shall see what your father will claim for his loyalties, or if he will lie."

"We should hang him instantly," Regan hissed.

"Leave him to my displeasure," Connley said. "Ban, you may go. You need not witness this."

"Thank you, sir, but I will stay." He wanted to look in Errigal's eyes and show the earl exactly what he'd wrought by never choosing Ban.

"Brave boy," said Regan, lovingly, but Ban knew this was not courage.

Just then Errigal dashed through the open doors from the courtyard, cursing the rain that plastered his hair to his face, dragged at his beard, and turned his leather coat dark in long grasping streaks. "What is this storm? Unnatural, I say." He looked to any of the others for an ally in commiseration.

They would not need to summon him, in the end, to his end.

"Not so unnatural as your actions," Connley coolly returned.

"What?" Errigal stopped short, shaking off his hair like a wet dog.

"You have betrayed us," Regan said.

Ban's heart beat hard enough to break. Every stab against his ribs fueled Ban's anger, drummed up his turmoil.

"No—never you, lady," the earl said, changing instantly to a penitent, his hands out and palms down. "You've heard of the shelter I gave your father, but surely you must know the old king needed it. I've only brought him to Hartfare, so he might find rest with Brona—this son of mine's mother. It was kindness to a king I have loved, my lord, my lady. That is all."

"Is kindness what made you write to Aremoria and offer allegiance against ourselves?" Connley asked, smooth and low as a wolf's warning growl.

"Filthy traitor," Regan said.

"Lady, I am none!" Errigal stepped to place himself nearer Ban, who noticed it with a sick sort of satisfaction. He fought against a terrible smile; he mustn't show his hand too soon, but remember when Errigal came to Hartfare and tore Ban from his mother, without a care to what Ban needed or wished; when he shoved his son onto a horse, taking him away from love forever, saying it was for their own good, that Ban was too low for Elia's glory; every fondly applied description of *base* and so many hearty, easy laughing *other sons,* as if Ban would cease to exist if his father were to do so.

Connley said, "You deny your words?"

Errigal broadened his shoulders, ignored the remnants of rain trailing down his face and beard, and lifted his chin proudly. "I do not; though I deny—only—that they make me a traitor."

"We thought you were our friend, Errigal."

"You betray us by siding with my father!" Regan said. "You betray even murdering, terrible Lear and the entire island by turning to Aremoria!"

Errigal pointed a thick finger at her. "You betrayed him, and yourselves, and this island first, lady, by casting your king out, by treating him as the enemy—him who was nothing but father to you! You put yourself opposed to Lear and goodness, and the stars themselves, and so *you* opposed this island and its crown."

"No," Regan said. "My sister and I are crowned here. By the stars and our own father's word, him who you obey like an unthinking dog."

Ban caught his breath. Surely Errigal would leave, attack, something, now—he could not stand for such talk. Ban's palms tingled for action. He realized he stood poised on the balls of his feet.

Errigal seethed through his teeth and said, "I would never allow a man— a father—to suffer as you have allowed it—it is cruel, unnatural as this storm! You are unnatural."

"Draw your sword," Connley commanded, drawing his own. "You will die tonight, at my hand."

Only Errigal wore no sword.

"Son—" Errigal said, reaching for Ban's.

Ban felt lightheaded, abuzz with lightning energy. He was the storm outside, and he gripped his sword, pulled it a handspan free, then stopped. He stared at his father's desperate face, at the uneven line where beard hung from cheeks, the damp corners of his big eyes, the handsome nose, his still-youthful mass of dark blond hair. How many times had Ban been so desperate, and his father refused to see or care?

Ban shoved his sword home in its sheath with a sudden, sharp snick. "I've seen no sign from the stars I should help you, sir."

This moment was the last drop of honey, the first whisper from a beloved voice. Worth every betrayal, without space for regret.

"Ban!" Errigal cried.

The Fox smiled.

"There is no place to flee," Connley sneered. "For my retainers are here, and yours will follow the Fox."

Regan said, "*He* is become Errigal, old man."

Anger drained from Errigal's eyes as he looked to his bastard. "Ban," Errigal said, his voice a husk of its old rich self.

"They are your sun and moon now, Father," Ban said, sickly triumphant, afire with revenge. "Your fate is in their star-sharpened hands."

He could not stay, could not remain indoors, sheltered from wild nature and the reveling wind. Turning even from the duke and his lady, from the hot, raging fire, from the warmth of the room and his own father, Ban the Fox walked out into the storm.

# ELIA

"Will we arrive soon, Elia? I don't know how much longer these thighs can hug this beast," Aefa called from behind her. They rode single file, for this track to Hartfare was narrow. Branches reached down for them, while ferns and sharp bushes reached up, making a constant scratch at shoulders, knees, boots, and their horses' backsides as they pushed through.

Rain drizzled through the thick black trees, heavy enough that Elia was glad of the hunter's hood, for her hair did not react pleasantly to being wet. Water drained down the back of the hood, occasionally pooling forward at the tip just above her eyes, then loosing a fat drop onto her breast. As with the ocean, this rain distorted the voice of the trees, and so she only could hear a jumble of the White Forest's words.

Elia lifted her hand to wave her understanding back at Aefa. The girl did not like horses, but she had kept her groans to a minimum, since this was faster than walking. They'd borrowed the horses and Elia's hood from Lear's own retainers, whom they'd met at the outskirts of the forest. The men had set up their tents there, until their king would emerge again. According to Captain Seban, the king and his Fool had been led into the forest by the Earl Errigal himself, only a few days past. They couldn't bring their entire force to Hartfare, and so there they camped on the plain.

Though Seban wished to send some guard with the princess, Elia insisted she did not need it, for she'd visited Hartfare before, and knew the way. At Elia's first blood, Regan had brought her, reluctant to travel so far without Gaela, but determined to give Elia what their mother had once given Regan.

Upon arrival, Brona had offered Elia a small glazed urn. The true gift had been the memory attached: of sitting in her own mother's library, just herself, the queen, and Brona. Dalat had given Brona this same urn.

That was the extent of the memory, but it was enough. Elia had felt a homecoming, and unexpectedly, felt loved.

Brona had hugged her, then hugged Regan, too—who allowed the embrace, surprising Elia more than anything. The sisters spent two days in the little village, under thatched roofs bursting with spring flowers, learning songs from the trees, drinking honey water and a very fine, delicate alcohol Brona promised she made only for new women and the sisters they brought. Those few days were the only time in her life Elia had spent with only Regan, without Gaela. She'd believed, then, that Regan had enjoyed it, too. When they returned to Dondubhan for the winter, however, Regan had become as cool and disregarding as ever. Though every once in a long while, she would seek out Elia, making a point to force her into an opinion on some thing or another, and Regan would, if often disdainfully, listen. But then came Connley.

Elia shivered as wind found a way into her cloak and set a chill to her spine. She flexed her hands, regretting her lack of gloves. But of course, the retainers had none to fit her.

She wished for her sisters to come here to Hartfare, so the three of them might peacefully determine what was best for Innis Lear, in this safe, warm, center. Elia worried that peace was more impossible than it had ever been, now that she had chosen to come home without consulting them first. She did not want their throne, but they would never believe it. Especially not now, when the island whispered its unhappiness to her, and called her queen. And what could Elia tell them about the king of Aremoria? And his spy?

Wind whipped suddenly, spilling a ferocious fall of rain upon them. Elia's horse jolted forward a few steps before settling, and she thought she spied the flash of fire glow through the bending, shifting blackness ahead. Elia smiled, despite the terrible evening. Hartfare was a good place. Her father was ahead of her, and sheltered, though she knew not how his mind might be. A warm hearth would allow Elia an easy chance to speak with him, comfort him, and perhaps smooth the terrible fissure between them. She was ready, if not to forgive, then to understand. And that was ever the first step.

The trees opened up, finally, revealing a rain-washed clearing. Thunder marked their entrance with a roar, and a flash of lightning on its heels cast the village they faced in a frozen moment of silver and fire.

Aefa pushed around and ahead of her, calling out to the village that their princess had come. Elia pulled her horse still, patting her soaked neck. Aefa managed to rouse enough people out in the rain to listen to her, saying she traveled with Elia Lear and requested someone to take them to Brona. There followed a flurry of very wet motion, and Elia was lifted off her horse, a cloak thrown over her, while the horses were led away into one of the nearest buildings. She and Aefa ran with their escort to the distant edge of the village, splashing mud and gasping as rain slapped their eyes and leapt into their mouths.

The door to Brona's cottage was propped open, promising warm, fiery sanctuary. Elia stumbled across the threshold, looking wildly about the room. There was the long, scarred oak table, there the hearth with its welcoming fire, over which hung a pot of soup and two pots of boiling water; the whitewashed walls and bundles of drying herbs dangling from black rafters, the scattered shadows up on the tangled underside of the heather thatching. There, the empty doorway that led to the mudroom and a privy out the back.

Her father was not here.

Wind slammed the door behind Elia. Lightning flashed, and suddenly the storm was a violent monster, a devourer. What had it already destroyed?

"Kayo?" called Brona, hurrying in from the rear, hair gorgeous and wind-tossed as ever, wool wrapped around her as a mantle. A wildness brightened her eyes, but the witch's face fell into a flash of despair before she tightened her expression. "Elia. I should not be surprised by this, given the talk of the trees."

"Are you all right? What's wrong with my uncle? Where is my father? He was supposed to be here." Elia clamped down on her own rising fear.

Brona shook her head "The old king ran into the wind, before the storm was so terrible. Some hours ago now. Your uncle Kayo and the Fool ran after."

Elia started for the door again, but Aefa was there blocking the way, windblown and waterlogged, frowning through long strands of hair plastered across her face. Aefa said, "I want to go after them, too. But that's madness, Elia! We must wait."

"Warm yourself here, and wait as Aefa counsels." Brona took Elia's shoulders with an urgency Elia did not feel was deserved. "None should be out in this. Not your fathers, nor—nor Kayo."

"Why?" Elia asked softly, hearing, or sensing, a thread of panic in the saying of her uncle's name.

"Your . . ." Brona stopped. She let out a breath, then said, "He is badly injured. I've been caring for him and it . . . he should not be out of bed at all, and much less so on a night like this."

"What happened to him? Will he be all right?"

"If he comes back safely, yes, perhaps. Or perhaps he will be blind."

"Blind!"

"Everything I *can* do, I have done." Brona met her gaze with such force of certainty, Elia let her eyes drift closed. For tonight, that was true of herself, as well. *Everything I can do, I have done.* But when the sun rose again, so much would rise with it.

"Your mother lives two cottages south of this one," Brona said to Aefa.

Elia said, "Go, see your mother, Aefa."

With a frustrated little press of her lips, Aefa nodded and dove back into the rain.

"Tell me how my father is, or was," Elia asked, as Brona sat her down beside the fire and began pulling off her hood and coat with quick, efficient movements.

"Lear is lost in himself, and in the stars inside his head, much worse now than at this time last year, or even from the start of summer," Brona said, after she'd stripped Elia of the wettest outer layers, and poured hot water into mugs for them both. Elia huddled in a blanket at the ancient wooden table while Brona pressed dry her hair and picked out the worst tangles.

"My sisters," Elia whispered. "They set him out into this."

"Your sisters . . ." Brona's hands paused, but the words continued. "Lear was on this path before Gaela or Regan did anything. It began long ago."

"Their choices did not help," Elia said stubbornly, gripping her clay mug, seeking the warmth as if she could draw it through her palms and into her heart.

"No, they did not help. They let anger and hurt drive them."

"They should be better, if they would be queens."

Behind her, Brona sighed. The scrape of the pick was gentle on Elia's scalp. "No, neither should wear the crown."

Elia turned in the sturdy old chair. "Why do you say so?"

Firelight found all the warmth in Brona's lovely face. In her hand she held the horn pick, and the loop of small amber beads unwound and free of Elia's braids for the first time in days. Brona stared rather bleakly at the fire and said, "Gaela abandoned both stars and roots, and believes in no authority but her own. And Regan is afraid of her own power, as she is lost to her own heart, too consumed by the magic of the island. Both will lead to no better ruling than your father's obsession with stars, without balance."

So the wind and trees believed, too. Elia sighed. "Gaela won't be swayed by this reasoning—she'll say Aremoria has no rootwater, no prophecies, and still is strong, does well enough to win every battle they've had, these last few decades. And she's right."

"Aremoria is not Innis Lear."

"I know, very well, what Aremoria is," Elia said irritably. "But then Gaela will also say she believes in Regan's power, enough for us all, that they make their own balance together, enough to lead those who would wish the stars to bear true and those who long for the roots."

"Gaela is incapable of balance!" Brona cried, flinging the horn pick to the ground with such force it snapped. The witch gasped for breath as Elia gaped at her, never having seen the woman so out of sorts. Then Brona put her fists hard against her hips. "I am sorry. I shouldn't—Kayo. It was Gaela who hurt him, Princess Elia. Your sister lashed out when he only tried to protect your father, and . . . he may go blind for it."

Elia's shock was drowned by the storm's sudden gust; it tore and crashed into the shuttered windows and rattled the front door. They were out in that maelstrom: her father and uncle. Aefa's father. She set her mug on the hearth and went to Brona, taking the witch's cold hands. "Everything we can do, we have done," she whispered.

Brona looked steadily at Elia, coming back to herself. Her cheeks were flushed. "There is more reason you should be queen instead."

"Oh, Brona," Elia murmured. She did not want to hear, not now.

"Neither of your sisters can bear children."

"Are you certain? How can you know?"

"Gaela, ever drastic, chose to make herself, and ensured nothing could be planted within her. While Regan never was given the choice. This is not star prophecy or wormwork, but simply the truth."

"Oh, poor Regan," Elia whispered to herself. Even so many years ago, when Elia had been a brand-new woman, Regan had made clear her desire to be a mother, and her awe at the processes.

Brona went to the door and pressed her hand against it as if to bear up the house with her strength of will. She whispered something Elia could not quite hear but she thought was a prayer to the island.

The storm battered the house, raging, then for a moment quieted itself. In the gentler melody of rain alone, Brona turned around. "Their truth leaves one option only. You, Elia, must be the queen, or Dalat's legacy, and the dynasty of Lear, will end. For your mother—for her line, for her hopes—you must."

"It's not a good enough reason alone," Elia whispered. "That I might have a fertile womb! It reduces me to only that, and I dislike it."

"It is important to consolidate power this way."

"In the eyes of men!"

Brona lifted her eyebrows.

Disgruntled, Elia grimaced. "I would like to . . . be a mother. One day. But not to rely on it, for the sake of a country more than even my own.

And we can't be certain I can conceive, because I've never tried. Maybe all three of us are cursed. Maybe this is the end of the kingdom of Lear, and the island will become something new. Maybe we never did belong here after all."

"Is that what you truly believe, that you and your sisters are not part of us? That Dalat did not make her heart into another root of Innis Lear?"

Elia stopped breathing. She stared at the blank tension in Brona's expression, feeling as though she were slowly tipping over an edge into some great writhing vortex of emotions. It would be so easy to give over to it, now.

Then she gasped and was solid again. "No," Elia said quiet, but firm. "I know we are of Innis Lear; this island was hers, and ours. It whispers in all our dreams. It is just so hard. Why is it so hard?"

"People make it so." Brona came to her and knelt upon the packed earth, touching both hands to Elia's knees. "I will help you. I loved your mother."

"As she loved you," Elia said, though it was merely a guess. "And my family . . . We *are* Innis Lear, and maybe healing our own divisions, the wounds in our past, can heal this island, too." Elia paused, ordering her thoughts. "I want . . . I want the island to be strong, the people to be safe and secure. I want a king or queen who loves our home and can protect it."

"It should be you, Elia."

The storm blew, hissing and screaming against the cottage. Elia could not hear words in the fury, but her breath shook out, full with fear. She touched Brona's hands. Elia could not agree, not yet. She did not know how to speak it; she did not know how to open her heart to so much vulnerability, when she had only just now relearned to open it at all.

# REGAN

THUNDER CRASHED OVER the towers of Errigal Keep.

Regan Lear seethed, her hands in fists, leaning forward as she stared at the once-Earl Errigal—this stamping bull of a man, her father's greatest support—flushed and red-splotched under his beard.

"Bring me my sword!" Errigal roared, loud enough to follow lightning.

Connley's breath was even, and Regan struggled to match his ease, despite the pulse of her heart under her jaw, the throbbing in her palms and temples. How dare this false, braying earl undercut them! How dare he turn to Elia! And *Aremoria*!

Her perfect nails cut into her palms with all their sharpness.

Ban the Fox had left, charged into the storm, and Regan wished to join him, to run and spin madly, to scream her rage with the wind and trees, and then harness all that power to her will. Take Connley and Ban both, put herself between them and the sky and the earth, dig and cut into herself, until Regan had her new life, or until she was dead.

But first, they would deal with this traitor.

A side door crashed open and a retainer burst in, gasping for orders from the raging Errigal. He skidded to a halt, looking between duke and earl.

"This man has proven a snake in the breast of Innis Lear," Connley said, holding his sword low. "Bring him a weapon to defend himself."

"Do it!" Regan snapped.

The retainer hesitated, and behind him others of the household slipped in, drawn to the growing commotion.

"Yours will do," Errigal said, holding a large hand to the retainer. As the sword was given over, the earl added, "I am no traitor, though a fool."

Connley pressed his lovely, hard lips together. "A traitor to me, who has always sought your support and friendship."

"Your wife betrayed her father, my king, long before I thought to act against you," Errigal said. "We have all first been betrayed by the stars themselves!"

"While my father betrayed the island beneath their blind eyes," Regan spat.

"And yet you wonder why you can't bear a child? It is punishment for all your conflict and undaughterly ambition. I've seen your star sign, I was present for your birth—"

Connley leapt forward, attacking with smooth grace. Regan gasped at the beauty of it, and gasped again at the clash of their swords.

Errigal used his greater weight, leveraging it to shove the duke back, but her husband was faster, younger, and he bounced free, turning hard with a new attack that the earl barely blocked.

Each steel strike rang in Regan's bones, vibrating with its own frenzied song. All around the hall men and women of the Keep had gathered, clutching one another and watching, too. The storm blew, and Regan whispered "*Destroy him*"; in reply the freezing wet wind shrieked in through the open great doors, slamming them back. It rushed at Errigal, spinning around him to disorient. He cried out, and Connley smiled viciously.

"This is no fair fight!" called out a rough voice. Curan the iron wizard, with his wife Sella holding his huge muscled arm in a vice grip. Curan's mouth moved again, with a hissing command, and the fire in the hearth flared.

Regan pointed at him. "I will flay your skin from your bones if you aid this traitor." The wind whipped away from Errigal, pulling his hair, and blasted Curan. The ironsmith stood like a wall and whispered something so that the wind fluttered and skirted softly around him.

Lightning struck and, two paces behind, thunder roared.

The duke and the old earl panted in the wake of the storm's anger, then the earl growled and renewed his attack. They battled hard, all striking steel and grunts. Errigal caught Connley's sword with his hilt, twisted, and hit Connley in the face. Connley fell to one knee, but turned, upright again even as Regan cried out, carving space with a good, desperate swing of the sword.

A pause as the two men faced each other again.

Regan said, "You would have done better to be ours, as your less loved son, Ban the Fox, has been. He will inherit this Keep, and be honored by us, by the queen myself and the king my sister. But swear yourself to me now, Errigal, and we will show you mercy."

"Mercy like you gave your father?" the old earl snarled. "You're an ungrateful, dry bitch, just as he said, all the better to have not been allowed to breed!"

Regan screamed, throwing herself forward, just as Connley drove his sword through Errigal's lower chest.

The earl flung his weapon wildly, slamming the flat of the blade against Connley's ribs. Connley fell to one knee and let go of his sword, which stuck in Errigal's chest: blood poured from the wound and spattered Errigal's chin as he stumbled back.

Regan rushed to the old earl, commanding another gust of cold wind to keep any retainers far back. The earl hit the wooden floor with a massive thud, and Regan leapt upon him, straddling his waist. Her skirts ballooned around them, and she leaned forward to grasp the hilt of the sword. She twisted it. The earl choked on a scream: it sounded exactly like the shriek of the ghost owl. Regan released the sword. Crawling up his body, she put her hands on the earl's face, hardly breathing—or perhaps breathing too hard, nearly out of her body. She curled her fingers. Sharp nails cut into the soft skin under Errigal's eyes. Regan said, "I should take these, old man, and prove how sightless you are, how useless and stupid, how extreme a fool."

The earl's handsome eyes brightened with tears before they spilled from the corners, and Regan, too, was crying suddenly, thinking of her father and this weak man's complicity in her persecution, and thinking of that lovely heart-faced owl she'd killed for nothing. With a scream, she tore her fingers down Errigal's face, scouring his cheeks.

Errigal twitched and his shoulders shrugged, caught in a jerky death dance.

"Go to those cold stars," Regan whispered. "Wait you there for my father!"

He died with her crouched over him like a spirit of vengeance.

Regan slid off, awkward suddenly and empty inside. The earl's blind eyes stared up at the ceiling, and Regan looked where they would have: nothing but air and limewash and the dark wooden beams. She shook with weeping.

"Lady!" cried Sella Ironwife.

The iron wizard and his wife knelt at Connley's side: the duke bent over his own knee, hands on his ribs. He coughed, his face contorting in pain. Blood spots flecked his lips.

Regan ran to him. "Connley!"

Curan carefully supported her husband, lowering him to the ground, then tore the duke's tunic and pulled up the bloody linen shirt. Connley's entire right side was billowing black and vibrant red with a massive bruise; a bloody gash stretched over at least the bottom two of his ribs, broken open from the weight of Errigal's sword. When Connley breathed, the shape of his ribs was not right.

Terror froze Regan, a cold panic that blinded her and stole her breath. "Connley," she whispered.

"Regan," her husband said, bloody and harsh. His left hand reached for her, and she grasped it with both of hers, dragging herself nearer to his heart.

"Bind him," she ordered. "Bind it well and—and ready a wagon, *now*." A flash of insight hung in her imagination: Connley submerged in rootwater, at the oak altar in the heart of Connley Castle. Sleeping, calm, healing.

Kissing his knuckles, she whispered, *The island and I will make you well again, beloved,* in the language of trees. Outside, the storm howled its disagreement.

BEFORE HE WAS Connley, he was Tear, son of Berra Connley and Devon Glennadoer. He'd been born when his parents were old, both of them in their fifth decade, because his mother, Berra, had been previously determined to marry the king of Innis Lear. She'd been wed to Lear's middle brother, without issue, and thus widowed when the man died. In desperate hope she put off all other suitors, even after Lear had married Dalat of Taria Queen, and for the four years after, while they failed produce an heir, and thereby legitimize the crown of the foreign usurper.

But Gaela had been born, and all the island knew the prophecy was real: Dalat was fated to be their queen for at least sixteen more years.

Berra had raged for three full months, then married the second son of the Earl Glennadoer and, after some struggle, got herself with child.

Tear was born eight months after Regan Lear. He did not meet her until the year memorial for her mother's death.

The great hall of the Lear's winter castle at Dondubhan was built of cold gray stone that vaulted higher overhead than any room Tear had been inside before. He could not help but be aware that to preside over this fortress had been his mother's lifelong goal. Massive hearths burned at either end, and a long stone channel ran down the center length, filled with hot coals. Servants replaced them regularly, scattering small chunks of incense that melted and released spice into the air. Candles dangled from chains along the walls and off the arched ceiling, though the highest were not lit. Berra told her son as they entered that the king had forbidden their lighting—because despite how the high candle flames would imitate stars hovering over their feast, lighting them required magic. And there was to be no more of that in the king's house.

She'd said it with no expression, but Tear knew his mother well enough to recognize the disquiet in her blue-green eyes.

At fourteen, Tear Connley was tall and slightly awkward, having not yet grown into his height. But none who looked upon him would doubt the regal lines of his jaw and cheeks and brow, nor the strength of his family nose. He was colored exactly as his mother: straight blond hair that tended toward red-gold, lovely blue-green eyes, and unblemished skin as smooth and light as cream. His lips were pink and sometimes the tips of his cheeks, too. If he smiled, he would be beautiful. But Tear rarely did.

He looked like a prince, which was why two people in this hall had already asked him if he was the young Aremore heir who had been sent by his father for the memorial. Tear tilted his chin down, both times, and said only, "No," slanting his gaze toward where the real prince sat, resplendent in orange and white like a summer's day, with only a finely embroidered strip of pale gray silk tied to his arm.

Abandoned by his mother, so she could more freely gossip and plot with her array of Connley cousins, Tear leaned his shoulder against the corner of a stone pillar, softened by time and darkened from hundreds of hands. He'd pulled his bloodred coat on to cover the mourning gray wool that he'd worn out on to the Star Field for the procession at dusk. Tear was beginning to be aware that the bolder color made him shine, instead of drawing him wan as it did his darker father. His mother approved, having raised him to use every weapon in his arsenal.

The great hall was crushed with people, most blending together in their mourning shades of white and gray, though some still wore jewels and silver that sparkled, in hair and at wrists or waists. Tear played a game with himself, trying to name every faction, and invent some plot for them to discuss. His own young cousins were mostly girls, and so they did not desire to spend time with him, given that he did not flirt or pretend to protect them. The boys were all ten years Tear's elder, thanks to his parents' long wait for children. Those boys had little interest in his cold quiet and used to call him his mother's daughter when they were younger and stupid enough to forget he would be their duke. Though Tear had hardly minded. They would be his allies when the time came, because he knew everything they wanted, and he would be in position to grant it, or not. And because he *was,* in many ways, his mother's daughter. She taught him very, very well, and he learned, adeptly and eagerly.

Someday Tear would wear the ducal chains; someday he would rule Connley and control the entire eastern edge of Innis Lear, down through the wealthy Errigal lands. Everyone on Innis Lear would love or fear him, or perhaps hate him. Anything, he thought, so long as their feelings were strong. His mother had told him, *Make the people want you for you, not your stars. Give them a connection to your flesh and blood and purpose, my boy. As we connect ourselves to the rootwater.*

He certainly wasn't following that advice while leaning apart from the crowd, so, taking a breath, Tear pushed clear of the column. He began a measured pace deeper into the room. He wound through clusters of adults, some laughing, some gossiping intensely with concerned faces. All were drinking warm wine from braziers hung over the hot coals. Tear took a cup himself and drank half of it down, despite knowing it would bring the pink out in his sharp cheeks.

His goal was the prince of Aremoria, Morimaros. Several years Tear's elder and here, his mother said, to court one of Lear's daughters.

Tear stepped up beside the prince, hoping his solemn expression lent age and wisdom to his features.

Morimaros nodded, dark blue eyes flicking across Tear's face. "From Connley?" the prince said.

Tear bowed. "The duke's only son."

"We hear fine things about your mind and ambitions, young Connley," said the Earl Rosrua's son, likely to take the title any month now. He stood at Morimaros's opposite side. "We'll welcome you to our ranks."

Again, Tear bowed, though more slightly. What he had heard of the heir to Rosrua was not to be repeated before any Aremore. "I hope Dondubhan is impressing you," he said to Morimaros.

"It is. Your people are very united."

*A strange response,* Tear thought, having expected to speak about the massive black Tarinnish or the spreading Star Field or the ancient, strong ramparts of the castle itself, the twelve-foot-thick walls or the watchtower. This was significantly more intriguing. "We are. It must be so in Aremoria, too."

Morimaros paused, as if realizing he'd been caught in an odd comparison. "I think . . . it is like the difference between our forests and yours. Here, you have fewer kinds of trees. Pines, oaks, and smaller trees in the south, but only the hardiest here in the north, where there are trees at all. They stand strong and alone against harsh circumstances, but still the forests are thick and immortal. Aremore forests have hundreds of kinds of trees. They do make forests—vast, amazing forests—but they are not so singular."

Tear understood in his gut, immediately.

But the Rosrua heir chuckled. "It's because our trees talk, you know, Your Highness. Like old women, leaning together and keeping everyone in line. But each a fishwife with an opinion to clutch at. "

An older man, whom Tear did not know, but who wore a belt with an Astore salmon stamped into the leather, said, "We do have some very foreign trees rooted here on our island. I believe, Prince, they're the ones you're most interested in."

Frowning, Tear decided to find out the name of this fool, the better to keep his distance. The daughters of Lear were daughters of Lear, not foreign trees.

The Aremore prince held his opinion, merely nodded.

"The eldest," Rosrua's son said—Alson, that was his name! Tear would make sure to remember now—"will certainly marry your lord."

Astore's idiot nodded. "Indeed. He and she have a tightness between them, and what man wouldn't want to bed her? She's magnificent. A stallion's prize."

All the men gathered, even Tear, looked toward Gaela Lear. She stood beside the tall chair in which she'd feasted, the stark white of her gown and the white veil drawn over her short hair making her skin gleam darker than ever. The expression she wore was equally stark: grief and disdain, both warring in her fierce eyes, though she spoke readily enough to the duke in question.

"He was fifteen when she was born," Alson said.

But Tear's attention was no longer free—caught instead, skewered by an arrow of fate, on the second daughter of Lear.

Regan.

She was beautiful. Half-hidden behind the elder, star-cursed princess, it seemed Regan stood with her shoulder pressed gently to the center of Gaela's back. As a support, or comfort.

Thin, boyish almost, except for the mature elegance of the quiet gray-and-white dress she wore. Silver shone at the princess's fingers and in her hair, at her cool brown neck. Red paint plumped her bottom lip and dotted in perfect arcs from the corners of her large eyes.

Regan Lear was flawless.

"Regan would be a good match for you," the loathsome Astore man said, attempting to engage the Aremore prince.

"How old is she?" Morimaros asked, though surely he knew.

"Fifteen," said Tear.

So he would be, too, in a few short months. "Excuse me," Tear murmured, slipping away. None cared.

He finished his cup of wine and retrieved more, as well as a second, for he'd seen Regan held a cup herself, dangled at the end of her loose arm, tapping gently against her thigh. It must have been long empty, for her to risk spotting her pale gown.

As he moved through people toward her, he saw her eyes never rested in one place for long. Regan studied everything, and twice tilted her chin up to murmur over Gaela's shoulder. Then the elder would look where her sister had been, before continuing her conversation with Astore, or one or two of that lord's nearby cousins.

Regan, Tear thought, fed Gaela information. Perhaps she was searching for something or someone in particular, or merely reported on what she could. The sister's close contact, the casual communication between them, awoke a gentle longing in Tear. What devotion. What communion. What love.

He reached their perch, finally, coming around from behind Gaela so the eldest princess would not notice him, but nor would he startle Regan. Her dark eyes caught his, but she did nothing to give him pause.

Through loud conversation, subdued laughter, the chaos of this feast, they did not unlock their eyes. Tear approached and held out the wine, and Regan took it, setting her empty cup to rest on the table nearest. As she did, he saw the tiny red sigil written against the meat of her thumb: a spell in the language of trees.

He saw it, and glanced directly at her face so she knew he did. Lifting his cup, he held her gaze again, staring at the swirl of brown and topaz in her eyes, at the tiny chips of blue ice. His breath sped up, and he heard the rush of blood in his ears.

She, too, raised her cup, and they drank, eyes locked together, as if their lips touched each other and not cool clay rims. As if it was a ritual, a glimpse of things to come.

Tear Connley wondered if prophecy could be read in the taste of bright wine or the wafts of spiced incense or the pounding of a young man's own heart.

He said nothing, but he saw her. He understood her.

And he would not forget.

# THE FOX

BAN LOST HIS horse in the raging storm.

First, they flew together over the rough, muddy earth, into the White Forest, where leaves were sharp slaps, and branches whipped his face and the horse's, where lightning turned trunks to silver columns of fire and the roar of thunder broke over the closer roar of bloated, flooding streams. He leaned into the horse's neck, fingers twisted in its mane, tight enough to cut off his blood, tight enough to make his hands numb, tight enough to keep his mind empty, only the throbbing reminder of the absence of pain.

Ban was eyeless with rage, like the wind, like the storm itself blowing over the forest.

So he gave the horse its head, and the creature ran fast and faster, crazed and speeding and wild. It screamed at a fallen tree, spun, and Ban wrestled it around again to the north. Or what he thought was north; into the wind at the very least, facing the storm head on and fearless, because he had nothing to fear anymore, nothing to lose.

And they came to a sudden gulley. The horse reared. Ban let go.

He fell, he slid, and his knees then hit the mud with a jarring impact. He caught himself against a tree, and his palm scraped raw on the jagged bark. The horse bolted.

Ban picked himself up and pressed on.

Rain pricked his eyes and lips; it soaked every layer of his clothes until he might as well have been naked. Still he moved forward.

Even beasts that loved the night did not love such nights as this.

He deserved it.

He needed it.

"Oh, stars," Ban said, tasting the bitter flavor of the words alongside the earthy taste of rain. Stars had nothing to do with this storm. It was all nature and menace. It ripped at his hair, tore the ends of his coat to tatters.

But he looked to the roiling black clouds, and thought, *I can out-scorn this wind and rain.* A storm like this pitied neither wise men nor fools, and Ban would not, either.

He stripped off his coat and tossed it to the mud. Laughed, harsh and high, but the sound was lost in the black, demanding, raging noise.

*White Forest, I am Ban the Fox!* he yelled in their language.

The ground slid away, and Ban fell down into a creek. His sword twisted in the belt, pinching his hip as he landed hard. He stood. Fast water curled around his shins, tugged at his ankles. Yet he stayed upright, his legs strong as the mountain even as a gust of wind thrust at his chest, burned tears from his eyes, and made his teeth ache. He bared them, grinning furious at the storm and unsheathing his sword.

Maybe he would die in this blustering, frantic night. But Ban did not think so. Worse had not killed him. This was not war. Island bears or lions from Aremoria or hunger-pinched wolves might hide their heads tonight; Ban the Fox would not.

He lifted his face to the sky.

*Ban Ban Ban! Ban the Fox!* the forest cried, thrashing.

The rain, the wind, the lightning and thunder could hurt him, but not truly destroy him. Not like his father might have, or the king of Innis Lear, those men who should have loved him and wanted him, expected the best of him. Instead of leaving it to foreign kings! This storm was not to be blamed; it was not unkind. For what was kindness but offering comfort where none was owed?

This storm was not his father. It owed him nothing.

Ban laughed and walked on, sword in hand.

Soon he stumbled and fell to his knees, dropping his sword. In the darkness, it vanished, leaving him to crawl forward through clinging ferns, and up to his feet again. Ban saw blackness and streaks of lightning-silver rain. He saw branches like claws. He saw rain dripping down trees in rivulets, and thought of crying.

His father might be dead now.

Ban wished this wind would blow the earth beneath him back into the sea forever. End all this. The end of the Lear line, the end of this very island. His own miserable life.

Heat prickled his eyes; it was tears.

Ban the Fox was crying.

He'd left his father to die. And worse, he'd deceived his innocent brother. He'd betrayed Mars, completely. His only friend. *And Elia, too,* his own secret voice reminded him.

Ban gritted his teeth; he closed his eyes.

It was over, it was done. Ban would not pretend all his actions had been justified. He was not more sinned against than sinning. He had loved a girl, and been torn from her only for being a natural boy in a world that only welcomed star-blessed men, and there a seed of destruction had planted within his heart, and here it burst out of his chest full-formed, with thorns and vines and bloodred blossoms.

Sinking to his knees in the muck, Ban knew that no matter what else, he was as wrecked as this island. He was no vainglorious, distant star, but a creature of earth; flawed, desperate, and with a heart so ready to be hurt it could feel nothing else.

Ban was a wild gale, all raw and screaming, attacking anything unwise enough to face him. He welcomed the taste of cold rain on his tongue, the storm mingling with those tears that coursed down his cheeks.

*Ban the Fox!* cried the White Forest; Ban responded with only a wordless howl. This was pure magic, wild and electric, blurring the air and mud into one chaos, a tempest so violent there was no difference between sky and earth, star and root; all was all, and he was part of it.

No hero, no good man, but a force of nature.

With his hands firmly in the mud, Ban pushed upright. There was no way to go but forward, on a terrible night such as this. He could only blow himself out with the storm.

# ELIA

IT WAS THE middle of the night, and Elia had yet to sleep. After a long discussion of queendom and rootwater and war, and it became clear there was no point waiting up for Kayo to return with Lear and the Fool, Brona had flung on a cloak and ventured outside. Elia tried to keep the woman here with her, but Brona had insisted, "I must check on the canvas over the garden, and one of the new families was having trouble with their roof—we've not managed to re-thatch it. Stay here and let me do my work. I will retire with Alis, or—or see if the trees will help me find Kayo. You will be queen; you must guard yourself."

It took every ounce of Elia's will to even pretend she might agree.

The storm sang to her as she lay alone on the straw mattress. The fire was low, popping around black and sun-red coals. Wind and thunder rattled the heavy wooden shutters tied down over the cottage windows and tore at the thatched roof. Elia curled onto her side, and the straw mattress crackled. She whispered a prayer for Lear, for Kayo, to the trees and wind. It cried back with every word, from every angle.

Elia needed to find her father, to speak with her sisters. As she'd said, her family was broken, and in breaking kept the kingdom unwell. That was what it whispered, that was the lament of Innis Lear. She needed to try to make them all see, her sisters and father, and Kayo and Connley and Astore, all: they were a family, and wouldn't Dalat have wished them together? The island did. Together, between the stars and rootwaters. It would have them whole.

They could not treat each other this way. If Gaela had blinded their uncle . . . if their father died in the storm . . . could anything be mended at all?

*Be everything,* the forest had said to her.

But *everything* was too much.

She tucked the blankets beneath her chin, stared at the shadowy silhouettes of drying rue and late roses, strips of mint, dill, starweed, and rowan berries. They hung in clusters and bouquets from the rafters, filling the cottage with a delicate perfume that held its own even against the ash of the fire and the wet, angry wind slipping fingers of peaty air under the door.

Elia closed her eyes. This dark cottage in the center of the storm was like the heart of an old oak tree, its damp, warm, black womb hollowed out for a nest, readied for a long winter's sleep. She'd huddled inside such an oak before, listening to its heartbeat, to the slow drawl of its dreams. There had been tiny green beetles and glittering dirt, the impossibly slow growth of roots, and the strong walls of the tree around her, reaching up and up into the night sky, a protective ceiling of black branches. And she had shared it with Ban.

*The Fox is my spy.*

A crack of wood and gust of wind startled Elia up.

She scrambled to her feet, blanket pulled tight to her chest. The cottage door hung open, and a man stood there. Lightning flashed behind him, presenting him as a solid black creature covered in streaks and droplets of water that glistened like the stars in the sky.

He stepped in. Wind picked water off his hair and shoulders, flinging it at Elia, as he struggled to shut the door against the gale.

It slammed closed, and there he braced against it.

This star-shadow man had on boots and a soldier's trousers, a linen shirt molded by water to his shoulders and back like a thin second skin. No coat or hood, no sword even. His black, choppy hair stuck out in thick twists and tattered braids, all of it heavy with rain. An earth saint, regurgitated by the storm.

Elia stepped forward. Her throat tightened; her fingers went cold and her face hot.

He groaned, his shoulders shaking like a sick man's.

"Ban?" she whispered.

His head hung as he pushed away from the door, turning. He stumbled, and Elia caught him around the waist with a grunt. Cold water soaked the long wool shirt Brona had given her to sleep in. She half dragged, half led Ban Errigal to the bed. "Sit."

He collapsed upon it.

"Get this off," she said firmly, struggling to lift his shirt. Clumsily, he helped. She pulled it over his head and threw it aside, crouching to begin the arduous process of untying the wrapped, tall boots. His breath rattled harsh in his mouth and teased the curls atop her head. Elia's fingers were dull and heavy, but she got one boot undone and tugged it hard. His hand fell against her hair, and Elia tilted her chin up to look through the darkness at Ban's face.

"Elia?" he whispered. Passion or fever or some desperate thing burned in his ghostly eyes. Ban did not seem so wildly beautiful as that day so many weeks ago when she'd last seen him. Tonight, he was desolate, young, and lost.

"Help me get this off," she said. "You need to be warm."

She focused again on the other boot, struggling to accept that Ban Errigal, the roots of her heart—and yet an Aremore spy!—was adrift, and breaking, and *here.*

After a moment, he obeyed her, removing his boots. "Now out of those pants," she said, going abruptly to the fire. Her hands were dirty with mud and bits of the forest he'd brought inside with him. She grabbed a handful of tinder and threw it into the hearth, then poked at the embers with an iron rod to wake them hurriedly. There was plenty of wood to feed it, if she could get it going again.

He stood up behind her; she heard a quiet rustle as he did what she'd instructed. Elia's breath was taut and fast, and as she listened she pictured it; pictured Ban stripping off his trousers and smallclothes, hopefully wrapping up in a blanket or something Brona kept, for surely he knew where such things might be found.

The fire's heat tightened the skin of her face, especially her dry lips, but Elia built it up, unblinking, no matter how the flames blazed in her eyes.

"Are you real?"

Ban's voice, so close behind her.

Elia dropped the iron rod as she stood and turned to face him.

He was naked but for the blanket around his shoulders like a cloak. Barely taller than her, barely broader, and bruised, scraped raw, and dirty. His brow furrowed and he watched her with those forceful mud-green eyes. Firelight caught in them: the flicker of a faraway bonfire through miles of black forest, a candle trapped at the base of a well.

"I'm real," Elia whispered, finally.

"I didn't expect . . . to find you here."

She stepped nearer to him. "Nor I you, but it is . . . right. This is where you're from, and the storm . . ." If it had brought them both here, was the island itself responsible? Here, the person she needed most right now. Ban was everything wild and cherished about Innis Lear: the shadowy trees, the harsh stone pillars, the windy moors and deep cutting gorges. The aching, curling waves of the sea. The danger and secrets. Of course he appeared tonight, reminding her what she needed—loved—about this forsaken place. Compared to the sun-warm coast of Aremoria and its equally bright, powerful king, Ban Errigal was everything she'd missed of her home. No matter his intentions, or perhaps even more because of them. Lies and secrets were part of Innis Lear, too.

"It brought us here," Ban murmured.

Elia kissed him, surprising them both.

She pressed her entire body to his, and grabbed his sopping, unruly hair. His lips were cold, but he opened them, and his mouth was hot.

Elia had never kissed anyone like this: hungrily and in a rage of sudden passion. It overwhelmed her, and she clung to Ban's head, to his neck. She kissed the corner of his mouth, sucked at his bottom lip. He tasted like mud and salt, and ever so slightly of blood. She wanted all of it, to consume him, to make him part of her, like the island was part of her.

And then Ban was kissing her back, truly and eagerly. His arms came around her, and Elia wrapped hers around his neck, leaning up onto her toes. The blanket fell away from his shoulders and flapped to the earthen floor. His skin was so cold, but he was hard and lean as a sword. She felt her belly against his, her breasts flat against his chest; but for her thin wool shirt nothing separated their skin. Elia could hardly breathe at the realization. Her fingers dug into Ban's shoulders, both excited and afraid.

She knew—from crude things Gaela had said, from Brona and Regan that week when Elia was thirteen, from listening to her father's retainers when she shouldn't have, from stories Aefa told, and her own cautious curiosity—she knew exactly what her body was asking for, and what the dangers were, what the joys might be. Elia slid away from Ban and said his name softly.

He studied her face, panting barely, just enough so she could see the pink promise of his tongue and a crescent shine of teeth in the firelight. "Elia," he breathed back.

There were so many years and lies between them. They were practically strangers, but for memory and hope.

It was enough.

She pulled him to the low bed, holding her eyes on his face because she was too panicky and delighted and inflamed to look anywhere else. He allowed himself to be led, to be shoved gently down. Elia climbed on top of Ban, stretching out along his whole body. It was so dark but for the glow of firelight, and her curls fell around her face as she leaned over him, making them a private chapel of hair and eyes, noses and mouths.

Elia kissed him gently. Ban tentatively touched her hair, petting it reverently as she kissed, as she brushed her lips on his again and again, like tiny sips, shallow gasps of love. He dug his hands into her curls until he found her skull and tilted her head before leaning up off the pillow to kiss her more deeply.

Then Ban sat up, carrying Elia with him.

Her legs fumbled to either side of his lap; she gasped at the feel of him, his skin, his strong thighs, his belly, the rough hair and flesh rubbing against her. Elia clung to him from inches away. Their noses nearly touched, and she could hardly look into his eyes for being so close.

"Elia," he said, and she felt his voice in every part of her: her name in his mouth raised the hairs all over her body, made her neck and arms and breasts shiver, her toes flex.

"Ban."

"Stop" was his next word, and Elia felt that, too.

She jerked. "I don't want to stop," she whispered. "I want this—you—I want all of it, and I know it's dangerous, and I don't know how exactly . . ." she shifted her hips forward, because maybe she *did* know how.

Ban pushed her farther away. "You don't know this is what you want."

"I do, though." Elia smiled.

This huge feeling was not grief or fury; it was warm, it enveloped her whole being. She did not want to diffuse it or let it go, but to instead let it overwhelm her. "I do know, as sure as I know anything. I want you, and this."

"It isn't what I want." His voice was scorching.

Elia froze, and so did the world. Even the fire in the hearth seemed to pause in its licking. In the next moment Elia climbed away from Ban Errigal. Her chest ached; she pressed a hand to her stomach against a blossoming nausea.

"Wait," he said.

There was no place for her to go. Elia stood still and held herself with her back to him, her mind empty because she refused all thoughts. Ban quickly rustled about, and then appeared wearing his damp, muddy pants to face her.

Because she was the daughter of a king, Elia Lear kept her chin high and met Ban Errigal's wretched, burning gaze.

He said, "I'm sorry. I didn't mean— I meant . . . El— *Elia*— I mean I don't . . ." He shook his head, his mouth turned into pain and sorrow. "You kissed me, and we almost . . . I've never wanted that, except with you. But I do. Want you. I want— I just want something for myself. Free of consequences. You."

"Yes," she whispered. She wanted it too: no plans, no future, no consequences.

"But I *can't*. I know what kind of creature a bed like that makes."

"Creature?" she said, her voice high as a sparrow's. "You're not the sum
of your birth and stars."

"You don't know what I am, what I've done."

Rory Errigal's image appeared in her mind, as did that of Morimaros,
Aefa, and the soldiers she'd seen in Aremoria, the world beyond this bed,
beyond Hartfare and Innis Lear. She did know much of what he had
done, and she wanted him. She knew what he was, and it was enough.
She reached for him.

He let her touch his face, even brought his hands up over hers.

"Do you hate me for being my father's daughter?" she asked softly.

"I could never hate you," Ban said, and his entire body shivered.

He kissed her gently, slow as a sunrise, and trembling. She felt tears slide
under her fingers where she held his face. And then he pulled roughly away,
a curse harsh on his tongue. He scrubbed at his eyes. A scratch on his forearm glinted red with fresh blood.

"Ban, I know what you've done. I know what you are. And I do not
hate it."

"I am what I made myself," he said.

Elia's cheeks remained hot, her body too aware of him; she was flooded
with embarrassment and desire still, and most of all, joy. Elia wanted to
make Ban feel better, be better. She wanted him to see what she saw, but
she didn't know how.

Grief or rage or love: why did Elia never have the right words to speak?

A queen would have them.

So that was what she decided to say.

"Everyone wants different things from me, and it is never enough: my
father wants that I be a star, only his, and not even my own; my sisters require that I submit to them, or to never have existed at all; Morimaros
wishes that I be his queen; and Brona and Kayo want that, too, but for
them! Even Aefa wants me to rule, if it makes me safe. You're the only one
who ever asked me to be something for myself. And there is a chaotic web of
danger all around us—war and spies, dukes and kings, and even just this
storm, this breaking island—and I don't know how to make any of it better.
I just know that I want to. I want to make Innis Lear strong, to help the
land revive and the rootwaters clear, and I want you to kiss me again, and
always."

"Why?" His voice cracked.

"Because I . . ." Her shoulders lifted; her voice drained away. "Because this is the only way I know what to say to you. We've never needed words."

"I think you're so beautiful, Elia, it hurts me sometimes."

It hurt her, too, the hearing of it. Morimaros had said she was beautiful, gently convincing. This was so different. With Ban it was a struggle. It was selfish to take and take.

Elia closed her mouth, stopped trying to speak. Instead, she pulled Ban back to the low bed. She sat on it, her head level with his waist, and untied his pants again. He held still, the long line of his muscled belly trembling, hands frozen at his sides. Elia focused on the work, and when the laces were free, she grasped the band of the pants and gently tugged them down over his hips. Her eyes flicked to his because she couldn't quite look at the rest of him.

Ban's lips parted. "Elia," he breathed.

"We're in the heart of the White Forest. Whatever we need, Brona can help with."

"She's not perfect with prevention," he said bitterly. "She had me."

Wrinkling her nose, Elia said, "Because she *wanted* you, Ban! And I want you, too. I always, *always* have."

His shoulders hitched as his breath went ragged, and Elia leaned back onto the bed, pulling the long shirt up her thighs, holding his gaze. All her skin was tight, and tingled: her lips, her nipples, the small of her back, and the damp well of her body, aching.

"Ban," she said.

He gave in, kneeling on the edge of the bed. Elia reached for him, and Ban bent over her. They scooted together, and Elia spread her thighs, pulling up the shirt to get it off herself. She had to wiggle where it stuck under her back, twisting her arms until it slipped up over her head, dragging at her hair. Ban did not help at all, propped over her on hands and knees. His breath was hot, skimming around her breasts and along her ribs.

In the dim orange firelight, Elia shivered. She touched Ban's chest: scars pale against his skin, some random, others in obvious designs of the language of trees. One of them spelled out his name, and Elia leaned up to kiss it, put her tongue there, making Ban groan.

He hardly moved, letting Elia do what she would, still hanging over her, every part of him awake and hot with desire.

She recalled Aefa's specific instructions: *Whatever else you do, make sure you're damp enough, if not from exertion and lust, then spit or grease or something, don't forget that, especially your first time. Try to relax! Not your strong suit, I know. I hope you'll have some wine.*

Oh, stars, and her friend was only a cottage away.

Elia smiled suddenly. Ban did not smile back, but something in his eyes brightened.

She touched her belly, and then petted the wild hair at the top of her thighs, at the crest between them, and slipped her fingers between the folds, showing him. "Ban," she whispered, using her other hand to caress his chin, nudging his face down so he would look.

With a little gasp, his entire body shuddered and he put his hand over hers, between them. At the first touch of his finger against her unbearably tender flesh, Elia whimpered, her hips lifting off the mattress. "Ban," she said again. More urgently, louder.

He shifted, panting, and carefully, shivering, they moved together, focused so precisely either would have been embarrassed to realize. Elia put her hands against his ribs, widened her hips, and whispered his name in the language of trees.

*THE NIGHT BEFORE* the island shattered, there was a raging storm.

Wind cracked the sky, drawing thunderclouds impossibly tall, like castles for lost earth saints, throwing black shadows over the whole island, coast to coast. All living on Innis Lear hid, tucked heads beneath blankets or huddled in nests or tree hollows, shivering, wretched; the sharp trick of lighting bit at tongues and fingernails and the napes of necks.

Those forced to venture out did so with clenched teeth and layers of protection, sticking carefully to known paths, holding hands, bracing against the ferocious wind and squinting through driving rain.

Those lost clung to anything they could find.

One let rain cut against her cheeks like cold daggers, preparing herself for what was to come. She was glad for such a roiling, starless sky.

One raced in such a terrible frenzy she could not feel the rain at all. It was only desperate tears, hot on her cheeks, and a storm of panic, lighting her from the inside.

One found, finally, the balance she'd long overlooked; branches stretching between all she'd ever loved. It was not a choice, or destiny. It was not storm nor sea nor rootwater well. It was only—always—a heart.

Another screamed for the stars to reveal themselves, cursing their distant impotence. How dare they allow a storm, a force of nature, to diminish them, to muffle their voices that should have called to him, should have whispered prophecy for comfort or action or—or anything! He would take anything now.

"Where is my wife?" he cried, and, "What have we done to her?"

At his side were two others, a foolish brother and a fraternal fool, lifting the man when he fell, stumbling through the storm with him, exhausted and heart-sick all.

The island held for a breath, gathering strength, pulling wind and power. The darkness overwhelmed.

The old man pushed on, or tried to, as fast as he could run through cold aches and the sheets of rain tearing through the canopy of trees. The light was shattered; there was no moon, and only the occasional burst of lightning that to dazzle his eyes: still, in each flash he saw her, his lost love, then she would vanish again into the black night.

In a meadow, the man spread his arms, yelling into the darkness that he could not be killed by a mere storm! Not without the stars' permission!

But the land didn't care. The island stormed. The island knew what this king had done, and not done, what he had betrayed—it knew his veins no longer bled rootwater.

He had lost all.

He had nothing.

No crown, no castle, no daughters, no wife.

The stars had abandoned him, even his most favorite star. He was nothing.

The island was all.

Roots, rocks, trees, vicious sky and clouds and rain—the fire of lightning. Between him and his beloved stars, slicing them apart.

*Nothing can come from nothing.*

The fools there, holding his elbows, wept and promised they would see him safe, but the old man knew what the island knew: this was an ending night.

Thrusting free of them, the once-king ran on. Flying, it seemed, over mossy wet earth, between trees that creaked and dripped, that bent in the rain. He did not breathe air but fire, choking on it, covered in water and mud.

*Lear!* screamed the storm. *Where is your crown?*

*The poison crown!*

*Lear!*

The storm drove him, with rain and wailing wind, with flashes of light, exactly where it wanted him. The massive black cathedral, ruined and reclaimed by the forest, the heart—the heart of Innis Lear.

The king had been here before.

*Lear!*

The thick wooden doors hung crookedly. He ducked inside.

The walls of the cathedral boxed him in, but the rain still poured down: there was no roof, and yet there were no stars. Music rose from copper bowls filled with rainwater; different sizes sang different songs. He smelled mildew and rich, fertile earth.

At the cross far down the aisle was the ancient navel well. Water pooled on the granite cap, and the rain splashed constantly.

He stared, breathing heavily through his slack old mouth.

The cathedral was so very dark but for a gentle glow like moon or star-light, which was impossible with the solid black sky above.

*Witness!* cried the storm.

The hairs on his neck and arms raised.

The once-king's world cracked again in an explosion of light and a roar of thunder.

Thrown back, he hit the stone floor with a cry.

Wind screamed, laughing, overhead, and through the shadows the once-king saw the smoldering navel well: the thick granite cap, scorched and broken perfectly in two. Each half had fallen away so the mouth of the well opened toward the sky.

Terrified, he got up and turned away. He squeezed outside again and ran. Mumbling prophecies to himself, he ran until his bones would break and he was truly blind.

The storm slowed to a churn. It stretched its cloudy wings.

Innis Lear sighed: cleansed, restored, and more than prepared for what came next.

# THE FOX

BAN TRIED TO let the whole world slip away, curled in a bed with a fire crackling bright and warm, and Elia Lear pressed to his back, her cheek to his shoulder, her arm around his ribs. And the storm blowing itself to sleep outside. He closed his eyes.

Could he find a way to take this moment and *make* it last? Nothing mattered when she was with him; nothing, besides her. It had always been so. The feeling was a seed of something Ban did not recognize, but craved. The pale promise of a morning when storms would clear, the sun would rise, and he would see a new future stretched before him like a golden road. Peace. The end of vengeance, the end of this tense imbalance of loyalty, not knowing where he belonged or who loved him. It had always been Elia.

They'd have to leave to be free of it all, to fully dig the roots of Innis Lear out of their hearts and blood, to strip away the clinging history of stars. Ban would marry her, travel with her far away from Innis Lear and past Aremoria, and find a place where they could be only themselves. Whatever they chose to be, without all this fate and history and obligation. A hired soldier and a goat girl. Or perhaps a farmer and an herbwife, or two shepherds. Shopkeepers or tailors or bakers or a blacksmith and his loyal wife, mother to their wild brood.

Anything but a bastard and a princess, anything but a star priest and a traitor.

Ban touched the back of her hand, where it lay relaxed against his stomach, her fingers skimming his skin in tiny strokes. At his touch, she stilled, and he flattened her hand beneath his. Was it even possible to purge Innis Lear from their hearts? Who *could* they be without stars and roots? "Elia."

"Ban," she replied, lips brushing his shoulder blade. Her sigh was soft and warm, skating down his spine to settle like a hot brand in the small of his back. He fought the urge to grip her fingers too tightly, to turn in the bed and press against her again, or to beg her without words to crawl onto his lap and move as she had before. To weave their spirits together again and again until she couldn't leave him even if she wanted to.

He opened his mouth, and words came out in a rush: "Go with me, as soon as the sun rises. Far away from this island. We'll start over, be only what we make ourselves, without pasts, together."

For a long moment, Elia was silent and still. Then she said, "But I am a piece of Innis Lear, and so are you."

"It's broken," he murmured. "Innis Lear. And we are broken, too. But if we left, maybe we could fix each other." Ban touched the ends of her hair, pulling the curls out and releasing them to bounce back.

She pressed her face against his shoulder; he felt tears. She said, "We have to fix it all."

"Why? Why us?"

Elia's voice sharpened. "Do you remember that beetle you dug out from under the stone in the Summer Seat meadow? It was iridescent green, with rainbows of blue and yellow? You put it on my finger like an emerald ring."

He nodded, voice stuck in his throat.

"I loved that silly bug. At first, after you were taken away, I searched for them on my own. I imagined, sometimes, when looking at the stars with my father, that the stars themselves were tiny bright beetles, crawling across the sky. The heavens were the same as the island mud, and all those stars my father worshipped were bugs like the one you put on my finger."

Ban turned under her arm until he lay on his back as she leaned over him. Firelight gilded her hair. Her eyes were deep enough to dive into. She was frowning, her brow furrowed by sorrow.

The silence dragged: something was wrong. He didn't want to ask; Ban wanted to exist here without the Fox, without questions and plotting, without everything he'd been made to be.

Her thumb stroked his collarbone.

"Elia?" he whispered.

The words tumbled out of her, then, hard and fast: "I know Morimaros sent you here, on his behalf. I know you've been an Aremore spy, and you intended to get the iron for Aremoria."

Shock silenced him, and behind it a wave of shame. Elia knew. But beyond that, Mars had told her: it was the only way for her to know. What else had they shared?

Ban opened his mouth, and nothing came out. The two of them in this bed, having been together like this, was another betrayal of that noble Aremore king. But Ban had loved Elia first.

"I . . ." Ban's voice was hoarse. He swallowed, reaching for some explanation that would keep her in his arms. "I . . . I needed Aremoria, and I needed his—his respect. I had none of that here, and even you . . . even you let me go. Being the Fox meant something, and I was recognized for it. Not as a bastard, but a soldier. A friend, even."

"I respected you. I needed you."

But an old hurt welled up Ban's throat and found its way out of his mouth. "You didn't write to me," he whispered like a child. "You never wrote to me, in all my time in Aremoria. I thought you loved me, but you let me go. Because your father told you to!"

"I shouldn't have. I am sorry, Ban. I did not know how alone you were. How . . . abandoned. No wonder you gave yourself to Morimaros, abandoning Innis Lear in turn."

"I didn't do it to abandon Innis Lear! I did it for *Morimaros*. Because he asked me, and because he treated me like I was worth asking."

Elia frowned, and Ban saw the struggle as she fought to hold his gaze. She, too, must be thinking of Mars now, while naked and sticky from sharing this bed with Ban. He desperately wanted to ask what was between the two of them, if they'd made promises.

Finally, Elia sighed softly. "I know Morimaros is good, Ban. Better than Connley, better than my father. But he's still the king of Aremoria. He wants . . ." Elia looked away again. "He wants to marry me, too, and I believe he has not lied about what he wants."

"Innis Lear. And you."

"Yes."

"He'll make himself the king of Innis Lear, if you marry him. Even if he swears not to lay siege, your sisters will take it as an act of war—Regan at least, who I've spent these past weeks with. And everyone knows Gaela looks for reasons to fight."

"So what should I do, Ban? Will my sisters hear me? They are poisoned with hate. I've tried telling myself they will listen, they have to, but with you here, now, like this . . . Ban. I am so very afraid that they will refuse me, drive me away again. Or worse!" Tears washed her eyes. "And what of Innis Lear? It is crumbling!"

"Regan will listen to me. I can protect you," he whispered, desperately.

Elia drew away, even as he held her naked in his arms. "Like you protected Rory?" she asked, carefully.

Ban flung himself out of the bed. He paced away, unsure where to put his hands, scuffing his bare feet on the dusty earthen floor.

Behind him, silence.

Hugging himself, he faced Elia again. She'd sat against the wall, legs drawn up under the quilt. Ban said, suddenly, hopelessly, "I think my father is dead."

"No," she whispered.

"Father was allying himself with you—with an invading force. With Morimaros. I told Connley and Regan. And I left him there, between them; they were in a killing mood."

"Oh, Ban."

"I'm not sorry. He never once put me first. My father did not defend me, and if he ever loved me it was less than he loved Lear, or himself, or those fucking stars."

"But you—"

"Errigal betrayed your sister, his queen, no matter why, or how, Elia," Ban said ferociously. "He pretended to be loyal to Regan and Connley, then went behind their backs to treat with Aremoria. He is a traitor."

"Done in by the same."

"I'm no traitor to *you*," he lied.

Elia scoffed, and wiped a tear off her cheek with a sharp flick of her hand.

"I never forgot you." Ban returned to the bed and knelt near enough to touch her if she wished. "And what I said before—I didn't do all of this for Mars. I did it for me, and for you, and because of the roots. I had to come home, Elia. You're right: we cannot leave. We're both part of this island. It's my blood and the air I breathe: even in Aremoria, it was always Innis Lear. I wished it could be anything else. I swear I did. I wanted it to be Mars, so much I believed it myself. But—I can't change who I am."

"Neither can I. I'm the daughter of the king, and I love him, I love Innis Lear. I have to help my sisters, and fix everything. Somehow."

"It needs to burn, Elia. This island is broken, and you can't piece it back together; you need to remake it."

"That can't be the only way. The roots have to be capable of regrowing. It's only been twelve years of breaking."

"No." Ban shook his head. "It's been longer than that, and the roots are not strong. They're weak and begging; the trees want to glory in themselves again, and in the hungry wind. They need heat and passion and sun, not just coldness and hesitation and stars."

"I came home and listened to the trees and wind for days, Ban Errigal. The trees have asked me for help, the way they want, and I will see it through.

I must convince my sisters to listen, too. Together we three must be able to find the right balance, the right weave to pull Innis Lear together again. We need a—a fulcrum, not a poison root. But first I need to find my father."

"You *forgive* him."

"Yes."

"I do not, Elia."

"I know." She was slipping away from him. Back to Lear, as always.

"Your father did this! And those like him, unwilling to cleave away from their rigid, starry ways, the ways they have no evidence serve the world best. What does it matter for my mother and father not to have been wed? Nothing except what men pretend it matters! What does it mean that I was born under a dragon's tail moon? *Nothing but what priests have decided it means.*"

"You hate him so much," she whispered.

"Yes."

"Then you will do nothing to help me." Her voice was dull. The passion, the eagerness from before had all drained away, and Ban did not know what to do.

"Understand, Elia, please," he said. He took her shoulders.

There it all came, blazing back. Elia's eyes widened, and she tore free of him, launching to her feet. "I do *not*. Why do you hate him so much?" She thrust her hands out. "Look at you! You are strong and famous! I heard your name spoken with respect in Aremoria, by the king himself! You did that—your actions made you a name outside of Errigal or my father! Earned you trust! Respect! So what if my father and yours scorned you as a child. It was cruel, yes, wrong, yes, but, Ban Errigal, *look at you*. You made yourself better than them! You could be so worthy of leadership and of love, but you can't do it. You *believe* what they said of you." Fury shone all around Elia, like a halo of lightning.

Ban said, terribly calm, "Because it's true. Here, there, everywhere I go I am a bastard, Elia. A spy and liar, and I am not good."

"You could be! I see better in you, and I always have. Take *my* word over my father's! Over *your* father's. I loved you, Ban, and I wanted your friendship, your heart—over anything else—and you wanted mine. So it didn't matter because I was just a girl, just a princess? The opinions of our fathers shaped you, but my heart knew better. Believe that if nothing else, you stubborn man."

Ban nodded, slowly, understanding a pit in his belly. "I believe you."

She threw herself at him, relief blowing out of her in a sigh. Elia hugged him, her mouth on his neck. "Good. Good," she murmured.

"But I can't help you save your father."

"Help me save Innis Lear, not my father. Us, our island. Our home."

They stared at each other for a long, dark moment. Outside the storm had calmed. Only the wind remained, blowing strong and steady through Hartfare, ruffling roofs, nudging at shutters and doors. It whistled down the chimney; their fire spit back.

"Ban, don't do this. Don't choose against me, not you, not now."

"Everything is a choice. You chose a long time ago."

Elia said, "No. Not love. Love is not a choice between different things like this. Love has to be growing, making your heart expand. It's not narrowing. I love you *and* Innis Lear. I love my sisters *and* my father. Not one *or* the other. You can be more—you can be what you were and what you are, and—and whoever you want to be."

Ban reached up and touched the corner of her mouth, slid his fingers along her jaw. "Your father sent me to Aremoria to get rid of me, because he hated me, whether because of my stars, as he told himself, or because he was selfish, and wanted you to himself. Do you understand? Such a man doesn't deserve your love."

"But he's my father still, and I do love him. I know you don't understand that, and I'm sorry. I wish you could. *I* deserve to love him."

"He rejected your love."

Her hand flattened over his heart. "I think . . . he tried to, maybe, because he was confused about the stars, or what he needed. He was afraid. He's dying and losing himself, and maybe it reminds him of losing her. Dalat. My father loved her more than anything. More than the island, more than us. That *was* his choice. And when she died he fell to pieces because there was nothing else! That's what comes of choosing to love something above all others, instead of widening your heart. If he'd loved stars *and* Dalat *and* my sisters and everything, maybe he wouldn't have broken without her . . ." Elia touched her lips to Ban's shoulder and whispered against his skin, "I won't love anyone so much more than everything else that I lose it all if that person is lost. If it makes your world smaller, it isn't love."

Ban shook his head and stared at the first subtle dawn light glowing at the window. "I would have chosen only you. And risked it."

"Choose me *and* Innis Lear! Choose me, and everything."

"That isn't how it works. Something always comes first. My mother chose Hartfare over me. My father chose Rory, always. Morimaros would never even consider me first; he must choose his crown and country. Even you chose your father, and the stars, rather than me, never made me first in your heart."

"I was a child," she whispered.

"I was, too."

"But we're not anymore. I can't love one person above all. Some things are bigger than just one heart, but that doesn't mean a heart can't love completely!"

"If you had let me, Elia, I would've given everything I am to you. That's all I've ever wanted: to be something that matters most of all for just one person."

"I can't," she whispered. "I can't leave everything for you, I can't . . . pick only you. I *won't*! I love you and I love Innis Lear, and if I must choose to put Innis Lear first it does not mean you don't matter to me, Ban Errigal. We're people, not saints, not stars; we have to move in some kind of structure. I can, *and will,* pick you and the island, you and my father, but I can't put you always before—"

Ban felt himself fall away from her. "Stop," he said, "I know you can't. I know it. No one ever has."

"Ban, that is an impossible thing you ask! I cannot separate your well-being from that of Innis Lear, or that of my father! It is all connected!"

"No, it isn't." His chest hurt, his eyes burned. "I know because Regan and Connley will always choose each other. Your father chose your mother, and then when she died he chose *you*. Over the island!"

"And look at what a disaster it was!" she cried, throwing out her arms. "No one thing alone keeps Innis Lear alive or its heart beating! That is not love! That is selfishness. That is pretending we are all only one thing. Only a star, only a woman, only a bastard. You're more than that, and I am, too: woman and daughter of a foreign queen and a star priest. I'm all of that. Take one piece away and the rest shifts and changes, just like . . . just like this island, or any land. If the stars are crying and lonely, the tide doesn't rise and the trees cannot speak! Or if the trees are all we hear, then there is no future or heaven for our dreams!"

They stared at each other across several steps of darkness. Fire at Elia's back, dawn at Ban's.

He did not know if the pain growing inside him was love or longing or something far worse. She was glorious. Bold and beautiful like her sisters, but stumbling in her passion, because it was new. He thought he was witnessing the birth of a star.

But a star was not what he needed. He was rootwater and poison, hissing wind and shadows. She was the first wink of holy fire that would light the sky for thousands of years.

Ban held out his hand, palm up. For a few brief moments at dawn, stars shone even against earthly sunrise, bright as butterflies or a meadow full of flowers—or iridescent beetles.

This had been their moment, and it was fading away.

Elia slid her fingers into his.

"I will choose everything," she promised. "I will *be* everything."

Ban thought of the storm. "I will be exactly what I have always been."

# REGAN

REGAN REMEMBERED ONLY three things from the night of her mother's year memorial: her father grasping little Elia's hand too tightly; the squelch of mud in the Star Field ruining the silk shoes her mother had given her, which were embroidered with the same blue Dalat had prized in the flecks of her middle daughter's eyes; a glass of cool red wine appearing exactly when she needed it most.

Long after the lighting ceremony, when they all returned to Dondubhan Castle for a mourning supper, Regan had kept herself at Gaela's side. She had listened to Gaela's vexed commentary with half an ear, studying all the players as they mingled in the dining hall with the rest of her attention. The two sisters had held the honor table themselves, for Lear had roamed the long room with Elia in tow, speaking only to his retainers and earls, the young Duke Astore and the old Duke Connley, and, surprisingly, their mother's young, handsome brother, from the Third Kingdom. Regan had despised the white-knuckled grip Lear maintained on Elia's shoulder, pressing the folds of her mourning gown askew.

With a little sigh, Regan had turned, catching herself at a pair of eyes the dull blue-green of old copper. The young man to whom they belonged had bowed and offered her a goblet, full of wine. He'd been no servant, wearing a vibrant red jacket over the gray-and-cream wool expected for a funeral, and a gold chain about his neck too rich for a mere retainer. His mouth was lovely, though thin-lipped, and his nose admirably regal, she had thought, fascinated. Cherry-gold hair flopped across his forehead, too unchecked. His pink cheeks did not flush further, though she had stared quite boldly. Regan then lifted the goblet and sipped proffered red wine.

It should've been the young prince of Aremoria attending her: their fathers currently negotiated the rules for later negotiating some possibility of marriage between them. But that prince had shown little interest in her.

"Thank you," she'd said, having a guess who this keenly handsome young man might be.

He'd smiled very slightly—as good at a cool smile as Regan herself—and said, "I am sorry for your loss."

Regan's throat had closed, and she'd struggled not to allow grief to wrinkle her brow. Only her eyelashes flickered. The young man nodded, then left.

A week later, she received a letter stamped with scarlet wax.

*I see you, Regan, daughter of Dalat,* it read in the language of trees.

It had been signed, *Connley, of the line of kings.*

Folding the paper, she'd pressed it between her breast and the warm wool of her dress. Eventually Regan had written back, and their correspondence went slowly, with no regular rhythm except that each took their own turn, never sending a new letter without receiving a response. There was little call for Connleys at Dondubhan or at the Summer Seat, for the perpetual tensions between them and the king, or them and Astore, but Regan had seen him again, finally, some year and a half later, this time broader in shoulder and with his bright hair smoothed back to show off that striking face. His red-and-black coat, tied tight over more expensive black this time, seemed to make his eyes burn. That gaze had found her where Regan waited with the remnants of her family, high on the Summer Seat rampart, and her chest rose faster—though she strove, again, to keep excitement off her face.

She had touched his hand later that afternoon, passing on her way out of the great hall when her father dismissed her and her sister, so that he and Connley's father, the duke, could argue without a woman's judging eyes. Regan's fingers had barely brushed the backs of his knuckles, and she'd held her eyes straight ahead. Then off with Gaela she went, though her sister had veered toward the barracks and Regan was left to wander to her chambers, cradling her hand between her breasts.

Words on paper had been their only courtship at first, along with tiny sketches of flowers or food or whatever thing was nearest Connley as he wrote to her. Regan returned pressed herbs for ambition and health, and advice on the best tea to soothe Connley's mother when she was dying of a wet fever, coughing and hard. When his mother did die, Connley asked Regan to come to the year anniversary, and she did, though with Gaela and Elia to make it a more formal royal affair.

It had been easy to keep her secret from Gaela, though Regan never explicitly decided to: Gaela never asked about such things as romance and men. Regan didn't mind these differences, for her sister would be a great, vicious warrior-queen and she trusted Regan absolutely, and so Regan would act as she needed in order to be Gaela's best support.

Alone with Regan in the shade of an oak tree where he'd brought her to share the ancient well of his father's bloodline, Connley had cried for his mother. Regan kissed him, but briefly, and he'd gasped. She'd kissed his tears away, and as his trembling hands cupped around her elbows, a shaking panic had filled her heart, for this was too big, too bright, and there was no space for brightness around Regan Lear. She was not allowed: there were no stars in her, only an empty, wide sky.

She had fled, and Gaela chided her for being missing nearly an hour. Regan easily convinced her sister she'd only lost time conversing with the wise grandfather oaks near the castle. It had been a retreat, as Gaela might have counseled upon facing an unwinnable battle, waiting to gather more allies to her side.

Not until after Gaela married her duke, and then after Connley's father had died, did the two lovers meet again. Six years since the fated goblet of chilled wine. Regan stood alone at her father's side, mostly, for her baby sister already inhabited the star towers, studying to become Lear's perfect pet. Connley was his own man, finally, duke in title and self, and could find reason to be at the Summer Seat if Regan would be, or north at Dondubhan, even braving Astore's displeasure to prove to Regan the depth of Connley loyalty, the lengths he'd go to just to see her.

The next kiss between them was anything but brief.

Regan remembered all their kisses, for they were as close to stars as she could get. A burst of light against a dark floral tapestry; bonfires kindled in a low feather bed; flickering quick as night-bugs, here and gone, there and gone, anywhere darkness lived; consuming and constant as a hearth fire.

Now his lips were cold and tasted only of blood. Around her, the wagon rattled and wind screamed. Lightning gave her cruel glimpses as the road vanished behind them: not fast enough. Regan huddled with her beloved under the thick canvas stretched over the wagon, holding his head against her belly, propped at the fore of the wagon bed. She tried to cushion her love from the wrenching travel, the rocking, hard cracks of the wheels.

There was not very much blood, yet Connley grew colder and colder.

He'd said, as Curan the iron wizard hefted him up, "Regan, be brave. There is something wrong inside me."

As they had loaded him into the wagon, Regan had commanded the Keep be held for Ban Errigal's return, and to yield for no other. She'd then climbed in with Connley, hushing him. *Save your strength, beloved,* she whispered in the language of trees. He was never fluent: she remembered so clearly his proud explanation that he learned to write her name and his, in just that way, because he wanted to impress her. No hint of chagrin to his tone, or guilt. The language of trees had grabbed her attention, because he had recognized her.

Wind blew, and a very soft, delicate moan parted her husband's lips. Regan smoothed his hair. Connley hated delicacy in himself, though he prized it in her. *Glass, my sharp wife,* he sometimes said, for she wore a mask that was smooth, clear, beautiful to behold. But it had cracked beneath long ago, and Connley knew where the perilous edges were; he saw them and loved them, though few others would admit a knife so deadly could be made of glass.

Her arms tightened around him, but he barely moved.

"Connley," she breathed, his name disappearing into the wind. The wagon tilted as they started up a hill, and Connley moaned again. His eyes moved; she saw a glint of them. Bending over him, she put her ear to his lips.

"Regan," he whispered, barely. She knew the sound of her name from his mouth, in all forms, but not this, not from a voice weak and hurting.

"Regan," he whispered again. "Don't lose yourself when I'm gone."

"Stop," she hissed.

She couldn't wait for the altars.

"Stop!" Regan screamed, slapping the front of the wagon. "Stop now!"

The driver pulled the horses back, and everything went still but for the wind. Even the punishing rain had ceased.

As carefully as she could, Regan shifted her husband to the wagon floor and began untying the canvas above their seat. When enough had been pulled free, she shoved it away: rolling black and vivid purple clouds pushed at the southwest edges of the sky, but in the east it was clear, stars glittering just like sharp shards of glass. *Not for me, not from me,* Regan thought, kneeling, holding the side of the wagon for support. Dark forest sprawled at the bottom of the hill behind them: this length of the West Ley Road poured through a deep valley between stretches of moorland. It was hours still to Connley Castle and her altar, that deepest seat of Regan's power.

"Lady?" Osli, from Gaela's retinue, stood still, silhouetted against the stars. She had aided Regan, she had driven the horses, she had kept the other ladies and retainers at Errigal Keep from following.

"Help me put him now against the earth."

With Connley spread against damp, yellow grass, Regan pushed Osli back and then took off her heavy outer dress. She knelt in wool shift and stockings to undress him, quickly, unwrapping his wound. He breathed slowly and shallowly, skin too pale, she thought, but the moon was behind the storm, and the sun too far away. Another storm, one made of blood and bile, had formed a violent bruise that covered Connley's chest, ribs, and stomach.

He was bleeding inside.

There was nothing she could do alone. Nothing any healer could do.

Water pattered off distant forest leaves. Wind glided more gently now over the moorland, teasing before dawn like a weary sigh.

*Save him,* Regan told the wind. *Tell me what to do,* she said to the earth. She brushed her hands on the grass, tugging. *Tell me. Help me.*

*He is dying,* the wind whispered.

*We cannot save him,* said the trees.

"No!" Regan cried. She tore up chunks of grass, then grabbed her own hair, pulling until it burned. Tears filled her eyes. She blinked hard, leaned over him so the tears fell onto his face. "Wake up," she said, and wrote *heal* on his cheek using the cool slip of her tears.

*Please,* she begged the island. *Innis Lear, I am your daughter, and I would give you anything to save him.*

Below her knees, the ground shifted. A small ripple, as if from a tide pool. Regan flattened one palm against the earth and the other over his sternum. Tendrils of earth crawled up his sides, like tiny worms.

*Saints of trees and stars,* she whispered, *birds of the sky and fire, worms of the dreamtime, lend me strength!*

Connley shuddered as the earth entwined him.

The sky brightened along the eastern horizon, creamy and gilded.

Regan grasped the small knife she'd plucked from her husband's boot and slashed the back of her wrist. Blood dripped onto his chest and she wrote *heal,* wishing with all her power that the rootwaters still flowed freely, that she could bathe him in the navel well, find the nearest star chapel and break it open until the island's heart-blood pumped out and over Connley.

Wind jerked at her hair, and she dragged her heavy overdress against Connley's legs, blanketing him up to his belly, keeping him warm.

Hidden inside the wind's voice was a sorrowful whisper: *Lost and fading,* it mourned already.

*Then I will die,* Regan cried.

This was the limit of earth magic, and star prophecy, too: neither could force a body to do what it was not capable of doing on its own. Roots might encourage, water direct, wind gift with speed, stars shine hope, but if something was too broken, not even the blood of the island or the tears of the stars could mend it.

Regan kissed him. She opened his mouth with hers, tasting the corners of his lips, the edge of his teeth, and he tilted his chin, sighing a harsh breath. Connley kissed her back. One hand found her neck, slid up to her skull, fingers dug roughly through her tangled dark hair. A spark—the last star Regan might ever claim. His grip tightened, then went slack as his arm sank slowly again. His breath softened. Hitched.

"No," she whispered, and the knife in her hand flipped; she aimed the point at her ribs, pausing just a moment to lift her voice to the wind: *My heart for his, my life blood for his, take it, take anything.*

Weight hit Regan's shoulder as Osli tackled her, knocking the witch to the ground and snatching at the knife with quick skill.

"No!" Regan screamed, and again, gasping, crushed beneath the other woman's weight.

"My lady would murder me if I let you die," Osli said. She tossed the knife far away, pinning Regan still. Regan tried to reach for her husband. Her fingers only grazed his hair.

"Get off me," she ordered, but in a quiet, desperate whisper.

The captain obeyed.

Regan crawled nearer to Connley, tucking her cheek against his shoulder from upside down, and wrapped one arm around his head.

Sunlight flashed in a long line at the horizon, a signal to the dying night.

# ELIA

DAWN BROKE THROUGH the storm clouds lingering over the White Forest, and the tattered, torn trees glistened with sun-pink drops of rain.

Elia opened the door of Brona's cottage for Ban's departure.

Though Elia only had wrapped herself in a blanket over the long shift she'd gone to bed in, Ban wore a clean shirt borrowed from Kay Oak's traveling bags, and a coat of his mother's that fit his shoulders. They'd done what they could with his hair, braiding pieces of it back from his face. Still he seemed wild, though that might have been his expression or those hollow cheeks. He paused, framed in the door. His eyes rested on hers, heavy with the weight of all that had passed between them.

But Elia felt grounded for the first time in years. She could see the paths they'd followed, and why, the choices they'd been forced to make for themselves and never for each other. Before she let him go, she needed only one more answer.

Elia folded her hands before her: not in pain, not holding some great, gnawing wound inside, merely regal and sure like the queen she was supposed to be.

She asked, "What do you want, now that this storm has passed?"

"I am the storm," Ban murmured. He leaned closer to her, until his forehead brushed hers and his words tickled along her cheekbone to her ear. "I want this island to crumble, and see what rises. Discover who can transform all the shattered power into something strong. Will it be you?"

"Stars and worms, Ban Errigal," she whispered, shivering.

"I had to come home because this is what I was meant to do. To pull Innis Lear apart. To show your father and my father and everyone who believes as they do how fragile everything truly is, and how wrong they have been."

"Am I wrong, too?"

Ban pressed her against the doorframe. Body to body. "What do *you* want, Elia Lear?" he asked, then kissed her tenderly.

She welcomed the kiss, relishing its warmth and simplicity, when nothing about this was simple. His lips, her tongue, their teeth and hearts.

Elia leaned back and said, "I want to save everyone."

"So we are opposed," he whispered, muddy green eyes too near her own.

"No." She touched his lips with her fingers, nudging him away. "I'm going to save you, too."

It was clear from the bleakness in his face that Ban did not believe her. Well, she would make him believe, just as she would make her sisters. "Go to Gaela and bring her to me at Errigal Keep. I will get my father and go to Regan. We will wait there, and when you and my eldest sister arrive, you'll see what I can do."

"I'll go to Gaela." Ban's lips barely moved under her fingers.

"Good." She began to kiss him again, but Aefa suddenly appeared.

"Elia," said a wide-eyed Aefa, approaching through the squelching mud with another woman behind her. "You—um."

"I must go," Ban murmured.

"Be well, Ban," Elia said. He nodded, then picked up his sword belt and left.

She had watched him go when they were children, crying, shoulders shaking with young agony at the injustice. He had watched her go last month at the standing stones: him blazing like a torch trapped in its sconce, her heart-frozen, numb.

Here was the third departure, and Elia was neither shuddering with agony nor stuck in place. She was ready.

And Elia was glad for last night's storm, glad for all its raw power that had thrust her together with Ban. She'd streaked across the sky last night, a star falling through the blackness, and landed where he'd been born, landed in the roots of Innis Lear, in this thicket of thorns and wild shadows. No matter what came next, threads of starlight had planted here, and Elia understood them.

At the edge of the woods a handful of moon moths floated, pale spirits darting in the flickering shadows, just where Elia could not quite see. In the gentle rush of a stream, Elia heard the hopeless echo of her starless sister's name, but the forest would say no more.

# THE FOX

THE RAVEN STRETCHED black wings wide, an arc of darkness against the bright green morning. It then leapt off a pile of stones and flapped past the forest canopy, into the keen blue sky. One cry for the wizard, and it vanished east, toward Aremoria and its king.

Ban sat hard onto the ruins he'd stumbled over, the leavings of some long-dead lord. Moss edged the crumbling stone foundation, and small ferns and patches of rose brambles grew in the cracks. He lowered his head into his hands. His skin felt raw, scrubbed over with shards of glass. That was the last missive Ban the Fox would ever send to Morimaros of Aremoria. He was not formed for order and service, for the soaring spires of clean, careful Lionis. Ban was wild, and this furious island owned his heart.

But he was sorry to hurt Mars. And selfishly glad not to be forced to witness the moment the king understood this betrayal.

Ban scraped his hands down his thighs. Ruins were what this island needed more of: places for the trees to swallow up towers and ramparts, for the navel wells to flood and nobody to count the stars for a hundred years. Raze Lear's castles to the earth, let them be reclaimed, and seed over the royal roads. Show the people of cold prophecy to fear this land they'd so quickly forsaken, the roots that had deserved to be better loved. Shove those standing stones into the ocean.

That was what Ban would do, if he were a wizard powerful enough.

Regan might let him.

Though Gaela might prefer to murder him instead.

He shuddered with the thrill of the idea.

Five years ago, when Ban nearly died in Aremoria, those compassionate trees had saved him, knitting him together and reminding him what power was. Ban had thought his mission must be to grow his reputation; he would become great, and then come home. To prove his worth, to show Lear and his father, and all of them, that Ban was more than any prophecy. To make them see him: he was a bastard, but by the worms of the earth and the cursed stars in the sky, he would be a powerful one.

Now Ban understood proving himself to those men meant accepting the very foundations of their star-addled beliefs, using the language they understood, taking up the very weapons that had been used against him.

But such things did not spur heat in his veins or give breath to his spirit.

He would go to Gaela Astore, as Elia had asked. He'd go, but he would show Gaela how to burn the island to the ground. Give the warrior what she needed most from him: his wild, natural power. And Regan trusted him; she needed him, she would agree. He would help them begin a new empire in a world not tainted by their fathers. He would say, *Yes, you should listen to Elia though she requests the impossible, and then hold her there between you as we destroy everything your father wrought. I have done this, twice over, for my own father is dead. And I have abandoned the only king who ever cherished me.*

If Ban could do it, they could, too. Now he was free. Free to be the island's champion—to bring magic and rebirth back to starved land. But his first mission was to seek vengeance for the ruination Lear himself had wrought.

The forest had agreed, and in proof had delivered Ban's lost sword, forged of whispering Errigal steel. A gift to aid his intentions. The trees and the wind had sung to him, leading him to the muddy hill where the sword waited, stabbed into the earth, glistening pure and clean in dappled sunlight.

Ban touched the hilt again now, and the sword sighed hungrily.

Something else sighed, too.

Not a tree, but—

Ban softened his breathing to silence and crept across a loamy sprawl of dead winter leaves, toward the sound.

Another sigh.

And another.

It was rhythmic. Someone—something—was asleep and snoring. An earth saint, Ban thought giddily, or perhaps even an old stone giant or forest dragon.

Ban's heart thrummed in his chest. He would not even risk a whispered inquiry to the trees. They'd brought him here; they knew of whatever awaited him and had not revealed it until now, like a game for them to play. Ban reached a soft, small meadow. The last of the rain was evident in the muddy grass, and in the heavy flow of the creek bending around the edge.

An old man huddled, sleeping against the mossy face of a granite boulder along the creek. He wore a tattered robe, and his hair was tangled and damp. His long face drooped in heavy sleep.

The earth tilted beneath Ban's feet. Blood rushed in his ears and he stood, stunned.

It was the king of Innis Lear.

Ban spun around, wildly, but there was no one else nearby. Birds chirped and the forest canopy shivered pleasantly, scattering tiny raindrops onto Ban's forehead. He stepped into the sunny meadow, one hand curled around the hilt of his sword. The other he lifted, palm out, as if the sleeping old man were a wild boar, a lion or deadly bear.

Ban approached slowly, and began to smile.

He could do anything to this foolish man, left alone in the heart of the forest. Slide this hungry blade into Lear's gut. Bash in his head with a jagged rock. Wake him with a whisper, before gently suffocating him. Ask the ash tree there to bury the king deep in the earth, until he was eaten by worms.

It would hurt Elia so very badly.

Ban ground his teeth together and hissed. But this old man, this awful once-king, deserved this and more, for all he'd done: not only to Ban, to his daughters, to his queen, perhaps—but even more for what he'd done to this island itself. The rootwaters should be free.

There might never come such a chance as this. But to murder him so secretly, without consequence, would do nothing for the island, prove nothing to anyone.

He bent and put his hand over Lear's mouth, to feel the small puffs of breath.

*Sometimes I cannot even breathe when he is near,* the king had said of Ban, dismissing his very existence with a wave. *The stench of his birth stars pollutes this air.*

And so Ban knew what it was that he would take.

A *WIZARD CROUCHED* between two young hawthorns at the edge of a clear, rushing creek. Bare to the wind and roots, he'd painted muddy lines onto his chest, in spirals down his arms and legs, and with a tiny knife, he now etched his name alongside that of a former king, glistening blood against his own skin.

The hawthorns shivered and shook with thrills; they'd not worked such magic in more years than they even understood. This was death magic, magic of the worms that fed upon their roots, magic that brought food to the world, decay and rebirth and an excess of fluid.

The wizard breathed into his palms, where the two shells of a walnut were fitted together, missing the meat. He replaced the nut with his own blood and a stolen silver hair.

*Breath and death,* he whispered to the nut in the language of trees, glad the daylight drove all the stars away, so they could not witness this. Or maybe they did: the wizard knew not. He only knew the blood of the land and the chatter of leaves.

*Breath and death,* he whispered again, and the hawthorns echoed it back to him.

The spell would be his last weapon, a comfort to him wherever he went. A safeguard, a triumphant laugh, a final word to be remembered by.

He would not be forgiven for this.

# GAELA

It was a cold, crisp morning when Gaela led her retainers out of Astora.

They headed north across the foothills to Dondubhan Castle, where her husband had already claimed the winter throne, and Gaela was eager to join with him. Two nights of angry storms had cleared out the remains of summer, scouring the hills of the last flowers and painting ice farther down the jagged peaks of the Mountain of Teeth, always a sharp ghost in the far distance. Her army marched quickly, a surging river of pink, black, and silver across the moors. They passed the Star Field silently, all eyes turned in respect, for even the least religious knew that this was where the kings and queens of the past rested, where stars and rocks came together to merge heaven and earth.

Gaela reveled in the cold wind, though winter itself she despised: layers of wool weighing her down, and the constant snow of the north trapping her inside, where there was little space to breathe or loom large. Tight quarters, sweat, pine-sharp incense, and fire all the time, wet socks from melting ice, all were oppressive and overwhelming, heavily laden with memories. Dalat had loved the winter, been fascinated by ice crystals and the patterns of snowflakes, sometimes even leaving open a window, and wasting wood to beat back the cold. She would wrap herself and Gaela and Regan in massive bearskins to watch the snow fall, so crisp and quiet.

This was before Elia arrived, loud and interrupting.

Gaela could not stand the smell of fur in the winter.

But it was not yet that darkest part of the year, and Gaela led her army to join with Astore at the seat of her childhood. Together they would push south to take back Lowbinn and Brideton, crushing Connley's arrogant claims while he sat in Errigal. If he would take the iron for himself, then Gaela saw no reason to let Connley think to keep any of the north.

Her only regret was leaving before Osli had returned from delivering letters in Errigal. But it was taking her longer than it should have, and Gaela could not wait.

Slivers of cold wind cut inside her throat as she breathed deep to call an order to move her retainers faster. Now that they'd crossed around the Star Field, their destination was visible.

The castle at Dondubhan embraced the Tarinnish, the largest, deepest lake on Innis Lear. Its name meant *well of the island* in the language of trees, and was one of the few words all still recognized. Even in the height of summer the black waters were cold with runoff from the mountains.

Gaela led her men from the karst plain of the Star Field down toward the marsh surrounding the lake and the river it fed. They met with the West Duv Road, narrow here, and built of stone to lift itself out of the muck to cross the Duv River over three thick stone arches. No more than two horses could walk abreast for the final hundred feet of the approach to the fortified first wall of Dondubhan. The wall rested on foundations as old as the island itself: a handful of massive blocks of blue-gray basalt gifted to the first people from the earth saints, pushed out of the roots in fully formed boulders and columns. If the stories were to be believed. Again and again, over generations, earls and kings had built the walls taller, adding an inner castle and fortified towers and longer arms of the wall to curl halfway around the Tarinnish. When the moon was brightest, the castle rock glowed, as eerie as swamplights or wandering spirits.

This afternoon, beside the dark blue and white swan flag of Lear, Astore's salmon crest flew from the tallest tower, snapping in the bitter wind. Men on the forward ramparts held up their hands to greet Gaela and her men, flying a matching banner. The drawbridge sat open, like a wide, wooden tongue, but her army was forced to wait while the iron-toothed gate was lifted for them to pass.

Gaela jogged her horse through the twelve-foot tunnel and into the fore-court, his hooves tapping lightly.

They rode to the center, and Gaela pulled her horse up, calling behind for her captain to halt and bring in only the first squad of retainers: the inner courtyard was filled with soldiers, blocking the edges so her men would not all fit as they should.

Her husband waited, astride, at the fore of his own men.

Sun glinted off Astore's chest plate, formed of three arched salmon in a trefoil. His helmet was hooked to his saddle, but otherwise Astore dressed in full war regalia, including the great sword on his belt. Fifty of his best men swept to either side of him, equally ready for battle. Behind him, the five thick blue towers of Dondubhan rose, shading him with their authority.

Impressed, Gaela nudged her horse nearer to his. "Husband, you'll leave me no time to don my own plates." She put a hungry smile on her face. "Though glad I am to see you so fine and ready to chase our great purpose."

Astore did not smile in return. His pale face remained rigid. "That will not be necessary."

Gaela narrowed her eyes. "You have not reclaimed the border towns without me."

"I will."

"But why?"

"You are my wife no longer, and have no cause to ride beside me."

The eldest princess laughed loud, for all these retainers to hear and take to heart. "Yet you are my husband, and thus married to the ascending queen of Innis Lear. But perhaps my father's mind has infected yours, and you, too, will betray the woman you've professed to prefer?"

"Get off your horse, Gaela." Astore flicked his gloved hand, and ten of his men dismounted, approaching her. She knew them all, had practiced with some. They willingly had called her their lady. Only two did not readily hold her in esteem.

"I will not," Gaela said, heart racing as she readied for battle.

With a small sigh and a tightening of his lips, Astore nodded. Then he said, "Detain her."

The men moved, and those of Gaela's command who had pushed into the forecourt shifted nearer to her in returned threat.

"Stop," Gaela ordered Astore's men.

They did. A few glanced nervously at their lord.

"Astore, what is your cause to take up this absolute folly?" Her mouth curled with distaste.

The duke said, loudly for all, "The lady's crime is treason against her father, for until Midwinter he remains the king of this island; and further treason against myself, her lord and husband."

"Oh, Col," Gaela said. The thrill she felt was nothing of terror, only anticipation. "I am Gaela Lear, daughter of kings and empresses, and these men around us belong to me and my island. Not to you—unless you are mine."

"Restrain her," Astore said, confident in his authority.

Standing in her stirrups, Gaela called, "Do so yourself, if you would be more a king than me."

Her husband lost all the remaining pink in his face, lips blanching straight and white as worms. With a sharp jerk, Astore pushed his horse right up to hers.

Gaela stared at his pale eyes and smiled. She swung down off her mount. Though not in full raiment, Gaela had traveled in dark leather armor and a mail skirt with heavy wool trousers. Hanging from the saddle was her grandfather's own broadsword. The pommel was shaped like a swan, and set with blue topaz in the simple cross guard. She strode the short distance to Astore's horse and gripped the ankle of his heavy boots. "Arrest me, if you are able."

He nudged her away and climbed out of his saddle. Because Gaela did not back off, he landed a hand from her, their chests aligned.

"I came here," Gaela said, "to lead a charge against Connley and take this north for *us,* husband, but you greet me as if you do not know me, as if you could be anything without me."

Astore gripped the handle of his sword in its piscine sheath. Softly he said, "You betrayed me, Gaela, years ago in deed, and now in defiance. Our marriage was a lie, and you have proved never to care for Astora or my people. You've cared only for your own ambitions. When my men sent word of what you did to the Oak Earl—your own uncle—I knew you'd lost yourself as your father did. I will join with the Kayo to take this island back for Lear. Elia will be a fine—gentle and womanly—queen for us."

Gaela said nothing: a prescient regret silenced her.

She was going to kill her husband this afternoon.

The thought made her dizzy, but she relished it.

Astore put his hands on her shoulders. "I will keep you very well, or even, if you like, arrange for escort to your mother's people. But here, near power, you are a danger to yourself and this entire island. And can be no fit wife for me, because of what you've done to yourself."

"You would put me aside in favor of drooling babies?" she murmured. "Choose children of your own line over ambition and a crown? Oh, I misjudged you, Col."

"Yes, you did. I have ever wanted that crown, and I mean to fight for it, still. But what is the point of a crown without a legacy?"

"Power, together, to make a legacy for every child on this island, Col." The depth of her disappointment in him surprised her, and that surprise stirred matching anger.

"You lied to me from the beginning. You never wanted me. You have never wanted any man. Though you professed to want a king. What kind of partnership is that, to have worked together based on such a lie?"

Baring her teeth in a mean smile, Gaela said, "I wanted a king—that much was true. But I have always intended to be that king myself, and toward that, on this cursed island, my stars provided a singular path. I have what I needed from you now, you foolish man, and I can finish the rest myself, without the need to share my crown."

"I loved you," he snarled, as if it would make a difference to her.

Gaela ended her smile. "I respected you, but no more."

His face blazed red with his outrage, and he yelled again, "Seize this woman!"

Gaela eyed his retainers. She met their gazes with her own severity. "No one here has the authority to arrest the ascendant queen of Innis Lear, Col Astore, but she can challenge you herself."

He put his hand again on the pommel of his sword. "I would die before I let you drag me down."

"Same, husband." Gaela reached, and the soldier Dig was at her side, putting her sword in her hand.

She did not wait, but swung it instantly, and with all the strength of her body. Astore barely blocked in time, stumbling. Gaela followed through with her shoulder, knocking him aside. He grunted, and before he could react, she drew the knife from her belt and stabbed it expertly between the buckles of steel plate, directly under his arm.

Astore's mouth gaped open, and he looked down at her hand on the hilt.

Gaela pulled the knife free. Blood gushed through the quilted wool of his gambeson, pouring red and hot. She had learned from him, that very first year, how to always find a mortal stab.

"You misjudged me, too, Col," Gaela murmured, opening her arm for him to slump against her. She caught him under his opposite shoulder, and carefully lowered Astore to his knees. "You always underestimated my ambition and my commitment. I would do anything for my crown and is-land, even let you paw at me, let you put your seed in me, thinking that it might ever take root. You've looked at me since I was a little girl like I was the thing to bring you what you wanted. But always you were the tool to bring me *mine*. I married you, and then I became you. Remember that as you die. Your honor is to have made the strongest king Innis Lear has ever seen."

Breath wheezed from his lips, but Astore couldn't catch enough air to speak.

"Men of Astore and Lear!" Gaela cried, standing with her dying husband against her hip, the murder weapon brandished and dripping a single long line of blood onto her wrist. "You have until his blood stops running to choose. Against me, and there will be a massacre here today, all the legacy of the fine Astore spirit become one of death and waste. Or *with* me, and we will ride out this afternoon to take all of Astore's ancient lands back in the name of our duke, husband to the new king of Innis Lear."

A gasping silence answered her first, and Gaela gripped her husband's neck, wishing for battle, hoping the men chose poorly, that she would be forced to throw Astore's body to the ground and let her rage free. To let herself go, to finally unleash and fight until triumphant or dead.

Her smile was fearsome to behold.

Astore held on to her hips, face pressed to her side. She stroked his hair, tugged it in the way she'd learned he liked, during their long marriage. But he was past such desire; he slid forward, blood spattering the packed earth as he slowly fell, but caught himself on his palms. His body shook with effort; Astore collapsed.

Several cries of sorrow rang out, but none leapt forward to attack.

More of Gaela's retainers had by now pushed into the forecourt, pressing hard and crowding.

"Gaela Lear!" yelled Dig in his bearish roar.

"Gaela Lear!"

"Gaela Lear!"

She held up her hand for silence. It fell, swollen and ready to burst again with further violence. Gaela shook her head in mock sadness.

Finally, one of the duke's first captains knelt, drawing his sword. He held the blade in one gloved hand, then kissed its guard. "Gaela of Astore and Lear!" he said, opening devoted eyes to her.

Gaela nodded regally, then crouched to grasp her husband's shoulder and roll him onto his back. He groaned. Blood coated his front and side. His chest hardly rose. Gaela touched his mouth gently, brushed her knuckles along his jaw. Strange how numb she felt, though a recognizable flutter of angry grief waited behind the coursing thrill in her heart. She would feel it soon: a sorrow of necessity, a lost ally. Men were fools, with backward priorities always turning their heads. Astore would have gained everything by letting Gaela reign as she wished, if only he had curbed his own desires.

Then the duke of Astore died, and his wife placed the knife that had done it across his heart.

COL HAD BEEN the duke of Astore since he was twelve years old, when his father died from a broken back during routine military exercises. It meant Col had been Astore a mere two years fewer than Lear had been king. He remembered the clear morning at the Summer Seat when the prophecy had been read, foretelling both the arrival and doom of Lear's true queen. And Col remembered his first sight of Dalat, her gentle warmth and lovely joy seeming so alien to the harsh moors of Innis Lear. He remembered her swaying walk as she left the star chapel, a wife and queen, and Col remembered where he had stood when he heard that her first daughter had arrived.

Even at fifteen years old, he'd known the screaming firstborn Gaela was his best avenue toward more power. Astore only needed to be patient and wait for her, discover what sort of woman she'd be, how best to use her, and then how best to win her to his side. Prop or partner, vessel or queen, Col held all options open as she grew. He was always generous with Gaela and friendly, ushering her toward Astore, though never too overtly, lest some other (particularly her father the king) think him despicable.

Initially he did not want her for himself, outside his heated ambitions for the crown. That at least proved that, while his vices might be numerous, desiring a child in his bed was not among them. No, it was only when her mother died, when Gaela came to Astora as a furious young woman, that he very suddenly and violently recognized her carnal appeal. So for half a decade more he'd worked with the information he gathered on her likes and dislikes, biding his time, teaching Gaela as a mentor, welcoming her to his retainers, waiting for her to approach him.

Tonight, she'd asked to speak with him privately, coming up at the end of the morning's training. Sweat had melted dust from the practice ground along the edges of her hairline, and she breathed hard from her sport. Her breasts heaved against the leather armor buckled across her front, and her eyes were wide and bright, a brown so deep and vivid Astore saw them in his dreams. When Gaela tilted her chin up and said, "I would have dinner with you tonight, alone, Col Astore, to discuss the future," he'd kept his smile tame, despite the immediate desire and triumph, crackling up and down his spine.

"I'll be honored," he said, knowing what she wanted.

Gaela Lear had turned twenty-one that winter, and it was time for her to be married.

Astore expected to be her husband. They'd not explicitly agreed upon it when she came to his lands, but there had been an understanding that in return for allowing her full access to his warrior retainers, to live with them and learn what they had to teach her of battle and weaponry, Gaela would one day owe him in kind.

As he was the duke of the largest, strongest domain in all of Innis Lear, the only way to pay him back would be to make Col king alongside her—as befitted her stars, which destined her to be reliant on another's strength.

So he met her as a king would, in his private dining room. Ready for her to submit to him, to repay his magnanimous patronage with a display of gratitude. Bold stone walls, decorated only with stately salmon banners; a warm, roaring fire in a hearth wide enough to roast a pig; long wooden table smoothly gleaming; two high-backed benches to either side of the single, narrow arched window that looked out over the lower yard and into the city of Astora beyond. This place was marked by symbols of his power, but not overwhelmingly so, not as the great hall would have been. Gaela was appreciated here, with room to weave in her own power and details. Col was vain enough to bathe carefully and dress even more so, despite usually bearing the trappings of fashion no mind at all. His best dark pink tunic that showed off the broadness of his chest and the strength in his arms, over black trousers that hugged his powerful thighs. He had his footman braid his hair in three furrows and trim his beard. Though he was not quite old enough to have fathered Gaela, it was a near thing, and he'd remind her of his might and virility wherever he could.

For several long minutes he debated bringing with him the duchess ring. In the end Col put it on his smallest finger; let her notice and be aware that he was just as ambitious as she. Then they could solidify any arrangements tonight: bargain and share drink, and she would take his ring, and he would take her to bed. Stars, but that would be glorious. Finally.

And in the small hours of the night, when he'd satisfied her and made her beg to have him, they would discuss the crown itself.

He allowed himself only a single short cup of his favorite Aremore wine while he waited.

Gaela arrived exactly as the sun set, entering on the tail of her name, as called through the door by the retainer on guard. Col did not usually keep one, being confident enough in his own ability to defend himself, but for this occasion, he'd thought it best to act as a king might.

She swept in wearing a bold, dark blue gown split at the sides so it appeared like a military tabard, and the arms quilted just as a gambeson would be. A belt of silver plates pulled all together at Gaela's waist, and cuffs of beaten silver clutched her forearms, more like gauntlets than bracelets. Streaks of white clay hardened swirls of her short black curls into a crown.

Col did his best to moderate the lust and admiration in his face, though he did not want to hide it: let her see she impressed him, and that he desired her in her martial beauty.

"Gaela," he said, standing and offering his hand. She gave hers, too, and he bowed over it, drawing her firmly toward him.

"Astore," she replied, and allowed him to seat her on one of the hard benches beside the window. Before he could do aught else, she continued, "I assume you intend to be my husband."

Taken aback, Col laughed. He did not let go of her hand. "I do, Gaela Lear. I assume you intend to allow it."

"It would be in both our best interests. I will be queen after my father, and you are his closest ally. He does not question your strength, your loyalty, nor your faith in his stars."

"All our stars," Col said. "I have seen yours, Gaela, and heard the entire life chart read at your naming. It fits well with mine. I commissioned a joined chart two years ago: we will have a unique partnership, and successfully achieve our destinies."

Gaela twisted her mouth and stood. It put her close to him, enough that he could smell the cool, earthy clay and a sharp soap lingering on her skin. He did not step back to make room between them. Her eyes were just beneath his. "One requirement for our partnership, Col: do not speak to me again of the stars."

He frowned. "Stars speak themselves and so should not be ignored."

"For men of Lear, those who would follow my father, perhaps, but I have never been served by stars, and neither was my mother."

"Ah," Col said, understanding. She was the daughter born to mark her mother's death, by those same celestial bodies. An aversion to such things was inevitable; he minded not at all, so long as she did not swing so far as to worship the mud. "You can make your own destiny," he said, to soothe her, and to prop her up.

A smile spread across her delicious, plump mouth. "I do, Col Astore, and I will make yours, too, if you join with me."

"Yes," he said, undeniably aflame at being told, instead of doing the telling. Discomfort rose in him, made rather delicious by the perversion. He put a hand on her waist, and she did not shy away, or even move. Instead, Gaela reached for his hand and lifted it so she could access the ring on his small finger. Still smiling, she tugged at it, and Col let her do the work, take this ring from him, and then slide it onto her own hand.

He ached for her, hot and ready, and he pulled her hips against his, pressing himself against her.

Gaela gasped softly, and Col nearly broke. He'd held himself in check so long, forced away these urges during the four years she'd been under his protection, while she trained with his men. Despite Gaela's flaunting of her strength, her intensity and the way she walked, spoke, and carried herself, as if already she owned him and all his retainers. As if she tempted him on purpose, was made to be his challenge. Col expected her to be ferocious, expected her to resist giving herself to him, and this tiny breath of submission was almost too much.

He dug his fingers into her hips, holding her belly against him. Even that gentle pressure burned up into his face. His cheeks would be red, he knew, his eyes hot. But he did not care if she saw, if she realized how badly he wanted her. Would she taste all of Innis Lear, or some foreign flavors, too? Her mouth would be hot as his, and her depths like a well of the island—his island, his well.

Col kissed her, and Gaela let him, still and only moving to put her hands on his shoulders for balance. She gave little, but Col pushed her mouth open; he kissed her with all his potency, reaching in with his tongue, dragging his lips against hers, wanting it all. Taking what he could.

In a moment, Gaela pushed back. She leaned her torso away, which pushed her hips more firmly against him. "Stop, Col Astore, and wait to touch me like this until we are united under the laws of Innis Lear and your stars. That is my second condition. That you stop yourself now, and we do not join in body until we are joined by ritual."

With ridiculous effort, he listened. "Gaela," he said, low in his throat, chiding and longing. But he smiled, because he liked her games and confidence.

"Col," she said, holding herself against him, as if she could read in his face just how much he liked it.

"Do you have a third condition?" He strove to sound conversational, not as if he was near to bursting.

"I do." Her hands climbed up his neck and she grasped his jaw, fingers in his beard. "Never rest until I am crowned. Destroy everyone in our path. Use all your power to put the crown in my hands."

"Our hands," he corrected.

"Yes."

"I will never rest until you are crowned, Gaela of Lear. You will be the most glorious queen in an age." Col meant every word, with every piece of his spirit and heart and body.

Gaela gifted him her wide, plump smile again.

He said, "I will set a date for our marriage."

"Do so. I will go to my sister, now, and return for it." A smile teased at her unteasing mouth. "That should make the wait easier for you, husband."

"I would . . ." He used his hands on her hips to push her to the side, so her behind pressed against the stone ledge of the window. "I would have the wait made harder for you . . . wife."

"I suspect things will be hard enough between us." With a twist, Gaela freed herself. She walked smoothly, as if unaffected, back to the long table and grasped his bottle of wine. Turning to him, she lifted the bottle. "To the crown of Innis Lear, which will be ours."

Col Astore believed her warning, and her promise, and relished both. Gaela bent her head with a play of obeisance—which only added to her haughty glory.

But he could see right through her, and in that moment, Astore knew.

*This woman is going to kill me.*

Nothing had ever felt more welcome, or more right.

# AEFA

AEFA STUCK CLOSE behind her princess, disconcerted at the way the White Forest parted itself before Elia, offering easy passage through its ferns and mossy old trees. Sun shone prettily through leaves turning yellow and fiery orange at their edges, and the breeze was cold but pleasant with none of last night's fury. Reborn wind, Aefa thought, free to be itself after the cleansing of the storm.

When Elia Lear had kissed Ban Errigal right in front of Aefa this morning, she'd been near sure her eyes would pop and she'd be blind forever. But her mother, Alis, hadn't seemed concerned, dragging the two girls inside to feed them since Brona herself had vanished before dawn. The moment Aefa and Elia were alone, off to wash up at the well behind Brona's house, Aefa had leapt on her chance.

"You need something to make sure Ban Errigal did not get you with child last night," she said as they picked their way around onion beds.

"Aefa!" hissed Elia, looking all around.

Triumph had surged through Aefa, and she'd raised her golden brows, then laughed once.

"I should bleed in the next few days, I think. We'll know quickly if there's anything to worry on."

"I want to know everything."

"So do I! About your mother—"

"You first. About *spending the night with Ban Errigal.*"

"Once I begin, I won't be able to stop."

"But you did . . . like it?" Aefa danced a little in place, giving in to the impulse to be nothing but a girl, gleeful and anxious and begging her friend to confide in her.

Elia nodded fast and covered her mouth against the press of her smile. When her eyes met Aefa's, though, Aefa could not deny the sorrow dragging at the joy. It cut at Aefa, and she took Elia's face in her hands. "Nothing that comes after has anything to do with it," she whispered. "If you loved it, and loved him, that's all that matters. Even if he is unworthy of you, which he is, the dirty traitor—no, no, listen!" Aefa smiled and kissed Elia lightly on the mouth. "Everything is terrible right now, except me of course, so even if Ban is one of the terrible things, last night he wasn't, so don't let go of that. Even later on when I tell you again and again that you should have considered doing that with the king of Aremoria instead. Promise?"

Elia had looked up at the first true ray of sun pressing through milky-golden clouds. "I promise."

And Aefa was certain she'd meant it. They'd washed, dressed, and eaten the breakfast Alis provided. Then Aefa had wound those amber beads back into Elia's hair; now here they were in the forest, gone after Brona, Kay Oak, and the old king.

"Aefa," Elia murmured suddenly, as wind tossed dappled shadows over her face, "I love you. You've been mine for years, and I've never acknowledged it, or acted it. I know how hard it's been, being my friend, when I offered nothing in return."

A thrum of pleasure zipped through the Aefa. Her grip tightened. "I adore you, Elia, and I think it won't be long before I admire you, too."

"I hope I earn it."

"Only you control that." The Fool's daughter pinched Elia's hip, but gently.

For nearly an hour they walked, toward the east. The forest whispered at them, through wind and singing birds, through the rustle of ferns and brushed tails, the buzz of crickets and chirping frogs. The gown Alis had found among Brona's things was a little snug in the waist for Elia; it had been previously let out at the sides, and hemmed hurriedly this morning to accommodate the princess's short legs. The unusual style did not matter, for its vibrant rust red color made it look velvet-soft instead of plain linen. Old turquoise silk laced it up the sides and the underskirt was a fine, warm cream. Elia promised she was comfortable, loved the discordant, bold colors, and the flick of the skirts as she kicked out with her boots.

To Aefa's eyes, she was a piece of the forest come boldly and uniquely alive.

With the forest's guidance, it did not take them long to find the king's camp.

Brona crouched at a small fire, roasting a spitted squirrel. Beside her, Kayo leaned on an old log, filthy from the storm and in a hunter's simple brown coat and tunic; only his very finely made boots suggested at his rank.

"Kayo!" Elia rushed forward, leaving Aefa to gasp at the earl's injury.

A bandage wrapped his head, crossing over his left temple, cheek, and eye. A vivid purple bruise streaked beneath his right eye, and there was blood in the white of it, making the gray iris seem to shine. Sweat glistened at his upper lip and brow. The bandage was bloody brown at the lower edge, as if the wound beneath had bled in the night.

He smiled when he saw his niece, but it was a smile of sorrow and nostalgia, the memory of a smile more than the fact of one. "Starling," he said, standing. "I will live."

"If he does everything else I say," Brona snapped.

"He will." Elia pressed her fingers to his forehead. "I think you're feverish."

Her uncle shook his head and murmured, "You're supposed to be in Aremoria."

"This is exactly where I'm supposed to be."

Aefa's father leapt up from where he'd lounged in restless sleep against an old stump. "You're here!"

"Dada!" Aefa threw her arms around his lanky waist, then hopped up to kiss his cheek. Lear's Fool looked gaunt and terrible, stinking like wet dog and sweat. "Mother will not approve of this appearance when you return."

"Maybe you can convince the king," the Fool sang softly, and let her go in order to hug Elia, too.

Kayo said, "If anyone can."

"Is he near?" Elia asked. Birds darted from one bright tree to the next, arguing over something.

"Past that hill of hawthorns." Kayo pointed weakly. "I'll show you."

"No." Elia lifted her chin and even raised onto her toes to get more in his face. "Stay with Brona and obey her as you would a queen. As you would my mother. I will not have you die of some fever."

Her uncle turned his head to the witch, Brona, who nodded, her mouth pressed in anger and distress. Aefa knew *she* certainly would do what that woman said.

Elia took off toward the hillock covered in twisted hawthorn trees. Aefa followed, unwilling to leave Elia alone for this confrontation, be it tender and forgiving or rotten and final. Beyond the hill, the forest opened onto a meadow where a small stream played over flat rocks, branching into tiny tributaries and keeping the grass soft and green. Sunlight shone down unmarred, and motes of leaves and earth floated amidst moon moths and brilliant blue butterflies that shouldn't have survived last night and the cold morning. Ferns clung in bunches between the narrow streams, almost like giant pillows. And upon them lounged Lear, the king. "Wait here," Elia said, but Aefa excelled at choosing the right commands to follow.

The king's feet were bare; scraps of a robe and trousers hung off his thin frame as he leaned back on his elbows, face turned with a smile to the bright sky and clear sun, like a basking cat, unaware or uncaring of his surroundings, lost in the pleasure of light. That shock of silver-streaked hair spread around his shoulders like a mane, and greenery was woven into a crown upon his head. Aefa recognized the feathered leaves and clusters of tiny white flowers: hemlock. It was a coronet of poison Lear wore.

"Elia," she whispered. "It's starweed."

The princess froze, no doubt worried he'd eaten some, or meant to.

"Father?" Elia said carefully as Aefa hung back to give the king some illusion of privacy.

Lear glanced up, his expression opening like a bright dawn. "Ah, pretty spirit, do come join me on this bank here."

Elia knelt in the damp grass beside him. "No spirit, sir, but flesh. Your daughter Elia."

The old king frowned. "My daughter went over the sea—I sent her there. But you do look like my wife, pretty spirit."

"Take my hands, Father. I am no spirit."

Aefa could hear the struggle in Elia's voice, and clenched her hands into fists, wishing to tear the difficulty away, or bear it instead.

The king frowned at his daughter. "Will you pull me into dreams? There are roots here, whispering. They would hold me under the earth forever, and as much I deserve."

"You hear the voice of the trees?" Elia whispered. She glanced to Aefa, and Aefa did her best to smile encouragingly. It was a good sign, for the star-touched king to be listening to the wind.

But a shudder pushed down Lear's body, and Elia grasped his cold, dry hands, bending to kiss his knuckles. The king pulled free.

"Let me wipe them," he said, clucking his tongue. "They smell of mortality."

Elia laughed, a small, helpless thing. "Yes, Father, they do."

He pursed his lips. "What do the stars smell of, do you think?"

His daughter opened her mouth, but shook her head in astonishment and ignorance. "I suppose they are clean smelling, like fresh water."

"My youngest smelled of goats," the king murmured. He closed his eyes, holding her hand to his chest. "Or some sharp, spicy oil her mother always wore. It spread to her baby skin, and I never remember a time she smelled like her own self instead of my darling wife."

"Bergamot oranges," the princess said.

"Oh, I should have told you, before you died."

"Father, I am Elia, your daughter. Not . . . Dalat."

It was hard even for Aefa to hear the name; she could only imagine the impossible effort it took Elia to speak it.

Lear looked at his daughter and seemed to see her finally. "Elia? Am I dead?"

"No, Father, I'm with you in the White Forest. Come with us, stand and go with me to Hartfare. You'll rest and be able to bathe, to eat and drink what you like. We will care for you—I will. I should never have left."

A frown marred his brow, made his nose seem overlong. All the wrinkles of his face bent toward the upset mouth. "I forced you away. I remember."

Elia nodded. "You did. But I . . . I love you."

Lear put his long, dry hands on her face, cradling it. "That is all you said before."

"It was not enough, then."

Aefa ground her teeth together but did not interrupt. That was the first lesson her father had taught her at court: to judge when to speak and when to be still. The most effective Fool—and friend—understood such a thing.

"I know, my love, I know, we never say enough." The king stared through Elia, seeing some other place. "I deserved nothing from your daughters," he whispered. "But I wished they loved me anyway. I could not tell them what happened— What? And take you away from them again? Lost once from life, and again from memory? But I see now—I saw in the storm, cold and hungry, oh so cold with nothing but myself, no stars, no love—how in being wrong I put on a mantle of rightness."

It was difficult for Aefa to follow his thoughts, but Elia held on to him, her expression listening, listening, as she did to the forest.

"But I loved you," he said, hands slipping off his daughter's face. The old king looked to the thin, trickling stream near his bare toes.

"Shh, Father," Elia whispered, putting her arms around him. She tucked her head against his shoulder. Aefa touched her own lips to keep silent.

"You trusted yourself," he said. "I did not trust anything but stars. I trusted them over us, over everything. Do you think they care if I trust them? Elia cares. Gaela cared, but not anymore. Regan . . . ah. It is too late, pretty spirit." Lear sank back, out of Elia's arms, and lowered himself onto the grassy hill again. "I should have trusted this, too." He fingered a leaf of the hemlock crown. "You weren't there, my star, but this is the island's crown. This is the island's star, these little white starbursts of poison. The king eats it, and drinks the rootwater. And the island keeps you alive; you belong to the island. That is how you become king. See? I have had poison, too, my love! I have had poison, too!" He laughed, shoulders shaking.

Elia drew her knees to her chest, hugging herself. For a long moment, Lear breathed and said nothing.

Aefa could stand it no more. She went to Elia's side and sat, leaning her shoulder against Elia's as the princess pressed her eyes against her knees. Lear had been freezing and hungry all night, Aefa thought; such suffering had stripped him to his most essential self, his nature revealed, and that nature was broken and trapped.

"He's been alone so long," Aefa whispered, and hugged her princess.

Elia asked, voice full of pity and raw need, "Do you think it's true? About the crown and the island and . . . my mother?"

But the old king interrupted with a sigh. "I should be blind, for all I have never been able to see."

His tender voice tore even at Aefa.

"Maybe," Elia said gently, unfolding herself to glance at him, "this is always what the stars saw. What was always meant to be. The two of us here, like this. Unnamed and uncrowned, Father, with our feet in the mud."

Her father laughed again, but gentler.

Elia put her palm to his cheek. "Maybe we had to go through this. I certainly did. To truly *become* your heir."

Lear stared at his youngest daughter, amazed.

"Maybe you did everything you had to do," she said. A sad smile bowed her lips: she had learned to couch the truth, and Aefa was both proud and stung by it. Elia said, "Be at peace. Maybe you did everything right."

"Maybe," he said, nodding his long head. The hemlock crown dragged down one temple, lopsided. He touched it carefully. "Did you know my daughter Elia . . . you, *you* would come in from an afternoon in the meadows and forest with a crown of flowers?"

Elia kissed him carefully. Then she glanced again at Aefa, and her lips trembled. Her eyelashes, even, seemed to shake. But Elia only said, "I remember."

# THE FOX

BAN THE FOX wandered his way north through the White Forest, a lightness to his step. If he could, in this dense forest, he'd run.

He might never complete his spell, but it was enough to carry the promise with him, a threat beneath his fingers instead of lodged, poisonous, in his heart.

Ban yelled his pride, leaping into the air, sharing his joy and his thanks with the trees. But instead of their fierce whispers, full of love—something darker seemed to echo back.

Wind crashed overhead, tossing the canopy. Yellow leaves rained down, and Ban stopped, closed his eyes. He could not quite grasp the words.

He swiveled, searching for water, or exposed roots: there, an elm leaned on raised earth, three roots curling through the grass like worms. Ban crouched by it, grasping the roots in both hands. He leaned down and whispered against the cool brown bark: *I'm listening.*

For a long moment, nothing changed. The snap of branches alerted him to the presence of a large animal. A very low crackle sounded nearby, small enough to be a slinking snake, just the brush of scale against deadfall, or a young rabbit hunched beneath ferns.

*Regan.*

The lonely name hissed on the wind, and Ban startled to his feet.

*Regan!* screamed the White Forest.

A wail came after, high and mournful.

*Regan Regan REGAN!*

*I'm coming,* he said to the wind. *Show me the way.*

*Ride,* said the elm tree, and the branches shuddered. From beyond them came a gentle, curious whicker. Startled, Ban said, "Horse?" He pushed around the old elm's roots and there it stood: the horse from Errigal Keep he'd lost in the storm. It—she—was ragged and still saddled; he ought to remove all the tack and rub her down, give her rest, but the wind snapped hard against the canopy.

*Regan!* The forest cried again.

Muttering an apology, Ban mounted and urged the horse after the wind.

FOR SEVERAL HOURS Ban rode, east and then slightly south, and then straight east again, galloping when he could to the farthest edge of the White Forest, where narrow fingers of it reached between high karst hills. He ate in the saddle, relieved himself only when he and the horse both needed water. In early afternoon they climbed one of the hills. The horse's hoof clopped on the naked stone, and Ban smelled salt on the wind.

Sun narrowed his eyes as he peered for some sign to follow. The wind blew steady and wordless, but moaned through the tiny crevasses in the karst. There would be sinkholes and caves here. There was little else about this part of the island Ban knew, except that if he found the road and turned north, by nightfall he'd be at Connley Castle.

"Regan?" Ban said plainly, then again in the language of trees.

Nothing but empty wind.

He squeezed his legs, and the horse walked on, picking carefully. An hour later, he smelled smoke through the shade of the valley. "Regan?" he yelled.

And after another few minutes, "Lady? Are you here?"

He stopped the horse and climbed down, wrapping the reins in one hand to guide her with him a few steps off the graveled road. Pine trees surrounded them, spicy and crisp, and Ban walked over a soft bed of fallen needles to touch his bare hand to the soft, thready bark of one.

*Sister,* he said, *where is Regan Lear?*

*Close, so close, but she will not speak to us, brother, we cannot hear her,* the tree whispered sadly.

Fear took his breath for a moment, but Ban still pressed his forehead to the tree and sighed a blessing onto her grove. *Still this way?*

*yesyesyes,* all the pines shivered and danced.

Ban couldn't think for the fear rushing through his veins to hiss in his ears. He moved on at his horse's side, pushing as fast as he could.

"Regan!" he cried again.

"Hello?"

It was not her voice, but another woman's. Ban dropped the horse's reins and hurried.

Even rushing he was still quiet, and thus startled the retainer who paced along the southwest perimeter of a small meadow camp. "Ah, shit!" she gasped when Ban appeared, wild, out of the trees. Helmetless, but wearing a rusty pink gambeson of Astore and mail sleeves, the woman went for the sword at her belt before recognizing him. "Ban Errigal."

"You came with messages from Gaela," Ban said. "Where is Regan?" He strode past the woman, toward a wagon unhitched from the pair of horses set to snorfling at what used to be long grass and clover.

"There, sir," the retainer said, but Ban had already seen.

Two unmoving bodies.

Regan curled beside a thicket of hawthorn roots, from which sprung a short, bent tree with no leaves, only dozens and dozens of bloodred berries. Her long dark hair was loose over her back and covering her face, spread in a fan of curls over Connley's chest.

The duke was dead.

His lovely eyes had not closed completely, leaving a slit of blue-green to shine in the light. Blood speckled otherwise bloodless lips, and yet more dried blood cracked against the splayed-open jacket, his torn shirt still half wrapped about him, along with a surprisingly untarnished bandage. One hand hid beneath Regan; the other lay at his side, palm open and empty.

Ban could not move. Not Connley, no.

*No.*

"Regan," he whispered, then noticed her shoulders shift very slightly with breath.

Sinking to his knees under the weight of stunned grief, Ban suddenly had a sick, confusing thought: his father might not be dead after all. Air passed Ban's lips and over his tongue, filling his lungs, but he could not feel it. Ban was choking on life, gasping and dull.

"She won't move," the Astore retainer said, pressing. "I can't get her to answer me, or eat or drink."

"What happened?" he managed to whisper.

"Connley and Errigal killed each other."

"He's . . . he's dead, then."

The retainer put her hand on Ban's shoulder. "Since last night. Though Connley lasted almost past dawn. Regan wanted to take him home. She was trying to save him."

Ban struggled to his feet and moved to the fallen couple. "Regan," he said, then knelt again, touching Connley's arm first. It was cool, and some stiffness of death had set in. Ban shook his head, protesting. The body should have been cleaned before that, or buried in roots. Regan could have—should have—asked the roots to take him, fresh still, for the worms of dreams and rebirth to feast upon. He said so, in the language of trees, but quietly. The hawthorn shivered; its roots rippled in agreement.

Regan clutched her husband's body, her taut, trembling arms the only sign she was aware of anything else in the world.

Ban kissed Connley's forehead. He could not press the eyelids closed.

Tears flooded Ban's throat. He leaned his forehead on Connley's, smelling sour death and urine and the full, bright scent of limestone and clay. Stars and worms, Ban was sorry. He shouldn't have left the Keep. He should have remained to see his father dealt with, remained and—and witnessed. If he had not been with Elia, might he have saved Connley's life?

Turning, he put his hands on Regan. "Lady, you must let go. Help me put him in the roots."

Nothing.

"Regan." Ban shifted nearer to her, wrapped his arm around her back, and brushed her cool mass of brown hair away from her face, gathering it together gently. Her eyes tightened shut at his care. She was peaked and splotchy, her lovely cheeks streaked with blood and dirt and tearstain.

"No," she whispered, as harsh as winter rain.

"Yes, Regan. Come with me."

She shuddered, then looked. "Ban?" Her voice was soft and lost.

He nodded and kissed her temple. He left his lips there, blowing warm breath into her hair. She shuddered again and in one swift move thrust up and seized him.

"Gone," she said, low in her throat. "There is no more of Connley at all, anywhere."

"I know," he said, holding her with all his strength. Using it to prop up his own heart.

The lady did not cry, but she held on to him long, as the sun moved away, the breeze lilted east to southeast, and shadows fell all around. Ban listened to the hush, to Gaela's retainer trudging back to the small fire and stirring it up again, evidence of her discomfort and attempt to give them privacy. Evening birds came out to sing, against the discordant tune of crickets.

"It's time," Ban said finally, stroking Regan's tangled hair.

They stood. Regan stared hollowly down at her husband, while Ban faced the hawthorn.

*Take him,* he said. *This is His Highness, Tear Connley of Innis Lear, a part of this island born, and part of it forever.*

The hawthorn shivered, tiny clusters of haws blinking in the twilight.

Regan said, *He saw me.* She gripped her belly hard enough to pinch her flesh through the shift she wore.

Roots lifted up from the earth, stretching, reaching for Connley. The shadows yawned, and the wind said, *With us.*

Behind them, the horses shied away from the trembling ground. Clay parted, roots looped up, grasping the duke's neck and wrists, his waist and thighs and feet. They pulled him down, into the earth.

Regan cried out wordlessly, up at the first stars filtering through the twilight.

Connley vanished, embraced by the hawthorn at last.

"I'm sorry," Ban said, staring where the duke had just been, longing to see that unique color of Connley's eyes once more, or marvel at the ambitious twist of his mouth. Regan heaved and nearly collapsed, but Ban caught her.

"It's my fault," he said, thinking of his cowardice at having fled the Keep last night.

The lady fell still against him. Dangerously still.

Blood sang in his ears: he was at her mercy, suddenly, beholden to a wolf who'd just lost her mate.

"No," Regan said, leaning away. In this newborn darkness, she was an eerie tree-shadow, a haunting spirit. Her crystalline eyes flicked to her husband's shallow grave. "This is the fault of our fathers."

The truth of it took his breath away.

And Ban could make both their fathers pay. As if everything had whispered and urged him to just this moment, with every breeze at his ear and choice in his heart, since the sun rose this morning. Or even longer. Since he'd come home from Aremoria, since he'd fallen in love with a star, since he'd been born.

Before he thought any deeper, Ban pulled the walnut from his jacket, dropped it onto the earth, and crushed it beneath his heel.

# ELIA

THE KING DID not wish to leave his meadow.

Elia urged their return to Hartfare before dark, but Lear sank stubbornly back against the earth, or pretended to be asleep, or simply ignored her. His eyes drifted up and up, always toward the pale blue sky, awaiting the absent stars.

Finally, Elia asked Aefa to return to Hartfare for dinner, to gather blankets and whatever else she and her father might need to sleep under the stars. The girl began to protest, but Elia smiled sadly and promised the trees and wind would warn her of danger. It would be a clear night, and they would manage until her return.

Aefa left at a run, and Elia sat down beside the king again. She said, "My Aefa will come back with blankets, with wine and some bread, and you and I will curl up to watch the stars be born. How does that sound, Father?"

He sighed contentedly, and leaned back onto the grass, and fell truly asleep.

Overwhelmed with affection, with fear and longing—and anger—Elia picked up his hand and clasped it in hers. He was so ruined, so wracked by madness and guilt, she shouldn't be angry. She did not have the luxury, though she wished, for a fleeting moment, that she could rage and hate him, as Ban had done.

Struggling for peace, Elia simply closed her eyes and whispered to the nearby ash tree. *I'm listening.*

*So are we,* the ash tree said, shaking a little so that three oval leaves drifted down to kiss the rushing creek beside them.

Elia remembered another ash tree, at the heart of her mother's garden at Dondubhan. It had been the queen's sanctuary against the harsh winters of the far north. Cherry trees had bloomed a blushing pink, and juniper had always been green, with tiny pale blue berries in the fall. But the ash itself had leaned over the queen's favorite bench. The morning Dalat had died, the first black buds had peeked out from the pale branches, later to bloom into deep purple flowers. Roses hugged the keep wall, the barren vines hooked against the huge gray stones. Elia, only eight years old, fled from her sisters to the garden, going first to the rose vines. She grasped one in her hand, squeezing the copper thorns until they hurt, until the curved spikes bit into her skin. The pain had focused Elia away from her churning stomach, and away from her uncertain but swollen grief.

A cold wind had blown gently through the evergreen fingers of the juniper, shaking its voice in sad little gasps to mirror her own muffled panting.

*Elia Elia Elia,* the wind seemed to whisper.

Her face had crumpled. She'd let free a wail, small as a kitten's cry, and closed her eyes. That morning, it had felt the only way: releasing the hurt a bit at a time, through soft cries and the pricks on her palm. Would pain melt out of her along with her blood?

"Elia," someone said.

It was no tree voice, or the wind, but a woman. Elia let go of the rose vine, but the thorns stuck in her flesh and she stopped.

Someone spoke in the language of trees. Elia could only understand, then, two words: *rose* and *you.* She did not move except to glance sideways.

A boy had stood there, not the woman who'd spoken before. He was her size, with ruddy cheeks and a thicket of black hair in tangles like a wild thing. His eyes were mud-gray and chipped with green. He repeated himself.

"I don't understand," Elia had said, tears in her eyes. "My sister only teaches me words that my mother wants to hear."

Behind them both, the woman spoke again. "He said the roses don't want to let you go."

Elia had choked on a cry, nodding and shaking. "My mother is dead."

The words themselves became the ocean of grief in her chest, and so Elia did not breathe for a long moment.

"I know," the woman said. She stepped to Elia, touching the princess's thin shoulder. It was Brona, the queen's friend, and witch of the White Forest. "This is my son, Ban. Do you remember him?"

Elia did not think she'd met the boy before, and she glanced at him more curiously. He did not smile or frown, only studied her with those large muddy eyes.

"I will ask them to let you go," he'd said finally, then whispered to the roses.

The vine shuddered and sighed, and the wind teased Elia's loose cloud of hair, without touching Ban's or his mother's.

And with a little extra shiver, the rose thorns released Elia's flesh. She'd pulled her hand back, and Ban snatched her wrist instead in his small, dry hand. Before she could speak, he had touched the smears of blood in her palm and drew three marks on the skin. "Thank you," he said, and then, *Thank you,* this time in the language of trees.

*Thank you,* Elia had repeated.

Ban tugged her hand and then pressed her palm against the bark of the nearby cherry tree. *Elia Lear,* he'd whispered.

Then the door to Elia's bedroom had crashed open, echoing through the empty garden, and her father, the king, called her name.

"Your mother loved you," Brona the witch had said as Elia pulled herself free of Ban. Elia backed away, shaking her head. There had been too much inside her, too many unnamed winds and currents still lifting, growing, pushing out and out to overwhelm her heart.

The boy Ban had vanished in a scatter of grass and fallen leaves, rushing away, and Brona had smiled sadly at Elia, then bent to pick something out of the roots of a cherry tree. She tucked whatever it was into her skirts and left, too.

Elia had turned to face her father, who strode blindly toward her, kicking his nightrobe and long blue coat in his hurry. His feet were bare. He'd picked her up under her arms and hugged her too tightly.

His hair smelled of Dalat's bergamot oil, and Elia had wrapped her arms around him, burying her face in his neck.

"Oh, Elia," the king had murmured, "Oh, my baby, my little star. You won't leave me. Never."

"No, Father," she'd whispered.

Hitching her onto his hip, though she was eight and wild and gangly, he'd carried her to Dalat's bench. They sat, Lear cradling Elia and crying, too. She'd gripped the edge of his coat, crusted as it was with embroidered stars. Dalat had let Elia sew three of them, up near the collar, and she touched one with her finger. The king shook, and Elia smeared her tears onto his chest.

"The stars promised this day would be as it is," the king had whispered, his nose in Elia's hair. His breath hissed through the curls to warm her scalp. "We can only give in to them, my star. They see all, and know what will become of all of us. You, you were born under Calpurlugh, the loyal and constant Child Star. My heart, my star princess."

Elia held tightly to him. The cherry trees bent around them, sheltering the princess and the king in their grief.

*Thank you,* she whispered in the language of trees.

"No." Her father sat up straight. A certain fire lit his eyes. "None of that."

Elia touched his cheek. The lines of his face pulled harder this morning, heavy with grief and age, and through her watery vision she saw a shimmer of gray in his short beard, just beside his ear. Like a spray of late starlight.

"No tree tongue?" she asked, confused. It had been the natural language of Innis Lear since the island rose from the sea.

"Nothing but stars now," the king vowed.

He took her chin in long white hands.

"The stars are all for Innis Lear."

THE STARS ARE *not all,* a much older Elia whispered now, in the language of her island.

She studied her palms for scars, as if their memory could repair the scars grown over her heart.

The king shivered and woke. He grumbled to himself, "The wind is not listening."

"It is," Elia said. "Especially while the stars are hidden by the light of day."

"They still watch us, always guiding our path," he argued, but without any heat.

Elia tilted her head back to search the sky. The sun had lowered beyond the western trees, and overhead all was creamy pink and sheer violet.

*The girl is returning, and more. Family,* said the ash tree.

Elia kissed her father's sagging fingers and stood. There, at the southeast edge of the meadow, they appeared: seven or eight folk from Hartfare, as well as all those promised by the trees. She waved, lifting onto her tiptoes. Aefa waved back.

A large fur was spread on the soft ground, and several woolen blankets. Elia got her father atop them, and gave him some wine. He nodded regally, as if the drooping hemlock crown he still wore was made of gold, as if his tattered robe were imported silk. Aefa pressed bread into Elia's hand, stuffed with sliced apples and pieces of cheese, and then after, a cup of wine, too. Dizzy and oddly at peace, Elia devoured it all, then went wandering along the creek, against the current. The water seemed to call her, babbling just under its breath. *This way, this way,* it seemed to say, though the words were not in any language she knew. More a tug at her heart, a rightness in her feet.

The sky dimmed, spreading violet and cream across the meadow, to the song of evening birds and laughter.

"Elia," the king called.

She went to him, kneeling.

"What will we see first?" he asked, tilting his head back. He reclined on his elbows and years seemed to melt away.

Elia lay beside him, so he could toy with her curls. As a child, she'd move her eyes as she searched for a star, certain that whichever was first sighted contained a message just for her.

Now, Elia knew from study and habit where stars would appear, their secrets predictable and universal. The Star of First Birds would be to the northwest, higher than the last time she'd watched for it. To the true north, Calpurlugh would appear, though it was autumn and so it would be the Eye of the Lion, not Elia's Child Star. If she looked east the Autumn Throne would rise, and the Tree of Sorrow, with its long roots. The trees in the west were too high for her to see the Hound, but she knew it would arc there soon.

The evening breathed cool air across their noses, and the king sipped his wine. Elia's cheeks were warm from hers already. She drifted, thinking of stars, and asked the wind, *Which direction shall I look?* It said, *We blow from the north.*

Elia turned her face with it and watched the southern sky through half-closed eyes.

"Ah, there is Lasural!" her father said, pointing to a single glint of light. "The tip of the Thorn. What do you see?"

"The Sisters," she whispered. "All five pushing out there in the south."

"Yes. So. Hmm. I suppose that is—is sacrifice for mine, a surprise of it, and for yours . . ."

"The wind blows from the north, so we should consider Lasural leading toward the Sisters."

The king of Innis Lear grunted. "The wind is—"

"Of the island, Father, it . . ."

Elia's answer trailed away as she heard a vast, sudden noise, a gathering noise, like the ocean's roar. She sat up, turning toward it: southeast.

A tempest of air and screams surged toward them, bending around and through the White Forest, tossing birds into the sky. It blew hard enough that Elia grabbed both the nearly empty bottle of wine and her father's wrist, squeezing closed her eyes, worried about which might do more damage if released into the shocking squall. Her hair tore and pulled; her skirts slapped hard.

Then the wind was gone.

Vanished, as if it had never been.

In the empty silence, birds struggled against the purple sky. Trees shivered, leaves tossing wildly, but slowly, slowly settling.

Elia let go her breath in a long sigh and put down the wine.

"Oh, Father, that was . . . that was too strange. Do you think the stars felt it, even?"

The old king said nothing.

She looked over to him, searching. Through the dim purple light, she saw her father reclined fully, lips parted, eyes still open. His hair was a wild tangle, twisted together with the half-torn crown of hemlock. His wrist was limp in her hand.

"Father?"

Leaning over him, she shook his shoulders.

Nothing.

He did not move. He did not *breathe*.

"Father!" she yelled. "Aefa! Kayo!" Elia grabbed her father's chin and looked into his faded blue eyes. But Lear did not return the gaze: his eyes were empty.

Elia gasped, and then did so again, knives stabbing her lungs. She held her breath and swallowed her terror. She put her cheek over his mouth. Waited to feel anything, for his tender breath to reach her.

She heard the pounding of feet as her uncle thundered closer, followed by all who'd camped nearby.

But there was nothing for them to do. Nothing could be done at all.

The king of Innis Lear was dead.

# Part
# FIVE

To Elia, daughter of Innis Lear,

I can no longer sit by, knowing what I have done. I have planted a canker in the heart of your island, and having heard from him a final word I must

To Elia, daughter of Innis Lear,

I hope you have found your father and are making progress toward your goals. I must tell you that Ban is—Ban has

To Elia, daughter of Innis Lear,

Ban has betrayed me. He sent a message, his final message, and he has chosen the island. Or you. I hope it is you, because that, at least, I understand. No, I

To Elia, daughter of Innis Lear,

Last night I went onto my balcony and listened to the Aremore wind. It tugged my attention toward the river, smelling of fire and crisp red leaves. Do you know that smell? I do not know what causes it, for there are no flowers now, but there is a shift in the taste of the air in this month. I have held a dead, curling leaf to my nose and smelled nothing. Yet, I associate it with this season, when the trees in Lionis burn red and orange. This season. Tomorrow is my birth anniversary, when we hold a grand festival in honor of Aremore. Some years it coincides with the autumnal equinox, though not this year. There will be a parade that lasts hours in the morning, throughout my city, and in the afternoon we open the palace to all, entertaining ourselves with players *and song, with applicants from my state library, hoping to impress me with their ideas. I wish*

*Elia, daughter of Innis Lear,*

*Elia,*

*Oak Earl,*
   *I hope this finds you, unhoused as you are.*
   *I have received word from Innis Lear and find myself determined to join you on your island. I must see through what I have begun. For not knowing whose eyes might see this dispatch, I hesitate to reveal details, except to say I will arrive at Port Comlack at the beginning of the dark moon week.*

*—M*

# RORY

RORY COULD RECALL, if he cast his memory back far enough, his youthful attendance at festivals on Innis Lear. The Longest Night was always a solemn occasion for vigils and for honoring ancestors and planting iron stakes at the front door if there were young children in the house. To keep away the hungriest earth saints. The summer solstice festival had been alive with laughter and dancing, costumes of feathers and wild fires; there'd been a harvest festival as well, when the hardest work of summer ended and everything was slaughtered for the winter. He'd celebrated that at the Keep with his parents, by burning sharp incense in all the rooms so the ghostly hounds of the earth saints could not smell properly to hunt anyone down, dragging them into the sky forever. In the spring there'd been a festival for all babes born that year, to name them and cast birth charts and share prophecies. That one Rory had the clearest memory of, for it had continued the most intact throughout his life.

Every festival on Innis Lear, when he contemplated them now, seemed purposed to bring light or laughter or togetherness like a shield over some darker, more dangerous promise. The earth saints will steal your children if you don't celebrate them! Watch out for the howling dogs riding the wind or they'll snatch you into oblivion! This summer we wear feathers and drink sweet nectar to become the birds of the sky, to balance in careful, ecstatic joy between the wind and worms—but beware leaning too far into the fire, or straying toward the darkest shadows! If you do not remember your name, you might never return to your body! And the star prophecies always, always worked to offer a path of hope against inevitable doom and death.

How strange it felt, then, for this Aremore celebration to be, as far as Rory could tell, nothing but pageantry and fun.

It was the king's birthday, and everyone in the country—certainly everyone in Lionis—was happy. Streamers colored rainbows across the sky, and petals fell like snow; whistles and tambourines played raucous music; the squares were filled with players and spiral dances and vendors with grilled meat and apple cider; the king himself had begun the day with a dawn parade that stretched from the outer gates of the city through the vibrant white streets, winding and cutting back on itself, until after hours and hours Morimaros had visited every neighborhood. He had smiled, laughed, waved, with his sister and nephew riding at his flanks. Behind came bright clowns and acrobats, then men and women in massive, glittering masks turning their faces into crystal moons like the beautiful earth saints of old; next giant puppets of paper and plaster, decorated with voluminous robes and crowns made of glass. These were the line of Aremore kings, stretching a thousand years. Behind rode any person with a horse who'd turned twenty-two in the year before, the age Morimaros had been when he inherited the throne. Some were noble, others merchants or those in a trade, or students from the great library of Aremore; some were even from the poorer neighborhoods, having banded together to hire a horse, or won the chance from one of the Elder Queen Calepia's charity funds. Even some foreigners joined in the parade: young men and women in the vibrant, striped scarves of the Third Kingdom; others in the ruffles of Ispania with their hair parted by jeweled fans at the tops of their heads; the furred and steel-gleaming folk from the Rusrike.

Rory's eyes still blurred from the glitter and spectacle.

He hovered now in the broad open front court of Lionis Palace, one of hundreds crowding the space. Near the arched double doors leading into the palace a dais had been erected, hung with brilliant orange banners. The king of Aremoria sat upon a white throne, resplendent in orange velvet and pristine linen. A crown of gold gleamed at his brow. Cup of cider in hand, Morimaros spoke with whomever approached—it was a long, winding line—for a moment or two, focused and engaged. Gifts accumulated behind him on the dais, accepted by the Twice-Princess Ianta and passed into the hands of lion-liveried attendants.

The cider flowed freely, dipped into cups from great barrels and cauldrons, and edging the yard were tables laden with all manner of bread and fruit, and cheeses molded into lions, as well as tiny candies and lion-shaped fondants. Folk pressed and laughed, waved at friends, and gathered around the pockets of musicians. There would be performers later: more players and puppeteers, clowns, and even a series of eager students who'd been granted the opportunity to present their king with new inventions or ideas he might implement.

Rory should've been perfectly at ease.

In Aremoria, when he roused himself to his habitual charm and natural—though now somewhat strained—affability, Rory was popular. He smiled at the servants and carried water for the girls bringing him a bath, then shrugged so casually at the shocked footmen that they couldn't bring themselves to judge him for not knowing his place. The captain of the palace guard, La Far, welcomed Rory to join him in morning exercise, and therefore Rory was accepted by the rest of the Aremore soldiers. At evening meals, Rory was solicitous of the noble ladies, earning their sympathy; what lords and husbands might initially direct suspicion upon him were mostly caught out by Rory's earnest engagement. He was simply one of those men for whom relationships and society came easy, as he was handsome, loving, and expected the best of all those he encountered. It all sprung from the confidence of place, from knowing exactly what status he held in the world, and the never-before-undercut assumption that nothing would change: he would always be safe, well-liked, and respected by his kin, his people, and his peers and betters.

Only now, it felt oddly hollow.

Dreams plagued him that the earth crumbled beneath his feet, as did this constant feeling that he was not where he was supposed to be. *Go home,* that voice told him, but folk he trusted most had asked him to stay away. His brother, Elia herself, the impossibly practical Aefa, Kay Oak, and even the good king Morimaros, when he had managed to find time to sit with Rory. They all had implored Rory to be patient, to wait until the time was right.

The insistence that he remain tucked away in Aremoria felt less like concern, and more as though Rory were being dismissed.

He continued to smile, to flirt and charm, to listen and converse sincerely, yet through it all the urge to be elsewhere distracted him like a constant itch, even ruining such a brilliant festival day as this.

Behind him a bird squawked, and he whirled sharply around, nearly spilling the too-full cup of cider in his hand. A boy stood there, and behind him a tall man holding a pole with a perch at its top. Tethered there was a parrot, head cocked and tail flared. Rory did not think the parrot appreciated all this spectacle. But he smiled at the boy. It was Isarnos, son of Twice-Princess Ianta, and heir to the throne of Aremoria.

"You're Ban the Fox's brother, aren't you?"

Rory managed to withhold the cringe. He turned it into a brighter smile instead. "Ban the Fox is *my* brother," he said, and winked.

Isarnos eyed him suspiciously, as if he did not understand the distinction.

Truly, there only was one in Rory's mind—or, he suspected, in that of any person from Innis Lear. But he'd become rather tired of the implication that Ban was better, more known here in Aremoria, even though it was absolutely true. Rory had fostered here for three years and had been perfectly adept at war, but he was always meant to return home to Errigal and be the earl. While Ban had been banished here and by hardship and magic earned a wild yet strong reputation even these civilized Aremore folk admired—if with a tinge of fear. Rory did not like being overshadowed by his brother's taller reputation, did not like being defined by Ban's achievements. He was used to being his father's son, the future Earl Errigal, as was natural and expected, and that was the definition of title, place, and self he understood.

This constant suggestion that he was second to Ban aggravated Rory and chafed at his pride now, as it never had before.

"I wish I had a brother," Isarnos continued.

"As you should!" Rory exclaimed, crouching to put his face slightly lower than the prince's. "Brothers are grand—when I was your age, my brother and I used to charge about ruins and play we were valiant warriors, or sometimes earth saints ridding the world of the massive old worms."

"Dragons!" Isarnos said. "Did you have dogs?"

"We did, sometimes."

"Can you do magic?"

Rory winced, letting it be exaggerated. "No, alas, I cannot do any magic, though Ban promised once to teach me some. Did he ever teach you?"

"I was too little, my mother said. But he showed me fire in his hand, and he could talk to my birds and the barracks kittens."

"That seems a very valuable skill. He ought to have taught you."

Isarnos pursed his lips and nodded hard. "How come your brother went back to Innis Lear? Why isn't he here with you?"

"He . . ." Rory paused. The exultant noise of the crowd washed over them, and the parrot flapped its emerald wings. "He's taking care of our father, and . . . and there are many things at home to be looked after. He's very good at looking after them."

"Wizards have to be. And brothers, too, I suppose."

Rory agreed, though it sank in, all of it—the itch to go home, his vanity and resentment—and he understood for perhaps the first time that Ban had every reason to never want Rory to reappear.

"I hope," he said slowly, "you'll get a good wizard of your own, when you're king. And that you'll count me a friend on Innis Lear."

The prince lifted his chin and stared at Rory with eyes a shade lighter than the king's. "But you're here. Will you go back to Ban and trade him to us again?"

Rory laughed—it was rather like a trade. "I might!"

And then he stopped cold. Though he was loath to admit to blame, he knew it had been his long-ago confession to his father about Ban and Elia's love that had banished his brother here. Rory had been at fault for pushing his brother out of Innis Lear, though it hadn't been his intention. Ban did not know—at least Rory did not think so.

*"Trust me, Rory," Ban said. "Go."*

*"Some villain has done me wrong," Rory murmured back.*

No, Rory refused the weave of that thought. His own banishment could not—*could not*—be Ban's fault.

But the courtyard reeled around him, and Rory felt the dizzying sensation from his dreams that somewhere he could not yet see, the city had begun to crumble.

"I have to—go, Your Highness," he said to Isarnos, and the prince's face fell, but he nodded.

Rory pushed into the crowd. There the royal guard lined the courtyard and watched from balconies for any danger; there the king's dais; there a tight circle of musicians with lyres and fiddles; there—there his own mother, a glittering, ginger bird in a huddle of Alsax and Rennai cousins. She saw him, too, and smiled politely: they had little enough to say to each other. Lady Dirbha Errigal had carved a place here in Aremoria, cut her Learish bonds.

He had asked, when she'd happened upon Rory last week at the Alsax townhouse, "Why, Mother, did you never come home?"

She had eyed him imperiously, shocked at his presumption. "And what?"

"Be—well, take your . . ." Rory had stumbled, for he'd not truly known the shape of his question.

Dirbha took pity on her son and said, "Your father breaks the rules. Why do you think you are here? He chose his bastard over his true-gotten son."

Rory had shaken his head. "That is not what happened! And I will go home, to be the earl, eventually. When everything is restored."

"Your father does not restore unless it suits him. He and I were bound together by the laws of Innis Lear, beneath the stars. That is how it should be, and yet, your father loved . . . *her* . . ."

"I loved you," Rory said.

Dirbha touched his hand. "It was not a lack of love that kept me away. I thought you knew. The thing that tore my title, my self-respect, my home from me was the bastard. That child was proof that my place on Innis Lear was nothing compared to your father's. Proof flaunted and then manifest. How could I trust your father's word, or his faith, or that anything he said mattered, if he would thrust before me evidence of how he only did what served his selfish desires? What is star prophecy if he manipulated it to his benefit? What is marriage but a battlefield if he strategized how to win? Marriage—love!—is no war. There should be no enemies, but only friends. Yet he made an enemy of my heart with that singular weapon."

"Ban," Rory had whispered.

His mother's entire body shuddered. The silence following had been a pretty one, tempered by music from delicate wind chimes ringing dimly through the window glass.

"I will not live in a place where I am so constrained, but the men around me are not," she'd said softly. "That woman—the witch—she lived her own life, but there were consequences for her, too. I hate her, I cannot help it, but she wasn't the one who broke his own laws. That was only your father, and all the others who looked away, who laughed or accepted his behavior."

"That still is not Ban's fault," Rory had whispered.

"No, it is not, but he remains the constant reminder of it."

Ban, Ban, Ban, it was all Ban: Rory hardly knew his own name when people looked at him and always saw the other. *Oh, it's the Fox's brother— What handsome men they have on Innis Lear— Have you heard, he was banished by his own father! Those people are strange! Superstition and star prophecy ruining lives—and their princess gone again, suddenly, will she return? She was too wild to be our queen—the folk of Innis Lear are better spies and wizards than kings and queens! The Fox's brother! Oh! This one could never hide—such hair! Will he, too, earn the confidence of our Mars?*

Rory's mother had spoken again, looking firmly into her son's eyes. "I can live with it all here in Aremoria, with the order and constraints that I could not bear under the colder, sharper sky of Innis Lear."

She'd asked Rory if *he* would stay, or if the claws of the island had hooked in his heart. *Will it ruin you?* his mother's voice asked in his crumbling dreams.

Innis Lear was his place. Rory was the heir to the earldom; he belonged there and wanted it. Elia had gone home because Innis Lear was hers. She'd been cast out by her father but not let it define her. What was Rory doing but playing a sorry victim? Even Ban had never let his bastardy or dragon's tail moon define him.

All his life, Rory had been promised his name.

But maybe he needed to go home and live up to it.

# THE FOX

WHITE-AND-GRAY BANNERS HUNG from the ramparts of Dondubhan Castle, crowning it with grief. The fabric snapped in the constant, furious wind. As they rode closer, Ban thought it impossible Astore should know Connley had died, and so decided they must be mourning flags in honor of another. Perhaps the soldiers recently killed in the fighting along the ducal border, or some minor retainer gone on in age. It mattered not to Ban.

Ahead of him, Regan Lear swayed with the rhythm of her horse's gait. Her back still held straight, never showing the weariness with which they all melted, having ridden hard the last three days from the eastern shores of Innis Lear here to the base of the Jawbone Mountains at the high north. A silent, rough progress they'd made, with Regan hardly eating, eyes sunken to purplish bruises, a permanent tightness to her mouth. Osli had braided Regan's hair into loops after the lady had torn out her first, more intricate style. But now the simple plaits hung bedraggled, and the hem of that once-fine gown was filthy, her embroidered slippers torn. Only her posture proclaimed Regan a queen. Ban and Osli fared not much better, for food had been scarce, as Regan hardly allowed them to pause to hunt while the sun shone.

The woeful party arrived, finally, having angled first to Astora, only to be told by retainers from Carrisk at the road's bend that Gaela had already led two raids, pushing at the Connley border, and now gathered her forces back at Dondubhan, another half a day north.

Ban should have been chilled to realize the trees had not whispered to him about the raids, nor gossiped about what death put mourning banners atop these ramparts. Except that the trees no longer spoke to him.

The wind blew constantly, voicelessly. It had never stopped since Ban cracked open the walnut shell, unleashing his furious magic.

Ban listened intently, but heard nothing in the sharp breeze: no angry snarls from the small hawthorns or cherries they passed, nor the shiver of voices in the long grasses of the moor. No calling birds or chattering crickets.

Nothing.

The voice of the island was simply gone.

He alone seemed to notice. Regan listened only to the dull silence of her own grief, and Osli focused on the processes of travel. If any town folk or farmers were afraid of or upset by the new silence, or by this constant, whining wind, they did not come looking to the roads for help or answers. Was it possible the island shunned only him? Ban the Fox, who had killed the king?

No, it could not be true. He had set this island free.

At dawn, Ban had murmured *Good morning* and received no response. He'd put his cheek to twisting gray roots and asked, *Are you listening?* He had called out to the rustle of branches that hid small animals, next to a formation of swans nestled at the frosty edges of a pond. None acknowledged him.

As they rode around the Star Field, Ban stared at the piles of island stones, at the altars covered in pale candles, at the trio of gray-robed priests casting a star reading in the center, bent and huddled and still as hoary statues. Could they feel the change in the wind, sense the dangerous silence? Soon he would have to tell them—someone—that the king, too, was dead.

Then Dondubhan Castle appeared.

Ban had not quite remembered the brutal grandeur of this fortress, nor the huge, rippling black waters of the Tarinnish. As a boy he'd been overwhelmed by its size, the number of families it could contain, and the power embodied in every large chunk of blue-gray stone. But Elia had lived here, and so Ban had loved it.

At the open gate they were challenged, until Osli called out their names and Regan lifted her face in a portrait of disdain. The beardless, clear-eyed soldier who spoke wore white on his sleeve, and said, "The lady will have to be informed of your arrival. None are allowed inside but her retainers, not since Astore's death."

Stunned, Ban glanced at Regan, who shuddered and clutched her reins tight enough the leather cut into her palms. Osli began to ask what had happened, but the lady Regan cut her off, caring nothing for another dead man.

"Stand aside," Regan ordered, suddenly livid and alive, and then pushed her horse on through the long, dark tunnel arch. Ban hurried after on his own steed; the stone floor off the tunnel gave way to a packed-earth yard.

Regan dismounted, tossing the reins to a soldier dashing up. "Take me to my sister. See these two loyal retainers fed and sheltered, then in an hour bring the Fox to us."

Ban slid off his horse. "My lady," he said, hoping to halt her. He'd rather go into this fortress at her side. But Regan pierced him with a look. She shook her head, and in the language of trees said, *I need my sister only.*

Bowing, Ban let himself begin to feel the hours of exhaustion, and cold, and hunger. It was a relief, too, to hear the language of trees after four days of silence, even from another human.

As Regan was led quickly away, Osli turned to him and said, "I must make my report to the commander and discover what happened. You'll do all right on your own?"

A tinge of humor was buried under her words, and so Ban summoned up a small smile. The retainer recognized that Ban had always been on his own, and would continue to survive it well. They'd discovered a tense camaraderie on the journey: nearly the same age, both outsiders on their chosen paths, dedicated to these royal sisters. Osli was as devoted to Gaela and therefore the lady Regan as Ban had once been to Morimaros, for Gaela, too, had given Osli the opportunity to make herself in her own image. Ban hoped, for her sake, that Osli never turned so capable of betrayal as he himself.

She offered her hand, and Ban clasped it.

A young man in Astore pink, but without the trappings of a retainer, fetched Ban and brought him into Dondubhan Castle.

Though the outer wall and barbican was a looming fortress of thick rock peppered with narrow-eyed arrow slits, inside, the castle keep itself spread much more elegantly, with dark wood and pale limestone arches and massive towers of blue-gray stone. It had glass windows as tall as Ban himself, and central trees planted in the interior that lifted high to give shade to the courtyards. Blue banners clung to the walls, most striped now with undyed wool for mourning. Ban was dumped in a lower-level room, one that he suspected by the stark furnishings was often reserved for star priests. Before the servant left, Ban caught his arm. "What happened to the Lord Astore?"

The young man grimaced. "Killed, by our lady," he said, before leaving swiftly.

Ban shook off his disconcertment and did his best, in the narrow quarters, to rinse his body and scrub dirt from his scalp. He had no razor, but thanks to Ban's maternal bloodline his beard never grew in thick, covering his jaw only softly with black hair, not too patchy, nor too unkempt. Keeping his mind as empty as possible, he warmed himself dry by the fire before reluctantly putting his dirty clothes back on. As he waited for his summons, Ban removed the little braids still stuck in his hair. He ran his fingers through for want of a comb, and bound it all back in a single short tail. Chunks and wisps fell around his face.

Ban paced, putting his thoughts in order: he must confess to having seen—spoken with—Elia, at Hartfare. That she was searching for Lear, and she wished to meet with both Gaela and Regan south at Errigal Keep, that she hoped still to find a plan for peace. Elia now knew of his former loyalty to Morimaros—his treason to Innis Lear. Ban considered confessing that, too, but whereas it hurt Elia, it would likely only inspire rage in her sisters. They would deal worse with the treachery.

Ban turned to the window and leaned out. The sky was a cold blue, clouds moving faster than they ought. This room overlooked the choppy Tarinnish, not the inner courtyards and garden lanes, and Ban was glad, since the dark and tumultuous waters did reflect his spirit.

He wasn't sure he could bear seeing the gardens and verdant nooks, the havens of his fearsome youth. Once in a garden here, Elia had whispered to him that she dreamed of him, that she saw him next to her always. And once they had kissed in the rose garden, near enough to prick their sleeves on the thorns where he had first laid eyes on her, near enough that the early buds had exploded into full blossom. Once, he'd put his head in her lap and let himself doze there; her fingers played against his bottom lip and tangled in his hair. Once Ban had been hopeful, and impossibly happy. Once, he'd not remembered to guard his heart.

And so of course, it did not last: there came the memory of the hardened face of his father at dawn, and the sneering, proud king, and the realization that she would let him go, that he would be forever alone.

Putting his forehead to the wall, Ban tried to empty his mind again. The cold of the stone seeped into his skin.

He must tell Gaela and Regan he'd killed King Lear.

It was a weight Ban could not quite shrug off. Not for loyalty or sympathy for the loss of a father, nor for regrets—this was by no means the first man the Fox had led to his death. No, he was glad the old man was gone, but Ban had not guessed that this utter, devastating *silence* would ever be the consequence.

Innis Lear itself grieved the terrible old man, despite his rejection of rootwater and magic, his injury to the land itself. The island wept and wailed, but still it did not *speak*.

The king's death should have been a triumph, a gleeful, malicious satisfaction sweet on Ban's tongue. Instead, his stomach knotted anxiously.

Finally, there came the knock to summon him. Ban leapt at the door, composing himself once more as he was led through the narrow castle corridors. Despite broad windows, Gaela's room was suffocating and closed up, brightened only by candles and firelight. The dark reds and blues and purples reminded Ban of nothing so much as the innards of a dying man, sprawled across a bloody battlefield. Perhaps that was exactly by design.

"Ban the Fox," Gaela Lear said by way of greeting, and he liked that she used the name he'd earned, not his father's bequest.

Ban had not been this near to the eldest daughter of Lear in years.

"Queen," he said softly, giving her back the title that she, too, had earned.

Both Gaela and Regan sat already in tall-backed chairs, wine in a jug and plenty of steaming meat on their plates. It smelled delicious. Gaela gestured with greasy fingers for him to sit, to pour himself wine. She swallowed her bite. "We did not wait, so please do not worry about any formality now."

Ban glanced to Regan, who'd bathed, and wore a dark dress of Gaela's, tied tight enough to pucker at the eyelets, and bound with a wide pink belt in order to fit her slighter frame. The lady's hair was braided simply in a loose crown, her face drawn still in grief. But her eyes were bright again. She nodded once to Ban, holding his gaze longer than was necessary; Gaela noticed this with narrowed eyes.

He could do nothing about that, and so sat, helping himself to the duck. Ban fed his suddenly voracious appetite while the fire crackled and wind blew hollow and high against narrow windows. Regan picked slowly at her plate, but Gaela finished and leaned back, and Ban knew it was a signal he should stop, too. He wiped his hands and drank deep of the dark wine. For courage.

The lady of Astore studied him, lounging back in her chair. Her dress was cut low and dyed so deep a purple it would be easy to imagine it only an extension of her skin. Some thick twists of hair, free of the white ribbons Gaela wore for mourning, had nestled against her neck and collar. "Well, Ban. You are the Earl Errigal now, besides a wizard, a soldier, and a spy. And my sister claims you're hers."

It was quite the opening gambit. Ban said, "Your sister Regan has won loyalty from me, and from the trees and roots, who are my friends. Her husband won me, too, by his own mettle and honor. Though I never thought they were at cross-purpose to you and your aims."

Regan smiled, the ghost of last week's sharpness in the delicate corners. "Never you and yours, Gaela. But your husband's, maybe."

Gaela held her gaze on Ban, never blinking. She was a ferocious dragon, born of these cold north mountains; he only a southern fox.

Showing his teeth, too, Ban said, "You were surely at cross-purpose with Astore, to kill him in the way you did."

Ban was dazzled by the fierceness of Gaela's regard, her grimace nearer a grin. "He betrayed me, and thought to rise higher."

Regan said, "As did the former Errigal. And our uncle offered Ban the same, once."

"Did he?" Gaela said silkily.

A flutter in Ban's stomach caused him to regret the greasy duck he'd eaten, and the wine went sour on the back of his tongue. He forced a nod. "I told the Oak Earl no. And I said the same to your sister Elia, herself, when she told me she would find—recover—and save your father, bring him out from the wilderness where he was cast."

At this, both sisters leaned forward. "What is this?" Regan asked.

The Fox held his hand still on the cup of wine. "The night of the storm, when I led my father to his death, and Connley met his own, I came across Elia Lear lodged in Hartfare."

"Elia is on Innis Lear." Gaela stood, towering over the table.

*I'm going to save you, too.*

Ban forced himself to speak. He would see out the plan, commit to this destruction. "She came to save your father, from you both, no matter the cost."

"Does she have Aremoria behind her?" Gaela leaned toward him, hands on the table.

"Not yet," Ban answered, heart pounding. "But she will summon him, if she needs to. Consider making him the king of Innis Lear."

"Over my dead body," snarled Gaela.

Regan closed her eyes. "What a fool our baby sister is, to set her sights so low."

"Aremoria will see the loss of your husbands as opportunity," Ban said, though it was only partially true.

A soft cry of distress escaped Regan's lips. Gaela gripped her shoulder. "We will find vengeance for Connley's death, sister," Gaela promised. "Take Errigal, and this entire island, for our own, in your husband's memory and for our glory. Elia will be sorry to come home for this challenge. She should have done as we said, and we would have made her choices easy."

Regan clutched Gaela's hand. The two shared a long, hot stare.

Ban lowered his gaze to the remains of duck and violent streaks of berry preserves.

"You look poorly, Ban," Regan said.

"I am reluctant to go against your youngest sister. To see her harmed, more than she might otherwise be. We were friends, once."

"But?" Gaela prompted, sensing his hesitation.

"I must—we must." Ban let all the years of loathing coat his voice. "Elia would forgive Lear everything."

Gaela downed her wine, licked a drop of it from the corner of her mouth. She came to him and grasped the shoulder of his tunic, dragging Ban to his feet. Regan joined them, taking his hand in her cold fingers.

Both his and Gaela's hands were rough and dry, muscled and scarred by swordwork. Regan's were smooth and elegant, with nails ragged from their travels, still honed enough to bite. Ban thought of Elia's soft brown skin, how it would blister if she went to war.

"You hate our father as much as we do," Gaela said. "I remember you, as a boy. He called you her dog. As if dogs are not loyal, not true."

"And you made yourself a fox," Regan continued.

Gaela said, "I made myself, too, Fox."

"He was sent away, Gaela, for the same reasons our mother was murdered. As heartlessly, as carelessly, as if so easily discarded."

If he did not confess to his part in Lear's death, it would never be known. The king died of age, of a lack of breath. It was none of Ban's doing. Yet he also greatly wanted the credit, to be included in the heat of their regard. And they needed to know it was done, that their way was clear. That Elia's hopes were already in ruins. "I have had my revenge," Ban said huskily.

Regan's nails bit into his hand. "Ambitious fox," she whispered, eyes stuck on his face, as if she would drown without him.

Before he could explain, Gaela said, "Do you swear to my cause, Ban the Fox, that which is my sister Regan's cause, as well?"

"I swear," he said, both believing it in that moment, and knowing it would not matter.

Neither woman knew how fickle Ban's oaths were.

Regan said, "You should marry me."

The air went still and heat spiked all through Ban, then Gaela snapped, "*What?*"

Regan detached herself from her sister and faced Ban. Though her hair was unadorned, and there'd been no trace of paint on her lips for days, that wintry beauty remained. "You are Errigal now, by our word. Become Connley, too," she said, cool and gracious. "Ban the Fox, general of Innis Lear's armies, all of them, beneath Gaela Astore of Lear. United by marriage and the roots of the island. Three impossibly strong lines of power between us. Our blood and our roots are suited."

Ban could hardly breathe. Elia had refused to run with him, to leave this island, to choose him for nothing but love itself. And here h⸺

choose him so boldly, proposing that their partnership would make the island stronger, that his presence would make *her* stronger.

Gaela studied her favored sister with narrow eyes. "You would have no mourning time. It might be seen as desperate."

"It *is* desperate," Regan answered, her gaze all for Ban. "But I will not let our father win now, even under Elia's aegis. I will do anything to end their bid, to end them. Connley is dead, but we will be queen, Gaela. He died for it, and there will be nothing can stop me now."

She drifted nearer to him. "Don't you desire me, Ban Errigal?" Regan whispered.

He parted his lips to answer—something, Ban did not know what—and then Regan kissed him.

Ban gasped against her mouth. He lifted his hands and found her elbows, then her ribs, as Regan seduced him with this slow, sensuous kiss. Cool shade and a slender, crystal waterfall; she was a refuge from bruising sunlight and battering wind, from the hungry salt sea and cruel constellations. It stirred him, but not like Elia. He thought of her, and it hurt to do so, more even than he had expected.

Gaela's deep laugh echoed, in the room and in Ban's gut.

Regan ended her kiss with a delicate lick, a taste of his teeth. Her hands lit upon his jaw, but her eyes remained dull and quiet. Ban could see her disaffection, despite the prowess of her kiss. She cared not for him, not nearly as she had for Connley.

"Connley would have approved," Regan said with a hush, as if she heard Ban's thoughts. She let her fingers stroke him as she lowered her hands. "I would marry you, Ban, and we would be well matched, though you are young, and in love with Elia."

Ban felt frantic, all at once: the terrified, cornered rabbit, not the fox.

"When it is all over, perhaps," Regan continued, glancing at her sister, not for permission but only agreement.

Gaela snorted. "Win this battle for us, Fox, and perhaps you'll be a duke for it, and shortly after a king."

"I will win it. For myself, and for you. But I will never be a king, nor even—a duke." Ban backed away from both, clutching his trembling hands at his sides as he bowed.

He remembered the messy passion with which Elia had kissed him. Insisting, making a home for him inside of her. Then the equally impassioned certainty with which she'd chosen against him, afterward.

Gaela returned to the table and poured them all more wine.

Ban took his cup from her hand. He drank it fast, and though Gaela smirked at him and made to speak, he was quicker.

"King Lear is dead."

"What?" growled Gaela. "What did you say?"

"The—your father. Your father is dead."

Regan grasped his jaw. "How do you know this? When?"

"I killed him," Ban said hoarsely, pulling free of the two women to stand as tall as he could, apart so that he might have a chance if they leapt to kill him. "The night Connley died. You raged and wept so thoroughly. I had Lear's breath in my hand, and I took it from him forever."

Gaela was shaking her head. "Magic? Is this only magic? You did not cut out his heart, or see him go cold?"

"No."

"How can you be sure, then? Are you as mad as he is? Shall I throw you in the bottom of my tower for this treason?"

Ban looked at Regan. "I hated him. But he was safe, and living, my spell waiting for your deployment. Then you reminded me. This was all the fault of our fathers: they have always been the cause of our misery. So they are dead now, mine and yours, both. We are *free* of them! We are beholden only to ourselves, no cursed stars."

Regan stared at him, breath shallow, the gleam of awe sparking deep in her eyes.

"Ban Errigal, *are you certain?*" Gaela demanded. Her dinner knife was clutched in her fist. "My father is dead? You killed him, truly? You robbed me, so easily, of my vengeance?"

"Listen to the island," Ban replied, trembling but sure. "Listen to this angry wind that has blown four long days and nights—since he died—and hear that it says nothing. If you can. Or ask your sister, and she will confirm. The island is silent even as it screams. There must be a king of Innis Lear. It longs for a head beneath a crown. It must have a ruler. Without a king, Innis Lear will die, or wilt, or—or the rootwaters will go dry, and the island will crumble into the sea if one of you does not take the crown now. Much faster than it has been doing, even under the fatal stewardship of that old, wretched fool."

Gaela's lips parted eagerly.

"The rootwaters," Regan murmured, drifting toward the window. "They'll accept me."

"You?" Gaela stalked after her, took her arm harshly, and spun her sister around. "Me. I will be king."

"Connley is dead," Regan insisted, as if it meant anything. Would prove something.

"No, you *are* Connley! And I am Astore. We are Innis Lear, sister, as has always been our intention. No stars. We will make our own meaning. Let us go now to the throne room and declare it so!" Gaela laughed.

Ban shook his head, knowing in his gut what he said was true: "The root-waters must accept you. The island. Not the people. Whatever ritual is done on the Longest Night, that is what you must do to win the crown. Then the people will follow, only after that. Even Elia will agree to support your claim, if the island accepts you."

Regan nodded slowly. "Yes. Yes, Gaela. Let us go together. Now. To the rootwaters of the Tarinnish. By morning we will be the queens of Innis Lear and nothing will stop us." She picked up her cup and drank all its wine, lifting her chin to reveal her tender, vulnerable throat. When she finished, the redness clung to her lips like blood.

Gaela lifted her cup in salute, and smiled.

Ban the Fox did not smile, because outside the wind blew voicelessly still.

# ELIA

THROUGH THE COLD **night came a summons:**

*Elia of Lear.*

*Elia.*

She'd been dreaming of something, but it was gone now, leaving only flowery vestiges in her memory.

Elia sat up in the small bed, awake.

Silence—but for the wordless wind and the crackle of straw as her own body settled.

*Elia.*

It was the trees.

Leaping to her feet, Elia grabbed her boots and shoved them on. Fumbling for her overdress, she was glad it laced up the sides instead of the back; Aefa stayed every night with her parents, and couldn't have helped tie anything tonight. The days had grown colder, so Elia grabbed the wool blanket from the bed and wrapped it over her shoulders before stepping outside.

Hartfare slept.

Overhead stars turned, winking and shimmering as if they crawled and moved of their own accord. Elia saw too many patterns, too many possibilities, the constellations weaving in and out of each other, rivers of stars and potential. She blinked.

The sky stilled.

Elia drew a deep breath of cold air. She listened, hoping to hear the call of Innis Lear again.

*Hello,* she whispered.

Wind blew in reply, flicking small, cold fingers against her messy crown of braids, teasing her nape until she drew the blanket tighter around herself.

*Elia,* said a few trees—those at the southwest of the village.

That was the way she walked.

For three days she'd lived in Hartfare, enduring as the island mourned. In all that time, the wind had not stopped howling and keening in sorrow, though Elia had cried herself out the first night. They'd brought her father here, to Brona's cottage, and washed him, put him in a simple gray shift. Elia had dotted his birth stars down his forehead with the white of star priests. She cast a final chart for him, too, based on the stars showing at the moment of his death: he should be interred when the Autumn Throne crested, a week before the Longest Night, the stars said. Nearly three months from now. And so with Brona and Kayo, Lear's youngest daughter had bound her father's body in cloth and settled him into a box built of oak, lined with flint and chips of blue granite. The once-king rested now back in the meadow where he'd died, guarded by a trio of his retainers until Elia was ready to have him sent north to Dondubhan.

Brona advised that Elia must consolidate her strength here in the south, and Kayo agreed, once he was able to speak again, after two feverish days when Brona fussed and worried the infection would take his other eye. The worst had passed, and he would see again, if dimly and incomplete. Aefa argued still that Elia ought to take residence at the Summer Seat, because it made a powerful statement. Elia had listened to them, but wished she was able to hear the trees' opinion.

Elia had promised to choose by the time the Star of First Birds awoke at dusk, inside the heart of the Throne. That would be within two nights. Then Kayo could send messengers to the Earls Bracoch and Rosrua, to the Earl Glennadoer, and to the retainers at the Summer Seat, that Elia was on Innis Lear. That the king had died.

She was fairly certain she would go first to Errigal Keep as she'd promised Ban, in hope that he too would keep his promise and bring Elia's sisters to her there.

They needed to speak together, even more now with their father dead. And Elia did believe Kayo when he insisted she should not go to Gaela, for it would appear that Elia was the supplicant, that she agreed to her eldest sister's ruinous claim to the crown. No, Elia must have her sisters come to her, it was the only way to establish any power in their dangerous triangle. Or hope to sway Regan on behalf of these most beloved wells and roots.

If only the island would counsel her, perhaps Elia would not feel so alone and unsure. But since her father had died, the voice of the wind and the trees had been nothing but a rush of air, a hiss of grief and pain, and the stars too seemed dim, hiding behind mournful clouds.

Brona said the island hadn't reacted so badly when the last king died. She'd only been a girl, but she remembered. There had been raining and storms then, too—though nothing quite like the great gasp of wind that had accompanied the moment of Lear's final breath. And never before could Brona recall this terrible silence.

But finally, tonight, the island called her.

*Elia.*

She moved more quickly, turning through the calm, dark forest in the direction she was beckoned.

Brona had guessed this, too. *Soon the island will show you how to be queen, if you keep listening. There is a bird of reaping that flies through all my holy bones, in the direction of the saint of stars. That is where the future is sanctified by the past, Elia, and life and death are nothing but different shapes of the moon. You will listen, and the island will know you.*

Her boots crunched over drying autumn leaves, and Elia could see everything before her: layers of gray and silver shades, the darkest purples and flashes of emerald when the sliver of moon caught a glimpse of her through the wind-tossed trees. A trickle of liquid starlight when she came across a stream, slipping and weeping around stones and swirling pools, splashing the eager roots that dug down the bank.

*Elia.*

She found a wall of sudden darkness, rising behind a hedge of rose vines and ash trees.

A real wall, built of very old granite and limestone, blue as the moon and creamy light. Black vines tangled and braided like wild hair all along the walls, darkening the stone, dry and wrinkled in many places.

It was the first star cathedral.

Lear had come here, a decade ago, and brought with him a round stone to close off the navel well. As he closed them all across the island, denying any power but that of the stars.

Elia's heartbeat slowed to a crawl, as if to join the creeping, dark pace of this entire world. She walked around the structure, thinking of the one time she'd come here as a child, before her mother died. Perhaps she'd been six or seven, holding Dalat's hand as they entered the grand cathedral, with both Elia's sisters at her side and a retinue behind. Lear himself had not been there, that Elia could recall, but most of the memory was a faded curl of smiles and bright blue sky. She remembered making pretty noises, softly touching the edges of a copper bowl half filled with water, and reading the poem marked into the north wall with her mother helping her form the words.

Now Elia found the doors open for her, though barely. As if they'd been closed tight, but something—the size of a deer or smaller—had shoved one side, leaving a crescent smear through the rotten leaves and mud piled against the outside. The thick wood smelled moldy, and she touched her hand to it, brushing gentle fingers against the rough corner and down to the iron handle. Splotches of lichen decorated both metal and wood, and Elia breathed deeply of the earthy wet smell as she slipped between the heavy doors.

Starlight seeped through the ruin. It never had known a roof, but now the effect was more haunting than holy. It felt like a place gone to seed much longer than ten years ago: half a century or more.

The benches and wooden chairs had split and been overgrown with not only moss, but tall and wispy grass. Abandoned nests from squirrels and doves moldered and fell to pieces in the old sconces and narrow shelves where earth saint statues and little altars once stood, most in pieces now scattered against the floor. Vines had grown across the southern aisle, and roses overtaken the entire eastern wall. A tree, an entire living ash, had broken through the floor in the west, pushing up and up with elegant limbs toward the night sky.

And there, in the center, stood the well.

The round granite cap Lear had once deployed in enmity had cracked down the middle, great stone halves fallen to either side like broken, tired wings. They leaned against the well itself, revealing the mouth to the night.

From the black waters came a soft, whispering song that smelled of decay and spring flowers.

Elia picked her way there, eyes stuck on the stone mouth, her lips parted so she could taste the air.

Water darkened the fissures between the rough rocks of the well. She touched her fingers to the dampness, and then touched her tongue.

Wet, healthy earth, metallic and heady.

*Elia.*

"I am here. Elia, of Lear," she said, her voice echoing softly all around. *I'm here,* she said again in the language of trees. *I'm listening.*

*Drink,* breathed the voice of the well.

She leaned over the edge, peering into the darkness. She saw a bare glint far below, but no rope nor bucket. No dipper with which to reach toward the water that glimmered and beckoned.

The darkness reached up toward her, and Elia felt herself falling forward. She slipped slowly down and down the stone channel toward the heart of

Innis Lear. Roots caressed her as she fell, and a soft bed of moss finally caught her, damp and soaking, gloriously bright green and smelling like springtime. Lights winked all around, waves lapping against a far shore, crystals in the black cavern, sparkling and laughing like stars but made of stone. Elia opened her mouth, and the moss lifted her up, giving her into the embrace of roots that tugged and rolled her through the island's bedrock, through the fertile mud fields and beneath stretching moorland. Trees whispered hello, worms caught at her hair, and the tickling legs of root insects kissed her in passing. She laughed, though earth pressed against every part of her, even her lips and tongue and eyes.

And then the wind came, and she flew up again, her blood soaring through her veins, her heartbeat a dance, a song, and Elia was not alone. She spun upright with a group of silver spirits, weaving through the flashing shadows of the White Forest. Where their toes tapped, mushrooms and wildflowers grew, and in their wake floated perfect heart-shaped moon moths, lighting a path.

A crown was gently placed on her head, woven of tiny white flowers, and Elia sat down on a throne of ancient blue-gray granite, worn smooth from a hundred queens and kings.

The crown fell apart, then, and petals tumbled down her hair and cheeks, landing in her palms and on her tongue. Elia swallowed, and a sharpness slithered down her throat, slowing her heart, turning her flesh to stone and her bones to water, until she sank into the granite seat, part of the world.

She sighed, and the island's wind sighed, too; she laughed, and the island laughed. When rain dripped onto the roots and leaves and peaks of the mountain, she wept.

Elia came back to herself slowly. Curled on the ruined floor of the star cathedral, pressed to the well, her arms pillowing her head. Sitting, she blinked: light in the sky told her it was morning, though whether a morning immediately following her midnight sojourn, or a morning a hundred years later, Elia could not immediately say.

She thought of dancing with the earth saints in her dream. A flash of white, a flit of bright shadow high above, startled her, and she looked up toward the spires.

It was no saint, but an old ghost owl; it drifted silently down toward her in a graceful arc. Elia got to her knees, watching with her breath held, in case by exhaling she might scatter the spell.

The fierce owl was beautiful, creamy and white with a pattern of speckles down its wings and a heart-shaped face, with solid black eyes calm on her own.

Held in its small, sharp beak was a crushed wreath of hemlock. Like the one her father had worn when he died, like the one that had disintegrated in Elia's dream.

The owl landed on the stone floor with a click of talons and dropped the crown at her knee.

She shivered, and listened to the island.

*Eat of the flower, and drink of the roots,* said the White Forest around her, and the wind blew the message against the four cathedral spires.

*Eat of the flower, and drink of the roots.*

Elia understood.

A bargain between herself and the island. This would make her the true queen of Innis Lear.

She carefully picked up the crown. *Thank you,* she said to the owl, bowing her head. It shrugged its folded wings.

And so Elia Lear knelt, as dawn rose over the star cathedral, across from the watchful owl, with a hemlock crown in her lap. Listening, and thinking. And wanting.

She did not wish to be the queen.

The sun rose, warming the sky to a pale blue. Wind growled and whined overhead, still longing for order, still sad over the lost king. The trees hissed and whispered, though not to Elia any longer. Everything waited. They would have her choose.

If she did this, she was the queen of Innis Lear.

Not her sisters, who would hate her and fight her forever.

If she did this, Elia could never again dream of only stars, or only a small taste of magic. She would be the warp and weft of the island's life, between the harsh land and the people.

*Am I the only possibility?* she asked, desperately. Surely there could be someone else, another who could take up this burden, someone to delight in the joys and the power. Regan would speak with the trees, accept this love, and Gaela was strong, ready for hardship. But would either woman listen to the heart of the island?

*Elia,* whispered the trees.

She did not want to make this choice.

Brona Hartfare had kept the rootwaters alive for twelve years. She deserved this honor, the allegiance of Innis Lear. And Kayo could be an excellent king by her side, raised as he had been to leadership, to mediation and economy. The island loved the witch. Loved both of them. Elia should bring the hemlock crown to Brona, and tell her the secret to getting rootwater running in her veins, to have the island see her and support her reign.

Then Elia could leave, could be what she'd always wanted: a priest, a witch. Or even a wife—she could find Ban, save him, take him from his hatred and anger: choose him, choose a life of magic together, simple and belonging and easy.

Was that the way to save everyone, to be *everything* and fail at nothing? To give up this power and responsibility?

Or was that only what she thought she wanted, because she was afraid?

*Elia*, whispered the trees.

*The witch is calling your name.*

*Your girl is calling your name.*

*We are calling your name.*

Elia stood and held the hemlock carefully in her hands.

*Sisters,*

*Our father is dead.*

*I send this letter in four copies, to find you either at Dondubhan, the Summer Seat, Astora, or Connley Castle, hoping to reach you in one of the corners of Innis Lear.*

*He died with me, suddenly, underneath a starry sky. I suspect you would prefer it had been painful, but he was at peace.*

*The island is not.*

*It longs for a king, and we must choose now amongst ourselves. We must be enough together to meet the island's needs. Come to me at Errigal Keep, and we will decide there, where the iron sleeps.*

*Regan, the trees told me of your loss—I am so very sorry that your husband, too, has died. I know you loved him. I am learning something of love lately, and I hope you are finding strength in Gaela as always, and in the presence of Ban Errigal, and in knowing Connley's bones will always be part of the stones and roots of Innis Lear, which were so loved by you both.*

*Your sister, Elia*

# AEFA

It bothered Aefa greatly that her lady still carried her crushed, dangerous flower crown.

Obviously it was hemlock, and the king had died wearing hemlock, and Aefa did not think anything symbolic or sentimental was worth the risk of Elia getting the poison on her fingers or accidentally swallowing some. Or worse just having it close to hand, and then deciding in one sad moment to die.

"I'm not suicidal," Elia promised softly when Aefa tried (for the seventh or eighth time) to coax the crown from around the princess's arm where she wore it hooked around her elbow like a large and deadly bracelet.

The reassurance was good, until Elia added, "Though I cannot promise to never eat it."

Aefa's huge eyes must have said plenty, because Elia hugged her and kissed her cheek and swore not to die by her own hand.

This was only marginally encouraging.

It had been four slow and worrisome days since the night Elia vanished and reappeared, and nearly a week since the fateful storm. Once Kayo could move, they'd traveled from Hartfare to Errigal Keep in a small, rather funereal procession, leaving the king under guard in the meadow where he'd died. They did not announce his death, but it was an impossible secret to keep on an island so tense, so ready to believe the angry wind was personal, an ominous message rather than mere late-season weather. The news seeped out, and by the time their party had reached the Keep, the doors were thrown open to them despite the order from Regan Connley that none be allowed to enter—none but her own people in Connley colors or those under the banner of Ban the Fox.

It was good to be in a well-functioning castle like Errigal Keep in the midst of mourning, because if the inner workings hadn't been so solid,

Aefa and her mother would've been hard pressed to keep everything running alone. They seemed to be the only two folk in all the world not brought low by sorrow. The Fool had been Lear's friend for twenty years, and Kay Oak wore a face like he'd lost a brother—with what was left of his face. Even Brona grieved, though for the dead Earl Errigal more than the king. Wasn't *that* a surprise. The Keep was full of mourning—for the earl and Connley, too. The iron wizard had ordered all the fires in the valley banked in deference, and the Keep's cook had organized a group of women to venture into the White Forest in order that they might bathe Errigal's body in rootwaters.

In the great hall, Aefa hummed to herself, an old wormwork prayer for new growth, while seated at Elia's feet with a length of dark blue cloth in her lap. She sewed a white star across the breast of the tabard, for Elia to wear when her sisters came: the colors of the house of Lear, but Elia's own standard instead of the swan. Perhaps a crown of stars or a spray of hemlock would've been more appropriate, Aefa thought darkly, but her skills with a needle were more suited to this large, basic pattern.

"This is an excellent idea," her mother Alis Thornhill, had said yesterday, when Aefa had been hunting around through old cloth in the storage room beside all the companion ladies' quarters. They'd chased out a last Connley cousin, who'd opted to flee north, but the rest of the Keep's women from highborn to low- had remained, making a welcoming home for their youngest princess. Alis had especially taken to Sella Ironwife, married to the Keep's wizard.

The women gathered in the great hall most mornings—the wind pounded constantly, dragging at the moors and snuffing out all fires but those carefully contained in hearths. They brought the day's work to their quiet, kind lady, watching Elia from the corners of their eyes as they chattered. The women certainly had a lot to say about Ban Errigal. They mused on his roots and his prowess, wondering whether he might stay on once his brother inherited the Keep—they assumed Rory would return home, innocent. Especially now that Elia was home, too. Surely Rory was soon to follow. Because Ban was gifted with iron, with all forms of magic both secretive and strong, most women refused to consider aloud that the bastard might have betrayed Rory on purpose. Though Aefa could tell by the glances shared that they suspected it was so.

Elia had taken up residence at the Keep just in time to get word from the Alsax: they were sending a barge to bear home a contrite and determined Rory of Errigal. The message suggested that the ship itself would arrive by the dark moon. Tomorrow.

Aefa slid a look up at her princess, who stared at her mending with a calm that almost seemed dull. But Aefa knew the pinch at Elia's brow that meant she was thinking hard, in layers and spirals, rather like the intricate patterns of the stars.

"You can talk out any plan, any wish, with me," Aefa had said, late last night, when she'd heard Elia turn over on the very fine bed the women of the keep had convinced her use in the earl's quarters. Aefa had cocooned herself in a pile of pillows and blankets in the servant's nook beside the massive stone hearth, near enough to hear her princess if she stopped breathing.

"I'm not ready," Elia had answered. "But when I am, I will. I promise, Aefa."

It required every ounce of Aefa's training and self-respect not to climb into the grand bed and shake Elia, or kiss her and lend comfort, or maybe pinch her until the princess laid everything out and shared. And if Elia had for even a moment lost all expression, had blinked and gone cold, Aefa would have done. She feared Elia would fall back into what she'd been before, the unfeeling star, the glass saint her father had molded her into. It had been Aefa's greatest worry, that Elia would lose all she'd gained, the strength and resilience and passion she'd recovered when she lost everything. When she'd begun to build her own stage upon which to stand. There was always the chance the princess would react to her own loss as her father had: by hiding in his grief and burying his rage, and then ruining everything around him.

Elia, though, had Aefa and Brona Hartfare and Kayo, and Aefa's parents, too (whom Aefa wasn't certain were in love any longer, but seemed to comfort each other and were sleeping together again, to her delight and trepidation). None of them would allow Elia to close herself off as her father had done in his refusal to listen—to his daughters, and to his island. And that Elia had been willing to chance new friendships and encourage confidences, to let herself smile and brighten this Keep's dark halls, promised that she had no intention of becoming her father.

Some of that, Aefa bitterly admitted, had to do with Ban Errigal. She'd never thank him for it, even if hope in him was the strongest thread widening the channels in and out of Elia's heart.

The star-cursed bastard.

Aefa jabbed her bone needle too widely, and sneered at herself. She'd better think of something else. Like the Aremore soldier La Far's very fine thighs. Except his eyes were so sad, and Aefa was ever surrounded by sad people.

She wished Elia would declare herself queen and let the consequences come.

She wished the wind would stop its angsty blowing, or she'd have to shave off all her hair to stop it coming unbound and sprawling across her eyes.

She wished . . .

A servant dashed in, fell to his knees, and hurriedly told Elia the barge had been sighted, far out on the turbulent horizon, with a sail striped in the orange, purple, and white of the Alsax.

"Thank you," Elia said, standing immediately. They would need to hurry, if they were to intercept Rory before he could hear the dreadful state of things from anyone else. It was, after all, Elia had said aloud, her responsibility.

Aefa folded her work and hoped that the wind on the ride wouldn't tear too much of Elia's complicated braids free.

Gulls cried loudly and salty water sprayed against the long legs of the dock as Aefa and Elia made their way along it. The amber beads in Elia's hair caught the sun between every fast-moving cloud, flashing with fire then fading dull again. She wore the vibrant red gown borrowed from Hartfare, laced with the turquoise ribbons. Though not regal, Elia stood as tall as she was able, and the tight gown showed off the roundness of her breasts and hips. Though who on the barge there was to impress, Aefa did not know. She was just grateful Elia had finally accepted she needed to always present herself powerfully.

Limestone cliffs hugged this deep cove, and the water was a brilliant turquoise due to the copper in the sand. A few boats rocked on the incoming tide, though most fishers and trade barges were out on the choppy sea. Noisy voices floated from the open building where a dozen men and women struggled to organize stacks of barrels and crates to be put on a ship to sail out with tonight's tide, down and around the coast to the Summer Seat. The dock master leaned outside his small watch building against a rusty barrel. Just off the water, where the limestone retaining wall held the sea back from the line of shops, flower and food stalls stood, mostly empty because of the incessant wind. It was the strength of a gale, a wild storm, but brought no rain or thunder. It was unnatural. Elia said the island was furious to have no king, and would continue until a new monarch was chosen.

The wind hissed over the water, throwing salt splashes up across the docks, staining the princess's dress. Aefa sighed.

Together, the two of them watched the barge approach. Rory stood at the prow, glaringly visible with his bright red hair. He lifted a hand and waved it wide.

The princess remained calm and still, but Aefa was glad to see Rory; despite his rakish proclivities, he was good at heart, and she thought he'd support Elia with his entire being, which would soothe feathers at the Keep.

The sail was lowered as the dock master used painted sticks to signal the barge to its usual berth. With oars, the barge maneuvered itself. It was a long, flat boat, filled with men, the rear stacked with crates and barrels. A few called out in Aremore.

"Our luck for the most beautiful welcome and finest of women!" Rory yelled through the wind as the barge tapped the side of the dock and sailors leapt out to tie it off. Elia held her hand to Rory and met his eyes, smiling back, but sadly. His hair was a disaster of windblown red spikes, and his freckles blended against the brilliant pink of his wind- and sun-chapped cheeks.

Aefa stood closer to Elia. They were going to break his heart.

"I'm glad you're home," Elia said.

Around them sailors disembarked, and a few strong-looking men in plain leather vests and coats, perhaps hired to guard the goods. And there was Eriamos Alsax, his brown hair just as wrecked as Rory's, but otherwise more put together. He'd traveled by sea all his life, Aefa supposed, as he greeted Elia with a touch of her hand and a bow, then winked at Aefa.

"Welcome to Innis Lear, Eriamos," Elia said. "I hoped to take a moment with Rory before going to the inn where food awaits, though you are so very welcome to join us and stay with us at the Keep."

"Thank you. Here is my sister Dessa." He turned: one of the sailors bowed. She was dressed in men's clothes, though making no effort to hide her womanhood. She smiled exactly like her mother, Juda, and her thick brown hair had maintained its curling shape during the voyage better than the men had managed. Rory offered Dessa his hand, and she took it easily, climbing out onto the dock to stand slightly too near him.

Aefa rolled her eyes fondly, but she was glad he might have some affection to hold him warm tonight, when he was mourning his father and realizing the treachery of his bastard brother.

"Welcome, too, Dessa Alsax," Elia said. Aefa could see her lady's strain as she maintained her poise. "I hope you'll be our guests at Errigal Keep tonight."

"Yes, home," Rory said. "With several unexpected additions!" Some mischief peeked from the corner of his smile.

"Rory," Elia began, but Eriamos cleared his throat and glanced at the contingent of guards. The young Alsax merchant indicated one of the soldiers who stepped easily from barge to dock. He was broad-shouldered and tall, turning to face Elia.

Aefa gasped like a child on her birthday.

This was no bodyguard or soldier for hire.

Standing before them was the king of Aremoria.

Morimaros was nearly unrecognizable in worn brown leather and regular gray wool. No brilliant silver pauldron graced his shoulder, nor the ubiquitous orange coat. His boots were scuffed; his trousers were old, soft leather. Nothing marked him apart from the rest of the soldiers. Even his sword was plain, sheathed in untooled leather and wood. His beard was gone, revealing a very square, very strong jaw and full, pink lips.

"Your Highness," he said carefully.

Elia thrummed with tension. "Morimaros," she murmured.

"Mars," he said. "Only that, now."

"Worms of the earth," breathed Aefa.

"It's safer," said the soldier behind him: La Far! Aefa contained her swoon, though she could not hold back a saucy wave. The man remained stoic and sad looking, with his blond hair back in a tail. "And I'm Novanos here."

Elia folded her hands carefully. "I did not ask you to come."

At the cool tone, Aefa stepped close enough to Elia that their hips touched. For comfort or caution, she would be there.

The king of Aremoria reached into his gray coat and offered the princess a very small folded letter. As he did, Aefa noticed the bareness of his fingers. He did not wear the Blood and the Sea.

Unfolding the letter, Elia glanced down, and Aefa unselfconsciously peered over her shoulder. It was one line, efficiently scrawled, but bold in words:

> *The island is as ready for you as I can make it. I will not be returning to Aremoria.*

Ban Errigal.

Truly, a bastard. And a traitor!

Rage coarsened Aefa's blood, making her rigid. Beside her, Elia crumpled the note in her fist.

"Elia," Rory said urgently. "Mars has come to offer his aid, his knowledge gleaned of our island from a commander's view. And he seeks my brother, as they once were close. Take me to my father! All of us, please. I'm hungry, and so tired of the sound of waves."

Closing her eyes for only a brief moment, Elia turned to Rory and took his hands. "Rory, please— I—I am so very sorry." She stepped so they were a hand's width apart. "Your father is dead, killed in defense of me, and you, and ever in service to my father. He died at the hand of the duke of Connley, who also is dead."

A long moment of silence stretched, broken only by gulls and yelling dockworkers. All blood drained from Rory's careless face, turning his freckles stark, and Aefa spied a contained wince on her princess's brow as the bereft son gripped Elia's fingers too tightly. "No," he said, sinking slowly to his knees.

"It was a noble death, and you are to be proud of him. He knew you loved him, at his end," Elia said.

Rory pushed his head to her waist, hugging his arms around her hips. She bent over him, her hands on his thick red hair, hushing his sudden gasp of grief, whispering her comfort, her apology, and allowing even her own grief, finally, to be spoken. A tiny tear slipped down Elia's cheek.

Aefa worried her lip as Rory shook, clinging to Elia.

"We are here to help," La Far said softly, at Aefa's shoulder.

"Good, because much of what needs fixing is Aremoria's fault," the Fool's daughter replied, without sympathy, and turned away.

# MORIMAROS

THE BOLD RED suited Elia Lear, as did her clashing teal ribbons, pulling disparate parts of her costume together into a whole: so Mars had thought watching her from the barge, as she stood, eyes calm, chin up like a queen. Even as the wind tore at her skirts and hair. She bore it without wincing, as if it did not cut tears in her eyes as it did his.

Now, watching her comfort the young Errigal as the others began unloading the barge, Mars was unable to look away from her: the compassion on her face before it disappeared because she curled over Rory, the warm brown line of her arched neck. He wanted to put his lips there, or at least his hand, to show her he would support her, or nothing more if she wished.

Though it was terrible that the Earl Errigal was dead, it was good Mars had come. He'd sent Ban the Fox to Innis Lear to promote discord, and Mars knew his spy's methods too well not to recognize the spiral of them. Errigal and his heir had been removed, putting Ban in the perfect position to take it all if he could convince someone to name him legitimate. How well the Fox did his work.

Mars clenched his jaw. Thinking of Ban turned his careful, meticulous thoughts to fire. Never before had he been betrayed like this, dismissed with so little explanation. *I will not be returning to Aremoria.*

It might as well have read, *I will not be returning to you.*

Mars had trusted that bastard. Given him every opportunity to achieve greatness. No one had expected so much of Ban as Mars had, and he'd been so very sure the Fox would rise to meet that expectation.

The king of Aremoria did not like this feeling.

He'd lost them both: Ban and Elia.

She did not even glance his way again.

Mars had thrown all aside to come here, just himself and twelve of his best men, men who'd served in the army beside him before his father died, when he was only Captain Mars, a soldier like them, fighting and aching to win and live and prove himself worthy. His mother had vehemently protested this scheme, but Ianta took his side, reluctantly, convincing Queen Calepia that Mars could not rule if he doubted himself. And he knew abandoning Elia Lear now would carve a doubt in his heart to last all his life. His sister did not know, still, of his relationship with Ban the Fox, and how tangled Mars's feelings were for the two islanders. Doubt, yes, and desire, and a stubborn determination to be selfish for once.

The king knew it was the core of his coming here: pure, selfish need. He wanted Elia, and he wanted Ban—differently, maybe—and if Mars must set down the Blood and the Sea to get them—or one of them—or settle his tumultuous yearning—so be it.

Elia Lear had come home to reign, and Mars had followed her to see if he could shed his crown for even a little while.

"You need a drink," the girl Aefa said suddenly to Rory Errigal, but she looked around to the folk still gathered, meaning them all.

Rory nodded against Elia—Mars unworthily wished to be the one pressed against her—and the princess helped him stand. She glanced to Eriamos Alsax and his sister Dessa. "We do have lunch at the inn. Come." Her impossibly black eyes darted to Mars, including him, and she led Errigal down the dock.

Aefa pursed her lips at Mars, unaffected by who she knew he was. "Come you, sirs." She flounced away, and Mars looked at Novanos, whom he knew to admire the perky, inappropriate young woman.

"Finish unloading," Mars quietly ordered his men. "Help the Alsax and act your parts. "

Then he and Novanos followed in the wake of Elia Lear. Novanos said, "It will be easy enough for them, for they play what they are: soldiers."

Port Comlack was as busy as it had always been, except for the frantic sense in the air, as if at any moment lightning might form out of the harsh, clear sky, and tear through town on this scalding wind. The inn where they were led was two stories wrapped around an inner court, but Elia went straight through the common room to a large table with benches on three sides. Sunlight and three great hearths lit the low-ceilinged room, heating it and casting out the briny smell of the sea. Six retainers stood along the rear wall, and a handful of regular folk chatted at a tall table, some eating hurriedly on stools by one flickering fire. Wind gusted against the shutters, riffling through the thatched roof overhead.

Elia sat Rory down and summoned immediate drink. She put her arm around his shoulder as though they were old friends—and they were, Mars knew, stamping down jealousy. He deserved her reprobation. Though he'd like to ask after Ban, to know if they'd spoken, or if she knew what had caused his Fox to turn away from Aremoria. From him. Had it been her doing? Would that make it easier to bear? What was the state of politics on Innis Lear? Where did Elia stand, and would she allow him to stand beside her? How did the wind scour the island like this, but bring with it no rain or storm?

"Rory, there is more," Elia said, raising her voice. "My father, too, is dead."

Shock clenched Mars's stomach. She said it so coolly, as if unaffected, except there was a slight tremble in her hand as she reached for a pitcher of wine and poured it into cups. Pressing one into Rory's hand, the princess put her back to Mars.

Aefa appeared before Mars and Novanos. "Well, sit down, sirs, don't hover. Or else go stand with the retainers, since that's your costume."

The girl was correct: Mars stood out like this. He nodded at Novanos, who nodded more gently at Aefa. They began to step away, but Mars said, "Aefa, I would speak with your lady alone, when it pleases her."

"It won't please her," Aefa said, ushering them to a different table.

Gritting his teeth for a moment, Mars put on a more concerned tone to ask, "What happened to Lear?"

"He was old," she said, as if the answer were obvious.

The king sat carefully on a stool, balancing his elbows on the rough table, and Novanos sat across from him. A serving girl set beer down for them, and Mars made a valiant attempt not to glower.

"What did you expect?" Novanos asked in undertone.

Staring at the pale bubbles circling the top of the dark beer, Mars shook his head once. The beer smelled like new bread. He glanced at Elia, still holding her arm around Rory Errigal. Mars hadn't spent much time with the young man, both lacking the occasion and disliking to be reminded of Ban. But he'd been told Rory was a flirt and quite good with his sword and shield. Two different girls in Mars's castle had fallen to his charms, and possibly one of Novanos's best soldiers. Ban had told Mars once that Rory took after Errigal, and it was easy to see. He touched Elia readily, and Mars forced himself to be glad the two friends had each other right now: he remembered too keenly the feeling of a father's sudden death.

He wondered how Ban had orchestrated it. And if the Fox had anything to do with the death of Lear. Mars would place a heavy wager upon it. But he needed more information before he could unravel this web.

Novanos tried the beer and grimaced. Mars smiled a little at the man's refined palate.

"You should at least attempt to relax," Novanos said. "Use this as the only freedom you're like to get the rest of your life. Enjoy the break from responsibility."

"I'm going outside," Mars said.

When his captain grunted in displeasure, Mars sourly added, "To enjoy my freedom."

Controlling himself carefully, Mars left the inn. He stood in the street, squinting up at the bleary sun and feeling like a spoiled child. The king of a beautiful, strong country, sulking as if he'd been sent away by his mother.

He'd wanted Elia to smile. To see him and be pleased, even if she strove to hide it. He'd wanted her to need him, despite those last words she'd said to him in Lionis, and despite that he'd lied by omission for nearly their entire relationship.

But her father was dead, so she couldn't. Even besides that, she had so many things to think about; Mars knew very well the sort of pressure she was under now, no matter what her intentions for Innis Lear. He understood better than any, yet here he was wishing her to be as foolish as he had been, to drop her responsibilities, and not prioritize her grief or her friend's grief and the loss of a strong earl, but Mars's miraculous arrival. It was childish of him, and beneath them both. She would never appreciate it.

Laughing bitterly at himself, Mars turned to go back inside and be patient. He would be here for her, however she would use him: that was his goal.

A dark-haired woman stood in his way.

Mars froze.

"Go with me," she said in a voice as regal as a queen's—if queens ruled shadows and dreams.

"Where is Elia?"

"You are not yet granted an audience with our lady, but go with me up the cliff. There is a path offering very dramatic views."

"Very well," Mars said, low and strangely unnerved. Heat prickled up from beneath his skin; the sky of Innis Lear was cold.

The woman nodded and led the way, her skirts swinging freely around her worn boots. She was not dressed as a noblewoman: the green of her cinched tunic was faded, though her skirts were layered and ruffled, like a distant cousin of Ispanian fashion. She wore no jewels but a few links of copper tied to her belt, and silk ribbons held back the wind-snarled mass of her hair. A plain black jacket, also faded, fit loosely and clearly had not been made for her, but for a larger man. Despite the mismatched clothing and untended hair, she was gorgeous. Her warm tan skin showed some lines of age and laughter around her welcoming lips. Mars was not so used to being attracted to people as soon as he met them, but there was a familiar wariness in her brown eyes when she glanced back to make certain he followed.

He did, a few paces behind, so as to keep from crowding her. She took quick, short strides through town, up the steep, snaking streets, and out of the cove. Some wooden stairs stained white by salt cut up off the main road, and she took them over and around jutting limestone capped with scraggly gray-green ocean grass. Wind blasted, shoving at Mars, but the woman seemed not to be affected; rather, the wind parted for her.

Mars concentrated on placing his boots carefully on the twenty or so stairs until they reached a plateau and a very narrow path, worn to limestone gravel against the grass and thin dirt. The woman climbed easily, mounting the bluff with a deep enough breath he could see her shoulders lift and fall. She waited, looking back, and when Mars joined her she began to walk again, meandering idly with her gaze directed out at the glittering sea.

Pale ribbons danced in the wind, loosening from her hair. It smelled of salt here, nothing more, because the wind scoured this place clean of all else.

After a quarter of a mile edging the cliff, the woman stopped and turned entirely to face the sea. "Can you feel the island's fury, Morimaros of Aremoria?"

He frowned and folded his hands together behind his back. This promontory of cliff reached farther out than the rest of the south coast, thrusting them high enough over the ocean that the crash of waves on the white rocks below was only a dull rush of sound. The wind battered at his back, as if to throw him over. "I feel the wind."

"Do you think it wants you here?"

To say what he truly thought—that it mattered not to him what the wind wanted—would cast this woman, and all of Innis Lear, against him. Mars only said, "I would like the opportunity to show I am an asset."

"What do you want?"

"To give aid to Elia Lear."

"Make her the queen?"

"If that is what she wishes."

The woman smiled, broad and knowing. "Did you wish to be king of Aremoria?"

"There are too many differences between our situations. I was always made to be my father's heir. Elia was not."

"Wasn't she?" the woman said sharply. "What do you know of how she was made?"

"Who are you?" Mars demanded. "That you speak to me this way?"

Her lovely black eyebrows lifted. "I thought you were only a soldier."

He sighed in frustration, and the wind seemed to huff back, shoving at him, tugging at the sword at his hip. Mars stumbled and turned to gaze inland, toward the northern moors, dark and silvery despite the glaring sky. "I am a stranger to you, and you challenge me without knowing me, regardless of my rank or name."

"You are no stranger to me; your name is on the wind, set there by many voices."

"Then you are a stranger to me."

"Why are you here, Morimaros?"

"To *help*."

"We do not need Aremore might."

"That is why I did not bring any."

"Your name, your presence, is more than enough. You are a living threat, and you know it."

"Then use me! Let Elia use me."

"Tell me: why are you here?"

The wind slammed so hard the grass hissed and roared like its own ocean.

"I want to help Elia."

"Why are you here?" Her voice lowered, and Mars felt it through the wind.

"I told you. Now give me your name, woman." He put his hand on his sword to stop the wind from slapping it against his thigh; too late he realized the threat of the gesture.

"Shh," the woman murmured, touching her lips and then holding her hand out flat toward the moors.

The wind settled.

That graceful gesture; her dark Ispanian flavor; the wary, powerful eyes: Mars saw her in double, then, one figure herself and the other his Fox. Ban was slighter, more desperate, but there was no doubt in Mars's heart.

"You're his mother," he said, stunned. But he should have guessed right away. Brona Hartfare, the witch of the White Forest. Mars felt a pang of dismay for noticing her beauty, as if it would let Ban down. As if the Fox's respect still concerned him.

She said, "And you're his king."

"Not by his word," Mars snapped, his only defense. "He chose you. Your island."

Brona studied him, not as pleased as she ought to be by the revelation. He thought of Ban, writing that note, sending it off, and could not help but wonder how easy a choice it might have been. Had Mars ever mattered to Ban the Fox?

The king turned swiftly away so she might not see the pain crawl over his face. *Ah, stars, Fox,* he thought, nothing but a name and a sorrowful curse.

"You set him here to pull the island apart—for your benefit. For Aremoria."

"I did." Mars barely managed to keep his voice from diving to a whisper. Not from guilt—he would not apologize for acting as a king, not to any but Elia herself. Yet this was Ban's mother, and speaking with her made him feel strangely closer to his Fox.

"Did you know how he would excel at it?" She seemed curious now, more than anything.

"I hoped he would. Lear was not a good king."

"You expect me to believe that was your motivation? The good of our island?"

Mars turned back to her. "It was a *part* of my motivation, and if you do not believe me, there is no point discussing further. All I have is my word, here on your island."

Brona Hartfare nodded. "I believe you. But what I've heard of Morimaros of Aremoria is that he is an excellent general, a liberal king, invested in the betterment of his people. It seems a king like that might have predicted my son's actions."

"I thought all his choices would point in my favor, because Ban would always be loyal to me."

Now Brona slanted him a look. Almost pitying. She said, "All Ban has ever wanted was for someone to be loyal to *him*. So while everyone allowed the stars to make these paths for us, for him—Ban became his own star."

Mars stared at her, understanding there was something in her words older than he could possibly come to terms with, more mysterious and strange than any man of Aremoria could fathom. But he felt the truth in them.

"What— Will you tell me what he's done? He's not here—with Elia. Where is he?"

The Fox's mother sighed. "With Regan certainly, and Gaela, too, most likely. Beyond that, you could say more surely than I what he is responsible for."

Mars heard the implication there perfectly: the witch meant Mars should know what he himself was responsible for. "I would have him at Elia's side," he said. "For that is where I intend to be, if she allows it."

"How unfortunate it is, King, that we cannot control the path of a storm."

There were a hundred things Mars could have said to defend Ban Errigal: that he was not chaos, that he had meant so much to Mars, that she should have cared better for her son, if she was so concerned with his behavior now. That the Fox had been determined and wounded, afraid and jealous and desperate for a friend, or a leader, or at least for a decent man to appreciate everything that Ban could offer, which was exactly what the king had been.

In the end, Mars said nothing.

Brona asked, "Do you love my son?"

"That doesn't matter anymore," Mars answered, harshly, for he had, indeed, loved the man. Trained him personally, lifted him up, trusted him! Simply enjoyed his thorny company. And missed him when he was gone.

She tilted her head and said, with the first lilt of maternal tenderness he had noted in her: "It matters to me."

That hurt the king, and he struggled not to show it. Instead he only nodded, and said, "I did. But I can no longer."

The ocean crashed below them, and the wind rushed past, twisting and tossing up dry grass in tiny whirlwinds. There came a moaning, a sorry cry, and Mars somehow knew it was the voice of Innis Lear.

BAN ERRIGAL WAS alone, and dying.

He gripped the tear in his gambeson, wishing he knew any words to whisper that might stop this gush of hot blood through his fingers. Words to knit flesh together, words to slow his heartbeat, or words at least to dull the pain until he could find a healer. But then, what did it matter if he knelt here to die; none would even notice.

He'd not even been given mail or breast plate, only this foot soldier's leather armor, buckled cheaply across his chest, and a quilted shirt. Nothing better for the bastard cousin from Innis Lear, foisted upon the Alsax though they'd rather have had his half brother Rory, the legitimate heir. Ban had not been given a choice, either.

A quarter mile behind him the sounds of battle continued: a constant rush of noise like the crashing of ocean waves or autumn winds through the White Forest's canopy.

This wound had come from a Diotan soldier, bigger than Ban—though everyone was bigger than Ban—who knocked Ban off his feet and tore away his buckler. As Ban had rolled against churned mud, reaching desperately for the small shield, the soldier had kicked him, then stomped down on his shield arm. The pain of a cracking wrist bone was enough to whiten Ban's vision and give the soldier an opening for a fatal stab.

Only the sudden arrival of another Aremore foot soldier saved Ban's life. The sword had skewed sideways, catching the quilted edge of Ban's shirt. It tore through the gambeson and into Ban's side, instead of his heart.

He'd scrambled away, leaving buckler and his own dropped sword behind, toward the edge of the battle. Ignored or unseen, Ban had made it free of the melee, head pounding and blood hot, with a roar in his ears that drove him to his feet again. Dazed, he'd stood, panting through clenched teeth, and stared at the slope of the battlefield. Aremore soldiers cleaved through the forces from Diota, winning. Cavalry to the southeast, foot soldiers pressing hard, all wearing the bright orange of their young king.

Ban wore it, too, under the leather chest piece. The long gambeson, thinly quilted, was dyed that sunrise orange, now streaked a brilliant scarlet.

He felt strength draining out of him along with the blood, and tucked his broken wrist against his chest.

*What am I doing here,* he wondered then, hazy from pain and weariness.

He took a step away from the battle, away from Aremoria itself. Pain surged from his sword wound; this would kill him. Hissing with every careful movement, Ban made his way toward . . . *peace,* he supposed dully. Shade and quiet.

If this were Innis Lear, the wind would tell him where to go, the trees beckon him with teasing secrets and the promise of help.

Ban walked too slowly. His boots crushed thick summer grass as the sun beat down, hotter than ever it did at home.

He had no home.

Blood soaked through the hip of his pants, sticking the wool to his skin. It trailed along his thigh, until Ban's entire right side darkened with thick, crusting blood. He was only fifteen years old, but he would die here, and nobody would care.

His mother, perhaps, for a moment might think sadly on Ban's fate, but then she'd turn her attention again to the people of Hartfare, her other strays and homeless witches, the lost and found of the island to whom Brona devoted herself even before her own son.

His father would cry false tears, wail with the singular passion for which he was known, and tell stories of Ban's young wildness: stories that always would deteriorate into a reluctant condemnation of his bastard stars.

Rory might miss his brother, but only long enough to play at avenging his death here against Diota.

And King Lear—

Ban stumbled, grunting as he caught himself on a sore knee, jarring his broken wrist. His skull throbbed. A blessed numbness had spread along his wounded side.

Ahead was a low, grassy valley beside the dark towers of a forest. Three cranky-looking hawthorn trees clutched the north, windblown slope. It was a good place to die. Small, sheltered on two sides by the roll of hills and one by the forest, and the other faced only the sky. Ban's vision blurred.

The king of Innis Lear would be glad he was dead.

And perhaps never tell Elia.

Ban drew a long, slow breath—it grew more difficult to breathe deeply. He walked toward the hawthorn trees.

A year ago, he'd have stayed alive for her. A year ago, when Elia loved him, and he returned it with a thrilling joy unlike anything he'd known before. Almost like balancing in the center of the land bridge to the Summer Seat, terrible cliffs dropping a hundred feet on either side to those tearing, wicked ocean waves. Almost like fire coming to life at the tips of his fingers, starlight and root magic joined in a singular spark of magic. Almost like that kiss.

Tears brushed off his eyelashes, and Ban realized he was crying. He slid a few paces down the slope to the dappled shade of the cranky hawthorns. Touching the hard wrinkles of bark, Ban left a bloody handprint. *Hello, hawthorn,* he whispered in the language of trees. Would trees in Aremoria know the words? Or did only trees of Innis Lear understand? Would they listen to a bastard if they did, even if he was also the son of a witch?

It hardly mattered. He was so very tired.

Ban sank to his knees, his shoulder against the trunk of the first hawthorn. Its roots curled through the sloping earth, hard gray snakes. Blood dripped from his wound, plopping against the roots and dusty ground in perfect tiny splatters. Ban blinked, and his tears fell, too. He sighed. This was the place.

The hawthorn shook its leaves, a long sighing response.

*Hello, little brother,* the tree whispered.

Relieved, exhausted, Ban laid himself down between the trees, head cradled in the crook of two roots. He kissed it, closed his eyes, and gave himself over to death.

He woke suddenly, from a dream of yellow flowers that floated in the air like bobbing butterflies, and gasped at a resurgence of pain. Blackness surrounded him, and not the blackness of a starless sky, but of closed doors and deep well water. He smelled roots and dank earth; a healthy, fertile smell. And blood, too, but fainter. His ears were muffled, his entire body cushioned by mud and roots cupped gently and perfectly around him.

As he slept, the hawthorns had made him a nest.

Or a grave.

He shifted but was caught by the heavy embrace of earth. A root hugged his left forearm against his chest, keeping the wrist secure. Another pair of roots circled Ban's ribs, pinching shut the leather vest and pressing together his yawning wound.

*Sleep, son, little brother.*

The words shivered through the ground, passed between the hawthorns.

*We hold you,* they whispered, shaping the language of trees rounder, louder and more tender both, to Ban's ears. Like a different dialect from the slick, intense whispering of Innis Lear.

*Thank you,* he said, attempting the same shapes.

Ban drifted, thirsty but whole. He thought of the starflower hollows in the White Forest, and Elia humming to the flowers, her black eyes bright with magic. The wind teased her to laugh, pushed her toward him. He thought of the garden behind his mother's cottage in Hartfare, of coaxing the sweet peas to curl and braid together along the trellis lines. Sweet peas spoke in staccato half words. Like night moths and cherry trees.

His dreams looped slowly: Elia here, a girl pulling herself out of the hollow of an oak tree, crowned with stars and beetles; King Lear next, towering like a column of cold fire, his touch withering the earth and stones of the island; Earl Errigal laughing so hard his cheeks pinked, pushing Ban toward Brona his mother, her hair tousled and her jaw mud-streaked because they'd been chasing each other though the White Forest, singing a whispered song to the trees. Elia again, always, and the shivering roots, chuckling wind, and rushing tide that grasped against the rocky beach. *Innis Lear.*

Memories, all, a tale for the Aremore roots, whispered through thin, cracking lips as he dreamed. And this land's story in return: bright green summer and the shuffle of red wheat, shaved from the ground for harvest; horses in an easy canter beneath shining soldiers and knights; the glorious sun colored the same as the royal flag tied to the top of a strong sapling oak; Aremoria's new king; winter snow a careful white blanket, and cozy fire that crackled but did not spark; caves beneath elegant old cities, stone mouths like natural wells, and lazy rivers braiding it all together in knots.

The magic was slow, the trees peaceful and reluctant to speak. Aremoria was not hungry like the roots of Innis Lear. Stars fell, forgotten here but as distant signals and pretty lights.

It was a comforting story. Ban would rest content if he slipped into death here in this cradle of earth and roots.

*Don't die, wizard,* the trees whispered. They nudged him awake with root fingers.

Ban opened his eyes.

Dirt fell into them and he blinked fast, tears welling protectively.

He listened.

Through the earth came the sounds of men. A stifled rhythm of talking, footsteps over Ban's resting place.

All the valley trembled with the presence of an army.

Ban whispered in the language of trees, *Yours or an enemy?* for he knew not any word for Aremoria or Diota that trees would understand.

*Enemy,* the trees told him, passing the word down and down.

A tiny insect crossed Ban's bottom lip, a beetle by the feel of it. He opened his mouth and caught it with his tongue. It crunched and he swallowed, unthinking. He was starving, and his tongue was sticky with sleep and thirst. So much so, he knew it had been days. Two at least, maybe three, since the battle he'd fled, desperate and despairing.

He'd urinated at some point. And now he needed water. That was his priority.

Ban was not going to die.

The realization surprised him, but only for a moment; then it felt right. This was not where his memories would end. Not here, away from the hungry island of Innis Lear. Not without seeing Elia again. There was too much to say. Too much to prove.

Ban turned his head carefully, and put his mouth against a root. *Water, I need water.*

The ground shivered, shifted so slightly no one on their feet above would notice, and slowly—ever so slowly—roots squeezed, channels were formed, and a thin trickle of water dribbled against his mouth.

Ban drank.

Overhead, the noise of soldiers settled. Night had arrived, Ban was certain.

He moved the fingers of his injured left hand. They did not protest, though they were stiff. The cracked wrist ached, but he would be careful. Slowly taking a deep breath, he tried to feel through the gash on his side. It hurt, crusted over with blood and scab. If he was careful, very careful, he could emerge and walk back to the Aremore camp. The trees would help hide him, and the earth. Warn him of danger.

*Do they sleep?* he whispered.

*Not yet.*

*Not yet.*

*Now.*

Ban smiled. *Please lift me up,* he said. *Carefully, slowly, silently as you can.*

The hawthorns agreed.

He was birthed from the grassy Aremore hill under cover of dappled, deep shadows. Earth rolled away, roots pulling back, other roots pushing him up and up.

Night was deep, the moon a useless crescent in the west.

Ban rubbed his eyes, leaving dirt on his face to cast him darker, a shadow of the land itself. He looked, and all around was a vast army, camped here in this protected valley. Firelight blinked between peaked tents, though banked low except in one or two places where soldiers sat awake to watch for danger. Ban crouched and asked the trees and wind to gently blow, not enough to alarm anyone, but just to cover the sounds of his escape.

Through aches and weariness, he stood. The three hawthorns hid him from most of the camp, though right here beside him, a tent had been built. At the top a pennant hung, limp but for the fluttering tip thanks to Ban's quiet wind. He recognized the bright white line of a Diotan commander's shield.

He should leave straightaway. He should make his careful way back to the Aremore army. His side hurt, and his wrist was broken. He needed to be cautious.

Or—

Or he might take advantage of his situation and find something valuable to bring back with him. Valuable enough that nobody would judge why he'd left the battlefield. Evidence of Ban's very specific value. He should count horses and men, find maps, or overhear a battle plan. Prove to the Alsax Ban Errigal was no useless bastard, but worth something. Matter to the Aremore army. Make a name for himself. And then prove it to his father, and even the king of Innis Lear. Ban was not to be ignored. He had power. Look what he already had survived with nothing but his words and blood.

The wind hissed, tossing hawthorn leaves together like applause. Ban smiled, this time hungrily, and stepped toward the enemy commander's tent.

# GAELA

GAELA STRODE JUST behind the gray-robed star priest, eager and nearly stepping on his old heels. It had taken several days to discover and summon this man, the same priest who had served at Dondubhan three decades ago, and once led a similar procession when Lear had come to take up the mantle of reluctant kingship. Unlike her father, Gaela was prepared. Her heart beat hard and steady, and every breath filled her from top to toe with vitality.

Tucked like a secret against the northeastern edge of the Tarinnish, the holy navel well connected to the black lake by a thin stream of water. The trickle only barely revealed itself, sliding around sharp pebbles and beneath ferns and long grass. At night, all was black, ethereal gray, and a deep, blunt, resounding green. Overhead, the wind dragged clouds across the stars in a sheer layer of silver, and so the sky seemed to ripple with emotion as their procession made its way around the lake.

Behind Gaela followed her graceful sister, who though still full of impossible sadness, was just as eager to be queen. They were accompanied, too, by that dark slip of a wizard, and Osli, with three more star priests and a dozen retainers for witnesses.

The star priest leading their party slowed as they entered the well's grove. He stepped aside for Gaela so that she might face the entrance. Massive, moss-covered boulders surrounded the grove, encircling it and creating a mouth of rocks and soft earth, damp and darkly green. Some trees grew here, lean as bone and gray as the moon. Few leaves remained, shivering in the omnipresent wind.

At the center, smaller blue stones created a pit as black as anything she'd ever seen. At the fore was a flat boulder, like a ledge, and another made a roof across two of the largest boulders to shelter this most ancient well.

The star priests moved to stand at each corner of the small grove, cupping the clay bowls of fire carefully before them. All looked to the oldest; a cragged and drooping old man with pale brown eyes and a spotted white face, who had stationed himself beside the well and now pointed at the clusters of tall spindled plants growing in the damp soil beside the well. "There is no ritual but this," he said. "Eat a handful of the blossoms, and dip your hands into the well to drink. Then, in the light of the stars, by the power of the rootwaters, you will be recognized as the rightful monarch of Innis Lear."

Gaela waited for the rest of her people to filter in around her, studying the flowers. The green stalks reached higher than her waist, spreading like fingers or thin, miniature trees. The leaves were feathery and green, and tiny white blossoms made starbursts and swaying baubles. She wondered why they seemed so strange, so out of place in this grove, when they were no more than a common weed, and weeds abounded in these northern reaches of Innis Lear.

"They should be blooming in the late spring," Regan murmured. "Not now. Now they should be dried seed heads. Might we, too, have blossomed here, my Connley?"

Gaela frowned, concerned for her grieving sister's state of mind.

"Death rattles," Regan's wizard, her Fox, murmured. Then, louder, his voice like ice, "It's hemlock."

"You would poison me?" Gaela turned with careful, coiled control to the old star priest.

Led by Osli, her retainers drew their swords, aiming furious blades at the four priests.

The old priest inclined his head and held her gaze. "It is the only way to gain the crown of Innis Lear, Princess."

Wind hissed across the tops of the low trees, tossing thin yellow-and-brown leaves toward them. It shivered the pines at the north of the grove. Gaela stared at the old man, wondering if this could be true.

"My father ate such poison?" Regan asked, strangely calm to Gaela's ears. Curious, almost wondering.

"Yes."

Ban the Fox stepped up to the edge of the well. "I believe it," he said in a taut voice. "The roots of the island and the blood of the king become united, sacrificing for each other. So one who would take the crown must take the poison, and then let the rootwater cleanse them, transforming death of the self into rebirth as the king. This is the way of wormwork."

"It is safer on the Longest Night, when the roots are strongest and waters blessed by the brightest, boldest stars. If fear pauses you now," said the old priest.

Gaela's skin chilled, and slowly began to tighten against her own flesh. Surely this was not fear, but fury.

Regan knelt by the star-bright weeds and brushed her fingers against the flowers. "So beautiful," she whispered.

"Put your swords down," Gaela ordered her retainers. She glanced to see it done, catching the gross tension on Osli's face. Her captain did not trust this magic, either, and she was loath to leave her lord so unprotected.

The rootwaters had never done anything for Gaela. Why should they keep her alive now? Gaela had rejected them again and again. Had rejected everything of magic, of star prophecy and the island. She intended her power for herself and her sister, not to share it with fickle wind, stubborn earth, prideful stars. Why should she put her life into—

The thought hit her like a ballista's bolt: Dalat had been poisoned *this* way.

Gaela had always suspected poison. She would never have been able to prove it had been her father's own hand, not just his fault—his requirement— his prophecy. Gaela had guessed, between the wagging tongues at court and her own ears, but never, until exactly now, had she *known how.* If this priest told it true, Lear had known of the hemlock here, as well as he knew his own stars.

Lear had poisoned Dalat to bring about the prophecy that she would die on her eldest daughter's sixteenth birthday.

The night before, the queen had been healthy, with an appetite and shining eyes. No fever or illness, nothing to claim her in the night so suddenly.

By dawn, Dalat simply had ceased to breathe.

Or so Lear had claimed. But he was alone with her during that night, and alone with her first thing in the morning.

If this hemlock grew so near Dondubhan, how easy would it have been to make certain she partook?

Gaela's shoulders heaved as she thought it all through, as she stared at the weedy hemlock, at the way the flowers looked like constellations. Of course it was such a star shape he would use; of course it was such a thing that he preferred.

Her heart burned with this new understanding. As if the island had collaborated in her mother's death, Gaela lifted her foot and brought it down upon one of the hemlock plants.

Regan gasped, and one of the priests grunted in protest.

"This will not happen," Gaela said. Her voice shook, from fury and a swelling panic. "I am changing the way this process works, changing ritual and the relationship between the crown and the land. I will not poison myself to suit dead ways of dead kings. I will be my own sacrament."

"It is supposed to be faith that guides the hand!" cried the oldest star priest. "To wear our crown, you must believe in the roots, in the island's blood and the prophecies of the stars!

"No." Gaela crushed more of the hemlock. "I am here for my own blood, which is of this island, and my own will, which shall be my only prophecy."

She drew out her knife and sliced at the green stalks, ripping up others and tossing them against the mossy boulders. Some leaves and petals fluttered down into the black pit of the well; lonely, fallen stars.

"Gaela." Regan clutched at her wrist. "I'll do it. I want to! Let me do this!"

"No. I won't allow you to be such a fool. And neither was our father, though he became one by the end. He would not have done this, hating the roots so, disdainful of all but the skies of his beloved stars. A coward, one who doomed his wife to save his own seat, but he'd never have wagered his own life. He lied, if he said he did."

The old priest shook his head frantically. "No, I was there. I saw it, then. He ate of the flowers, and drank of the waters, before he grew dizzy and collapsed. Lear went still for a long hour as the stars wheeled overhead, and then the king opened his eyes, and the stars shone upon his awakening."

"A pretty story." Gaela did not care.

Tears glittered on Regan's cheeks, and she knelt beside the well. "I don't mind if it kills me, Gaela," she whispered. "The reward is greater, to be what we always wanted. What Connley wanted. I would be made full—new."

"How dare you offer to abandon me," Gaela said, so low in her throat she could hardly believe it was her own voice. "Remember who you are, Regan, and who I am, and what we are to each other. What we will be to this land."

Silence fell all around, but for the constant pressing wind, and Regan's hard breathing. Gaela put her hand on her sister's neck. She was sympathetic; she hated for Regan to weep, to hurt so badly and desperately, but Gaela was angry, too, furious that Regan felt so bereft without Connley, when they still had each other. And Regan could still try for a babe, perhaps with the Fox, his seed surely more cunning than Regan's dead husband's, and enough power between them to spur life.

No other love should be able to drag Regan away from Gaela! As if they could not be all to each other, beyond the ways of men, and their rules, and their stars. No.

"Regan," she said, resolute but not unkind.

Her sister's head nodded, wearily.

"Ban," Gaela ordered, "hold my sister up."

The young man took Regan's elbow and leaned her against his chest. His eyes were bright, slightly too wide, and he murmured softly into Regan's ear.

Gaela then faced their enrapt audience and forged onward.

"My sister and I will stay here for some time, and when we emerge, we will be crowned. You, men, you, priests, listen to me: I am the rightful king of Innis Lear because it is who and what I am, what I have built myself to be, what I should have been from birth. My father was the king, and his father, back two hundred years to the first king of a united Innis Lear. And my mother, so enamored of our roots and stars, was buried here, and she has become this island, anointing my own natal claim. This crown is my legacy. I have ingested the poison of life these last twelve years, and my sweat has watered these lands." She leveled the old priest with her boldest gaze. "My blood *is* the island's blood, do you understand me?"

After a moment, Gaela swept her stare to encompass the entire company assembled in the holy grove. Regan, still against Ban the Fox, followed her sister's gaze.

Many nodded immediately: Osli and three other retainers, whose faces were firm and already lit in awe, knelt. Some thought hard, then glanced at one another, and back at her again, before going down on their knees, too. The shaking priests were cowed by the display, and followed the others' example. Except for one.

The old priest was stone, in body and in regard.

Gaela said, "I will cut you down if you prefer."

"This is not the way, Your Highness," he said. "You are right about everything in your history, and what you have earned, but still the island must know you, before giving its people and roots and breath over to your care. You must give it your blood; you must drink from its roots. You must face the stars above. It is not that you are less if you don't, but that the wind, the water, the island will not—"

"Choose, priest," Gaela said. "The island might wait, but I won't."

He slowly, painfully dropped to his knees. Frustration made his jaw hard and his wrinkled lips thin as he placed the bowl of oil and fire at her feet. "My queen."

Because she wanted to, she kicked out, catching the discarded sacred bowl with her boot. The oil splattered, and fire destroyed the rest of the hemlock.

"Queen is my sister's calling. Now, I am king."

AS THE SUN rose, Gaela sat in the throne of Innis Lear, there in the great hall of Dondubhan. Regan held herself carefully beside the throne, resting in a narrow, tall-backed chair nearly as regal. Both women were dressed and decorated voluptuously, in the midnight blue of the line of Lear. White clay dotted their brows and red plumped their lips. Star tabards fell across both laps. Gaela wore a heavy silver coronet and held a sword across her thighs. Regan cupped a silver bowl of water from the Tarinnish, a thin diadem of intricate leaves upon her brow.

Dawn slid gray-pink light through tall windows as men and women of Dondubhan and Astore offered vows and gifts to the new monarchs. Unease and hope mingled in a tense, airy soup, for most in the hall did not approve of the timing, yet they wanted nothing so much as for Innis Lear to prosper once again. And here, now, arrived a chance for restoration under their new queens.

Ban the Fox had knelt first, in the winter blue of the Errigal earls, and sworn his loyalty to Gaela, then Regan. They had named him before everyone, not only as earl but as the first root wizard of Innis Lear's new age.

That had further spread out gossip and hope, like threads of lightning.

Retainers and messengers were sent to the corners of the island, beckoning for the lords to come to their queens on the Longest Night, for the heads of towns and castle stewards to come. There to witness all three daughters of Innis Lear together: the rulers crowned and their priestly sister set to her place in the star towers.

Gaela studied the face of every man, woman, and child who knelt before them, composing to herself the letter she would write to Elia. The defenses she would mount against Aremoria immediately, the summons and plans for sea vessels, the enlisting of unlanded men and women, and the tithing of the landed. The urgent business of the western coastal road, adjustments for depleted grain to the south. Her father's body would need to be brought to the Star Field. The star towers would be shuttered if they did not make prophecies to suit her needs, despite whatever choice Elia would come to make about her own future. All the wells might be opened if local folk so desired, but Gaela would first send a mission into the heart of the White Forest, perhaps led by the Fox himself. They would need to find the ruins of the ancient star cathedral where the navel of the island drove deepest, that inspiration of the old faith and the way of kings long dead. And that—that well Gaela would fill to the brim with sand and salt.

The only power on Innis Lear would be her own.

Hours ago, in the darkest moment of the night, just before they left that poisoned grove, Ban had spoken, holding Gaela's sister carefully. His words were a warning, and a challenge:

"Elia would swallow the hemlock, and the rootwaters would save her."

Regan had closed her eyes, lost to her selfish pain, but Gaela had smiled. "She will not, and they cannot. For I will stop her first."

*To Elia of Lear, and any who would be her allies:*

*We crown ourselves here at Dondubhan, where the kings of Lear have been crowned for seven generations. The island is ours: I who am Gaela King, and I who am Regan Queen, for the king who was our father named us his true heirs, and as we have made the necessary rituals of our people, so shall we rule.*

*If you would meet us on this island, be it as subject to her king. We shall appear on the plains of Errigal on the Fourday of this month's dark week. There you shall submit to our rule. If you choose otherwise, death or exile will be the only way forward. Copies of this letter fly to every corner of Innis Lear, so that all understand our first decree, even so that the very wind and roots understand.*

*Your sisters and rulers,*
*Gaela King of Lear*
*Regan Connley of Lear*

# ELIA

FOR THREE DAYS Elia had awaited her sisters at Errigal Keep. She moderated the line between Lear's retainers and those of Errigal still loyal to Ban the Fox, meeting those she could at Rory's side. He knew all the women and servants and the families of his father's retainers, and they welcomed him, even when Elia cast suspicions upon Ban. She spoke twice, for long hours, with Curan Ironworker, the wizard, gleaning what information she could on the recesses of the forest and the changes in the song of the iron marsh, as well as asked him questions about Ban. Elia had made herself available to all, as best she could, letting go of her old instincts to withdraw, to remain apart. She was not a star, she told herself, but a woman. A sister. A friend. A princess, as well as a star priest. A daughter still, and one day, she hoped, a mother, though she was not with child now.

Nor yet was she a queen.

With the crushed-hemlock crown circling the crook of her elbow, Elia went to the ramparts in the evenings to see the first stars, to mourn her father alone and allow herself to feel anger toward him and all the mistakes he'd made. To explore the unfamiliar fury burning in her heart: that he'd put Elia in this position, and brought the island so near to ruination. But in many ways, the stars had ruined him, too. They had been Lear's everything, perhaps more so than even Dalat, and surely more so than himself. That singular focus had made him weak. If the stars were always to blame, there was no way to hold oneself responsible for anything.

And Elia understood the answer was not to do the opposite: to obey the island roots unthinkingly. She could not eat the flower and drink the water on the island's word alone. Ruling Innis Lear should be a partnership, a conversation, and she would not rush the moment, though she believed one would come.

There were many conversations to have first. The morning after Rory'd arrived, Elia tended the dead Earl Errigal at his side. The body had been laid out in the cellar, washed and dressed, with his sword and chain of earldom. Elia held Rory's hand while he breathed through great pain, and when he calmed, she asked, "Why are you here at my side, Errigal Earlson?"

His full name startled him, and he wiped under his eyes. "My father—" he said thickly.

Elia took the earl's chain off the dead father's chest. "I mean, why did you come home, why are you with me? Your brother is gone to my sisters, and they will take this chain from you for defying them, and give it to Ban. They have already declared it—you've heard what the iron wizard said was Regan's order."

"It's mine," Rory said. "Maybe Ban should have been my father's heir, because he's oldest, or because he's smarter than me, but he isn't. I am. I want it."

"Your stars are suited to it."

"They are."

"Why not go to Gaela and demand your rights of her?"

"Gaela alarms me."

Surprise widened her eyes.

Rory pressed on, distraught, "She doesn't . . . Do you know anything about war games? Gaela wins them, but always the same way. Even when her specific tactics vary, the strategy is the same. It is always an aggressive one, always driven and determined, but she cuts losses without a thought. She is a great commander, but a queen should not leave fields trampled behind her every time, nor use a village as a point of play. They're homes, and they matter beyond winning that single battle."

"And Regan?"

"Regan is a witch, not a—a queen. Maybe with Connley, she might've . . . but not alone." He winced at the sound of his prejudice. So like his father's, and he seemed to know it.

"And me?" Elia murmured.

"I trust you," he said, as if it were that simple.

"Rory."

He smiled, flirting just a little. "I've loved you since we were children, and I've seen you. You always made us stop to say hello to anyone we passed when we played. You knew their names, everyone."

"You do that, too."

"I'd probably make a good king, then," he joked.

But a moment fell between them, and they stared. Elia wondered what would happen if she married him right now, today. An old friend, a soldier, one of her father's favorites, the heir to Errigal iron. A man she could control better than her other options. It would rearrange many pieces of this dangerous puzzle.

"If you ask me, Elia," Rory said, low and serious, "I will say yes. But you shouldn't."

"Tell me why."

"We shouldn't do things that will hurt more than they heal."

It broke her heart to hear the regret in his voice, and Elia realized she did not want to know what caused it.

He told her anyway. "It was my fault they sent Ban to Aremoria, that spring."

"How?" she whispered. "It was my father, afraid of Ban's stars, and thinking Ban was unworthy of me."

"I told *my* father . . ." Rory glanced at the slack face of the body laid out beside them. It was a gruesome location for such intimate talk. "I told him that Ban loved you, and that the two of you should be married, and then we'd all be happy. It was only a week later that—" He stopped.

Elia covered her mouth and turned away. "You didn't know," she said, muffled by her hand. She forced it down to hang rigid at her side and repeated herself.

"It doesn't matter. I didn't think. About much at all. And if Ban did know, or realized it . . ." Rory sighed. "I deserve that he's returned the favor. Though I won't—I won't just submit to his revenge."

"No." Elia turned back and offered Rory the earl's copper chain. "Take it."

Rory kissed her temple and refused, grief thickening his tongue. "When this is over, either I or my brother will put it on. Only then."

When the sun set each night, Elia crouched with Brona to cast holy bones. While Brona read the cards and bones, Elia would read the position of the stars. Together they wove stories of skies and roots: the first night came a tale of loss, where the stars dominated all and soon there was no place for the birds of any world to land.

The second night the story was about Kayo, who was in love. That story was a spark of warmth, a reminder that affection could still blossom and grow on Innis Lear, even in the past six years. Elia found herself teasing Brona, happy. Kayo himself admitted it in the morning, and admitted, too, that he'd asked Brona to marry him before and the witch's answer remained always patience. "She will need to be patient with me now," her uncle said, his hand hovering over the bandage on his face. The wound healed slowly, and Kayo had to be gentle with it or an infection might spread and blind him in his other eye, too. That Gaela had done this to him, so viciously, with such disregard, put Elia firmly in agreement with Rory: Gaela would make a terrible queen, even regardless of the island's will.

Last night the bones and stars had told of a queen slowly being born.

Elia avoided the king of Aremoria completely: he and La Far lived with the retainers to keep knowledge of his identity shrouded in as much secrecy as could be managed. They did as her father's retainers did, so it was easy to keep her distance. If she spoke to him, Elia was certain she would do irreparable damage between their countries. She did not forgive him—she could not, if she was to be queen of Innis Lear. But she did wish, some moments, she could find the strength to confront him, and then together they might commiserate over their hopes and fears regarding Ban the Fox.

Waiting put an edge to her voice; she could not relax. Neither did the island. Wind ravaged them, always, until only those who accustomed themselves to the noise were able to sleep. It begged and screamed wordlessly, but for the occasional cry of her name. Even under the brightest autumn sun, birds huddled in the crooks of tree branches and horses resisted leaving their barn.

She took several men to the navel well of Errigal Keep and pried off its cap. The well burped up a gasp of wind that ought to have been rancid but instead smelled like wine, sharp and sweet and heady. *Drink,* whispered the well. *Eat,* said the wind.

The hemlock crown had lost all its scent, and most of the petals had fallen in Elia's wake. Aefa seemed relieved, but there was poison in the leaves and stems, too. Any part would suffice. And if she needed it, the island would show her where to find more starweed.

But Elia would not eat it, not yet. Not until she faced her sisters. She refused to take action that could not be undone.

And then the letter came, in the hand of a messenger in pink, who tore into the Keep sweaty and desperate.

Elia was in the great hall, seated at a long table near the hearth, peeling and chopping onions with women and boys from the kitchen. The stinky, tearful work was made better by the poetry and songs of the folk, who'd spread out here at her invitation because of the space and warmth; the gale outside had turned frigid.

Eager, ready, Elia opened the letter immediately. She read it, then again.

She sank to the rush-covered floor, sitting in a pool of bright red skirts, and read the message a third time.

Aefa knelt beside her and read the letter, too.

"Worm shit," she said.

"Aefa." Elia took a deep breath. "Aefa, send everyone away, and bring me Kayo, Brona, and Rory. And Morimaros. I would speak with them."

"Morimaros?"

"This is the business of kings and queens. It is time."

While Aefa hastened to comply, Elia hauled herself to the tall-backed chair just beside the hearth. She lifted the hemlock crown from the seat, sat herself, and settled the crown onto her lap. She read the letter again. *Death or exile will be the only way.*

Ban had failed her, refused to bring her sisters here. This stank of his destructive work: turning family against itself, lighting sparks for war to burn everything to ashes instead of nurturing growth, instead of protection.

And her sisters threatened to kill her.

Elia closed her eyes. She did not want to feel the betrayal. Not this time. Better to turn cold and still, better to breathe the emotions away, to diffuse them into air and mist.

But no. She had to feel in order to fight.

Tears flicked down her cheeks, and she did not break. She put her hands on the arms of the chair, leaned her head back, and let herself be hurt. And angry. And so very sad. All the whirling emotions gathered around her heart, squeezing, lifting, and she wept quietly as she waited. Tears dripped off her chin to tap the letter itself.

Her sisters claimed to be queens, but high overhead the wind threaded itself angrily through the stones of the keep, blowing frustration down the side of the mountain. The island disagreed. They had not made the bargain.

Warmth from the whispering fire enveloped her; she tried to pull comfort from it. The shuffle of folk leaving with onions and knives had vanished, replaced by the sure footsteps of those summoned. Elia left her eyes closed.

"Elia?" Kayo said.

She stifled the urge to leap up and offer him aid. Instead she smiled sadly. "I have news from my sisters."

Chairs were moved, and a bench, too.

Kayo settled in a heavy chair to support his weary body, and Brona sat beside him on a stool; Aefa, Morimaros, and Rory shared a bench. Rory leaned forward, elbows on his knees, eager for her word, though with a slight frown as he could see how she'd been affected. Morimaros positioned himself nearest to her on the bench, and his gaze branded her with its weight. Kayo shifted and opened his mouth; Brona touched his knee to quiet him. His bandage was pristine: no yellowing from the witch's tonics, no blood.

"They will be here to speak with me in two nights," Elia began. She no longer wept, but the evidence was clear on her cheeks, if not in her voice. "They have crowned themselves at Dondubhan, so many months before the Longest Night, flaunting the conventions of Innis Lear, and demand I submit to them here, or go into exile. Or die."

Rory yelled wordlessly. Kayo grunted as if in pain. Brona closed her eyes. Morimaros held his expression reserved.

"I have asked you all here to advise me, as a council to a queen. My proven allies all, but for you, Morimaros. No matter how you came, you are the king of Aremoria, and I expect you to show it."

He nodded, jaw clenched.

It was not an impressive group, Elia suddenly thought: Kayo never a warrior, so gravely wounded and near blind, Aefa her Fool, a half-deposed earl, and the witch of the White Forest. Though Brona was powerful, she rarely looked it. There was something, Elia supposed, to that tactic.

"What will happen if I submit?" she asked. "If I give in to them and be what they would have of me: little sister, star priest. Inconsequential. What is the worst that would follow? What consequence?"

"You will not," Kayo said, gripping the arm of his chair shakily.

"This island will break," Brona answered, as if her lover had not. "Gaela cannot rule Innis Lear. She is as bad as Lear himself, and worse than her late husband, Astore, for she embraced her path with wholeheartedness as fanatical as your father's. She is the continuation of Lear's rule, not a break from it, no matter what she believes. A zealous refusal to listen is no better than a zealous devotion to the stars."

Elia agreed, and saw Rory nod vehemently. But she said, "Maybe Innis Lear is destined to break."

Kayo leveled his niece with a vivid frown. "You do not believe that."

The pain in his voice seemed physical, and Elia looked at Brona, worried she ought not to have summoned her uncle from his sick bed. But the witch nodded, though her brow wrinkled and she put her hand to Kayo's back, caressing in soft circles.

Elia met her uncle's open, unwounded eye, and said, "Ban believes it. He said Innis Lear should burn to ash. That it is the only way to remake the island better. I've seen nothing in the stars to suggest otherwise. And the roots are determined to tear us apart, with ill crops and wailing wind."

"Is that what you want?" Kayo asked.

"No." That, at least, Elia knew. "I want Innis Lear to thrive."

"So you cannot submit."

"This is yours, Elia," said Rory, as he had claimed Errigal for himself beside his father's body. "Don't give it away to your sisters."

"How should I fight them? Should I cast Innis Lear into civil war? Raze the island with war machines and drown the rootwaters in blood?"

Kayo said, "Rosrua and Bracoch will be with us."

Rory said, "Rosrua today, Bracoch tomorrow. If we fight, it will be near equal in numbers."

"With the island on your side," said Brona.

Elia looked at Morimaros, who had remained silent.

"Aremoria will eventually go to war with Gaela Lear on the throne," he said, roughly as if he'd not spoken in days.

"But not with me."

"That is not what I want from you."

"You would take me, marry me, and scour Innis Lear of my wretched family? Give Ban and Gaela what they want? Destruction for his part, war for hers?"

"It is an option. If the island must break, make it break in the shape you want."

"I don't want it to break at all."

"Something will," he said, hands fisted on his thighs. "Do not let it be you."

Elia stood, furious. The hemlock tumbled down her skirt to the stone floor. "So I should let my sisters destroy themselves? And all my island?"

"It would be a slow destruction, if you submit," the king said. "Gaela could rule for years, until someone rebels, or until famine or this cursed wind drives the people against her. That might be sooner than I think. There are no heirs, and will never be, from what I understand. So under her crown the island is doomed. But if you went with me there would be time."

"Time. To think, to plan, you mean. On your own behalf or mine? To analyze and find alternatives to submission or death. Exile is the safe choice."

Morimaros pulled his mouth in a small grimace. "I want you too badly to pretend objectivity."

"I appreciate the honesty," she said flatly, even as Aefa gasped and Rory widened his eyes. For a moment, Elia had forgotten she was not alone with the king of Aremoria. To recover, she asked, "If you were me, would you retire? What would you do?"

"Fight."

Elia sucked in a breath. He had not hesitated a second, despite it going against his own advice for her.

Morimaros said, "This is your country, your island, and you love it. If you can lead Innis Lear, the people and trees and all of it, to something better than your sisters, mustn't you? If people will follow you and fight for you, choose you, if that is your gift, how can you run? How can you submit?"

Heart pounding, Elia asked, "Is it my gift? How do I know?"

The king tilted his face to hers; she stood over him, hands clenched at her sides. He said, "Will people come for you? I have. Kayo did, and your father's retainers. These earls Rosrua and Bracoch with their armies. This witch, who holds more power than most. Are there more? Will your wind summon them, and the roots pass the call? What makes a king or a queen, besides the will of the land and the people together?"

Elia backed away from the intensity of his gaze. She knocked the backs of her thighs against the tall seat beside the hearth and looked to the witch of the White Forest for escape. "You are powerful, Brona, and have thrived all this time. You gather people to you; you create sanctuary; the roots and stars trust you. You would make a better queen than me."

Silence fell. Elia glanced at the wretched, dead crown of hemlock at her feet. She knew what she believed in her heart, but she waited to hear what Brona would say.

Rory and Aefa both fidgeted. Kayo held Brona's hand but said nothing, and by that Elia thought he agreed, or at least would not argue either way. A remnant of his upbringing, to let the women in his life decide for themselves.

Morimaros's jaw was tight.

Finally, Brona said, "It is not my name the island calls."

Closing her eyes in relief, in sorrow, Elia nodded. She understood. She agreed. "The island won't have Gaela, either. Brona is right: my sister can call herself king, and all the people of Innis Lear can follow her, and the island still will not submit. She would have to tame it with fire and iron, and I cannot imagine Innis Lear would endure it. And Regan might once have been able to survive the ascension, but no longer, with her withered heart."

"Survive . . ." Aefa's clever eyes darted to the poison circlet on the ground. "What aren't you telling us, Elia Lear? You don't mean war; you mean something else. What is it that would kill your middle sister, were she to try to rule?"

"I know how to become queen," Elia replied softly, glancing around at all her allies. "In a way that not even Gaela can stop, not without killing me herself."

"The Longest Night ritual," Brona said.

"Do you know what it is?" Elia asked.

"No."

Kayo said, "Talich at Dondubhan does. The old priest who led your father through it. He married them, too, your mother and father."

Elia knelt and lifted the hemlock crown. *Eat of the flower, drink of the rootwater,* she said in the language of trees. She repeated herself for her allies, aloud and in their own tongue: "Eat of the flower, drink of the roots. That is all." She took a deep breath. "I swallow the poison, and the rootwaters cleanse me of it, and so is the bargain between crown and island set. My blood becomes its blood, and its blood mine."

Her uncle let go of Brona abruptly, shaking his head. He put his hand to his bandage, grimacing.

But Brona touched her mouth, and nodded *yes*. She understood in her gut, as Elia did.

"You can't," Morimaros said, and Aefa shot to her feet.

"I agree with the king!" the Fool's daughter cried. "Poison, Elia, you can't think it, who told you that? Was it Ban? Was it Regan? Think where the message came from and mistrust it!"

"The island told me," Elia said.

Rory put his arm around Aefa. "It sounds like magic. It sounds like the oldest earth saint stories and festivals." His voice was full of wonder, and dread—but also hope.

"I—" Elia nodded. "Thank you for your counsel, all of you. I am going to meet my sisters in two nights. I will bring a crown of hemlock, and between the three of us, before the night ends, there will be a queen of Innis Lear."

"One of you will do as the island bids." Aefa's distress heightened her voice.

"Or all three of us," Elia said soothingly, feeling calm and cool—but it was not the distance of stars, it was the strength of certainty. "In two nights, we shall meet them. And it will be done."

"Ban will be with them," the king of Aremoria said suddenly.

"Yes."

"I want to go at your side. I need to."

"I will allow it," she replied, and then left them all, without another word. As was her right.

Outside the great hall, Elia turned in a full circle, unsure where to go. But of course, the answer was high toward the stars.

Up and up she went, through the old part of the Keep and into the black stones of its most ancient tower. The stairs narrowed, and Elia climbed higher, until she reached the pinnacle, ascending through the trapdoor and into the bare sky: this platform, with barely room for two or three men, had been built for a watch in the days when kings ruled only pieces of the island, constantly on guard for attack.

Stars gleamed; she could see them in every direction, though wind cut harshly from the southeast. Elia sank down against the crenellations.

Tilting her head back, she stared into the night, tracing the shape of blackness, not the points of light. She resisted all thoughts, flattening her mind into nothing more than the patterns between stars. No signs revealed themselves, and Elia discovered no hidden meaning; long ago star priests had suggested the void beyond the heavens was the origin of chaos, the home of pain and love, of all wild instincts. That it had been the coming of the stars that brought order into the world.

Footsteps on the narrow stairs below the platform roused her.

It was Brona, lifting the trapdoor.

"Did I upset everyone, enough so they sent you to chide me?" Elia asked.

But the witch said nothing, staring at Elia with a strangeness, a hesitancy. "Say what you've come to say," Elia ordered gently.

Brona lowered herself to sit beside Elia and stared across the small tower at the opposite stones. "Dalat, your mother, took hemlock and died of it."

A great, raw pulse of fear drained Elia of all warmth, and she remembered that morning suddenly: her mother's dull, dead gaze, her father's choking grief, her sisters' fury, and Gaela's accusation that Lear had poisoned her. Elia shook her head. "No, Father would not have done that. I cannot believe it."

"Dalat did it to herself."

Elia's lips fell open, as if she could taste the delicate petals of hemlock. "She tried to be the island's queen?"

"No," Brona said. "No, it was not for that. She did not intend to be saved."

Elia's tongue dried and her gorge rose. *No.*

Brona continued gently, "Dalat loved you, and your sisters, and even your father and this country, so deeply that she died to preserve it. She died to keep everything alive, to hold your place and your father's authority."

"No," Elia said, pressing away from Brona. "She . . . the stars . . . she would not have done that. If she loved us."

"If the prophecy concerning Dalat's death had proven false, everything your father had built would have crumbled. Not only his personal faith, but his rule and the provenance of his crown. All would have questioned you. Connley's mother and Earl Glennadoer would have questioned your entire bloodline, and Dalat's very presence on the island. Everything, don't you see? If your mother had not . . ."

Elia stared at her small, brown, trembling hands. Dalat had killed herself? For politics. For stars. To stop war. To protect her daughters and her people. *Oh, Mother,* she said to the wind.

"Elia."

She needed—she needed to breathe, to think through this. Three long, deep breaths were all she allowed herself. Each shook. "It was not my father," she finally said.

"No, Lear did not know her plans."

Elia shook her head, opened her mouth, was silent, and then tried again. "Why didn't you tell my sisters, at least? So they would know, and not hate him? Why didn't *she?*"

"Dalat did not want you to know," Brona said. The witch sat straight, old grief bowing her mouth. "She wanted all of you to have faith in the stars and in your father, too. She thought—she thought her death would bring you all together. Make you stronger."

Elia laughed pitifully and looked up at the sky. Wind blew hard enough to blur the constellations. "Oh no. She trusted none of us, not even my father. Her husband! She did not—did not let us be her family."

"It was bold, brave even, to take her own life for the island. To remove the uncertainty, prove that your father and his ways were true. I admire that . . . a singular choice, one that changed everything, solidifying the power of the crown."

"It didn't work," Elia said.

"It could have. The choices your father made afterward are what ruined it: Lear alienated his daughters, and as king he adhered to such a strict form of star worship he cut out all other avenues. If he'd merely kept his faith, and continued to rule—without closing the wells, for example—if he'd striven for connection with his daughters . . . maybe Dalat's sacrifice would have been successful."

"She should have trusted him, and told him."

"Maybe, but Lear was always so impulsive. He might have stopped her and ruined her plans."

"Because he loved her! He might have given her to the rootwaters to save her."

Brona frowned.

"You truly never knew of the hemlock ritual?" Elia asked, feeling accusatory but not caring. She might accuse the whole world tonight.

"I did not." The witch's brow crumpled, and tears shone in her dark brown eyes. "I'd have brought her rootwater. She might have died on Gaela's birthday, then been reborn."

Compassion pierced Elia's heart, but she was crying again, too. She glanced toward the stars. Would they ever have comfort to offer her again? No longer could she imagine them pure and righteous, nor even bright, crawling beetles. What if the prophecy had been written: *On the night of her first daughter's sixteenth birthday, the queen will be reborn?*

It was such a similar prophecy. Depending on the wind, or roots. Depending on the entire shape of the sky.

"Are you going to do it?" Brona asked.

"Yes," Elia said. "To give myself entirely to the fight, I must transform. But I will offer my sisters the same chance. I will not make my mother's mistake, or my father's."

"I will follow you to the very end, Elia Lear, and not only because I loved your mother."

Elia nodded but closed her eyes in dismissal. She wanted to be alone with the night. Brona's steps creaked gently on the old wood, and the sound of the trapdoor closing settled the shadows in Elia's heart. She breathed, listened to the angry night, and said to the wind, *Thank you.*

*Eat the flower, drink the rootwater,* the wind snarled back.

"How did my sister die?" Kayo whispered into Brona's hair.

He stared at the valley of candles and stars—Dalat's year memorial, where the family she'd lost mourned—and it came to him that he should take Elia away from here, away from this island that had killed Dalat, before it sank into his niece's bones, before she was too much a part of it. The old empress would welcome another daughter for her line.

To answer Kayo's question, the witch of the White Forest turned to face him, and the star field cast her in fire, a salamander woman, a dragon with lips and curls and deep, sorrowful eyes. "Come," she murmured nudging him farther away. "I have a message from Dalat, come."

Breathless with surprise, he obeyed.

Brona led him back, along a winding route, through the moonlit field of stone and starfire. Near the trees again, she stopped. She took both of his hands; hers were cool and dry, gentle. "What know you of your sister's marriage, as it relates to how the island viewed her queenship?"

Frowning, Kayo said, "The marriage was foretold by the religion of the stars, and Lear never questioned it."

"Yes. And they loved each other."

"So it seemed to me," he agreed. Kayo remembered the way Dalat had watched her older husband, and how their heads leaned together always, sharing conversations and secrets and caresses.

"Before Dalat came, another woman was to be queen. The daughter of the old Duke Connley was married to our king's elder brother. Connley had believed the marriage contract would survive the deaths of Lear's brothers, but he underestimated Lear's devotion to the stars."

A hot flutter began in Kayo's stomach: this was aged politics, and he had asked Brona for the story of Dalat's death. "This Connley—I remember him."

"Do you remember the rest of the marriage prophecy? That Lear's destined wife would give him strong children, rule beside him well, then die on the sixteenth anniversary of her first daughter's birth."

"She did," Kayo whispered again.

"She did." Brona smiled. It was a dangerous, flat smile.

"I did not believe in it! Or I would have been here. I thought . . . I didn't think of it when I left because it was *ridiculous*. Stars do not know such things—they are merely lights in the sky!" Kayo pulled away from her. "How can you—"

"Listen, Kay Oak of Lear."

It was not his name. She said it, though, with raw certainty, and it echoed in his skull like a spell. Brona had, with four words, rooted him here.

He was rigid. He did not want to hear more. He could hardly breathe.

"Two years ago, rumors reached Dalat's ears: if the queen did not die on her appointed day, she could not be the woman the stars had ordained. If fate's finale proved wrong, what of the start?" Brona's voice was hollow now, but not soft. She was angry.

Kayo understood.

The moon flashed behind a swift-moving cloud, then was bright again. Time sped, it seemed to him, and the island trembled.

Brona said, "It was not only Dalat in danger, do you understand? It was her daughters and their entire legacy. There might have been war if Connley had convinced enough people that Dalat was not the true, star-ordained queen. And if she was not, how could her daughters be true? How could their foreign blood belong to Innis Lear? Do you see? If Dalat did not die . . ." Brona shook her head. "But she did."

"Was it— Was it Lear?" Kayo could hardly bite out the words. "Did he murder my sister for his stars?"

"Lear would do nothing. He knew of the brewing danger, but he was ever paralyzed by heaven. He said again and again that Dalat must have faith, because she *was* his true queen—their daughters, *his* daughters—and the stars would offer satisfying answers. *Hold with me,* he said, *have faith with me, we will do and be as the stars require. For that is what we must always do.*"

Kayo tried to crouch on the ground for balance in this dizzying, swaying world, but Brona held him upright.

"If I had been here," he said, "I would have protected her—you should have! And . . . he did not protect her. He—"

"Now, Kay Oak, listen to me." Brona knelt, and he collapsed with her. They faced each other on the rough moor, and Brona closed her eyes. She drew a deep breath.

Kayo's eyes burned; his heart pounded in his ears and wrists and temples. All the sky was darkly silver.

And Brona Hartfare shocked him to his soul by speaking in the language of the Third Kingdom, "*This is my choice, son-of-my-mother. I make it for myself, your mother's-daughter, and for your sister's-daughters, and I ask that you accept it now. I ask that you give yourself to them, to their protection, for they will need your heart-strength and generosity. Never tell them of my choice, but keep them well. Son-of-my-mother, I love you.*"

Kayo dragged himself free with a cry, turning away as if to retch. But there was nothing, nothing inside him except grief and regret. He gripped the roots of a strong tree, bending against them.

Brona's hand found his shoulder.

He squeezed his eyes shut, and tears leaked through his curled lashes.

"I have said these words, Kay Oak, every night and every morning for a year and three days. The island's roots and the wind of our trees know what Dalat of Taria Queen and Innis Lear has asked of you. It knows what she asked of herself."

Kayo did not think he was as strong as the daughter-of-his-mother. He barely felt Brona's touch as he dug his fingers into the cold earth around the oak's roots, as if he could grip the very heart of this dangerous, unforgiving island. To strangle it, to bury himself, or only to grasp hold, he could not say.

*THE SISTERS MET* in a pavilion erected over the rocky Errigal moor, built of canvas in the neutral gray colors of death, with massive torches flickering bright against the black sky.

Innis Lear raged, tossing flags and leaves sharply, grabbing at anything not tied down. The wind stung the eyes of retainers and servants, tore at the horses' manes, rattled tack, and shoved wagons. Half the tents could not be put up, taking thrice as many men to hold and stake down, and even then the gale blew harder.

The youngest princess had sent word, offering instead the shelter of Errigal Keep, but the eldest denied it. *Let the skies scream at our meeting,* she said to the messenger.

And so they arrived.

Wind gusted from the north, drawing the cries of the island in its wake, from the mountains, karst flats, cliffs, meadows, and moors, arrowing toward the iron marsh, toward the daughters of Lear.

Gaela Lear had brought with her an army twelve hundred strong from Dondubhan, with more following at a slower pace—though some from those barracks had deserted, running here to the daughter they knew best from her time at the northern star tower, and out of friendship with Rory Earlson. The Astore army camped in a wide, flickering fan to the west, right up to the edge of the White Forest. To Regan's bloodred banner five hundred from Connley had joined, and the Earl Glennadoer as well, with his mud-and-feather-painted soldiers.

Toward them from the fortress of Errigal Keep came the party of the youngest Lear daughter, all in the midnight blue and white of Innis Lear itself, dotted throughout with the wintry pale blue of Errigal. Her force was the smallest, a bare two hundred from Errigal and the surrounding farmland, but four hundred and then three hundred more had arrived today with the Earl Rosrua and Bracoch. Plus their dead father's hundred loyal retainers, not a one of whom had broken toward Gaela and Regan.

The wind roared, tearing at hair and tabards.

None could predict what might happen this night, not with all the holy bones in the world at their feet.

Elia Lear stopped at the base of the pavilion to glance at the canvas roof slapping hard in the wind. "Why do my sisters hide from the stars?"

Of course Lear's youngest did not need to hide from the sky because she was a piece of it: her silver chain mail glittered like a shirt woven of stars, and her dress was cream and gray like a priest's, but from shoulder to knee a tabard hung in a rich dark blue, vibrant enough to catch the light, and at her breast a single, blazing white star.

All who saw her understood: Elia Lear would not submit.

Kay Oak stepped to her side, leaning heavily on an old oak cane. The wound on his face was revealed: a swollen gash sewn with pale thread, a path of moonlight across his brown face. It marked out the earl's left eye, and the surrounding bruise flared like a deadly dark flower. Beside him stood the witch of the White Forest, and with her a dozen women of Errigal and Hartfare, then the old king's Fool, iron wizards, and more. There came the cragged Earl Bracoch, and the younger Rosrua, with Rory Errigal holding the chain of his father's title instead of wearing it across his chest; the youngest man's eyes hunted only for his bastard brother.

At Elia Lear's other shoulder stood a gilded man, beardless, dressed like a noble retainer also in Learish blue: the king of Aremoria.

"We do not hide," Gaela Lear answered her youngest sister, stepping to the fore of the pavilion. The self-proclaimed king of Innis Lear wore vibrant purple and red, with shimmering chain mail falling off her shoulders like wings. A sword and scabbard encrusted with gold and garnets hung heavily from a belt at her hips. Her hair was sculpted into a spiral crown with pale clay. That same clay dotted down her temples and cheeks in the mockery of a star pattern. Beautiful and striking, she embodied the Star of War, with all its promise of victory and glory and strength.

And Regan Connley was the matching Star of Death, in a white gown with scarlet trim and collar. Red paint colored her eyelids and her bottom lip, and streaked across her cheeks in violent lines. Her hair was loosely drawn back under a white mourning veil that ruffled and shivered in the wind like a furious waterfall. The simplicity only exaggerated her dangerous beauty.

With them stood the Fox of Innis Lear, in a dark gambeson and dull armor, his sword whispering at his hip; he was a shadow of war, a wizard's secret form. He stared at Morimaros of Aremoria, in Elia's dark blue, sword at his side but lacking crown and royal ring. The king's eyes scoured the

Fox with the penetrating force of the furious wind, angry, wounded, and worst of all: disappointment.

Gaela said, loud enough to be heard by all, "As agreed, come inside: we meet as rival sisters, not enemies." With her middle sister in perfect alignment, they stepped back to welcome the youngest.

The Oak Earl gripped Elia's elbow. "Change your mind," he was heard to say, low and firm.

"I will not," she said back, only a whisper in the wind, but he knew, and slammed his cane into the rocky moor.

The youngest princess left him behind, for only two would enter with her: a triangle complete, to face her two sisters and their wizard.

Elia stepped inside, followed by Morimaros of Aremoria and Aefa, the former angry and strong, the latter clutching to her chest a cloth-covered prize.

The noise of the wind changed, from desperate wailing to a dull, distant roar, as if those six stood inside the heart of a seashell, protected from the crashing ocean. Iron stands rose like spears in each corner, lifting plates filled with candles head-high. Chairs waited, but none sat upon them, and all ignored, too, the low table with dark wine and bright stone cups.

Gaela appeared amused at her little sister's choices of seconds, but Regan eyed Aefa and her bundle suspiciously. Ban the Fox concentrated on his breathing; he'd not expected his former king to join them now.

"Sisters—" Elia began.

Regan interrupted, "You are bold to bring Aremoria with you. Have you fallen for his charms, baby sister?"

"We thought," Gaela said, "you would prefer our offering." She turned her gaze to the Fox, who stared at Elia.

"I have business with my old friend, the Fox," Morimaros said threateningly. Elia held her hand to him, and he did not step forward.

The wizard said, "I ended our business."

"That is not your right," said the king.

"Morimaros," Elia said. "This, now, is our turn to speak: my sisters and I. You are here on our sufferance."

He bowed his head, though did not remove his gaze from his Fox.

Gaela smiled broadly at Elia. "You have found some iron in your worm-soft bones, or else been blessed finally by our imperial ancestors."

"Circumstances have tempered me," Elia replied.

"Then," said Regan, "swear to us and retire to the star towers."

"No."

"No?"

Elia held out her hand, and Aefa Thornhill lowered her arms from her breast. She held a pillow, its prize covered with a thin blue cloth. The girl took a fortifying breath and picked the cloth up by a corner, sweeping it away to reveal a crown of freshly woven, slightly crushed hemlock. In the flickering orange candlelight, the starburst blossoms seemed to catch fire.

Regan gasped softly, eagerly, even, and Gaela laughed dark and loud.

"You are resourceful, Elia," the self-annointed king, her sister, said. "Did Brona show you this? Or did the trees themselves whisper their secrets to you? Was it because you *listened*?" On the last word, the wolflike grin turned into a sneer, though Regan beside her seemed almost wounded.

"The trees," Elia said. "You know what this means, then? We should eat it, and drink from the navel well, and be the queens of this island together."

The three sisters stood at three points, the bright stars that formed a constellation of disaster.

Wind shoved at the north wall of the pavilion, pushing the canvas taut.

"You think it would only save you," murmured Regan. "That our island loves you best of all, little sister. That we are unworthy, because you do not understand our way of loving. You have ever avoided your own choices, and now you make the island seek vengeance on your behalf."

"No, that is *not true*. I do not want either of you to die. I want all of us to survive—to live, together, as we have not in so many years."

"Then submit," snarled Gaela.

"I would survive," Regan said. "The island loves me, as it loves you, only more, for my Connley's bones are our roots now."

Elia reached for her sister, but stopped. "I am so sorry he's gone, Regan. I know you loved him."

The middle sister's face turned hard as crystal.

Gaela stepped nearer and put one hand on Regan's shoulder; the other she made into a fist and settled threateningly against Elia's. "This is a waste of our time."

"If you are to be queens of Innis Lear," Elia said, "you must be part of the island, sacrifice your own selves to gain its trust, the trust it waits for you to show. Are you afraid of something our father was brave enough to undergo? If you would be the queens of Lear, this is how the crown is claimed."

"I claim my own crown. Our father was not strong enough to do so. He was weak, and terrible. Magic did not help him."

"He denied all but the stars; that is why the island turned on him, as it will turn on you if you reject the roots."

"I do not need it. Let the wind rage—eventually it will stop, when it understands I dominate." Gaela spread her arms, displaying herself.

Aefa thrust out her chin. "You cannot defeat the very rocks you stand on."

"Quiet, Fool," the eldest sister ordered.

Elia closed her eyes briefly, then leveled her gaze upon Gaela. "Are you less brave than our *mother?*"

"*What,*" snapped Gaela.

Regan hummed, low and soft, discordant with the wind.

Elia took Gaela's wrist. "Dalat has everything to do with this, with us, with what we are. This is how she died: as a queen. With one action to protect us and uphold the star prophecy. She ate poison, and did not let the island save her."

"No," Regan whispered.

The eldest laughed like a snarling wolf, tugging out of Elia's grip. "I don't believe this. It was Lear's worship of star signs that doomed our mother."

Elia nodded. "Yes, but because she chose to let it, she chose to strengthen the people's faith in the stars—which was faith in her. Don't you see? Dalat's legacy depended on that prophecy being fulfilled."

Regan shook her head, *no no no.* "She loved us, and him. No one who loves like that would keep such a thing secret. Connley would—" The middle princess stopped suddenly, going still and certain and cold. "It is not possible."

"She was wrong," Elia said, glancing between her sisters. "She should have told us, told our father. Trusted him. But he lost her, too, haven't you ever thought of that? He adored her, and his heart tore apart when she died. Have you no sympathy for that?"

"I crushed sympathy in myself long ago, little sister," Gaela said.

"I do, though, have sympathy," their witch-sister answered. "But no more for him than for myself or my sisters. No more than for the roots and wells of Innis Lear that he forsook! His pain does not excuse his actions."

"Nor yours, Regan," said Elia.

Gaela shook her head. In a voice sharp and regal she said, "I do not believe this, but even if I chose to, how would it change anything at all? It does not make me want to eat these death flowers, especially if my mother died of the same. You cannot manipulate my heart, out of desiring my destiny. I have always been meant for the crown. I have strived all my life to make myself into a king. I will not apologize for what I have done to achieve this, and none shall take it from me because of stars or trees. It is mine. I am the oldest and strongest. Peace will come from me."

"And all my strength is hers," Regan said. "Why do you not give over yours as well, Elia?"

The youngest breathed hard, struggling for calm. "I would have, before you went just as mad as Father, mad with violence and hatred, disregarding Innis Lear itself. I cannot allow the island to crumble beneath my feet for your arrogance and ambition."

"You're ambitious, too, Elia," Ban Errigal said. The wizard had been quiet, following his queen's command.

The sisters turned to him like a fearsome, three-headed dragon. Elia said, "To bring everyone together. To save everyone."

"To forgive," he sneered.

Morimaros of Aremoria spoke pointedly to the Fox, "Sometimes we forgive others because it keeps our own hearts whole, not because they deserve it or for any thought of them."

Ban's nostrils flared, but Aefa yelled, "Stop, all of you! This is a family squabble that will tear the roots from the earth and pull the stars from the sky if you allow it!"

"Yes! Don't you see?" said Elia. "This happened because our family shattered, and if we come together again we can fix it together."

"What would that look like? You married to this king? Always a threat at our east?" Gaela smiled a dark smile.

Regan petted Elia's cheek before her little sister could shy back. "I like this rage in you, baby sister. Perhaps you can join with us. But you must give up your Aremore king, and these fantasies about our mother, and let go of thinking Gaela and I do not have Innis Lear's best interest at the fore of our minds. If the rootwaters mean so much to you, as they do to me, I will eat this poison, and Gaela will be my king."

"No," Gaela said stubbornly. "We do not need the imagined approval of the land. It is ours."

"Ban will tell you," Elia said, latching her gaze onto the Fox. "You know, Ban Errigal, Fox of Aremoria, of Innis Lear, of whatever side you steal. Tell them, if they trust you so well, that they must bargain with the island."

"You cannot use him against us, either," Regan said, silkily. She dug her fingers into the Fox's hair, curling a fist against his skull. "Ban is ours. You gave him up, his great strength and power, but we will not."

The hemlock blossoms trembled as the Fool's daughter stamped her foot. "How can you do this, Ban Errigal? Elia has loved and defended you beyond all reason, while you have betrayed all of us some time or another. How dare you stand against her?"

"How . . ." Ban bared his teeth. "Here are two queens who admire me for myself and give me a purpose I am suited to. Who do not treat me as a bastard, or a tool, or someone who never, *never,* can be an equal. They are *my* equals! They do not hold themselves apart from me."

"You hold yourself apart from us," King Morimaros said, quiet with intensity. "I made you my friend."

"How do you come to be here, Aremoria?" Gaela asked. She stepped to the king: the black princess of Lear was nearly as tall as the foreigner. "What is your game?"

"I am here to support Elia for the crown. That is the will of Aremoria."

"It will be war, then."

"No!" Elia put herself between them, a hand on the king's chest and one flat out to Gaela.

Morimaros met Gaela's hot gaze over Elia's head. "You will lose against me."

The eldest sister did not smile, but behind her hard expression came a ferocious joy. "You cannot take Innis Lear. It has never been yours, and never will join with Aremoria again."

Elia shoved hard at both. "Stop, now. This will not be war. We must— we *must*—eat of the flower, and drink of the rootwater. That will decide, without bloodshed, without dividing our island."

"Yes," hissed Regan.

Gaela whirled to her middle sister, thrust out a hand, and grabbed her arm. "Collect yourself, sister."

In the quiet, the wind gusted again, streaking under the tightly staked walls to tear and tease at their ankles and skirts. Candles snuffed out.

*Fire,* said Aefa Thornhill with a snap of her fingers, and five of the candles lit themselves again.

Through the dim orange shadows, Morimaros of Aremoria advanced. "Ban Errigal. Our business is bloodshed." The king grasped the front of Ban's gambeson, pulling it into his fist. "I challenge you. Fight me, if you think you are worthy."

Gaela Lear laughed.

"To the death," added Regan, dark fascination in her tone.

"No," the last princess said, calmly.

But the king ignored her. "If I am defeated, Innis Lear will see no penalties from Aremoria. Novanos, called La Far, will make sure of it."

Ban stared at Morimaros.

The silence grew heavy with monument.

The Fox had betrayed everyone; all knew it to be true. He was a shadow, a wormworker, a traitor, a spy. A bastard. He knew the secret paths behind sunlight and slipped through cracks, understood the language of ravens and the tricks of trees. He could see how, with one act, he could change everything here, destroy and re-create with a word.

And so, the wizard drew a shaky breath. He said the only thing he could: "Yes. But if I am defeated, you all three eat of the hemlock crown."

Wind slammed into the pavilion, shrieking, whistling like triumphant horns.

In the following stillness, Gaela glared in Ban's face, grabbing his chin. "What did you say, Fox?"

Elia pressed a hand to Morimaros's chest, hard, as if she could force him away from the rest.

"I said," Ban repeated, loudly in the dark chamber, "we will fight, and if I am defeated, you let the island choose its queen, and all swear to lead no army against her."

"I can fight my own battles for the crown," Gaela said, frowning.

"This is what a king would do, Gaela Lear. Champions fight for them; they do not make their own war. Are you a warrior or a king?"

"Stop this!" cried Elia, but Aefa touched her shoulder.

"This is the best," Aefa said. "No war, very little danger. Only two men at risk."

"More than that is at risk," the princess gasped.

Regan circled her fingers around Gaela's wrist and squeezed so the eldest released Ban's chin. He swallowed, staring past both sisters at Elia. As if devastated by hope.

"So," Gaela said, nearly a growl. "If Morimaros of Aremoria wins, little sister, you will have your desire that we eat the island's poison. But if Ban the Fox wins, your Aremore king will be dead, and your allies will disperse. Rory Errigal will return to Aremoria forever. Kay Oak will be struck down for disobeying my banishment."

Elia's entire body had gone rigid. Her voice trembled with strain as she asked, "What of me? What will you ask of me?"

Gaela studied her baby sister for a moment, and then smiled. "You will marry Ban Errigal, and your children will be my heirs."

The youngest princess looked at Ban the Fox with eyes spinning betrayal and wild panic.

And the wizard said, in the language of trees, *It gives you everything you need to save everyone.*

*Not you,* Elia replied in the same.

Of all there, only Regan the witch understood their words, but her heart did not care any longer.

*You must,* Ban said.

Elia opened her mouth, hesitating as she stared at him, and the entire world paused with her. But the world cannot hold still for long. She breathed deeply. "I accept."

Her sisters clutched hands, pressed their lips into matching grim smiles. "As do we," Gaela King said.

"At Scagtiernamm," Regan Connley added. "Where the wind and trees can witness. Just when the sun rises."

*Dawn,* Elia Lear whispered in the language of trees.

The island beneath their feet seemed to shiver, and the wind made an obeisance of gentle, laughing huffs against the death-gray pavilion.

# THE FOX

BAN ERRIGAL'S ENTIRE life had led to this.

Elia looked directly at him and said, "I forgive you."

There was no possible response he could offer, desperate as he was to remain standing, to hold himself together.

She turned from Ban and to her sisters, inviting them all and their captains and whatever men would fit to shelter in Errigal Keep and its yards for the long, blustery night to come. Gaela agreed.

Then, very like a queen, Elia marched out of the pavilion with both Morimaros and Aefa at her heels.

The two eldest Lear sisters surrounded Ban, who felt himself entirely stunned by the swift current of destiny.

Gaela's face was murderous. "You'd better win, Ban the Fox," she said.

Regan kissed him, soft and scraping. She left her cheek against his to whisper, "The island will choose. Nothing else matters now."

"I will win," he lied, meeting Gaela's eyes. "I will go ready those men who can move, to join Elia in the Keep."

Their permission given, Ban hurried to do so. It took the greater part of an hour before he was on his way with a full contingent of men, behind the two queens and Earl Glennadoer, with Osli at his side, and upon arrival at the Keep, nearly another hour to settle all in their places. The wind blew, softer than before, but still urgent and waiting. He swung his saddlebag over his shoulder and strode inside.

But alone, Ban reeled still, and could not yet go to his old rooms. He leaned into the whitewashed wall, and said Elia's name silently, no voice behind it.

The future of Innis Lear was rooted to his life or death. Him, and him alone. Ban the Fox, bastard of Errigal, would determine who wore the crown.

Was this glee and triumph building like a scream inside his chest? Or despair?

It would not do to dwell—not with so few hours left in his possession. Ban dropped his bag and hurried around the corner, where he caught a passing servant and asked after his father's body. Wrapped and oiled, the earl had been laid out on a slab of worn granite in the cellar. Curan Ironworker and Captain Med had seen to it in the absence of both Errigal sons.

Ban went on alone, hurrying down the stone stairs with a shuttered lantern.

Usually the cellar smelled of earth and water and candle smoke, and a slight sourness, though Ban had not visited in years. Today, it burned with pine and strong myrrh to cover the inevitable stink of death.

Layers of dark linen wrapped the broad body, still daunting and wide, despite the sunken betrayal of slow rot. There was nothing to see but the shape of his father, so quiet in death. The lantern Ban had brought cast shadows over everything. His own shadow lengthened, stretching unnaturally across the slab altar and Errigal's body.

Ban's father had been dead for twelve days.

His lantern's light wavered, and Ban realized he was shaking.

"I wondered if you would come here," Rory said from the deep shadow beyond the first row of dusty wine.

"Brother," Ban said.

"I am no such thing to you, am I? Have I ever been?"

"I'm sorry." It gave Ban no relief to say it, thought his regret was true. Ban *was* sorry—sorry that Rory had been hurt and that Errigal had died as he had, that his brother would have wanted nothing so much as to die in their father's stead. And he was sorry that Rory was now looking at him with such disgust. But Ban was not sorry for his choices, though he suspected he should've been. He was not sorry their father could no longer carelessly parade through life, untouchable as the stars he'd so worshipped. It was Errigal's choices, too, his misplaced trusts and spoiled passions, that had brought the old earl to be here, lying coldly in this underground tomb. His sons at war.

Rory snorted and emerged into the broken light. He put his hand on the chest area of their father's body and lifted a bottle of wine to his lips. It sloshed loudly; most had already been consumed.

The brothers stared at each other over the corpse. Ban set his lantern on the altar and reached out for the bottle. Rory smacked it into his hand.

Ban drank, eyes never leaving Rory's blotchy, angry face.

Rory took the wine back. "Am I supposed to hope you live or die tomorrow?"

"Die, I suppose," Ban said viciously.

Rory flung the bottle against the wall; it broke into three pieces, then hit the stone floor and shattered further. Rory breathed hard, while Ban did not even flinch. "Sometimes I hate you," Rory whispered.

Ban nodded.

"I didn't deserve this," Rory said.

"I didn't do any of it to hurt you."

His brother only pressed his mouth in a grim line. "You'll die."

The cold agreement of his guts finally bent Ban's knees; he crouched and put his hand to the floor for balance. "I think so, yes," he hissed, unable to find a voice.

His brother knelt beside Ban and shoved him, then caught him and grabbed his shoulders. "You have to fight, you shit, you fox, you—you *bastard*."

The word hit Ban harder than it might've, a bite under his heart, because in all his life Rory had never flung it at him. "I will fight," he snarled into his brother's face.

"Good. But you'll lose."

"What do you want?" Ban cried, wrenching away.

"I don't know! I . . ." Rory fell back onto his behind, put the heels of his hands against his eyes. His fingers curled like claws. He heaved a deep breath and then dropped his arms. "I have always been generous to you, always loved you completely."

"I did not doubt that. I only . . . do not know how . . . I was not made for love." Ban shrugged, trying for indifference, but it was a jerky, offended motion.

"I know that is a lie. On your last night at least, do not lie. You were loved in Aremore. Did you never see that? The king—but . . . You were loved. And you loved Elia. I saw it when we were young."

"It only broke things," Ban whispered.

"I'm sorry for that. For my part in it."

Frowning, Ban gripped his brother's arm. Even not understanding, he could give Rory this: the illusion of forgiveness.

Rory nodded heavily and climbed to his feet. A tear caught in his eyelashes and glinted in the lantern light. He nodded. "Fine. Good then. I'll—I'll grieve you, you know. When you are dead. Had you not killed our father, I might have named my heir for you, the uncle who should have taught him to make swords and climb trees and drink beer. Who should have—should have . . ."

Ban slowly stood, too, and gave in to a sudden impulse: he hugged Rory, and said, "You could name a daughter after me, then."

His brother's arms came around him, too tight, tight enough to kill. Ban held his breath and did not struggle until Rory's embrace loosened into something real. Rory whispered, "No, I don't think so."

"I understand," Ban whispered back.

Rory released him, backed away, and said, "Goodbye—good night."

The earlson left, and Ban did his best to banish all thoughts: of his brother, of the morning, of the last week or years or—

The Fox stared at his father's withered body. He went to the broken wine bottle and slid the largest pieces together with his boot, then picked them carefully up. Cradling the shattered glass, Ban climbed the stairs out of the cellar, and made his way to his own room.

# MORIMAROS

MARS BARELY SAW the corridor in front of him as he strode through Errigal Keep. He slid his hand along the stone wall, but his vision was a blur of blue-black wrath, and fear, and guilt.

His name was called behind him, and he ignored it the first time. The second time it was said sharply, and he paused, leaning into the wall. It was Elia's voice, Elia Lear come after him.

She ducked around him, putting her small body between him and the heavy stone wall. Her dark eyes were glaring, now they were alone, her mouth bowed in displeasure. Anger, even. She put both hands on his chest and pushed.

It did not budge him at all.

"How dare you take this onto yourself, Morimaros," she said furiously.

"It had to be done," he said back, just as upset. He curled his fingers around her wrists, squeezing with careful control. "Ban Errigal was mine— my soldier, my spy—and now mine to show justice."

"Revenge, you mean!"

A retainer passed, solicitously ignoring them.

The king took deep breaths in an attempt to rein in his emotions. But the air was thick, the corridor narrow, and beautiful Elia so close. His throat narrowed, too, and his chest clenched. He had to breathe. Mars jerked away and dragged Elia with him. She walked stiffly as he led her outside into the cold night. Soldiers camped everywhere, shadow bodies, impossible to tell apart. Around the long dark wall of the Keep he and Elia went, and to a corner where the outer fortification and the castle joined. There he stopped, turned her, and tucked her against the sheltered corner, blocked the wind with his body. He gasped for air, head fallen back. The night sky was blissfully huge and clear, the stars bright.

"Breathe, Morimaros," she said gently, unlacing the ties at the collar of his dark blue Learish tunic. She freed his throat, then slid her hands up to his smooth jaw. After a brief touch, she dropped her hands and sighed angrily.

"Elia," he said, low and longing.

"You acted the king—it was *my* negotiation. You undercut my authority."

"No! I was a man—your man, to fight for you. Like the Fox himself said: kings use champions to fight their battles. Let me be your champion."

"It should have been my choice; you should have listened to me. If you were my man, my champion, you would have stopped when I said *no*."

Mars opened his mouth to argue, but couldn't. He snapped it closed again, clenching his jaw in renewed anger—at himself, at the Fox, at all of them.

"I should send you away. Now. Before dawn can come and—"

"No, Elia, please."

She crossed her arms. "Would you even go? If I commanded you to get your men and go before dawn, sail away so I could deal with this on my own, would you? I do not think so. You are not very good at taking orders."

He stared at her, wanting nothing so much as for her to touch him again. His shoulders heaved. His thoughts fled through a maze of possibilities: the answers he could offer, the actions he could take, and what she would do, then his response, and on and on and on. It all turned to tragedy. For himself, and for ruined Ban Errigal.

In the end he said nothing.

"I thought so." Elia's arms relaxed until she held them still at her sides. "Then tell me, why did you do this? Challenge him?"

"I did it for you."

"No, you did *not*! You did it for *you*. So *why*?"

Mars burst out, "Because I had to! Because he betrayed me. He was mine, my soldier and spy and—and my friend, and he threw me aside!"

"He was mine first. And before that he was his own, and his spirit belongs to Innis Lear. None of us are yours, Morimaros. We do not do things as you do; we have rootwater and poison in our blood and that makes us strong. This is not your island. It is *mine*."

His hands shook. His heart, too. He'd not felt helpless like this since he was a small child. Not even when his father died and Mars had slid the Blood and the Sea onto his finger. "I *know*," he said. "But you're right, I don't—I don't know how to be other than a king."

"You don't have to. You can't, and we shouldn't have pretended otherwise."

The grieved wisdom in her eyes filled Mars with longing again. To bundle her away to some safety, to tear her from all of this so she never had to carry this kind of weight. The kind of weight that made a king promise to kill his friend in a few short, dark hours. Nausea crawled up his throat.

Mars swallowed it painfully and whispered another truth. "I loved him."

"I know." In the darkness it was difficult to see; only a flicker of distant light from the Keep and torches lit along the ramparts overhead offered any break in the night. But her eyes shone, sharp and black and teary. "Please don't kill him."

The words cut between them; Mars stepped back. "He might kill me instead."

Elia surged forward and grabbed his face—too hard. She dug her fingers around his jaw. "Don't let him do that, either," she commanded.

Mars felt the breath of her words slide along his chin, and he finally kissed her.

He kissed her slowly and desperately, as if her lips were his destiny, shaping him with every glancing touch or press or bite. An inexorable progression from who he'd been before, to who he would be now.

She hardly moved at first, except to allow it, then her clutching fingers relaxed and she touched his cheeks gently. He lifted her by the elbows and pulled her firmly against him, tasting the salt of tears on her mouth, the tang of lip paint, her softness, and then her power when Elia suddenly kissed him back.

Wind slipped around her and tugged at him, coiling around his neck, fingering his short hair and eyelashes. It giggled and whined. Elia slid her hands down his chest, grasped at his arms, at his ribs and waist, shifting and moving exactly like the wind she was.

Mars held her head in his large hands, kissing her until he needed to breathe. Then he leaned back enough to catch her blurry, fluttering gaze. She licked her lips.

"I love you, too," the king of Aremoria said, hoarsely. And, "Do you forgive me?"

She's said so much to Ban at the pavilion: forgiven him, her blessing and condemnation both.

Elia asked, "Should I forgive the man or the king?"

Slowly, Mars shook his head. He was both. Always.

"I will do what you tell me to do," he said, touching a thumb to her bottom lip. "Whatever that is. Anything you order, right now." He ran his thumb along the soft skin, then let go. His entire being longed to hold her closer, to beg Elia for what he wanted, to sink onto his knees before her, even as a king. "And forever from now, I will be honest with you—even if it makes Aremoria and Innis Lear enemies, for politics or trade or anything. I will tell you the truth."

"Mars," she said carefully, as if tasting the flavor of the nickname. "And Morimaros. Man and king."

"I wish we could be only one thing, choose only one thing."

Elia said, ferociously, "I don't want to be chosen above all things, one thing most of all. I want to be a part of someone's whole."

He was silent a moment, studying her. "Do you remember all those weeks ago, at the Summer Seat, when you said I was the Lion of War and as such always apart from your Child Star? That they could not exist in the same sky, because of how they are created by the shapes around them?"

She nodded.

"What would happen if the eye of the lion were named Calpurlugh? It is only semantics; it is only what some old man said long ago, that makes such a thing impossible."

"New shapes," she murmured glancing up at the sky. "You want to make new shapes."

"I don't know what else a king is good for," he said ruefully.

Elia Lear took his hand, the one missing its royal ring, and drew a long breath. She tilted her head toward the wind as it teased wisps of her curls free at her temple and ear. She said, "Fight for me at dawn, Morimaros of Aremoria. I will be ready, with a crown of hemlock."

# AEFA

NO ONE NOTICED Aefa hang back from the procession that made its way through the darkness toward the Keep. And none noticed her wander to the crowded great hall where a fire blazed in the massive hearth. Folk huddled here in pairs and family groups, whispering, drinking, lulling children to sleep. They shared blankets and tossed bits of food at the hairy dogs, everyone stuffed together against the cold wind outside. Waiting.

Aefa continued to carefully hold the hemlock crown on a spill of midnight blue wool. It shivered with her breathing, and she did not know what to do with it.

Sighing, Aefa dragged herself over to the thronelike chair beside the fire. She collapsed onto the floor, scooting her bottom against the fresh rushes until she leaned against the throne. Legs crossed, she gently placed the crown in her lap.

The poison hemlock was lovely: fresh, tiny white flowers in clusters, shooting out in starbursts off a central, pale green stem with small violet blotches. Elia had braided the stems together, over and over, until the crown itself was a gangly, intricate circlet of nothing but constellated flowers.

Aefa skimmed a pale finger against some petals, barely able to feel their soft response. Her thoughts were filled with a gentle awe. This pretty, natural thing was the kingmaker here. Poison. Death and rebirth through the cold rootwaters was what made kings on Innis Lear. If her best friend weren't facing it, Aefa might have smiled at the simplicity.

In order to earn the trust of the island, one had to trust it with one's life.

Aefa shut her eyes. Elia was willing. Elia was being so brave about it, or in denial—there was a trait that showed strong in the Lear bloodline. But no, Aefa believed Elia meant this faith with all her heart.

If only Aefa did.

Perhaps it would be easier to take the leap herself, to entrust her life to the rootwaters, than it would be to watch Elia eat this poison, to watch her grow numb and fall, to be desperate that the waiting waters would purge the poison from her blood and Elia would open her beautiful eyes again and say something tender about whatever she'd seen, while she had been briefly dead.

Aefa had to clutch at her own hands to keep from flinging the crown into the fire. Every part of the plant was deadly, Brona had warned.

A log in the hearth popped, startling Aefa. She laughed at herself, but sadly. She was terrified of the approaching dawn. Ban Errigal and Morimaros of Aremoria facing off, likely killing each other; then the sisters eating this poison crown and letting the island choose.

Aefa expected the king would win, unless the traitor cheated somehow, and perhaps that would negate everything. No magic, no slick treachery allowed.

Thank all the stars and worms of earth Elia was not pregnant with that bastard's bastard.

Closing her eyes, Aefa wondered if the princess needed her yet, if Elia had returned to her rooms, or if she was with the king. Worms, but Aefa hoped she was with the king. Convincing him to win, to fight hard, saying whatever she needed to say and doing whatever she needed to do.

Very unlikely.

Aefa jumped to her feet, crown in one hand, her skin protected by the thin blue cloth, and hurried after her friend.

Elia was nowhere to be found. Not in her bedroom, not up on the lookout tower. Aefa wandered at a decent pace, not to worry anyone, but searching thoroughly. She saw Rory Errigal storming up from the cellar, and she saw Regan Connley drift down the corridor away from where she'd been placed to sleep.

As it grew later, Aefa returned herself to the bedroom she was sharing with Elia. Just as she reached the doorway, the princess appeared there, too, eyes cast downward as she walked slowly along the thin woven rug keeping warm the hall floor.

"Elia," Aefa said softly.

The princess's eyes flew up. Though some curls stood rampant about her face, free of the loose braids Aefa had put in earlier, Elia looked the same. Untouched. No: her lipstick was gone, smeared down to nothing but a flush of color on the left corner of her mouth.

That sight made Aefa's heart pound. "Come," she said, shoving open the door. It was grandly appointed, though small, and Aefa dropped the hemlock crown on a cushioned chair before kneeling at the hearth to stir up the fire.

Elia walked to the center of the room and stopped. "Aefa," she said, very low and haunting.

"I'm here." Aefa flung herself up, coming before her princess and taking her hands. "Tell me."

"I kissed the king of Aremoria," she said, sliding Aefa a sorry almost-smile.

"Finally!" the Fool's daughter danced in place to cheer up her friend.

But Elia's smile trembled. "I am having trouble letting myself feel it all."

Weaving their fingers together, Aefa made sure her face was bright and open, ready to listen.

"There is so much, and all of it conflicting. I—I cannot fall down and wail," Elia said. "I cannot yell or sob or even rejoice. Those are not things a queen does. But I also . . . I know better than to shut it all away, to wrap myself in blissful numb nothings. Not anymore."

Aefa bit her lip, then nodded. "I understand. I think . . . Well, there is more possibility between falling and flying wild. You do not have to be only either a cold star or a fiery explosion."

"How do I find balance when my heart is aching to burst?" Tears hovered in her black eyes. "Someone I love will die in the morning. Ah!" She caught back a gasp of pain, widening her eyes so as not to blink and force the tears to fall.

"Hold on to me." Aefa tugged Elia nearer and put the princess's arms around her waist, then wrapped her own arms around Elia's neck. She took a deep breath. "Rain is not always a storm. The wind does not always howl. Sometimes death is quiet, or love is peaceful. There are little things."

"Fire can be a candle flame," Elia whispered.

Aefa hugged her tightly, smelling the rich bergamot oil, the tart remnants of paint, sweat and warm skin—every Elia smell except charcoal smudged from a freshly drawn star map.

The princess pulled away, but held on to her friend's hands for a moment. She stared into Aefa's eyes, as if searching for something, and then smiled a very little again. Elia's brow remained pinched, her wide eyes teary. Then she let go of Aefa. *Fire,* she whispered in the language of trees, and snapped her fingers.

Tiny orange flames flickered to life. They danced in the air, two of them, around and around, as if orbiting each other.

The light put warmth back into Elia's eyes, and Aefa felt like crying, too.

The princess drew her hands closer, and the flames drifted into one, joining with a tiny crackle. Elia allowed her face to crumple and tears to fall, but she did not lose the thread of magic, did not stop her even breathing, despite the weeping.

With Aefa's help, cupping her hands around the flame to block the breeze of their motion, they walked to the hearth and knelt, adding their magical flame to the comforting fire.

# REGAN

THE BED WHERE last Regan had slept with her husband was too wide, too cold, too lonely.

Better that she sleep against the earth, wrapped in the roots of a cold hawthorn tree, or ancient oak.

Wind rushed against the windows, skittered against the sharply pitched roof, and whistled down the chimney. The small fire flattened but held on to itself.

One of his long jackets lay folded over the back of a tall chair. Bright, gleaming red. "Connley," she murmured.

But the wind outside hissed back her little sister's name.

Gasping, Regan swept out of the room, past surprised attendants. She covered her ears with her hands, nails dug into her scalp. "No," she moaned. The island should mourn with *her,* call her *husband's* name.

Though Gaela was the first recourse of her heart, Regan was angry with her elder sister, too. As they'd come to the Keep, Regan had been desperate for privacy and a glass of wine, to discuss Dalat, breathless with the need to wonder with her sister: Was any of it true? What Elia said? Regan's heart had struck a wild rhythm, her free hand curled into a fist so tight her knuckles ached. Had Dalat eaten the king-making poison herself?

But Gaela had turned a ferocious snarl on Regan and said, in the most drastically even, low voice, "No, it is not possible."

Then her best, strongest sister had stalked away, leaving Regan truly alone.

But it *was* possible, if the trees believed it, if the wind screamed it, if—if poison was the true way forward on Innis Lear.

Regan's breast heaved. The tingling, cold edges of panic pressed close, and she ordered one of the women trailing her to take her directly to Ban Errigal.

She did not knock at his door, just opened it, finding the Fox beside the hearth, where a small altar was spread and fire burned in a fist-sized iron cauldron. Three candles were lit, additionally, at the window, and a pile of broken glass glittered on the small table beside the bed.

Ban himself was already undressed, crouched in a long, loose white linen shirt that fell to his knees. His sword belt hung from the only chair and his boots stood tall beside it, along with the rest of his fine warrior's clothing and equipment.

"Lady Regan," he said.

"I would not be alone tonight."

Silently, Ban came to her and offered his hand. The lines of his face were stark in the haze of candlelight. She allowed him to lead her to his bed. There he knelt and helped her out of her short boots. Perched at her feet, he lifted his head up. "Is there anything you need? Water, wine? Should I help with the overdress?"

His voice was soft, softer even than his forest eyes or lovely mouth.

"Overdress," she murmured, and touched the places it laced under her arms. She raised them, and he worked quickly at the silk ties. Together they lifted it over her head, and Ban folded it carefully over the back of his chair. She shut her eyes as tightly as she could, and a flash-memory of Connley's folded red coat waited in the dark.

"Please take some of the pins out," she said next.

He obeyed, gently sliding his fingers into her coiled hair to find plain, dark horn pins. Removing enough so that the three thick braids fell around her neck and shoulders, he settled the collected pins beside the pile of broken glass on his table. Then Ban glanced at her eyes; Regan nodded, and he got into his bed.

Climbing in after, Regan put her head on his shoulder and her hand over his heart. Ban stared up at the shadowed ceiling, and they both listened to the wind shrilling against the ramparts. He was smaller than her husband and she did not fit so well against him.

What would Connley think of this? The duel, the hemlock, the stars and wind and love and death and . . . everything? Her hand curled into a fist again, the knuckles whitening. Regan did not wish to watch another duel. It would bring visceral memories of her love: the line of his shoulder, the gleam of his teeth, the passion shifting the color of his blue-green eyes. Regan's breath had thinned; she was panting. Near hysteria with no warning.

"Regan?" Ban whispered.

"I wish Connley were here," she whispered into the darkness. Ban hugged her, touched her hair as she trembled.

"It would all be different if he were," the Fox said.

"Not the hemlock crown."

"No," he agreed.

"My sister would not lie about our mother."

"Elia would never."

"But I—I should be comforting you, Fox. You fight in the morning."

"I don't need it."

"Is that a lie?"

"No."

"Aren't you nervous? Will you sleep?"

"I won't sleep, but I . . . am not nervous yet. That will come. And, Regan, I am glad you are here." Ban drew a shaky breath. "No one should be alone the night before battle. I have been, once, hiding in my dugout, waiting to send a signal. I knew the fighting would soon begin, but not the hour, I knew I would rage and kill, I knew . . . but there was no room in my hole for sword or shield, so I would have to acquire my own from the enemy. Those were the worst times. Alone and knowing little of what is to come. So this is better. I know who I face, and I know when, and why."

"*Do* we know why?" Regan whispered. "Some moments lately, I don't remember."

"For love," he said. And there was his lie.

*For love,* the witch whispered back, in the language of trees.

# GAELA

GAELA LEAR STOOD outside the door through which Brona Hartfare slept. It was mere hours before dawn, and Gaela had yet to put her head to pillow.

Errigal Keep was a warren of new and old rooms, and tonight Gaela had wandered all the corridors and ramparts, from the deepest cellar to the tall tower platform, avoiding this confrontation, hoping to purge her rage and upset. But nothing had ever been able to do such a thing. She'd been born furious and riled. It was her lifeblood.

Had Dalat wondered why? Cared or not cared? Loved Gaela for that very ferocity or been afraid of it?

Had her mother killed herself assuming Gaela would be strong enough without her? Why hadn't there been a final message or word she'd given Gaela to remember, the rest of her lonely star-cursed life?

So many questions, the largest of which hummed and begged in her pulse: *Why why why?*

Gaela pounded on the witch's door.

"Brona," she demanded, low and urgent.

In a moment she heard a shuffle and the door swung open. Brona waited in a loose robe, but she was unrumpled and clear-eyed.

Gaela shoved in. "Was there nothing she said for me? Why did she trust you and not me? I was sixteen!"

"Gaela," the witch said, but Gaela had already stormed past her, toward the dimly glowing hearth. Spread over a heavy black cloth were all twenty-seven holy cards and a scatter of bones and polished rock.

"Tell me," Gaela insisted.

"Gaela," Brona snapped.

Unused to such command, the eldest daughter of Lear glared, but she saw then the source of Brona's upset.

Kay Oak struggled to get out of the bed, naked, with a bandage covering his eye. He groaned, and Gaela felt a thrill of anger and guilt. She ground her teeth together. "Get out, Uncle, before I remember my proclamations about your banishment."

Brona went to his side, grabbing a shirt and helping him into it. As they dressed him, Gaela worked to slow her heated blood. Kayo moved stiffly and leaned hard on the cane Brona handed him once his boots were on. "Be gentle with yourself," Brona murmured.

"Try to rest, love," Kayo said. He moved carefully toward the door but stopped before Gaela. "First-daughter-of-my-mother's-only-daughter, your future rests on the death of Brona's son, so do not treat her poorly tonight."

Gaela had forgotten that. She blinked, scowling. "Did you know? About Dalat?"

"I told him, a year past her death," Brona said, nudging Kayo away by the shoulder and putting herself in Gaela's line of fire.

Kayo left, slowly, feeling the way into the dark hall with his cane.

Alone with the witch of the White Forest, Gaela suddenly felt trepidation.

"Come, sit." Brona knelt by the hearth, slid all her cards into a stack, and shuffled slowly.

"I don't want a reading."

"I know. I'm asking questions about my son."

"That isn't my fault."

Brona glanced at Gaela from beneath her lashes, her face tilted toward the cards in her lap.

"It isn't." Gaela plopped down on the hearth rug and crossed her legs. She leaned forward, peering through the gentle orange light at Brona. "Ban the Fox made himself."

"As you did. Do you think those things disconnected?"

"I think my mother had a hand in making me, in ways I did not know until tonight."

The witch nodded and flipped over three cards: two from the suit of trees and one bird. Gaela could not identify them further.

"Well?" Gaela asked when Brona flipped three more cards, then three more, but remained silent.

"I thought you did not want a reading."

Baring her teeth, Gaela said, "I want to know why my mother trusted you, and not my sisters. Not me."

"She did trust you, Gaela. She trusted you to protect Regan and Elia and grow into a strong queen."

"She didn't say goodbye."

"In some ways she did."

Gaela pursed her lips. Her neck ached from the weight of all her hair coiled atop her crown and the layers of clay sculpting it in place. She ought to have rinsed it clean and smeared these decorations off her cheeks. Flattening her hands against the soft wool of her skirt, she carefully asked, "Did my mother leave me a message? Did she say anything about me?"

"She loved you, Gaela. She said to Kayo that this fate was her choice, and he must understand that. So, too, must you."

By now Brona had spread all twenty-seven cards atop her cloth, in five circles that spiraled atop each other, so only the top layer of cards was completely visible. The steady glow of embers cast them in umber and shadows, the roots and feathers and bright stars, the splashes of water and several moons in several shapes. Splatters of blood and new-budding flowers. "What will you do, in the morning?" Brona asked, placing the bones down one at a time, instead of tossing them in a scatter.

"Be king."

"If my son lives."

"You sound doubtful. Have more faith, Brona Hartfare. Ban is wild and vicious, and—though not easily—he might defeat the steady, predictable king of Aremoria."

Brona stood abruptly, scattering the cards. "You will never give up the crown."

Standing, too, Gaela said, "Should I?"

"You made a bargain."

"And I will find a star prophecy claiming only I can rule, else Innis Lear will fall to ruin. Something even my baby sister cannot disprove. Is that not how it's done by kings on Innis Lear? Besides, what else could be done with me? Kill me? I think not. The island needs me. Worry not, Brona. I will rule, and Elia will make your son happy enough. Both of them at my side, for what other choice will they have?"

For a long moment Brona studied Gaela, and the warrior queen held the witch's flickering gaze.

Then Brona lowered her eyes. "What choice, indeed?" she murmured, then turned to the narrow table pushed against the wall.

Gaela watched as Brona chose folded paper pouches and a stoppered vial, adding a pinch of this and drops of that into two clay cups. She brought them to Gaela and handed both to her. Gaela sniffed: sweet and soft, with a hint of spice.

The witch fetched a bottle of wine and poured some into both cups. She took one and raised it. "To the queen of Innis Lear, then."

"Those past and future," Gaela agreed. She drank the wine. The spices filled her nose, making the flavor strong and bright. "This is good."

The witch smiled softly, licking a drop of wine from the rim of her own cup. "My own recipe. It is even better warm."

"Have you no warming pot? Our next cup should be so."

"You might set the cup against those embers: it is strong enough not to crack with the heat."

Gaela downed the wine, then poured more, settling her cup just inside the dark stone of the hearth, tucked where the embers might heat it more quickly.

Brona held her own cup between her palms, nestled in her lap. They both were quiet, listening to their shared breathing, to the tender shifts and cracks of the red-hot embers. Gaela wondered if Dalat had shared such wine with Brona, long ago. And she wondered if she would remember the color of her mother's hands at all, if she herself did not share it.

"Gaela, do you understand at all what your mother sacrificed for?" Brona asked, as tenderly as the fire.

When Gaela went to speak, she became strangely unsettled, for her words arrived reluctantly. Gaela had never been reluctant in all her life. "Us. Family. Her life and . . . future."

"Dalat changed the entire island, with only a small vial of poison."

Something in the witch's voice caught Gaela's heart; it skipped and started again. "She—she . . ." Gaela's tongue felt heavy. It was very late, and she needed her sleep. She blinked slowly.

"It was the act of an earth saint," Brona whispered. "A choice worthy of worship. This island has never forgotten Dalat of Taria Queen. Nor will it forget you."

"No . . . it . . . will . . ." Gaela rubbed her face. She sighed. She was so sleepy. "Not."

She tilted toward the hearth, but Brona caught her, an arm about her royal shoulders, and drew Gaela against her.

Brona gently helped her fall, whispering quietly to the fire and the wind, a blessing for Dalat's eldest daughter.

# TWELVE YEARS AGO,
## DONDUBHAN

It was not unusual for the queen of Innis Lear to be seen wandering the halls of the winter seat well before dawn. The guards and castle folk had accustomed themselves to it, and assumed their foreign mistress slept poorly, or still followed the Third Kingdom tradition of rising early to be blessed by their luminous God. None minded, for insomnia was not so strange, and she was kind to them, and thoughtful, though often distant, as if her thoughts preferred to reside with her daughters, or drift with the wind, or perhaps keep themselves to memories of a sun so hot none of this island could quite imagine it.

This morning, the queen seemed more present, right there with them in the dark Dondubhan corridors, touching the stone walls, dragging her fingers along the seams. She watched her bare toes curl against the newly laid rushes: evergreen juniper and the first long-leafed sea grasses of spring. She breathed deeply, as if relishing the cold, damp northern air, the thin scent of low hearth fires, and the first hint of fresh rye seeping up from the kitchens.

This morning, the queen also seemed melancholy.

In an hour, the dawn would break on her eldest daughter's sixteenth birthday.

The past week had been tense: less laughter, and the music forced in the hall. Gaela had stomped in her soldier's boots and Regan pulled too hard when she separated locks of Elia's hair to braid. The king held their youngest daughter too tightly, and watched Dalat as if she might fall without warning into the deep black waters of the Tarinnish. Elia had asked her softly, twice, *Mother, what is wrong with everyone?* And both times Dalat cupped her daughter's warm brown face in a hand as black as night, smiled, and replied only, *Tomorrow is your sister's sixteenth birthday.*

The queen could bring herself to say no more.

*For my birthday this year,* Elia had said, *I would like my own set of holy bones. Like Regan's, and Brona's. There are nine holy bones, and Father says nine is the exact number of stars in the Lion of War, which is the constellation surrounding my birth star. And I will be nine years old.*

*Our Calpurlugh,* Dalat had murmured, gently pinching Elia's cheek. The queen had recalled her youngest daughter's last birthday, when all she'd asked for was magic. Brona had braided tiny white flowers into Elia's hair— starweed, as dangerous as any prophecy—and with a whispered word in the language of trees, the flowers burst into silver-white fire, exactly like a crown of stars. Elia had been pleased, but this terrible idea had blossomed in Dalat's heart.

This morning, the queen chose an indirect path for her wandering, to mimic her usual ramble though the castle, but she knew her goal. Finally, when she reached Gaela's chamber—not so far from her own as she'd made it seem—Dalat touched her hand to the smooth wooden door. A castle guard noted her from several paces down the hall where he was posted, and she smiled. His eyes politely flicked away.

Entering quietly, Dalat shut the door again behind her. Her first child maintained a sparse outer room, to discourage entertaining or comfort of any kind. Still smiling, the queen walked past the simple chairs at the cold hearth, a pile of leather armor, a stool stained from boot polish. Gaela did so prefer caring for her own tools. Pride lifted Dalat's smile wider.

Both her first and second daughters slept in Gaela's bed, and though she'd expected it, the image of Gaela curled protectively around her sister Regan wiped the smile from Dalat's mouth. She closed her eyes against a swift cut of grief.

Dalat went straight to the window. The heavy winter shutter had been pried open and set on the floor, leaning beneath the sill. Damp wind spat at her, and no wonder her girls huddled beneath a heavy bearskin, imported from the Rusrike. The queen tightened the knot holding her robe closed. She put her hands on the stone sill and leaned out, but the walls of the castle were so thick that even bending fully at the waist her head barely peeked past the edge. Below, the sheer drop angled straight down to the Tarinnish's black waters. Beyond, the foothills of the Jawbone Mountains. She could see miles and miles of the north island. None could approach this way without being seen. It was desolate and silver under the late horned moon and the scatter of winter stars. In the distant east, Dalat spied a hint of velvety blue. She breathed deeply, her stomach pushing against the corner of the window.

In the Third Kingdom, the sun would be up already, for the days were longer there. Her people would be breakfasting, spilling crumbs of biscuits and drops of last night's wine onto the sand to honor God's creations.

She hoped God would forgive her.

Putting her back to the window, the queen gazed at her daughters. She had tried to teach them about God, but not as earnestly as she might've. One zealous parent was enough for any child. And her people's God was also the stars, after all, and the earth; God did not need or beg worship, but only sought love. So long as her daughters loved, they knew Dalat's God. And these two would always love each other, of that she had no doubt.

She knelt at the side of Gaela's bed, wishing she did not have to say good-bye. But here was the flaw in her husband's faith: when there was proof to be had, its lack could kill. Dalat had heard the whispers, the threat to her children: those stars decreed she was the true queen of Innis Lear, and the true queen would die on her daughter's sixteenth birthday.

If she did not die, she could not be the true queen.

It was a suffocating paradox. Die, or her legitimacy died. And with it her daughters' future. Her husband's faith.

Dalat pushed a puff of curls back from Gaela's temple and kissed her cheek. Her husband had not wanted Dalat to bear any daughters, as if that on its own would defeat the prophecy. Four years of marriage passed before Dalat had stopped trying to convince him otherwise, and took the matter onto her own shoulders. From the moment she'd told him of their child, the king had been afraid. Even small moments of happiness were overshadowed by his fear. That was the greatest tragedy of it all, to Dalat: every father should know joy in his first child.

Dalat had loved Gaela with all of her soul to make up for it.

That eldest daughter slept with her lips just parted, so even in the dream world everyone could see her teeth. Regan's eyes flickered under her lids, one hand beneath her cheek, the other fisted in the blanket. They'd spent all the previous day together, with Elia, too, and Brona Hartfare, who knew everything. Who waited alone right now at the Dondubhan well, writing prayers into the water, reciting Dalat's promise to herself and to the wind and roots of Innis Lear. Dalat understood the magic of this place, though had never claimed it. The island would embrace her daughters if they allowed it to: Gaela, a piece of iron already, still forging herself; Regan, who reached as the wind reached, thirsty as roots for life; Elia all joy, a little piece of luminous God.

They would protect one another, and, she hoped, their father. With her death, the king would need them, turn to them. Gaela would understand her father's faith in the stars was true, finally, and he would see this was none of Gaela's fault. They could love each other, and they only fought because they were so similarly stubborn and set in their own righteousness. But when Dalat died, they would come together. And Regan and Elia.

The queen bent across her eldest and pressed a kiss to Regan's mouth, which frowned now in her dreams. Her mother's kiss smoothed the girl's lips. Regan relaxed, and the dream slipped away, leaving only peace.

Dalat left them to sleep the rest of the night away.

She nearly did not go to Elia's room.

Her baby. Curled at the foot of her bed in a twist of blankets, Elia's hair was impossibly tangled, for the little girl rejected her cap and picked it all free of its braids nearly every night. Dalat climbed into the bed and grasped Elia's waist, dragging the girl against her belly. Elia groaned and snuggled closer. "Mama?"

"Yes, baby." Dalat buried her nose in Elia's curls, smelled the dirt and sweat under that sheen of bergamot. Elia was eight years old and should have been getting over this childish disregard for bath time, but it was so sweet when she still snuck into the jars at Dalat's mirror and overused the expensive oil from the Third Kingdom. To smell just like her mother. Dalat laughed happily, squeezing her.

Elia's eyes popped open. "Mama!"

"I'm sorry, baby." Dalat kissed Elia's head. The queen shut her eyes and hummed a few notes from an old desert prayer she barely remembered, until her daughter had been quiet and still for many long moments.

Dalat did not make another stop. She'd said her farewell to Brona last night, and could only hope those ladies she'd befriended these past twenty years, and the retainers' wives she loved, and especially her companions from home, would understand. Understand, and watch out for her babies. Understand and hold this kingdom together with her husband, despite how terrible his grief would be.

She'd left the vial of starweed in their bedchamber, to force herself to go back to him, else Dalat feared she'd have taken it outside, not found the courage to face him as she died.

The king of Innis Lear snored softly in the light of a single wide candle. Though it had melted to a stub, it still managed to flicker over the volumes of star charts he'd been reading before sleep. His head tilted to the side in his repose, one hand on his chest, the other flung over his head, with two fingers twined in his long brown hair. He did that, twisting strands around several fingers as he pondered something, like wool around a spindle. It was so rich a brown, his hair, thick and dry and waved. Sometimes Dalat found single silver hairs and plucked them, eliciting a hum of irritation from him: he wanted their proof of age and wisdom, for he was, after all, halfway through his sixth decade, and old. *You must think younger, to keep up with me,* she would say in turn, and drag him to bed for a romp. Dalat teased that she alone kept him in shape, for without her, he would hunch over a book or slump in his throne, disaffected and bored with all but the stars.

Quickly, before she could change her mind, Dalat went to the small table that was her own, covered in slim books of poetry and her letters. She unstoppered the thin vial and drank every bit of the slick poison. Then she took it to the window and dragged open the heavy shutter. Lear stirred at the noise, but Dalat ignored it for the moment. Below her bedroom window was a small garden of sturdy fruit trees and juniper. She tossed the vial at the trio of gnarled cherry trees, where Brona knew to collect it in the morning.

Light in the east turned the central tower of Dondubhan Castle into a black silhouette. *I will be air, and I will be rain, and I will be dust, and I will be free,* she thought to herself, another old desert prayer. Maybe Dalat would see her own mother again, soon. Maybe death would feel like dry desert wind.

Returning to the bed, she slipped out of her robe and under the wool blanket with her husband. Pillowing her head with her arm, she lay on her side to study him. There already had been wrinkles at his eyes and mouth when she first met him, stepping off her ship and onto this rocky island. She'd come from the Third Kingdom via five foreign ports, meeting kings in all, and eating new foods and singing new songs. But the look in his warm eyes, blue as a shallow lake in a face pale as melon rind, caught her immediately and never let go. He was so much older than she, with a purity of passion like she'd never before known. Nothing got in the king's way when he set his heart on a thing, especially when that thing came as a mission from his stars.

Dalat had been glad to be such a mission. Destiny was romantic, and not something the Third Kingdom empresses put much stock in: hard work and loyalty made queens, they said, not prophecy. But there was little room for adventure without faith.

The queen of Innis Lear sighed. Here she'd had twenty years of destiny, and she would not go back and change a moment. Dalat kissed her husband. "Gaelan," she murmured against his mouth.

He had refused for so long to speak of this moment; now she would give him no choice. This they would experience together; he owed her that, because he loved her. Because his stars and his enemies had built this cage around her. She would kiss him as she died, exchange vows of love once more, and then he would know that his faith in the stars was true and right. He would keep his faith and be able to love their daughters. Without her. Be both father and mother.

Her fingers tingled: the poison would numb her and put her to sleep, Brona had promised, and she would die in a daydream.

"Gaelan, wake up."

Her husband frowned, groping for her. She guided his hand, and he woke as he found her. "Dalat," he whispered, eyes unfocused. He licked his lips, blew a long breath, and rolled his shoulders, all with his hand gripping her waist.

"Dawn is here." Her voice wavered.

"What is . . ." The king sat up swiftly. "Morning. Gaela's birthday! My love—Dalat. You're alive."

Her smile was tired. Dalat felt heavy, her limbs slow as cold honey. "I love you," she said.

Gaelan gathered her against him, eager to push their bodies together. "I love you, more than everything."

"Hold me . . . tightly."

He obeyed, and stroked her braids, his mouth at her ear as he said, "I have thought, over long nights, that if you did not die, if your heart still beat this morning, if your spirit was as glorious as ever, we should rename you only my wife, and make Gaela our queen. She could be ready now, to make the bargain. That would fulfill the prophecy well enough for all the stars. A new queen, reborn, and crowned with her own name, her own glory. The old queen's death symbolic. And it ties neatly with star and moon cycles of death and rebirth."

The king leaned back, smiling proudly, triumphantly, until he saw the tears in Dalat's eyes. The slackening of her mouth. "Dalat?" he whispered.

"You did not tell me any of that. You . . . wouldn't talk to me," his queen managed. Her chest hurt. And her stomach. "I asked you, and I asked you, in so many ways this year, to . . ."

"What? This? I did not—could not risk changing anything with words!" Gaelan curled his long fingers around her bare shoulders. Her head lolled, but with a great strength of will Dalat lifted it again.

"My heart was strong enough," she whispered, horrified, so very heavy now, and scared. "I only die because I thought there was no other way. For my—us." *I thought you would never bend. I thought . . . my daughters would be torn to pieces by Connley and—and Glenna—Glenn—and . . .*

"No, you aren't dying. You're here, with me. What is wrong?" Gaelan shook her, then released her shoulders to grasp her head. The queen's arms flopped against the bed.

"I thought you were too afraid to lose me, or else lose your stars. I thought you would never make a plan in case they failed." Was she saying it all out loud, or only trying to? Dalat could barely tell. But Gaelan's face contorted as if he could hear her. "So I made a plan on my own," she said.

This time when her head dipped back, Dalat could not lift it.

"No!" the king cried, laying her down. He bent over his wife. He slapped her; when her head turned from the force it did not turn back.

Her eyes drifted shut. His frantic, beloved voice faded in and out as he argued with her, as he demanded to know what she'd done. His lips on her mouth, her face, his wet lashes brushed her cheek. The damp kiss of tears. Or gentle rain. Or

# ELIA

THE NIGHT CAME to its end when the roots of the Thorn Tree vanished under the western horizon, while its branches still stretched toward the seven constellations that in this hour of this month were known as the Mantle.

Five hawthorns huddled in a line down the lee of the rocky slope, protected from the harshest sea winds. The trees had given Scagtiernamm its Learish name: *Refuge of Thorns.* It was a portentous place and time for a star reading, in the Refuge of Thorns, beneath a sinking Thorn Tree constellation, before the Salmon nosed up or the Star of Fourth Birds burst visible as a trailhead for the following sun.

Elia trudged up the moorland alone.

As she walked, she asked the world, *Why is there no language of stars?*

The wind shivered her eyelashes. *What do you think your charts and numbers have been?* asked the nearest hawthorn tree in a creaking, hissing old voice.

*The stars speak a silent language,* she murmured.

*Yes.*

*Do they care about us here?*

Neither the wind nor the roots replied.

"Why should they care?" asked Ban Errigal.

It seemed she was not the first to arrive.

He stood in the line of hawthorns, fully armored in leather and mail, with a faded gambeson and a sword in his belt that babbled a stream of words Elia did not quite understand.

There'd been a fire beside his feet recently; a thin trickle of smoke rose still. Two fingers on his right hand were blackened by char. Elia smelled blood—a sharp complement to the salty wind.

"No magic," she said, stepping nearer. "Only you and your sword against him."

"I know," Ban said. "I will not cheat. I will not pull out a dagger from my boot and cut him when he expects honor."

Elia bit her bottom lip: Aefa had painted it red again, and Elia could taste the sharp flavor. She said nothing.

Suddenly, Ban whispered, "You'll be a good queen."

"Don't die, Ban," she replied. Her fingers flexed, but she did not go nearer.

He said a word too softly for her to hear, and a breeze wafted around his ankles, teasing at the thin smoke. Ban kept up his gentle whisper as the smoke turned in a circle, braiding strands of itself in and out and around, lifting away from the smoldering embers in a silver ring.

Elia listened to the wind, to the babbling sword at his hip, to the eager fire voices and the hawthorn roots, all interested, focused here: she said *fire* and snapped. Tiny flames caught in the air. Elia dotted seven of them around the edges of the rising ring.

It spun slowly between them: a crown of fire and silver smoke.

Wearing the beginning of a smile, Elia glanced at Ban. But the little flame jewels flashed, linking together and flaring bright. The crown turned entirely into fire, white-hot, and then nothing.

Elia gasped, its heat a strong memory left on her cheeks.

Ban the Fox watched her with his ghost green eyes, challenging and sad.

The crunch of footsteps and a low murmur announced the arrival of the others, and the two wizards turned away from each other.

Dawn was delicate purple light, and thin clouds streaked across the remaining stars.

Here was Kay Oak, leaning heavily against Alis Thornhill and wincing at everything, while Aefa and her father the old Fool softly teased a riddle between the two of them. The retainers spread out all around. There came Curan Ironworker and his wife from Errigal, with some other Errigal retainers, and finally Rory, looking more stoic than ever before. And folk from the Steps as well as retainers from Connley and Astora, from Port Comlack: soon near a hundred had gathered here, forming a circle several people deep.

Morimaros and La Far pushed through, with seven of the Aremore soldiers they'd brought to the island.

The king of Aremoria was glorious in his full mail shirt, with a polished steel pauldron cupped around his shield shoulder and plate armor collaring his neck beneath the lowered cowl of a mail hood. Plain leather buckled a sword in place, and a simple blue cape hung tossed over his sword arm. His gambeson and trousers were deep blue, the gauntlets tucked into a belt of stunning white. His hair was newly shorn, just a shadow against his skull, and his jaw was as bare as it had been since he arrived.

His expression was still, distant, like it had been at the Summer Seat all those weeks ago, when Elia had convinced herself he cared nothing for her at all. But now his blue eyes pinned her in place, and she thought of his hand on her back, his mouth, and how he'd smiled in Lionis when he'd told her the story of the Mars's Cote balcony.

Innis Lear could destroy this man, as it destroyed all things.

Elia looked for her sisters. They were not to be seen, nor Brona Hartfare.

She frowned, but Morimaros said, "It is dawn. Are you prepared, Ban Errigal?"

"Where are my sisters?" Elia asked, seeking all around.

"Regan went to find Gaela two hours ago," Ban said softly.

"Gaela was with Brona," added Kayo.

Because this was Innis Lear, a star priest stepped out of the crowd. "A blessing for the dawn, Princess?"

She looked at Aefa, then at the duelists.

The two men stood opposite each other, facing across gravelly flat moor. La Far held a round buckler for Morimaros to use as a shield. Across from him a haggard Rory had moved to Ban's side, speaking softly to his brother and offering him the same weapon.

The traditional dawn star blessing was an ululating prayer to the invisible daytime stars.

*Oh hidden stars,* the invocation went, *unseen as luck is unseen, as the wills of the saints are unseen, as love and honor and hope are unseen, be with us though we cannot mark your place with our mortal eyes.*

"No," Elia said softly.

"My lady?" the priest asked. It was one she was familiar with, a younger priest grown up entirely under the reign of King Lear. His surprise widened his eyes, caused the white tattoos dotted like constellations down his cheeks to shift and twist.

"I will offer the blessing," she called, then said, in the language of trees, *Hail the roots of Innis Lear.*

Her voice did not shake, but the earth below her feet did; it trembled beneath all of them, rattling stones, brushing grass together, shivering the pebbles and shaking tiny beetles and crickets up into the air. Wind kissed everyone: lips, eyes, cheeks, hands, whatever piece of skin waited open and free to the sky. "Hail the stars in the sky," she called, repeating it in the tree tongue. "And hail our hearts in between."

*And hail our hearts in between.*

"My heart is broken."

Everyone turned toward Regan Lear as she appeared.

She walked through the crowd, her dress dragging behind, the hem tattered. It was her underdress, and a robe over it, not a gown. Hair fell loose in tangled brown waves, curling around her jaw. Regan blinked; a sheen of tears made those dark eyes as large as navel wells. Red lines were painted down her cheeks like bloody tears.

"Sister," said Elia.

Brona Hartfare came behind, gaze steady on Regan's back, as if the witch's willpower alone held Regan upright.

"Begin this duel," Regan commanded, raising a hand to point at Ban and then Morimaros. "Fight for the crown of this island, fight for betrayal and hearts and the roots and stars. *Fight!*" She screamed the last word, and it rang up and up into the air.

Something was wrong, and Elia could hardly breathe. "Where is Gaela?" she asked.

"She is beyond witnessing this now. *Fight!*" In the language of trees, Regan added, *If you do not fight now, Fox, it will all be for nothing. Fight!*

Ban Errigal drew his whispering sword. Morimaros did the same.

Heart pounding, Elia stared.

Regan came to one side of her, Brona Hartfare the other. Regan touched Elia's shoulder, gripping it hard as an eagle's talon. "This is how my heart broke, little sister. So too will yours now, one way or the other."

"Why do you relish it so, Regan?" Elia whispered.

Her sister did not reply.

Brona touched Elia's other hand, offering comfort. Elia took it, glancing at the witch. The washed morning light showed Brona's age in fine wrinkles, in some strands of silver winding through her lush curls; they reminded Elia of the Elder Queen Calepia who wore her white age like an elegant crown. One of those mothers would lose a son.

Elia clutched Brona's hand. "I am so sorry."

"For my son?" Brona asked lightly. "I have always known his blood would spill here, to water this island."

"Where he belongs," Elia whispered.

Brona put her free hand over her own heart, as if to say, *Here is where my son belongs.*

To Elia's amazement, her sister, too, put a hand to her heart, and tears slipped down her cheeks.

Then Morimaros lifted a white-gloved hand. "*Esperance!*" he roared, and attacked.

# THE FOX

THE ABRUPT ATTACK made Ban throw up his buckler to desperately catch the charge: it rattled through his bones, the jar of Morimaros's greater mass and strength. Ban leapt back, turned, and sliced with his hissing, giggling blade.

It was only an initial spar: striking, blocking, their grunts and wrenching movements the focus of these hundred folk. They parted quickly and stared. Mars breathed evenly. This was not at all like those fights in Aremoria, the autumn Mars and Novanos had mentored Ban. This was so different: the look in the king's eyes was not encouraging, but hot and deadly.

Mars darted out with his sword. Ban parried, they turned, engaging too dangerously for Ban; unbreakable though the blade might be, he'd lose his sword if they crossed. Ban kicked, stomping the heel of his boot to Mars's thigh. The king cursed and staggered back. Then he feinted, drawing Ban out, but the Fox was ready and stuck with buckler instead of sword, knocking Mars's off center. They clashed, and Ban's feet slid in the gravel. He did not dig his sword under as he'd been taught: that was a killing blow.

Instead he swung with the pommel, hitting Mars's face. The king smiled grimly and spat blood. "You make those death strikes, Ban. Fight me like you betrayed me: with no thought of my heart."

The Fox opened his mouth to speak, but Mars dove at Ban, who barely escaped. He turned and slammed his buckler into Mars's sword, but Mars's buckler skimmed his gut just as he spun away. The blade of the king's sword cut along Ban's arm, dragging at the mail shirt. Ban tucked in, slicing back.

Another flurry of strikes and blocks, Ban giving ground under the strong onslaught, until he fell to one knee. He gasped for air and struck back with his sword. His buckler was gone, his left hand numb. Ban needed another shield, or hammer, or even a knife, but there was nothing. This was single combat, not melee.

He got up, bruises screaming.

Mars threw away his buckler, too, in a fit of fairness that had Ban sneering.

"Was it kind or sporting, what I did to you, Mars?"

"I am not like you," the king answered.

Ban laughed wildly, choking on it. "You could never be!" His vision swam; he staggered and barely caught himself. He'd taken a knock to the temple; he couldn't recount when, but the throbbing, the blood sticking down his jaw, was proof.

Both men fell silent and still, but for their heaving shoulders. A crow called, laughing as only crows laugh.

"I loved you," Mars finally said, bleakly.

"And I you," Ban answered.

The king scoffed. Tears or sweat streaked his bare, handsome cheeks.

"It was not you that I meant . . ." Ban shook his head. It did not matter; Ban could not defend his heart. There was nothing to say, no value in it or truth, anyway. "Again?" he offered instead, raising his whispering sword.

It would be the end, he knew; shieldless, he did not stand a chance.

"Surrender, Ban," Elia called from the edge of the spectator circle. "Give in. Please."

Ban did not even glance at her; he couldn't. He attacked once more, with a cry.

He was finished, hurt, and so there was no surprise when Mars batted him away easily. Ban kicked, grabbed at Mars's sword arm, then spun and shoved his shoulder into the king's back. Mars went down, caught himself and rolled, and Ban chased after, sword raised. Mars lifted his legs in order to kick Ban away with hard boot strikes. Ban dodged, and stabbed, but shifted at the last moment, penetrating mail, but only to skim Mars's ribs.

Blood flowed, and Ban couldn't see through his sudden wash of furious tears.

He lurched away. He should surrender. He could stop. Especially if he refused to win this fight! If Ban couldn't bring himself to take the kill strike, he should give in.

But no. No. He was Ban the Fox, soldier, spy, and little else. He would die here, on this battlefield.

With a terrible groan, Ban attacked again. They engaged, and Mars threw Ban back, slicing his sword in a glorious arc that caught Ban's arm.

The limb shocked into hot pain, then numbness.

Ban tried to clutch at it, but his fingers stuck too tight around his sword, melded in pain to his aching arm. The Fox swung again, but it was slow, so slow. His sword hissed furiously.

Amazement, and something like peace, blossomed in Ban's heart when, at last, Mars's sword found its mark.

The blade slid into Ban's flesh over his heart and just below his left shoulder, a rod of lightning through his body. Blood burst down his chest, soaking even his back. Mars jumped forward, dropped his sword, and grabbed his Fox against him.

They fell together to their knees; Ban's name on the king's bloody lips.

Ban heard nothing else, only his name, again and again. He opened his mouth to say—nothing.

There was nothing.

He thought,

*here I am at last.*

# REGAN

REGAN LEAR TURNED away from the battle and walked north toward the White Forest.

Always, always she had been the second daughter of Lear. Gaela's younger sister. The middle, the princess, not the heir, because her glorious older sister would rule. Regan was the pillar for Gaela's wounded, raging heart, a web of iron roots dug deep into the earth of Innis Lear to hold Gaela high.

Regan did not know what to be, without her elder sister.

But Gaela was dead.

So Regan walked, and walked. The wind gusted hard at her back, pushing her along the way. *Good, yes*, Regan was glad the wind agreed this was the way to go.

Back to the earth, to the heart of the island. To a spring, or a grove of ash trees. Always ashes had been her favorite: slender and gray, at first, but spreading and gorgeous as they grew strong. The whisper of their leaves was always a delicate song.

Why did she feel so cold? She shivered hard, as if ill.

All Regan could hope for now was a bed of roots, a cool, damp nest in which to close her eyes and simply stop. Fade into the earth as if she'd always been a part of it. Where Gaela would be soon, and Connley already waited.

Regan was a worm of decay, twining about the forest roots, always between death and new life, but never quite alive. Everyone around her died; perhaps it was the reason she could bear no child. There was not enough life in her.

Her sister's cheek had been so cold.

Regan shuddered again, and the wind trailed sharp fingers down her spine.

"She asked for the poison your mother used," the witch had said softly. "I did not expect her to drink it."

It had not seemed a thing to believe, and yet, there was the proof of it before Regan's eyes: Gaela laid out by the hearth in Brona Hartfare's room, sleeping, dead.

Regan had clawed her skin until blood dripped like hot tears down her face, and pulled Gaela's dagger free of the sheath at her thigh. Brona had leaned away, but Regan did not strike. She'd touched the cold blade to her palm, then the back of her hand, dragging the tip up her wrist and over her sleeve, leveling it at her own heart.

But the sun had nearly risen, and Ban the Fox waited for her in the Refuge of Thorns. Regan had kissed her cold sister and gone out onto the moor to find her other sister, dull and alone. The dagger loose in her hand.

Shouldn't she feel more?

Now the duel was over, too, and Regan walked. For a few minutes or an hour, or a day or a year, she lost the scale of time. There was such emptiness inside her.

*Regan, pretty Regan,* whispered the wind.

She replied not at all. The wind had given her nothing. The roots had given her nothing. She'd never had any reason to ask the stars. Only Gaela had loved her, and then Connley.

Ban the Fox might have, but he was dead. So was her mother. Her father, Lear, dead. All her enemies were dead, but all her family, too.

"Regan!"

The witch ignored the sound of her name, even from her baby sister's voice, and walked on, her pace the same, toward the edge of the forest. Her slippers skidded on the rocky slope, and Regan crested it, stumbling down into the forest valley. Blue sky shone down on the black and gray and white forest, scratched here and there by scarlet and orange because it was so late in the year. Beautiful, the brilliant colors of death. On Innis Lear they wore white for the dead, but death was so vibrant. It was a sun of colors. Gaela was bold, and now she was dead. Regan had always been cool and shaded. She was still alive.

Not for long.

The shadows of the White Forest overcame her, and Regan lifted her gaze to the trees. *Where the ash?* she murmured in their language, and the wind pushed her forward.

"Regan!"

The second daughter of Lear entered the slip of ash trees and brandished Gaela's knife.

"No!" Elia caught her arm, jerking her around. "Regan!"

Blood and tears striped Regan's face; her loose hair crackled with wind and energy. "My sister is dead," she said in a hollow voice.

". . . Gaela is dead?" Elia breathed.

"I was not so strong as her, nor so glorious."

The girl, the little princess, moved carefully closer, staring at the dagger in Regan's hand. "How?"

Regan shut her eyes. "Gaela drank Dalat's poison."

Elia swayed, struggling to remain on her feet. "No."

Dry, cracking grief shook Regan's bones, and she showed her teeth in an anguished grimace. "I will not live without her!"

"I know, sister! I know!"

Regan bit her lip, turning it gray then breaking the skin. Blood leaked free.

"Listen to the wind, Regan, to the island and these roots, please. They love you, this island loves you, I love you—you are not lost, we are not lost!" *Listen,* Elia begged, *ash friends, speak to my sister, this is Regan Connley of Lear.*

The grove of ashes shook and shivered, whispering Regan's name.

She closed her eyes. *I know,* she said to them. *I am roots, I am the roots of this island, I am born of you, and formed of nothing else. Nothing is born from me but wormwork!*

Elia knelt before her sister. "We have each other, we can still . . . we can still be better . . . a family."

"A family! Our family is dead. All poisoned, with flowers or magic or stars. My Connley, dead. Gaela, dead. Our mother, too. Ban the Fox, dead—and you should be glad of that, *sister.*" Regan grasped Elia's chin and took aim. "Our father's murderer, slain now by your valiant king of Aremoria."

"What?" Elia wrenched herself away.

"Ban Errigal killed his enemy, our father."

"No, Father was old, and in despair! I was there: his heart simply stopped!"

"By magic. A wizard with the ear of the wind and the love of the roots, and the hatred of our father." Regan laughed wildly, recalling the panicked, terrible moment when Connley was dead and Ban had glowed, incandescent with rage. He had dropped a nut from his pocket and crushed it, and all the wind of the island had begun to scream.

Elia shook her head. Tears clung to her short lashes, and she flailed at Regan, trying again to steal the dagger. "It isn't true. Give that to me, Regan!"

But her sister pushed her back. "You tried to save him, last night. You love him, still." She laughed more, but it was weak now, almost sympathetic. She knew what it was like to love too much and yet never be able to change a thing. Regan pressed the bloody scratches on her cheek again until they seeped, like the tears of Saint Halir, the spirit of hunters. Then she put one bloody hand against Elia's and said, *You will be alone, and for that I am sorry.*

"Regan," Elia whispered back.

"I will not miss you," the witch said, lifting the small jeweled knife, "but you must remember us to your children."

"Please, sister. Regan."

Regan turned the knife upon herself. The point found her skin, just over the collar of her ruined gown. "I will take my mother's way, too," she said with a small, hysterical laugh. "The rootwater cannot save me from this! Soon, Gaela, soon, Husband, soon, Mother, soon, all my poor babies!"

*Stop her,* Elia begged of the island. She grasped Regan's wrist, clinging to it. *Wind, stop her. Be my ally. Ash friends, trees, stop her. Love her!*

Regan lashed out at Elia's face; pain burst in Regan's hand and Elia folded quite suddenly. Regan took a deep breath and repositioned the knife.

The witch no longer listened as Elia begged the world, groggy, dragging herself up against a tree. *Save her, please. Please.*

The earth shivered.

Around Regan, roots pressed up, rolling the ground like ocean waves. Fingers of mud reached, worms of earth grasped Regan's skirt, tugging at her. Regan looked down in surprise, blinking tears and blood.

*Regan, queen, witch, lover,* shuddered the whole of Innis Lear, opening its arms.

The ash trees bent toward her, their roots lifting, churning, walking the trees up out of the earth and nearer to Regan Lear.

*Yes,* she murmured.

Gaela's knife fell from Regan's hands.

An ash shoved Elia out of its way as the youngest daughter of Lear tried to hold on to her sister.

Seven ash trees gathered close to Regan, wrapping her up. *Queen, love, Regan,* they whispered as she slumped and wept, as she dug her hands into their golden leaves and their roots wound about her ankles. The trees twined themselves together, a braided tower of ashlings, closing Regan off from everything but their cool, dark center. They wanted her, and refused to give her up.

Then she was gone, leaving her last sister behind.

Wind ruffled the last autumn-yellow leaves, tossing them down onto Elia Lear like a benediction.

TWENTY YEARS AGO,

THE SUMMER SEAT

GAELA CROUCHED ON her hands and knees in the center of her bed chamber. Her arms shook and her shoulders heaved. She squeezed her eyes so tightly shut it pulled at her scalp.

Her sister crept slowly into the room, even younger and slighter. Regan was not afraid of Gaela, but afraid of whatever in the world had caused this uproar. The fur and blankets had been torn from the bed and crumpled across the floor. Ashes from the fire and chunks of black coal were strewn over the hearth. The small weapons rack lay crashed on the ground, spears and elegant knives scattered hard. A tapestry in the bold patterns of the Third Kingdom had been torn off the wall; threads and rags of it were pinned high still, tatters drifting in the ocean breeze that slipped salty and cool through the narrow window.

Gaela had ripped off her little leather vest, too, a gift from their father that was very like a soldier's leather chest piece. She'd scoured it with her nails, then grabbed one of the spearheads and slashed at the leather, cutting it in ugly stripes.

"Gaela?" whispered Regan, kneeling beside her sister. She smoothed her pretty skirt and held her hands folded in her lap, waiting for Gaela's signal.

A great sniffle and then a following sob were enough; Regan wrapped her thin body around Gaela's back, hugging with all her might. She hummed and murmured, pressing her cheek to Gaela's shoulder.

For a long time, Gaela cried, in silent, painful gasps and sobs, her tears stuck in her throat. She fisted her hands against her knees, then slammed them into the now ragged rug, again and again, until Regan caught them and held tight. Gaela shoved her away and then scrambled after, grabbing Regan into an embrace. "I'm sorry, I'm sorry," she hissed, horrified at hurting her sister.

They leaned together, Gaela's bloody knuckles smeared against Regan's soft palms, foreheads touching, eyes closed.

"Did you know about the prophecy?" Gaela asked, in a bare breath of a whisper.

"There are so many."

"About Mother's death."

Regan stiffened, wary.

Gaela struggled to breathe without trembling. "The stars say she will die on the sixteenth anniversary of her first daughter's birth."

"No." Regan pulled back to stare at her sister's face. Studied the stain of tears and pink, swollen eyes.

"I heard Satiri say it, and she doesn't believe it, but they were talking about the baby. That it doesn't matter if it's a boy or a girl, because what matters already happened. She already has a *first* daughter."

"Satiri doesn't like prophecy, maybe she misheard."

Gaela shook her head. She rubbed her eyes with the backs of her wrists. "Satiri doesn't mishear, and she doesn't gossip. I turn sixteen in eight years."

It was twice as long as she'd already lived.

"I should die instead," Gaela said. She released Regan and reached for the spearhead again: a spade of iron, the tip jagged and sharp. She put it to her neck and pressed, but Regan took hold of her wrist and dragged it away.

"No, you can't. You can't do that."

"Better me than our mother."

"It won't stop it, if that's the prophecy. Say again what Satiri heard."

*"The queen will die on the sixteenth anniversary of her first daughter's birth."*

Regan pressed her lips into a line, thinking, her eyes flicking between her sister's. "You have to live, Gaela. With me. I need you—I don't have my own stars, you promised to share with me yours. And—and that prophecy is about the day of your birth. You already were born, Gaela," Regan said with gentle, cold certainty, disturbing in a girl of only six years. "It's too late."

Too late.

Gaela stared at her little sister, breathing hard and fast. She'd already killed her mother, before she even knew she could.

This occurred to her like a tiny seed: if she'd already done the worst, it didn't matter what terrible things she had yet to do. So the eldest daughter of Lear gripped her sister's hand, and promised never to let go.

It was too late for anything else.

# ELIA

No one stopped her as she wandered back toward Errigal Keep, dazed, bloody, with nothing but an ornamental knife in her drooping fingers. As Elia entered the front court, she was not recognized quickly, because of the slump of her shoulders, and her tangled, half-braided hair. Her skirt trailed behind her in tatters, the front hem muddy and tripping her, but she did nothing to lift it up.

"The queen," someone murmured. But she could not be. Not now, not yet. Elia angled toward the side of the Keep; she needed to get to her room, wash up. No, she needed to find Gaela—no, Aefa . . . or . . . Her thoughts scattered. Her pulse pounded, and every thread of wind beat with the same rhythm, as if Elia herself were the core. *My sisters!*

A man ran toward her; she stopped to wait on his urgency. What could matter? Her sisters both were dead. She was the only remaining daughter of Dalat and Lear. Elia blinked. Her eyes were dry, her entire body dry as a mountain peak. Had Ban—

Morimaros of Aremoria reached her, gently panting. Behind him careened Aefa, running full tilt. Blood marred the king's face, making his eyes sharp as blue fire. He'd shed his plate armor, down to crusty gambeson and trousers. Blood stained the collar of his shirt, and she wondered miserably it if had ever been any color but red.

He grasped her shoulders, said something of his relief.

Aefa flung herself into Elia, knocking her from Morimaros. "Gaela is dead! We did not know if Regan . . ."

Elia nodded, allowing the hug, arms limp and stolen dagger cold. "Regan, too."

Aefa yelled for water, spared her friend a warm kiss, and dashed off to find Kay Oak and tell him the queen had been found.

The king of Aremoria said her name again. He touched his fingers to her cheek, extremely careful around the blossoming bruise. "You're otherwise uninjured?" he asked softly.

Elia could hardly catalogue the extent of her wounds, so myriad, so small, and internal they were, slashes to her heart.

After a bruised silence and several steps, Morimaros spoke again. "You said Regan is also dead?"

"Gone, at least," Elia whispered. She did not know if death had come to her furious, mad sister, or peace, or only soft darkness.

Morimaros studied her, then cupped her elbow. "Ban is going to die."

She gripped the little knife tighter. "You mean he's not dead yet."

"Soon." Morimaros took Elia's other hand. "The day is yours, lady," he said, and what began as a hesitant, sad voice grew in strength and volume. "This island is yours, too, Queen Elia of Lear."

It shook her.

Around them soldiers and retainers knelt. Elia's heart trembled as she tried to speak, or offer a mask of stately grief at least. But the knife was in her hand, and she burned to use it. As men said, *Hail queen,* and *Elia of Lear,* and *Long under the stars may she reign,* Elia stared at Morimaros's weary blue eyes. "Take me to Ban, before he dies." She strode forward without an answer from him, but made herself glance and nod to the lines of soldiers, turn her empty palm out to them in thanks and acceptance, in blessing.

Morimaros led her into the Keep, but suddenly Rory Errigal was there, crying her name. She did not give him anything. Rory smoothed his fingers over the aching side of her face where Regan had hit her, but she fisted a hand against his mail and shoved at his chest. "Not yet," she said. "Take me to Ban."

The earlson hesitated, concern streaked over his freckled features, but gave in with a reluctant nod.

No one stopped her after that.

Ban the Fox lay dying in his bed. Rory called softly for Brona to come out. She did. Her apron was streaked with blood, most of it dry, and she smelled of the iron stuff, and of sharp herbs, too. "Elia," she murmured, glad and surprised.

"Let me through," Elia said.

Instead, Brona put her arms around Elia, hugging her tight. Elia did not move to pull away or to return the embrace. She stood and accepted Brona, and the woman touched their cheeks together, nudging Elia's mass of hair aside so she could whisper, "He is not so dire and dying as I've led them all to believe, Elia. It is very bad, and he's broken, but I have some little hope.

If they know he might live, they'll put him in shackles. That weight will kill him surely."

Cold understanding stiffened Elia's limbs: Brona believed her to be an ally in wishing for the Fox's survival.

She nearly laughed. But Elia had room for only one feeling in her heart, and sympathy, humor, love were none of it.

She went inside.

The fire was low, and only listless sunlight filtered through the dark, shuttered windows. Elia firmly shut the door behind her.

His breath was a crawling, shallow rattle.

Elia slowly approached, her steps silent across the thin rug. Unlit candles were set upon a low table, a pile of discarded weapons hugged one corner, and holy bones and their cards were spread in a half circle beside the smoky hearth.

His eyes were closed, his skin yellowed and sunken beneath stark red scratches and a flowery bruise. He'd been washed, his hair slicked back, and his shoulders were bare; torso, too, until the thin blanket pulled nearly to his navel. A great, bloody bandage wrapped his chest and right shoulder. Ban Errigal was a garden of bruises and cuts shiny with salve.

The entire place smelled of sweat, blood, and clear, sharp medicine.

Seeing him infuriated her.

Her hands shook; she swallowed bile and sniffed great tears away. Her jaw clenched. This was what she'd been driven to, this moment in this dark room, just the two of them, him dying, her . . . she did not know. No longer sister, no longer daughter. A wizard and a queen.

A queen of all this: Her father—dead! Her sisters—dead! And for what? For this rageful creature. Pitiful, and still alive.

Elia hitched her skirts up and climbed over his body. His lips curled, and he hissed painfully through teeth, wincing, and his eyelids fluttered. *Mama?* he seemed to mouth.

She straddled his waist and leaned down to put the edge of the knife under his chin.

The touch of cold steel snapped his eyes open.

"Look what you've done to me," she whispered.

"Elia."

Her name thick as a prayer on his tongue.

She choked, eyes burning with tears. "Regan is dead. And Gaela is dead. And my *father*! You murdered him! But you're not sorry. You would not change a thing!"

Ban did not blink or look away. He did not deny he'd killed King Lear.

When he swallowed, his throat leaned into the dagger. "My choices brought me here, and yours you. I am what I am, what I have always been."

Her mouth contorted; the edges of her sight rippled. "I loved you more than anyone," Elia whispered. "Yet you are the one who taught me to hate! Not even my sisters could do that! It was *you*."

The blade pressed harder. His chin lifted, but there was no place for the Fox to hide. He did not move his arms, or tense; he did nothing to escape.

"You loved me," Ban whispered, closing his eyes.

Elia trembled. She readied herself to take revenge, to slice this blade across his neck, to kill him as her father had been killed. Swiftly, some beast to be put out of its misery.

And he did look miserable. His eyes opened again, and he met her gaze with something calm, relieved in them. "I am glad," he said, thickly. "I am glad to die at your hand and no other's, Elia. Queen of Innis Lear."

Tears plopped onto his chin.

Her tears.

She threw the knife across the room and collapsed against him, ignoring his small cry of pain. Elia curled her fingers in the blanket, tore at it, though it would not rip. She had to do it, or she might hit him, scratch at his bandages and see his wound gape anew, bite his bruises, beat him and make him hurt the way she hurt. She squeezed her eyes closed, ground her teeth against the shaking sobs.

Ban did nothing but breathe and then he lifted his less-injured arm to put his hand on her cheek.

It calmed her in a gut-wrenching flash.

Elia kissed Ban, like it was the last thing she would ever do: hard and angry, smearing tears with lips, fast and desperate.

Then she got up, and she left.

He said nothing to stop her, though his right hand shifted, fingers curling like he could catch her invisible traces and pull her back.

But Elia was gone; it was only a long-awaited queen who emerged from that dark embrace, who pushed out into the brightly lit corridor, where all her people waited. The light dazzled her earth-black eyes. She paused, touched a hand over her heart, and called for the hemlock crown.

*IT BEGINS* WHEN the new queen of Innis Lear admires the glint of ice crystals upon the standing stones; how each point bursts into silver strands, reaching for the next, connecting the frozen stars with interlocking lines of frost. Her breath appears as it passes her lips, given body by the chill of winter, and as she did when she was a little girl, she plays with it. She puffs air out in rhythm with her heart, then blows a long, thin stream, mouth tugging into a smile.

Moonlight silvers the flat hill upon which the trio of stones rise out of the moorland like ancient priests—or, she thinks, like three brave sisters. She walks to the smallest of them, fur slippers crunching gently over icy winter grass. Her glove is a white mark against the deep gray stone, and slowly, slowly, heat from her body spreads to the frost, melting it in an aura.

To the north the horizon blisters with bright firelight from the fortress of Dondubhan, where the Midwinter celebration lifts the Longest Night into glory and hope, where all her people still sing, drink, and dance. Where the king of Aremoria waits, summer gold and patient, for the queen to return, and the half-blind Oak Earl smiles at his new wife, and Rory Errigal wears a new duke's chain, shirt stained from excess wine. Their queen should be there, she knows, and she will be. But this last atonement must to be served, this final moment to bury the remains of war and suffering and broken hearts.

It's her lady Aefa and the weary retainer La Far who cover her absence at the festivities, both of whom can understand her need for privacy, though only Aefa knows the true cause of it. This is a secret shared only by three women in all the world: Aefa, Brona the witch, and the queen of Innis Lear.

The queen scrapes her hand down the smallest standing stone. She tilts her head back to peer at the moon and its skirt of brilliant stars as it hovers over the rugged top edge of the stone. In her cream-and-gray gown, she might be a saint herself, a reflection of the Star of Sorrow, for the queen wears mourning clothes: no colors or dye, only the natural shades of wool.

Even her coat is white fur and soft tan leather, rustic and unfashionable, but it hardly matters to her. She's tied up her own hair with plain string, and for jewels only agreed to the silver circlet crown and a necklace set with diamonds the Aremore king gifted to her.

"Elia," says a quiet voice behind her.

She breathes her misty breath against the ice of the stone, and turns.

The man is only a shade, a lean figure in a black coat, hood raised, sword at hip. A traveler's pack slides off his shoulder and slumps against the ground. He steps nearer.

The queen says, "I heard Ban the Fox finally died in Hartfare, despite his mother's best care."

"He did," comes the low reply. "And in Hartfare we heard the queen will not marry Aremoria after all."

A smile glazed with bittersweet humor pulls at her lips. "This morning the star priests presented a new royal prophecy: This queen will never marry, and the father of her heirs will be a saint of the earth."

"Mars is good enough to be an earth saint," the man says.

The ache in her heart is nothing but a shadow of passion, lacking all rage. She can carry it, though it feels like swallowing ice. "When she came for her own wedding, Brona brought me a long box of bones and ashes. I will bury them in the deepest part of Innis Lear, so her son will always be part of my island's heart. But you, I—" Her courage breaks, and she quickly turns her face away.

He appears there, holding her jaw in cold, bare hands. He lifts her chin, and she feels her strength return as she looks into his ghostly, familiar eyes. His face is thinner, sharper, wild and biting.

She takes a breath and says, "You I will not see again."

"Not on this earth, not in this life," the shadow whispers, as if it is all the voice left to him.

The queen brings her hands up between them to tug the gloves from her fingers. She lets them fall to the frozen ground. Drawing nearer, she touches his face, thumbs gentle at the corners of his mouth. "Go," she breathes. "And be something new."

"Promise me something," he says, tilting his head against her left palm.

Her brows rise, willing to hear him but not to swear unknowingly.

"When you bury the Fox, do it on a night with no stars."

She brushes her thumbs over his mouth, nods, and releases him.

The shadow-man leaves, pausing only to scoop up his bag before walking far off, to vanish in the sparkling blackness of this Longest Night.

The queen kneels, her back to the smallest standing stone. Its chill, and the ice of the earth below, seep into her body. She leans her head back so the silver crown taps the rock, and she closes her eyes to the fine moonlight.

Stars shine, and the moon too, turning the frosted grass and low hills of Innis Lear into a quiet, cold mirror, until heaven is below her, around her, and everywhere.

# Acknowledgments

Thanks to my AP English teacher, Pat Donnelly, at St. Teresa's Academy in 1998, for first helping me explore my hatred for King Lear.

As always with writing, this book would not exist without the support of friends and peers, especially: Julie Murphy, Bethany Hagen, Justina Ireland, Laura Ruby, Anne Ursu, Kelly Jensen, Leila Roy, Sarah McCarry, Kelly Fineman, Dot Hutchinson, Robin Murphy, Lydia Ash, Chris McKitterick, Brenna Yovanoff, Dhonielle Clayton, Zoraida Córdova, Ellen Kushner, Racheline Maltese, Joel Derfner, Delia Sherman, Karen Lord, Stephanie Burgis, Tara Hudson, Rebecca Coffindaffer, Sarah Henning, Robin McKinley.

Thanks to my family, always ready with a hug or wiseass comment. Usually both.

My editor Miriam Weinberg went above and beyond with this book, pushing me and trusting me beyond all reason. I'm forever delighted to have your wit, talent, and passion in my life and work.

Also thanks to everyone at Tor who has been welcoming and worked tirelessly for me, especially Anita Okoye, Melanie Sanders, and Lauren Hougen, and Irene Gallo and the design team for this powerful package. I submitted the first novel I ever finished to Tor, back when I was still in high school, and was *thankfully* rejected. But it's a dream come true to see that logo on the spine of a book I wrote.

Eternal gratitude to my agent, Laura Rennert, who has never given up on me, and all of Andrea Brown Literary Agency for such abundant support even during this dark time line.

And thanks to my wife, Natalie C. Parker. It's the first time I can legally call you that in published acknowledgments, though you've been at the heart of them all.